THE CANTERBURY TALES

Harriet Lee (1757–1851) and **Sophia Lee** (1750–1824) were born in London, the daughters of two actors. After their mother's death, Sophia looked after Harriet, their brother and three other sisters. With the profits from her comedy, *The Chapter of Accidents* (1780), she set up a girls' school in Bath which she and Harriet ran successfully from 1781 to 1803. Sophia wrote another play, *Almeyda, Queen of Granada* (1796), which closed after only four nights despite the fact that her good friend Sarah Siddons was cast in the leading role. She also wrote novels, including *The Recess* (1785) and *The Life of a Lover* (1804). Harriet Lee published two novels, *The Errors of Innocence* (1786) and *Clara Lennox* (1797), and two plays, *The New Peerage* (1787) and *The Mysterious Marriage* (1798). The sisters began writing *The Canterbury Tales* in 1797.

Harriett Gilbert is the author of six novels, *I Know Where I've Been*, *Hotels With Empty Rooms*, *An Offence Against the Persons*, *Tide Race*, *Running Away* and *The Riding Mistress*. She is the author, with Christine Roche, of *A Women's History of Sex* (Pandora Press, 1987).

MOTHERS OF THE NOVEL
Reprint Fiction from Pandora Press

Pandora is reprinting eighteenth-century novels written by women. Each novel is being reset in modern typography and introduced to readers today by contemporary women writers. The following titles in this series are currently available:

Self-Control (1810/11) by Mary Brunton
Introduced by Sara Maitland

Discipline (1814) by Mary Brunton
Introduced by Fay Weldon

The Wanderer, or Female Difficulties (1814) by Fanny Burney
Introduced by Margaret Drabble

Belinda (1801) by Maria Edgeworth
Introduced by Eva Figes

Patronage (1814) by Maria Edgeworth
Introduced by Eva Figes

Helen (1834) by Maria Edgeworth
Introduced by Maggie Gee

Secresy; or, The Ruin on the Rock (1795) by Eliza Fenwick
Introduced by Janet Todd

The Governess; or, Little Female Academy (1749) by Sarah Fielding
Introduced by Mary Cadogan

Munster Village (1778) by Lady Mary Hamilton
Introduced by Sarah Baylis

The Memoirs of Emma Courtney (1796) by Mary Hays
Introduced by Sally Cline

The History of Miss Betsy Thoughtless (1751) by Eliza Haywood
Introduced by Dale Spender

A Simple Story (1791) by Elizabeth Inchbald
Introduced by Jeanette Winterson

The Canterbury Tales (1797/99) by Harriet and Sophia Lee
Introduced by Harriet Gilbert

The Female Quixote (1752) by Charlotte Lennox
Introduced by Sandra Shulman

The Wild Irish Girl (1806) by Lady Morgan
Introduced by Brigid Brophy

The O'Briens and The O'Flahertys (1827) by Lady Morgan
Introduced by Mary Campbell

Adeline Mowbray (1804) by Amelia Opie
Introduced by Jeanette Winterson

Memoirs of Miss Sidney Bidulph (1761) by Frances Sheridan
Introduced by Sue Townsend

Emmeline (1788) by Charlotte Smith
Introduced by Zoë Fairbairns

The Old Manor Home (1794) by Charlotte Smith
Introduced by Janet Todd

The companion ot this series is *Mothers of the Novel: 100 Good Women Writers Before Jane Austen* by Dale Spender, a wonderfully readable survey that reclaims the many women writers who contributed to the literary tradition. She describes the interconnections among the writers, their approach and the public response to their work.

THE
CANTERBURY TALES

HARRIET AND SOPHIA LEE

Introduced by Harriett Gilbert

PANDORA

London   Boston   Sydney   Wellington

This edition first published by Pandora Press, an imprint of the Trade Division of Unwin Hyman, in 1989.

Introduction © Harriett Gilbert, 1989

All rights reserved. No part of this publication may be reproduced, stored in a retrieval system, or transmitted in any form or by any means, electronic, mechanical, recording or otherwise, without the prior permission of Unwin Hyman Limited.

PANDORA PRESS
Unwin Hyman Limited 15/17 Broadwick Street, London W1V 1FP

Unwin Hyman Inc
8 Winchester Place, Winchester, MA 01890

Allen & Unwin Australia Pty Ltd
P.O. Box 764, 8 Napier Street, North Sydney, NSW 2060

Allen & Unwin NZ Ltd (in association with the Port Nicholson Press)
60 Cambridge Terrace, Wellington, New Zealand

British Library Cataloguing in Publication Data

Lee, Harriet, *1757–1851*
 (Mothers of the novel).
 I. [The Canterbury tales. *Selections*]
 II. Title III. Lee, Sophia, *1750–1824*
 IV. Series
 823'.6
ISBN 0–86358–308–3

Typeset in 10 on 11 ½ point Ehrhardt
Printed and bound in Great Britain by
Cox & Wyman Ltd, Reading

CONTENTS

Introduction by Harriett Gilbert	*page*	vii
The author's address to the reader		xv
Preface by Harriet Lee to the 1832 edition		xvii
Introduction		xxi
The Clergyman's Tale. Pembroke		1
The German's Tale. Kruitzner		110
The Scotsman's Tale. Claudine		230
The Landlady's Tale. Introduction		270
The Landlady's Tale. Mary Lawson		281
The Friend's Tale. Stanhope		323
The Wife's Tale. Julia		360

INTRODUCTION

They weren't without arrogance, the Lee sisters. In her preface to the 1832 reissue of their story collection *The Canterbury Tales*, Harriet, the younger of the two authors, made clear in what ways she considered the work to have been a formal innovation.

'I think I may be permitted to observe,' she writes with the poise of someone who knows that she may observe what she likes, 'that when these volumes first appeared, a work bearing distinctly the title of "Tales", professedly adapted to different countries, and either abruptly commencing with, or breaking suddenly into, a sort of dramatic dialogue, was a novelty in the fictions of the day.'

This is hardly the voice of a woman alarmed or defensive at having made it into print. The majority of the Lees's forerunners may have shown their writing only to friends, or published it under assumed names for fear of losing their female 'character'; by 1832, however, not only was Harriet confident that the *Tales* were a popular and critical success but the place of women in the world of English letters had changed to a considerable degree.

What had happened was that the novel had been through a golden age. For half a century, from approximately 1780 to 1830, it had been, at one and the same time, the most popular, talked-about literary form and – because it was still very new – constantly vital and innovative, pushing and testing the limits of what it could achieve.

And in that period, unlike today, it was women who'd written more novels than men. Previously kept to the fringes of literature by their exclusion from knowledge of the classics, politics and religious theory, they'd poured in to this brave new form – in which theory could emerge from the observation and understanding of actual behaviour

Introduction

and develop directly with reference to human psychology – all of their energy and talent. It was they who had played the decisive role in determining the novel's structure, preoccupations and imaginative range. Indeed, although it is impossible to say which author wrote the *first* real novel, Mrs Aphra Behn is a strong contender for England – with her story of a noble slave, *Oroonoko*, published in 1688.

Through the following decades, as the form staggered on with uneven, toddler-like steps, there were certainly gifted men to offer it a hand. Daniel Defoe's *Robinson Crusoe* was published in 1719, Samuel Richardson's *Pamela* in 1740, Henry Fielding's *Joseph Andrews* in 1742.

At the same time, however, more and more women were defying the old expectation of their sex and helping the novel on its way. If their names don't come leaping unbidden to mind, it might be as well to remember the men – critics, academics, even publishers – who have subsequently hidden their achievements. But Penelope Aubin, Mary Collyer, Mary Hearne, Arabella Plantin... these are just some of the women pioneers whom Dale Spender in *Mothers of the Novel* (Pandora, 1986) has rescued from the grave into which they'd been tossed by traditional literary history.

For the half-century during which the Lees were creative, even male literary historians are forced to admit that women made the running. In his fine but not noticeably 'feminist' *Novels and Novelists* (Windward, 1980) Martin Seymour-Smith has devised a table called 'Major Works of Fiction': for the period from 1780 to 1830 he lists seven novels written by men and *ten* written by women. The latter consist of six works by that mistress of the form Jane Austen, Charlotte Smith's *The Old Manor House*, Ann Radcliffe's *The Mysteries of Udolpho*, Maria Edgeworth's *Castle Rackrent* and Mary Shelley's *Frankenstein*. Indeed, the pre-eminence of women was such that men of the period often felt it useful – for the first and last time until this decade – to publish their fictions under women's names and in what they believed to be a 'womanly' style.

Having said all this, I ought to make it clear that novels were still not approved of by the establishment. Written in the main by women and 'tradesmen' (in other words, not by gentlemen), they were seen by members of the ruling class as vulgar, trivial, morally subversive, absurd... in short, were accused of much the same vices as pop, for example, or TV today. Critics may have covered pages debating their merits; the public may have hurried to borrow them from the newly-formed lending libraries (purchase was often out of

Introduction

the question: a novel could cost as much as 13*s* 6*d*); but the old guard sneered and shuddered and wrinkled its nose.

Of course, then as now, its accusations were sometimes totally justified, but the flailing lack of discrimination was caused not by judgment but alarm. Even the best written, most intelligent, wittiest and best constructed novel was derided; even the most imaginatively daring, the most psychologically or socially perceptive. Because, even more than its clumsier sisters, *it undermined the status quo*.

Not only did novels give the middle classes (and, by the way, their servants) access to a world of ideas that had previously been governed by scholars and aristocrats, but often such fictions would be set in contemporary surroundings, would discuss current class and sexual relations and, centrally, current morality – all of this largely from the point of view not of upper-class men but of middle- or 'trading'-class women.

Such subversion! And it had the same effect – popular excitement on the one hand, establishment disgust on the other – as youth's invasion of the cultural domain in the 1950s and 1960s, or as women's *re*invasion of that sphere in the early 1970s.

This revolution was already rumbling when a couple of actors, John and Margaret Lee, gave birth in London to the first of six children, a daughter. It was 1750 when Sophia took breath – and among the books published the previous year had been John Cleland's novel *Fanny Hill*, Sarah Fielding's *The Governess* and, by Sarah's older brother Henry, *Tom Jones*.

How soon it was before Sophia became aware of such literary happenings it is, by now, impossible to know, but the circumstances of her childhood were such as to turn her eyes firmly in that direction. First, as I've said, she was the child of actors (her father a theatrical manager besides), which gave her an automatic admission not only to the worlds of literature and art, but probably to a wider, more liberal society than most of her peers.

Second, the Lees were never wealthy: a condition with which it is common for women to cope, where possible, by using their pens. And third, when Sophia was still quite young, the death of her mother not only compelled her to care for her younger siblings – Harriet, three other sisters and a brother – but almost certainly brought her much closer to her father. And this man, of whom little else is known, provided Sophia with an education at a time when women were usually left to scavenge for one where

ix

Introduction

they could – an education which was, in turn, passed on to the younger Lees.

Similar backgrounds produced a great many women writers of the late eighteenth/early nineteenth centuries: the need to earn a living, most obviously; but also the access to a father's erudition, worldly experience, creative support – combined with the withdrawal of a mother's understandably cautious and restraining hand. As Eva Figes has pointed out in *Sex and Subterfuge* (Macmillan, 1982), Maria Edgeworth, Fanny Burney, Charlotte, Anne and Emily Brontë all lost mothers early on in their lives.

This was not an *unambivalent* advantage. Paternal support and encouragement could gradually transform into shackles, with the need to please Daddy deterring the novelist from following creative paths of her own. (Maria Edgeworth was especially hobbled by her father's involvement in everything she wrote after the inventive *Castle Rackrent*.) Equally, a lack of money, the need to maximise royalties, could blinker a writer's imagination while spurring her productivity. That Sophia and, eventually, Harriet were freed from the worst of these double binds was due to a stroke of good luck: the very first work that Sophia had published was an overwhelming commercial success.

It was a comedy, a play called *The Chapter of Accidents*, and was published and produced in 1780 when Sophia was 30 and Harriet just 23. Gathering her profits, the older sister immediately founded a girls' school in Bath, invited Harriet to help her run it, and thus provided the two of them with an income for a couple of decades – provided them also with enough free time, between the teaching and the housekeeping, to develop their literary careers.

And develop them, adventurously, they did. Sophia it was who took the next step by publishing, in 1785, what is generally considered to be among the first historical novels, *The Recess*. Set in the reign of Elizabeth I, it used the then little practised device of mixing invented characters with such real-life figures as Mary Queen of Scots, Leicester, Norfolk and Sidney.

The following year, both sisters hit the bookstands: Sophia with a romantic novel called *Warbeck* and Harriet with *The Errors of Innocence*, a novel written in letter form and specifically critical of women's position in society. Then followed plays, with varying success: Sophia's tragedy *Almeyda, Queen of Granada* ran for only four nights, despite the fact that her friend Sarah Siddons, one of the century's most celebrated actors, was cast in the leading role; Harriet's comedy *The*

Introduction

New Peerage didn't do badly at all, but her *The Mysterious Marriage* was never produced.

It took until 1797 for Harriet's second novel, *Clara Lennox*, to appear; but that year was far more indelibly marked by the publication of Volume One of what was to become the sisters' crowning achievement: their jointly-written collection of stories *The Canterbury Tales*. Hugely popular, praised by the critics (including the poet Lord Byron), it eventually spread to five volumes and is, indeed, an impressive creation. Even those stories reprinted here, which represent something like half the original, range widely beyond what is normally considered the province of eighteenth-century women writers. Love and marriage most certainly feature, as do the niceties of social intercourse, but also revolution and war, murder and illegitimacy, history and ethical debate. And, as Harriet so proudly claimed, the form really was an innovation: paced to the speed of a three-act play as distinct from the leisure of a three-volume novel, if not quite the compact short story of today it was certainly one of its precursors.

Similarly, it looked back to the novel's roots. In her preface to the re-print of 1832, Harriet explains the collection's title thus: *The Canterbury Tales* were 'first called such merely in *badinage* between the authors, as being a proverbial phrase for gossiping long stories; certainly with no thought of blending them with the recollection of our great English classic [Chaucer]'. And surely there's some truth in the stories' owing a debt to fire-side narrations; yet merely by letting us know that she is familiar with Chaucer's great verse work (which the scholar Thomas Tyrwhitt had rescued from semi-obscurity just 50 years before) Harriet is also showing off both her education and the *written* lineage of her tales (a point reinforced by Sophia with her use of the Chaucerian 'yclept' for 'called' in her introduction to Volume One).

For the sisters were neither of them 'primitives': 'naive' artists of a quirky charm who might have been working in any culture at any period in history. As much as the far more famous Jane Austen (whose first book was published in 1811), or their contemporaries Maria Edgeworth, Fanny Burney and Ann Radcliffe, they were working consciously within and against a tradition. The Lees were, in other words, knowing experimental writers: as energetic and pushy as, for example, Fay Weldon, Angela Carter or Kathy Acker today.

The fact that they were developing a new and vivacious art form does mean that *The Canterbury Tales* don't possess the polished perfection of

Introduction

some later novels or short stories. 'The Clergyman's Tale', Sophia's main contribution to the present edition, is in fact pretty raw and rumbustious, more a galloping farm horse than a thoroughbred pony. As complicated in its 131 pages as any three-volume novel – with a maze of stories within stories within stories that can leave the reader feeling dizzy – its kidnappings, disinheritings, deaths, discoveries of long-lost relatives kick up every cliché of expression and sentiment going.

Through the dust, however, there emerges a theme which the rest of the collection develops: essentially, the middle-class conviction that 'virtue' derives not from birth but education. 'He, who was a fountain of knowledge,' sighs 'lovely Agnes' of the brother who gave her what education she has, 'graciously accommodated himself to my uncultivated capacity. Mutual love soon led us to unbounded confidence; and, while he flattered me with softening his soul, I gradually imbibed from it that high spirit of virtue, which, while it enables us to rise above the little evils of this little world, insensibly prepares us for the better.'

Harriet's 'The German's Tale' takes up the theme with more sinewy hands. This story – the one by which Byron was particularly impressed and on which he based his tragedy *Werner, or The Inheritance* – tells of the eventful journey home, through war-ravaged Silesia, of an exiled, spoilt and self-satisfied young nobleman. Parallel to his physical journey runs a journey towards understanding: notably, as he moves from being a dissolute and undutiful son to the painful responsibilities of fatherhood.

At one point in the tale, when Kruitzner has just taken lodgings with Michelli, the father of his future bride, Harriet writes: 'Michelli felt himself indeed interested alike by the situation and character of his new acquaintance, in whom he was surprised to find a degree of intelligence and knowledge not often to be met with even in those of maturer years; and, under the influence of a first impression, he placed to the credit of nature, and a love of study, what was in fact the result of a highly-cultivated education.' Contained in this sentence is far, far more than Sophia's simple equation: education + love = virtue. Harriet not only distinguishes between such 'culture' as the ruling classes could scarcely fail to acquire and the learning which those less privileged must work at, and out, for themselves; she understands also how easy it is, at first glance, to confuse them.

Introduction

Indeed, not only 'The German's Tale' but 'The Scotsman's Tale', 'The Landlady's Tale', 'The Friend's Tale' and 'The Wife's Tale' are alive with Harriet's perception and intelligence: her understanding not just of human nature, its contradictions and complexities, but of group psychology, the politics of class, sexual politics, philosophical debates and international events. (If, from her novels, you'd never guess that Jane Austen lived through the French Revolution and the Napoleonic Wars, Harriet Lee leaves you in no doubt that she did.)

And, yes, she is a fierce moralist: education should *not* be treated as a luxury; privilege should *always* be accompanied by duty; men who treat their young wives as accessories are little better than murderers; men who abuse unmarried women, then desert them when pregnant, the same... She is also, however, a restless stylist and formalist: her voice diving close to melodrama, then flying with wit and amusement; her pen nib scheming the debating points of 'The Friend's Tale' (nurture versus nature) then spattering anger and frustration at men with 'The Wife's Tale'.

Perhaps best of all is the way in which her insights, rages and laughter reach us so clearly – across almost 200 years – like the limpid ring of a glass that's been hit with a finger and goes on ringing.

Listen to this, from 'The Landlady's Tale':

He was one of those rattling sparks, sir, who dash on in life without looking to the right or the left, through a long lane of the maimed and the blind, whom they have made so; till, being come to their journey's end, they are obliged to cast their eyes back, and see the sad spectacle of human misery.

Or this 'lawyer joke' from the end of 'The Wife's Tale':

'And why did you not say at first that you came upon a good errand?'
'What could possibly make you think that I should come on any other?'
'Bless my soul, sir, I took you for a lawyer.'

Enough. Read the rest for yourself.

THE
AUTHOR'S ADDRESS
TO
THE READER

If you find my day-dreams as agreeable as I have done, we may henceforth recite Tales without going to Canterbury, and travel half the world over without quitting our own dear fire-sides. Should you be good-naturedly disposed, you will not inquire minutely where the travellers were picked up by whom the following stories are related; but will continue to ramble on, with me, through the regions of imagination, without much anxiety as to the object of the journey, provided the road prove but pleasant.

PREFACE
BY
HARRIET LEE

Some perplexity having arisen from the insertion of two names in the title-page of 'The Canterbury Tales', it was observed to me, that to prefix a short explanatory address, ascribing each tale to its distinct author, would be desirable in the present edition of them among the 'Standard Novels'; and I readily comply with the suggestion, since it allows me opportunity to make such mention of her who is not more[*] as may prove acceptable to the curiosity, or, perhaps, to a better and gentler feeling, in the reader. If I introduce particulars relative to myself, I hope they will be considered as belonging to the general subject.

The outline of the work was exclusively mine, and afforded me a convenient prospect of pursuing or discontinuing it, as circumstances might permit. I wrote the four first stories with great ardour and rapidity, chiefly to indulge the pleasure I always found in writing; yet, it must be owned, not without a latent, and (author-like) an increasing, hope that I might be fortunate enough to please the public. The stories were printed in one volume as soon as finished; and my hope was not disappointed, since the success of the work was such as to render a continuation desirable. For this, however, I was not altogether prepared; but a previous arrangement, made between my eldest sister and myself, afforded an auxiliary whose acknowledged talents left nothing to fear from the coalition, but that the second party might, as is often the case in coalitions, entirely supersede the preceding one.

---

[*] Sophia Lee, who died March 13th, 1824.

Preface

Sophia Lee, as the author of 'The Recess',* and of the comedy called 'The Chapter of Accidents', already held a distinguished place in public favour. The richness of invention, and the versatility of talent, which characterised those efforts of her pen, were again displayed in 'The Young Lady's Tale, or the Two Emilys'; and in 'The Clergyman's Tale, or Pembroke'. After contributing these, and the introduction inserted in the first volume, she declined taking any future share in the work, and left the additional volumes, whatever their number might prove, to me, 'in whose mind', as she smilingly observed, 'thick-coming fancies allowed no room for further copartnership.'

An interval, however, still elapsed between the publication of each succeeding volume: not from lack either of inclination or materials to proceed upon, but that 'carking cares', and necessary occupations, engaged the hours of both sisters; the eldest of whom had, from a very early age, supplied the place of a mother to the younger branches of her father's family, and became their after-guide in such active duties as left little leisure for the indulgence of a literary propensity. Nor was this a trifling sacrifice on her part; since her first works enjoyed such popularity as might have engaged a less affectionate character in a very different career from the simple one of domestic life. Taste and feeling, however, still retained their influence, and were shown in many poetical trifles, – written, indeed, without a direct view to publication, but from which I venture to select and present one.

SONG

Say, what is love? a fond day-dream,
Where nothing is, but all things seem;
Where souls in tender trances lie,
And passion feeds upon the eye.

A thought now soothes, and now alarms;
A sigh, a tear, a folly charms:
Why, Reason, why the slumber break?
Ah, spare the agony to wake!

These lines, musical in themselves, received additional grace from an air which was composed for them by the eldest of the accomplished daughters of Mrs Siddons.

---

* The first English romance that blended interesting fiction with historical events and characters, embellishing both by picturesque description. 'Cleveland', written, as I believe, by the Abbé Prévót, had precedence of all.

Preface

I now bid adieu to recollections that might engage me too far, and hasten to finish my much less interesting prosaic detail.

The publication of a third volume would probably, I thought, end 'The Canterbury Tales'. Yet a fourth appeared, containing the story of 'Kruitzner'; and the favour which that story found, both with general readers, and form the distinguished few whose mere approbation is fame,* brought forward 'More last words', – to quote the appropriate motto to a fifth volume. With this, 'The Canterbury Tales' closed; first called such merely in *badinage* between the authors, as being a proverbial phrase for gossiping long stories; certainly with no thought of blending them with the recollection of our great English classic.**

Before I finally dismiss the subject, I think I may be permitted to observe, that when these volumes first appeared, a work bearing distinctly the title of 'Tales', professedly adapted to different countries, and either abruptly commencing with, or breaking suddenly into, a sort of dramatic dialogue, was a novelty in the fictions of the day. Innumerable 'Tales' of the same stamp, and adapted in the same manner to all classes and all countries, have since appeared; with many of which I presume not to compete in merit, though I think I may fairly claim priority of design and style.

H.L.
Clifton, January, 1832

---

* That with which Lord Byron honoured it was very long after.
** Chaucer.

INTRODUCTION

There are people in the world who think their lives well employed in collecting shells; there are others not less satisfied to spend theirs in classing butterflies. For my own part, I always preferred animate to inanimate nature; and would rather post to the antipodes to mark a new character, or develop a singular incident, than become a Fellow of the Royal Society by enriching museums with nondescripts. From this account you, my gentle reader, may, without any extraordinary penetration, have discovered that I am among the eccentric part of mankind, by the courtesy of each other and themselves – yclept poets: a title which, however mean or contemptible it may sound to those not honoured with it, never yet was rejected by a single mortal on whom the suffrage of mankind conferred it; no, though the laurel wreath of Apollo, barren in its nature, had been twined by the frozen fingers of poverty, and shed on the brow it crowned her chilling influence. But when did it so? Too often destined to deprive its graced owner of every real good, by an enchantment which we know not how to define, it comprehends in itself such a variety of pleasures and possessions, that well may one of our number exclaim, –

> Thy lavish charter, Taste, appropriates all we see!

Happily, too, we are not, like *virtuosi* in general, encumbered with the treasures gathered in our peregrinations. Compact in their nature, they lie all in the small cavities of our brain; which are indeed often so small as to render it doubtful whether we have any at all. The few discoveries I have made in that richest of mines, the human soul, I have not been churl enough to keep to myself; nor, to say truth, unless I can find out some other means of supporting my corporeal existence than animal food, do I think I shall ever be able to afford that sullen affectation of superiority.

Introduction

Travelling, I have already said, is my taste; and to make my journeys pay for themselves my object. Much against my good liking, some troublesome fellows, a few months ago, took the liberty of making a little home of mine their own; nor, till I had coined a small portion of my brain in the mint of my publisher, could I persuade them to depart. I gave a proof of my politeness, however, in leaving my house to them; and retired to the coast of Kent, where I fell to work very busily. Gay with the hope of shutting my door on these unwelcome visitants, I walked in a severe frost from Deal to Dover to secure a seat in the stage coach to London. One only was vacant; and, having engaged it, 'maugre the freezing of the bitter sky', I wandered forth to note the *memorabilia* of Dover, and was soon lost in one of my fits of exquisite abstraction.

With reverence I looked up to the Cliff, which our immortal bard has, with more fancy than truth, described. With toil mounted, by an almost endless staircase, to the top of a castle, which added nothing to my poor stock of ideas but the length of our virgin Queen's pocket-pistol, – that truly *Dutch* present: cold and weary, I was pacing towards the inn, when a sharp-visaged barber popped his head over his shop-door, to *reconnoitre* the inquisitive stranger. A brisk fire, which I suddenly cast my eye on, invited my frozen hands and feet to its precincts. A civil question to the honest man produced, on his part, a civil invitation; and, having placed me in a snug seat, he readily gave me the benefit of all his oral tradition.

'Sir,' he said, 'it is mighty lucky you came across *me*. The vulgar people of this town have no genius, sir, – no taste: they never show the greatest curiosity in the place. Sir, we have here the tomb of a poet!'

'The tomb of a poet!' cried I, with a spring that electrified my informant no less than myself. 'What poet lies here? and where is he buried?'

'Ay, *that* is the curiosity,' returned he exultingly. I smiled: his distinction was so like a barber. While he had been speaking, I recollected he must allude to the grave of Churchill: that vigorous genius, who, well calculated to stand forth the champion of freedom, has recorded himself the slave of party, and the victim of spleen! So, however, thought not the barber; who considered him as the first of human beings.

'This great man, Sir,' continued he, 'who lived and died in the cause of liberty, is interred in a very remarkable spot, Sir. If you was not so cold and so tired, Sir, I could show it you in a moment.'

Introduction

Curiosity is an excellent great-coat: I forgot I had no other, and strode after the barber to a spot surrounded by ruined walls; in the midst of which stood the white marble tablet, marked with Churchill's name – to appearance, its appearance, its only distinction.

'Cast your eyes on the walls,' said the important barber: 'they once enclosed a church, as you may see.'

On inspecting the crumbling ruins more narrowly, I did, indeed, discern the traces of Gothic architecture.

'Yes, Sir,' cried my friend the barber, with the conscious pride of an Englishman, throwing out a gaunt leg and arm – 'Churchill, the champion of liberty, is interred *here*! – Here, Sir, in the very ground where King John did homage for the crown he disgraced!'

The idea was grand. In the eye of fancy, the slender pillars again lifted high the vaulted roof – *that* rang with solemn chantings. I saw the insolent legate seated in scarlet pride. I saw the sneers of many a mitred abbot. I saw, bare-headed, the mean, the prostrate king. I saw, in short, every thing but the barber, whom, in my flight, and swell of soul, I had out-walked and lost. Some more curious traveller may again pick him up, perhaps, and learn more minutely the fact.

Waking from my *rêverie*, I found myself on the Pier. The pale beams of a powerless sun gilt the fluctuating waves, and the distant spires of Calais; which I now clearly surveyed. What a new train of images here sprang up in my mind! borne away by succeeding impressions with no less rapidity. From the Monk of Sterne, I travelled up in five minutes to the inflexible Edward III. sentencing the noble burghers; and, having seen them saved by the eloquence of Philippa, I wanted no better seasoning for my mutton chop.

The coachman now showed his ruby face at the door, and I jumped into the stage, where were already seated two passengers of my own sex, and one of – would I could say, the fairer! But, though truth may not be spoken at all times, upon paper one, now and then, may do her justice. Half a glance discovered that the good lady opposite to me had never been handsome, and now added the injuries of time to the severity of nature. Civil but cold compliments having passed, I closed my eyes to expand my soul; and having fabricated a brief, poetical history of England, to help short memories, was something astonished to find myself tugged violently by the sleeve; and not less so to see the coach empty, and hear an obstinate waiter insist upon it we were at Canterbury, and the supper ready to be put on the table. It had snowed, I found, for some time; in consideration of which, mine host

Introduction

had prudently suffered the fire nearly to go out. A dim candle was on the table, without snuffers, and a bell-string hanging over it, at which we pulled; but it had long ceased to operate on that noisy convenience. Alas, poor Shenstone! how often, during these excursions, do I think of thee! Cold, indeed, must have been thy acceptation in society, if thou couldst seriously say –

> Who'er has travell'd life's dull round,
> Where'er his various course has been
> Must sigh to think how oft he found
> His warmest welcome at an inn.

Had the gentle bard told us, that in this sad substitute for home, despite of all our impatience to be gone, we must stay, not only till wind and weather, but landlords, postilions, and ostlers, choose to permit, I should have thought he knew more of travelling; and, stirring the fire, snuffing the candles, reconnoitring the company, and modifying my own humour, should at once have tried to make the best of my situation. After all, he is a wise man who does at first what he must do at last; and I was just breaking the ice, after having nursed the fire to the general satisfaction, when the coach from London added three to our party; and common civility obliged those who came first to make way for the yet more frozen travellers. We supped together, and I was something surprised to find our two coachmen allowed us such ample time to enjoy our little bowl of punch; when, lo! with dolorous countenances they came to give us notice that the snow was so heavy, and already so deep, as to make our proceeding either road dangerous, if not utterly impracticable.

'If that is really the case,' cried I mentally, 'let us see what we may hope from the construction of the seven heads that constitute our company.' Observe, gentle reader, that I do not mean the outward and visible form of those heads; for I am not amongst the new race of physiognomists, who exhaust invention only to ally their own species to the animal creation; and would rather prove the skull of a man resembled an ass, than, looking within, find in the brain the glorious similitude of the Deity. – An elegant author more justly conveys my idea of physiognomy in saying, 'Sensibilities ripen with years, and enrich the human countenance, as colours mount into a tulip.' It was my interest to be as happy as I could; and that can only be when we look around with a wish to be pleased; nor could I ever find a way

Introduction

of unlocking the human heart, but by frankly inviting others to peep into my own. – And now for my survey.

In the chimney corner sat my old gentlewoman a little alarmed at a coffin that had popped from the fire, instead of a purse: *ergo*, superstition was her weak side. In sad conformity to declining years, she had put on her spectacles, taken out her knitting, and thus humbly retired from attention she had long, perhaps, been hopeless of attracting. Close by her was placed a young lady from London, in the bloom of nineteen: a cross on her bosom showed her to be a Catholic, and a peculiar accent an Irishwoman: her face, especially her eyes, might be termed handsome; of those archness would have been the expression, had not the absence of her air proved that their sense was turned inward, to contemplate in her heart some chosen, cherished image. Love and romance reigned in every lineament.

A French abbé had, as is usual with gentlemen of that country, edged himself into the seat by the belle; to whom he continually addressed himself with all sorts of *petits soins*, though fatigue was obvious in his air, and the impression of some danger escaped gave a wild sharpness to every feature. 'Thou hast comprised,' thought I, 'the knowledge of a whole life in perhaps the last month: and then perhaps didst thou first study the art of thinking, or learn the misery of feeling!' Neither of these seemed, however, to have troubled his neighbour, an Englishman, who, though with a sort of surly good nature he had given up his place at the fire, yet contrived to engross both candles, by holding before them a newspaper where he dwelt upon the article of stocks, till a bloody duel in Ireland induced communication, and enabled me to discover that, in spite of the importance of his air, credulity, and a love of the marvellous, might be reckoned amongst his characteristics.

The opposite corner of the fire had been by general consent given up to one of the London travellers, whose age in infirmities challenged regard, while his aspect awakened the most melting benevolence. Suppose an anchorite, sublimed by devotion and temperance from all human frailty, and you will see this interesting aged clergyman: so pale, so pure was his complexion; so slight his figure, though tall; that it seemed as if his soul was gradually divesting itself of the covering of mortality, that when the hour of separating it from the body came, hardly should the greedy grave claim aught of a being so ethereal! – 'Oh, what lessons of patience and sanctity couldst thou give,' thought I, 'were it my fortune to find the key of they heart!'

Introduction

An officer in the middle of life occupied the next seat. Martial and commanding in his person; of a countenance open and sensible; tanned as it seemed by severe service, his forehead only retained its whiteness; yet that, with assimilating graceful manners, rendered him very prepossessing.

That seven sensible people – for I include myself in that description – should tumble out of two state-coaches, and be thrown together so oddly, was in my opinion an incident: and why not make it really one? I hastily advanced, and, turning my back to the fire, fixed the eyes of the whole company – not on my person, for that was no way singular – not, I would fain hope, upon my coat, which I had forgotten till that moment was threadbare: I had rather, of the three, imagine my assurance the object of general attention. However, no one spoke, and I was obliged to second my own motion.

'Sir,' cried I to the Englishman, who by the time he kept the paper certainly *spelt* its contents, 'do you find any thing entertaining in that newspaper.'

'No, Sir!' returned he most laconically.

'Then you might perhaps find something entertaining out of it?' added I.

'Perhaps I might,' retorted he in a provoking accent, and surveying me from top to toe. The Frenchman laughed – so did I; – it is the only way when one has been more witty than wise. I returned presently, however, to the attack.

'How charmingly might we fill a long evening,' resumed I with, as I thought, a most ingratiating smile, 'if each of the company would relate the most remarkable story he or she ever knew or heard of!'

'Truly we might *make* a long evening that way,' again retorted my torment the Englishman. 'However, if you please, we will wave your plan, Sir, till to-morrow, and then we shall have the additional resort of our *dreams*, if our memories fail us.' He now, with a negligent yawn, rang, and ordered the chambermaid. The two females rose of course; and in one moment an overbearing clown cut short 'the feast of reason, and the flow of soul.' I forgot it snowed, and went to bed in a fever of rage. A charming tale ready for the press in my travelling desk – the harvest I might make could I prevail on each of the company to tell me another – Reader, if you ever had an empty purse, and an unread performance of your own burning in your pocket, and your heart, I need not ask you to pity me.

Introduction

Fortune, however, more kindly than usual, took my case into consideration; for the morning showed me a snow so deep, that had Thomas à Becket condescended to attend at his own shrine to greet those who enquired for it, not a soul could have got at the cathedral to pay their devoirs to the complacent archbishop.

On entering the breakfast room, I found mine host had, at the desire of some one or other of the company, already produced his very small stock of books, consisting of the Army List, The Whole Art of Farriery, and a volume of imperfect Magazines: a small supply of mental food for seven hungry people. Vanity never deserts itself; I thought I was greeted with more than common civility; and having satisfied my grosser appetite with tea and toast, resumed the idea of the night before – assuring the young lady, 'I was certain, from her fine eyes, she could melt us with a tender story; and that the sober matron could improve us by a wise one:' a circular bow showed similar hopes from the gentlemen. The plan was adopted; and the exultation of conscious superiority flushed my cheek. I declined being the first narrator, only because I desired it too much: and, to conceal from observation the rage for pre-eminence burning in my heart, I made a philosophical and elegant exordium upon the *levelling principle*; ending with a proposal, that each person's story should be related as numbered lots might determine. On purpose to torment me, my old competitor, the Englishman, drew number one; the second lot, however, fortunately was mine; the third the Frenchman's, the fourth the Old Woman's, the fifth the Young Lady's, the sixth the Officer's, and the venerable Parson had the seventh.

I had now only one hope, which it must be owned was that the first speaker might *prove* as dull as I thought he looked. When, after a modest pause, he totally discomfited me by saying, 'that as he had been a great traveller, and in his various peregrinations had seen and heard many extraordinary things, the one most present to his memory should serve for the occasion.'

And now, courteous Reader, with some palpitations of the heart, I give up myself and my companions to your mercy. Forget me not when my turn comes, though it is that of the Traveller first to address you!

THE CLERGYMAN'S TALE
PEMBROKE

> Let your gentle wishes go with me to my trial; wherein if I be foiled, there is but one shamed that was never gracious; if killed, but one dead that is willing to be so – I shall do my friends no wrong, for I have none to lament me – the world no injury, for in it I have nothing; only in this world I fill up a place that may be better supplied when I have made it empty.
>
> *Shakespeare*

At a county meeting of Warwickshire gentlemen in the month of August, a proposal was made to shoot game in North Wales during the season next ensuing. Among those who joined to form the party, was Mr. Pembroke; a gentleman by situation entitled to lead in any pursuit he adopted, but without the least taste for the one in question, save that it was exercise. He had too feeling a mind not to discover that the associated company, with the train of servants, dogs and horses, must be intolerable grievance to the rustics, who had yet dared not complain. Game the party rarely could find; but the riotous enjoyment of luxurious suppers, and a boundless indulgence of the bottle, made the major part of the company what is rather indefinitely expressed by the term *jolly* – a mode of felicity it had never been the fortune of Mr. Pembroke to partake: - he often, therefore, stole from his associates, to seek in the sequestered and wild scenes around him an indulgence more congenial to his taste, and to ponder on a strange though common calamity that empoisoned the lot so many of his neighbours were for ever tempted to envy.

Mr. Pembroke was a younger branch of that celebrated family, which not valuing itself more on antiquity than achievements, had always proudly refused to bury *name* under *title*. A retired and literary taste, early discovered by Mr. Pembroke, had made his father, whose fortune was scanty, destine this son for the church; and after a due progress he was sent to Oxford, to finish his studies and take orders. With the solemn considerations of his future life, romantic visions often blended in the heart of the young man; and his circle of society was so confined that a cousin of his own name, as poor as himself, soon became their object. Nature had not been as niggardly as fortune to the lovers; therefore, in mutually pleasing, there was no other difficulty than the sweet doubt which it is almost happiness to know, though it is absolute felicity to end. A remote prospect of preferment was, however, all that flattered their wish of uniting; and till that uncertain good should be theirs, the enamoured pair cherished a tenderness which, while it governed the heart of the young lady, guided and elevated that of him she preferred. By the singular whim of a very distant kinsman, and a happy coincidence of both Christian and surnames, it was pointed out to Mr. Pembroke that he might claim, under a will made ere he was in existence, the large possessions of the famous, or rather infamous miser, Henry Pembroke of Farleigh – a lonely cipher in creation; who lived unbeloved, and died unlamented; having gratified the poor but single pride of his nature, in erecting, merely to fill up his hours, and tax the strength of those labourers whom he scantily paid, a magnificent mansion, the very worst room, in which he thought too good for himself. Hardly had he accomplished this sole labour of his almost animal existence, ere death enclosed him in a much smaller habitation; and he left his large possessions as an estate in fee to the lawyers rather than to his heirs, so questionable was his whimsical testament. By a happiness in his fortune, rather than any peculiar right, and the professional exertions of a counsel not more eminent for talents than a generous use of them, the young Henry Pembroke established his claim; and had no sooner taken possession of Farleigh and its domains, than he gratified his heart, and married his cousin. And now, then, he was surely happy. Ah, no! he soon became painfully sensible that the speck scarce seen in a character when contemplated through the medium of partiality, and at a distance, forces itself for ever on the eye when the object is contagious; and, when that object is beloved, in time spreads over even the heart. Mrs. Pembroke no sooner found an ample fortune added to that name she regarded with a childish veneration, than she buried a thousand merits under a single failing. Lovely in person, accomplished, and sensible, with a benevolence of nature that made her to everyone whom she thought inferior to herself a ministering angel, as such was she worshipped by her poorer neighbours; while to her equals, or superiors, her air became repulsive, her manners almost forbidding. Her husband was the last person to discover this foible, but not even he had influence enough over her to correct it. Happily, though the vicinity of Farleigh supplied many genteel associates, it had not any family entitled to dispute consequence with Mrs. Pembroke; of course she lived amicably with all, and beloved by many of her neighbours; but whenever the season for visiting London recurred, her miseries annually recommenced; and her *rights* in society became the only subject of her conversation, the unremitting cause of domestic contention and rage. By this single foible, she not only kept herself and servants, but her husband, on an eternal fret. After a thousand contentions that made Mr. Pembroke blush, and a thousand impertinencies which he was sometimes in danger of being obliged to defend, his lady declared the modes of a London life insupportable to her, and gave up her town-house as a needless expense. With a fond predilection for domestic society, and a right to every indulgence that fortune can give, Mr. Pembroke was, therefore, condemned to pass the few months he necessarily attended the house of commons in a paltry confined lodging in London, while the remainder of the year he spent in a home so magnificent as to make him but the more sensible of the folly he suffered by. Nor was the arrogance of the Londoners Mrs. Pembroke's only affliction. A few years after her marriage she began to suffer the *family* grief; and not having yet borne a child, she was obliged to conclude the noble name she inherited, for many generations renowned, would never be continued by herself. No medicine did she leave untried – no mineral water untasted, that was recommended as likely to enable her to bring an heir to the *ancient house* of Pembroke. Eighteen years had elapsed in vain hopes and new experiments, when, to the equal astonishments of herself and husband, Mrs. Pembroke was obviously pregnant. Farleigh was immediately half pulled down, and new nurseries adjoining to her own apartments erected for the expected stranger, with every modern improvement which architects recommended, or her reading had suggested. The appointed time made Mrs. Pembroke mother of – a girl. Hardly had she gratitude enough to thank God for her own safety, or a living child, so mortified was she at not having borne a boy. Her husband, surprised to see himself in reality a father, felt no want of a son, while clasping the infant Julia to his bosom; and the mother at length reconciled herself to the cruel disappointment. Miss Pembroke was committed to the care of her nurse and maids, with an almost regal parade: – before she could walk, her anxious mother lost whole sleepless nights in considering what other misses she could with propriety visit; and, before she could speak, who it was possible she could, without derogating from her birth, marry. Mr. Pembroke was soon made sensible it was not proper for him at all times and seasons to run in and out of the apartment of Julia; and he had generally the ill luck to be too early or too late in seeking her company in the garden; for the apprehensive mother kept a watch even upon the sun, lest he should rudely visit the delicate complexion of Miss Pembroke.

Accustomed soon to submit to what he could not approve, the liberal mind of the father saw in this childish pride and weak anxiety a thousand dangers growing with the infant. With more eagerness than he ever prayed for one child, did he now implore the saving blessing of a second, that the hopes and attentions of his wife might at least be divided: – of this he, however, found no probability; and he too fondly loved the mother of his Julia to pain her by a secret or illicit attachment. – *Julia*, therefore, *her Julia* – *Miss Pembroke* rather – to all human appearance was the sole heiress of Farleigh: – the doating mother daily assured the servants of this: they circulated the assurance among the neighbours; and all with one voice enforced it to the very child when her mind became equal to comprehending the term.

Accustomed to ruminate on these domestic errors, and probable evils, Mr. Pembroke, as he grew into life, acquired a pensive abstracted air, and a habit of wandering alone. During this shooting excursion nothing had occurred to call forth the social principle, still less any partial sensibility, in the generous soul of Mr. Pembroke, and his thoughts insensibly sunk into their habitual channel. He found himself thoroughly tired; and taking his horse early one morning, he separated not only from his friends, but his servants, to follow without choice the path before him – it led to rich and solitary scenery; yet the hanging cots of the peasants on ridges of the mountains sometimes added the softer shades of life to those almost savage. The woods soon sheltered him from the observation of his jolly party, and he found even loneliness enjoyment. Yet the beauties of nature, which his eye dwelt upon, only shared his contemplations with his own peculiar destiny; and even while his senses luxuriously partook of pleasure, his heart was pinched to the core by a hopeless, a secret vexation. To have Julia, his lovely his amiable Julia, fostered in arrogance, while yet too young to rise into dignity, was indeed a cruel reflection. Yet how was it to be prevented?

The rude path worn by the cattle on the side of the mountain was overhung at intervals by red crags of rock, and at others by wildly spreading oaks; while here and there an humble hut exhibited the promise of society, which it could hardly be said to supply: from these the playful babes ran in and out, almost in a state of nature, and seemed, like the blossoms around them, to ripen on the breath of heaven. While gazing on a cluster of these young ones, it suddenly crossed Mr. Pembroke's mind that could he obtain, or purchase, a boy, by presenting it to his wife as his own, he should at once indirectly check the weak pride that shocked him, and by limiting her hopes of Julia's fortune, oblige her, in the education of a child so dear, a little to attend to his opinion. He recollected with surprise and pleasure that he was alone, and it was the first time for many years he had ever been so. Secure, by this means, that no prying domestic could publish the truth, he resolved to attempt obtaining an infant boy, to whom his patronage, and a liberal education, would eventually make an ample amends for the maternal endearments of which he must necessarily deprive him.

At this juncture a fine chubby-faced boy peeped over a crag just above his head, and shouting, gaily clapped his hands, and ran away. Mr. Pembroke hastily alighted, and hanging the bridle of his horse over an antique stump of a tree, mounted the rude steps cut in the rock, and soon saw at the door of a miserable cot a little withered old woman knitting; while, in the house, one of the same sex, but younger, was distributing a scanty breakfast to five children, of whom the boy in question seemed to be the third. On finding he was neither the youngest, nor the elder, Mr. Pembroke was persuaded he would prove the one with whom the mother would soonest consent to part: – he therefore addressed the poor woman in the most ingratiating terms; but was in a manner confounded on finding she did not understand him, and replied in a tongue to which he was no less a stranger. He now tried to engage the regards of the children; won them to play with his watch-chain; and placing its appendage to the ear of each, delighted in the innocent surprise which they all united to express in the same unintelligible manner. Even their mother modestly drew near to survey the ticking wonder; and Mr. Pembroke saw with astonishment that his own country could afford beings as wholly unversed in the improvements of polished life as the savages of America. Of gold and

The Canterbury Tales

its importance the poor woman had, however, a vague idea, by the air with which she surveyed a well-filled purse which he had inadvertently put up when he left home, and till this moment found a troublesome companion. Gladly throwing it into the lap of the careworn matron, he thought his view accomplished, and the boy, whom he now took in his arms, hence forward his own. Here he, however, erred. Nature, most active in the most ignorant, made the mother, when she learned from this action his design, fly into a transport of fear and fury: throwing back the purse, she appeared ready to second her incomprehensible oration with blows; Mr. Pembroke, therefore, judged it wise hastily to remount his horse, and pursue his way down the path of the mountain. As is natural, in all cases of disappointment, he sought, and found, every possible argument that might console him. 'How,' said he, 'had I obtained this boy, could I ever have gained his affections? What babe have I ever loved like my own sweet Julia! Nature, true, though indefinable, in all her operations, binds the parent to the child, and the child to the parent, by a ligament too fine for human art to form, or break. Yet, could I once have a son, how sweetly might my remaining years pass away – in guiding, guarding, loving him, as well, though more rationally, as my wife does her daughter.'

Mr. Pembroke's attention was suddenly detached from these contemplations by the exquisite beauty of the solitude into which he had at length sunk. The road was cut through a woody dell; while jutting hills on either side half embowered him in variety of verdure, slightly tinted with the early hues of autumn. This beautiful road meandered in its course like a river; and the enclosing hills changed their appearance at every step his horse made: now clothed to the round tops with velvet verdure; now only broken crags of richly shaded rock; now overhung with lofty woods. The dewy freshness of the morning improved the romantic charm of the scene; for while the one enchanted the sense, the other refreshed it. That intuitive elegance and refinement, which enables some minds to give half the graces they discover, made Mr. Pembroke check his horse; and sweetly loitering at every new turn, survey with regret that which he could no longer continue to behold. He was now in the very depth of the dell. An antique grey rock seemed cleft by the club of some giant, and, hanging over his head, discharged a mountain-torrent, which, foaming across the way, rushed along a stony moss-grown bed, with a meandering course similar to that of the road. More curiously surveying the impending rock, he perceived a plank thrown as a bridge over the fall of water, from one point of stone to the other, with a slight balustrade; but so tottering and aerial appeared the whole construction, that Mr. Pembroke rather concluded it to be an object from the window of some unseen dwelling than erected for any accommodation to man. Goats hung browzing about the bridge; and the whole wild scene struck him as so picturesque and interesting, that, alighting, he rudely sketched the outline in his pocket-book, resolving to employ the evening in finishing the drawing while yet the objects lived to his imagination.

Again on horseback, the turn of the ground shut from his eyes the road and brook that had so charmed them. He had, not, however, proceeded far on his way, when he was roused by a deadly shriek of a human voice. He started – listened – but it was not repeated. Convinced that he had not passed any vestige of a human habitation, he was again proceeding, when a strong conviction that the cry could not proceed from an animal, struck on his recollection. The mere possibility that the bridge had endangered some human being, made him feel it his duty to return and satisfy his mind. The pool formed at the foot of the rock, by the fall of the streamlet, was so overgrown with bushes, that it was not easy for Mr. Pembroke to penetrate through them; but how did he rejoice in his humane exertion, when he found that it would save the life of a fellow-creature. Close under the rock, on its face, he beheld a child, either stunned by the fall or choked by the water. With the crook of his whip he caught the petticoats of the babe, and drew it near enough to take it up. Laden with the precious burden, he again forced his way through the brake. The usual means soon made the infant disgorge a quantity of water, and its kind preserver tenderly chafed its little hands and temples. Yet he feared his cares were too late, as the only signs of life he could discover were a faint warmth, and almost imperceptible motion about the heart. Apprehending its little head was hurt, he threw up a profusion of rich auburn ringlets which hung over a face that, though burnt by the sun, appeared a model of beauty. A slight contusion was discernible on the temple of the lovely boy, for such Mr. Pembroke found his *protégé* to be. Happily he had in his pocket a hunter's bottle of brandy, which his wife ever carefully ordered his servant to put there; and pouring a little of it down the throat of the child, he used some to bathe the swelling. Still the lovely infant continued motionless. Mr. Pembroke anxiously looked for some vestige of a dwelling, but in vain: never was scene more solitary! He hallooed; but the echo of his own voice was the only sound which reached his ear. Distressed at the idea that the precious babe might die for want of proper assistance, he now lamented having dropped his company and servants. And who could the sweet boy be? Lovely as a babe of paradise, yet clad in the raiment of poverty; – even his little feet were without shoes, and cut by the flint of the rock. While exerting himself to wring the infant's wet clothes, ah! whispered his heart, if Heaven should have heard my prayer, and given me this boy to accomplish my view, how happy will I make him! It is plain, whoever this child belongs to, his parents can hardly maintain him; yet Heaven, that denies me a son of my own, has given to these peasants a Grecian Cupid. But while I thus commune with myself, may I not suffer the blessing to escape me, and the babe to perish for want of a surgeon? Mounting his horse again, with the lifeless child before him, nestled close under his coat, Mr. Pembroke hastened onward, vainly hoping that each turn of the road would bring him to a village or town, and no longer finding any charm in sequestered scenery; but after descending another irregular mountain, he saw only a barren moor, across which the road lay. His patience was nearly exhausted, when happily, nature did her own work, and relieved him from all fear on the infant's account. The brandy which the little creature had insensibly imbibed threw into his cheeks a richer crimson than usual; and opening at last a pair of beautiful black eyes, he stared confusedly at Mr. Pembroke, and, bursting into tears, demanded vehemently some unknown person, in the same unintelligible tongue that had already embarrassed his protector. That gentleman now seriously reprobated the supineness of the clergy, and the negligence of the schoolmasters, who ought long since to have made English the only language in the King's dominions; yet satisfying himself, from this mark of infantine ignorance, that the boy his heart already adopted was, however, eminently endowed by nature, only the son of a herdsman, he no longer made it a question whether he should hence forward call him his own. In his diurnal stores he had some biscuits and spiced bread, with which he sought to calm the little agitations that a moment produces, a moment disperses, at the happy age when reflection points not the pang. Of the first the babe partook with a heartiness that showed his breakfast had been scanty; then, playing with the rest, he would in turn feed his benefactor: at intervals, hiding his lovely head under the protecting coat, then archly peeping it out again with smiling irresistible confidence and fondness. This child *may*, perhaps, love me, cried Mr. Pembroke, pressing him yet closer; – yes; this child *will* love me, for he is too young to be sensible of any tie stronger than that my heart now forms between us. 'Precious smiler!' added he, kissing the beautiful eyes of the endearing infant, 'thou shalt be my own Henry – my Henry Pembroke! – I will join thy hand to Julia's as a brother; and to the last hour of my life shalt thou find father, mother, friend, in the man to whom Heaven itself surely has given thee!'

Every moment confirmed this generous resolution. Those short sobs and imperfect moanings of the interesting babe, that seemed to spring from the probable loss of a maternal bosom to lean on, now gave way to exquisite delight. Mr. Pembroke almost fancied a horse must be a new object to his *protégé*: yet, soon familiar with it, the child threw one of his graceful limbs over its neck; and with sweet mimickry he too would manage it, he too would stroke its mane, and lavish fond caresses; till, quite tired out, his little head sunk against Mr. Pembroke's bosom, where fatigue soon threw him into a deep sleep.

In this situation, the travellers rode into a small town, where alighting, Mr. Pembroke retired to a chamber, and putting with his own hands the sleeping Cupid to bed, he hastily summoned both a surgeon and a tailor; the former having declared the contusion trifling, and the limbs of the babe unhurt, the latter measured him as he slept for a masculine habit, which, for a double payment, he agreed to sit up all night to make.

The wish of knowing who the child at intervals yet moaned for had wholly vanished from the mind of Mr. Pembroke, since it now included a discovery of his origin, which, strangely qualifying with his own conscience, he secretly determined *not* to know. Every person in this inn spoke Welsh, for which reason he would not suffer one of the servants to come into the chamber, rather choosing to sleep with the babe himself. The flood of tears, and new demands of the child on missing some one, when he first waked, were at once, however, forgotten, when Mr. Pembroke produced his fine new Boy's habiliments in the morning. Wholly taken up with this important change and acquisition, the babe displayed a grace and manly spirit that bound his generous benefactor for ever to his fate.

A postchaise was ordered, into which Mr. Pembroke lifted his little treasure, and hastily drove towards Warwickshire; having sent back a Welsh lad to order home his suite from the mountains. The apprehension he at first had of the child's addressing strangers now gave place to a degree of surprise, at perceiving the terror he always showed on the approach of unknown persons; when he never failed

The Canterbury Tales

eagerly to fly to those arms which fondly folded him, grateful for the generous confidence.

It was not till the travellers were fairly out of Wales that Mr. Pembroke found himself at leisure enough to consider the difficulty of disposing of the little creature, for whose future welfare he had voluntarily made himself wholly responsible. He, on reflection, diverged from the line to his own house to put up at the Swan at Stratford-upon-Avon, which was among the demesnes of Farleigh. Mrs. Fenton, who, with her husband, had long been among his tenants, was herself a mother, and readily took to her good graces the little unintelligible Welshman. She summoned both her sons from school to play with and teach him English. Mr. Pembroke found, on examining those boys, that they were in so good a train for education, as to determine him to place Henry with them, and the same master. That the lovely child might have a right to the name he was resolved to give him, Mr. Pembroke requested Mr. and Mrs. Fenton to answer for him at the font, where he himself attended, and saw the interesting stranger registered by the name of Henry Pembroke. The good folks at the Swan melted into tears when they found the squire was 'so main good to his little by-blow.' Mr. Pembroke, with hardly less emotion, recommended him to their kindness, and implored Heaven to render him affectionate and grateful to his *fond father*. Having seen the sweet boy provided with every necessary, and established a strict intercourse with Mrs. Fenton and the schoolmaster, his benefactor departed for Farleigh.

An absence so unusual as the first surprised Mrs. Pembroke; its strange continuance at Stratford distressed her: nor could she forbear mingling some reproaches with the welcome her heart yet gave her husband. Julia knew only indulgence, felt only joy, and, hanging round the neck of her dear, dear papa, implored him to stay with her for ever and ever. The tender father felt shocked at recollecting the mortifying check her mother's error must subject to endure. Not that his tenderness for his daughter had suffered any diminution; his liberal heart was large enough to contain both Julia and the interesting Henry.

He was so near Stratford, that he had often occasion, and always opportunity, to visit Henry; nor did he ever see him without renewing his thanks to Heaven for singling him out to save so striking, so superior a creature. The affectionate boy was told the arms he flew into were those of a father, and soon found English enough to impart to the beloved visitor all his little joys and sorrows; but with the

Welsh language he seemed to lose all recollection of those to whom he had spoken it. In reality, the age he had now reached, with the change in his dress, the variety of scenes and objects, together with the busy though uniform duties of a school-life, had at once effaced whatever had been impressed on his infant mind, which was in too crude a state to know more than wants when Mr. Pembroke found him; whose generosity cherished those first into wishes, which his fondness delighted to gratify. The more dear the boy became, the more difficulty did the nominal father find in avowing that title, lest he should be obliged to withdraw to a certain degree from the endearments of the child, or see Mrs. Pembroke's jealousy and disgust embitter the sweet boy's life, and perhaps his own. Almost forgetting the object he at first had in view, he half resolved to bury the secret in his bosom, and by educating Henry at a greater distance from the family, keep his existence for ever from his lady's knowledge.

The question was, however, only one to his own bosom: for not a being around him was ignorant of the claim he had given the young Henry to his name; nor did any one doubt the child's natural right to it. The groom sent the tidings through the maids to Mrs. Pembroke's and Miss Julia's own women; who felt so much indignation at finding the latter had a rival in her father's affection, as to venture hinting this painful tale in Mrs. Pembroke's hearing. Though pride made that lady command them both to be silent, she could not, alas! 'unknow' what they had told her: – the conviction sunk deep: for even her neighbours, as if impatient to convince her that she had no more power to fix her husband's faith than themselves sent her in one day three anonymous letters; various in spelling and style, but agreeing in matter. Each separately told her that Mr. Pembroke spent his whole time at the Swan at Stratford, where he kept a pretty bar-maid and had by her a bastard son. The pride which made Mrs. Pembroke a troublesome member to society prevented her from becoming a torment to her husband: she burnt the letters without mentioning them, silenced the servants, and conducted herself with a dignified mildness towards Mr. Pembroke. But though the torch of jealousy was turned inward, it was not extinguished: the cruel flame preyed on her very vitals. Constraint, sadness, nervous complaints, tremulous anguish, at length proved to the husband that his wife had found or felt the secret, and it became the least pain he could give her to avow it. A word on her part concerning his absence drew from a heart all her own the preconcerted tale by which he was resolved to abide: –

'a hunting match – a country inn, a light, but lovely girl, who was determined to seduce him; – intoxication – a moment of folly – an age of repentance – an angel boy whom the mother had died to give birth to, and whom it was his duty to love and provide for.' Mrs. Pembroke heard this recital with a variety of emotions: – the man of her choice – the delicate, the refined Henry, – he whom alone she loved, – had then been capable of a gross and vulgar inclination, and for a low and vulgar woman too! – strange! incomprehensible! A moment's thought, however, reminded her that this vulgar creature was dead, and she had no longer the mortification of sharing her husband's affections with such a rival. But then the child was yet living. Heavens! and could Miss Pembroke be levelled one moment in the heart of her father with the offspring of a bar-maid! Mr. Pembroke's penetrating eye saw in that of his wife the whole chain of her ideas; and as it was only necessary to moderate her pride, he soothed her heart with new vows of faith, no more to be broken – of love that should last for ever. She, something fretfully, replied, that since the thing had happened, and could not now be otherwise, she should forgive him: though much she wondered that he could forgive himself. What would *he* have thought, had she for one moment descended to turn her eyes from himself to his groom? She hoped, however, that it did not form a part of his view to educate the poor wretched infant on a footing with Miss Pembroke. Should the boy hereafter turn out well, she might, perhaps, be brought to countenance him; and she should get her uncle in the Indies to push his fortune there: but that must be on the express condition that he never attempted to take the name her daughter and the heiress of their house bore, since that could only be perpetuated by her husband's assuming it. 'Do you recollect, madam,' cried Mr. Pembroke, coldly withdrawing the arms that a moment before fondly clasped her, 'that you speak to the father of Henry? – Forget not either that I can give a child so beloved more than the name of Pembroke: correct this intolerable arrogance in yourself – check it early in Julia – educate her more humbly than heretofore; and when I see how she adorns the vaunted name of Pembroke, I shall better know what share of my fortune to bestow on the dear boy, who has no friend on the earth but myself. I shall not trouble you to procure him the patronage of your uncle: he will not need any, while Heaven spares him a father.'

Confirmed by this conversation in the propriety of checking the aspiring haughtiness of his wife, Mr. Pembroke no longer sunk the name or supposed rights of Henry among his own family and dependents: – he soon found it right to remove him to a more expensive and improving school, where, under a clergyman of the first manners and information, he saw the youth rapidly acquiring all that could either qualify him for society, or embellish it.

Accustomed, at length, to admit a tie to which she found it impossible to object, Mrs. Pembroke's tenderness for her husband returned in all its force. She sighed to think that Julia had a partner in her father's heart; but satisfied she herself had not any, she relied on his acting generously towards his legitimate child. To judge what was to be expected, she hinted a wish to 'see the poor unhappy boy.' A word was sufficient: for Mr. Pembroke longed to make his Henry an inmate at Farleigh: and despite of prejudice, his lady soon saw in all their force the charms and mental graces of Henry. 'That I should ever wish to have been the mother of a bar-maid's son!' cried Mrs. Pembroke, turning to throw herself into the arms of her husband. 'But is not this lovely child the son, too of my Henry?' The little Julia, enchanted to have got a brother, she knew not how, entwined her arms every moment round his neck, and he amply returned her infantine caresses.

Henry from this moment became a part of the family; and as Mrs. Pembroke promised never to refer to the misfortune of his birth, and faithfully kept her word, it was wholly dropped among the domestics. Mr. Pembroke heard from that time more of his daughter, and less of his heiress; nor was this tender condescension in the partner of his life lost on him. He no longer held up Henry to her as the rival of Julia, whose rights he regarded as inviolate: always declaring that her brother should, at a proper age, embark in whatever liberal profession he might prefer, and derive no more from himself that an income would give him safety in launching into life.

The amiable Julia, as her years increased, saw the situation of Henry in a more interesting point of view. Her maid, affectionate but ignorant, had early informed her of her own advantages, and the humiliation annexed to her brother's birth. Far from exulting in her superior rights, as Julia grew old enough to estimate, she learnt to blush for them; and took delight in giving the lead on all occasions to Henry, from whose more improved understanding she derived infinite advantages. This was, indeed, a recompence to her father. What could he desire, but to see this generous principle actuating the soul of his Julia, and the son he had adopted so worthy to excite it? The purest peace and pleasure seemed to have fixed their abode at Farleigh, when an unforeseen occurrence put them both to flight in a moment.

The day that gave Julia to the world had been, from its first return, annually celebrated in a sumptuous manner by her fond mother. That which made her fourteen demanded more than usual consideration, and all the neighbouring young families were invited to a *fête champêtre*, at which Julia with her brother were to preside; while the various parents formed a separate party. The latter were yet in the dining parlour, when Master Vernon rushed in with a swelled forehead and a bloody nose, to claim his mother's protection from the fury of Henry. The youth in question followed, though apparently without any further hostile intention. Mr. Pembroke, vexed at seeing the pleasure of the young ones thus broken in upon, and particularly hurt by this breach of hospitality and decorum on the part of Henry, threatened hereafter to call him to a severe account for the insult to Master Vernon. 'I know of none, father,' returned Henry, 'committed by me. Master Vernon, because he was a great hulking fellow, thought he might haul and kiss Miss Pembroke, whether she would or no. She called on me to protect her, but he would not let her go – so I knocked him down – that's all.' 'No, that is not all,' cried his sobbing antagonist, whose face his mamma was tenderly dabbing with her cambric handkerchief. 'Well, if I must tell the rest,' sullenly added Henry. 'I must.' 'Ay, do young man,' said the incensed Mrs. Vernon, in a flame: – 'my Frank is the gentlest, dearest creature in the world!' 'He knows how to give a provocation, though he does not know how to take a punishment.' rejoined Henry. 'I am sure, angry as my father seems he would not wish me to allow any body's son to call his a bastard – a base-born brat.' What became of Mr. Pembroke at these words? He pressed the indignantly glowing face of the gallant boy to his bosom, while his own was suffused with even a deeper scarlet. Mrs. Vernon completed the distress of both by a coarse-minded apology for her dear Frank's coming out with this unlucky truth. The bright eyes of Henry, now fixed in astonishment at the *éclaircissement* and now flashing fire at the manner of it, turned from his father to the lady, from the lady to his father. Seeming at length to recover utterance – '*Am* I then indeed a bastard, sir?' cried he to Mr. Pembroke: – 'only tell me that – *am* I indeed a base-born beggar's brat?' 'This matter must be discussed hereafter,' returned that gentleman in a faltering voice, and with a disorder that struck conviction, like a dagger, through the heart of Henry. The tears which his pride had hitherto suppressed, now fell in torrents from his eyes: – he raised them and his innocent hands in speechless reproach to heaven; then fondly clasping his father, ran abruptly out of the room.

The necessity of appeasing an ignorant woman, with other attentions to his guests, had a little withdrawn Mr. Pembroke's thoughts from this painful occurrence, when now Julia, with hardly less perturbation, made her appearance, to inquire of her father where he had sent Henry; as the whole young party waited only for him to begin the ball. This question produced a general alarm, but no information. Henry, after a minute inquiry, was not to be found; – the gaiety of the day vanished with him – Julia cried herself sick – her mother was solely intent on soothing her – Mrs. Vernon, miserable at her son's disfigured face – and Mr. Pembroke, half distracted, lest the high spirit of Henry should produce any further ill consequence. All the servants ran different ways, inquiring for him; but the gardener, who particularly loved, was determined to seek, till he found, the truant. The probable protectors of the boy were not so numerous as to perplex those in pursuit; and Henry's humble friend at once traced him to the Swan at Stratford.

Mrs. Fenton with great surprise greeted the faithful inquirer, and informed him Master Henry was at that moment fast asleep; having arrived early in the morning (he too probably walked half the night), with swoln eyes and blistered feet. He then immediately embarrassed Mrs. Fenton with questioning her closely about his birth. Her answers were, however, far from soothing his feelings, or satisfying his pride. He stood a while quite aghast and silent, then sadly sighed, and faintly repeated, 'The illiberal scoundrel was in the right, and I have no friend but Almighty God! – to him them,' cried he, falling on his knees in a passion of tears, 'do I commend myself, and abjure any other father!' Mrs. Fenton now persuaded him to bathe his weary feet and retire to bed.

The gardener, holding it wise to stay with the youth, had at once despatched a messenger to relieve Mr. Pembroke's anxiety; and Henry, on awaking, learned from his sorrowful friend Mrs. Fenton, that the trusty Thomas had been sent to attend him home. 'No, madam,' replied the gallant boy, 'I have no home – I know not how to blush before my Father's servants! If he was ashamed to marry my mother, it is a punishment imposed on him to blush before the son, to whom he has given an ignominious being!' And blush Mr. Pembroke did; for, though in another room, he lost not a syllable of the noble boy's spirited language. So elevated a pride could not but add to Henry's merits in the eyes of his benefactor; yet how was he to soothe it? He sometimes meditated disclosing the whole affecting truth: but would the youth, who could not brook ranking as an extraneous branch of a noble and affluent family, endure to be told he sprang from beggary, and was reared by compassion? Perhaps, the fear of losing his hold on Henry's affections, rather dictated this caution to Mr. Pembroke than the apparent consideration for the youth's pride; since even while unresolved what to tell, or what to hide, he hastily broke in, and catching the dear exhausted youth in his arms, was choked with a variety of emotions. Henry ardently clasped his only friend, without daring to lift his pious eyes to his face lest they should behold there the shame of a parent. 'I complain not, my father,' sobbed he, clasping Mr. Pembroke yet closer: – 'no, bitter must be your feeling already, that you gave me not a right to the name you never denied me. Yet this insulted, illegitimate Henry knows not how to dishonour it. An indignity like that of yesterday I never can again endure. *Name* I now too certainly know I have not; but a determined spirit sometimes rises above the injustice of fortune, and makes one for itself. That I may be enabled to return to you without blushing, let me have your blessing, your prayers, my beloved father – never till that hour shall I see Farleigh – never more behold my sister. Yet tell our Julia I will strain every nerve to learn how in future to protect her from insult, – myself from ingnominy.'

Mr. Pembroke flattered himself that in a few days these irritated feelings would subside, and he should recover his influence with the youth. On the contrary, a fixedness of conduct took place in Henry of the first transports of anger, which impressed his nominal father as something almost unnaturally noble. When further urged to go home, – 'Never, my father,' returned the gallant boy, 'till I have been a soldier; – I will be only a soldier – discard me not unblessed – bestow on me a sword, and leave me to carve my own fortune.

Mr. Pembroke soon found a resolution that never seemed to enter the youth's head, till this unlucky brawl, invincible. The irritation of immediate injury subsided; but a melancholy, insurmountable, determination succeeded. It was at length agreed that Henry should no more be urged to revisit Farleigh, and his benefactor accompanied him to London; in the vicinity of which the youth was placed at a military academy of eminence. Henry had too true a taste for science in general to confine himself to tactics; and his early days were so devoted to literature, as to fill his mind with whatever might make his future life, distinguished and happy.

It was now discovered by Julia that she wanted more eminent masters than the neighbourhood of Farleigh afforded; and the delicate state of health Mrs. Pembroke suddenly fell into made all the punctilios she had formerly insisted on in London no longer of importance in her eyes. The family again passed part of every year there; and Henry had soon the sorrowful but sweet indulgence of blending his filial tears with those of Julia for the approaching fate of her valuable mother. That no secret anxiety might imbitter the hour of mortality, Mr. Pembroke generously executed a deed of trust, ensuring all his possessions, after his own death, to the darling daughter of both allotting to Henry only a small estate of five hundred a year: the right of survivorship, should Julia die without issue, he, however, wisely secured to him. The near approach of death, that awful levelling principle, had almost wholly removed from Mrs. Pembroke's mind the poor pride by which it was once actuated; and the high spirit of Henry had impressed her with a very partial regard for him. – 'Ah, madam!' cried that youth, when first they met in London, 'I knew not till the moment of insult half my obligations to you; but can I ever forget them?' – He knelt; and, kissing her hand, pressed it with reverence to his heart. 'And Julia too!' added he, remembering well he owed no less to the sweet girl, hanging over him with increased fondness, from recollecting that she had been the innocent cause of the indignity which drove him from Farleigh. 'Is it possible,' sighed poor Mrs. Pembroke, 'that this noble creature should be the son of a bar-maid?' 'Alas! that this charming Henry should be my brother!' faintly then would murmur her daughter.

Each time the family returned to London, they found Henry considerably altered and improved: his carriage, formed by military exercise even in tender youth, became manly, – his mind imbued with knowledge, firm. Mrs. Pembroke found, in the painful necessity of preparing to part for ever with her husband and daughter, new motives for valuing the youth to whom they were both so precious. She every-day, every hour, commended to Henry's care, his fondness, his protection, the gentle girl already growing too dear to him. Softened and impressed by her sick mother's address, the agitated Henry sometimes flew to Julia, who, throwing herself freely into his arms, left on his cheek tears that sunk into his heart. New to emotion, he often flattered himself that the suffocating throbs of such moments were only due to the occasion; while at others, prolonging the sweet

17

The Canterbury Tales

embrace, he blushed at having dared to do so, and almost resolved to shun for ever the exquisite temptation.

Mrs. Pembroke expired at Farleigh, bequeathing to Henry a sum of money, which the marriage articles had left at her own disposal; her magnificent watch; and a mourning ring, on which was engraved 'Remember.' Henry looked on it, and thought she had seen into his soul. It felt like the ring of Amurath. With this memorial of kindness came letters from Mr. Pembroke and Julia, fraught with that and sorrow: both equally conjured him to sacrifice the disgust he had to Farleigh to the love that summoned him thither; and, by his return, animate the home thus suddenly become desolate and cheerless to its possessors.

Henry was apparently about eighteen; and had gone through his military exercises with a spirit, strength, and skill, that secured him from all future indignity: nor did he now excuse himself from returning only because disgusted; though still he felt it was impossible he should forget the mortifying, the illiberal insult, of young Vernon. Impossible that he should reach the place his heart told him he was entitled to hold in society by any thing but his own exertions – alas! his pride he would gladly have sacrificed to his sister's request, had not the quickened pulsation in every nerve, whenever the thought of Farleigh occurred, told him the alarming truth, that it was Julia he would constantly see, Julia he would ever hear, Julia alone his soul desired. 'Oh, no! tempt me not,' cried he, ere he broke the seal of every letter, – 'tempt me not, fairest of creatures, my best beloved! never must I visit Farleigh; at least not till I have conquered the feeling that alone makes existence worth having.' On the contrary, the youth implored for liberty to serve abroad; and Mr. Pembroke at length consented. To purchase him a commission, that gentleman, with Julia, again came to town: the cheek of Henry burnt with indignation at the proposal. 'Is honour, then, bought and sold, my father? Such honour a son of yours must disdain. Your Henry must own to his own exertions the rank he obtains: let me serve the gallant Wolfe as a volunteer, for that only will I be.'

As such young Pembroke was presented to the first commander of his time, now on the point of undertaking the memorable expedition against Canada. Minds like Henry's claimed his distinguishing regard; nor was it ever wanting to the worthy. The magnanimous general, struck with the glowing grace of conscious integrity that marked alike the youth's carriage and address, flattered both father and son with

The Canterbury Tales

the happiest predictions of the future fortune of the volunteer. Mr. Pembroke and Julia accompanied Henry to the port, – the one fondly loading him with advice, the other no less fondly imploring it from him; nor did she once interrupt him, but with an assurance that every word he uttered was indelibly engraven on her heart.

Pure and elevating sense of duty! of what privations art thou not capable? With dauntless heroism this youth tore himself, thus early, from the only two beings in creation who had an interest in his welfare, a claim upon his feelings. Julia was unconscious of the power vested in the talisman which hung upon the heart of Henry, when, on seeing him anxiously contemplate the rich curls of her auburn hair, as they playfully fell over her mourning habit, she instantly cut off the most beautiful of them all; and, opening a spring behind her father's picture, enclosed there the precious treasure, then threw the chain from her own neck over that of Henry. He pressed the invaluable gift to his lips, – he pressed, too, with a soft sigh, the lovely hand that gave it; then hastily glanced his eye on his mourning ring, and murmured emphatically the motto. Impatiently he rushed to the arms of Mr. Pembroke, and with a desperate resolution flew into the boat that bore him to his military companions.

What a sudden, what a chilling change did Henry find alike in the scene and in his fate! Delighting in all the sciences, but an adept only in that of the heart, the young volunteer knew none of the little arts of life, still less did he know those of war. He was yet to learn that where one man bears arms from the love of glory, thousands seek in them a mere profession: but his discernment was too acute for him not to discover that a volunteer is understood to be another term for a military Quixote, and that he himself was considered by all around him rather as an indulgent son of a rich man, who could only by experience be cured of a whim, than as a bold and unsupported individual steadily pursuing a single and a great object. The elevated mind of his commander enabled him to form a juster calculation: and Henry soon won from the heroic Wolfe marks of confidence, and instances of trust, that gratified his feelings, and fixed his services.

In the tedious and unpromising campaign, the glorious leader had 'room for meditation even to madness;' and few around him caught from his eye with the quickness of Henry the impulse of his mind: but the situation was too important, the doubts too awful, for either to speak. Yet, if a service of danger occurred, it could be said that

The Canterbury Tales

> Henry was ready ere he called his name,
> And though he called another, Henry came.

So happy was the youth in executing the orders given him, that the General soon offered him a commission. Pardon me, sir, returned the volunteer, I have not yet deserved it: – these few words made such an impression upon the gallant Wolfe, as in other circumstances would have ensured his fortune. Rising thus without rank through the smile of the General into consequence, young Pembroke insensibly changed from a humoured boy into a military phenomenon. It became the fashion in the camp thus to treat him, and the home despatches spoke the same language. Mr. Pembroke now never visited the secretary's office, or bowed at the minister's levee, but that he was not congratulated on the glory which Henry was acquiring even in his nonage.

A pleasure like this was perhaps necessary to compensate to Mr. Pembroke's heart for a chagrin even his beloved Julia gave him. Hardly had she appeared in elegant life, ere she attracted so much admiration as to ensure her a choice in most families entitled to match into hers; but not one lover would Julia condescend to favour. To see her happily married was the great object with her father, and his own judgment soon inclined him towards a gentleman, who had such a disadvantage to encounter in the mind of Miss Pembroke, as hardly left him a chance of being estimated by his merits. This unlucky lover was young Vernon, who, when a rude spoiled boy, had, by a gross speech, driven Henry from Farleigh. His ripened understanding made him unable to remember the moment without blushing. The weak misjudging mother who had cherished his faults was long since dead. A liberal education, and just turn of thinking, had rendered young Vernon in person, mind, and manners, no less than fortune, a match so entirely unexceptionable for Julia, that she now shed almost as many tears at finding him without a fault, as she formerly did for the consequence of his gross one.

Although Mr. Pembroke knew not how to exert authority in a point so delicate, it was so near his heart, that he resolved to add to his own influence that of Henry. He enlarged on the altered and superior character of young Vernon, and called upon the candour of his darling son to dismiss from his mind any little selfish recollection of the boyish quarrel between them, and to second his wishes for this match in his correspondence with Julia: assuring him that, should she be won to accept Vernon, he would find in her husband a brother and a friend infinitely to be respected and valued. 'Vernon the husband of Julia!' – discordant was the sound to Henry's ear, – odious the words to his eye: and if she must enrich the hand of some man, did the world afford no one worthy of her but Vernon? Could his father forget, then, that this youth first rendered him an exile, an alien from that mansion in which he now insolently sought to dwell, and dwell there the lord of Julia – perhaps her beloved. Spleen, jealousy, a thousand humiliating imbittered reflections crowded into his bleeding heart. The letter of Julia was yet in his hand, – the seal unbroken: – he paused in trembling anxiety, then threw it disdainfully from him, as if assured that he should there read only a confirmation of the merit, the triumph, the felicity of Vernon, and shrink under the cruel sense of his own insignificance, his isolated state in society. The young mind generally makes the most of its misery ere it deigns to doubt whether it has not exceeded. Henry, worn out at length with fretting, suddenly reproached himself with caprice; and, kneeling with tender devotion, took up the rejected packet, and kissed the characters which the fair hand of Julia had traced; rapidly passing his eager eye over a long letter without once catching the name he detested. Ah! no, the delicate Julia would not wound his sensibility, or quicken his recollection, by telling him of the pretensions of Vernon. She wrote only of himself, – implored for long letters, a little to enliven the dulness of Farleigh, which grew every day more intolerable now he was out of all possible reach. She concluded with telling him, that a little touch of the gout their father had been seized with, had enabled her to engage a neighbouring physician to order him to Bath; from whence she hoped to persuade him to set out on a tour through Wales, where it was her secret object to discover some romantic solitary abode, like that they had often imagined together, where she would, if possible, reside till he should return crowned with laurels, once more to dwell with them at Farleigh.

And now the soul of Henry overflowed with wild undefinable tenderness. Alone, in the wilds of Canada, he enjoyed a pleasure so perfect, that many a long life has been spent in unlimited indulgence without affording the voluptuary such a moment. 'No, Julia,' sighed he, as fancy sobered into reason, 'I cannot, dare not, return to Farleigh: – born to live *for*, it is not my happy fate to live *with*, you: yet, oh! had it been young Vernon's.' He now resorted to his clarionet; and running imperfectly over the favourite airs of Julia, almost believed he heard her soft applause. A hoarser voice, however, broke the reverie.

'I once, young gentleman, played that instrument better than you can.' Henry, something surprised, raised his eyes to a silver-headed surly veteran, nicknamed in the camp the Misanthrope. So seldom was his taciturnity broken, that he seemed now only to have transferred it; for Henry gazed on him in silence. 'You do not manage your stops well,' added the stranger, with more conciliation of tone. 'Will you who thus criticise have the goodness to improve me?' returned the youth, respectfully tendering the instrument. 'How should I play?' gruffly returned the old man; 'do you not see that my right arm is useless?' Henry's sympathetic glance atoned for his oversight; and his new friend then more mildly added, 'I may put you in a better way for all that.'

The stranger did not over-rate his musical skill; for in a very short time Henry touched, by his advice, yet more exquisitely, the clarionet. Nor did their intercourse end there. The retreating dignity of the war-worn veteran was calculated to impress a nature like Henry's. 'Although you never till now noticed me,' said the old man, 'I have sat hours in the woods to listen to you. Your instrument I was once thought to excel on; and music is still,' added he, sighing, 'my passion – my only passion.' 'And I will play whole hours,' politely added Henry, 'to give you the pleasure which you can no longer give yourself.'

Henry, though accustomed to military banter, and equal to returning it, was, however, something surprised at seeing a gay young officer at the mess lift up his hands and eyes when he conveyed a slice of beef to his plate. Unable to interpret this without inquiry, the whole party pleasantly answered, that they concluded he must have renounced all such gross sinful food, now he was got so great with old Pythagoras. As this banter could apply only to the lame and interesting veteran, – and Henry kept up the subject to learn all the young men knew of his history, – that was comprised in a few words. Cary, he understood, had from early youth been an officer, but of a fickle turn and melancholy temper, which had made him often change commissions to see new service; till having from a wound in his right arm lost the use of it, he sold out; and, living contentedly on a very little, had travelled from curiosity almost over the whole world. Enthusiasm inhabits not the heart while the affections are uncherished; but, destined to form a part of every nature, it then passes into the understanding. A long residence in the house of Bramin on the banks of the Ganges had inured Cary to the pure and simple habits of that sect, insomuch that he no longer tasted animal food, and was said to believe in their doctrine of the metempsychosis. 'You have seen his two fine spaniels?' said the relator, on concluding his story. 'They are too beautiful to be overlooked,' returned Henry. 'Curse me!' added a raw ensign, 'if I don't think the queer codger fancies them his near relations; for he made a devil of a row when I had one of them stolen, and shut up for a couple of days, just to see what old Brama would do when he missed her.' Alas! thought Henry, how severe must have been the unknown affliction which has thus bewildered a brain rational in all other instances. 'But the best joke of all,' cried another flimsy wit, 'is, that the comical put, though he has only one hand, would as soon use that to fire one of us off at the mouth of a cannon as to take a pinch of snuff; and what polite reason does he give, think you? Why, he says it may perhaps be a kindness, as we shall then get a new form; and we shall have devilish bad luck if we should ever become any thing worse than we now are.' At this speech Henry's muscles relaxed unconsciously into a smile, and he felt his partiality for Cary increased.

As soon as the hoary veteran found that a youth universally courted took pleasure in tracing him through the solitudes he rather sought, because he knew not where to meet a congenial mind, than from misanthropy, his harshness of character wholly disappeared. It was Henry's generous wish to steal into his confidence, that from finding the point whence his reason diverged (for even he thought it at intervals wandered), he might gradually, perhaps, bring it back to the path of right. Although profoundly silent on the sorrowful past, this tender consideration had a charm for the abstracted Cary; and chance soon cemented to friendship an acquaintance which chance had so oddly begun. The attachment had the sanction of General Wolfe. He had selected Cary as an engineer, a post to which his long experience eminently qualified him. Often did the friends lean on a cannon, and confer by looks, as the heroic General sought to smile off in social intercourse the heavy weight of the war, so plainly depicted on his ingenuous countenance.

Environed with variety of dangers, and confined to narrow boundaries in the region of sylvan beauty, the impatient English wasted of necessity those precious days that could not now be many, in petty skirmishes and vain efforts to bring that enemy to battle, who securely entrenched, knew much might be lost, but nothing gained by this measure. The high and valorous spirit of General Wolfe could not brook retreating without a conflict; and every passing hour pressed on him the recollection of the approaching one, when nature periodically, in Canada, locks up all her treasures beneath mountains of snow and masses of ice. With gelid breath she there binds to solidity the impetuous rivers; and for the emulation and envy of proud man, constructs magnificent bridges of materials so frangible, that the sun-beams might annihilate them; yet over these for months pass and repass busy multitudes, utterly regardless of that wonder which they annually witness.

The suffering of mind that allows now of communication usually preys upon the constitution, and General Wolfe found himself with a malady medicine never cured. It was now only he knew the value of Henry Pembroke's devoted regard; who watched over the important invalid with the spirit of a man, and the softness of a woman: dear remembrances from home, however, lightened the hours, and the letter of Julia, a thousand times read, still excited in Henry the same delight.

LETTER

'Castle St. Hilary'

'A little volume from our precious volunteer has been at last sent hither after us. Henry is well. – Oh! what a weight did this take from both my father's heart and my own. I pass over all your masterly and beautiful descriptions, my beloved brother, of the country, for I can only be interested or entertained when you speak of yourself.

'Ah! Henry, are you still, then, fond of a camp? Have you forgotten us, in the pride of attaching the regard of your glorious commander? Why oblige us alike to adore him? In vain you argue on the impossibility of your safety being risked, while it is the interest of the French to avoid an engagement, and the choice rests with their General, not yours. Rumour, my dear Henry, sad and serious rumour, shows the fallacy of this opinion: had you a leader of a common character, you would be certainly in no danger; but that many-headed monster the public, without capacity to judge, or information to ground judgment on, already questions the conduct of your General, and he has too heroic a soul not to prefer glory to life: at least, thus have you taught us to believe; how then, can I be at ease?

'Yet I think my anxiety is abated, since we got out of the gay scenes of Bath; where my poor father lived through each day only by the expectation of the newspaper of the preceeding one; and my very soul was harassed with the insipid conjectures of my pump room companions; who often lost, in the sight of a new face, or a new bonnet, all recollection of Canada, and the war.

'Yet let me distinguish one among the many, so charming, that my heart made almost a friend of her, and my father's almost a wife. Nay, start not, my Henry! our father is only a man, and Lady Trevallyn seems something more than a woman. Made *for*, and a little *by*, the world, the high air of *ton*, and finish of beauty, have not destroyed the warmth of her heart, or the enchanting *naïveté* of her manners. She has tried hard to make me as fine a lady; but I have still my old trick of blushing, either at my own faults or other people's. I do not accuse her of plotting on my father's heart, observe, for she reigns in too many to make that of a man of his age or rank an acquisition; but I soon took notice he never left home when she was there, and that was almost continually; for we lived next door to each other. The mansion I date from is hers, or rather her son's, where she has promised us a visit. – Ah! should fortune send our Henry to us at the same juncture! – why he too would be chained to the car of Lady Trevallyn; and I must thank one of her school-boy sons for gallanting me about. She is neither too old nor too wise to be entertained with flights of imagination, by vulgar souls yelped romance; and after I had drawn one of my usual pastoral wild pictures of a Welsh retreat, in which I meditated burying both my father and myself, during your absence, she assured me, that Castle St. Hilary was the very dwelling I had by intuition described: save that its antiquity was such, that 'were Samson now alive, and should take any exception either to the building or the company, a single shake of his would pull it about our ears. The rocks were already so sociable as to nod at each other over our heads; and the waterfalls as incessantly melodious as heart could desire. The anchorites of the mountains were, indeed, rather more numerous than we might like; but, luckily, they went on four legs; and however magnificent their beards, neither troubled us with their lectures nor their company.' I liked the description, and my father the lady: a blind bargain was struck between our family stewards; and when our lovely widow, with other water-fowl, took wing for Weymouth, we set out on the tour of Wales.

'Pray, did you ever suspect our father of turning author? – or has he newly taken up the idea? His travels through Wales, I am convinced, he must design shortly to treat the public with; ornamented with drawings by a young lady, for her own amusement: for had I not had my portfolio and pencils, I know not how I could have passed the long intervals of his absence. With feet still tender, and a gouty cough, never did he espy from the chaise-window a shady dell or winding road, but John was stopped, and he must explore it. A stony brook became as sure an attraction to him as if the nymph of the stream had been braiding her green locks, and waiting for him by appointment at its source. At length we reached this sweet abode – this solitary castle. Erected, in the eye of fancy, as we look up to it from the road, on the very boundary of creation; one seems with pilgrim devotion to deposit all human cares and follies at the foot of the mountain it stands on, and find here a kind of resting-place between earth and heaven; to which it so nearly approaches, that I sometimes fancy I see my guardian spirit, as each neighbourly cloud breaks, and surely breathe something of celestial peace and purity.

'Had I my beloved Henry for a guide and protector, I would run about these mountains like a chamois, and not leave a spot unvisited. I know not what the charms of Canada may be, but do not think we need go so far to find all our visions of beauty, and retired felicity, realised. At least come and journey through Wales with me before you decide. Let your eye wander here through the rich foliage of the woods that till the hollows, then lift them to the grotesque summits so far above you – climb as though you were scaling heaven, and you will look down on the village of St. Hilary and its castle, as bee-hives in a garden, while one rude mountain seems to shoulder another, far as the eye can reach, – a sea of green billows fixed into solidity by the fiat of the Almighty. How the soul feels at once its force and its feebleness in contemplating scenes like this! the mysterious image of immense power overshadows us, and imperfect humanity can only glorify by silence the Creator of all things, and wonder a mite should have that privilege: – to this sublime spot I resort when I can reach so far, and often conjecture whether my dear Henry sees at the same moment a scene as grand, or feels a sensation as pious.

'This ancient seat preserves all its family honours without giving you the idea of any thing frightful or gloomy. There is a simplicity, a kind of lovely homeliness in its interior, like the heart probably of the founder; who cases that in iron as well as his castle only against the enemy. To his friends and his poor both were alike open. The Gothic gates and uncouth statues in the outer hall make me expect, every time I enter, a greeting from Prince Llewellyn, or at least Owen

Glendower, while other harpings than those of my own hand seem to ring on my ears. A table, like that of King Arthur for size, solidity, and polish, appears in perspective; but we have not been so lucky as to encircle it yet with true knights – even of the shire.

'The gardens, I own, do not please me. Battlements of yew, and fortifications of holly, ever offend taste; and a considerable tract of ground is ornamented with every diversity of verdure, under the daily torture of the shears of the gardener: at their extremity you behold the ruined but beautiful gate of a desolated priory: – pass that, and all is enchantment. No weeds are to be seen within the sacred enclosure – sweet shrubs and plants have been nurtured in every favourable spot – each mouldering pillar is enwreathed with jessamine – the Gothic fretwork of the windows seems bound together by a treillage of roses and woodbine – the cloisters, yet in tolerable preservation, supply a walk ever dry, and enclose an orangery; – I thought myself in fairy land. The dear sociable soul who thus gave a charm to ruin, a grace to imperfection, has filled every niche with a comfortable seat, always calculated for two persons. This silent solemn scene by moonlight is almost too touching for sensibility, while one fancies the fragrant and beautiful flowers are springing from the fair and pure bosoms of nuns now no longer beating with vain hopes or fears – as mine still does. Would you think I should find another treasure beyond? – but of this I will not speak, that I may have something left to surprise my Henry with when he comes here to visit us – for here till he comes will I stay. Nay, perhaps I shall not then quit St. Hilary. Abhorred be Farleigh, while my brother refuses to dwell there! – yet my father bids me enjoin you still to direct your packets to his own seat, as the most certain mode of conveying them to us. Adieu! beloved Henry; remember of what importance you are to your father and your poor Julia, and take care of yourself for our sakes, if not your own.'

The conviction this epistle gave Henry, that Julia had determinately flown from the addresses of Vernon, and sought to seclude from the world those charms that fixed all whom they attracted, was, perhaps, necessary to invigorate his soul in the hour that called for all its strength. That momentous one was now at hand when the glorious Wolfe resolved upon conquest or death; nor knew that to him they would be one and the same thing. In the daring enterprise that hero meditated was comprehended so many various exertions of human powers, as showed that he relied on finding in each fellow-soldier a nature like his own; and Wolfe well knew how to impart his native energy. When the solemn hour of embarkation came, the troops ascended the boats appointed to fall down the river St. Lawrence, with the firm step of valour and of virtue. Each eye, having first besought its God, was turned with awe and admiration towards the dauntless leader, who, with circumspect mein, but sublime determination, marshalled the silent soldiery. Henry Pembroke stood near him, and had the envied honour of being bade to do so in the field of battle.

Day closed ere the little flota launched upon the rapid tide, which, to each thoughtful mind, seemed to bear them like time rolling onward to eternity. The stars alone, more silent than the troops, shone with a pure radiance peculiar to the cold atmosphere. The winds now rushing through impending woods of growth immemorial, that cast their deep shadow on the water, seemed like a furious host of congregating foes; and now lost behind the rocky heights, nature's proud bastions, which the floating troops were soon to scale, allowed them in passing to hear the careless whistling of unsuspicious sentinels, who were not warned, even by a whisper, that an enemy was at hand.

How glorious, how triumphant was their landing, though fierce and desperate the conflict! Impatient in the dreadful onset for artillery, General Wolfe commanded Pembroke to fly to the pass, where, by exertions almost beyond human strength or skill, the seamen were drawing the cannon up the precipices, and urge the engineers to point it. Hardly had Henry repeated this order to Cary, ere the fusee of an ambushed Indian enlisted in the cause of France, laid the youth at the feet of his friend. In the fate of an army an individual is usually forgotten, and Pembroke had been trodden instantaneously to death, but that Cary caught up his body, and throwing it over the only cannon, called to the spirited tars who were on the point of descending, in a voice of thunder, to save the brave volunteer, the favourite of the General. They halted a moment; then, with adroitness peculiar to themselves, interlaced the slings by which the artillery had been dragged up, and laying the bleeding Henry in this rough cradle, rushed down the rocks, impatient to renew their vigorous efforts for their country's service. A young midshipman, stationed on the river, received the apparently lifeless charge from the sailors; and, as he dared not quit his post, Henry must have bled to death, had not the elder brother of the little officer been led by affection to share his danger: no rigid duty interfered in his bosom with that

The Canterbury Tales

of humanity; and on hearing who the sufferer was, he hastened with him to the camp.

One universal burst of joy, of sorrow, of generous ennobling tears, ran through England at the news of the conquest of Canada, – at the death of its conqueror: in vain was the rich territory gained, in vain an army preserved; – Wolfe, even in the arms of victory, had fallen, and each man seemed to lose in him a son – a brother – a friend: ah! each had lost even more, when the adored object of national gratitude lived not to enjoy its rapturous effusions.

News like this every where out-ran the post, and soon was known even at the remote Castle of St. Hilary. The generous tears with which Mr. Pembroke and Julia embalmed the lost hero were, however, strangely blended with uncertain alarm for Henry: but the newspaper was not come. It at length arrived, but gave no relief to the anxious readers. The post, they flattered themselves, would end their fears: it followed, but brought no letter: a second came, but not a line did it convey. Silent though ungovernable anguish seized at once on Mr. Pembroke and his daughter; but the mutual misery burst into words as well as tears, on the proposal of posting to London for intelligence. The fragile Julia instantly lost all feeling for herself, and travelled night and day with her father; who hastened to the War-office, where he found that Henry, being a volunteer, had not been included in the return of the killed and wounded; though that one fate or the other had been his was indubitable. The distracted Mr. Pembroke could hope for farther intelligence only from the officer who brought the despatches: that gentlemen, however, recollected nothing more than having seen the youth by the side of the General at the onset. A pre-eminence so glorious Mr. Pembroke immediately felt might easily become fatal, nor wondered Henry was overlooked when Wolfe expired: though, under other circumstances, his wounds might not have been mortal, or his death unmentioned.

Oh! that Julia, when his heart-rending account reached her, could have taken wing and crossed the seas to Canada; then would she have explored every bloody spot of the well-fought field, nor once have rested till, living or dead, she found her beloved brother. Her afflicted soul now imaged him for ever exposed to the birds of the air and beasts of the field, till grief was wrought up in her to the highest pitch by the accumulation of horror.

Yet not to its highest pitch was it wrought up in Julia, for she knew not self-reproach – that was the portion of her disconsolate father;

who too late bewailed having appropriated the blessing which Heaven bestowed on other parents, without being content with the precious one it gave exclusively to himself.

To the inhabitants of Castle St. Hilary a sad and uncheered winter commented. Not one of all the inquiries concerning Henry had produced the smallest information; and therefore those who loved him were destined long to endure every misery of conjecture, unrelieved by hope. It had been much Mr. Pembroke's wish to return to his own house, but the bare mention of Farleigh always threw Julia into an agony of grief: for there still to her eyes stood the dear, insulted, indignant boy, as when he was driven from that happy home, only to seek in another country an untimely grave.

From Farleigh, however, at length was forwarded a box that the ship marks showed to have come from Canada. The sight of it renewed the lamentations of Mr. Pembroke and his daughter. Ah! what could a box bring them? save the loathed uniform of the lost Henry, or those various treasured trifles which remembrance so endears, that only with life we resign them. Painful as must be the certainty, doubt could not be endured. Some rich furs, and a letter in an unknown hand, were all the contents of the box. With trembling impatience Mr. Pembroke tore open the latter, and Julia turned away, that he might not observe how she sickened at the signature of Vernon. Yet even the slightest glance had carried to her heart a doubt, a joyful doubt, that once more drew her eye to the letter. Had she indeed seen there the name of Henry? Ah! too sure her sense had not deceived her: – at once the paper, so lately abhorred, became dear – invaluable. It told her that Henry yet lived, and lived by the generous cares of Vernon. Words never spoke the gratitude that now throbbed at the heart of Julia. She raised her hand in rapture to heaven, and had the luckless lover been his own reporter, freely, gladly would she have allowed that hand to drop into his, and have thought the long desired blessing too poor, too trivial an acknowledgment of such a service.

The long silence of Vernon he excused by relating the deplorable state of Henry, who had been but very recently pronounced out of danger; and such was, while he was writing, the severity of the season, as to make it quite uncertain whether he could put this letter into any channel by which he might lighten the sufferings of the family at Farleigh. His best chance was by committing it to an Indian, who knew how in the severest season to perform his periodical perambulations: and if he executed his trust well, Miss Pembroke would with this news

The Canterbury Tales

receive some rich furs, which he entreated her to wear as a mark of his devoted respect. He slightly hinted that her rejection only could have make him quit England; which he did in company with his younger brother, then first sent into service, in a frigate their particular friend commanded. In knowing it was destined for Canada, he the more readily embarked, as he had always had the vanity to fancy that could he meet the gallant son of Mr. Pembroke, he should now find means to gain that friendship he had long known how to value. They had indeed met – but how? In the tumults of the onset at Quebec, while standing by his brother, the young volunteer was in a moment laid at his feet, drowned in blood, and without a sign of life. Humanity alone would have claimed the exertions which sympathy quickened. Great, however, was the difficulty of getting the youth conveyed to the English camp, nor, when that was accomplished, could he command the assistance of a single surgeon, who were all on appointed duty. During this anxious interval the blood of Henry continued to flow, till every vein was exhausted. It was then found that the ball had entered at the right shoulder, and, as the arm was extended, had torn its way through, till at the elbow it was apprehended to have touched the bone, and the surgeon was urgent for amputation. Vernon's opposition prevented this, and eventually saved the arm of Henry; but the effusion of blood caused a low and tedious fever, producing a dangerous degree of weakness, and a continual wandering of intellect, though his voice was almost too feeble for utterance. The memorable and immediate conquest of Canada gave the whole army those comforts they must soon have grievously wanted; but so alarming was the state of young Pembroke, that nothing but the severity of the season could have warranted the removing him to Quebec. At length that became the least of two dangers; and having the aid and concurrence of a respectable friend of the sufferer's to whom his welfare seemed hardly less dear, he had ventured this measure. It had the apprehended consequence of a relapse. The perpetual sickness, faintings fever and delirium, returned with added violence; nor could they for many days hope that Henry would ever struggle through his sufferings. During this period frost shut up the river, and left no certain means of communication with England. In his cares, however, was now associated a worthy veteran whom the merit of Henry had attached to him and who was always, when reason reigned, recognised by the eyes of that youth with peculiar pleasure; which had become a great relief to Vernon himself, as his brother had unfortunately taken the measles at Montreal, and he was obliged either to leave the orphan his parents' dying injunctions had given to his care at the mercy of strangers, or commit Henry to the charge of his venerable friend Cary. He had yielded to the most pressing duty, and was now setting out on a dangerous journey; having made every possible provision for the welfare of Henry, whom Cary promised never to leave. He concluded with giving the address of that gentleman, whom he exhorted Mr. Pembroke to treat as an old friend. With affectionate wishes for the return of Henry to England, he hinted a hope that, whenever the youth should learn to whom he owed his life, Julia would deign to use her influence with her brother to accept those cares as a small atonement for that error of his boyish days which he could never recollect without blushing.

'And now our Henry has surely had enough of war!' sighed Mr. Pembroke, as he folded the letter: – 'enough, too, has he won of humour; and if ever, my Julia, our arms again enfold the wanderer, hard shall he find it to escape them. This noble Cary too! how will my girl recompense him, and young Vernon?' 'By loving one half as well as I do my father, and the other half as well as my Henry,' said Julia, pressing her cheek against her father's 'Only half as well, my Julia?' urged the generous parent. Julia sighed, but gave no other reply.

Several letters, fraught with the same happy news that had been sent by different channels, reached, in the course of a few months, Castle St. Hilary. At length one from Cary informed them, that though Henry's wound was nearly healed, either that, or some unknown cause, had produced such a delicacy in the habit of the youth, as threatened a consumption; and had made the physician order him to hasten into the milder air of his own country. A letter of the same date from Henry himself, however, spoke not of any malady; but breathed a spirit of melancholy, the more alarming, as it seemed impossible for Mr. Pembroke to trace it to any cause. The soul of Julia impulsively assigned the true one; and when she urged her brother, by every power which affection holds or gives, to hasten home, she delicately insinuated that Vernon was not in England, and the gates of St. Hilary were still closed on lovers of every description.

It was but too true, that as the wound in his arm closed, that in the heart of Henry became empoisoned. As soon as he had power to converse, the grateful sensibility of his nature led him to inquire whither the gentle assiduous stranger to whom he felt so much indebted had vanished, and who he was. The warmth of Cary's heart threw him off his guard; and although it had been Vernon's express request to

The Canterbury Tales

have his name concealed, lest it might revive painful recollections in the mind of the sufferer, Cary not only declared that, but was diffuse upon the merits of the man by whose generous cares alone Henry lived to make the inquiry. That youth felt as though again struck to the ground. A thousand times he bewailed the ineffective aim of the ambushed Indian, which allowed him to survive one wound, only to precipitate him to the grave by another not the less mortal because unseen. Vernon appeared to him the chosen favourite of Heaven, since thus permitted to crush with obligation the wretch who first through his means knew misery. Well could the youth calculate the hopes this hitherto rejected lover would be entitled to cherish; for had he not, in Julia's eyes, now fully extended his boyish offence? Alas! might not even he himself be called upon to ratify, approve, the lover's claim; detail virtues he could not deny; amplify those kindesses it was death to him to have received; echo every plaudit of an admiring circle; and, finally, be obliged to witness the union horrible to his idea, but to which it was impossible he should object: for he, even he, felt that Vernon had deserved Julia.

While the unspeakable sorrow took these painful forms in the bosom of Henry, he would often, in silent agony, throw himself upon the ground, and tear the hair in handfuls from his head; giving Cary the dreadful apprehension that his intellects were failing. A thousand times did that friend entreat him to unfold the cause of these horrible transports. A thousand times did he claim a generous, an unlimited participation of this inexplicable anguish; but, alas! it was among the exquisite miseries of Henry that he could not disclose them. This stifled jealousy soon dried up every soft sluice of affection, and with corrosive power ate into the very heart of the unrecovered youth – a deadly canker on the fairest fruit of humanity. His long fits of melancholy abstraction were now only broken by convulsive starts, and internal struggles! which made his eyes shoot fierce and furious glances on mere vacancy. But nature cannot long endure such suffering without showing its effect; and those checks, on which health had promised once more to spread her roses, now daily became more and more hollow, and pallid, even to ghastliness. Short shivering sighs alone indicated that he breathed; and the gloomy languor of his half-closed eyes showed how seldom they knew the renovating blessing of repose. It grieved poor Cary to the heart to watch the daily desolation of such a fine creature; and to know that there must be some deep-seated cause, both from the

suddenness and rapidity of his decline: yet he remitted not in his efforts to obtain the confidence he almost dreaded. Devoured as Henry's spirits were by cruel recollections and nameless fears, he was yet open to the impressions of sympathy; and conceiving some confidence due to such unwearied kindness, he tried to mislead his anxious friend by a partial one. He ventured one day to disclose the least of his griefs in the mortifying story of his obscure birth, which left him through life at the mercy of the world, or rather the victim of its cruel prejudice; while he had neither acceptation in it, fortune, or those ties of affinity more dear than all. 'And causes an evil light as this a grief so mighty?' cried Cary, turning on him keenly eyes that struck through his soul a reverential sense of suffering and of sorrow he had never known before. 'Oh, world! thou maze of never-ending wonder! thou wilderness of still shooting calamity, how various, how complicated, how fanciful are thy woes! This boy here, indulged almost beyond his wishes, holds himself licensed to groan, and rend his hair, only because he wants thy empty title to those blessings which he accepts or rejects at his pleasure! Ah! what then should I do. Might I not be sanctioned in still scattering these grey locks on the winds of heaven, and drenching even yet the earth with the tears of these withered eyes, so long only fountains of sorrow, when I remember – '
A deep convulsive sigh suspended speech in the veteran.

There is something so impressive in the grief of advanced life, when the suffering mind soars to dignity, that those yet younger, awed into silence, hastily gather back into their own unexperienced bosoms each little selfish complaint, and almost blush to have ventured any. Henry felt this powerfully; and, in turn, became the supplicant for confidence and unreserve.

'Long, long and many are the years,' sighed the agitated Cary, 'since these lips were unsealed to mortal man? and why should they now be so? No, it is not possible for me to unfold my fate even to you – yet the impression of recollected misery which thus shakes me teach you, young man, no longer to magnify those little present evils, that you many hereafter find to be but the lightest links in the vast chain of human calamity which encircles the earth, and may one day enthral each faculty of your soul. It is not what we have, but what we lose, which stamps the fate of man, – you might have had all, all you wish, and been at last as very a wretch as I am. Fond parents, – lineal honours, – ample fortunes, – the wife I adored, – offspring no less lovely, – did Heaven in lavish bounty bestow on me; yet here I stand

The Canterbury Tales

impoverished of all these blessings, single in creation, – uninterested in the fluctuating multitudes by whom I am surrounded, – uninteresting to them. Whether these bones shall be inurned in the proud vault of my forefathers, or whiten on the plains of Canada, no one knows, no one cares. Yes! you perhaps, would give them decent burial; and these faithful animals,' concluded he, pointing to the two beautiful spaniels affectionately couching at his feet, 'with an attachment unknown to sophisticated man, would, perhaps, stretch themselves in death on the grave of him who loved – who fed them.'

When grief loses sight of its greater objects, and retreats either into self, or such as are inferior, it may be wrought to disclosure. Henry seized with animated sympathy the occasion, and at length conquered the repugnance his friend expressed to descanting on the story he had already briefly capitulated.

'When I consider the great bond and duties of morality,' sighed the dignified old man, 'I own I ought not to hesitate – selfish is the navigator who burns the chart of his voyage, when so many must doubtfully follow the same course. From the errors of my youth, may you, Pembroke, learn discretion, – from its miseries a patient endurance of your own appointed lot. Yet there are things I must detail which it is agony to think of: – let your generous, glowing heart give proportionate value to the confidence.

'I am the only son of a baronet, who was the head of an ancient family, and the sole heir of an entailed and ample estate. My father, who unhappily had not known the advantage of a liberal education, could never be persuaded that it was essential to a gentleman. Among the causes of his aversion to literature was a love of money ill suited to his condition in life; but thrift is a common fault, I believe, in uncultivated minds, which seek a poor occupation (for man cannot live without some) in petty calculations. My mother, having no other child, could not endure to part with me; and therefore valued herself on saving my father's money by instructing me in my native tongue. By their mutual care I was so consummate a blockhead, that at nine years old I could hardly read a chapter in the Bible. In this happy state of ignorance I should probably have grown up, could my mother have kept me always at her apron string; but I was now too stout for her to manage, and too cunning to impart to her how I passed the intervals of absence. A narrow escape I shortly after had of breaking my neck, by riding a vicious horse, without a bridle or saddle, put it out of all doubt that to some control I must be subjected. My father, with his usual parsimony, only calculated where I could get most learning for least money; and my mother, how she should keep me near enough to cocker me with cates continually, and have me home every Sunday. At length it occurred to them both that our worthy clergyman, who was blest with a son two years younger than I was, whom his father's care had already made the best scholar in the country, would be a most excellent preceptor, if he would take me to board.

'Cramped circumstances, and clerical dependence, are never so severely felt as when they subject persons of merit to such troublesome encumbrances as I must necessarily have proved: yet the excellent man was obliged to receive the compliments of his neighbours on the honour of being intrusted with the young esquire. When I recollect, among a hundred ways I had of being irksome, the daintiness of my appetite, which taxed the good people's circumstances to supply their table with delicacies for me they denied to themselves, I wonder they did not hate me. Study I soon found detestable; and as I was already able to maintain my argument against my father, I did not mind letting my tutor have the best of it; for he was to live by his learning, and I by the wisdom and economy of my progenitors. Seldom came a day that a worthless gamekeeper, to hide his own depredations under those imputed to the young squire, did not entice me from the parsonage; and its worthy inhabitants were often in a state little short of distraction, lest I should have come to any accident: so early can self-will and the pride of life reign, where parents fail to rectify both by due government and proper tuition. I should doubtless have grown up an ignorant clown of fortune and family, had my poor mother lived, for never did she fail to intercept the necessary complaints which my tutor sought to convey to Sir Hubert's ear. The mistaken good woman, however, died when I was about twelve years old, and with her I lost a thousand foolish fond indulgences I heavily missed. My father now often heard how unruly I was, and seemed, in becoming a free man, to have acquired a new importance in his own eyes. Among the reasons he gave me for "turning over a new leaf," as he termed reformation, was, that except I amended, though now an only son and heir, I might not always remain so. The latter I, however, knew to be a mere threat; for every servant, as well as kinsman or friend, had already assured me that I could not lose my inheritance by his having twenty more children. Happily for the peace of my own soul, a change in my conduct was effected by a better motive than the fear of losing a fortune – a conviction of my own ignorance. I began to find the taste for literature which my young friend Llewellyn early displayed, had not only given him an acceptation in society that made me blush to take place of him, but diffused through his manners an elegance seldom found in mere scholars, while it tinctured his life with that exquisite power of enjoyment which a regulated and informed mind, united with a glowing imagination, alone can give. Llewellyn was thought poor, dependent. No, he was rich – for he was master of himself; and I, the esquire, was poor and dependent; for I had an empty head and an ungovernable temper, which threw me upon the mercy of all around me.

'The moment a young man first discovers his own fault is the one that determines his character, since he must ultimately sink under that he does not at once resolve to rise above. I was not however too old to redeem past time; and Llewellyn soon did more for me than his father had ever been able to do; who, good old man, exulted to see me sensible of his son's superiority, but in proportion as I gained my tutor's affection, I lost my father's. His table was often surrounded by illiterate, assuming persons, whom even I could confute on a thousand occasions; and though I had now sense enough to speak with modesty, I was soon found guilty by ignorant eldership of being too young to be in the right. Sir Hubert one day bluntly informed me, that he expected me to learn, and not to teach; hinting that he had some thoughts of clipping my wings by marrying again. It was shortly after obvious, that a lady newly widowed had made up her mind he should do so; but of this I took no note.

'A brother of my mother's, who had passed his youth abroad, and risen in the army to the rank of General, now came down to spend a month with us. He expressed great astonishment at finding his nephew near six feet high, as well as himself, and still more that he had no profession. As he sometimes kindly regretted not having a sergeant with him, who could teach me to move like a gentleman, I took an occasion to show him that the inside of my head made a better figure than its outside; and he was no less suddenly amazed at my knowledge, which to him appeared pre-eminent. His ignorance was of the good-natured kind, that buds forth into wonder; and he really supposed I should be a phenomenon at college, whither he insisted I ought immediately to go; but as he was not much more generous than my father, this admitted of debate. At length they agreed to squeeze out enough conjointly to equip me for, and maintain me at Oxford; but I had sufficient feeling to languish to share the advantage with

Llewellyn. It was almost ruin to his father to engage in such an expense; but the youth had set his mind on academical honours; and the pride of showing this beloved and gifted son to all the wise professors, was a temptation that my worthy tutor could not resist. He therefore, agreed with his wife to starve their appetites, and feast on the rising fame of their son.

'The General himself conveyed us to Oxford, and there set down two raw striplings never before out of the nest they were fledged in, to *feel* the world rather than to *see* it. To how many wants did a single week make us sensible! – how many wishes grew out of those supplied wants, and how endless soon became both! The known circumstances of my young friend, as well as the right turn of his mind, gave him an advantage over me, in permitting him to limit his expenses. But for the only son of a rich baronet to affect economy would have ensured general ridicule and contempt; while the same extravagance would have been produced by fear, instead of frankness of temper. I, however, did not affect prudence; but almost withdrawing from the studious Llewellyn, committed my conduct to the guidance of those who were only less modest, not more judicious than myself; by whose advice I so fully profited, that in a year I amassed a list of bills as long as my father's rent-roll, and incurred a censure from the Vice-Chancellor. Obliged a little to feel and reflect, the affectionate Llewellyn would, no doubt, have suggested some method to retrieve my imprudence; but I was ashamed to consult one whose virtue tacitly reproved me; and, "what does he know of life?" was the cry of all my inconsiderate companions. When I imparted to them my distress, they shouted with laughter. Was I not an only child, and therefore the heir of my mother's fortune, no less than my father's entailed estates? The young spendthrifts had a copious acquaintance among the Jews and money-brokers in London. By their recommendation I drove up my new curricle thither, and found that so much admired, the town so agreeable, and the sons of Israel so accommodating, that my visits to London more than once made me in danger of expulsion at college. At the time I ought to have finished my education, I had not one penny left of my poor mother's portion. To bury the sense of chagrin, and go off in a blaze, I gave a dinner at the Thatched House to all the Cantabs of my acquaintance, and thence adjourned half drunk to a masquerade, where I was soon found out and surrounded by a bevy of light ladies, among whom I had a very large acquaintance. Before us we saw a stalking figure of Guy Vaux, prying into every corner.

He took my fancy, and I began to hunt and quiz him. He suddenly stopped, raised his little dark lantern, and, turning the light full on my face first, from whence I had taken the mask to cool myself, removed his vizor, and whisked it round to his own. I beheld my uncle the General, and became sober in a moment. Here ended my town career, and many a sour lecture followed; though I really think his telling me he first knew me by my inveterate country tone vexed me more than his informing my father of all my follies, who abruptly recalled me.

'Impoverished of what fortune I could call my own in my father's lifetime, humbled and disgraced, I returned to a home not more endeared by the daily lectures I had for living an idle life, when I had never known profession or employment. A large demand on Sir Hubert, from some of my accommodating London money-brokers, incensed him to the extreme. He flatly refused to pay a guinea for me, and bade the hardest of wretches do their worst, which was in reality consigning me at two-and-twenty to the King's Bench and ignominy. I remonstrated, entreated, promised in vain. He saw all his coffers plundered, and his old oaks levelled in imagination; and solemnly swore I should learn by want the value of both. After a little time he, however, cooled, and made me a proposal which riper years and more observation would have guarded me from listening to, but which, at my time of life, and under such a pressure of circumstances, was readily accepted: – it was to join with him in cutting off the entail: not that, he said, he should eventually deprive me of my birthright, nor, as I was an only child, did it appear likely; but that I should by this step put it out of my own power either by early intemperance or extravagance to let myself be plundered of my patrimony. The plea was, though arbitrary, fatherly and prudent; the sum offered more than enough to relieve my feelings, by acquitting me to every creditor. The lawyers went to work, and the entail was regularly docked.

'The lightness of heart that followed the payment of my debts, was, however, something damped by seeing my father appear openly as a wooer of the widow lady I formerly mentioned. In fact, I had soon reason to fear the late measure was suggested by her as a preliminary to her marriage; thus securing to her children, should she bear Sir Hubert any, by the influence she might obtain, the rights of eldership. I felt all my own indiscretion, but I uttered not a word. I soon saw a second bride take the place of my poor mother, who bore not the least resemblance to her; – proud, vain, selfish, and ill-tempered to all but her husband, the new wife knew well how to manage him by an affected fondness, while she vented on me that spleen I excited only be being my father's son. My first severe blow in life now fell on me. I was sunk to insignificance by my own faults merely; and to complete them, had assigned away, like Esau, my birthright for a mess of pottage; but I had not, like him, the heart and blessing of my father. My stepmother became with child, and Sir Hubert doubled his idolatry. The coldness of both consequently increased to me; and even the domestics, by an utter inattention to my orders, showed that they understood me to remain only on sufferance in the mansion of my fathers; where empty pockets seemed to threaten me with eternal humiliation. How I could long have borne this situation I know not; but on representing it in part to my uncle the General, he sent me a commission in the army; bidding me come up to him, and leave Sir Hubert to enjoy at full his delectable fit of dotage: he concluded with some of his usual harsh, coarse comments on those follies that had given my father an excuse for a second marriage. Ere I left home I saw a sister added to our family; and observed that her sex had been a severe disappointment to both the parents. It seemed a little to turn Sir Hubert's affections again towards me; for he assured me on parting, that the future yet depended on myself, nor would the dear stranger cause any material alteration in his views, if I from this time behaved with prudence, honour, and feeling. Thus, however, did not my uncle and I part; for when he found that I had put it in the power of a second wife to step between me and the estate unalienably mine, had I been but rationally selfish, he became outrageous with passion, and gross in his expression of it: he at once adjured me as a spendthrift, and ridiculed me as a fool. In taking leave of England for Minorca, I had, therefore, the pleasant conviction that it contained not one human being who cared if I ever returned to it or not, and hardly one whom I on my own part wished again to see.

'The impressions of youth are, however, naturally as versatile as impetuous. New scenes and new objects easily dissipate painful remembrances. My present profession and associates pleased and amused me. The garrison, though limited as to numbers, was in a healthy situation, and the officers men who had mostly seen service, and learnt discretion. I loved music, and studied it; passing my time agreeably enough, till the regiment was ordered to the West Indies. Though my pay was certainly too little to maintain a gentleman, I always found it very difficult to wring from Sir Hubert's grip those remittances that were indispensable; and had only one consolation for present inconveniences, – that I had never said or done, since we parted, aught that my father could construe into an offence; and my lady mother had never borne him another child. The change of climate soon brought on me that desperate fever which often rages in the islands, and is so fatal to Europeans: it very nearly left Sir Hubert without an heir. I was a whole year recovering: my pecuniary demands, of course, became greater; and whether my father distrusted my accounts of a sickness so lingering, or his wife stood between him and humanity, I know not, but I often felt the pressure of poverty in a degree which he ought never to have suffered his son to have experienced; and which might again have driven me to desperate or mean resources, had I not profited so far by my past errors and follies as to endure patiently. Yet the evil hour sometimes comes upon us, however wary; and a single one finished my ruin. The liquor of the country always inflamed me almost to madness; and having, in some dissipated company at a tavern, exceeded the little I usually allowed myself, I fell in with a party playing high – this fatal fever of college came over me. I felt in my pockets, but they were empty, and known to be so. My companions derided my prudence: – I no longer knew what I did, when I desperately offered my only stake, and played away my commission. The frenzy of intoxication was succeeded by a misery I remember even now with horror. I had seconded the arts of my stepmother, authorised the parsimony of my father – in fine, disinherited myself. To complete my tortures, a note was brought me from a military friend, advising me, on the pleas of bad health, to request leave of the commanding officer to return home, and immediately to sail in the fleet now under weigh for England; as he was grieved to inform me that I could not appear without a general slight which no individual can, either by resentment or apology, get over; and that would for ever stop my career in the army: though I was so much beloved, that all the regiment would defend my honour if I went home as sick.

'Sick indeed I was, sick of myself, life, every thing, and to what a home was I now to return! where I was unwelcome even before I knew myself to be penniless, and dishonoured. The tumults of my mind during that memorable voyage never shall I forget. How often was I tempted to bury myself in that tumultuous deep only more perturbed than my own soul; but my cup was not yet full, – much, much of bitter, and one drop of heavenly sweetness yet remained to be poured into it. I turned my unwilling steps towards the house of my father, without daring to apprise him of my arrival, lest he should shut that and his heart alike against me. I discharged the chaise ere I came to the last turnpike, dreading lest a hue and cry of joy should run before me only to aggravate my humiliation and misery. The evening was closing as I passed a thousand well-remembered spots and persons; but I felt as a criminal, and skulking along knew that my arrival would gladden no one heart in creation. At length I approached the garden. Oh, happy spot! where once in innocence and peace I revelled on the present, not considered the past or future. There once hung my infantine swing between two lines. There once proud of my boy's apparel, I gaily leaped my pony. There once I saved a frozen beggar, and my mother fondly blest me for it. I – I – myself was now become a beggar, and who should bless, should save me? I turned my lonely steps towards the church, and stretching myself upon the vault where that poor mother lay in happy ignorance of my misconduct, I implored heaven by her sainted spirit to accept my penitence, and soften the heart of my father. After this sad oblation, I ventured to present myself at the door: a cry of delight ran through the domestics, who had at that moment forgotten I was no longer to be considered as their future master. Nine years had elapsed since I had set eyes on my father, who was grown by infirmity more than so much older. The dear man was sitting bolstered up in a fit of the gout. I sunk at the feet of the venerable, though harsh, parent, and nature asserted her power in both our hearts, by almost audible pulsations. Hardly could I gain voice enough to murmur out, "Father, I have sinned against heaven and before thee, and am no more worthy to be called thy son!" This awful address, springing from a true sense of error, carried with it all the force of the following sacred impressions, and disarmed parental wrath: the feeling became too mighty; he threw himself on my neck in speechless agitation, and both almost died of the tender pang of re-union. A thousand pious ideas were blended with nature's fond transport, and having called up incidentally all that could operate in my favour, I found my fault, if not overlooked, so lessened, that I had little difficulty in prevailing on Sir Hubert to forgive it. Thus, by true contrition, I suddenly felt, after an interval of so many erring and miserable years, that I had at once recovered virtue and a father.

'A beautiful child was now summoned; for her mother, most luckily was abroad on a visit, who, with sweet endearment, entreated me to love Caroline. It seemed impossible to avoid loving so engaging

The Canterbury Tales

a creature; who, in the innocence of her little heart, called upon papa to admire her "fine officer brother;" and by the involuntary flattery of childhood led me to believe that there was yet something left in me which the guileless might love.

'This tender reception and generous pardon doubled the tie of nature, by binding my very soul to my father. His lady on returning beheld with astonishment her Caroline on my knee, entwining her arms round my neck; while Sir Hubert, with almost equal fondness, surveyed his son and daughter. I withdrew, accompanied still by the little charmer, who would not part with me, as well to save my own shame, while my father revealed my fault as to avoid his lady's cold looks, and, perhaps, cutting comments. The last I did not escape, for though he spoke low, and even, I though, humbly, she replied in a high and acrimonious voice, "And is all this rejoicing then, Sir Hubert, only because your worthless son has disgraced himself, and half ruined you? Pardon me, if I do not partake so singular an exultation." By what way could I hope to win a woman like this? Had it been possible, my extravagant fondness for her daughter must have subdued her enmity. Adored as Caroline was by both her parents, I soon learnt, I think, to love her better than either did; and certainly much more wisely: for I found she, like myself had been allowed to run wild in her childhood, and her naturally fine understanding was as uncultivated as her temper was unformed. Sick of the world, and willing to be wholly forgotten by it. I thought now only of indulging a love of literature and music, and cheering my father's age by my company, while I lightened to him every care. It seemed a generous return for his liberal forgiveness to become the preceptor of Caroline, and the novelty and distinction of the thing took her young fancy; while it bound me to certain daily acquirements of limited knowledge, which I could only instil by first studying. As the little ingenuous heart of the sweet child unfolded itself to the cares and affections of mine, I found a strange void in my own, which I had never till now felt, or at least reflected on. The exquisite delight this little creature gave to us all rendered me suddenly sensible of the charm of those natural ties by which we impart and double our being. Alas! it was not at large I made this observation; every throb of my heart told me that there existed one, and only one, with whom it could realise the fond – fond visions of domestic bliss, that now daily floated before my fancy.

'Although Caroline had no governess, I saw in the house a young creature, whom I knew not how to class with the servants; yet she appeared not at our table. This interesting, lovely young woman was called Agnes; and the fear of fixing attention on either her or myself made me unwilling to speak of her, even to Caroline, who had the common propensity of children in running to her mother with whatever she heard, while her observation was singularly acute for her years. It was very rarely I could cast a glance on the lovely Agnes; yet though I reproved my own vanity for the thought, I could not help fancying her eyes demanded something of me, which her blushes showed she would not claim. Her dress was always of the most common materials, but it was not possible for any thing to look common on Agnes. Her fragile form rose just above the middle size, and was turned with the grace of the Medicean Venus. Her arms and throat were of a pure and delicate whiteness. Her dark hair broke in rich curls over her expressive brows; and her large black eyes had a retiring modest charm I never saw in any other. Even now,' exclaimed Cary, glancing his wild looks intensely forward, 'the angel stands before me, with that touching meekness, that bending grace, which might have won the world – as it, alas! did me. Those beautiful those modest eyes were further shaded by a large straw hat tied with black. Her vesture was of some soft mourning muslin, which sweetly enfolded her fair form. I looked at Agnes, and wondered no more how my little sister became so amiable and graceful.

'Notwithstanding a certain interest we silently took in each other, I saw this charmer would not depart from the respect due to herself; or easily might she have fallen in his way who passed half his life only in looking for her I grew alert in observing every thing in which she might have but a remote concern; and seeing with what elegance the flowers were daily disposed in the room when I was accustomed to instruct Caroline, I doubted not but that the snowy hands of Agnes gathered and arranged them. I might have waked the lark from that moment, though till now a sluggard. I ambushed myself at peep of day in the flower-garden, and was soon repaid by seeing Agnes enter it.

More sweet than May herself in blossoms new!

'I had never yet been able to indulge my eyes with looking enough at her, – Ah! did they ever look enough? and, remained in the green-house till she came there to add a few geraniums to the fragrant contents of her basket, which she nearly dropped at sight of me; but she recovered her self-possession in a moment, and rather received

The Canterbury Tales

and returned my address as one who was entitled to, and expected it, than as a young creature whom I either pleased or honoured. I hardly knew what to call her, and delicately hinted that her Christian name was already familiar to my lips, but that I had never heard the one I should add to it. "Is that possible?" cried she, half smiling: but the painful consciousness suddenly followed of how completely she must be sunk, when her very name was annihilated; and the rosy blush, that almost absorbed the startling tears, gave new animation to her delicate beauty. "Yet am I pleased, sir," added she, "with what severely humbles me: for rather would I know myself without consequence, than conclude a gentleman without feeling: and I own I have not as yet thought that your distinction; since you deigned not to recognise the little playfellow of your youth, once the object of your indulgent kindness – the sister of your friend Llewellyn." The lovely Agnes could not resist the recollection, when a youth so dear to us both was mentioned: "Ah! sir, added, she frankly extending her hand, as asking sympathy, "the loss of that invaluable brother has almost killed us."

'I knew too well that the hopeful son of my tutor had died just as he was on the point of attaining the long-looked-for promotion, which was to have given affluence as well as honour to his family; and my only reason for omitting to visit the parsonage, was a fear the sight of me brought up with the lamented Llewellyn would revive the bitter sorrows of his parents. I implored the sweet girl to pardon me a stupidity which I could not pardon in myself, and reminded her that she was hardly the size of Caroline when I went abroad. "I know it well," returned she; "but you, sir, are not grown, though I am: yet you too are altered. Have you forgotten your expensive parting present of a gold locket with Llewellyn's hair? I wear it still." She drew the treasure from the fairest of bosoms, and hallowed it at once with a kiss and a tear. Envied, envied benedictions both! "And now, if you indeed have pardoned, tell my your story, my sweet girl. Llewellyn would wish it told to the friend of his choice." "The short and simple annals of the poor," returned the enchanting Agnes drying those eyes that in a moment again overflowed, "may be comprised in a few words. You, sir, already know the narrow income of my father, and how many almost necessary indulgences he was always obliged to deny himself, that he might give my brother the education both thought so essential. To see Llewellyn's rapid progress, and general estimation, made us all ample amends for domestic privations, and the prospect of his rise in the church gave happy hopes of future affluence.

You left me, I remember, running a little wild thing about the house, assisting as I could in family affairs. A sister of my mother's, who had married in Bristol, came to see us when I was near twelve years old, and took me back with her, that I might daily attend a neighbouring school, where by ingenuity and diligence, I profited more than my family hoped. I was about fifteen when my aunt became a widow, and her entangled affairs obliged her to send me back to my parents. Limited as had been my means either of observation or improvement. I was struck on returning with the humble style of the home which I before thought it Paradise to dwell in. Hardly could I be convinced that my parents had not contracted these expenses, they, alas! had never any means of extending. I should have found the daily task of lightening my mother's labours a cheerless duty, but had not Heaven blessed me with a fraternal friend in Llewellyn, who, born to endear every scene he graced, entered, at the intervals he could absent himself from college, his father's humble roof, with a tender reverence that made all our cares be absorbed in pleasure. Astonished at finding his little sister suddenly sprung up into a young woman, he sounded the depth of my intellects, and calculated my acquirements. With a fond distinction of the little merits he found in me, he made me insensibly conscious of those I wanted; and he, who was a fountain of knowledge, graciously accommodated himself to my uncultivated capacity. Mutual love soon led us to unbounded confidence; and, while he flattered me with softening his soul, I gradually imbibed from it that high spirit of virtue, which, while it enables us to rise above the little evils of this little world, insensibly prepares us for a better. Felt I now the sting of poverty? Ah, no! I saw pleasure was to be found every where by the good; and that the mind, cast by contracted circumstances upon itself, throws out wild shoots even in a chilling atmosphere, which can amply supply the loss of those indulgences the sunshine of prosperity only can bestow. My delight was reading; and my dear brother always selected for me such books as he thought would form and fix my taste; making me in his absence, write comments on those I then read, which, on his return, he would peruse, delighting to rectify my judgment when it erred, and if he found it correct, gratify me with that pure applause which nurtures every noble faculty of the mind. How blessed were the days we thus passed together! Had I a sorrow, it was lost in his society; had I a joy, it was doubled by his participation: but a pure creature of a better world could not long endure to be of this. It is a little more than a year ago that he returned, with a cold and cough

The Canterbury Tales

upon him, which none of us supposed dangerous, till the hollows of his youthful cheeks showed the ravage it was making in his constitution. He was ordered to pass the winter at home! Oh! how long, how dreary did that winter appear, as I watched the wasting of his graceful form! The efforts made to remove the disease only, I fear, took from him the strength necessary to encounter it. As the spring came on we fancied he amended. What an ecstasy ran through the family! My father insisted that he had suffered from confinement, and so often urged him to try the air, that he at last complied. Never can I forget the day that, as I entered the garden, I saw him feebly coming down the walk! The depredations of the disease were never so visible: – my heart died within me. On casting his eyes forward he perceived me at a little distance, and lifted them to the sun with a wan smile of tender resignation. Oh God! what a smile! – it almost killed me. I flew to give him my arm, glad to escape the sight of that face, more dear to me than any thing on earth. Horror was as prevalent as grief whenever, from that moment, I was obliged to fix my eyes on it: yet if I could hear, without seeing him, his harmonious voice gave me ever the sweet familiar pleasure peculiar to family friendships. The desperation of his case was at length past concealment: he alone bore the conviction with fortitude. Five weeks did I and my poor mother watch, with unclosed eyes, by his bedside; till at length his celestial spirit exhaled in piety and peace. Heavily, most heavily, we wept – heavily must we ever weep on the grave of Llewellyn! When we became able to look out of ourselves again, we had sad leisure to discover that the poverty which my brother's illness had increased, his death perpetuated. Our pride, our pleasure, our promised affluence, all, all had expired with Llewellyn. Alas! in addition to my share of the general calamity, I had a hoarded portion of my own to groan over in secret. My companion, friend, instructor, bosom counsellor, was no more! The books we had studied together lay yet around me, but I could only drench them in my tears. The precepts of this beloved brother I still seemed to hear; but I had no longer voice to repeat, or spirits to apply them. My poor parents began to apprehend that the solitude I affected would prey upon my health, and rob their age of its last prop, when my lady, who sometimes visited us, with an air of benevolence proposed, that, to amuse and employ my mind, I should take charge of Miss Caroline. In the universal dejection of the family each sought not, therefore found not, that comfort which had heretofore reconciled us to an humble lot. My parents too were painfully sensible that they could not provide for me, should I lose their protection, and that it was wise to accustom me to maintain myself. The offer was therefore accepted, and six months ago I came here as the governess of Miss Caroline."

'The lovely Agnes suddenly paused, struck with, as I concluded, a delicate consciousness that she could not proceed without shocking my feelings; as the situation in which I found her showed too plainly the fallacy of her parents' expectations. I implored her, however, to pursue her story with frankness; hinting that she could hardly tell me anything of my lady mother which would be new or surprising.

'"At my first coming, then sir," resumed the interesting girl, "I had a thousand lectures given me, both concerning my own conduct and that of your sister, all of which it was not less my inclination than my duty to be governed by; but, I know not why, I was never able to convince my lady that I sought to make her will the rule of mine. Miss Caroline too, lovely and innocent, is yet inquisitive and unruly. A thousand little tales she continually ran to her mother with; nor could the dear thoughtless child guess at their cruel consequences to me. I, too had often occasion to complain of her, for either ridiculing or defying an authority which I rarely exercised, and always with great tenderness; but I had the mortification to be told, either that the child was in the right, or I had not taken the proper method to amend her fault. It had been premised, ere I entered upon the office, that to dress, work for, and attend on Miss Caroline, should be among my duties. I blush to tell you that those are all now remaining. The servants have long known me insensibly levelled with themselves. My parents stipulated that I should dine in the parlour; but my lady, two months ago, informed me the indulgence made Miss Caroline pert, and that I must dine with her in the room appropriated for teaching. This arrangement did not satisfy my pupil, who had influence enough to resume her place in the parlour; but mine was never more allowed me. The additional trouble of supplying me a solitary meal was soon rudely neglected by servants, who finding me ranked with themselves in all other instances, saw no cause for dinstinction in this. Thus, by insensible degrees, while anxious to fulfil every duty to God, my parents, and my benefactors, did I find myself a mere superfluity in life, a nonentity, or rather an encumbrance; and long am I likely to remain so, as my lady is willing to escape the odium of sending me back to the dear parents who fondly fancy I am happy in her favour; nor dare I add to their distress by humbling them yet more with this recital, especially as I well know Sir Hubert, in the days of my brother's severe sickness had lent my father a sum he is unable yet to repay; and it would kill him to bear the weight of an obligation to the family who could forget he was a gentleman, no less by birth than profession. In troubling you, sir, with this detail, I rather sought to awaken your friendship than pain your feelings. Your better judgment and kind heart may, perhaps, enable you to find some method of getting me sent home, without any further evil having resulted from a vain experiment."

'You may guess, my dear Pembroke, from the impression the lovely Agnes had already made on me, at the effect of this simple yet touching recital; but though I promised her my aid, I never attempted to keep my word. I would sooner have parted with my life than the angelic Agnes. This promise, therefore, only tended to beguile her into confidence and intercourse. The dislike I ever entertained to my stepmother now arose almost to aversion. Caroline was nearly included in the same feeling; and since she could set at nought the mild influence of the lovely Agnes, I resolved to maker her sensible of one she could not over-rule: but she was gentle, and all her little faults were of her mother's making. The sweetness with which she obeyed me showed that at once, and won my fondest affection.

'As it was impossible for me long to appear ignorant either of the residence of Agnes with us, or her name, I foresaw I should find it very difficult to avoid becoming suspected of a passion for her; but, from the moment my heart had found this precious hoard of secret happiness, I knew how to bend it to my purposes. I affected a studious, sedentary life; would hardly see any body, or notice those whom I saw; passed almost the whole of my time in the library; and left about, for the eye of the observing, rough copies of translations from several of the Latin poets, which appeared to be the cause of my abstraction. Some few moments – and they were very few – I yet found to offer up my soul's devotion to Agnes; for I no longer affected to second her wish of returning to her parents; and though she still continued to talk of it, I thought, by the hesitation of her voice, that this effort of respect to her family and herself would cost her heart too dearly to be put in practice. The wish gradually died away. The painful humiliation of her present state she began to endure with more patience, – with the soft endeared submission of silent tenderness. Although she almost lived on air, (for dinner, I knew, she never tasted,) she improved in loveliness, by the rich glow and varying graces which the pulsations of the heart ever diffuse incidentally over the person.

'Utterly secluded from a world that I had in my years of vanity been told I well might grace, poor and dependent, my days elapsed in an exquisite trance I should have cursed the man who wakened me from. Can human life afford an enjoyment comparable to those we feel when we devote ourselves, by silent and delicate attentions, to the dear object of our choice, – the single being in creation? But if, by a peculiarity of circumstances, we are able to make those attentions understood by her, while they are inexplicable to the rest of the world, we surely taste the most refined felicity our imperfect nature is capable of knowing. You are fond of the clarionet: oh! with what pleasure, on learning my Agnes loved it, did I spend whole months in mastering the instrument, though she could only catch the notes as she walked in a distant wood with Caroline.

'Sweet, sweet was the labour, with my own hands to embellish the spots she was fond of! How often have I, O God!' cried the agitated historian, throwing back his grey locks from his sunburnt forehead, and lifting his large dark eyes with impressive wildness to heaven, 'the very recollection of those days is too mighty for this weak brain, this swelling heart! Agnes – my angel Agnes is for ever vanished! The lovely visions that "were around her as light" alike are vanished. The awful darkness of the soul is fallen upon me; and long have I wandered – long must I wander, alone and benighted, though this busy world. In my widowed heart,' pursued he, drawing from his bosom a packet sealed with black, which, with eastern solemnity, he put to his head, his eyes, his lips, and his breast, 'be all the remainder of my sad story buried – with my Agnes!'

The animated sympathy and tender consolations of Henry could hardly recall the veteran from the deep reverie into which he then fell; and it was a considerable time ere he resumed his recital.

'A creature like Agnes, gifted with an intuitive sense of decorum, far, far, beyond that which is the bond and grace of polished society, no sooner saw my weakness and felt her own, than she nobly made a law for herself, and deprived us both of the pleasure we almost lived on – the sight of each other; at least all the kindness and confidence that endeared it. This was effected by a very simple means; for she now never separated, night or day, from my little sister. Apprised both of Caroline's shrewdness and loquacity, I hardly dared speak to either when they were together, and vainly studied how to find one without the other. My only chance was that of quitting the dining parlour early; for well I knew Agnes was then a wanderer somewhere, and Caroline by her mother's side, which she never left till cloyed with fruit and sweetmeats. I therefore affected to become more and more deeply absorbed in my literary pursuits; often came in with a pen in my hand, and snatching it up the moment the cloth was drawn, ran again to the library. This I did long enough to assure myself that no one would follow to interrupt my studies, or rather to discover my absence from them; but finding I was considered as a mere bookworm, I one day ventured to explore the whole house and its vicinity, without being able to discover my charmer. Not even her own little apartment escaped my search; but as if by magic, Agnes daily vanished till Caroline left her mother. Had I not, when a schoolboy, known every room and closet in my father's mansion, I should have concluded she had found some secret place in it with which I was unaquainted; but that, I was convinced, could not be.

'It was just possible that Agnes might, in this interval, reach the parsonage, and return; and not doubting but that I must find her with her father and mother, I ventured to call even at this unusual hour upon them. Agnes, however, I saw not; nor could I learn that this was her time for paying them her duty. Almost in despair, I turned again towards home; but seeing a servant, who might mention having met me, I passed, to avoid him, into the churchyard, and was hid by its wall. Suddenly my ear was there greeted, and my soul revived by the sound of an organ, for my mother had bequeathed her own to the church. I approached, and through the door caught the angel voice of Agnes, rising in sad yet sweet accordance. I remained in the porch, and listening intently, found that it was the funeral anthem and dirge she was performing, to the memory of her beloved brother, there buried: – "If there was any virtue, if there was any praise, he thought of these things," A requiem at once so holy and so tender, "rapt me in Elysium."' I ventured not to sully with an earthly love the sacred image impressed at that interesting moment on her pure soul; But daily resorting to the porch, lived on the sound of her heavenly voice, till a monument, which I had for some time bespoke, should be placed over the grave of Llewellyn. When it arrived, I had for the time it was fixing up permission, that she might resort thither and indulge her taste, while she freely practised music. I seized the opportunity to take an impression of the key on wax, and rode many a mile ere I ventured to have one made.

'The little mark of respect and friendship I had shown Llewellyn offended my father, as another of my romantic and idle extravagances; but it wholly won the generous heart of Agnes. In what brilliant tears did her eyes over swim when they afterwards met mine! with what melting softness did she address me, even though Caroline was by! how did she pursue with fond regard my very footsteps!

'I waited my opportunity; and one day, while she was divinely touching the organ, I softly opened the church door, locking it again, and cautiously leaving my key within. I hid myself, till I was convinced by her descending, that she was alone. Softly and reverentially she paced up the aisle, and sunk on the grave of her brother in silent prayer: nor for him alone did the angel pray. Sorely she sighed, and pressing her hand on the purest of human hearts, gave me reason to believe myself included in orisons so touching: – a sigh even more impassioned burst from my bosom: starting, she turned with terror round, and felt relieved on seeing only me. "Rise not, my Agnes," cried I, sinking alike on my knee, "nor let one fear disturb you, – a fiend alone could give you any: see not in this unauthorised intrusion aught but the fond wish for your society that militates against a mere decorum, nor dares offend your purity. Here – before the alter of God, and kneeling upon the the tomb of your brother, I swear – solemnly – deliberately swear, never to give you a pain I can spare you – never to tinge that lovely cheek with a blush for any fault of mine." She regarded me with a dignified silent seriousness, implying belief; and stretching out my hand with her own yet linked in it, towards the alter, she accepted the vow, and we mutually bent to heaven to confirm it. "Nor is this,"' added I, "the only vow I mean to pledge to you, my Agnes: – here, here, I once more swear to give my hand to her who holds it – to my Llewellyn's lovely sister – to Agnes only." A beautiful flush rose to her cheeks, but I had ratified this vow on her lips, ere she had recollection enough to reject it.

'Thus in a church was the soft silence of our love first broken, – in a church was it daily confirmed. What precious hours did we steal to pass at the grave of Llewellyn; with an innocence his disembodied spirit might have witnessed, and a delight well worthy of it. The ruin but too probably attached to my marrying Agnes made her inexorable to my entreaties; and the advance years and increasing infirmities of my father rendered it likely that I should soon be master of my own resolutions. But what young heart can live upon the cold uncertain future? I was persuaded that we might venture a private marriage;

The Canterbury Tales

and the caution we had hitherto observed would sufficiently guard us from suspicion. Agnes shrunk from the idea; and even if I dare judge for myself, and act independently of my father, so would not she. Obedient even in thought to those who gave her being, she resolutely refused to marry without her parents' consent; and that, she assured me, I should find not less hard to obtain than the approbation of Sir Hubert. I was too much bent, however, on calling her entirely my own, not to revolve all possible ways of inclining the venerable pastor to my purpose; till a bold and desperate project sprung up in my heart, which I ventured not to impart to Agnes, yet deliberately resolved to risk. I told her that her own father should marry us. She treated this as mere banter, but knew not what to make of the determination of my manner. I exacted nothing more of her than a promise not to visit home till she should be summoned thither; and, with a confidence which she could not account for, assured her that summons should call her to church as a bride. Confused, perplexed, and anxious, she gave me the promise I required; but knew little comfort while so uncertain a plan was in agitation.

'I now resorted daily to the parsonage, with a look so self-reproaching and disconsolate, that the good man became very urgent with me to impart its cause. When I had sufficiently awakened his sympathy, I ventured to hint to him a passion that I had cherished to desperation, but I named not the object: – his pale and agitated looks told me I need not. He greatly did his duty, by exhorting me to forget the object, however lovely or amiable, so ill suited to me in fortune. I interrupted him by declaring myself incapable of such base desertion. I owned I was already wedded – irrevocably bound by ties of honour which the church might confirm but could not cancel. He lifted his trembling hands to heaven, "And the unhappy girl has yielded?" sighed the tender father. I remained silent, but soon passionately sinking at his feet, conjured him to remember that the choice rested in his own bosom; and Agnes was my wife if he would only give her to me. Shame, pride, and piety, struggled severely at his heart; but our agitation and high tone soon added a third person to the party too delicately alive to female honour or disgrace not to side with me: – I mean the mother of my angel. Our joint entreaties at length wrought upon the worthy man, and he consented to marry me privately to his daughter. Oh! cruel state of woman in society, when a mother was obliged to consider that act as honourable and generous, which, had the fault been real, would only have been the poorest

The Canterbury Tales

kind of reparation. I blushed to be treated with tearful gratitude by the matron whom I had thus wounded.

'It was, however, almost impossible to prevail on the offended father to address one line to the child he thought so culpable; but I assured him that unless he did he would never see her more. At length, with bursts of mingled shame and sorrow, he snatched a pen, and wrote, – "Meet me at the alter – at the altar only can I meet you." I caught the pen from his hand, nor would allow another word to be added. Hardly could I control the fond, the glowing exultation of my heart in having thus insured its only wish. The distress of the parents I knew to be temporary and imaginary, – the happiness I had thus gained long and exquisite.

'Agnes looked now on me, and now on the billet, in mute wonder, hardly crediting the hand to be her father's; but the transports of my joy were a full confirmation. A moment's reflection proved that I could neither have will nor power to deceive her; and I soon had the exquisite delight of seeing her young heart participate the sweet perturbation of mine at our approaching union.

'I wrote to implore the anxious parents not to betray my confidence by one unkind look at their daughter; and named the day and hour, when with the clerk, and one faithful, though humble, friend of their own choosing, they should expect us in the church. I had consented she should return, when once married, to pass the day at my father's; where she was to obtain leave to remain a week with her own. I was in waiting for my lovely fluttered girl in the porch of the church; and her father stood ready at the altar with his book and surplice on. The sad solemnity of his greeting shocked and surprised Agnes. Conscious through her whole life only of virtue and filial reverence, she could not account for the stern and chilling air with which he went through the awful service. The floods of tears that fell from her mother's eyes had not the same effect, for her own flowed abundantly. The benediction of both parents, which followed that of Heaven, was faintly and imperfectly bestowed on her; while to me it became cordial and animated. The father then hastened to depart, as having by a powerful effort over himself got through a painful duty; and my beauteous Agnes, hurt and appalled she knew not why, trembling and alone retrod the steps that brought her.

'Oh! think what a lingering day of torture remained to us both; – to be in one house, yet wholly estranged: to have gained severally the treasure above valuation, without daring to avow its possession: the

The Canterbury Tales

sun, that I more than once imagined a second time stood still, at length sunk in the west, and the day finally closed. Caroline's tongue, which I thought would never cease, was at length silenced by sleep. I walked in the wood beyond the garden, till the lover's friend, a bright moon, showed my timid lovely bride, softly closing the small gate upon herself. I sprung forward to claim her as my own, and folded her to a heart as entirely hers now as at that blessed moment. When she spoke to me of her father's wrathful looks in the morning, I enjoyed the pure felicity which I was going at once to dispense and to feel; and opening the jessamine-covered wicket of the parsonage, I sunk with my bride at the feet of her humbled and afflicted parents, imploring them to pardon the only artifice by which I could have won their sanction to our union. I bade them fold to their virtuous bosoms a daughter as pure as when she was first pressed there. Oh! what a tearful joy was theirs at this blessed news. My fault was forgotten, more than forgotten – hallowed by their bursts of grateful affection. Agnes, again astonished, sought by turns in the eyes of each an explanation. Comprehending at length the artifice I had adopted, never did she appear so transcendently lovely as, while her looks reproved her parents for believing me, and her blushes so sweetly vindicated her own purity. The world affords not four such happy beings as encircled that little table, though on it was only "a feast of herbs." The father's hand had given me Agnes in the morning; the matron hand of her chaste mother now bestowed her for ever on the happiest of mankind.

'How little may constitute felicity to tender hearts you will judge, when I tell you that mine knew no drawback save a fond desire I had to see my Agnes released from subordination, and elevated to her own place in society; but she bore all the inconveniences of her subjected state with a meekness so noble, that it doubled my adoration, while the sweet mystery of our marriage gave to the wife all the charms which fear and anxiety bestow on her whom we are impatient to make so. What under other circumstances we should have thought a misfortune, we were now obliged to consider as a blessing, for, after a while, we saw no prospect of becoming parents.

'The contented manner in which I had appeared to sit down for life at home, was, however, not very satisfactory to my lady mother, who saw, with deep chagrin, that Sir Hubert, as his years and infirmities increased, turned over to me all his correspondences, accounts and whatever claimed exertion either of body or mind. Her own mean, selfish temper made her incapable of hoping to find generosity from

The Canterbury Tales

me, should Heaven suddenly recall my father; and she determined to keep the power wholly in her own hands, by once more driving me from my peaceful harbour into that world where I had been wrecked already. How she wrought upon my father, who certainly had no mind to part with me, to purchase another commission, I know not. The first word I heard of the matter was its being presented to me. A sentence of death could hardly have shocked me more. By some previous prejudice, he construed my visible repugnance to serve into want of manly spirit; and briefly informed me, that infamy in the army, and contempt among my friends, must follow my declining the purchase he had made for me. I remained almost in a state of distraction, and avoided immediate decision. My wife became my consoler. She tenderly urged my compliance, though it must leave her unprotected, save by her infirm and humble parents. The dread of exasperating Sir Hubert, and aiding the dark machinations of my stepmother, who evidently wished to get me disinherited, which must plunge my sweet Agnes in eternal poverty, alone induced me to hesitate. I was no sooner found to do that, than volleys of letters came every day, either to Sir Hubert or myself, from all our meddling relations, insisting upon it that my resuming my station in the army now in actual service, and showing my courage, could alone retrieve the character I had lost in the West Indies, where it was hinted I was spoken of rather as a poltroon than a spendthrift.

'This ignominious representation roused every particle of man in me, and in an evil hour I accepted the commission, though to have driven a plough upon the estate which I was born to heir, and have dwelt in a cottage with peace and Agnes, would have been preferable. Alas! not one of those blessings was ever more to be my portion. She too, made up of soft affections, had implored, entreated me to consent; for to know me at once defamed and disinherited would have sunk her early to the grave. A thousand times was I on the point of avowing our union, and carrying with me the treasure of my life. But I was going to a camp, to share hardships, and risk dangers which my Agnes knew not how to calculate; nor dared I describe to her tender heart the various horrors of the scene. Yet oh! that she had known them, and claiming all her rights in and over me, we had together shared the vicissitudes of war, the discomfort of poverty. Oh! that I had risked every misery but the one I must to the latest moment of existence groan under.

'My compliance being obtained, Sir Hubert, resuming an air of paternal kindness, gave me a solemn assurance, that his will secured

The Canterbury Tales

to me those rights of heirship he had vested in himself only to guard them; nor should he ever alter it while my conduct was prudent and dutiful. With his customary severe thrift, he, however, neither gave nor allowed me more money that was indispensible to my situation; nor could I, in parting, much enrich the angel whom my love had bound to endure the subjection of my father's house. To me it had been, from the hour of our marriage, lessened, as my proud soul already called it her own. The proximity of her parents, however, assured her of tenderness and protection, nor did my absence rob her of any good, save my poor self. Her thoughts on this sad separation I understood only by her tears; for Agnes knew not by weak complaints to imbitter duty, still less by entreaties to interfere with it. Briefly let me say I left my love. Oh! that I had left life and her at the same miserable moment.

'I found my regiment ready to embark for Flanders; and soon after I arrived there had occasion enough to show that I neither wanted courage nor conduct. The fluctuations of the war caused me to lose many letters on which my existence seemed to hang. Those that reached me gave me a dreadful alarm for the life of Agnes: as from the time of my departure sleep and appetite had fled her: but all my fears soon ended in the sweetest hopes: for I found she was likely to become a mother. Yet this pleasure of perpetuated being, which pervades all ranks alike, was damped to me by the recollection of her peculiar situation under the roof of a man incapable of pardoning her want of fortune; for that was the only want which malice itself could impute to Agnes. I eagerly exhorted her, ere suspicion could arise; to quit not only my father's house, but that of her own: and, ever observant of my will, she answered that her aunt had come from Bristol, on the invitation of her parents, to consult upon the safest and best mode of conduct she could observe: they had agreed that she should follow her aunt thither: in so large a place she should be secure from notice, and might not only lie in, but safely reside there till I should return to England. For this, however, a small supply of money was necessary, and that she was obliged to look to me for. In the certainty of obtaining it, she had, however, already expressed a wish to be dismissed to my lady; who had only required to stay till another attendant should be found for Caroline; and this, as she could not leave the country till a remittance arrived, would be no inconvenience. Alas! this letter found me as poor as herself; but the delay made me almost frantic: it was the death-stroke of our happiness; for ere I could aid

The Canterbury Tales

her removal, came another which I have not lost. Read it yourself; you will have no difficulty, so beautiful is her writing: hardly was her hand, or even her heart, more so.'

LETTER I

'Life of my life, how shall I find language or strength to tell! – yet vainly should I attempt to conceal, what from others will reach you with every aggravation. Oh, Hubert! beloved husband! why did we ever part? or rather, perhaps, why did we ever meet? since not allowed to add to each other's happiness. Could I in your arms find support for this weak and trembling frame, – on your bosom repose this aching head, in your heart blend grief with grief, I might perhaps gather courage to endure the fate which I have not been able to avoid. Driven with the grossest indignity, the most heart-wounding contumely, from your father's house, I return to the hitherto peaceful dwelling of my own, only to put all peace to flight. Sinking into the earth, I dare not ask consolation of my parents; for I, alas! am become their affliction. Bowed to the grave almost with the weight of my sorrow, their eyes now shun mine. What have I left in life but you; and you are far – far away from the wretched Agnes!

'Alas! my love, I deserve not your indirect reprehension – I make not evils for myself; and your tender exhortation had all the effect you wished. I bewailed no longer the situation I was in. I saw myself, as with a tenderness most elevating you call me, "the breathing temple of a human soul." I despised the weakness that made me brood over a poor apprehension for my own safety, in a moment of suffering invariably the lot of woman, while my Hubert, without any fear, daily, nay hourly, risked a life a thousand, thousand times dearer to me than my own. I found my health amend daily; and yesterday, only yesterday, rose in better spirits than I have known since we parted. One week more, and I should have been quietly enfranchised from my worse than Egyptian bondage, but, alas! my love, Heaven had ordained it otherwise.

'The weather has, I fancy, of late been very oppressive, for I have often found myself strangely faint; yet not so faint but that I could conceal it. Yesterday a large company was expected to dinner, and Miss Caroline was very anxious to be dressed with nicety. I failed not in exertions to please alike herself and her mother; but I was worn out with fatigue, both were so fanciful. I had occasion to fetch your sister some gloves from my own room; and there cast my eyes on your dear packet, enclosed from my father. I tore the cover off to assure myself of that I already knew, and kissed all of your writing that ever reached my eyes – the direction: – for, fearing to keep my lady waiting, I put the letter eagerly into my bosom, and hastened back. What was my surprise and vexation, to find Miss Caroline completely undressed; and all her beautiful long hair, that I had spent an hour in curling, combed quite out for me to dress again. The impatience I felt to read your letter, the trembling that always seizes me when I receive one from you, the ill-humour of my lady, and the eternal whims of Miss Caroline, altogether, made me feel ready to sink every moment. Perhaps the heat of the sun, which was on the room, and they had not consideration enough to observe that as I stood it shone almost full upon me (for they kept me all the while standing), might occasion the disorder. Miss Caroline was at last ready. My lady was just going: – one moment more, and I might have lived or died without any human creature's being apprised of my fate; – but that moment was not mine. A strange sensation of giddiness suddenly seized me; and reeling, I caught at Miss Caroline's chair, but wanting power to hold it, I dropped upon the ground. It was, I believe, a long while before Mrs. Margam could bring me to life again; but I saw I had been removed to the long window-seat in the gallery, where the casements were thrown open. I was shocked too at perceiving my clothes loose, and that I was in a manner undressed. The fear of the housekeeper's remarks was for a moment my only one, – but in another I missed my letter, and that thought was a bullet shot through my brain. No need had I to enquire for it: – a glance informed me it was in my lady's hands, and that Sir Hubert was raving like a madman. I wonder I did not at once drop down dead with terror, or that our poor infant survived so agonising a pang. I fell into violent fits, from which I had hardly a chance of recovering; for at intervals I saw the servants, who were before in a manner round me, standing aloof, as though your poor Agnes had shed pestilence in her very tears. I had no choice but to speak the anguish of my soul, and implore the compassion of my lady: this brought Sir Hubert forward. I will not further shock you, my love, by descanting on his unkind, I may say unmanly, treatment of me. Alas! he held in his hand the positive proof that I was your wife; yet he spoke of me as a light wretch – nay a very vile, abandoned one – for why should you not know the truth? As such he bade his servants turn me out of his house. His wife, coarse and violent as himself, deigned not

The Canterbury Tales

to listen to my supplications; nor, though a mother, had she any pity for my situation. The servants, I believe, felt for me, but obedience is the habit of their lives. Suffice it to say, that your best beloved – your wedded wife, your innocent, helpless Agnes, was spurned from your father's door as the most vicious of her sex; and it was shut for ever against her. My head was so weak, my heart so agitated, that I for some moments doubted whether this extraordinary event could be real or not. Alas! I found it but too certain, and tried to totter towards the parsonage: but I could get no further than the seat by the stile, under the last elm in the avenue; and here I wondered anew at my own misery! nor could guess what would next become of me. I thought till I was past all thinking; for my poor father, alarmed at some flying report of the servants, was hastening to inquire what had happened, when he saw me "wounded and bruised by the way-side." He who never could see a stranger so, and pass by, rushed to his poor daughter, and his pious tears revived my drooping nature. "Open *your* paternal arms, dearest, best of men," cried I; "for if you too spurn me, I must instantly expire!" He clasped me to his bosom, and I thought our hearts would alike have burst under the old elm. He tenderly led me home, where already the whole neighbourhood was gathered: – some to report, some to inquire, some to pity, but all to satisfy their insupportable curiosity, without any compassion for our wounded feelings. Among them shortly after appeared Sir Hubert's steward; and by owning a commission to me, released me from my importunate visitants. "He was," he said, "ordered to tell me, that if I had the discretion to avoid attempting to intrude myself on a family that would never admit any claim to be vested in me, I should be treated with favour; and my child properly provided for." My father turned his back on the sycophant, and quitted the room. The man continued to advise me at least to appear compliant, till Sir Hubert should cool. But I saw that to give myself up for a day, was to forfeit all estimation for ever; nor could I suppose that you would have wished me thus to act: – would you, my love? All the little recollection the dreadful shock had left me, went simply to forming my conduct, according to what I thought your honour required, and your conscience would dictate. My father had, in the interim, however, decided for us both; as he now re-entered with the church register in his hand. "Go, sir," said he, "to Sir Hubert, and tell him, such is the power of integrity, that no human insult can reach or humble it. Tell him my daughter has been for some time his own, not by my choice but that of his son;

and let him timely consider how he shall answer to his God, if he by cruel treatment shortens her days, or robs his child of the blessing of becoming in his turn a father. For me I have not forgotten I am in his power: – for his own soul's sake, let him not abuse it; for I must risk that when my duty is in question. I have, sir, already taken all the neighbours you met here with me to the church, and there shown them this regular authentic register of a legal marriage. Look at it yourself, and tell Sir Hubert I leave it open to the inspection of the whole parish. Since we have only virtue, let us fully establish our claim to that."

'You know how commanding an air my father can assume, though his manners are simplicity itself. He took my hand, and conducted me to my room, leaving, without a look, the mean agent of a mean proposal to stay or go as he pleased.

'Once alone, – the violent perturbation of personal suffering and indignity abated; – oh! how acute were my feelings for you! I, I then, who adore you, have innocently robbed you of your natural inheritance, – for to obtain that for her daughter has ever been the object with your stepmother; and Sir Hubert, cruel as I found him, has, I believe, long hesitated to gratify her, from a conscientious rather than affectionate motive. Sometimes, too I dread your imputing my sudden deprivation of sense to mere ill-humour, rather than weakness. Yet when did you ever affix an unkind construction on aught I did? And in this cruel instance recollection was lost; for some constitutional pang overcame me.

'My mother's grief surpasses my own; and she has not youth to bear up under it, nor a distant beloved husband to divide her thoughts. She had ever, you know, such a regard to the opinion of the world, has been always so highly esteemed, that, to know all tongues are busy with our names, while humiliation is our portion, will I fear, shorten her days. Perhaps, too, the recollection of the debt due from my father to yours adds apprehension to her distress. Yet, however, his passion might lead him to injure or insult me, Sir Hubert cannot surely deliberately wreak his vengeance on an upright minister of God.

'Dearest, best of fathers! I *will* be comforted – at least I must soothe mine with the hope. He came suddenly upon me, and found me blistering, as you will see, this letter with my tears.

'Husband of my heart! love not your hapless Agnes the less for the poverty she may bring on you; and it shall be the business, as it is the duty, of her life to lighten it. Let us once more meet, my Hubert! and we will share one fate for the rest of our days.'

'I was engaged in very severe service when this killing letter reached me. I wonder, in the distraction of my feelings, that I did not put my head before a cannon in the moment of explosion. Honour itself could not have kept me in Flanders, but that I immediately saw the die was cast, and my return could only supply fuel to the flame which humanity might quench. From my father I had soon after a letter: he reproached me with intriguing under his roof with a worthless girl, and insulting both her family and my own; bade me write to her to accept his bounty, and not aggravate what was past by pretending I had married her, or I should ruin both her and myself, for he would wholly disinherit me in favour of Caroline. I saw a worldliness in this letter that showed my stepmother had prompted it; and a kind of reluctance in the conclusion that induced me to be very cautious in my answer. I replied; and vindicated myself from the imputed insult to both families by avowing my marriage, with the means by which I over-ruled the scruples of my Agnes's father. I entreated Sir Hubert to consider, that if either of us had been culpable in seducing the other from duty, it must be I; yet at thirty-two to fix my choice was surely pardonable, and to sanctify it could not disgrace me. I implored him, by every tender impulse which had made my birth and that of Caroline dear to him, to consider the rights of the babe who was soon to be added to his family; and by protecting the innocent and suffering mother, entitle himself to the eternal gratitude as well as duty of his son. To this filial address I had no answer; nor, in fact, from that moment, did I ever receive a single line from my father. I had the ill fortune to lose my baggage, and of course many letters, necessary as well as dear to me. Of the few that remain this is the next.'

LETTER II

'If it will joy your heart, my best love, to know that I am yet well, take joy; for I am still able to tell you so myself, although I am so altered that I am almost glad you cannot see the shapeless Agnes. My father has ever been the tenderest of comforters, and I must now very soon have another, so dear – oh, Hubert! how dear! I sometimes sit and wonder if the babe will be like you. What a treasure to me, who have no picture of you, should I hold a living one in my arms! and I can talk to that of its father, from morning to night, without tiring it.

'My appetite returns with my peace of mind; and I eat a hearty dinner now every day, though so long out of the habit of it. Nothing reconciles us to the inconveniences of poverty like experiencing the miseries of grandeur: poor things as we are, to sacrifice so much comfort to pride. Could I have resolved to inhabit my own humble home, I should at once have told my parents how my lady treated me, and then they would have sent for me back again ere you returned from abroad; and I should not have been in your way every day, and all the day. And would I have had it thus? I dare not ask my selfish heart; for, early used to endure poverty, I might perhaps have gladly compounded for that to be the wife of my Hubert; but when I reflect I may rob him of affluence – that is the sting.

'Grieve no more, my life! that you cannot send me money, – in our humble situation, a little suffices; and now I see that the neighbours are convinced I am your wife, I do not so much wish to leave home. My poor mother cannot bear I should be without her aid; and, indeed, I am such a tender, timid thing, I know not what would become of me if I left her. My father, finding Sir Hubert's hatred of me inveterate, thinks my quitting the country might make the birth of your son, if a son it should be, disputable: he therefore says the whole neighbourhood shall be able to testify the child is ours. Yet it is irksome to encounter cold looks from those whom one has been accustomed to live well with; and though many of our neighbours have a regard for us, none dare smile when their landlord frowns. I could, on that account, prefer going to my aunt; but the will of my father was ever mine, till I found a dearer lawgiver in my husband.

'I could tell you something enchanting of your sister, if I was not afraid of wounding, of humbling you; yet ought any thing to do that which springs from right feeling? The precious child contrived to send me a hurried, but very affectionate letter, to say how sorry she was that she might not come and see me; and that she had teased her godmother out of almost a whole piece of cambric to dress her doll, in hopes it would make a robe for the baby; and this present accompanied the letter. She adds, too, that it would delight her to be a godmother herself, only I must not tell anybody of it - *they* would be so angry. By this she implies both parents: so they talk of us sometimes, you find. If it is a boy, she wishes him to be called Edmund; yet gives an odd reason for the choice – that she overheard her papa say, he hoped I would *not* give my brat that name. Sir Hubert must have some reason: let me know your will, that I may not err.'

'This innocent and kind letter of my sister's, in showing the generous feelings of her nature, endeared her much to mine: her hint, too, appeared of importance to our little one, it if proved to be a boy. The first son of my parents, who died at seven years old, – before, in fact, I was born, – had been called Edmund; and, like other short-lived children, remained on record as a model of perfection. In the hope that as his thoughts were yet on us, my father would relent, my mind became more composed; which was absolutely necessary to the closing of a troublesome wound that I had never dared to own I was suffering under, while I had the painful addition of cramped circumstances: for never, from the moment I avowed my marriage, did my father remit me a guinea. The blessed news I soon received – that my Agnes had made me one, and, with a lovely boy, was doing well – left no other misery on my mind than that of absence. Oh! how I longed at once to enfold in my arms the unknown babe, and my suffering angel! See what she says.'

LETTER III

'Yes! I hold now in my fond arms the blessed image of him ever in my heart: clasp our lovely boy, my Hubert! in imagination, to the bosom he sprung from; and bow to the God who has borne me thus safely through so many trials, even though your eye is not on me to cherish, your voice is not near to invigorate, my languid nature.

'My mother would fain persuade me that I am too delicate to nurse our darling myself; but God surely never made that woman a mother who is really unequal to the first duty of the maternal character. Sweet little fellow! as he lies at my bosom, his moaning, short-breathed satisfaction is music to my ear, and rewards me for the determination I have shown.

'It is impossible to tell you how much kindness I have received from many who are afraid to avow the part they take in our welfare. Presents have been sent often from I know not whom; baskets of delicacies have been found in the orchard; the poor old butler, your nurse's husband, brought me some of the fine rich sack your father values so; and said, that if Sir Hubert hanged him for it, he would not know his young master's lady want. He begged so hard to have a look at the babe, that my mother prevailed on me for one moment to suffer her to take him out of my sight. The worthy soul clasped him in his arms; and, falling on his knees prayed to Almighty God to bless the sweetest child he ever set eyes on. Do you know, the precious crowed as he looked up in his face, my mother tells me; indeed, the angel hardly ever cries. Alas, my babe! I have shed tears enough for both of us; and my poor, poor mother does little else. She never sleeps either, and looks so broken and wan! Ah! if I have gained one blessing only to lose another! But my restless sensibility may be too much alive: let me hope we have passed the roughest part of our journey; and though the hut where we rest ourselves is low and humble, we have only to get you among us, and to reconcile our minds to the future, when we may look down upon Sir Hubert and his selfish lady.

'Caroline, in quilted satin, sent me two guineas *for her godson*. Darling creature! who was ever more generous? It was, she says, her all.

'On Sunday, my father means to church me as Mrs. Powis, where he will publicly baptize our boy, by that name, and Edmund with it; though I am not sanguine on the influence of sound over him in whom feeling is annihilated. Oh! my love, that I had but you to countenance and support me!'

'How heavenly a disposition is seen in this letter, through which we may discern that my angel and her boy felt daily every distress but the bitter one of absolute want; and not from the least of her humiliations could her husband save her – killing recollection! Again too was I plundered of my baggage, and a chasm of a year appears in our correspondence, while still the war raged, and left me no hope of revisiting England.'

LETTER IV

'Oh! what a joy, my Hubert! Why are you not present to share it? Dearest of husbands, these poor arms are lightened, as well as my heart; our little man walks! – ay, walks alone; and is so full of his own mightiness – so proud of it. He took his grandfather's stick this morning, and tried to shoulder it, as I had in play done; looking

The Canterbury Tales

up at me with a smile so like your own. Oh! what a tearful pleasure was it to gaze on him, my Hubert! I am tempted every word I write to tell you how very beautiful he is; but as all the people round us say he is my image, I am ashamed, though in my eyes he is your picture in miniature. Were his proud grandfather only once to behold the cherub, he surely would relent; for when I look on him, I feel convinced that no parent can resist the impetuous gush of natural affection. Were this afflicting war once at an end, and we had you with us – did your father, I again say, see the sweet child in your arms, all would be well; but I have no power to move him – perhaps no right to expect it. In the sad uncertainty of your return I am nevertheless brooding over a project of my own, that I will not communicate till I know the result; and my smiling babe is to be the principal agent. Every day do I give him a lesson of love – at the spot to where first I learned it. Ah! know you not that it was the grave of our dear Llewellyn?

'Your remittance, my best love, is come to hand. Alas! I am sure you deny every thing to yourself for our sakes. I have now time for employment; and do not you blush that I have obtained some? You know I am a nice needle-woman, and I have neither my dear husband nor Caroline to work for. You have no idea how fine a young creature your sister grows. Her present governess is a Frenchwoman, who scowls at me and my boy, as though she were to have Sir Hubert's estate. I dare not venture on his immediate precincts, but I wander almost every day to the chestnut grove, and weep as I wistfully survey the temple above, where you used to stand with your enchanting clarionet, and steal my heart through my ear; for you had many, many ways of making it all your own. Oh! how dreary appears the spot, where I no more can behold my Hubert! – and it is I who have robbed him of his inheritance! – I who keep him in exile! – I who live but in his sight! One day as I was toiling up the hill, Miss Caroline espied me from the sundial on the terrace, and not heeding the commands of her governess, who passionately jabbered French, flew through the little garden gate, and, reaching me, clasped and kissed her godson with infinite tenderness. She sweetly too called me by your name! – delightful was the sound from your sister. "Is this a hat for Sir Hubert's heir?" cried she, throwing off disdainfully that which our boy wore. Do you know, the darling looks at it ever since with as much scorn as his aunt did, and never more would put it on? You need not be afraid that I shall make him too humble, though you compliment me with being so. I rank him by your degree, not my own, and only value myself as the mother of my Hubert's son. All my girlish apparel I have given up to deck the dear one. Ah! what can add to his beauty?

'I wish I could relieve your mind about my poor mother, but she has never been the same creature since my day of disgrace; and grows now so thin and weak, that, unless you return to revive her spirits, by recalling her hopes, I fear she will droop even to death: yet she so doats on our boy, that I really believe she forgives us both all the tears we have made her shed, whenever he climbs up her knee, as she sits perusing the Bible; and, stealing her spectacles, holds them over his own lovely eyes, and most sententiously hums, as though reading; imitating my father's sonorous voice: and then, we all, you may guess, smother him with caresses. Ah! he is a sad pet, without your assistance.'

LETTER V

'Alas! my Hubert, I have now done my very utmost to move your father, and have failed. I suffered neither pride nor the sense of humiliation to interfere with my duty. If poverty is to be the portion of our lovely boy, as well as ourselves, let him always remember that his mother humbled herself to the dust to obtain for him a better fortune.

'Yet surely, if Sir Hubert had but one spark of humanity, not to mention feeling, I could not have failed; for well our little smiler acquitted himself in the trial. It had long been my idea, that, could I venture to take my child to church, and be sure of his remaining quiet, the pious impressions incident to the awful place and duty would co-operate with the strong pulsations of nature to produce in your father some tenderness to my boy, if no pity for his unfortunate mother. That no displeasure to me might induce Sir Hubert to stay away from church, I have long done so; and contented myself with praying at home, till I could trust to my influence over my sweet child to keep him quiet. During the last three months he has been capable of observance, and every day have I taken him to the grave of Llewellyn; there, without witnesses, has his mother imposed on him the painful penance of silence: this for a great while the animated cherub neither understood nor approved; but finding all his winning ways, and little efforts at talking, produced no return from me, except my pressing a

The Canterbury Tales

finger on my lip, he gave up the point, and grew habitually silent – though he wondered why, as I guessed by his sweet intelligent eyes.

'On Good Friday, as the season when every Christian is thrown solemnly on his conscience and his feelings, I called upon mine to carry me through my determined duty. I waited till the whole congregation was collected; and Sir Hubert, his lady, and daughter, were all in the great seat; when, to the general consternation, with my eyes humbly fixed on the ground, and my deserted son in my arms, I came into the aisle, when I suddenly trembled so that I feared I could not walk up to it. My poor father, whom I had not apprised of my intention, lest he should construe it a scheme, and unsuited to the sanctity of the day, was already in the reading desk, and had begun – "If we say that we have no sin, we deceive ourselves." His voice faltered at sight of me, and a momentary pause in the service rendered the sentence he had pronounced peculiarly impressive. Having tottered to the grave of Llewellyn, I sat down upon the flat raised stone that covers him, just under the dear eternal token of your generous friendship, the marble monument. I took off, as the solemn place required, the interesting babe's hat: and thus showed his lovely eyes, and all the rich curls of his hair. I thought more than once that Sir Hubert looked askance at him, but it became not me to watch his eyes. I was employed in observing that the darling broke not in upon the solemn order of the place. Twenty times was he going to speak aloud, when a look of mine corrected him; and imitatively pressing his pretty finger on his rosy lip, the precious would archly smile, and hide his beloved head on my bosom. The sweet Caroline thought not, I am sure, of prayers; but her mother disdainfully turned away, nor once vouchsafed a glance on me, or my Edmund. Every other eye in the church was fixed on us both.

'The service over, Sir Hubert (which indicated he was disturbed in mind) rose hastily, to go out. I likewise arose; and, with my boy in my arms, must, you will recollect, almost touch him. The darling child, as if intuitively to second me, reached out his little hand, till it brushed his grandfather's shoulder; and, in admiration of his scarlet laced waistcoat, cried out, "Oh! fine!" Think whether it was not a dagger to my heart to see Sir Hubert shake him off in a manner, and hurry out of the church. I almost fainted; but my father, solemnly blessing me, bade me begone, and leave him to his duty: and now, my love, I despair indeed; for if our sweet boy moved not at a moment like that Sir Hubert's heart, less than an angel never can.

The Canterbury Tales

'To spare my poor parents seeing the excess of my grief and disappointment, the next morning I wandered to the solitary spot under the hollow of the hill, where you used so often to study; and there stayed reading and weeping, and weeping and reading; – your letters, I need hardly add, thus employed me. Our rosy cherub had just found, the early produce of the spring, some tufts of primroses; and gathering handfuls of them, brought the treasure to me, and enfolding some in every letter, made signs to me to seal each; and, with exultation, added – "Send papa." This tender reference, at so early an age, to my feelings, and a beloved though unknown parent, strangely blended my sorrow with delight. I was caressing the lovely creature, when I heard voices very near me, and, raising my eyes, saw two ill-looking men with guns in their hands: the inveterate hatred of his grandfather came suddenly into my mind. I started up, and, with my child in my arms, ran like a wild thing till I reached old Mary's cottage; – I hardly thought it possible I should run so far, for our Edmund now grows heavy. The men yet loitered, but, Heaven be praised, we escaped them. Should my boy be either killed or kidnapped, life would become an insupportable burden to me: – never more will I go out of the reach of assistance. When I told this alarm to my father, he seemed to think my own danger greater than my son's; but I am his child, Edmund mine. Oh! when will you come to protect us both?'

'The next letter informed me of what I had long fearfully expected – the death of my dear love's mother; and heavy did she find the loss. It added likewise to the pecuniary embarrassments of her estimable father. To complete our misfortunes, I was a second time severely wounded at the battle of Dettingen, and taken prisoner. The exertion of valour which exposed me to this evil was, however, highly spoken of; and death had been so busy there, that it was hardly a distinction for me to rise. Promotion of the most honourable kind was mine: and my uncle, the General, still alive to military glory, broke his long silence with a kind letter; enclosing, with the coarse observation that my father was probably as close-fisted as ever, the blessed relief of a bill for a hundred pounds. It came, however, too late to save my arm, which, by the ignorance of the surgeon appointed to attend me, I lost the use of; and I had been too poor, till now, to call in other advice: my very soul was cheered, however, in remitting half the money to Agnes, in a letter her father received, but not herself, for, oh! this was the answer' –

69

LETTER VI

'Unhappy husband! – visited of Heaven! – too severely do I share, to soften as I would, the calamity which it is my dreadful duty to communicate. The comfort of my age – my darling Agnes – is lost for ever! – your precious boy too is for ever gone! Let us humbly hope her reason failed ere her own rash hand thus cut short lives so precious. Spare, spare me the horrible particulars of an indubitable fact. Again has the grave of my Llewellyn been opened. Alas! that some pious hand had laid ashes there, ere I had survived to read the funeral service over the last of my race! But I resign myself to the will of God: – ask comfort of him, my son – he alone can give it to you.'

'Oh no! – nor God – nor man – nor time – nor circumstances have ever given it to me!' cried the agonised Cary, eagerly snatching the letters to bury them again in his bosom, as if with them he there could have again buried their contents. 'Such was my frantic desolation of mind, that the enemy rather chose to give me back without a cartel, than take charge of such a wild wretch. I found letters announcing a legacy from the General, adequate to my future wants; and in the flaming anguish of my soud I vented to my father all I felt. I told him, I think I told him, that "I would spare him the added sin of disinheriting me – I disinherited myself! I renounced with horror the poor plot of over-valued earth, where my Agnes, driven by his inhuman neglect to despair, had sought with my boy an untimely grave. His ample possessions were only that in my eyes; and a distant land should inhume my bones, where he could never trace me. Since his inhumanity had rendered me single in creation, he should find that he had lost for ever his son in the horrible hour when I lost mine!" Before it was possible my purpose should be defeated, I had lodged my legacy in the Dutch funds, under the name I have ever since borne, after which I sailed to America. From that period I have been a citizen of the world – without tie, connection, correspondence, hope, or wish. The only mitigation of suffering I have ever found is motion; and had I not full power to ramble and ruminate, I should soon become a lunatic. That horrible calamity I have, however, escaped: for all the singularities that mark my conduct are the fruit of reflection, and of an intelligence.' Cary paused, with a bewildered air and with increased solemnity added, 'Henry, I love you much – I have permission – that power—' Again he abruptly paused, and cast his eager, expressive eyes every way around, as if to mark if aught human were within ear-shot. From the vacated Indian hut, into which the friends had retreated to rest themselves, Henry did the same; and struck no less with the sublime solitude they had reached than the affecting visionary with whom his soul was so powerfully assimilating, he sighed. They were standing on a rocky height, having rounded one yet more elevated, which shut from their view the town and harbour. Above and below, far as the eye could reach, rolled in majestic windings the river St. Lawrence; while a hundred rills, formed by the melting snow, shone silvery to the sun-beams, through as many inlets of the rocky banks. The enormous woods behind them, coëval apparently with time itself, haughtily seemed to shake off the white burden of premature old age, and blend the budding verdure of spring with icicles but half dissolved; while the tufts of mould upon which they trod, threw up, in almost wasteful gaiety, rich half-brown flowerets, even though on their neighbouring masses of pointed stone the chill frost lay yet unmelted. This union of contrarieties in nature Henry felt to be like that between himself and Cary; but for man there is, alas! no renovation on this side of the grave. 'I shall go to him, but he shall never return to me,' murmured the sympathetic youth. Even these imperfect accents waked Cary from the deep and mysterious meditation into which he had fallen; who thus resumed his discourse: – 'Think not, my young friend, that it would have been possible for me thus long to have dragged on existence, had I wholly lost Agnes. Oh no!' added he, striking his breast, while with exultation he raised his tone of voice, 'mine is an enviable, a triumphant lot. That purer part of my lovely wife, her disembodied blessed spirit, in its sublime essence, deigns yet at intervals to hover over me in hallowed visitation: nor can I reconcile to your comprehension the appalling foreknowledge I find of her approach. The adored vision is at once glorious, indistinct, incomprehensible, shadowy, chilling, formless. Though this ethereal intercourse is the sole delight of my life, imperfect mortality ever shudders to meet it; and a dreadful struggle, as of death, announces to me her approach. Almighty power!' exclaimed he, springing passionately forward; but in a moment shrinking back, he had hardly breath to utter '*Now! now!*' – when, withering as it were in the arms of young Pembroke, he added faintly, – 'I feel her now, in every fibre, in every aching pore! – Cold, cold, humid, earthy!' Large drops of sweat started upon the forehead of the impressive visionary, and there seemed to congeal. The playful muscles of his lips stiffened in mystical reverential silence, and his fine eyes became mere orbs without expression. By a painful effort he rose from his supporter, and voluntarily prostrating himself on the cold ground, waved his hand as choosing to be left there. Henry Pembroke, in almost equal horror, wept to see

> – 'That noble and most sovereign reason,
> Like sweet bells jangled thus, and out of tune.'

But to shrink from the martyr of sensibility was not in his nature. On the contrary, fully convinced that the malady thus cherished must be incurable, Henry hardly felt himself less bound by that than the ties of gratitude to the interesting sufferer, over whom he had in all other instances an almost boundless influence.

Cary at length arose as from a trance; and having on his knee devoutly offered up a silent thanksgiving, turned to Pembroke, in whose young eyes still swam tears of tender compassion. Wiping from his forehead the cold drops that yet hung there, the fond visionary raised his brows with an almost celestial complacency, while his eyes even lightened with ecstasy, and on his sun-burnt cheek sprung up a rich glow that gave life to many a trace of long-buried manly beauty. Pembroke, on seeing the soul thus break through the cloud of human calamity, beheld in the grand creature before him a seer of ancient days; and now surveyed the scene, and now the man, with a wonder that made him almost envy so elevating a malady, and for ever impressed on his memory the hour they thus passed together on the rocky heights of Canada.

'The suffering you have witnessed,' said the recovered wanderer, in a solemn and collected voice, 'is, you know, temporary; but the pure peace it breathes through my nature long and lasting. This holy indulgence was, however, so sudden, that I feared it was to reprove my communication; but the angel sanctions it. – I would have known how you obtained such grace, but I had no answer. Doubtless, the sympathy of your generous nature touches hers; though to you she will never be revealed. Ah! no, that awful distinction is mine – mine only. You may, perhaps, witness more of these trances: – let me warn you ever to retire in devout silence – break them not, I charge you, lest over-wrought nature should make life vanish with the spirit that suspends it.'

The holy kind of calm that followed the intellectual error of Cary a little reconciled Henry to it; but he secretly resolved for ever, if possible, to avoid these temporary suspensions of mental, and, perhaps, corporeal life, that he felt it impossible to behold without a suffering hardly inferior.

'With a restless mind, and speculative eyes.' concluded Cary, 'have I, since I quitted the army, traversed almost the whole known world, guarded in savage regions, supported in desert ones, visited in such as are not utterly defiled by cruelty, and the train of execrable human passions, by the spirit of my angel. Many years did I reside on the banks of the Ganges, among the pure of heart – among the Brahmins; and that I might win their regard, I accustomed myself to diet in their manner. My heavenly visitations at that period became so much more frequent, that I resolved never again to render myself the tomb of any creature that had once known life. But this abstinence sprung not from supposing that the ethereal spirit, lodged in man, though sullied by imperfection, or stained by vice, can never be condemned to grovel in an animal. Oh! no, I had an awful conviction that it takes a higher flight: if my love for these faithful creatures,' pointing to his two beautiful spaniels, 'has countenanced this supposition, know that it was by command I took – I cherished them: it is not for me to enquire, but to obey.

'Believe me, Henry, it belongs only to little minds, and such as move in a narrow space, to be decided, and opinionated. The further we extend our progress in life, and the more we observe upon society at large, the more cautious do we become of pronouncing judgement on others. All countries, nations, and sects, either naturally or accidentally, differ: yet I have always found this infinity of modes of thinking and acting so justifiable, whenever I listened to the parties immediately governed by them, that it appears to me, the only conclusion we can fairly draw from the little we gather in our journey through life, is, that so much must ever remain unknown to us in the material, as well as immaterial world, as renders human wisdom in its amplest extent only enlightened ignorance. It is not, therefore, the man who knows most, but the man who makes the best use of his knowledge, that is entitled to our admiration: he who, disdaining the vain parade of science, simplifies all his talents and acquirements into virtue and benevolence, is, whatever may be his country or opinions, 'the noblest work of God,' He darts not, it is true, an eccentric course, like a comet, whose rays, as evanescent as they are bright, excite wonder and apprehension, but are without utility: no, like a fixed star he holds his place in the host of heaven; and while he benignly illuminates his

The Canterbury Tales

own sphere, he is at once reverentially beheld, and understood, by all who live within reach of his influence.'

'What a piece of work is man!' sighed Henry to himself; – 'yet this is one well worth saving. Yes, Cary, I will struggle hard to bring back to reason a mind so glorious in its wanderings; – you, too, shall see, and share, the benevolence of our father.'

The volunteer was yet a mere novice in knowledge of the world, and naturally credulous; he therefore easily persuaded himself, that his visionary friend had too fully relied on a letter, which, however decisive, was not circumstantial. Could he, therefore, once induce Cary again to revisit his own country, the part of it which contained his lost treasure would soon be discovered: and, perhaps on enquiry, some information might occur to lighten his sense of the calamity, if not restore the lamented object.

Among Cary's objections to returning, Henry soon found that the dread lest his ethereal visitations should not be as frequent, was predominant: yet great was the struggle between the living and the dead, in the too susceptible soul of the supposed misanthrope. Long unused to the tender intercourse of friendship which he now daily held with Pembroke, and relieved from the weight of his own secret by a confidence that so endeared the person trusted, Cary knew not how to resist the importunate entreaties of the grateful, the affectionate Henry, to go with him, – to share for life his heart – his attachment – his situation. The anxiety with which Cary had watched Henry during a dangerous and long confinement, had centred his thoughts and feelings so much in the youth, that he felt a dread, a horror, at the idea of being suddenly left in the worst of all solitude – that of the soul; – again to traverse the vast wilds of America, and once more to mingle with savages only, whose nearest approach to society is the not offending against it. Long conflict of this kind soon brought upon the interesting visionary one of his trances, in which he fancied the beautiful spirit bade him accompany Henry. The youth was just on the point of embarking and seized the moment to hurry away with him the friend whom he knew not how to lose for ever. In the close intercourse which a ship necessarily induces, Henry easily discovered by what means the powerful imagination of Cary had been bewildered; for he found his abstinence excessive, and his use of laudanum immoderate. Sometimes the youth was tempted to throw his friend's medicine-chest overboard; and at others to qualify the drug with water: but Cary was so worn out with confinement in the

The Canterbury Tales

narrow limit of the vessel, and so shaken in mind as they approached England, that Henry ventured not to lessen the veteran's only relief till both should be more at ease.

The thoughts of Henry during the whole of the voyage had been wholly devoted to the dear object of his fondest affections. Reduced, and exhausted in constitution, – worn, and wan in look, – his heart had not lost any of its energy, and each quick throb bore through his secret soul the name of Julia. Was he sure he could see in this much loved creature only a sister? Was he sure, if Vernon should be with her, that he could conceal the misery of his mind? Alas! he was not sure of any thing but the tumult of expected pleasure, tempered with dread.

Mr. Pembroke, apprised of the delicate state of Henry's health, and the probable time of his arrival, had sent an easy travelling chaise, and two trusty servants much attached to the youth, to wait his landing at Portsmouth. Their well-known faces instantly brought the dear familiar charm of home, the sweet remembrance of his boyish days, before the young volunteer. He was never tired of seeing, or of asking from them a thousand little domestic occurences, which correspondence, even when unreserved, conveys not. In these cheerful and eager discussions Cary could not possibly be a party, and insensibly his misanthropy recurred, with the idea of loneliness and desertion. England had for him, too, its overwhelming train of recollections; but they breathed no enlivening spirit into his nature, and he almost sullenly sunk again into himself. Henry saw this with compassion; but as it was for the veteran's own relief, not any personal gratification, that he had brought him over, he thought it best not to be too quick sighted. In truth, he was no longer master enough of his own faculties to withdraw them from the dearer objects to whom he was now rapidly approaching: – fast as post-horses with relays could carry the friends, they drove to Castle St. Hilary; and the ease of the carriage made Henry propose to his companion proceeding by night as well as day. Cary made no objection, but added continually to his dose of laudanum as his fatigue increased. At the grey dawn of the second morning, after winding up a high mountain, the carriage stopped. Through the gates Henry's eager eyes perceived, in a lighted hall, his father hastening, newly arisen; and the lovely Julia in her nightcap and robe-de-chambre. In a moment he shot into their arms; and the sweet tumult of melting emotions absorbed recollection. The altered countenance, and thin person of Henry, then awakened all Julia's anxious feelings; and to see his arm yet in a sling shocked his father. The gouty limp of that excellent man

The Canterbury Tales

touched the affectionate heart of Henry; but the rich roses of Julia's cheek gave him sweet assurance sorrow was yet far from her heart; consequently that she knew not love. In a momentary intermission of exquisite delight, the recollection of Cary flashed across the mind of Henry; and shame, at the consciousness of having wanted feeling, as well as politeness, tinctured his complexion with a bloom as lovely as Julia's own. 'My friend, Sir!' cried he, starting up, - 'where is my friend?' – 'Call him *my* friend too,' fondly returned Mr. Pembroke, 'whoever he is; and a very dear one, if his name should be Cary.' On enquiry, Henry became yet more distressed; for he learned that the veteran, in alighting from the chaise, had slipped down, and greatly hurt his ancle, which the housekeeper was chafing; as he would not allow any one to interrupt the re-united family, in the moment of so joyful a meeting. With Julia in his hand, as his apology, Henry in a moment flew to the side of the veteran; who gazed on her with a wild and boundless admiration: while to the cordial greeting of Mr. Pembroke he gave but little attention, and no answer: nor did he even attempt to silence the reproaches with which the ingenuous youth loaded himself. Henry was struck with the secret dread of an approaching trance; but the assiduous softness of Julia soon lessened this apprehension. She had long used herself to every endearing care of her father in his fits of the gout; nor did she think the man who nursed, and perhaps saved Henry, less an object of her attention. On her knees she would bathe the hurt leg, while in mute wonder Cary regarded her; and with her own soft snowy hand she bound up the injured ancle. It was with difficulty they could prevent the sufferer, though still silent, from adoring the gracious vision, for such he seemed to imagine her.

The servants newly arrived having, by this time, circulated among the rest how rapidly the travellers had posted, Mr. Pembroke no longer wondered that a man advanced in life should be exhausted; – it astonished him that the injured constitution of his dear Henry could sustain such fatigue: yet the exertion of the heart always has its due weight with the heart. Sentence of bed was immediately passed upon the travellers by Mr. Pembroke; and a most happy slumber closed, after so many years of voluntary exile, the eyes of Henry beneath the paternal roof: for to his own satisfaction had he supported the painful pleasure of again enfolding Julia to his bosom.

Each following day, for many ensuing ones, seemed too short for the various details, inquiries, and narrations of each incident that had individually occurred to Mr. Pembroke, Henry and Julia. Cary was for a fortnight necessarily confined to his bed, by an inflammation on the muscles of the leg. Henry and Julia, hand in hand, came constantly to spend some hours by him; and the pleasure he took in their company brought again to being those latent charms and merits, which he would not equally disclose to Mr. Pembroke; who saw with astonishment the partiality of both his young folks to the man whom he thought a repulsive misanthrope. The rest of their time the young people passed in visiting the wild and singular scenes around St. Hilary: while, still untired, Henry always wanted to see something Julia alone could show him; hear something Julia alone could tell him: and, by those little exquisite artifices that the heart so well knows how to suggest and vary, obtained almost an exclusive monopoly of Julia's company.

Mr. Pembroke, accustomed to every benignant exertion of friendship and hospitality, held its first principle to be leaving his guests to think and act for themselves. After, therefore, a few cordial visits to Cary, with liberal offers of such comfort as an affluent and social home can supply to a solitary wanderer, he considered that gentleman as a part of his family: though not without wondering how it was possible a being so solitary, rugged, and eccentric should have fixed the friendship, and touched the feelings, of Henry; whose own manners and conduct were marked by singular elegance and refinement. To indirect inquiries on this head, Henry gave his father only the general answer that his friend had not been always thus unsocial; and that he owed his life to a tenderness a similar occasion would always call out; though at other times it was chilled by recollected misfortunes. The sad detail Cary had given him, the youth held to be too singular and sacred a confidence ever to pass his lips without that friend's previous concurrence.

It was soon known through the family that the stranger, as he never tasted animal food, sat not down to the dinner table. An additional roll, and a couple of hard eggs, were, therefore, usually sent to his apartment with his breakfast: after which he almost always disappeared, and ate his hermit meal in some haunt of the mountains. The close of day, however, brought him home again: and if Henry was accompanying Julia with his clarionet, as was their common employ, while Mr. Pembroke played chess with Mr. Benson his chaplain, Cary would choose the most remote corner of the saloon, and listen in silence till the music ended; – a civil good night was all he then uttered. This conduct sometimes distressed Henry; more especially as he had robbed himself of all right to remonstrate from the moment he conferred an obligation. The motive that induced him to bring the incurable sufferer to England, still, however, impelled him to follow, soothe, court him: but Mr. Pembroke, not bound by the same delicacy to endurance, nor the same confidence to sympathy, daily bewailed the hour that Henry had first met this forbidding inmate; and was often painfully struck with the idea of a predominating affection in meritorious exertions of mere humanity from the youth to his friend. The pungent pang of his earlier days then came over him again; and he fancied it at times impossible to be truly loved by another man's son.

In the delightful hours of unreserved communication, while Julia was pointing out the various scenes of solitary beauty around to her brother, each alike indirectly sought to trace the future plans of the other. Alas! they were of necessity ultimately the same; – elegant pursuits – unwearied and equal attention to their father – a life of celibacy, and the constant society of each other, comprehended their views, and seemed to bound their wishes.

Mr. Pembroke, who had resided in Wales, at once to indulge Julia, and use every means in his power to discover the parentage of Henry, having failed in the last object, and regained the society of the youth under circumstances so honourable to himself as might obviate all his former objections to Farleigh, suddenly found himself tired of St. Hilary; and complaining of the air of the mountain as too sharp for a gouty habit, had the pleasure of being urged by Henry as well as Julia to return to his own mansion. Thus satisfied of the harmony that would hereafter reign in Farleigh, he would have set out for home immediately, had he not been in expectation of a visit from Lady Trevallyn; who had promised herself, in the company of Mr. Pembroke and his family, a pleasure which she could not otherwise find in a place where domestic affairs must nevertheless bring her. Julia observed, that were they ready to depart when this charming friend came, they might all set out together; and perhaps tempt her to stop awhile, on her way home, at Farleigh.

The beautiful month of June was already begun, and its close was the appointed time for the visit of the engaging widow. A season like that would make any place pleasant; and since Henry was for ever to leave St. Hilary, he was resolved to make the most of his short term there. All the morning, therefore, he usually spent in riding or rambling with Cary, and the afternoons with Julia; while Mr. Pembroke, in the hope that Cary would either take up his abode in some cave on a mountain, or, in following the family to Farleigh, associate according to the modes of civil life with them all, endured the present plans, though they sometimes left him alone till late in the evening, except for the company of Mr. Benson, who attacked him at his favourite game of chess, and often kept him up to a late hour.

One night, having waited till twelve without complaining of fatigue, though riding had almost overpowered her, Julia became exhausted and faint; and Mr. Pembroke, reproaching himself for inattention, hastened her to bed; then, with all the family, retired. Henry having, however, been agitated by hearing Julia speak in terms of high esteem of young Vernon, could not calm his heart enough to think of sleep. He therefore attempted not to go to bed, but paced a long while about his chamber. The silence of the night was only broken by an owl, which hooted from the tower of the church, once belonging to the priory it adjoined. Henry had been listening to this dreary musician from the casement, when drawing his head in, he heard so deadly a shriek as to transfix him almost to the spot. The first thought of a tender heart is ever on the object most dear to it; and Julia in danger was the sole idea that occurred to Henry, though how, or by whom, he could not imagine. With a pistol in his hand, and his sword under his arm, he flew towards her apartment, which was a suite of rooms at the end of the long gallery farthest from his own. Each step he took, however, lessened his fears; for he became convinced that he left the sound behind him. He now doubted whether he should not rather alarm than relieve Julia, did he knock at her door; but with now her eye, and now her ear, to the key-hole, she was already stationary there; and, well knowing the sound of his step conjured him to wait a moment, when she would bring a light she always burnt, and lessen her own apprehension by going with him. The dreadful and unintelligible shrieks continually increased; but Julia, catching his arm as he rushed forward, told him she knew the voice to be that of her woman, who slept almost over Henry's own apartment. As they passed through the higher galleries together, each chamber door exhibited a head variously capped; but not one showed the whole body belonging to it. The screamer proved to be struggling in strong fits; and Henry, though of a muscular form, found he could not confine her without further assistance. The servants, summoned by Julia, and emboldened by seeing a light, emerged. The room was soon crowded with curious half-dressed figures, whose voices made them known rather than their faces. The poor Abigail, after a variety of applications, came a little to herself, but obstinately hid her head under the clothes, and trembled

The Canterbury Tales

that the bed shook with her. Julia twenty times demanded if she did not know who spoke, ere she answered. 'Oh yes, Madam! I know you well enough; but it is *there* – I am sure it is *there*; and I shall die if I see it again!' – 'See what?' cried Henry. – 'Oh, Sir! look about; cannot you see it? can nobody see it, then, but me?' – 'What are we likely to see? or, rather, what do you imagine you have seen, Lucas?' said her lady. – 'Oh Lord, Madam! what you may all see, though, perhaps, I am the only person to have this warning; and this may be a call to me only. I little thought of my turn coming so soon.' – 'What call, what warning, is this poor thing talking about?' cried Mr. Pembroke, who, ailing as he was, had limped up stairs. 'My good girl, tell us what has thus frightened you? what have you seen?' – 'Oh, my dear good Sir! I am glad you are come. Send for Mr. Aubrey and the church Bible; for I dare not look up. I saw – as sure as you are alive I saw – the ghost!' – 'Saw what, girl?' exclaimed, angrily, Mr. Pembroke; while every servant, by an involuntary leap, had removed further from the bed; and all, with a stifled groan, ejaculated, 'Lord in heaven forbid!' – 'The ghost!' after a pause, said her master; 'do any of you know—' – Oh yes, Sir! we all know,' cried a dozen voices at once. 'Well, at any rate, speak one of you at a time. Jenkin, you are an old servant at the castle; what do you know, and who is the ghost?' – 'Why, for a matter of that, Sir, there be a power of them, as they tells I; for numbers of folk have seen deadly strange sights here, though, for my part, I never met with any thing: but, for noises, I must say – however, Mrs. Lucas seems to have something on her mind. Pray tell his honour what sort of a shape the ghost appeared in to you.' – 'I will, Sir, I will,' cried the terrified Lucas, raising herself in her bed, and looking as wildly and wistfully round as if she suspected the ghost of the cowardice of skulking behind the company. 'Sir, I must say, I was in a heavy sleep; for I never had a thought of a ghost. Indeed, Mr. Layton had talked me – Lord forgive my presumption! – out of the notion; for he says he reads all the wise men of old, and knows there's no such thing: but may be the world is worse than it was, for too sure there are ghosts now-a-days. So, Sir, as I was saying, I cried myself to sleep, not thinking – Lord, he knows – of a ghost; but a good-for-nothing, false-hearted – but,' bursting into tears, 'I will not trouble your honour with my own affairs.' 'No, do not, just now, there's a good girl,' returned her master. 'So, sir, I waked up in a moment, with the notion of somebody pulling the bed-clothes; so I spoke in a snappish sort of a way, for I made sure it was a frolic of the maids; and I was heavy to sleep again, when, all of a sudden – the Lord protect us! – there came, close to my ear, such a hollow groan! I opened both my eyes wide in a moment; and though it is not yet full moon, the nights are so light that I saw–' 'What? what?' in an agony of impatience, re-echoed every voice. – 'A tall, very tall, thin figure of a woman, holding open the curtains, and looking – oh, dear! – as if she was just stepped out of her coffin; and I gave such a squall!' 'Yes, as waked the whole house,' cried Julia. 'But are you sure it was a woman?' without ceremony, exclaimed all the terrified servants. 'Because, you know, when it appeared to Rees Howels—' 'Oh!' interposed Mr. Pembroke, 'let us have but one ghost at a time; and I thought just now we had only one, at least as our own peculiar property; for you called it, by way of distinction, *the* ghost; but, as Jenkin justly observes, why should you think it a woman, Lucas?' 'Oh, dear sir! because she had on a long trailing dress of white, pinked all over like a shroud; and her cap was tied under her chin with a knot of white satin riband, as Miss Julia's is at this moment.' Henry could not resist a side glance at Julia's *coiffure*, and wondered how even a ghost should look ill in what made her look so uncommonly pretty. Mr. Pembroke found hs inquiries had opened a new vein of conversation only to himself; nor did he think he had any probability of extending his own conviction to the rest of the company. Finding, therefore, that Lucas would not be left alone, the heads of the house retired to their own apartments; and all the female servants remained where they were, fortifying each other in their fears by an exact detail, in twenty various ways, of all the odd noises, singular figures, and supernatural incidents that had cause the Castle of St. Hilary to remain so long untenanted; agreeing, at last, that it was a monstrous shame Lady Trevallyn should cajole poor Mr. Pembroke into living here, without communicating what she probably had never heard – the miraculous legends of St. Hilary.

The poor frightened Lucas had, however, so bruised herself as to be confined to her bed for several days: during this time she never varied in her evidence, nor repeated it without trembling and horror; in consequence of which half the beds in the house were vacated as the maids walked off in pairs, and the men stole into each other's rooms. With this social arrangement, oiling the locks, adding new bolts, and treating the ghost much as Londoners do an expected thief, the servants flattered themselves that the lady-apparition was utterly excluded, and things fell into their usual train at St. Hilary.

The Canterbury Tales

Mr. Pembroke now despatched several of his own old servants to Farleigh, that all might be ready, should Lady Trevallyn agree to accompany Julia thither: and as she was daily expected, he began to consider what orders he had for the domestics around him; and when the footman one morning brought breakfast into his study, where he usually took it alone, at a later hour than the young people, he bade that man send the butler to him. Mr. Pembroke, though in no hurry, thought he must have employed one of Joab's messengers: the bell again brought, however, the same servant. 'Did I not bid you send the butler to me?' 'Yes, your honour, I told Mr. Hopkins so, but he says as how he is busy and can't come.' 'Well, if that is the case, Thomas will do, send him.' Another long waiting ensued, followed by another application to the bell. The same man unwillingly answered. 'Well, and where is Thomas? Is he busy too?' 'Why, your honour, Thomas is the most busier of the two; for he is looking up all his things, to give an account of to Mr. Hopkins, who is calling over the plate.' 'Well, Hopkins and Thomas are great plagues both, with their precise ways: however, I can talk to the coachman the while – let Samuel come to me.' Alas! no Samuel appeared. Again the bell in a peal announced the wrath of the ringer; and again, with a face yet more dismayed, the same servant more slowly entered. 'Why you are all past tolerating!' exclaimed Mr. Pembroke angrily: – 'must I go to my coachman, or my coachman come to me?' 'Why,' cried the fellow, as if overjoyed at the proposal, 'if your honour would be so good as to step to coachy, he will take it main kind; for his head's all of a confusion like, and he is in the harness-room, looking over the bridles and saddles.' 'And pray, may I know how this sudden fit of exactness came over you all?' 'Why, your honour, as there is no sleeping in this house for any but you great quality, we poor folks cannot live by keeping our eyes always open, so, please God, we all means to sleep out of it this blessed night.' 'That's a civil intention, truly; and for what reason, I pray?' 'Why, I know, your honour won't believe me; but last night, as I am a living man, we all saw the ghost! Nay, pray your honour, it is no laughing matter; for our Marget says the fright has turned one side of her hair all grey like a badger.' 'Nay, if this is the case, I wish some of you may not be better acquainted with the tall thin lady that you choose to own: but since she has found her way into the butler's pantry and the harness-room, in defence of my own property I shall summon the ghost into open court: set the old justice's chair in the hall, and bid every creature that has seen this spirit attend. I should have left the aërial lady,' concluded he with a laugh, 'to glide about the garrets unmolested; but apparitions that pilfer spoons, and filch bridles, ought to be made examples of.'

This tale, that at first appeared as a jest of some kitchen wag, now wearing the air of imposture in a wider extent, excited Mr. Pembroke's contempt at once and displeasure. He resolved to sift all the parties, and convict the knaves on the evidence of the fools. His inquiry for Henry and his friend, who were, he was told, upon the mountains, brought Julia to him, who begged to be of his jury, as the trial of a ghost promised to be new and entertaining. They found, it is true, the justice's chair in the hall, but not one creature attending. 'I told you, my love, how it would be, ' cried Mr. Pembroke, peevishly; – 'numerous as our scared fools are, no two of them, you find, can agree in their account of this business. Why, where are you all?' concluded he, opening a door that led to the inner hall. 'Here, your honour!' replied a whole choir of discordant voices. 'And why do you not attend me where I ordered?' 'Oh, Lord! your honour, do not ax us to come there,' cried the coachman, just popping in a jolly round face, white as his close-curling wig with terror, 'because – because.' 'Because what, fool?' cried his master. 'Because, Lord forgive us all our sins! that is the purcise place the apparation do hold his revels in, as we knows to our sorrow.' 'So it is a *he* after all. Come in for a pack of fools, and I will insure you from the company of the ghost, who will never venture into mine I think I can swear.' 'Why, to be sure, I never heard as any thing have appeared to your honour yet; and I hope you will never be so misfortunate as to see any thing badder than yourself, as we poor souls have, worse luck ours.' 'Is that possible?' said Mr. Pembroke, smothering a pleasant smile: – 'come in, I tell you.'

And now, holding each other's hand, as children do when playing thread-my-grandmother's needle, a whole set of gawky fellows crept slowly in; and by their number convinced Mr. Pembroke, that unless he could quell the insurrection raised by the ghost, he should not have one bumpkin left to saddle his horse or set his breakfast. Nor did the string consist merely of the men; last, as the most timid, followed all the maids; save Mrs. Lucas, whose testimony was fully established already by her midnight tête-à-tête with the aërial visitant. This long string of foolish and appalled faces so struck Mr. Pembroke, that he burst into an immoderate fit of laughter, which lengthened to ghastliness the countenances around him. 'It was,' they whispered one another, 'so presumptuous!' 'Well,' cried he, trying to recover himself, 'which of this numerous assembly saw the ghost?' 'Oh! all, all!' echoed the whole body. 'Indeed! then one ghost has, I find, more courage than my whole family. And pray where might he catch you all so pleasantly together?' 'Here, in this very spot!' almost groaned a fellow, of a height and size to have recommended him to the King of Prussia's tall regiment, while he stood quaking like a schoolboy over whom the rod impends. Something seriously surprised, Mr. Pembroke now demanded, 'Is there any of my servants who did not see the ghost?' 'Only old Mrs. Sleaford, and she is always poring over the Bible, and Mr.Layton, your honour's own gentleman, and he says there is no such thing, for he is a philosopher of the new school, as he calls it, and a new school it is: for he says as how he understands mathephysicians, and reads Bacon; for my part, I only eats him.' ' And pray when did this apparition take you all thus by surprise?' 'Exactly at twelve last night: – we can't mistake the hour,' said the butler, with a sagacious nod, 'we all know it for a particular reason.' 'And if your reason, Hopkins, is not a profound secret, tell it to your master.' The butler pursed up his mouth importantly, and fixed his eyes with peculiar meaning on a rosy wench, who hid her face directly with her apron. During this inquiry it had struck Mr. Pembroke, that however the philosopher of the new school might meditate mischief in the family, it could not be of a ghostly kind; for he, it was plain, had denied the existence of spirits, and had been sent the morning before to a town at such a distance that he was not yet returned; and must bring some papers to prove that he went, which would clear him of this imposture. This meditative silence on both sides gave a serious air to the business. Among the servants it was obvious something was to be told, that impeached somebody; and honour to each other seemed to preclude sincerity to their master. Luckily, Mr. Pembroke just then recollected, that mercy is the better part of justice. 'Come, my lads,' said he, 'I see you all have had a dreadful fright; and so I will not be angry at any prank that has brought with it so severe a punishment – speak out.' This anmesty, however, encouraged not any one to become spokesman. 'Hopkins,' resumed Mr. Pembroke, after a pause, 'I know you for a sensible man – tell me what brought you all together in this hall at so late an hour last night.' Hopkins turned an eye of self-importance on the sheepish fellows around him, which intimated, you see our master knows how to distinguish a man of merit; and clearing his harsh voice, began, 'Why, please your honour,

The Canterbury Tales

the wisest of us are fools sometimes, as you will say of your humble servant, when I tells all. Evan, our groom, goes a sweethearting to – Lord, Win, don't blush, and look so foolish – master, and miss Julee, has more sense than to think it a crime to have a mind to be married. You must know, sir, our Evan has hung back a little, and we all found out – that I shall not tell – no matter how – we all found out as how Win was to go, last night, into the garden to sow hemp-seed.' 'And to all human appearance the most useful thing she could have sown in my garden,' sarcastically observed Mr. Pembroke; 'but how came this to enter her head?' A rising tee-hee ended in a stifled sort of universal groan, and fearful Lord have mercy upon us! 'Bless your honour!' continued Hopkins, 'why I thought every child knowed that: she was to go out exactly as the clock struck twelve, and throw the seed over her right shoulder – no, her left – was it her right or her left?' 'Prithee get on, and let her throw it over both shoulders rather than fail.' 'Well, then, she was to throw it over one of her shoulders, we won't say which, and then she was to see the man she is to marry, coming after her with a scythe in his hand.' 'A scythe,' interrupted Mr. Pembroke; 'a ring I should have thought more to the purpose.' 'So we thought, your honour, it would be fine fun if Evan, his own self, would go out; and Owens offered him the lent of his scythe: but Evan was so hen-hearted that we could not work him up to it, and it is God's mercy we did not; for I am afraid it will go hard with the poor lad, he takes on so. Desperate bad he has been all night, and says it is a judgment on him, and that Win saw his own apparition; when, Lord, he knows the figure was no more like him than an apple's like an oyster.' Truce with your similitudes, good Mr. Witwoud,' said Mr. Pembroke, significantly smiling at Julia, 'and get on with your tale. You very prudently then, I find, set my gates open at midnight; and I may be glad nothing worse than a ghost came.' 'Why, sir, there was no chance of any thing else coming, nor that neither: or, icod, we would have shut the gates fast enough: but we were all full of fun, for, being Midsummer eve, I had handed about a little of the best ale, your honour: and not a soul of us all once thought of the ghost – that is, not the real ghost; and you will say that is the more wonder, as we axed him in a manner to frighten us; and, to do him justice, he did not need to be axed twice. Well, as I was a saying, we were all *perdue*, peeping through the crevice there of our own hall-door, for I had put out the lamp within, and left the little one burning here on purpose; and by-and-by we sees poor Win creeping along, with the seed in her apron, and one hand there, holding it ready: so what does we all do, John, and Thomas, Coachy, Owens, Evan, Rees Howels, Jenkin, and all the maidens, but steal out into this big hall, and divide behind the gates, as they were thrown back, that we might sally forth upon poor Win and make fun of her. Presently we heard the poor soul panting, and running, as if the devil was behind her, as, indeed, he was; and when we all jumped out, she was so deadly flustered that she dropped down, as though she had no life in her: and while we were in a puzzle what this could mean, we heard an odd heavy underground sort of a noise as if coming in. Lord, I thought every soul of us would have swounded, like poor Win! for, sure enough, we all remembered, too late, that we had been playing with edge tools, as the saying is. Tall Thomas happened to be first, and he was as weak – as weak as a thread paper, so down he fell; and all of us after him, just like a pack of cards when you send the jack of an errand.' 'So, after I have listened to your preaching all this time, I find you saw only the set of fools I now see,' said their master. 'Ay, marry did we,' exclaimed the whole tribe; 'we saw a tall, tall outlandish horrible figure, just in the first porch – he had eyes like two flambeaux, and would have made six of our coachy, fat as he is. Oh! Lord, how we trembled, prayed, and hid our faces. He went round the hall with the same unsufferable lumbering noise, and as slow as King Pepin in the puppet-show, only he did not carry his head under his arm; and after that he very coolly stepped up into his place again. To be sure, we were all rare ninnies when we came into the hall not to take notice he was out of it.' 'His place!' cried Mr. Pemroke, gazing around, without being able to guess at their meaning; 'where, pray, might this big gentleman's place be?' 'Why, *there*, sir,' cried Magos, the handsome dairy-maid, in a shrill pipe, that might have frightened the ghost, as it did her master. '*There*, sir!' was echoed by the whole train; and, turning round, Mr. Pembroke saw their trembling fingers were all pointed towards a grim gigantic stone statue of an ancient Briton, who had a counterpart on the other side to support the well carved oaken gallery, once the seat of the minstrels and harpers, when the feast of knighthood was held in this hall. The outrageous superstition and extravagance of the servants entirely overpowered the gravity of Mr. Pembroke and his daughter; while the whole train, shocked at this new provocation to their midnight visitor, knelt around, and offered to take their oaths that they saw the figure mount up there again – while their appalled faces showed an expectation that they should be justified by the descent of one or other of the fierce Britons, from whom they never long removed their eyes.

Mr. Pembroke would have concluded the men drunk, if men only had been the parties; but the vehement declarations of the women perplexed him. With all the mildness of reason, when it condescends to ignorance, he argued on the improbability that disembodied spirits be permitted to quit a state of either blessedness or punishment, only to add to our follies, or our fears; and still more how incompatible would be such a re-union of our separated natures, when we know the grosser part to have become dust and bones, and the customary garments in which fancy enwraps its own vision are always indisputable under lock and key, in some chest or wardrobe. To this rational representation, modified, as Mr. Pembroke supposed, to their capacities, no one attempted to give an answer. 'He was,' they all cried, 'very wise and very good, and well, they knowed, never did any thing should prevent *his* resting in his grave, but that was not the case with some folks; and if he knew half the tales they did about this old castle, he would not wonder.' 'If ever I know any thing to the prejudice of the dead, ' interrupted Mr. Pembroke authoritatively, 'one of that body shall rise to tell it me.' 'Well,' they all cried, 'they had nothing more to say: but, for their parts, they had rather live in a barn, and have it all to themselves, than in a castle full of gold and diamonds, if they must pop on a ghost, or a goblin, at every corner: therefore, if his honour pleased, they were all ready to go. 'At any other time Mr.Pembroke would, in mere vexation, have indulged them, and posted away to Farleigh himself; but while hourly expecting Lady Trevallyn, it was impossible to go. For could he affront her with the information that his servants had dragged in imagination her ancestors from the grave, and circulated reports always odious, and frequently injurious? Were he able to quiet this one alarm, he thought it probable that he should either trace the trick – for a trick he fully believed it – to the right author, or quit the scene of action before the ghost had courage to come forward again. He therefore resolved to try a last experiment with the obstinate ignorant race around him. 'Well then,' concluded he, 'since I cannot convince, I do not wish you to remain here in apprehension: as to the poor foolish girl whose hempen spell conjured up a phantom, that I wish had its produce around his neck, it is not fair that she should lose her place, and her husband too; so tell Evan if he has a mind to make a match with Win, I will give them five guineas to begin the world with.' This bounty of five guineas electrified the whole family: each eye forsook the statues, on which all had been hitherto fixed, to consult that of the person it liked best: and coachy edging up to the cook, who receded not, observed, that, 'since his honour was so generous to Win, who made them all like to lose their places, by running husband-hunting at twelve o'clock at night, he hoped he would remember other folks might like to be married quite as well as Evan.' Mr. Pembroke half smiled at his own ingenuity; and, hinting that if they would marry, and live well together in their places, they should all have the same compliment, a few words settled the matter; and couple after couple, with a nod (the respectful salutation of that country), walked off: till only Magos, the dairy-maid, who was the beauty of her own circle, remained; and that only because she held herself so high, for tall Thomas passionately implored her to take him and the five guineas. To be left alone was, however, more than her spirits could long stand. 'To pe sure,' she said, 'cee little treamt ven cee refused my Lord Trefallyn's valie, and Tavy Jones the sopkeeper, and Mr. Auprey's own clerk, cee soud ever take up with a footman: however, a lifling husband was petter tan a ted gost at any time, so cee thanked his honour,' and, with Thomas, added to the matrimonial cavalcade. Julia, retiring, congratulated her father on so ingeniously making every one forget the ghost. He might have said, except himself, and poor Lucas; who, from her fright, and being crossed in love, seemed to be in the way of increasing the family of ghosts at St. Hilary.

Peace being now restored in the parlour, and Hymen reigning in the hall, Mr. Pembroke looked out impatiently, as evening came on, for Henry and his friend, to advise with them on the best means of detecting this daring imposture. Understanding that on coming in they had adjourned to the library, Mr. Pembroke joined them there. The nature of Cary was softened by a day of almost unremitting attention from Henry; and, hearing that Mr. Pembroke wished him stay, and consult with him on a point of importance, he attempted not, as usual, to retire. When Henry heard his father's account of the general alarm, and its supposed cause, he cast a look of deep chagrin on Julia, and compassion towards Cary; well knowing, that to discuss the invisible world would wake to him 'the nerve where agony is born.' It happened, however, at this juncture, that his mind had taken that high and solemn tone which impressed on all around him a native grandeur, and firmness of character, calculated to enforce his opinion, which he had always a fund of observation and reading to support. Far from adopting Mr. Pembroke's idea, that this was an imposture among the domestics, the veteran enlarged on the possible intelligence of one world with the other, in a flow of eloquence and information that Mr. Pembroke had seldom or ever heard; and with an almost divine complacency. Awe-struck with his elevated visitant, the moment that gentlemen chose to be known, Mr. Pembroke no longer was surprised that the young heart of Henry, yet in the glow and energy of passion, unfolded itself in the warmest affection towards a being to whom he almost bowed. The sweet Julia, drawing her chair closer to her brother's, whispered him, that she wished they had been so vulgar as to have danced among the happy hymeneal party; for this glorious friend of his had strangely shaken her nerves, if not her understanding. Henry, who best knew the wild charm which a disordered mind gives to whatever it can at all connect, still recommended the considering the whole ghostly business as a trick; unless they should have, in their own persons, any cause, to think otherwise: and since the hall was the scene of apparition action, instead of going to bed, he proposed, that his father, Mr. Benson, and his friend Cary, should, with himself, secretly assemble there at midnight; and throwing the gate open, leave a lamp burning, while they sat in silence and darkness in the dining parlour; this figure, if palpable to touch, should thus, if they saw it, be the most frightened of the company. To this plan none of the gentlemen objected; and, for that night, and two following ones, they watched, but in vain: all was profoundly quiet. They all then agreed, that Cupid had taken in masquerade the figure of the enormous Briton, and Hymen, in the shape of Mr. Aubrey, had laid the spirit.

On the day before Lady Trevallyn was to arrive at St. Hilary, Mr. Pembroke began to fear that he should not, as he had purposed, leave it in her company; for some little cold which his midnight watching had given him occasioned those flying twinges of the gout that usually fore-ran a serious fit. The partiality he had for the society of the sprightly widow made this idea particularly vexatious: to drive off the apprehended evil, he took a medicine that sometimes had that effect, and retired early to his own apartment. In the restless, irritable state he was in, Henry became the sole object of his thought: such is the power of conscience, destined thus to counteract error by an equal sway in the heart with its fondest feeling. Yet had he exerted every effort to discover the singular spot on which he saved the half-drowned child in vain. Whether he should venture to communicate this circumstance to the youth, or whether such a confession would not wholly attach

The Canterbury Tales

him to Cary, for whom already he showed a reverence and affection equal to that he, when thought his father, obtained, was a question often agitated in his bosom, but never decided. After lying awake till he found himself feverish and exhausted, he dropped into a sleep, heavy but not refreshing. In the dead of night he was roused from it by a groan, so deep and hollow, that it seemed to issue from a soul in torture. The remembrance of the awful discourse on life, death, and immortality, in the library the other evening, flashed with all the force of powerful but disjointed ideas across his mind; his pulses beat in a manner audibly; his spirits faltered; his limbs were without motion: in a room that communicated with his own his valet always slept, and a lamp was burning there, which, through the door that stood ajar, cast only a faint and streaming light across a part of his chamber. He now, though with an appalled and trembling hand, drew aside the bedcurtain, when a figure, all in white, seemed as it were to grow out of the floor to an amazing height: sight and hearing instantly deserted Mr. Pembroke; and, when he at last recovered both, he fixed hs eyes on Henry, with his valet holding him, and Julia half undressed, bathing his temples with hartshorn and other volatiles. With bewildered looks he gazed around, but had presence of mind enough not to declare his cause of alarm. He only inquired who had waked his son and daughter, and how they came there. Layton said, 'that he had been startled with his groans, and hastened to call Mr. Henry: Miss Julia heard his voice, for he obliged to speak very loud to the young gentleman through the door, and was so frightened she would come too.' 'Did you find my door open or shut?' inquired Mr.Pembroke, with a trembling voice and anxious glance around. 'Shut, sir, I think – I was in such an alarm I really cannot be sure how I found it.' 'Consider a moment, it is of a great importance.' Henry, by an expressive look, suggested to Julia that their father was certainly delirious. 'No – no,' sighed Mr. Pembroke, shaking his head, 'I am as rational as you are: – I heard as plainly as I did the rustle of these damask curtains, when I drew them aside to look at it' 'What, my dear – dear father, did you hear?' exclaimed Julia. 'Nothing, my sweet girl – go to bed – you will get a sad cold.' Henry, however, would not quit his father till commanded; and then made Layton watch by his bed-side in the arm-chair: a greater trial could hardly have been devised for this philosopher of the new school; as Mr. Pembroke, who ever till now disbelieved in the return of spirits, had certainly indirectly owned having seen one. Neither he nor his master could close an eye

The Canterbury Tales

the remainder of the night, though wholly unmolested. 'Poor harmless wretches!' said Mr.Pembroke to himself, while recalling the terror of his servants, 'how I laughed at, and discredited your report; yet why to you should the dead return? – you never stole – you never basely appropriated the child of other parents. – Alas! those whom I vainly have sought in this world were early sent, perhaps, by broken hearts to the other, and now hover round me and the noble boy they can no longer claim.'

With daylight, however, the vigour of the mind, to a certain degree, always returns. That Mr. Pembroke had heard and seen something, he was assured; but, as he could hardly shape into any form the indistinct image that yet soared before his eyes, the possibility of imposture again recurred. Magnanimously resolving to impute to himself the weakness he had censured in others, he ordered his chamber-door to be left unfastened, that he might take his chance for another visitation; which, thus prepared for, he thought he should meet with manly courage.

Mr. Pembroke's taciturnity to his family, however, availed not; for Layton had, early in the morning, published an account of his groans, his wild inquiries, and the long reveries in which he still was plunged. 'Master himself has seen the spirit, then' – 'that comes of being foolhardy; – 'I wonder whether he spoke to it,' – was the talk of one servant to another; while all, with anxious inquiring eyes, examined the pale and pensive countenance that no longer heeded them. The shock of the night had, however, relieved Mr. Pembroke from present danger of the gout; for, at the sound of Lady Trevallyn's carriage, Henry was hardly quicker in the offer of assistance than his father. 'I have a hand for an old friend, and another for a new one,' cried she, extending a pair, white as snow, to Mr. Pembroke and Henry, which the latter respectfully kissed, in token of his gratitude for offered friendship. – 'Julia, my dear! I have a hundred embraces for you. I hope,' she added, in an inaudible whisper, 'you have made up your mind to letting me be your sister-in-law, though you was so ill-natured that you would not have me for a step-mother: I really think I shall never be able to get down my abominable, frightful native mountain, in any other conveyance than a chariot drawn by doves; and as they are apt to mistake their way, I think that fine blackeyed Henry of yours – Henry, I think, you call him – most undertake to guide them.' That youth, who was already enchanted with the intelligent countenance, elegant figure, and prepossessing manners of the lively widow, was wholly won by the affectionate caresses she lavished on his sister. As Mr. Pembroke led her into the saloon, she turned aside a moment to lean upon Julia's shoulder; then dashing away the tears her sweet eyes were surcharged with, she reached out her hand to Henry. 'Come, you creature! be but half as agreeable as you look, and I will endeavour to lose the painful remembrance of many a scene long past, and many a friend for ever vanished; but every object I look on brings so much to my mind.' Again she swept away the tears with her white hand, as if she would not be a fatigue to her friends; and, running to Julia's harp, struck a chord. – 'Oh, you sophisticated mountaineer! A French harp in the land of David! How do you think Taliessen, Modred, and the rest of the brethren who sit in the clouds above here, will take the compliment? Come, let me try if it will give me a native strain for the genius of our mountain;' and, with exquisite skill and taste, she played, 'Of a noble race was Shenkin.'

Pleasure and affection, in all their beauteous iris hues, now diversified the hours to the younger two; while Mr. Pembroke blended delight with a gnawing recollection of what he ought to do, and what he might have to dread. His silence and abstraction suggested to the delicate mind of Lady Trevallyn, that she had not been as attentive to him as she used to be when Henry was far away. Starting up, she seized the chess-board; and placing it on the table Mr. Pembroke sat by, 'Now will I lay my life, papa, by that air of gravity, you fancy I have done flirting with you, since I have got this fine young fellow to amuse me: not at all. I intend to keep you both in play. To show my amazing regard, and how often have thought of you since we parted at Bath, I made an idle wretch teach me so much of this game that I shall beat you most unmercifully if you do not look about you; so be upon your guard.' Sitting down at once to chess, she made gay signs to Henry and Julia that speech on her part would be treason; while Mr. Pembroke gladly engaged with such a charming opponent in the amusement that most withdrew his thoughts from one dear but oppressive subject.

Henry now impatiently expected the coming home of Cary, that he might dispose him to please and be pleased with their fair guest, who already was curious to see him: with the close of evening he usually returned; but it hardly closed at all, so brightly rose the moon, now at its full. Julia took her work-basket, and whispered Henry, that in so sweet a night it would be delightful to walk, and meet their solitary friend. Fain, fain would he have had her company; but politeness obliged her

The Canterbury Tales

to stay at home. Thinking no spot so likely, by this light and at this hour, to attract a visionary as the ruined priory, Henry bent his steps thither; but, though its solemn beauty charmed one sense, and the profusion of plants and flowers gratified another, it was not the haunt of Cary. Sighing that Julia was not with him, the youth wandered onward.

The ruins of the priory were of great extent, beside that part so sweetly embellished, and carefully preserved by the lords of St. Hilary: they ended in the village, whither Henry now betook himself; for though society was shunned by Cary, poverty he constantly sought, and relieved with an unsparing hand, as though it held the widow's cruse of oil. Henry called to mind that his friend had taken the address of a maimed labourer, who had sent in the morning to ask aid at the castle. The sufferer he easily found, and assisted; but heard no tidings of Cary. Having in vain search protracted his stay as long as he thought he could, without being deficient in politeness to his father's guest, the youth turned to hasten home through the shortest path. This led by the parish church; which, though long since separated from the priory, proved they had once been united, by the Imperfect fragments of massy walls which every where presented irregular projections, overgrown with ivy; that alone held, or appeared to hold, together the tottering and ragged abutments. Suddenly Henry missed a little favourite dog of Julia's, whom he had courted to follow him; and calling aloud, the creature ran out of the porch of the church, but as quickly ran back again. Invited by a bright moon, and a door half open, Henry followed: a bold projection of the ivy-bound ruin left the chief part of the church in solemn shadow; but that only gave effect to the radiant beams of the moon, as aslaut, from a painted window over the communion-table, they shone full on a recumbent figure Henry at first concluded to be marble. A second glance showed him it was Cary; thrown negligently at his length on the slab of a raised tomb, his elbow resting on that, and his head on his hand. The injured arm lay on the neck of one faithful spaniel, who, like a conscious favourite, with eyes fondly fixed on his master, had crept almost into his bosom. His companion, with equal but humbler devotion, remained couched at his feet. That fine care-worn countenance, which Henry's eyes ever loved to contemplate, was solemnly inclined upward. On the sound of approaching steps he, by a hasty turn of his head, threw back those grey locks that hung in their usual 'careless desolation;' and the moon-beam showed the tear which he hastily dashed from his cheek, while his eyes struck fire at the intrusion. Henry was shocked: he stopped reverentially, and gazed as though on a man of other days, – a vision of the mournful sons of Ossian. Hardly could he resist the impulse to fall at the feet of so singular, so grand a creature. Cary, seeing who it was, started up abruptly, and walked away with him. 'You will discover all my haunts in time,' said he, in a broken moody kind of voice: – 'I was always fond of a church by moonlight.' Henry was too well acquainted with the usual tone of his friend's mind in scenes like this, and felt too much awe in his own, abruptly to propose his joining a social party; where, if he added not to the gaiety, he must infallibly cast a gloom. He led, however, to the invitation, by speaking of the lively and elegant Lady Trevallyn; declaring that he had never seen so fascinating a creature, and regretting she was a dozen years older than himself, as the only reason why he was not wholly enchained by her. He then came upon his commission, and urged his mournful friend to attend to the entreaties of Julia, and join the company, 'What can be so natural as your finding a handsome, lively woman, pleasant company!' sighed the veteran, wringing affectionately the hand of Henry. 'Go, enjoy the charms of life while yet it has charms: but remember, dear lad! our compact in America; and do not, from mistaken kindness, insist on my being happy any way but my own.' He was near a deep thicket when he spoke, and turned into it abruptly; nor did Henry venture to pursue him.

The sound of the piano-forte and harp, made Henry, on re-entering, sensible that he was wanted. His clarionet was produced, – the candles were put out, – and to the light of the moon they had what Lady Trevallyn called 'a dear romantic concert,' where memory gave one part, and taste the other. The castle clock chimed twelve ere any of the party were tired; but Lady Trevallyn then cried out on Julia for keeping town hours; and declared she had never sat up so late in this part of the world before.

Mr. Pembroke ordered his door, as he had pre-determined, to be left unfastened, and bade his valet retire to his own room: who, in spite of the philosophy of the new school, would not have been sorry to have joined the happy hymenial party, and had a spouse of his own, either to share or relieve his fears. Worn out with restlessness, Mr. Pembroke descended in the morning; and condoled with Lady Trevallyn on seeing her swoln eyes and pale cheeks show that she had not rested better. 'I had but a poor chance of sleeping here, my kind friend,' returned she, 'at any rate; and that I lost by the idle prate of your servants to mine. I find you have frightful and strange stories concerning our poor old mansion, – mortifying ones to me. No,' added she, sighing, and turning her thoughts inward, 'we are an unfortunate but not guilty family; and it is dreadful thus to rake up the ashes of the honoured dead.'

Mr. Pembroke, incensed at the intolerable impertinence of his servants, sought to soothe her wounded feelings. 'Ah! my dear sir,' said she, with a melancholy smile, 'how shall we seal up the loquacious lips of people who can never know the truth, and are, therefore, so fruitful in invention? I can only shorten my visit.' Julia then acknowledged having stayed at St. Hilary merely to receive it; and pressed the charming widow to let the whole family attend her to Farleigh. Lady Trevallyn saw that to deny was to involve them in the censure she cast on their servants, and therefore acquiesced. 'One visit here I must, however, pay,' said Lady Trevallyn, 'and only one – I can go to good Mr. Aubrey almost directly; and then, my sweet girl, let us immediately leave this hateful place; which was the scene of misery during my youth, and will become a cause of contention to the last hour of my life. Ah! Julia, you too have a great fortune; but your wise father will not do as mine did, who threw me away merely to save that: – they married me when I was little more than a child, only for fear I should be capable of the delicacy of choice; and Lord Trevallyn almost forgot I was ever to be out of my nonage. Time made me a woman, and my husband made me a wretched one: – he never treated me with confidence or kindness; and always expected a new gown, or a kiss, should appease all the pangs of a generous and tender heart, that found itself unvalued. In reality, he had married me only to unite the two finest estates in the county, – but my poor father at last grievously disappointed him, by settling this on my second son; from whom the elder, possessed by his guardians with the idea that he was wronged in the arrangement, threatens to claim it, as soon as he comes of age: and, what is worse, my counsel say he can do it, and leave my sweet Cecil penniless. But this is a wretched way of passing our time, my Julia; and if I frighten you into a vow of celibacy. I shall have a legion of lovers in arms against me.'

Miss Pembroke, finding they were almost immediately to depart for Farleigh, left it to her father to attend Lady Trevallyn to Mr. Aubrey's, that she might give due orders through the family: and Henry, by a hint of hers, set out on an uncertain peregrination after Cary; anxious to apprise him of this hasty determination, and induce him to accompany the family.

Although Mr. Pembroke did not hesitate to escort Lady Trevallyn, the rector was to him a stranger. Age and infirmity had prevented Mr. Aubrey from waiting on him at the Castle, and he was himself subject to cold, therefore avoided a chilling country church. Mr. Benson had always officiated at the Castle. How much did Mr. Pembroke regret having been governed by a mere form, when he saw the interesting venerable rector of St. Hilary: who, bowed by age, raised his silvered head with a patriarchal dignity, as by the assistance of a stick he rose out of his arm-chair to greet Lady Trevallyn. She sunk gracefully at his knees, as to those of a revered parent, in silent tenderness: a mutual gush of sorrow, too poignant for words, made Mr. Pembroke feel his company an oppression to them. He, therefore, opened a glass door, and passed into a small but beautiful flower-garden, which led to a second, filled with roots and vegetables. Beyond he saw a paddock with a cow; and an orchard invited him on the other hand.

Many years were gone by since Mr. Aubrey and Lady Trevallyn had met, and much had they to say: but hardly had they entered on an interesting subject, ere dismal out-cries for help came from the orchard. Mr. Aubrey could hardly move, and the lady would have been of no use. The servants, who luckily waited with Mr. Pembroke's coach, ran, on hearing the cries, nimbly onward; and soon, to the horror of those in the parlour, returned almost as hastily; bearing Mr. Pembroke streaming with water, and in a manner lifeless. Lady Trevallyn entreated they would bring the lady in; but conforming to the orders of Cary, who was with them, the servants carried the lifeless Mr. Pembroke to his own coach; into which the veteran, equally wet, jumped, and it drove rapidly away to the Castle. Lady Trevallyn took a hasty leave of Mr. Aubrey to follow on foot, attended by his servant.

Julia she found in a state little short of distraction. Henry and Cary were employed in stripping the body, and using whatever means might restore it to life. The latter, inured to the contingencies and inconveniences of the world, was always prepared for them. He therefore produced a lancet, and instantly opened a vein in Mr. Pembroke's arm; which bled, though with difficulty. Henry hastened to lighten with this news the apprehensions of Julia, and anxiously implored Lady Trevallyn to sustain the sorrowing daughter. The activity, recollection, and tenderness of Cary, had done almost everything that could be done for Mr. Pembroke before the doctor and surgeon arrived. But, alas! a misfortune had happened that Cary could not be aware of. The chill of the water into which Mr. Pembroke by accident slipped, had seized

The Canterbury Tales

on nerves so delicate, and together with the gout flying about in his habit had caused a paralytic seizure, from which it was possible he might recover, but merely possible: his speech was gone. What an affliction was this for his children! – what a surprise to his servants! who found in this event a confirmation of their extravagant notions; and not one now doubted but that the disturbed ghost announced the present calamity.

Julia and Henry united to implore Lady Trevallyn, since she could neither share their duty, nor lighten their sorrows, to consider her own immediate comfort, by quitting this detested Castle, into which, Julia, in bitterness of grief, every moment exclaimed, she had brought her father only to die. But they did not know the warm and generous heart of Lady Trevallyn; who scorned to indulge a selfish pride or feeling, where friendship was concerned: and useless as she must be, and odious as she found the place, there would she stay, to share the anxieties which she was not able to relieve.

A long, long night passed away in medical and vain experiments; while the streaming eyes of the kneeling Julia, fixed on the almost motionless orbs of her father, vainly sought in them recognition.

In the course of the following day Mr. Pembroke came enough to himself to recollect his deeply afflicted children, as by looks, and vain efforts to speak, he showed; but not a distinct sound could he utter. A few hours more made his consciousness of the imperfection of his organs a misery indeed: especially when he turned to Henry: who duteously was stationed on one side of his bed, as Julia was on the other. Her hand he clasped incessantly in his cold and clammy one, as if no feeling but affection remained towards her; while on Henry he fixed looks of such sad and anxious intelligence, that the youth involuntarily laboured concerning himself. Oh! what fervent prayers did he put up, that the sufferer might be able to tell him the secret, though both were to die one hour after. Julia, however melancholy her situation, had only a father to lose – Henry in his father felt that he was to lose his fate.

On the third morning, when worn out with watching, and utterly without hope, Henry and Julia were, as usual, listening to the disturbed breathing of their father, they heard his well-known voice imperfectly say, 'Who is there? – 'Your children! your miserable children!' both answered on their knees, and bathing his hands with their tears in a moment. He cast a fond parental glance on their haggard looks, and soiled habiliments; well knowing how to estimate the love that would not allow them to leave him for an hour. 'My beloved children,' faltered the good man, 'life is always brief, – mine has nearly flown from me in a moment: nor know I now whether heaven will leave me another. I have much to do; and must do it well. Let me discharge my mind first of its greatest duty. I am sorry Mr. Benson is already gone to Farleigh; but send and entreat Mr. Aubrey to officiate. The state I am in warrants the liberty; and, till he arrives, leave only a servant in my room, that my agitated feelings may not rob me of due recollection.'

Oh! with what gratitude to Heaven did Julia impart to Lady Trevallyn, and Henry to Cary, this favourable change. The veteran had not once left his room since the sad accident which he alone preserved Mr. Pembroke from perishing by. The place was among his haunts; and, on seeing that gentleman reel into the water, he instantly plunged in himself; nor could a man less strong, or less courageous, have borne him up so long, or called so loudly for help.

Painful as the venerable Aubrey found the religious summons, it was his duty to obey, and he had long learned to conquer every emotion inconsistent with that. He found at the bedside of Mr. Pembroke Lady Trevallyn seated, and the two young people devoutly kneeling. All three, with due reverence and tearful anxiety, united in the holy rite, which, with determined sanctity, the infirm Aubrey administered. A short pause afterwards, the sick man required to collect himself. He then ordered his whole train of servants to be summoned, who, now persuaded that he was the culprit who had roused the dead from their graves, entered with fear and trembling – wondering what crime he had to confess. Mr. Pembroke cast his eyes over the groups and missing Cary, would have him called. Henry foresaw it was possible that he might not, so summoned, attend, and therefore undertook to invite the veteran himself. Even he seemed not likely to succeed; for though, where he could be of use, Cary would have contended with every element to effect his purpose, where he could not be of any, he held it an oppression to be urged to come. Henry, however, so implored him, that he yielded to weakness, not reason, and followed the youth. Lady Trevallyn, as they entered, cast a curious eye on the sun-burnt visage of the stranger; but he gave her opportunity for nothing more, by abruptly hastening to a corner of the room yet darker than the rest, where he might witness all that passed, without being himself a party.

Mr. Pembroke, apparently much revived by the pious duty he had performed, attentively surveyed the anxious and inquisitive faces surrounding his bed, and more articulately began: – 'The solemn rite, my friends, by which I have just sealed my faith in a better world, and made my peace in this, will, I hope, fully convince those present that, though my organs of speech are not perfect, I am in full possession of my understanding. A general conviction of this is necessary, to give credence to a painful and extraordinary disclosure I have for some time mediated, but may no longer be silent upon, lest an important secret should suddenly go down to the grave with me.' He paused, as wanting breath; but his eye had been too intently fixed on Henry to leave any doubt either in the youth's bosom, or those of the spectators, that the secret, whatever it might be, related solely to him. Was it happiness or misery? thought Henry. An ague shook him at the mighty question of his own soul. He had knelt by Julia's side, to save the sick man turning from one to the other; and now, as if to ascertain his hold on Mr. Pembroke's affection, would divide with Julia the fond parental grasp of the cold hand, or thus enfolding hers with it, sought perhaps to make an equal claim to both. 'The circumstance my soul labours with is so singular, so unexpected,' slowly resumed the sick man, 'and its consequence will so astonish – ' He had overstrained his newly recovered and weak powers, nor could he utter another syllable. Expectation sat on the sharp arch of every brow. A single breath drawn might have been heard, and each person present hung on tiptoe over the one before him. A little cordial revived the invalid, and he again pursued his discourse. 'Henry, my dear Henry, it is you who must now fortify your mind; for I am under the direful necessity of at last owning that you are no son of mine.' A deadly paleness increased for a moment on the cheeks both of Henry and Julia; when a glance each half-raised, and neither wholly ventured to fix on the other, enriched their cheeks alike with a bloom that sweetly interpreted the emotion within. Julia then dropped her eyes on the ground, and Henry turned his with deep intenseness on those of his languid friend, as though he would through them drag forth the discovery his failing speech thus painfully prolonged. 'Imagine not, beloved Henry,' continued Mr. Pembroke, 'that it was to lower your pride, or wound your feelings, I mediated this solemn acknowledgement. It is a relief I am obliged to give my own conscience; and I call upon the God, whose mercy I have recently supplicated, to witness that I never saw your mother – that you came a helpless stranger to these arms and therefore can be no son of mine. But I have told you this, my Henry, only to make you so.'

A burst of delight, even to agony, that overflowed the bosom of the youth, as he fell in a manner prostrate before his boundless benefactor, was too mighty for both. Mr. Pembroke, when able, drew his daughter fondly towards him, and tenderly whispered – 'I have for some time guessed at my Julia's objection to matrimony – has she any now?' The subdued but soul-touched Julia, lifted her modest eyes from the bed-clothes, in which dread and uncertainty had caused her to bury them, and her look made the gracious inclination of her head needless. By an irresistible impulse Henry caught her in his arms, and her cheek found a sweeter resting-place on his shoulder; while the fond father made an effort to seal, with his blessing, those sacred, those delightful vows, each beating heart was for the first time making to the other. 'I have been aware this moment would come for some time past,' said Mr. Pembroke, to the venerable clergyman, 'though I foresaw not the awful circumstance that was likely to have shut me from my portion of delight. Take this, sir,' and he gave Mr. Aubrey, a special licence: 'open again your holy book, and this very moment unite the hands of this young couple – now, while I have life to give them to each other.'

Henry, at a hearing so blessed, sprung from his knees, as though light enough to soar up to heaven; and eagerly raising, with most endearing tenderness, the abashed and trembling Julia, looked to Lady Trevallyn, who kindly advanced to support her. From that fair friend's finger he softly drew the wedding ring, which his fond eyes contemplated in unspeakable rapture. The aged Aubrey once more arose, and, assuming his surplice, opened at the marriage ceremony. What a moment! The sick man again uncovered devoutly his head – the servants sunk in solemn silence upon their knees – and Cary, at some little distance, arose with that impressive air of dignity by which he was always distinguished when himself – shaking disdainfully from his cheek the mark of an incurable sensibility yet melting at his heart.

A few, a very few minutes, to the astonishment even of the immediate parties, united for ever two lovers, who one hour before had never breathed a sound like impassioned tenderness, although in secret they mutually consecrated to celibacy the heart neither dared to give to the other. Oh! how sweet were the blended tears of gratitude and delight, that each poured over the generous but failing hand that had united theirs! In natures, finely touched with the pure spirit of heaven, it is hard to discover which feels most gratification – the obliger, or the obliged: yet, in her father's eyes, it added a charm to

The Canterbury Tales

the many comprehended in Julia, to perceive that she would not have it remembered she made at once the fortune and the happiness of Henry; who, on his part, proud only with the mean, felt it but as an added enjoyment to owe every good to Julia and her bountiful father.

A little time stemmed in each bosom its conflux of passions, and the fair Julia suddenly recollected the very singular circumstances under which she had been married. She cast a surprised eye on her *robe de chambre*, nor did she forget her little morning cap; but glancing over the dishevelled hair and careless attire of Henry, she thought she had never seen him look so handsome; and though woman enough to prefer propriety, she was angel enough to know that virtue makes it.

'I have now,' resumed Mr. Pembroke, 'my beloved children, acquitted myself of half my duty – and only half: had I ventured this discovery one week ago, my Henry, when I had told you that I was not your father, I should have been obliged to add, that in the whole world I knew not where you might even seek that fortunate man – for never in a course of years could I discover even the spot where I saved you. An elucidation almost supernatural, though it may eventually shorten my days, clears up this mystery.'

Henry implored the generous man not to exhaust himself in a vain attempt to add to perfect felicity; since, in making him really his son, and the husband of his adored Julia, he had crowned his every wish; nor would he seek in new affinities but doubtful blessings.

'However pleasing this glowing transport may be to my heart, my Henry!' returned, with a sigh, Mr. Pembroke, 'it adds a keen pang to the many my conscience has for years given me; since I have selfishly appropriated a good which Heaven bestowed on others, who may have deplored through life your loss. Yet a liberal education your parents could not have afforded you; for you will probably find them, my son, among the poorest of the poor; and it will be your happy fortune to make their latter days easy. I did not convene all these domestics as mere spectators of my discourse or conduct; but because there must be some among them that can end our doubts the moment I give them a detail of the means by which you became mine. Eighteen years ago I was parted from my company, and rode through a solitary dell in this country, where it was the will of Providence that I should save the life of this youth, then a little creature in petticoats, and entirely alone: the love I had for him made me delay so long inquiring to whom he belonged, that when I did, either my ignorance of the name of the particular spot, or some unaccountable change in the face of the country, rendered it impossible for me to trace his parentage. I had for many years totally given up the hope, nor would I rob him of the sweet ties of natural affinity as my own son, unless I could have ensured to him a larger, as well as juster portion of natural affection: yet my heart and my conscience have always been at variance on his account; and it was only by resolving to give him my Julia, that I could find out how to reconcile them. When I accompanied Lady Trevallyn to Mr. Aubrey's the other day, I saw in their eyes a wish for unreserved discourse that made me through delicacy, wander into the parsonage garden: beyond it was an orchard; and, towering over the fruit-trees, at the extremity I discovered a singular circle of irregular stones, which appeared to me to be a Druidical monument. Astonished that so remarkable an object in a prospect should be no where visible from the castle, I advanced to survey it more accurately. I then saw it was naked rock, washed bare by time and storms. It was not, however, less a curiosity for being natural; and I ventured down between a cleft in the stones, where steps were cut to a pool of water, wide and deep, where I guessed the family drew their daily supply. Though the ground became declining and slippery, I reached the verge of the water safely; nor would my feet then have failed me, had I not suddenly cast my eyes on the object where Henry very nearly lost his life; and mine would that moment have terminated, but for the instantaneous plunge and vigorous exertions of his melancholy friend; though how he got there I know not. The object I mean is the rude and singular bridge which crosses the cheeks of rock where the water overflows, and forms another pool below: from that bridge the sweet child must have fallen when I dragged him out of the lower water.'

'Almighty God!' cried the venerable Aubrey, sinking feebly on his knees, and raising his eyes and hands with meekly impressive devotion to Heaven, 'thou who never utterly forsake those who humbly rely on thee, let the gratitude of thy servant become acceptable in thy sight! – less for restoring this youth to the name and honours of his ancient family, though great in that is thy mercy, than for relieving my aged heart from the weight of misery, the dread of guilt. My darling child was then only unfortunate, not sinful: she sunk into the pool in the maternal act of attempting to save her lovely boy, and rose a spotless angel to thy presence! Blessed art thou in what thou givest and what thou takest away! Son of my beloved Agnes—'

A deep convulsive groan, silenced the excellent man; and, from its resemblance in sound to that which Mr. Pembroke heard in the dread of night, seemed to him a summons from the other world. He hastily signed to the servants, who drew open the bed-curtain, and all eyes fixed at once on Cary – pale, agonised, heart-wrung; yet making, with outstretched arms, his speechless claim to Henry. The name of Agnes had told all to the affectionate youth: he flew to his father's knees, and received his head upon his bosom. 'Son of my angel Agnes! ever intuitively the object of heart-broken joy, 'have I,then, thus strangely, thus blessedly, found thee! Life flows back too rapidly, and chokes me with excess of happiness – I feel the debility of very childhood. Yet proudly now, my Edmund! I resume the long abjured name of Powis, since I thus give it to thee, – since even the grave restores half of my buried treasure. Yes, I now behold without abhorrence this mansion; for it will henceforward have a master who might grace a throne. Julia! generous Julia! you are become the lovely owner of this borrowed home; and, with Edmund Powis, must bid us all welcome here.'

'And have I no claim to make?' interrupted Lady Trevallyn, with enchanting sweetness. 'Unkind brother! to suffer us all so long to number you among the dead! Henry,' added she, affectionately holding out her hand, 'you loved me when I had no claim upon your heart – love me not the less when you know me for your father's sister.'

'Father ever revered, ever beloved!' cried the veteran, dropping with deep devotion at the feet of Mr. Aubrey, – 'reproach not my silence. Had I loved you less, I should long, long since, have sought you; for I have existed only in the precincts of your dwelling, – have lain whole days by the side of the pool that engulfed all my worldly hopes and yours: but could I dare to present to the lonely, venerable father of Agnes, the wretch who had in her loss utterly impoverished him? Take, then, in this precious boy, my only, my rich compensation. And you too, glorious minded Pembroke! must, in the right of this our mutual son, pardon me those harsh, repulsive manners, I dared not alter. To have yielded but a little was, to a nature like mine, to have yielded all; for I am a frail wretch, compounded of extremes. Neither in this house could I venture to mingle in society: total abstraction alone could save me from discovery. Had I not lived, though I know not why, on our Edmund's looks, I should instantaneously have turned with abhorrence from this gate when it opened not to me as its master. Great indeed must be my involuntary paternal tenderness, to induce me to wander about my natural home so long, a disinherited outcast.'

'Brother!' cried Lady Trevallyn, bursting into tears, 'treat not so hardly our poor father's memory; whom, without cause, you now condemn. You have not, perhaps, perused his will: it was made, we afterwards found, on the day following that when your lovely and pious wife, so sweetly and humbly, presented your son in the church to those eyes that never would, till that moment, see him. Conscience and religion seconded so judicious a claim on Sir Hubert's feelings, and, destroying all former wills, he then made the one which we some years since established. It gives you, it is true, a limited income, and no power; but to your child the whole of the estates are bequeathed, without restriction, should he reach one-and-twenty. My second son was, if Edmund dies, to become the next heir; but I was not then marriageable, nor did I ever think I should rear a second son, for I lost three in as many years; so that I thought Heaven visited on me the sons of my forefathers. When Edmund, with his mother, was for ever lost, the cry of the people was against our poor father's cruelty, in driving her to such despair; for, alas! no circumstance ever came to light to lessen the horror and misery we all felt in supposing the desperate act her own. Your father suffered, I believe, almost as much as Mr. Aubrey. Never, from that moment, could he endure to be seen: he thought every finger made him its mark – every voice whispered, as he passed, execration; and, too surely, much of evil he knew not was, from that lamentable period, imputed to him. Your letter from Flanders, whatever its contents, was a death-stroke to your father: never, from that hour, did he utter your name; but I have seen, from involuntary recollection, many and many a tear stream in silence down his aged cheek. The horror he had of the rocks and waterfall (till then, you well know, his favourite object, in our view from the back of the castle,) made him order the poplar plantation to be enlarged that now shuts it quite out; and across the dell he threw a wide stone bridge with a high parapet, which, choking up the road below, made the wood unite; and it is now so shot up, that those who are not previously told can never suppose that they are passing over a bridge at all. Thus, but for an almost miraculous intervention of Providence, which gathered together on this only spot all the parties concerned, might Mr. Pembroke have left the country, utterly ignorant of the long-sought dell, though daily crossing it. It was a great surprise, I well remember, to us all, that Edmund's body could never be found; since that of his dear unfortunate mother was soon dragged up, holding still in her hand his little shoes, which she

The Canterbury Tales

no doubt was going to put on, when, escaping from her, the heedless babe ran to the spot which cost her a life she would not have wished prolonged if he had perished. But the pool is seated in the solid rock, which has many fissures; and it was concluded some one of them had been wide enough to engulf a child so young.'

'Alas! had I not been poor even to distress,' sighed Mr. Aubrey, 'I would have had the water drained off: though I doubted not for a moment that the precious child was lodged where his mother was found: but, alas! I had not the means. Yet, though the sweet sufferer had long been lonely and unhappy, she had always seemed patient and pious. Terrible was it to me to be obliged to conclude that she had at last despaired. How brightly did the sun shine on the dismal morning! I had a small patch of corn yet uncut on the far side of the mountain, and our only servant was sent at break of day thither. Before I followed I just looked into my poor girl's room, and saw her with the babe at her knees, hearing him his prayers in Welsh, for she had taught him no other language, that she might give him the more chance of winning Sir Hubert's affections. I kissed them both, and gave Agnes, with my blessing, such comfort as my God gave me. Alas! I returned to a desolated home – from that moment ever solitary and cheerless.' 'If I had stayed but one day longer at St. Hilary,' said an old waiting-woman of Lady Trevallyn's, 'I might have told something – though not much neither; and then one never dares to speak to one's betters of their sorrows, though one's heart is ready to break for them. That very morning my old lady had discharged me, only because, as she said, Miss Caroline was too fond of her servant; and so, God bless her, she is perhaps at this blessed moment, for she took me again as soon as she married. I was a light body then, all but my heart, and that Heaven knows was heavy enough. Jogging behind Jerry over the side of the mountain that looks down upon the parsonage, I was gaping every moment back at the castle, when, all of a sudden, I heard a most dismal screech, and the echoes there made it quite fearful. I looked down upon the orchard, and saw Master Powis, for so we all called the sweet child, though Sir Hubert would not allow of it, running along as hard as he could set foot to ground, and his poor mamma was in full chase of him, in, as I then thought, a desperate passion; but I doubt now, sweet young lady, it was only of terror. However, Jerry and the horse jogged on, and I lost sight of them both among the apple trees in a moment. The coach was just setting off for London, and I had been months there before I heard of this melancholy misfortune. I little thought till now that it was the very day I went by, or I would have spoke – not that my speaking would have done any good.'

'Misjudging woman!' interrupted the silver-headed Aubrey, 'sincerity ever does good. it is at least the solemn acquittal of our own consciences. From what horrors of mind would you have saved both me and the hardhearted Sir Hubert, could we have been sure that the lost Agnes had not been impelled by despair to fly in the face of her God, and drag down my grey hairs with sorrow almost to the grave!'

'Let us not destroy the universal satisfaction of this blessed discovery,' said Mr. Pembroke, 'by reverting to miseries which no care of ours could prevent, and all have so severely suffered by. And now, good people, you may retire. Go, prepare the marriage dinner, which the whole neighbourhood shall partake. And since you are assured Castle St. Hilary has rather been the seat of misfortune than guilt, let me never from this moment hear of another ghost or goblin.'

In full persuasion that this discovery would give repose to the dead as well as the living, the domestics withdrew, impatient to publish whatever they had been told, and open the cellar, alike for the recovery of the heir, and the marriage of Miss Pembroke.

'Of ghosts or goblins in this place we never more, I believe, shall hear,' said Sir Hubert, sighing; 'for could I have dissipated the general alarm without implicating myself, I could have told you three nights ago, that the perturbed spirit, who walked the castle at midnight, was not my father's, but my own. Recollect my extraordinary situation, and this will not surprise you. When the entreaties of my beloved son won me, against all my prior determinations, to return with him to England, I knew none of his family – cared not for them or their residence. We found Mr. Pembroke's carriage and servants waiting for us as Portsmouth; and the impatience of my darling son urged him to post night as well as day. I was almost overwhelmed with fatigue, while, buoyed by youth and tender expectation, his constitution failed not. The servant who rode before us paid all the charges; we therefore drove through the towns without heeding them; and I naturally supposed Farleigh, where I had been accustomed to direct my letters, must be the mansion to which we were thus eagerly posting. I had sunk into a stupor that had all the effect of sleep but its comfort, when the chaise slowly began to ascend this mountain; nor do I know how long it continued to do so, as I was half roused only by its stopping. I saw Henry leap out, and happy, happy strangers fondly flew to claim him; while I, unnoticed by all, uninteresting to any one, prepared cautiously to alight. The grey dawn was now peeping; and as I set my foot upon the step of the chaise! Had he arisen from the grave and stood before me at the gate, hardly could I have felt more sensible the shock! My intellects, my knees, my very life seemed to fail me! I was in this state borne into the breakfast-room, and, on reviving, found myself seated in that lost father's well-known gouty chair. Too complicated were my feelings to admit of description. The pangs of filial love – the consciousness of being an alien – the conviction that the honours of my family were no more – when the mansion was tenanted, and I, I myself was become a stranger in the house I was born in! – an accumulation of distracting feelings almost made a maniac of me. Whether to spring up, and at once execrate, abjure the scene of so many sorrows, or, for the sake of the generous youth whom I had so far followed, bury the knowledge in my own bosom, was the struggle – a tremendous struggle I found it! – The servants, having no idea that my suffering was mental, imputed my sighs, my groans, my inward agony, only to a hurt on my ankle, with which they aroused Henry. Bringing this angel of light in his hand, and followed by her benignant father, the beloved youth flew to inquire into my ailments, and by the generous softness of his nature, bound me for ever to the scene of my misery. Julia too, by I know not what charm, arrested my attention. Never, since I last looked on Agnes, had my eyes dwelt with pleasure on the face of woman, till they fixed on that of my Edmund's beloved: – I was tempted to worship her as a vision of heaven. I knew not how to bring so sympathetic, so angelic a being, down to the level of mere mortality. During my confinement, often with my son did his lovely bride watch by my bedside, and soon they divided all that remains of an exhausted heart. So powerful was their mutual influence, that I began to fancy it a mournful pleasure to wander round the domains which I ought to have inherited. The first peasant I met at a word informed me of all that I could wish to learn; for to what rustic was the death of the lovely Agnes and my infant heir unknown? Having obtained this important agonising recital from an unobserving stranger, I shut myself up in almost impenetrable gloom and abstraction: devoured by bitter recollections each surrounding object fed. Nor did I dare to impute my flight from society to its true motives, for that would have drawn every eye upon me, and made me now the object of idle wonder, and now the wretch of importunate kindness. Solitude became my only safety, silence my resource. Mr.

Pembroke, with his usual indulgence, allowed me to pursue that course which my son told him was habitual; and I again procured a key to the well-known church, where I passed days and nights on the cold stone that covers my angel and her brother. The pool where she perished was another of my haunts, and that I found to be wholly my own; for never foot approached it, till Heaven, in its own good time, sent Mr. Pembroke thither. With a burning brain and bleeding heart, it was not very likely I should get wholesome rest; and my comfortless nights generally elapsed in vain visions of the past. Sometimes, in all the secrecy of our bridal love, and the bloom of her virgin beauty, I seemed to clasp my Agnes to my unswerving heart; and then, no doubt, I unconsciously arose, and softly paced, as I once had been used to do, to the chamber my wife occupied; for that was the one in which Miss Pembroke's maid first fancied she saw the spirit. When more dreary images took possession of me in my sleep, I am apt to suppose I trod at midnight the path to the church, wrapped, perhaps, only in a loose gown; for I sometimes found myself in the morning chilled, worn, and weary: – from thence, I imagine, I must have been returning, when the servant took the alarm, and gave it, by their extravagant descriptions, which were 'the very coinage of their fears.' The other night, though of the intrusion no one complained, I fancied I knelt at the bedside of my father; and, ere I reached my own, by some strange chance or noise awaked: after which I considered; how I should avoid in future causing this frightful alarm.'

'It was then, *you*, Sir Hubert,' said Mr. Pembroke, after a pause, 'whose midnight visitation so shook my nerves, and seemed even to me of another world. 'Thus conscience does make cowards of us all!' Yet happy, perhaps, was it that you threw me upon mine, which never from that moment allowed me rest or comfort till this hour – an hour that has, I think, enriched every body but this sweet lady's second son.'

'What my Cecil must lose in wealth,' returned Lady Trevallyn, 'his elder brother and I shall gain in peace; for it is dreadful to see your children, when blessed with enough, unnaturally struggling for too much! – yet Lord Trevallyn was taught by his father to consider the preference mine gave to his brother as an act of weakness and injustice: he has, therefore, always declared his intention of trying his claim by law; and as to lose the inheritance of Powis would leave my younger child destitute, I have had the first legal opinions on the tenure by which it is held for him. All agree that there is an error in the wording of my father's will, which must give the whole property to his next heir. Most strangely is that heir restored to us in his only son; and long may Sir Hubert Powis enjoy, and fully may he bequeath the estates of his ancestors!'

'Your Cecil, my Caroline,' rejoined Sir Hubert, 'shall rather gain than lose by the re-appearance of his uncle; for I will at once equally divide between him and my own Edmund the accumulated rents of the intervening years, as an immediate provision for both: nor shall more be wanting to my nephew's future welfare: – we will teach him that a little wealth will suffice, with content and virtue: the riches of the East cannot save those from poverty who are without them.'

The blessing of heaven, from this moment, descended on all the relatives so fortuitously assembled at Castle St. Hilary. Sir Hubert Powis, restored to his rank and rights, soon lost, in the endearing habits of social life and exercised benevolence, those wild trances which solitude and sorrow had dignified as supernatural. With Lady Trevallyn, and Mr. Pembroke, he formed one family, under the direction of Edmund and Julia. They all three bore as sponsers to the font the infant son of that amiable pair; and the venerable Aubrey lived to baptize another heir to the Powis name: then, full of years and honour, he was contentedly gathered to his Agnes and Llewellyn.

THE GERMAN'S TALE

KRUITZNER

———

>   ——— What is't that takes from thee
> Thy comfort, pleasure, and thy golden sleep?
> Why dost thou bend thine eyes upon the earth,
> And start so often when thou sitt'st alone?
> Why hast thou lost the fresh blood in thy cheek?
> Oh! what portents are these?
>
> Shakespeare

Towards the end of the month of February, in a winter memorably severe, a man, his wife, and their son, a boy not seven years of age, arrived at M—, an obscure town on the northern frontier of Silesia, within the estates of the Prince de T—. A fever that attacked the husband, together with an unexpected and heavy fall of snow, impended all further advance towards Bohemia, their ostensible place of destination. The malady proved dangerous; and the resources of benevolence (for the travellers were suspected to be indigent) would have been soon exhausted in a petty German district, not abounding in religious foundations or opulent neighbours.

The town, though in itself extremely insignificant, had been raised to temporary consideration some years before by the residence of the Prince, who had chosen to pass on that spot the period of a political disgrace; and his departure had again reduced it to its original obscurity. the inhabitants of M— might with great justice be divided exactly into two classes: the poor, who *were* proud, and the poor who were not. The former dwelt in a small number of ill-built houses confusedly huddled together, and dignified with the title of a Bourg; where, under the claims of a sort of antiquated and worn-out nobility, they indulged in arrogance and sloth. The latter, who were distributed over a long, straggling, and half-ruined suburb, were mere bourgeois, with wants and ideas equally contracted to their satisfaction: nor had the two classes any thing in common but that selfishness and torpor which is the general result of ignorance.

Frederick Kruitzner, for so the stranger was called, and his unfortunate family, continued, therefore, to languish during more than ten days, unnoticed by any body but their host; who so far concerned himself about their future fate, as, in the progress of that time, to have made up his account that the said Kruitzner should not die in his house; for which reason he deemed it would be most convenient speedily to remove him from it. For reasons, doubtless, however, more merciful and wise, Providence had decreed that Kruitzner should not at that critical period die at all; and though this conviction seemed to give but little satisfaction to any human beings, his wife and child excepted, it is probable that in the region of eternal blessedness, which is to be occupied with minds, not bodies, the grateful and pious expansion of theirs would fill a larger circle in the sphere of existence than the souls of twenty – ay, a hundred – such being as their host at M—: which hundred, indeed, stripped of their portly corporeal clothing, would, perhaps, have formed collectively so small a mass as might almost seem to demand the eye of Omniscience to discover any soul at all.

Be that as it may, Kruitzner, after having just looked, as it were, into the chasm which nor ray, save that of Faith, ever yet penetrated, suddenly found the vital springs once more in motion. The severity of the season, however, was still such as to preclude the possibility of passing forward with safety: had it been otherwise, Kruitzner, though recovering, was yet too weak to undertake a journey of such length: it was even suspected that his resources no longer permitted him to attempt it. Yet had he not hitherto appeared to be absolutely destitute; and there was that in the countenance of Josephine, his wife, which announced a magnanimous confidence in the future rarely to be found in decided and habitual poverty. Josephine was, indeed, of a cast of woman not often seen. It would have been difficult to say she had perfect beauty; but she had looks that might have awed or won a world. They had indeed even actually won, to a certain degree of interest which he was not accustomed to feel, the Intendant for the Prince de T—; and as that quarter, or rather suburb, of the city in which his highness's palace stood, contained several houses adjacent to it not tenanted, and, indeed, from the long absence of the Prince, hardly tenantable, though they had once been splendidly filled, the Intendant,

The Canterbury Tales

who was not unacquainted with the fears and wishes of Kruitzner's host, had for some time revolved in his mind the magnificent project of permitting the invalid and his wife to shelter themselves under the roof of one of these: judiciously calculating that the tax of gratitude he should thereby impose would, most probably, be paid precisely in the manner he would himself desire: namely, by the death of one, and the life of the other; or if, contrary to probability, both should happen to live, he trusted that future contingencies might reward him in some way for this extraordinary act of bounty.

It could not be doubted but the overture was received with that sensibility it seemed to demand, and which the forlorn situation of the parties was calculated to inspire them with. On the evening of a very rainy day, therefore, the invalid and his family, constrained by hard necessity, and the cold countenance of their host, departed to take possession of their new, or rather old, habitation. The few ruined conduits that ran through the town poured black and muddy torrents into the river, and a pale streak of crimson on the horizon announced the setting sun, the influence of which had suspended the storm; while, through the windows of those houses that had glass ones, the faces of their inmates were indistinctly seen, alternately drawn thither by the wheels of the Intendant's crazy calèche, under shelter of which he had graciously offered to convey Kruitzner to his new abode. With much satisfaction their host saw the family depart; not without receiving, from their small resources, a payment sufficiently scanty, indeed, though all they could bestow, in acknowledgment of his services. Josephine, with a heart relieved by the conveyance she had found for her husband, pensively followed him, holding her little son by the hand: sometimes wading with difficulty through the mud; at others, covered by the water which streamed from the houses; and anxiously watching the calèche, as it jogged on at a pace not much quicker than her own.

It was among the advantages of their new accommodation that they had permission to fetch wood from the Prince's stores; and, perhaps, there are few persons who do not know the cheerfulness of a blazing fire. If any such there are, let them take a walk, like Josephine, through the moist atmosphere of a low, comfortless town; and if, like her, they happen to sit down afterwards with a beloved husband and child round the social hearth, they will, probably, not envy the first monarch in Europe his courtiers, his lustres, or his carpets. Happiness! indefinable good! – perhaps best extracted from misery! —Ah, could we but keep thee!— Yet Josephine *did* keep thee – for the night at least: for she possessed certain materials in her own bosom to which thy precious ore, though not inseparable from, naturally adheres. – Not so Kruitzner! *his* slumbers were disturbed both by sleeping and waking visions, to which, perhaps, the impression of external objects on the organs of sense as much contributed as the yet uncertain state of his health. For the first time, after a tedious confinement, he had that evening seen daylight and the sun. He had believed he should never see it more, and to his dim eye it had all the effect of a new object. The breath of heaven, too, had blown upon his face; and recollections, long torpid under the heavy hand of sickness, were awakened in his heart. During the tedious vigils of the night, he surveyed with wondering and curious eyes the tarnished splendour of the bed and room into which he was thus strangely thrown; and though superstition peopled it, not to him, as it might have done to those of his neighbours who knew the stories attached to it, that gloom which is haunted by 'the ghosts of our departed joys' needs no other spectre to fill it.

In the solitude and obscurity of their spacious and comfortless mansion, days and days now past over the heads of Kruitzner and his wife. Deep snow, in the interim, capped the high mountains which separated them from Bohemia; floods inundated the country; cold chilled the human species; and it seemed as if the vital principle contracted hourly into a narrower circle, till the little town of M— became the point at which it stopped. On those days, when the sun broke through the cheerless atmosphere, Kruitzner was occasionally seen turning up the ground in the garden for the few winter roots that it afforded. It was observed that he was still pale, even to sallowness; that he had powerful features, a brow marked by sorrow, and an eye of no striking effect in his countenance, unless animated by some sudden emotion, when it darted forward a fire that seemed like new-created light upon the world. From his own habitation he never stirred; and, as that habitation was of no very good report in the neighbourhood, he was a little troubled with visiters. Sometimes, indeed, the wife of the postmaster condescended to look in upon Madame Kruitzner, when the Intendant favoured her with a seat in his bone-setting conveyance. On such occasions the good lady, who had only three faults, – pride, curiosity, and the love of talking, – seldom came without bringing to the little boy pots of conserves, sugar-cakes, and such other housewifely presents as cost nothing to the donor and gratify the appetites common to children. When this happened, she did not fail, however, to observe, though by stealth, the keen air of impatience with which the boy would devour her cates; accompanied sometimes with thin slices of bread, which his mother cut for him; while his father, who rarely spoke, would lean his elbows on his knees, and, covering his face with his hands, only now and then cast wild and eager glances upon his wife and child. These temporary starts of sensibility excepted, Kruitzner was sombre, abstracted, and frequently employed in writing. Yet to whom his letters were addressed remained a profound mystery; – the good lady, though she took care to question her husband duly on the subject, not having been able to extort the smallest information from him. For though Weilburg, such was the name of the postmaster, was not excellent at keeping a secret, he was at least more discreet than to confide it to his wife. In this instance, however, his merit was small, since, in fact, there was, as far as letters were concerned, no secret to keep: Kruitzner's, if indeed he wrote any, never being known to reach the post-office.

Mr. Weilburg was, nevertheless, a man of no little importance in his department: he was believed to be rich; his wife claimed a sort of remote and left-handed relationship to the Prince himself; and had been even noticed before her marriage by a certain Countess who had formerly occupied the very house lately lent on sufferance to be Kruitzners. Of this Countess strange things had been reported when she was alive, and strange things continued to be reported now that she was supposed to be dead. She was strongly surmised to have been the chère amie of his Highness; and, as fame related, had, in a fit of jealousy, destroyed herself, in one of those very apartments the Kruitzners then inhabited. Other reports, indeed, averred that, far from committing any such unchristian-like act, she had accompanied the Prince in his berlin on the road to Vienna; but as she certainly had not been seen to depart from her own roof, and as an air of mystery had been, perhaps, voluntarily thrown over the business, in order to save a half-ruined reputation, the whole disgrace was judiciously transferred to that which could best bear it – namely, the house; which, to a certain degree, stood proscribed. That under such circumstances, Madame Weilburg should become a visiter there, seemed a little extraordinary: but it is possible that she had either judgment or authentic information enough to know the futility of these suspicions: – or, it may be presumed, that, having once tasted the pleasures of grandeur and luxury in that very house, and seeing in Josephine an extraordinary as well as fascinating character, both of form and mind, she did not think it improbable that circumstances might bring back the days which were past.

To Mr. Wielburg the person only of Josephine was yet known; though he might almost be said to have the hearts and heads of the whole little community of M— in his possession; since his authority in the post-office made every thing that was interesting to either pass through his hands. Those who have been present at the opening of the bags, and delivery of the letters, alone know what a scene of perturbation and anxiety such occasions present, even in peaceful days; but in time of war, as was then the case, how many hands are stretched out, how many cheeks are flushed, how many hearts palpitate with hope, or sink with despondency! The names of a son – a brother – a father – a husband – a lover – tremble, in imperfect and half-suppressed sounds, on the lips of the standers-by; yet no decided one escapes: the strong convulsions of the mind most sensitively shrink from observation, and each retires into himself to devour the pang or the joy of the moment! Even in the town of M—, insulated as it seemed in creation, a cipher, only swelling that great aggregate termed society, these feelings were confusedly understood; and they frequently led to developments of circumstances or character, by which Weilburg knew how to profit. Nothing of this, however, had yet occurred in the case of Madame Kruitzner. She had at first attracted his notice by a certain exterior of grandeur which he was unable to comprehend. 'This woman is nobody,' said he to himself, whenever he saw her at a distance, in her snow shoes, her close pelisse lined the common skins, and her fur cap, marking her fine brow, and the correct outline of her features; while the little Marcellin at her side showed in his blooming countenance the exact miniature of hers; – 'this woman can be nobody, who is thus able to encounter the severity of such a season! Yet what a step! what a walk! one should swear it was a coronation, instead of the business of a domestic, that she is engaged in!' Madame Kruitzner, meantime, wholly unconscious of the comments that were made on her, with sober and persevering equanimity always attended the arrival of the courier, and always hitherto in vain. Now and then, indeed, she was observed to drop a tear when the child complained of cold or fatigue, which he never did till they were returning: for, by a sort of affectionate sympathy, the elastic step of the mother seemed to invigorate her young companion.

A certain confidential communication that passed at this juncture made the inquiries of Madam Kruitzner more accurately observed

115

than before. To the two important characters of postmaster and intendant the town added a third, seldom omitted in any district however small, namely, a lawyer; – or rather one who called himself such: for the more honourable part of his fraternity would probably have alike disclaimed his pretensions and his practice. He was a busy, officious sort of personage, who knew almost every thing better than law; and exactly among that servile class of his profession who are employed to embroil a cause – an occupation which the dishonesty of their clients, not less than their own, renders, it is to be feared, full as profitable as that of ending it. But though Mr. Idenstein (for such was his name) professed to live by his talents, those who knew him best were inclined to think it was by the exercise of one only – the talent of being useful. It proved, however, in this case, as in many others, a host in itself; for it made him always an acceptable guest at the only two good tables in town, the Intendant's and Weilburg's; which, as he was needy, was an advantage he failed not to profit by. To the Intendant he particularly addressed himself, in the hope of obtaining his countenance, at some future period, towards a more important and advantageous establishment than could be found at M—; where, although the spirit of litigation abounded, the body and sinews were wanting. The Intendant, on his side, was liberal of *promises*; for he had, in reality, no intention of parting with Idenstein: having himself, as he often declared, more occasion for law (for he very properly seldom termed it justice) in the management of the Prince's concerns than almost any man within the district. Idenstein's employment in Weilburg's house was of a lighter nature and one better suited to his taste; for it chiefly consisted in retailing all the intrigues of the neighborhood to his hostess; which, as he was not malicious, but only credulous and vain, he often did with some pleasantry, and without interpretation from her husband – a sly, quiet, stagnant sort of character, more apt to listen than to talk; and one who thus, under the appearance of a dull taciturnity, concealed a disposition no less frivolous and inquisitive than that of his wife.

Various inquiries, supposed to be set on foot by a great man, now directed the attention of this respectable trio to Kruitzner and his family. There was, indeed, no certainty, and, in some respects, little probability, of their being the objects of the inquiry; but idleness and curiosity had marked them out as such. The persons concerned in forwarding it were at least assured no ill consequence could result to themselves; nor was any one amongst them of a character to advert to

The Canterbury Tales

the evil it might produce to others. Sly conjectures, craft observation, together with a sort of petty activity, formed the habit of their minds; and this habit spontaneously directed itself to every thing where there was the smallest appearance of mystery. That of want is, alas! too painful to be initiated not to bid them shrink with reluctance from the discovery. Kruitzner and his wife, lulled into temporary security, nevertheless believed they had, in their present condition, no other evil to contend with: nor had it hitherto occurred to them to suspect, that, while they were striving to snatch all the repose that poverty and sorrowful recollections would allow, the snare was secretly winding around that threatened finally to destroy it.

That repose, precarious as it thus was in its nature, was indeed every day fading from their grasp, even while they were yet ignorant that any one was at hand to tear it from them. Their retreat at M—, which had in the first instance promised them little else than a grave, appeared, from the circumstances in which they were placed, to shut them out almost as completely from the rest of the world as if they had really been buried there. Stationed within that narrow limit, and devoid of the means either to advance or recede, they found themselves in the most frightful of all solitude – that of the soul: and though there is a principle in nature, and a still stronger in love, which obliges us to rejoice, despite of past calamities, in the recovery of a being whom death alone seems capable of sheltering from future ones, yet did the faint pleasure of unexpected convalescence daily give way, even in both, to the most racking inquietude. The good genius of Josephine (for on her a good genius still attended) had, nevertheless, so far favoured them, that the only letter she had ever sent from M—, written immediately on her arrival there, and at the critical moment, as it seemed, of her husband's fate, had, by means of the obscurity in which she was then plunged, fortunately escaped the cognizance of Weilburg; who, except on occasions of interest or curiosity, seldom executed his employment in person. The mere superscription of that letter would have enlightened more effectually than his own ingenuity, or even that of his assistant, ever succeeded in doing: but it had been carried to the office late at night by Josephine herself, thrown hastily into the bags, and the answer to it – the important and anxiously expected answer – never arrived.

Sanguine as the parties concerned in the present scrutiny respecting Kruitzner and his wife might originally be, they had very soon opportunity to perceive that there was either little to discover, or that the discovery would not be easily made. The habitual reserve of his character had, from the first, afforded small hope of success: and in hers there was a generous plainness and candour that defeated, even without intending it, the little arts of a sophisticated and frivolous mind. It was in vain for Madame Weilburg to observe – 'that the delicate hands of her acquaintance were never fitted for those humble offices in which she was employed.' In vain did the good lady wonder, 'that Madame Kruitzner had not profited by the kind dispositions of the Intendant, to solicit some appointments for her husband in the household of the Prince;' even her happy prognostics upon the promising countenance of Marcellin were thrown away. Josephine was little likely to be touched with the coarse flattery of one whose penetration into her condition of her character was so small: and though a grateful sense of some trifling obligations, together with a natural indulgence to the foibles of others, taught her, on these occasions, to practise an extraordinary self-command, it was not possible for her always to disguise that restlessness and impatience which springs from an agitated heart.

During the first days of this intercourse the Intendant himself frequently made one of the party; but he had just that sort of understanding which informed him he was of all men living least calculated to answer his own purpose of winding into confidence. He had gained possession of his situation soon after the Prince quitted M—; and having originally taken up all the shreds and patches of self-importance left there by his predecessor, he found it impossible to lay them down in that degree which the haughty and repulsive manners of Kruitzner demanded; him, therefore, he soon most cordially hated: nor did the pleasure he really found in seeing Josephine indemnify him for the mortification his pride received in the society of her husband; he, consequently, discontinued his visits, or paid them very rarely, and at hours when he believed he should not encounter the latter; – turning over all exercise of ingenuity that respected him to Idenstein, whose subtle and pliant manners eminently fitted him for the task.

Kruitzner, though of a more complex character than his wife, was yet, however, of a more vulnerable one. Neither humiliation nor adversity had succeeded in eradicating from his mind certain proud and turbulent feelings, which, though by necessity rendered passive for the moment, were ready instruments in the hands of those around him to accomplish any purpose of craft. Nothing but a profound conviction of the danger and hopelessness of his situation rendered him impenetrable; and it was easy to discern that there were springs in his soul by which he might still be governed. It had not been the lot of those who sought yet to discover them, however; and it was even plain that, if they ever did so, it would be more the work of their fortune than of their talents: yet little conciliating or conciliatory, as were the general habits of his temper, they were not always equally intractable: for, to the forlorn and desponding heart, however cautiously it may be guarded, there will still be moments in which the voice of flattery sounds like that of friendship. Idenstein, who had address enough to perceive this, was at infinite pains to improve those moments; and be failed not, whenever they presented themselves, to pour forth such general and desultory effusions of philanthropy as he supposed calculated to make a deep impression on the mind of his hearer: that he did make, however, seemed far from answering the purpose designed by it. Kruitzner was, indeed, frequently roused to momentary attention: something like hope would, on those occasions, kindle in his eye; but a still stronger feeling seemed almost immediately to quench it. He would gaze and listen with the intentness of a man who is desirous to receive as a truth what his mind, nevertheless, rejects; till, both the powers of hearing and sight being at length absorbed in some remote idea, he would start from his seat, rush into the garden, and remain there till the departure of his guest.

Idenstein had sagacity enough to conclude, that he who flies from the danger of betraying himself is more than half way in the net; and after one of these broken starts, he one day ventured to follow him. Kruitzner was standing on a small eminence that commanded the distant mountains, and looking earnestly towards a particular spot. The snow, which had fallen so late in the season, had rapidly thawed before the increasing heat of the sun; traces of vegetation were obvious throughout the whole country around; and a thousand streams, swelled suddenly to petty torrents visible both in the valley and nearer hills, brightened the prospect.

'You are fond of this view, I think?' said Idenstein, who had frequently seen him on the same spot.

'It looks towards Bohemia,' replied Kruitzner, motioning that way with his hand: – there was something singularly mournful in his tone: – he wore, too, 'a countenance more in sorrow than in anger.'

' True – you – you are going thither?' again rejoined his inquisitive companion.

'I *was* going thither.'

'And why do you not pursue your journey?'

Kruitzner started.

'Are you not afraid to ask?' said he, fiercely. – There was something so odd in the question, and so odd in the manner in which it was put, that Idenstein felt for a moment not wholly devoid of the sensation imputed to him.

'Dare you solicit my confidence?' continued Kruitzner, in the same tone. Idenstein, though his nerves had not quite recovered the attack upon them, yet brightened up at the word confidence, and muttered something expressive of more than a civil assent.

'Take it then in few words – I am poor' – The countenance of the inquirer again fell. Of all Kruitzner's concerns, this, in fact, seemed to him the only one that did not require to be told; and it was, unquestionably, that he least desired to hear: he ventured, however, to express his regret on the occasion; and to add, 'that he was himself precisely in the same predicament.'

'I thought so!' said Kruitzner, with bitter irony: 'I had heard that the acquaintance of a poor man are always discreet enough to be poor too.' – Idenstein, who had really spoken truth – not, indeed, for its own sake, but because it happened to dictate the answer most common and convenient on similar occasions, felt rebuked. During the short pause that succeeded, he had, however time to recover his presence of mind, and to perceive all the difference of situation between the man who avows his poverty, and of one who only suffers it to be guessed. He believed he saw himself touching a critical moment, from which much would be gained or lost to the future; and the recollection that he acted under the Intendant gave him courage for what was to follow. He thought, moreover, and not without reason, that he perceived remote traces of irresolution in the countenance of Kruitzner.

'Poverty,' said he, fixing his eyes, therefore, on his companion, and raising his voice with an oratorical emphasis, 'is, like all other evils, merely comparative! I may consider myself as poor, yet be in a condition to show my regard by assisting another. – A small sum' – Kruitzner suddenly changed colour, and the violent palpitation of his heart was distinctly visible – 'a *very small* sum,' continued Idenstein, 'I think I could command.'

'Let it but enable me to accomplish my journey,' said Kruitzner. – He paused, and his voice was smothered.

'Whither would you go? – and who is the person I am thus to oblige?' – Kruitzner hesitated; an indistinct apprehension crossed his mind; and the grossness of the man who could thus abruptly question him presented itself in glaring colours: but sad necessity, and newly awakened hope, struggled in his breast with a force calculated to silence every opposing sentiment.

'Wish not, my kind friend!' said he, at length, after a silent conflict, and in a subdued tone, 'to know what it would be painful for me to tell, and of no avail to you to hear. – If you dare trust me, accept my promise that you will neither trust the powerless nor the ungrateful. – I have no other security to give.' – That he proffered was by no means in Idenstein's way to receive; but short as his progress towards confidence had been in comparison with his expectations, yet as he found he was not likely then to derive further advantage from the conversation, he was content to accept the terms proposed – having previously succeeded, however, in explaining his offer down to so *very* small a sum, as nearly dispelled his own fears, and completely annihilated the momentary gleam of hope he had kindled in the bosom of his companion.

Inconsiderable as was the assistance Kruitzner thus obtained, and inadequate towards the purpose he so earnestly desired to accomplish, it was yet such as the cruelty of his fate utterly forbade him to reject. Since his residence at M—, he had known privation and poverty in a degree which, far from having felt, he had never before even witnessed: penury itself now approached; and as he had not supposed it possible that the cold hearts of those around would induce them to lend any succour to a man who dared not sufficiently solve the enigma of his own life to proffer a hope of payment, the desperation of his fate pressed so forcibly upon him, that the interference of Idenstein seemed little less than a miracle. As the fervour of this impression, however, wore off, his knowledge of mankind taught him to look in that for the cause; and Idenstein quickly perceived that he was now, in turn, become a subject of much anxious observation to his new friend, who, for several days after, never saw him without striving to find in his looks and demeanour traces of some sinister design. In this, however, the penetration of Kruitzner was foiled. Idenstein had naturally a kind of pert frivolity, that wore the appearance of artlessness; he was, besides, too much on his guard to allow any motive to be discernible for his actions save that he announced; and Kruitzner was at length induced, or, perhaps, was willing to believe, that he had really excited a sentiment of disinterested kindness in the bosom of a man, so utterly distinct from himself. this conviction taught him a little to unbend. He did it, as he thought, with circumspection; but it was not in the impetuous character of Kruitzner to reason accurately, or to guard himself at all points. His real necessities, his sanguine disposition, the dangerous habit of relying on his fate, soon divested him of his caution; and though he still preserved an inviolable silence with regard to past events, he omitted to direct his penetration to the future.

Idenstein was careful not to throw his new acquaintance off his guard. He now changed his battery; and, perceiving he could not allure to confidence, waited the occasion for exorting it. He had no doubt he should succeed; and, therefore, took pleasure in the pursuit: for it was among the silly foibles of his own character, to sport, as he believed, with those around him; to dupe them, while they were arrogating superior prudence; and to enjoy his triumph. It was a character that cost him dear in the end; and, even in its progress, often rendered him a contemptible and unrewarded puppet in the hands of others. In this instance, however, he was only one out of three, neither of whom suspected the length or importance of the clue they were unravelling. The ingenuity of Idenstein, aided by his apparent insignificance, was not, however, unsuccessful. The victim plunged deeper and deeper into the snare: and, so well did his crafty adversary understand how to tempt his wants by the display and loan of petty sums, that the unfortunate Kruitzner at length started as from a dream; and, in finding himself a debtor, became suddenly sensible to a new and undefined misery, of which, amid all his calamities, he had hitherto been ignorant. Dissimulation or fear was alike uncongenial to his nature; but he perceived the absolute necessity of practising the former, and he strove to regulate his conduct by that conviction. Idenstein was not, however, deceived: what followed between them became, therefore, a contest of cunning, in which the latter had all the advantage. It was in his choice, at any time, to rouse the proud spirit of Kruitzner to a point of defiance that should put him within his power, and it was not seldom that he touched upon the experiment. He was not wholly without a personal apprehension, however, that taught him to forbear in time: while Kruitzner, on his side, strove no less sedulously to avoid a crisis so dangerous, and secretly cherished the only hope he had now for a long period been able to entertain – that of accumulating, by means of this forbearance, a small hoard that should supply the necessities of his wife and child, while he himself undertook the desperate project of pursuing his journey to Bohemia on foot. How great would have been his surprise to have known that this scheme was perhaps the only one which all parties, could they have penetrated it, would have favoured! Yet such, as far as the junto at M— was concerned, was undoubtedly the case.

By comparing the inquiries that had reached them, with their own observations, this sagacious circle had, at length, satisfied themselves that Kruitzner and Josephine were in reality above the condition they avowed; and busy Imagination had eked out their small share of discernment, with a conclusion that one or the other sprang from a family of rank, and was become liable, by a disgraceful connection, to its resentment. Had Madame Weilburg been consulted, she would at once have pronounced the transgressor upon his hereditary honours to be Kruitzner; in whose person, though faded, there were yet sufficient traces of dignity and grace to arrest female attention: but the jury on this occasion were men; and they, with one voice, pronounced Josephine to be unquestionably the culprit. Enlightened partly by their own suggestions, and partly by her eyes, they saw beauty, grandeur, and all, in short, that was really to be seen in her – except virtue: and, as she was not *their* relation, they were inclined to think that a non-essential in her character. In fact, poor Josephine, though very unconscious of the obligation, certainly owed something to their suspicion of her wanting it: for, though each would individually have had little reluctance to consign Kruitzner to hard diet and a dungeon, there was not one of them could, without scruple, determine on giving up his companion. Of these sentiments the Intendant was the leader. Her exterior charms, more than any interest created by her situation, had first induced him to step forth in her favour; and this circumstance was so far fortunate, as it shielded her on every occasion from the wanton insolence of Idenstein, who attributed views to his employer more decided than the indolence and coldness of his nature really prompted him to pursue.

The project which Kruitzner had continued to meditate, he at length confided to his wife. Those only who had known the previous events of her life could tell the heartsickness it was calculated to excite. Yet such was the peculiarity of their fate, that remonstrance would have been cruelty. To be able together to withdraw privately from M— seemed little short of an impossibility; that she and her child should pursue the journey on foot, was wholly such. There was not the remotest hope that Idenstein, or indeed any human being, would assist them in undertaking it: – so far the contrary, that both were sensible mystery or suspicion had attached itself too much to their fate to allow the circle in which they lived voluntarily to lose sight of them. Yet the importance of the journey was no less felt by Josephine than her husband: she was deeply sensible that he had never loved any human being as he loved her; nothing, therefore, but despair could have induced him to thinking of quitting her; nor, on her side, was there a consideration on earth, save that before her, which could make her consent to their separation. Yet, in addition to the exquisite suffering attending such an event, she felt she had another trial to encounter, which the habits of Kruitzner's mind did not even lead him to suspect: in a word, that it would require an almost invincible fortitude to remain in the house they then inhabited, with no other companion than Marcellin. Superstition had, nevertheless, little or no share in her repugnance. The report of Madame Weilburg, who was never weary of talking about her late 'dear and beautiful countess,' had sufficiently persuaded her hearer that the story related of the latter was, if not wholly ill-founded, at least false in its catastrophe. She had, in fact, gathered enough to be assured that the Countess was still in existence; nor were the opinions and character of Josephine, even at the worst, such as inclined her to tremble at the dead. Had they been so, the interior of the house, marked by a depressing and faded magnificence, distributed into intricate offices, once crowded with domestics, now dark, still, and lonely, would have been sufficient to have appalled her. It was in itself a body without a soul – a region whence every thing vital appeared strangely to have fled. But the fears of Josephine were of a nearer and less chimerical nature; and originated in the situation of the house, which was at the extremest verge of a ruinous and half-unpeopled suburb: a spacious garden extended behind from the prince's grounds to the high road, surrounded by a wall extremely dilapidated, and so low in many places as almost to invite intruders; while the neglected state in which the whole had long been suffered to remain, gave it an appearance particularly rude and solitary. That wing of the house which was nearest to the town, adjoined to a mansion that had formerly been possessed by the retinue of the prince; it was now uninhabited, and formed a gloomy barrier between the palace and the habitation of Kruitzner. No sound, therefore, that issued from the latter, could be heard by any human ear; nor was it possible to summon a protector thither: yet was the house every where so slightly barred, either because the narrow circle of the town secured its neighbourhood from depredation, or that the numerous train of the

Countess rendered precaution unnecessary, that any night wanderer might without difficulty enter it.

Kruitzner had himself assented to this observation, when made by his wife during the early days of their abode there. But misery is an exclusive feeling, and leaves no room for meaner and subordinate ones; the circumstance had, therefore, faded from his mind as altogether immaterial: nor, while enclosing Josephine and his child in the same apartment with himself, did he believe he had any thing to apprehend, or to lose. Beyond that apartment and the adjoining saloon, of which they also taken possession, a long range of rooms extended – spacious, and chiefly dismantled. Marcellin, to whom the general appearance of the house was not very inviting, had at first found some difficulty to reconcile himself to so cheerless a residence: curiosity, however, led him soon to explore it; nor did he fail to return on these occasions with strange tales to his mother, either of noises that were in fact caused by some remaining articles of furniture accidentally displaced by himself, or dungeons, which proved upon examination to be nothing but cellars and recesses. His parents sometimes smiled at, and sometimes chid him. Josephine, in particular, who had often occasion to prove the fallacy of his fears, had at length ceased to heed them; and as the boy, though not without the capricious cowardice of his age, was, on the whole, of an enterprising character, he had ceased to heed them also.

If, under these circumstances of real or imaginary danger, terror at any moment assailed Josephine herself, the consciousness of their poverty forbade her to cherish it. Even at the worst, Kruitzner was ever near her – active, intrepid, and manly; but of his protection she was now on the point of being deprived: and, however small the temptation her situation offered, either to plunder, or offence of any kind, it is still the lot of woman to fear the evils of wantonness and levity, – evils, which the very certainty that she must fear, and, whatever her vigour of mind, may be unable to repel, often tempts the wicked or the thoughtless to inflict! Josephine justly distrusted her won fortitude when the voice of Kruitzner should be no longer near to encourage, or his arm to shield her; when the very apprehension of the sufferings he was encountering might unstring her nerves; or the possibility of his eternal absence overwhelm her heart with despondency. Yet the trial, fearful as it appeared, she believed must be encountered; and what was indispensable she would have despised herself had she wholly shrunk from. Collecting, therefore, the stronger powers of her mind, she resolved silently to abide the issue, whatever it might prove, with resolution.

The frame, however, is not always able to sustain the struggles of the heart. A just mode of thinking, and a happy temperament, had done much throughout life for Josephine; but they could not do every thing; and, despite of her efforts, her cheek announced to Kruitzner that all was not well within her bosom. His own feelings interpreted hers. Days of painful irresolution succeeded on both sides, during which their deep abstraction, and the heavy rains which continued incessantly to fall, rendered them insensible to the total solitude in which they had been permitted to live. Marcellin was not so inattentive. He was extremely tired of the wet weather, which kept him within the house, and very much surprised and angry that nobody came to enliven it. The first gleam of sunshine was a moment of transport to him: he skipped twenty times in a quarter of an hour to the door, and, at last, bethought himself of requesting permission to pay a short visit to Madame Weilburg, whose closet, he was secretly not without hopes, still contained some of those good things he had been accustomed to find there. Marcellin, however, like most of his age, forgot his promise of returning as soon as he was out of sight. He was right in suspecting the cakes and sweetmeats were not exhausted. He got more than his portion, and saw besides such a number of entertaining sights, as put home entirely out of his head. His stay, indeed, so far exceeded his usual limits, that his parents began to be alarmed. Josephine was already anxiously near the door, and her husband was preparing to seek the little stray, when he suddenly jumped in, wild with spirits and indulgence, – 'Weilburg and his wife were dressed so fine! – the Intendant was *so* busy! – – Mr. Idenstein too was there! the Prince's own coach was going out! and if his parents would but look out of the window, they would see it bring home the stranger to the palace!' While Kruitzner and Josephine smiled at this prattle, which was blended with a thousand gay and infantine caresses, the innocent child wound it up, by pronouncing, in the name of *the stranger*, that of the being on earth most hostile to the safety and respose of his father.

Josephine, who saw the change in her husband's countenance, had hardly time to silence the transports of the boy, and hurry him, with her, into another room, when Idenstein entered – adorned, indeed, as had been described, in holiday foppery, and with a repetition of the same hateful intelligence. He addressed himself familiarly to Madame Kruitzner as she passed him, and coldly to her husband. They had

The Canterbury Tales

differed when they last met, and Idenstein apologised, with an air of conceited importance, for an absence which he secretly knew to be acceptable, Kruitzner, whose mind was at that moment a chaos of perturbation and surprise, was little disposed to consider their relative situations, or how far worse his own had insensibly become since he entered M——: impoverished, indeed – but no man's slave – for he was then no man's debtor! – personal insult or degradation, in any possible shape, he had never known, and, if the late transactions with Idenstein had sometimes inspired a transient and painful feeling that resembled the latter, he had banished the idea from his bosom as one to which death itself would be preferable. With such habits and sentiments, roused as they now were by the most poignant recollections, the frivolous being before him became almost as completely annihilated to his eyes as to his heart. Idenstein, possessed with his own self-importance, did not easily discover this: but when he did, he well knew how to harrow up the proud spirit that could teach it him, by an abrupt and insolent demand, which it was impossible to satisfy.

Kruitzner, forced thus hatefully back upon the misery of the present, again shrunk into himself, with an indignant pause, and questioned his soul upon all the possibilities of the future. He was now every way taken in the toils. A few hours alone, probably, intervened between him and the formidable enemy he had hitherto successfully avoided. That he could no longer do so, he had every reason to suspect: – but, at the very best, the situation in which he was involved with Idenstein (the barrier being once broken between them) exposed him to humiliations which he found it impossible to endure. – To make good his long-intended departure on that very night seemed the only method of escaping them; and dangerous, therefore, as the attempt might prove, both to himself and Josephine, there was no longer any alternative but to hazard it. This resolution made, the tempest of his soul gradually subsided: a kind of desperate stillness seemed to lock up his faculties. – He half-smoothed his brow; dismissed, though with some difficulty, his troublesome companion; and, closing the doors even against his family, sat down, in solitude and gloom, to meditate throughout the evening on the future fate of that wife and child whom he was thus driven by cruel necessity to abandon, and to calculate by what further suffering he was himself yet to expiate the wanton follies of the past. – Such was, now, the forlorn and hopeless situation of a man, who might, at one time, have said, with Anthony,

> —— 'I was so great, so happy, so beloved,
> Fate could not ruin me; – till I took pains,
> And work'd against my fortune: – chid her from me,
> And turn'd her loose: – yet still she came again.
> My careless days, and my luxurious nights,
> At length have wearied her!'——

He who had announced himself at M— simply as Frederick Kruitzner was by birth a Bohemian, and of the first class of nobility. Under the obscure name he now bore, he had buried that transmitted to him through a long line of illustrious ancestors, and which his father had hoped to see descend untarnished in the person of his son. Those hopes had long since vanished: and, before the period at which Kruitzner arrived at M—, Count Siegendorf had ceased to inquire whether or not he had a son in existence.

The Count himself, though his character was in the end not wholly free from a certain degree of austerity grafted upon it by afflicting circumstances, was naturally noble, generous, and humane. He was not without the pride of rank; but it acted only in a certain sphere. His moderation rendered him dear to his inferiors, in an age when subordination was vassalage, and every lord a petty despot. He was not young when he became a father, and he looked with the peculiar fondness of one who had hardly hoped to be such, on the son whom a dying wife doubly endeared to him. In the education of the young man nothing was neglected that was either honourable or useful: nor were his talents such as to disgrace his preceptors. His boyish days, if they gave not assurance of any eminent power of mind, were yet marked by quickness of apprehension and feeling; and in his rapid progress towards manhood, his father believed he saw the promise of an honourable life. The person of the young count was early formed. The hardy exercises to which he was habituated, rendered it vigorous and manly. His features were fine; his voice was commanding; his eye then sparkled with that flame which now burned so dimly in the socket; and he had a loftiness of demeanour which seemed the expression of a noble soul.

To this character of person, that of his mind, however, did not correspond. He had rather pride than dignity; and, unhappily, that very failing, which, when it springs, from the consciousness of noble descent, sometimes becomes the source of noble actions, had on him a very opposite effect; – for he was proud, not of his ancestors, but of himself. His mind had not energy enough to trace causes in their effects. The splendour, therefore, which the united efforts of education, fortune, rank, and the merits of his progenitors, threw around him, was early mistaken for a personal gift – a sort of emanation proceeding from the lustre of his own endowments, and for which, as he believed, he was indebted to nature, he resolved not to be accountable to man. By feelings like these, the grand principles of filial duty and affection could not but be early undermined; and, reasoning progressively upon this system, every new distinction which advancing life necessarily brought with it to a young man introduced under auspices so favourable, nourished the latent fault of his character. He never stopped to inquire what he could have made himself, had he been born anything but what he was. He was distinguished! – he saw it – he felt it – he was persuaded he should ever be so; and while yet a youth in the house of his father – dependent on his paternal affection, and entitled to demand credit of the world merely for what he was to be – he secretly looked down upon that world as made only for him.

The crimes, however, by which such a character might have been stained were fortunately most congenial to his: the love of pleasure was the great spring of his soul – a passion little remarkable at a very early period; for at a very early period the circle of his pleasures could not but be narrow: nor were boyish sports the objects of serious reprehension. But when nature and education seemed to have done their part, and the important one of man was to commence, how was his father shocked and astonished to find all that should have led to generous emulation or heroic virtue perverted solely to the purposes of self-indulgence and voluptuous dissipation. Willingly, however, did the tender parent allow for the force of temptations which youth seldom wholly withstands. He depended on the innate virtues of his son to arrest their progress after a certain period, and on his own paternal authority finally to subdue them: but the young count, wanton with prosperity, was little disposed to pause in the career of his pleasure; and the first pointed reprimand of his father conveyed to the latter that most afflicting of all pangs – a conviction that his reprimands would for the future to fruitless. With trembling uncertainty he ventured to probe deeper into the heart of his son, and learned to shrink before the fearful apprehension of seeing himself despised there. It was now time to assert his own claims; – Bohemia was on the point of plunging into a bloody, though hazardous war*, and by her rejection of the

---

* Commonly called the War of Thirty Years

Austrian yoke offered to the brave and independent a sphere of action calculated to awaken every nobler energy of the soul. The state had not yet, however, summoned all its supporters: they were called upon by turns individually; and their collective force was reserved for that period when all hope of a peaceful adjustment should be frustrated. Count Siegendorf had been among the first of those who armed their vassals: he now proposed to draw them into action, eager to execute a plan he had long meditated of intrusting the command of them to his son, persuaded that he should, in so doing, afford him an occupation gratifying to the turbulence of youth, and which, as it had been that of his ancestors, their example would teach him to fill with glory.

The young man was both naturally and habitually intrepid. The avowal of this determination was, therefore, received by him with unfeigned satisfaction: and he pressed forward the preparations for his own departure to the camp, with a zeal that once more invigorated the half-extinguished hopes of his father.

Again was he received in a new circle with those flattering testimonies of regard on which he was so well disposed to rely. Much was expected from him, and much, therefore, in advance was granted to him; but he had not been long with the army before it was discovered that glory was in his eyes only another mode of pleasure, and not exactly of the kind he most coveted: he was, besides, self-opinionated enough ever to believe he might pursue it his own way, and arrogant enough to assert his opinions; in the persuasion that those who controverted them had, as was indeed sometimes the case, no other advantage over him but that of which he always denied the validity – experience. Under these circumstances he could not be deemed a good soldier; and such was the nature of the war, that the cause he did not serve his influence and example were calculated to injure. Of his personal courage, indeed, no doubt was entertained, for he had frequently given proofs of it equally useless and rash: but the diminution of his followers, and the impoverished state of his finances, were particulars, that, as they could not be concealed, soon brought home to his father the conviction that he was no longer to be trusted as a leader. Complaints extorted from all superior to him in command daily confirmed this. The Count knew too well his own importance in the state, to believe any member of it would thus speak of his darling son, the heir of a powerful domain, unless impelled by the strongest necessity. That necessity continually became more urgent, and the complaints more importunate. The young man, relying on his personal merit, and full

The Canterbury Tales

of an arrogant self-sufficiency that left him little disposed to weigh what was passing around except it pressed upon his pride, was far, meantime, from being aware of the storm that impended: it burst, therefore, like thunder, when an authoritative mandate absolutely took from him all future command or influence over the vassals of his family. This mandate he was sufficiently inclined to dispute: but he now, for the first time, began indistinctly to perceive, that, whatever might be his own estimation of himself, he had not yet made progress enough in life to enter the lists of honour or responsibility with his father. A confused sense of shame, blended with a suspicion of error, passed rapidly across his mind; but it was a troublesome sort of feeling, and he dismissed it as such.

The Count, nevertheless, had not thus mortified or degraded his son, without preparing somewhat that might soften the blow. He had secretly solicited, and obtained for him, a command in the army, which, though of infinitely less importance to the state than that he had lost, was not ill-suited to his rank in life, and secured to him the opportunity of recovering the estimation his indiscretions had robbed him of. And now then all again was well in the mind of the youth. He observed to his companions 'that he had lost a command given only by the indulgence of a father; – or rather, one which he might consider as the claim of his birth: the rank he had just received, though less distinguished, was therefore infinitely more honourable. It was bestowed by his country – it was a proof of his desert! – a proof that he commanded fortune, and might henceforth defy her frowns!' – He was nearer the experiment than he expected. The post in which he was stationed stood exposed in a particular manner to the attacks of the enemy. A furious alarm was given during the night. The duties of his situation demanded every exertion of promptitude or valour; but he was buried in a licentious debauch, and incapable of acting. The post was lost – his honour tarnished – the furious resentment of his countrymen could no longer be controlled: – he was dismissed, by the general voice, from all employment, and banished to his estates: the lenity extorted by his rank alone moderating an indignation that might have led to consequences the most fatal.

And now he began to suspect that he did not command fortune. A fierceness dormant in his nature and ever roused when her personal feelings were offended, impelled him to some desperate act of vengeance, and rebellion. But against a nation – a father! a father whose almost unlimited indulgence could not fail to inspire him with some affection, though it extended not so far as to place parental feelings in balance with his own! – no remedy, no alleviation, presented itself. In the first transports of a soul, thus rent, as it were, with contending passions, he thought not –

> To throw away the worser part of it,
> And live the better with the other half;

but, fixing at once upon the most desperate resolution, he collected a quantity of gold and jewels, more than sufficient for a temporary provision, and, attended only by two servants, passed into Saxony. Alas! he little knew the lingering banishment to which he condemned himself.

In the first tumult and agony inflicted by this event, Count Siegendorf would willingly have made almost any sacrifice to recall his son. Unhappily the greatness of his efforts only confirmed in the latter the idea of his own value in society. Placing to the account of general regret and estimation that which was, in fact, simply the effect of parental fondness, he conditioned, he protracted, he wavered, till the resentment of the Count was at length roused to temporary alienation: he took the field himself, to atone for the misconduct of his son, and the softer feelings of nature insensibly died away before the increasing tumult of war. Nor were the pleasures of a gay and luxurious court less adverse to them in the bosom of the young man. He now, for the first time, felt himself wholly uncontrolled. His resources were great, his reception every where splendid; his personal accomplishments and lavish expenditure created him flatterers, if not friends: there was only one spot in the world where he had ever heard rebuke: to that spot, therefore, he daily felt an increasing reluctance to return; for he was not wise enough to know that the language of unqualified panegyric is always that of indifference or insincerity.

Time, however, which alike dissipates the illusions of the flatterer and the flattered, at length began to strip the son of Count Siegendorf of the lustre in society that title had hitherto given him. He had been received there at first as what he really was – a dissipated, turbulent, and inconsiderate young man: it was now suspected that he would prove a profligate one. His former character excluded him from the society of the rigidly virtuous: the latter seemed likely to degrade him to a class much below it. The worldly wise, the prudent, the proud, alternately began to shun him: these, however, did not fill the foremost line of the circle in which he lived, and he missed them not. An evil he deemed infinitely more serious now seemed to menace him: his pecuniary resources were drawing to an end, and he saw no mode of repairing them, but by a step at once so humiliating to his self-love, and adverse to his habits of life, that he could not resolve to take it. His letters to his father were answered by remonstrances, which, though they sometimes awakened a tender sentiment of regret in his heart, were insupportably painful to his pride. That pride at length found another hope on which to rest – hostile, indeed, to the interests of his country, but eminently favourable to himself. The Austrian power had every appearance of being restored throughout Bohemia; an event which, if it took place, would necessarily bring with it the disgrace of those who had disgraced him. To this hope he now almost anxiously looked forward, for he had hovered too long in Saxony, the banners of which were already displayed in the Imperial cause. He even debated with himself whether he should not join them, and give to his own return the air of a triumph: – this, however, a secret sense of honour and filial duty forbade. He therefore quitted the court of the Elector, to carry his dissipation and follies elsewhere; but he did not fail to sound his father with respect to his plans, and to hint to the latter the security he might at least derive to himself by the apparent secession of his son from a cause likely to prove unfortunate.

To projects half disgraceful, and, as he believed, wholly illusive, Count Siegendorf listened with disdain. Three years had rolled away without producing that reformation which his incessant and repeated indulgences taught him to expect. His fortune had been every way drained; but he had spent it gloriously in his own person, and unworthily only in that of his son. He now loudly and vehemently proclaimed his intention of renouncing that son, if he delayed to return to the paths of honour: – he did delay, till reconciliation was no longer practicable, and the whole weight of his father's indignation was ready to fall upon him. As he had reason to know that his personal liberty would be endangered through the steps taken by the latter, who secretly moved every foreign state by turns to give up a young man who thus disgraced his own, he changed his name, and became a wanderer on the northern frontier.

Here he at length painfully learned that he could no longer command fortune. Fortune! – alas! he could no longer command even the meanest of her votaries. All resources from his father were finally cut off: his own, estimated by his habits of expense, were nearly

The Canterbury Tales

exhausted; the irritation of his mind had united with the dissipation of his life to impair his health: a tedious and consumptive malady preyed upon it; and he, who three years before had thought the world was made for him, now began to believe he was only to occupy that small portion of it allotted to the humblest individual. The virtue yet lingering in a heart not wholly hardened or corrupt, induced him to resolve on sparing his father the final pang. He altered his route, and continued to wander through several towns of Pomerania and Lower Saxony – frugal, less from necessity than from absolute indifference to all that had once seduced or allured him. He was at length obliged, by increasing weakness and indisposition, to stop at Hamburgh. Though once living only in the tumult of conviviality, he had no longer strength or spirits to support the noise of a house of public entertainment; hiring, therefore, an apartment in a remote quarter of the town, he began to deliberate whether he should await death, or firmly advance to meet it. It was at this crisis his guardian angel first interfered; spirit of peace and honourable poverty was in the air he breathed, and soon communicated its invigorating influence to his heart.

The apartments nearest those of the Count were inhabited by a man of the name of Michelli; a Florentine by birth, and of a family which, though not of the first rank, was yet noble. Born indigent, but with a taste for the sciences, Michelli had pursued them with avidity under the greatest master of the age. But as he had not talents or protectors to shelter him from that persecution to which even Galileo finally became a victim, he was obliged, at an early period of life, to quit his country. He carried with him an only daughter, and fixing his residence where he believed he might with safety pursue his tastes, supplied the narrow circle of their domestic wants by his ingenuity in making mathematical instruments. The invention of the telescope, yet in its infancy, had already excited the wonder and admiration of the learned; and though far from having attained that perfection which the masterly skill of future genius was to produce, it had thrown a new and almost supernatural light over the regions of science. To give it those powers of which he believed it capable was the constant aim and employment of Michelli. but while anxiously, and even industriously, tracing the progress of knowledge, the philosopher had yet in his moments of leisure an eye for the human countenance, and a heart for human feelings. The young invalid, consequently, did not pass unnoticed by him. He perceived that he was friendless and unknown: it was precisely his own situation in society; and, without

The Canterbury Tales

officiously obtruding, he sought therefore the occasion of obliging him. To those simple courtesies of life which spring spontaneously from the heart, the young man, amidst all his varied experience, had yet been a stranger, and they made therefore a singular impression upon this. Insensibly he permitted civility to advance into slight, but social intercourse; and it was on one of these occasions that he first beheld Josephine. Though then in the very bloom of youth, she was hardly so handsome as she afterwards became. She had the Italian dignity of features, a chaste simplicity of manner, together with an understanding which it seemed the peculiar privilege of her heart to develop, and which, like her person, received from that its last and most touching charm. Her beauty was not overlooked by the Count, but his heart and his passions were alike joyless and inert. To his palled imagination life was already vapid: he believed he had exhausted its prime sources of pleasure – love, friendship, and flattery; yet he did not quit the humble hearth of Michelli and his daughter, without carrying away with him the recollection of faces and voices which, though they spoke not absolutely the language of either, yet seemed in sweet alliance with all.

A subject of contemplation, whatever might be its nature, was but too likely to banish Sleep from a pillow she had lately seldom deigned to visit: morning, of consequence, found the young man considerably worse than he had been the preceding evening; and Michelli, who missed him at the hour when chance usually brought them together, somewhat suddenly entered his chamber. A faint pleasure kindled on the cheek of the Count, not unmingled however with a less generous feeling, accustomed as he had ever been to respectful attendance and distant homage, his proud and repulsive spirit nevertheless stood abashed before a man who, though not wholly unacquainted with ceremony, used it only as the substitute for regard, and, in very simplicity of manners, dismissed the one as soon as his heart received the other. Michelli felt himself indeed interested alike by the situation and character of his new acquaintance, in whom he was surprised to find a degree of intelligence and knowledge not often to be met with even in those of maturer years; and, under the influence of a first impression, he placed to the credit of nature, and a love of study, what was in fact the result of a highly-cultivated education.

In the hospitable and humane attentions of her father Josephine almost equally shared. Her heart had never yet obeyed any impulse save that communicated by his; nor did she attach either value or importance

The Canterbury Tales

to those little offices of kindness which she was now induced to show. The exterior of the Count had not made that impression on her which in his brighter days it probably would have done. She had not seen him often, however, before she discovered that he was interesting and aimiable; but sickness had robbed him of the graces of his person, and corroding reflections preyed on those of his mind: both gradually began to re-assert themselves. – Contemplated indeed thus,

――― 'In his calm of nature,
With all the gentler virtues brooding on him,'

it would have been hardly possible to believe that he had been so lately the victim of intemperate pleasure and ungovernable passions. Far, indeed, was Josephine from suspecting it: the languor and melancholy that preyed upon him she imputed solely to affliction or ill health; and she insensibly began to look with tender and increasing sympathy on the sufferings of a man who had knowledge to command respect, and endowments that seemed to give him a claim to distinction.

If the society of the Count was daily more agreeable to Josephine, to her father it soon became nearly indispensable. Michelli corresponded with almost every man of science in Europe: but as the narrowness of his circumstances made heavy demands upon his time, his daughter frequently became his amanuensis. This office was at first shared, and at length wholly engrossed, by his young acquaintance. The Count, besides being skilled in all the modern languages, wrote Latin with a fluency and correctness far exceeding the abilities of Michelli himself; nor were his acquirements contemptible even in those branches of knowledge to which the other more particularly applied. The intercourse of mind, therefore, became every day cemented between them; preserving just those shades of difference which distinguish the disciple from the master: and if the modern Alcibiades fell short in talents and graces of the Grecian one, he was at least hardly less zealous or docile in his temporary pursuit of wisdom.

By a singular transition, the son of Count Siegendorf was now become a familiar guest at the frugal board and fire-side of Michelli; and never did days pass to him so delightfully. His understanding there daily improved; his temper harmonised; the vigour of his person returned, – his passions, acting for the first time under the impulse of reason and virtue, gave just energy enough to his manners to mark the features of his mind; and, finally, – in the contemplation of all, – the heart of Josephine was irrecoverably lost.

During the state of convalescence and languor that had preceded this period, love was a passion that had rather stolen by degrees into the bosom of the Count than imperiously asserted a claim there; but its influence was not the less powerful. It now reigned despotically and unrivalled. In proportion as the inquietudes of passion began to seize upon him, he adverted, however, with more acute anxiety to his own real condition in life. Could he even have resolved to trample on the most sacred laws of hospitality or gratitude for the indulgence of his inclination, he felt that nothing short of systematical and consummate hypocrisy could afford him the remotest probability of success. The love of Josephine was a generous, tender, and genuine feeling, that looked out in her eyes, and spoke in her voice; but 'no thought infirm altered her cheek:' – it was a feeling that would have gone through the world with a deserving object, and encountered without shrinking every sorrow that world could inflict; but it would have withered before the breath of disgrace. The Count, without being exactly able to calculate its force, yet felt its nature; and was deeply sensible that such a woman must be at once resigned, or honourably secured. Yet that his father should consent to such an ill-assorted union was an idea so extravagant, that he dared not for a moment indulge it; and hers, though he might be tempted by the moderation of his wishes to bestow his daughter on an obscure and deserving young man, would most unquestionably withold her from the libertine son of Count Siegendorf: one whose character, when known, would inspire no confidence, and whose age and rank would easily enable him to break through any tie sanctioned by his family.

A temporary gloom again clouded the features and mind of the Count; the question had been, indeed, decided in his own bosom from the moment it became such; for it had never yet made a part of his character to contend with any passion; much less did it now, when to yield seemed a virtue: but the manner in which he should present himself to Michelli; and the point still more difficult to decide, that in which he should address his daughter, became the constant subject of his meditations, and once more banished repose from his pillow. He now watched Josephine with such impassioned eyes as taught her soul timidly to shrink into itself, and present to his anxious imagination and quick feelings an exterior of coldness that almost drove him to distraction. With a perturbed heart, he at length ventured to sound the opinion of Michelli. The philosopher paused upon it – like a philosopher, – or, as the Count rather thought, like the executioner who holds his axe suspended over the neck of the criminal. he answered at length, however, with his accustomed simplicity and plainness. He had conceived highly of the talents of the young man; he had no reason to doubt his conduct; of his family he was but little solicitous to inquire; for the story of misfortune and emigration presented to him at the first period of their acquaintance, when, as it seemed no interested purpose could possibly be served by it, he never suspected could be other than true: but he was a philosopher of the later ages; and though he lived chiefly among the stars, he was aware that a little terrestrial provision was necessary towards the support of a household, however simple its plan. To this objection the young man was already prepared with an answer. Previous to his explanation with Michelli, he had the precaution to convert many valuable jewels into money, which he lodged safely in respectable hands; and though, as the son of Count Siegendorf, poverty had long threatened him, he was not indigent when considered only as the future son-in-law of Michelli. For the first time in his life, too, he now ventured to hint that he had talents – education; – and was rendered modest enough by love to be surprised when he found the plea admitted. Michelli referred him finally to his daughter; and, in so doing, seemed to the over-wrought mind of the Count to sign his death-warrant. He did not long, however, continue thus diffident; the passion that animated him soon found or made its opportunity; and Josephine was too much overwhelmed with the consciousness of her own feelings to be able to conceal from him that he was beloved beyond his most sanguine expectations. – Michelli soon after bestowed the hand of his daughter on the heir of Count Siegendorf, without knowing that he was raising her to a rank the proudest in the city would have envied; – that he was consigning her to a fate the humblest might pity.

Time did not render the Count indifferent to the blessing thus conferred. It continued to revolve: he became a father, and, in becoming so, the recollection of his own was forcibly awakened. For near six years all that had passed on his native soil had been to him a blank; he now looked often on Josephine and his son, and anxiously wished that he could have transported them thither. Alas! the dangerous wish was one day to be most fatally indulged; the tranquil and philosophic case in which he lived, nevertheless, for a considerable period subdued it; but it returned with accumulated force, and acquired every hour fresh activity from a thousand remote and incidental feelings, which, however, all tended to one object. The radical fault of his character was yet far from being extirpated: for whether under the influence of virtuous or illicit passions, whether revelling in the courts of princes, or living in the bosom of frugality and temperance, his own pleasure, or his own indulgence, was the invariable guide of his actions: and even at a crisis, when he was willing to believe that filial duty and honour gave rise to his returning sensibility, it was strangely compounded of that pride and self-love which the purifying angel had not yet wrung out of his heart.

After long and deep reflection, he at length ventured to address his father. His letter was couched in mysterious terms, but they were those of contrition. That he had still much to be forgiven was evident; yet such was the confusion of his mind while writing, and his consciousness that in his union with Josephine – prejudice apart – he had nothing to blush for, that his expressions seemed to announce him proud of some unexplained offence, and more disposed to assert his rights than to atone for his follies. He had, however, no cause to suppose the letter reached its destination. The apprehension that his personal liberty might be endangered by a discovery of the place of his abode induced him to send it through a very circuitous channel, and war raged throughout all Germany with too much fury to excite any reasonable surprise at its failure. It was long, nevertheless, before he persuaded himself it had failed. The interval was filled with impatient expectation – broken starts – deep reveries in which his wife could have no share, and which insensibly stole him from her arms and her society. She often perceived a strange anxiety and perturbation in his countenance that irresistibly communicated its influence to her heart; but though she had no reason to doubt his love, there was at those moments a haughty and repulsive fierceness in his temper that alike threw soothing and expostulation at distance.

Where the error of her choice had been Josephine was at a loss to discover, but she felt she had erred. Gifted as her husband appeared by nature – graced by education – passionately attached to her – suitable in years – and accordant in tastes, – she yet became painfully sensible that she was mismatched. Long indeed might she have sought the cause; for no feeling in her own bosom had ever yet taught her, that a mind ill at peace with itself must inevitably scatter a blight on the minds of all around.

But Siegendorf was at length no longer master of his emotions or his secret; of the whole circle of human failings, deceit was the one least congenial to his nature; and in a furious conflict of self-reproach and impatience, he poured out at once to Michelli and his daughter the extraordinary story in which they were so deeply involved. Astonishment seemed for a time to suspend the faculties of both. Michelli, alarmed, flattered, and grieved, hardly knew what was the predominant sentiment of his mind. Alas! Josephine knew too well that of hers. A dream of grandeur and magnificence did, indeed, transiently glitter before her eyes, as the phantoms were presented there; and she perceived, by the detail of her husband, that all of either which ambition could covet was probably included in her gains: it was for her heart only to calculate its losses; and that at once told her the immeasurable difference between them. She had given her hand to a man gifted, as she believed, by nature beyond his fortunes: she perceived, on the contrary, that she had united herself to one who debased them. In the simplicity of her first choice she had been every thing to her husband: – she was now only one of many objects, and perhaps in the end the least valued. Ill-omened did the exchange appear to her, from content to magnificence: and, for the first time in her life, the very softness and diffidence of her nature made her unjust; for she imputed all the singularity of his late conduct to repentance, and all his repentance to her own want of desert. Judgment and consciousness, however, soon rectified the error of the heart. Without trying the past by what might probably be a fastidious refinement, she perceived that it was her duty to extract happiness from the future. The conduct of her husband rendered it evident that she had been passionately beloved by him; and when she weighed it with his past life and modes of thinking, she saw with modest wonder how greatly she had been esteemed. There was no reason to suspect that the sentiments she had once inspired could possibly be extinguished in his bosom, even if they had undergone a temporary suspension; they might yet, therefore, be rendered a source of happiness to both: or rather, she felt that if they became such to him, her own would be sufficiently ascertained.

Those feelings and perplexities, which had been very indistinctly expressed by the Count, presented themselves meantime at full to the cool judgment of Michelli. It was clear to him, indeed, that the letter had probably never reached Prague; but it was not easy to determine whether, if it had done so, the event would have been fortunate. He perceived at once the only evil that had escaped the imagination of Josephine – the possibility of her husband's making his peace at the expense of her honour. All that a tender heart could picture to afflict itself hers indeed had for the moment presented; but nothing that could degrade the object of its fondest affections: nor would even the voice of her father have been heard on that subject without incredulity. Michelli spared her the grievous and humiliating idea, by addressing himself, where he believed he ought, to her husband. But he had yet known only half the character of the man to whom he spoke. That fiery and rebellious spirit, which brooked not control from his own father, revolted to its first nature at the remotest thought of it in hers. Conceiving at once all the extent of Michelli's surmises, however cautiously they were expressed, the Count was not just enough to feel that his own deceit had incurred the indignity, and he resented it with the same turbulent disdain that so often marked his conduct. Michelli was justly roused to anger. They parted on ill terms. The Count retired to his own apartments to deliberate, and his determination, as before, was fatal to his honour.

To abandon Josephine or her child would never, probably, in his worst moments, have occurred to him; for he was not a villain; if the man who always first considers himself can be securely deemed otherwise. In this case, however, it was a crime to which he had not temptation; for he fondly loved her; nor was he less attached to his son. Even for Michelli he had the most unqualified esteem: but of the mode of making either of them happy or prosperous his imperious temper directed him to constitute himself sole judge. – Among various methods of subduing his father's heart, the Count had ever deemed one to be infallible - a personal appeal. It was a project he had long secretly mediated, and almost resolved upon; but to which he now believed it impossible that, under the impression Michell had conceived of his designs, he should consent: nor could he be assured that Josephine herself, guided by her father's judgment, would not vehemently oppose his departure. – To effect it, therefore, within four-and-twenty hours seemed the only easy method of effecting it at all. Little preparation was necessary, and hardly any thing but secrecy indispensable. Night was already far advanced. He stole softly to the chamber of his wife, and perceived that care and long watching had at length buried her in a profound sleep. He kissed her, and might have exclaimed with Othello, –

> 'Oh balmy breath! Almost thou dost persuade
> Justice to break her sword!' –

for justice, by a strange perversion of his better reason, he believed it, thus at once to punish the injurious suspicions of Michelli, and, by the most summary proceeding, attest his own honour. Morning at length appeared, and found his resolution fixed. He forgot his first fatal flight from his father; he forgot the instability of his own character; he forgot every thing that ought to have restrained him, and in an evil hour he passed the gates of Hamburgh!

The Count had not, however, proceeded many leagues before tenderness and a more correct sense of equity began to struggle in his bosom. He half suspected his own measures of being precipitate: he was at least sure they admitted of misconstruction. He pictured to himself the overwhelming grief of Josephine, and even the silent consternation of her philosophic father. Though unable to resolve on the humiliation of returning, he stopped at the nearest post town, and from thence wrote to his wife. All that language could convey, either tender or generous, was expressed in his letter. Most earnestly he conjured her to guard both her health and peace unimpaired till his return. He presented his absence to be such as he really hoped it would prove – beneficial and temporary. He committed their beloved boy to her wise and maternal protection, with fatherly fondness and unlimited confidence. It was their united claims he solemnly protested that he was journeying to secure, and his own filial duties which, though late, he was about to fulfil. He concluded with drawing a flattering picture of the affluence and felicity which a reconciliation with his father would ensure their future lives: nor did he, now that the momentary resentment he had felt towards Michelli was partly subsided, omit to make that honourable mention of him to which, by his virtues and relative situation, he was entitled. Such was the letter of the Count! Alas! when language without being insincere grows thus eloquent, the exquisitely discerning heart too often traces in it only the overflowings of a conscience yet unseared, that thus compromises with itself, and spends the wholesome vigour of the mind in exhausting and deceitful effusions of sensibility! – If such were the feelings of Josephine, obedience, that saddest or most sweet of duties, yet taught her to conceal them. She calmed her brow to Michelli: she took her son with aching fondness to that bosom which her husband had deserted; and strove to find in rectitude and hope a balm for evils she saw no rational mode of remedying.

But, whatever might be the sincerity of the Count in the tender professions he made his wife, – and in those he *was* sincere, – the reflections that writing naturally tended to produce had insensibly rendered him less sanguine as to the success of his own projects.

Those reflections now told him, that from the moment he set foot in his native country he could no longer consider himself as a free agent; since even if his past transgressions did not render him amenable to that country, of which the crisis when he quitted it made him doubtful, he was at least certain that the limits of parental authority would be enlarged to the uttermost by that of the public: and to what, should his father prove inflexible, might not such authority extend? – it might bear him for ever from Josephine and his son; it might oblige him to violate every tie either sacred or delightful; and render him of necessity the very villain Michelli had more than half suspected he would prove. What plea had he to offer that might obviate these probable evils, or subdue as once the resentment of a father whom he had so long either neglected or defied? – simply the influence of his presence, and weight of his promises; and now, for the first time, his self-love vanished before the idea of the former, and his self-delusion before that of the latter. At every pause in his journey he looked back with more restless anxiety on those he had left, and forward to those he was approaching. Pride, honour, love, every thing dear to him, was included in the event; and where the stake is so mighty, he must be a daring adventurer indeed who trembles not to cast the die! – A circumstance wholly unlooked for at once gave a new colour to his fate.

The Count's journey was of necessity tedious and indirect, as the horrors of war every where obstructed or followed him; his route, therefore, included the town to which he had requested that the answer he had flattered himself with receiving from his father might, under a fictitious name, be addressed; but the channels of correspondence were at the period ever uncertain, except in great commercial cities: the distracted state of the country rendered them still more so; and, as near two years had elapsed from the time he had written, his inquiries, hitherto fruitless, now seemed almost irrational; yet that restlessness which still attends incertitude induced him to renew them. The postmaster paused a few moments; examined a small drawer that appeared full of discarded papers, and then, to his astonishment, produced a letter, the superscription of which he instantly knew to be the writing of his father. Could that father have seen the breathless impatience with which he tore it open, he would probably have fallen on his neck, and believed he had indeed found his son again. The date of the letter was not very far back; and the first lines of it expressed surprise at that of his own, which appeared to have been nearly lost, and very long retarded. A tender inference was, however obviously to be drawn from the various precautions that seemed to have been taken to preserve the answer from failing: it was written from the camp.

Count Siegendorf passed over, in gentle but dignified terms, that part of his son's letter on which he could not rely: but though he had, unhappily, little confidence in his professions, he spoke with sensibility of the returning consciousness of duty and honour which dictated them. He demanded, however, to be informed most explicitly of the nature and extent of the offences he was called upon to pardon. 'The narrative,' he observed, – and the observation was not made without an expression of the most impassioned regret, – 'now included the events of years; but on his part he was prepared to temper the severity of a judge with the indulgence and patience of a father. As he was not aware of the reasons that had induced his son to change his name, he highly praised the delicacy that led him to renounce, rather than continue to disgrace it. He adverted in strong, though broken starts of tenderness, to the hour when that name might resume its first splendour; but he peremptorily forbade him ever to appear in his native country till such an hour arrived. Finally, he touched upon his son's pecuniary resources, and desired him to name the spot whither those remittances might be made, which his exigencies could not but require.'

And now again the heart of the young man beat high with habitual self-applause and congratulation. Plunged as he had just before been in a gloom almost approaching to despondency, with a sensibility yet aching under the recent loss of all dear to him, and an imagination prompt to magnify every possible evil. he rushed at once into the contrary extreme. Far from seeing in his father's letter what he justly might, – a mind self-balanced, and prepared to make, if necessary, a desperate sacrifice to honour, – he dwelt only on the tender passages of it; and believed he discerned in them a thousand struggling though half-suppressed feelings, which his answer, for he answered it on the spot, would he flattered himself, render unconquerable.

The enthusiasm of the moment could not but dictate more of promise than detail. He avowed, indeed, the circumstances of his marriage, and the birth of his son; and he was careful to satisfy the pride or the prejudices of the Count, by an assurance that the family from which Josephine sprang was such as did not attach disgrace to his own. The remainder of the letter consisted of a solemn asseveration of his sincerity; of the temperance and simplicity established in his modes of life; and of the unshaken fidelity with which he meant to fulfil all his engagements. The tenor of the whole was, indeed, well calculated to raise the hopes and expectations of a fond parent to the most sanguine pitch: it was dated from the spot on which it was written; and he concluded by saying, that he should pursue his journey as far as Cassel, 'there to attend the further orders of his father, and to receive testimonies of his kindness in any way he should deem it suitable to offer them.'

The event which had thus intoxicated his heart remained to be related to Josephine. Why could he not press her to his bosom? – read in her eyes the sweet participation of his hopes, and communicate them by that intuitive and sympathetic power which leaves language so far behind! He was sensible that the letter he addressed to her, though the honest effusion of his own heart, was not such as could create unmixed pleasure in hers. The glaring colours with which his imagination painted the future were calculated imperceptibly to throw into shade the retired and humble happiness of the past; and, by a peculiarity with which he had tinged his own fate, he felt that he could not exult in the distinction he was to bestow, without involuntarily taking something from that he had received.

Refinements which are only the effect of capricious sensibility do not often produce much real disquiet. His was 'the perfume and suppliance of a moment.' Again the awakened consciousness of youth and prosperity began to beat in every pulse: nature, as he pursued his journey, seemed to have changed her aspect to him; the forms of pleasure floated indistinctly before his eyes, and a tumultuous crowd of long-buried sensations and habits revived in his bosom. In the security of receiving remittances from his father, he drew out of the hands of the banker at Hamburgh that little provision lodged there for his wife and son. His pride loudly demanded an indemnification for the privations it had long undergone; and, unfortunately, it soon received one too ample. He had hardly presented himself at Cassel before he was recognised by several young men of his own rank and age, in the service of Landgrave, for the son of Count Siegendorf; and as it was not doubted, from his appearance and expenditure, that he was licensed in the past, all the seductions of dissipation and bad example were held out in the present. A memorable period succeeded! – youth, habit, self-indulgence, again too fatally prevailed; – and the husband of Josephine, ten thousand times more criminal in that character than he had ever been before, relapsed into those vices which had already made a wreck of his honour and his peace. Amidst the excesses which now threatened finally to destroy both he was even indiscreet enough to forget all the importance attached by his father to the renunciation of his name. He did not indeed formally resume it; but he was sufficiently willing that his rank should be understood; and it was too necessary a claim in the circle he mingled with, not to become generally so.

Three months rolled away in excesses which he persuaded himself were venial, as he was fully resolved the summons from his father should end them: whenever that arrived, he solemnly promised his own heart to abjure all pleasure incongruous with his duties – to live only for Josephine and his family, and to limit his follies for ever. It was so long ere any intelligence reached him from Prague, that he almost began to doubt some second delay, more unexpected than the first, had attended his letter. The answer to it at length arrived, and his follies were, indeed, for ever limited; – but unhappily, by no forbearance or virtue of his own. Contrary to his expectation, the packet was addressed to him by the name and titles of his family; as though the flaming indignation of his father disdained all concealment, and was willing to announce itself at the fist glance.

Count Siegendorf, in the most pointed terms, and such as bespoke him well acquainted will all that was passing at Cassel, at once renounced a son to whom it was evident no promise was sacred; 'who had flattered his hopes only the more grossly to betray them; who has sported with the name of his family again to disgrace it; who was alive to no feeling of duty, no principle of honour; and whom time and misfortune, far from reforming, had only taught duplicity.' He enjoined him, as he valued his liberty, never again to venture within the limits of Bohemia, much less dare to appear in his presence. He concluded with saying, that, 'worthless as he feared the scion might prove of such a stem, he was nevertheless willing to receive the little Conrad, and secure for him those claims he was born to, under the express condition that his parents should see him no more. That if they acceded to these terms, he would remit to his son an annual provision; but if otherwise, he disclaimed him for ever.'

From the day this letter was received, the character and manners of the young Count seemed to undergo a total alteration. He believed himself grossly injured by his father, and he conceived a resentment likely to end but with the life of one of them. His mind, untuned for pleasure, for ever revolted from it: he remained several weeks buried in meditation; at the expiration of that time he departed abruptly from Cassel, and wrote to Josephine to meet him, with Conrad, within a few leagues' distance of Hamburgh. The fate he had prepared for himself weighed heavily upon his soul, and seemed at once to have absorbed all its softer feelings: there was not justice enough in that soul to level the accusation where it ought to have fallen; and he regarded the event as unprecedented and intolerable. To remain for life only the son-in-law of Michelli was an idea that even his darkest contemplations had never presented to him; yet such was now the probable conclusion of his fate. The manner of his father's letter left him without a doubt that he would, if further irritated, execute the resolution he announced, and, vested with that power the states would easily put into his hand against a son they did not esteem, make over the honours of the family to the collateral branch, which centred in Baron Stralenheim; a native of Franconia, and nearly allied on the female side to the house of Siegendorf. The simple but hateful, medium his father had proposed could alone, therefore, stand between him and final ruin. But how was Josephine to encounter a blow every way thus cruel? or how was a husband to relate to her the fatal consequence of his own accumulated indiscretions? It is among the great evils of misconduct to harden the heart, and it had hardened that of the Count. Yet on this side he was not yet invulnerable. Another motive, however, even more urgent than any yet considered, impelled his decision. Circumstanced as he now found himself, it was not possible for him to replace the sum which, relying on the liberality of his father, he had imprudently lavished. Yet that sum, lately deemed so insignificant, was mighty now in his account of life. For was he to return to Hamburgh a poor dependant on the bounty of Michelli? Or could he become a hireling, and give to his wife and child the scanty bread of poverty? Misery – inevitable – intolerable misery, – seemed to environ him on every side. but there was a point in his character at which it ever repelled the arrow from himself, though at the expense of all around; even now, in the very crisis of self-condemnation and shame, concentrating, as it were, to that point all the harsher and more stubborn feelings of his nature, he prepared to meet Josephine and Michelli with a demeanour that should alike exclude expostulation or reproach, by showing that his decision, whatever it might prove, would be irrevocable, and that he would be responsible for his conduct to no being but himself.

He had only to see Josephine to be convinced that he might have chosen, if a more upright, yet a no less indulgent judge. – She, as well as Conrad, was in deep mourning, and he learned, with that acute and unexpected pang which ever attends the death of those we believe we have injured, that Michelli was no more. The philosopher died as he had lived, in peace with God and with mankind. Dismissing his resentment against the Count, he left him the sole goods he had to bequeath – his daughter, his pardon, and his blessing. In parting with Josephine, however, even the gentle and stoical habits of his temper were almost inadequate towards supporting the firmness of either. To her bosom he had long since communicated all the pure and noble qualities of his own: he had nothing more to give! – they parted, therefore, as those who were to meet again, and to know each other by the sympathetic influence of the virtues and affections. – The Count was not insensible to this short and simple detail: but it was now no season for indulging the softer sensibilities of life. With Michelli was buried the last hope of saving Josephine and her son from impending separation: for so desperate had been his own plans, that he had more than once thought of silently renouncing both, and, by plunging into a military career, however obscure, either save himself from the disgrace that seemed attached to existence, or the guilt of voluntarily ending it.

Again the tender influence of Josephine was employed in expelling the corrosive reflections that preyed upon the heart of her husband. Rising vigorously with the occasion, she endeavoured to recall both to his imagination and her own those brilliant pictures of the future which he had himself once presented to her. They were now, indeed, to be realised only in the person of their son; but would they be therefore less valued? Conrad, removed from their protection, would be but the more dear to their affections. On her part she could resolve, with matron firmness, to resign him to a fate prosperous beyond what the cruelty of theirs allowed them to hope they could bestow; and if their own were less dazzling, she tenderly reminded her husband of those days when magnificence formed no part of their plan of happiness. The Count listed in silence: he strove to assent; he would willingly have concealed from every human being that he could not without reluctance resign, even to his son, that place in society he had in his own person so wantonly thrown away, nor give to his father a blessing of which he was to deprive himself. The mind of Josephine was too acute, however, not to discern the latent rankling feeling. But she buried the consciousness deeply in her own bosom, and with it all those afflicting sentiments which the character and conduct of

Siegendorf could not but create. – Conrad was something more than eight years of age, when he was at length delivered up to the care of his grandfather: the latter was punctual to his engagements; and though the income of the Count was limited, it was such as supplied every demand, save that of luxury.

The career of dissipation now closed: – and so silent was the progress of life, that time and fate seemed stationary. Josephine could still indeed occasionally beguile the hours of her husband; but neither time, nor circumstance, nor love itself, ever restored to him his former character. He was habitually morose and abstracted; animal spirits and youth no longer danced through his veins, and he had no store of pleasurable ideas that should supply their place. Occupied in gloomy meditation, he turned his eyes incessantly back to the brilliant horizon of his early life, and murmured at the span to which it was contracted. The birth and growth of another son somewhat meliorated these feelings; but, by a strange perverseness in his nature, the Count never loved Marcellin with the fondness he had shown for Conrad; while Josephine, on the contrary, seemed anxious to indemnify herself for the loss of one child by cherishing a double portion of fondness for the other. – The secret storm of the passions at length slowly subsided in the bosom of her husband; who, fixed in his fate, fallen from his fortunes, soured to the present good, and only at intervals stealing from her eyes that gleam of sunshine and of hope they ever communicated, presented to indifferent observers merely a common character and a common lot.

But though the years immediately succeeding that gloomy one which seemed to fix the fate of the Count passed thus apparently in abstraction, they were secretly marked by various transitions of sentiment and feeling. As the colours of the past became less vivid, his mind dwelt with more deep and intense contemplation on the prospect of the future. In the death of his father he still saw the probability, the almost certainty, of a change in his situation that could not but restore to him his natural rights, by leaving no other competitor for them than a son, whose tender age would ill calculate him for a contest. Count Siegendorf was now far advanced in life, and had never been vigorous: a day, an hour, therefore, might settle the great account between them – but days and hours fly not according to the calculations of man! – insensibly they swelled into years, and brought with them no change. The young Count felt his confidence in the future diminish. That very circumstance which he dared hardly own to himself he desired, might no longer assure to him the inheritance which alone could render it desirable. Years still continued to revolve, and the event of the future became daily more problematical. At length that proud and rebellious spirit which forbade him to make any farther effort with his father, chiefly, perhaps, because he believed the authority of that father must soon inevitably terminate, gave way before the probability of its devolving to a son fast approaching manhood. He contemplated with bitter and ceaseless regret the still increasing interval during which some favourable moment might doubtless have been found to sooth an indignation his forbearance had perpetuated, and recall to himself feelings now probably centred for ever in another object!

It had been among the voluntary engagements of Count Siegendorf, to inform Josephine and her husband if Conrad were either sick or dead. – No such intelligence ever reached them. He was well then! – he was great – perhaps happy! – No tender yearnings recalled the memory of his boyish days! his parents were to him as nothing ! – he made not any effort to see – to hear of them! – they languished in obscurity, and in a fondness that knew no fruition, while he revelled in every thing that fortune or fondness could bestow! – If these reflections corroded the heart of the father through a thousand avenues, they were not excluded even from the tender, and generous one of Josephine. At a crisis when her husband's peace was at stake, she had, indeed, heroically dared to part with her son; – but to lose him for ever brought with it a pang that shook her utmost fortitude. For the first time in her life she envied Count Siegendorf; and, like her husband, looked with longing and anxious eyes towards that only spot whence both were alike excluded.

During the latter years of the Count's residence at Hamburgh, it was among his additional grievances that the man whose name had been held forward to him on an occasion which he could never remember without bitterness of spirit, had taken up his abode in that neighbourhood. Baron Stralenheim he had reason to know was the person formerly deputed by his father to watch over his actions, and restrain them, if possible, by the hand of authority. Years had passed since that time, and there was no reason to suppose that Stralenheim had any longer an influence over his fate. But the resentment and disdain once conceived against the latter had engendered a deep distrust in the mind of the Count. No two beings on earth could seem however more distinct from each other than they now appeared to be. The Count had never since the period of his marriage, and even some months preceding it, borne his own name – the fatal period excepted which he had passed so indiscreetly at Casel, where, though he claimed it not, it was generally given him. He was not sure that the Baron knew his assumed one; and certainly the residence of the latter at Hamburgh seemed to have no reference to his: yet it was singular that he should reside there! the circumstance of his doing so, for he was a man of stately and reserved habits, came to the Count's ear by what nevertheless appeared to be a mere accident.

In the household of the Baron there was an Italian of the name of Giulio; a Piedmontese, who had resided many years at Hamburgh during the life of Michelli, and though in an obscure situation, and not precisely of the same country with the latter, yet, being a man of ingenuity, was very well known to him. Josephine, to whom every one was in some degree dear that recalled the memory of her father, never failed to notice Giulio when he fell in her way; and when that did not happen, a sentiment of grateful respect induced him sometimes to inquire after her. On this man the Count fixed a suspicious eye; but he saw him very rarely, and nothing appeared in his conduct to justify the idea of his being a spy.

The strange and inexplicable feeling which superstition terms presentiment was nevertheless singularly allied to reality in the case of the Count. The residence of Baron Stralenheim had in fact that very reference to his which he suspected; and could he indeed have looked into the bosom of time, he would have known the latter to be of all existing beings the one most portentous to his future life! Of this they were alike ignorant: nor was it possible that either should yet suspect the dark shadow they were mutually to cast over each other's fate! Giulio was nevertheless no instrument in the hands of the Baron, who was even unsuspicious of the opportunity that offered of making him such. Stralenhiem was a man of a phlegmatic character, and a narrow mind. He had spent one half of his life in the service, because fortune had placed him there; but he had no taste for glory; and he had retired to spend the remainder in the country, with as little taste for that. He loved, however, the petty dignity attached to his family and alliances; and surveyed with much satisfaction a Gothic chateau situated in a marsh, and flanked with avenues of worm-eaten timber, because its precincts were his own.

From this dream of solitary and insignificant grandeur he had been suddenly waked some years before by a remote expectation of the inheritance of Siegendorf: the magnitude of the object was such as might have roused a more torpid mind; and it accorded too well with the propensities of his, not to call forth all his attention. His hopes had, however, been frustrated before they could reasonably be termed such. The Count, ever indulgently learning towards his son, had almost instantaneously repented the measures dictated by temporary resentment, and had therefore withdrawn, as he believed, from the hands of Stralenheim all power of injuring him. But Stralenheim was a man of cold and deliberate purpose: not easily kindled to pursuit, but tenacious of his object; and as he perceived the Count to be wholly devoid of suspicion respecting him, he had address enough craftily to retain the power, though he could not calculate exactly when or how he should use it. The adoption of Conrad had appeared a far more fatal blow to his hopes than any reconciliation with Conrad's father: yet even this did not wholly extinguish them; for he was of a temperament that enabled them to be permanent, without being active. Imposing on himself, therefore, just as much restraint as should keep him within the sphere of the young Count, whose assumed name was the very one that exposed him to danger, Stralenheim waited patiently the slow aid of time and occasion. – Such was the enemy that hung over the head of the unhappy Siegendorf! an avenging instrument, as it seemed, in the hand of Heaven, ready forcibly to impel the scale of misery downwards whenever error or misfortune should drop their weight into the balance. – An event that had nothing to do with the calculations of either party seemed precisely at this period on the point of overturning those of both.

Twelve years had rolled away since the departure of Conrad. The income of the Count had been regularly paid in the interval; and as he relied on its increase whenever his father died, either by the accession of himself or his son, the caution of Josephine had never been able to prevent his expending it even improvidently. With a feeling that partook at once of incredulity and amazement, he learned that it was no longer to be remitted to him. His father then was dead! – no! – the prohibition was signed by his hand. The eyes of the distracted son perused the billet, and his memory too well authenticated the writing. That cruel fever which afterwards was incorporated with his constitution seized at once upon his pulse – his brain – his heart! long and painful was the struggle between life and death – but the vigour of constitution prevailed: he at length recovered, and found himself almost a beggar! An act of cruelty so extravagant as that of impoverishing an only son, could not, however, be without a motive. No excesses had now disgraced the tenor of his life, no arrogant assumption of name that of his family. At a crisis when the bitterness of despair had nearly overwhelmed Josephine, these considerations had nevertheless inspired her with fortitude enough to take the only step that could avert it. Blending the dignity of her natural character with the sensibilities of a wife and a mother, she ventured, in language rendered exquisitely touching by the occasion, to address that respected father-in-law whom she had yet never seen. She wrote also to her son.

The sullen despondency which first seized the Count on his recovery, yet yielded to a feeble impression of hope on having the measures pursued by his wife. He consented to live; but his imagination bounded the term of life, though he refused it not as a temporary gift. As yet, indeed, he believed it to be an uncertain one from the mere languor and feebleness which succeeded indisposition. He was dosing one evening on a small couch Josephine had drawn for him to the fireside, when, roused by an indistinct murmur of voices, he raised his eyes, and perceived that she was talking with a man in the anteroom. A second glance showed him it was Giulio. Agitated by the association of ideas which had long haunted him with respect to the latter, be inquired his business; the man was abashed; the languid air of Josephine, so different from that which was habitual to her, had already inspired in him an embarrassment common to timid and uncourtly minds, not accustomed to set the feelings of others at defiance: he was conscious of intrusion, and, in a voice of apology, explained his errand: it was simply to inform Josephine that he was on the point of returning to Italy; to inquire if she had any thing that demanded his service there; and modestly to request, as a token of her regard, a few mathematical instruments of little value, that had been made by Michelli. Again the Count was struck as with some inexplicable relation to his own fate in so sudden and unexpected a departure.

'For what reason,' he asked, 'did Giulio, at that crisis, quit Hamburgh?'

'Baron Stralenheim had dismissed his household, and was about to undertake a long journey.' – Josephine found the self-possession which her husband wanted, and inquired, though not without some emotion, – 'Whither?'

'He was not quite certain; he believed it was to Prague; he was at least sure it was as far as Bohemia.' – The silence that followed this reply was unnoticed by Giulio, who saw in the questions put to him nothing but a condescending civility that strove to efface the coldness of his first reception; it was his part, he conceived, to show that he felt it so, by prolonging the conversation.

'Baron Stralenheim,' he continued, 'is neither very communicative nor very generous. Were he the latter, he would probably not dismiss his suite: for he is going, I am told, to take possession of the rich inheritance of Count Siegendorf.'

'Siegendorf is alive!' exclaimed the agitated Count, in a voice which he found it impossible to control.

'At least – his grandson,' added Josephine; and she too faltered, struck with a thousand painful recollections; and with the cruel possibility of even that being a doubt.

'The Count himself unquestionably is dead,' replied Giulio: 'the Baron seems to think little of the claims of his grandson, whose legitimacy he says is dubious; the inheritance is at least worth a struggle – and he is not, therefore, the man to part with it.'

To the heart and imagination of the Count and his wife these few words summed up the history of years; perhaps of all that remained to them in existence: they touched at length, then, the final point at which they were to stand or fall; and how did it find them provided for the contest? – sick – miserable – impoverished! – blighted, as it appeared, by a father's dying curse – since his last cruel prohibition was hardly less; and forgotten by that only being on whom they could rest a hope. For what was become of Conrad? why did he not now seek them? was he the victim of some secret machination on the part of Stralenheim? or was he revelling in the inheritance of his father, and unconscious of the storm that impended over himself? – Whatever might be his fate, his character, or his sentiments, it was at least evident that his parents were as necessary to his future welfare as he could be to theirs: since what besides their personal appearance could legitimate his birth against the claims of a crafty and powerful competitor? One only doubt invalidated the importance of these mighty questions; and that doubt was quickly removed, for a very short inquiry authenticated to the Count the intelligence of his father's death; Giulio having received all his information on the subject from Stralenheim's secretary, who had himself read the letter from Prague that announced it.

In the tumult of contending hopes, fears, and sorrow, that naturally took possession of the bosoms of Josephine and her husband at a crisis thus important, it afforded at least a gleam of satisfaction to the latter to perceive by the open communication of Giulio, and the surprise as well as interest he expressed on finding his hearers someway implicated in it, that his visits had certainly no connection with any project entertained by Stralenheim: the latter, therefore, it was possible, might be wholly ignorant in whose neighbourhood he dwelt; it was highly to be desired that he should remain so: Giulio was therefore strictly cautioned on the subject; and, as the immediate departure of the Count and his wife seemed the only step likely to ascertain their security or rights in life, it became necessary to consider by what means the journey could be undertaken. Bitterly did the Count now lament his own habitual extravagance, and his reliance on a future that had so often deceived him, when he felt that it had robbed him of those supplies which on the present occasion were absolutely indispensable, and, united with his sickness, had left him worse than poor. The sole method that presented itself of providing for the expense of a long and dangerous journey was by parting with every valuable they possessed: in so doing they made, indeed, no great sacrifice, for they possessed nothing that they believed would be henceforward either necessary or useful to them; but the manner in which the business was to be transacted was a circumstance of far more difficulty than the business itself; and in this they had again recourse to Giulio, whose condition and modes of life rendered his personal service no degradation. Through his means they privately converted, though to a great disadvantage, every thing that could be easily disposed of into money; after which, taking such precautions as might enable them to appear like travellers in an humble but decent rank of life, the Count and Josephine at length turned their steps towards Bohemia.

In the Palatinate and Upper Saxony war raged with a fury the effects of which were not to be calculated: and though Swedish and other troops covered the north, they were less hostile, and, not being actuated by civil discord, less bloody than elsewhere. No method, therefore, of reaching Bohemia appeared so certain as that of passing into Siberia; which, for the most part, united in the same cause with the latter, and at all times strongly incorporated in its policy and views, afforded the safest passage to emigrants of different descriptions. The Count was, on the whole, sufficiently acquainted with the country; and, though yet feeble, and ill able to sustain a journey of such extent, he was not less impelled by the necessity of the occasion to undertake it, than invigorated by the persuasion that his suspicions with regard to Stralenheim had been those of an irritable mind; and that, in reality, the latter neither knew him under his assumed name, nor kept any watch over his footsteps.

The security in which the Count believed himself was, nevertheless, the precursor of danger. Stralenheim was informed of every material step taken by the former; and he was well pleased to see him quit Hamburgh, where it would have been difficult, if not dangerous, to make any attack upon his personal freedom without the most unquestionable authority: whereas, in the insignificant towns through which he must necessarily travel, that with which the Baron had armed himself might, by the power of gold, be made to act in full force: and as it was particularly authentic within the territories of the house of Brandenburg, it was the purpose of Stralenheim to attach him near some fortress within that limit; where being himself a military man, he did not doubt but he should find such connivance as might enable him, if not to effect the Count's confinement for life, at least to secure him for a period sufficiently long to give his adversary every advantage he could desire.

Ingenious as craft may be, it is perhaps never so much in danger of being defeated as when it encounters the suspicious timidity which results from a consciousness of error, and a premature knowledge of life. The Count, throughout the progress of his journey, had little else to do but to think and to consider. A singularity that occasionally marked the interrogations put to him at different barriers, together with observing the countenance of an individual who had crossed him more than once, again awakened the latent jealousy of his nature. He had too much at stake, and was become habitually too profoundly meditative, not to guard against the remotest danger except such as was merely personal and accidental, to which he was ever indifferent. That he now looked to was of a more important nature: he could not, indeed, ascertain that there was any; but he suspected it, – and to suspect it was enough. At a point of his journey, therefore, when a deviation from it could least be guessed at, he suddenly struck through the by-roads of a forest, once more changed his name to that of Kruitzner, and felt assured that he had, for a time at least, escaped all pursuit. Here, however, ended his good fortune. The way he had taken was circuitous and fatiguing; his health was again attacked; his little means daily diminished; subsistence, hope, life itself, seemed hourly fading from his grasp, and he was set down in the obscure shelter afforded him by his host at M—, with only the last lingering sparks of either remaining.

Afflicting as his fate there continued to be, yet in his calculations with regard to the Baron he had fortunately not been deceived: the route he had taken was one through which the latter had neither directed his inquiries nor his measure; but Stralenheim, though foiled, was not easily defeated: he well knew the Count's method of travelling was too humble and economical to carry him further than certain regular distances, and on this he had reckoned even at the time of his departure from Hamburgh; for though he had not quitted that city till several days after his competitor, of the rapidity of whose proceedings he had not been sufficiently aware, he was convinced that the influence of money would bring him soon within track, and enable him to be near enough to enforce his measures whenever he judged it prudent to set them in motion. In this, however, the Baron made a false estimate of his own character, for he was not generous; neither, though persevering, was he active: his journey, therefore, was not pursued with the celerity he expected; and though he had sufficient reason to know he kept his object in view, he did not come up with him. The address with which the Count changed his name and route arrested the progress of the Baron, who was then at Frankfurt. It was of the first importance to him that the immediate heir to the estates of Siegendorf should be prevented, for a time at least, from appearing on his patrimonial lands, either to assert his own claims, or to establish the validity of his son's: if, therefore, he had wholly escaped the Baron, the journey of the latter was useless, and afforded too little ground of hope to induce him to continue it; since the inheritance it might be easy for him to take possession of, it would be impossible to recover. To these considerations all others gave way, and Stralenheim necessarily remained stationary till tidings of the fugitives should reach him.

Confused accounts of persons answering to the description of those sought, though differing in name and other trifling particulars, seemed at length to ascertain that the Count and his family were within a certain limit. Had the Baron been profuse of his rewards, he would probably have traced the precise spot; but as those rewards chiefly consisted of promises, few of his emissaries imparted more than half of the little they knew; some because they had cunning enough to foresee they might sell their discoveries to more advantage by degrees, and others because their avarice was not awakened by the hope of any advantage at all. Of the former description were the junto at M—, but Stralenheim had learnt enough to be assured his victim could not be far off. Preparing, therefore, without remorse, to authenticate by every specious form of justice the severity of his proceedings, he resolved to secure his person on the first possible opportunity; and he persuaded himself this could be done with more perfect facility, as the mandate announced no heredity distinction or title of the Count; but, noting him simply by the name he had borne at Hamburgh, left him not the little chance of profiting by an attention almost invariably shown to rank.

The season, however, was daily less favourable to the increasing impatience of Stralenheim. The frost had been succeeded by a rapid thaw: the Oder overflowed its banks, and the smaller rivers that discharged into it had carried away their bridges. There were still here and there fords, over which the peasants indeed ventured to pass; but it was not seldom that even they found the undertaking both difficult and dangerous. To all remonstrances on that subject, however, the Baron was insensible: the life of a soldier had habituated him to hazards of every kind; and he believed that he had only to add more horses to his carriage, and take other trifling precautions, to ascertain his safety. The postilions, in obedience to his command, plunged, though with reluctance, into the stream, and it was soon obvious that they had not exaggerated the danger. The horses, as well as those who guided them, nevertheless, struggled vigorously against it, and at length succeeded in reaching the opposite shore; but the force of the current had hurried them beyond the precise track: the bank to which they approached was steep and dangerous; it was, besides, undermined by the violence of the floods in the effort of climbing it the ground gave way, – the horses lost their feet, – the weight of the carriage impelled it violently backwards, – it overset, – and all the hopes, views, and schemes of the Baron were on the point of terminating for ever.

Two strangers, who had but lately gained the shore, were witnesses of the scene, and, perceiving the danger to be imminent, plunged, with some hazard to themselves, into the water. The last effort of the Baron, on perceiving his situation, was to open the carriage-door, and attempt to throw himself out. He had so far succeeded, that his rescue was accomplished with less difficulty than it otherwise would have been; and though he was to all appearance lifeless, the assistance given by the strangers was not vain. Many peasants also now hastened in aid of the latter; and by their united efforts, not only Stralenheim, but his attendants and baggage, were preserved from the stream. He was conveyed to a habitation not far distant, and every attention shown him which the circumstances of the time and place admitted. Once more restored to the consciousness of what was passing around, he became sufficiently convinced of his own rashness to be grateful to those who had preserved him from its effects. They were travellers like himself, and, like himself, some what too daring; for their own situation, a few moments before, had been little less critical than his. One of them announced himself to be a Hungarian; the other a native Saxon. The appearance and manners of each, especially those of the latter, bespoke him above the vulgar rank; and the Baron surmised they might both probably be Austrian, who, from motives of justifiable prudence, forbore to avow themselves as such. The danger they had so gallantly encountered in favour of a stranger loudly demanded his gratitude; and as he found, on inquiry, that their journey was nearly in the same direction with his own, the most useful and obliging mode of testifying it was to provide for the general safety by making them his associates, at least till such time as the subsiding of the waters should secure either party from future difficulties. After a moment's hesitation the strangers accepted the proposal.

The Baron, however, in escaping the stream, had not escaped all the consequences of his plunge there. Violent feverish symptoms announced the probability of future suffering. The house to which he had been dragged afforded no accommodation or comfort to alleviate it. He recollected, precisely at this juncture, that he was within the estates, and not far from the palace, of the Prince de T—, under whom he had served; nor did he hesitate to profit by the occasion. His name, though not his person, was known to the intendant at M—; the rank he announced secured his reception; and thus, at length, without any previous plan or knowledge on his own part, was the Baron set down within three hundred yards of the man whom he had travelled so many leagues in search of. Thus, too, were the misfortunes of the unhappy Count brought to a climax, when the name of all others most hateful to him dropped from the lips of the innocent Marcellin; and when the report of Idenstein confirmed the alarming intelligence that '*the stranger* arrived in the prince's coach at the palace' was no other than *Baron Stralenheim*.

The singular coincidence of circumstances that brought the latter thither could neither be known nor guessed at by the Count.

The Canterbury Tales

Stralenheim so lately at Hamburgh, now close upon him in a devious road, was but too rational a confirmation of all his former suspicions. That the Baron sought him he could no longer doubt: whether he knew he had found him he was yet to learn; but that his own departure, if it was to be accomplished at all, must be undertaken immediately, even under the miserable circumstances of performing it on foot, could not but be certain. From the long and deep meditation into which he had been plunged after Idenstein quitted him, he was first roused by the timid embrace of Marcellin, whom his mother had sent to take leave of him for the night. Siegendorf, who felt the cruel probability of its being for ever, strained the boy to his bosom with a melting fondness which he was not in the habit of testifying; while the child, who feared that he had in some way innocently transgressed, lavished caresses on his father that almost looked like presentiment. Josephine herself did not enter: she knew the temper of her husband ever disposed him to indulge the first bitterness of his feelings in solitude; and if she did not sympathise with, she at least had habituated herself to respect that proud sentiment which forbade him to unveil the secret recesses of his heart even to her. She was besides willing to free both, before they again met, from the interference or observation of the child. Siegendorf continued to listen to the voice of the latter, as it reached him from the further room, till the sounds died away; when lifting his eyes from the fire, on the embers of which they had been long fixed, he saw the moon already risen. She was to be the sad and solitary witness of his intended journey. He could neither resolve to take leave of Josephine, nor to depart without doing so; and rather from a mechanical desire of motion than any settled plan, he walked out of the house.

The night was cold: a bleak and boisterous north wind had arisen, and impelled volumes of dark clouds rapidly across the sky. He turned towards the high road, which was at the extremity of the garden wall, whence it sank into a woody hollow, at that hour peculiarly sombre. It suited his frame of mind, and he pursued it for somewhat more than a quarter of a mile; when the wood shelving away on both sides, presented the open country, and presented at the same moment, to the great surprise of the Count, a view of that inundation with which the late rains had covered it, – the whole landscape seeming to form a sheet of water, over which the moonbeams played with a radiance that at once ascertained the fact. To her friendly light he was evidently indebted for his safety, if not his life! – but his mind was not in a tone so to consider the dispensation. He turned sullenly back, and, continuing his walk round the wild and lonely outskirts of the town, came at length within reach of the hum of men: – it was hateful to his ear. His eye involuntarily glanced towards the palace. Many of the apartments had lights in them, and throughout the whole there was an air of unusual festivity and mirth. 'I also lived in Arcadia*,' murmured the Count, as he traversed the streets, impatient to hide himself from every human eye. Contrary to what was usual, they contained many idlers, who were passing home, or elsewhere; and from their talk, as they crossed him, he learned that the Intendant had, by the command of the Baron, ordered dancing and a supper. Siegendorf was not more than 500 yards from his own abode, when he was rudely jostled by a man who passed him; and turning round he perceived it was Idenstein. In the humour the Count felt himself, life, though it were his own, or that of any other human being, was vile in his eyes; but he secretly despised Idenstein, and judged his own personal strength to be so much the superior of the two, that he hardly deigned to resent what he nevertheless suspected to be an insult. He only stopped, and asked Idenstein 'if he knew him?'

'I can't tell any body that does, Mr. Kruitzner, except, indeed, it may be *one!*' returned Idenstein with a marked and insolent sneer. The tone in which he spoke, together with his general appearance, convinced the Count that what he had considered as an insult, might as probably be the effect of inebriety. But who was the *one* that knew him? there was something in the words too accordant with the chain of the hearer's thought to escape his attention. He, nevertheless, walked on in silence, though he perceived that Idenstein still kept by his side, and, in a voice of intoxication, continued to mutter something, like a man who is confusedly pursuing the thread of his own ideas.

'The question may as well be settled here,' said he, at length, laying his hand roughly on the arm of the Count. The latter raised his eyes, and perceived they were precisely opposite one entrance of the palace.

'What question may be settled?' replied he, fiercely shaking

---

* Il y a un paysage de Poussin où l'onvoit de jeunes bergères qui dansent au son du chalumeau: et, à l'écart, un tombeau, avec cette inscription, 'Je vais aussi dans la délicieuse Arcadie!' – DIDEROT, *sur la Poësie Dramatique.*

A landscape of Poussin's respresents a group of shepherdesses dancing to the music of the pipe. In the back-ground is seen a tomb, with this inscription, 'I also lived amid the delights of Arcadia!' – DIDEROT, *upon Dramatic Poetry.*

The Canterbury Tales

Idenstein off.

'Whether you are really the man Baron Stralenheim is in search of, or not!'

The indignant Count, now driven alike beyond all measure of patience or of prudence, and believing, from the motion of Idenstein, that he intended again to lay hands on him, seized the latter forcibly by the collar, and, throwing him to a distance with no little violence, saw him fall at his length on the pavement. What injury was likely to be the consequence he neither knew nor cared; but before he closed his own door, he perceived more than one person issue from that of the palace, and, by the moonlight, believed he distinguished the Intendant to be amongst them.

The wildness and abruptness with which Siegendorf entered alarmed Josephine even more than his absence had done. Hardly had he indistinctly, and in a few words, given her to understand the cause of both, when they heard the house door open, which the Count had not had the precaution to secure, and the voices of Idenstein and the Intendant, apparently loud and threatening, below. Frantic with passion, the Count looked wildly around him for some weapon of defence: he believed himself on the point of suffering personal indignity, and every gleam of reason or of prudence vanished before the idea. The distracted Josephine conjured – implored him to retreat before the storm. In the last moment of desperation his eye glanced upon a large and sharp knife which lay on the table near and with which she had been cutting bread for the child's supper. Siegendorf siezed it with an earnest grasp, as if with it he had seized his fate: then pausing irresolutely for a moment, he at length turned from the door towards which he had advanced, and passed abruptly through another in the opposite direction: – not less determined than before, but like a man who, feeling he has power in his hands, is become less desperate.

Idenstein and the Intendant staggered in almost on the instant, both evidently in a state of intoxication; and Josephine, who a few moments before thought she could have encountered a host, turned pale and faint before the image of brutality. The violence of her emotion, however, presently subsided, when she discovered the Intendant to be in fact only boisterously merry; and that the purport of the visit, as far as either party could make themselves understood, was to reconcile the difference between Idenstein and her husband. Vehemently did she now long to recall the latter – to dissipate the frenzy of his mind by convincing him that what had lately passed was a mere frolic of intoxication, and to restore to it that balmy hope which seemed to have fled the mansion. It was impossible, however, to venture upon a step thus dangerous and delicate; and she found herself fortunate beyond her expectations in being able to sooth the beings before her into temporary quietness, and finally to retreat.

Her gentle voice then prepared to tranquilise the bosom of her husband, and she trod in search of him with a light and rapid step along the apartments. They were dark and solitary! She then concluded that he had quitted them through some of the various detached doors – all, however, were closed, and, as usual, slightly secured! – A wonder, vague – undefined – alarming, seized upon her, and she hastily passed forward through the house, but Siegendorf was nowhere to be seen in it. An open window, at length, attracted her notice, with some heavy furniture near, by which, though the casement was high, it might be reached. She could not with certainty recollect whether she had closed it, as was her custom towards evening, and with an anxious eye she surveyed its exterior distance from the ground; the descent was dangerous in the extreme; but it was not wholly impracticable; and the cruel apprehension that Siegendorf, impelled by the agitation of the moment, had accomplished his meditated purpose, and really departed for Bohemia, at once assailed her. Even this, however, became now the least of her terrors: the deep abstraction and gloom in which he had been plunged throughout the evening – the frenzy of rage that seemed to have succeeded it – the fever which she well knew beat in his pulse – and the actual hopelessness of his fate, armed, as he unhappily was, with the means of ending it, all united to inspire her with the most gloomy forebodings. Every hideous form of suicide presented itself to her imagination: she rushed breathless through the apartments, starting as she entered each, with the expectation of what it would present to her, yet impatient to explore the next. In the irritated state of her nerves and spirits, strange phantoms began to swim before her eyes, and unreal voices sounded in her ears; incapable, at length, of further struggle, she returned to the chamber of Marcellin, whom her agony and terrors had awakened; and, laying her wan cheek against the rosy one of her child, lost all consciousness of suffering in temporary insensibility.

For what period of time this lasted Josephine was unable to ascertain: but she was not yet sensible to the pulsation of returning life, when the sound of her own name seemed to recall it; she opened her eyes – the boy, supposing her asleep, had again sunk into slumber in her arms, but the flashing and uncertain blaze of a light, now burning in its socket, showed her husband standing by the bedside. He might well have been mistaken for one of those forms of suicide her imagination had painted: his eyes had lost the fury which lately animated them – his cheek was wholly colourless, as though the blood had indeed 'all descended to the labouring heart:' – in one hand he held the knife which had been the chief source of her terrors; the other was pressed forcibly within his bosom. Josephine attempted to offer him hers: he laid down the knife, folded his arm gently round her, and, drawing her towards him, related in a low and smothered voice the story of his absence. – It was, alas! little calculated to remove from her heart the horrible weight with which it was oppressed!

Siegendorf, in rushing so hastily from an encounter with those whose blood he secretly feared he should bring upon his head, had retreated to the last apartment of the range – it was a chamber: here he made a desperate stand, and, placing himself against the wainscot, prepared to plunge his knife deliberately, though not without warning, into the bosom of the first man who should attempt to lay hands on him; the vigour with which he pressed against that which supported him, suddenly caused it to give way; he looked round with surprise, and perceived it was not an accident, but the effect of some spring which he either touched or stood upon. It was no moment for deliberation! – he passed hastily through the aperture, and, without considering how he should return, closed the panel. He was immediately involved in total darkness: his extended arms, however, informed him, as his eye had indistinctly done, that he was in a gallery of no considerable width; floored, perfectly dry, and, as he believed, carpeted: the strangeness of the event filled his mind with painful curiosity, and he continued to advance more rapidly than in a cooler moment he probably would have ventured to do. Suddenly the ground, by some extraordinary impulse, seemed to shake beneath his feet; but before he had leisure to question the cause, it announced itself – for confused sounds of distant conviviality burst upon his ear, and snatches of music assured him that he was in the neighbourhood of dancers. The mystery was solved at once: it was clear that, having traversed the house which immediately adjoined to his own, he had reached the interior of the palace; and the various stories related of the Countess and the Prince passed in a moment across his recollection with the force of authenticity. While he continued to think, the sounds died away –

he left them behind him, and found he touched the extremity of the passage. The spring, invisible on one side, was palpable at once on the other; encouraged by profound silence, he gently pressed it, and found himself precisely where the previous calculation of a moment might have told him he would find himself – in the state-chamber of the palace, and the bed-room of Baron Stralenheim!

Astonishment, approaching to stupor, chained up the faculties of Siegendorf; yet an instinctive impulse of self-preservation made him grasp with ferocious boldness the knife he still held. The apartment was extremely spacious, and magnificently hung: a bed of purple velvet, fringed with silver, stood under a canopied recess on one side; on the other was a cabinet of curious wood, ornamented with precious stones, and richly-mounted: lighted tapers were placed near, and letters, as well as other papers, confusedly scattered over it; but the object which at once arrested the attention of the Count was several rouleaus of gold that lay ranged beside them. – Lastly, near the fire, abhorred by his eyes, and now fearful indeed to his imagination, was Stralenheim himself, stretched in an easy chair, and buried in a deep sleep.

The dæmons of desperation and cupidity seized at once upon their victim in every form of temptation which ingenuity could devise. Poverty – insult – a dungeon! – a despoiled inheritance – a helpless child, and a despairing wife, passed in gloomy perspective before him. How should he, who had never known what it was to contend with one imperious wish, now stem the torrent of all? He believed it almost a duty to free himself, for the sake even of others, from the abject penury which seemed to include every evil. His hand was on the gold, when Stralenheim moved. Siegendorf fiercely raised the knife: happily the motion of the Baron brought with it no consciousness – he merely turned his face from the light which incommoded him. The Count, after gazing on him for a moment, hastily thrust into his bosom that portion of the gold which was nearest, retreated, closed the door, and, in the dreadful perturbation and disgrace of the occasion, breathed out an imperfect ejaculation to that God who had providentially saved him from being a murderer!

This was no tale of comfort to the ear of the heart of Josephine! It brought too close to the latter that afflicting doubt she had so often banished from it – on what point of her husband's character she could finally depend! She saw him driven from error to error – from temptation to temptation – still yielding – still repenting – and where would be the last? Sacrificing every thing by turns, either

165

to false calculations, or ungoverned passions: his father – his wife – even his honour! at least that pure and secret sense which seemed to her its essence. Murder had already become amongst the almost inevitable temptations of his fate! She ventured not to pause upon the ideas which thus irresistibly forced themselves upon her mind. Other considerations, far subordinate, indeed, but sufficiently important in their nature, were open to the observation of both. Of what use was the gold thus dangerously and unjustly acquired? It could not extricate them from their entanglements at M—; it could not even be offered to Idenstein! – it could buy them nothing! – It could obtain them nothing! – It was as dross in their hands – or even worse – since, but to be suspected of possessing it, would bring forth at once accusation and proof! would throw them inevitably and disgracefully into the power of Stralenheim, and give to his most vindictive measures the sanction of law – alas! almost that of justice! These, and similar considerations, had, in the tumult of his thoughts, wholly escaped the attention of the Count. In possessing himself of gold, he had, for the moment, believed he had possessed himself of every thing: but it was not so! far otherwise; for he felt that he could not purchase his liberation, even though he were to make the last humiliating sacrifice of every manly principle. Dissimulation, falsehood itself, would be of no avail towards accomplishing that purpose. Though his real condition in life was an enigma, it was well known that he could have no resources at M—, and the only shadow of deceit he had received no remittances by letter. The Count then, far from having palliated even the obvious and coarser evils of his fate, had, in fact, only added to them; since the flight which his poverty did but threaten to impede, his newly-acquired wealth forbade him to attempt. For what, should suspicion be awakened, might in his absence be the probable fate of his wife and child?

In reflections like these the little that remained of night soon fled away, and morning brought with it appropriate fears and sorrows: for now Idenstein might again obtrude upon them! That he was an instrument in the hands of the Baron his own wanton insolence had effectually testified; and that he could be formidable without that circumstance they too well knew. The senses and the heart of Siegendorf seemed at length, however, dull to apprehension of every kind. He resigned himself with a sort of sullen despondency to his fate; and if his pulse underwent any change on hearing the voice of the Intendant, his countenance did not announce it.

The Intendant was languid and heavy with the excesses of the preceding evening: it was evident, nevertheless, that be came to observe and to scrutinise, though he strove to veil the intention. A few moments' conversation was sufficient to convince both the Count and Josephine that their visiter knew nothing of what had passed in the chamber of Stralenheim, who, finding himself unusually ill the night before, had taken a large quantity of laudanum, and was not yet stirring. The observations of the Intendant, therefore, went only to the same point with those of Idenstein: both were now fully persuaded that Kruitzner and his wife were the parties sought by Stralenheim, and each equally desirous to know the value of the secret before he finally parted with it to his employer: nor was the Intendant without a curiosity to discover – what he perceived the policy of the Baron had hitherto studiously withheld – the names and condition of his intended victims. His visit, therefore, was long, wearisome, and, as is often the case with such visits as mean every thing, seemed to mean nothing. It obtained him no information; and he at length retired, as little satisfied with it as those had been to whom it was made. Neither the Count nor Josephine, however, heard without a silent sense of self-congratulation, that Idenstein suffered to severely from the effects of intemperance as to leave no probability of his quitting his chamber till late.

The departure of the Intendant seemed to promise a momentary respite of persecution; but the hope was illusive: a voice to which they were not familiar, heard in parley with Marcellin, attracted the attention of the Count and his wife soon after their guest had quitted them: the child ran hastily into the room, and announced a stranger, who inquired for the Intendant. Siegendorf advanced with no less rapidity: his soul seemed to forbode that it was Stralenheim, and to dare the encounter. The stranger, on his part, either supposing the child did not understand him, or that the rank of the persons on; whom he intruded dispensed with ceremony, entered almost at the same moment. He was a much younger man, however, than Stralenheim, and of a more noble appearance. His eye fell first on Josephine: he paused, looked earnestly at her, and from her to the Court; repeating, not without hesitation, the question he had before asked: faintly was it replied to; for almost before the sounds could escape on either side, the eyes and palpitating hearts of each present had asked and answered a question far more important! Josephine and her husband believed it possible they might mistake – but the stranger

The Canterbury Tales

did not doubt! he knew, and in a moment recognized his parents! – It was Conrad!

With a burst of agonizing joy the mother threw herself into his arms; nor did Siegendorf feel less acutely the sudden and inexplicable throb of nature, increased, too, as it was, by every circumstance of time or place that could add to it. To have found him! found that son so long and so anxiously wished for! and at a period so critical, seemed little less than the immediate interposition of Heaven! nor did the particulars that attended it appear less a subject of perplexity and wonder than the event itself: that Conrad should have been the deliverer of Stralenheim – the companion of his journey – an inmate of the same house, was a coincidence of circumstances so extraordinary as almost to be incredible! Of the wonder, however, Conrad himself was wholly ignorant, till it was now hastily and vaguely communicated to him. The mere circumstance of meeting the Baron had to him nothing remarkable in it: the service he had rendered the latter had arisen from the impulse of the moment; for he neither knew, nor believed, even when he was told, that he had rescued an enemy or a competitor. Nurtured as Conrad had been in fondness and indulgence, no menace of a rival heir had ever offended his ear; no name, but that of his father, had ever been announced as standing between him and his inheritance. All that was necessary to be known appeared to him, therefore, sufficiently ascertained when he beheld his parents; nor did the tumult of their mutual joy seem a season for other explanation. How sweet were the emotions with which they listened to that hasty one the moment allowed Conrad to offer on his part! With what delight did they hear that the son against whom their hearts had so often murmured, had been wanting in no duty or affection: that he had voluntarily and even rashly quitted the splendid lot assigned him, to seek those whom childhood had endeared to his memory, and either share with them, or renounce his own pretensions in life.

Ages would have seemed too little for the story each was now obliged to comprise in moments. How the future was to be regulated, and whether, thus fortified with double claims, it would be advisable that they should openly and immediately defy the power of Stralenheim, or, silently withdrawing, establish their own rights on the spot where his rank and influence would be comparatively insignificant, were questions too mighty and important to be easily explained to Conrad, or, when explained, to be determined upon. Till they were, profound silence was alike the interest of all. How easy was the restriction! with hearts once more kindling to hope, and recollections absorbed in the transport of the occasion, the Count and Josephine felt no want, no wish but to gaze and to listen. All they had lost – all they had desired – all for the pursuit of which they had steeped themselves in poverty and sorrow, vanished before the feeling which had now taken possession of their bosoms: while Conrad, pressing to his the little Marcellin, buried his face over that of the smiling boy, and seemed to have found in this new and unsuspected tie a tender medium, through which to announce his own sensibility.

Josephine, however, anxious that no premature discovery on the part of Stralenheim should blight the prospect of the future, was earnest to send her son from her. Conrad only mused at her remonstrances, and smiled at her fears.

'Stralenheim,' said he, 'does not appear to me altogether the man you take him for: – but were it even otherwise, he owes me gratitude not only for the past, but for what he supposes to be my present employment. I saved his life, and he therefore places confidence in me. He has been robbed last night – is sick – as stranger – and in no condition to discover the villain who has plundered him: I have pledged myself to do it – and the business on which I sought the Intendant was chiefly that.'

The Count felt as though he had received a stroke upon the brain. Death in any form, unaccompanied with dishonour, would have been preferable to the pang that shot through both that and his heart. Indignantly had he groaned under the remorse of the past, the humiliation thus incurred by it he would hardly have tolerated from any human being; yet it brought home to him, through a medium so bitterly afflicting, as defied all calculation. At the word *villain*, his lips quivered, and his eyes flashed fire. It was the vice of his character, ever to convert the subjects of self-reproach into those of indignation.

'And who,' said he, starting furiously from his seat, 'has entitled you to brand thus with ignominious epithets a being you do not know? Who,' he added with increasing agitation, 'has taught you that it would be safe even for my son to insult me?'

'It is not necessary to know the person of a ruffian,' replied Conrad indignantly, 'to give him the appellation he merits: – and what is there in common between my father and such a character?'

'*Every thing*,' said Siegendorf bitterly, – 'for that ruffian was your father!'

Conrad started back with incredulity and amazement: then measured the Count with a long and earnest gaze, as though, unable to disbelieve the fact, he felt inclined to doubt whether it were really his father who avowed it.

'Conrad,' exclaimed the latter, interpreting his looks, and in a tone that ill disguised the increasing anguish of his own soul, 'before you thus presume to chastise me with your eye learn to understand my action! Young and inexperienced in the world – reposing hitherto in the bosom of indulgence and luxury, is it for *you* to judge of the impulse of the passions, or the temptations of misery? Wait till like me you have blighted your fairest hopes – have endured humiliation and sorrow – poverty and insult – before you pretend to judge of their effect on you! Should that miserable day ever arrive – should *you* see the being at your mercy who stands between you and every thing that is dear or noble in life! – Who is ready to tear from your name – your inheritance – your very life itself – congratulate your own heart, if, like me, you are content with petty plunder, and are not tempted to exterminate a serpent, who now lives, perhaps, to sting us all! – You do not know this man,' continued he with the same incoherent eagerness, and impetuously silencing Conrad who would have spoken: – 'I do! – I believe him to be mean – sordid – deceitful! You will conceive yourself safe because you are young and brave! – Learn, however, from the two instances before you, that none are so secure but desperation or subtilty may reach them! – Stralenheim in the palace of a prince was in my power! – My knife was held over him! – a single moment would have swept him from the face of the earth, and with him all my future fears: – I forbore – and I am now in his. – Are you certain that you are not so too? Who assures you he does not know you? – Who tells you that he has not lured you into his society, either to rid himself of you for ever, or to plunge you with your family into a dungeon? – *Me*, it is plain, he has known invariably through every change of fortune or of name – and why not you? – *Me* he has entrapped – are you more discreet? He has wound the snares of Idenstein around me: – of a reptile, whom, a few years ago, I would have spurned from my presence, and whom, in spurning now, I have furnished with fresh venom: – will *you* be more patient? – Conrad, Conrad, there are crimes rendered venial by the occasion, and temptations too exquisite for human fortitude to master or endure.' The Count passionately struck his hand on his forehead as he spoke, and rushed out of the room.

Conrad, whose lips and countenance had more than once announced an impatient desire to interrupt his father during the early part of his discourse, stunned by the wildness and vehemence with which it was pursued, sunk towards the close of it into profound silence. The anxious eyes of Josephine, from the moment they lost sight of her husband, had been turned towards her son; and, for the first time in her life, she felt her heart a prey to divided affections; for, while the frantic wildness of Siegendorf almost irresistibly impelled her to follow him, she was yet alive to all the danger of leaving Conrad a prey to reflections hostile to every sentiment of filial duty or respect. The latter, after a long silence, raised his inquiring looks to hers; and, whatever the impression under which his mind laboured, he understood too well the deep and painful sorrow imprinted on her countenance not instantly to conceal it.

'These are only the systems of my father,' said he, continuing earnestly to gaze on her. 'My mother thinks not with him?'

Josephine spoke not: there was an oppression at her heart that robbed her of the power. Conrad covered his face with his hand, and reclined it for a moment on her shoulder.

'Explain to me,' said he, after a second pause, 'what are the claims of Stralenheim, and why he is thus formidable to us.' Josephine was ill able to undertake the task: she felt it a duty, however, to expel, if possible, from the bosom of her son, feelings alike disgraceful and injurious to his father; and to exonerate the latter, as far as circumstances would permit, from that censure to which his intemperate passion had subjected him. It was not easy, however, so to relate the past events of Siegendorf's life as deeply to interest a noble or an upright mind. The candid and tender Josephine, therefore, almost betrayed the cause she strove to serve by an effect of that ingenuousness which was natural to her, and which she too evidently struggled to suppress. She detailed, with as much simplicity and exactness as the time and particulars would allow, the circumstance by which Siegendorf conceived himself to be within the power of Stralenheim; the events that occurred at Hamburgh, the intelligence of Giulio in which Conrad had so deep a share, and every agitating and distressing occurrence that had since preyed upon the temper or feelings of his father. Lastly, she painted that critical point at which he now stood with respect to the Baron, and all the possible evils that might result from the persecution of the latter.

The countenance of Conrad gathered into increasing attention as she continued to speak; and he became, as might well be expected, profoundly meditative, when he perceived the new light her narrative threw over the fate of his family. *That* showed him at once the mighty stake for which Stralenheim had so deeply schemed, and all the hazard of the present conjuncture: what he had believed to be little less than madness in the discourse of the Count was, however exaggerated by the irritation of his mind, yet grounded on the most alarming facts; and unwilling as he himself was to pain his mother by the avowal of any corroborating circumstances, he was yet secretly sensibly that, in the progress of his own intimacy with Stralenheim, he had reason to surmise that the latter was in pursuit of some enemy whom he had both authority and inclination to crush. In this secret Conrad had hitherto felt little interest; he now perceived that he had the deepest. While revolving it, he was bewildered with the recollection of that new entanglement the Count had so lately made for himself; and saw, too evidently, that, were it possible to defeat the great aim of Stralenheim by a united and open defiance, which yet they had abundant reason to doubt, there would still remain the probability of a discovery that could not fail to overwhelm them with shame and disgrace. Among the Prince's household there might be many who knew the communication between Kruitzner's residence and the palace: possibly the Intendant himself. To guard the secret of the Baron's losses was, therefore, the only method of defeating suspicion: nor was this altogether so hopeless an undertaking as it appeared; for Stralenheim, when intrusting to Conrad the particulars of the robbery, had himself doubted whether prudence did not rather require him to bury it in silence, than insult the domestics of his Highness by a charge which he might find it impossible to substantiate. This opinion Conrad had combated; and the conduct of the business had, in consequence, been finally submitted to his discretion: a word from him would, therefore, perhaps still determine the Baron to silence; and aware, as the former now was, of the innocence of those before suspected, he might utter that word without dishonour or insincerity.

The disposition of Conrad differed widely from that of his father: it had less passion and more decision. The difficulties with which he was encumbered faded, therefore, as he continued to meditate on the means of removing them. While listening to the Count's discourse, it had appeared to him all confusion, mystery, and chimera: he was at length master of the subject: he saw in its clearest and strongest light, free from the passionate irritation of Siegendorf, or the softer perturbation of Josephine; though not without those attendant feelings that peculiarly marked his own character. His countenance, therefore, cleared, and he had the air of a man who, relieved from a wild and tormenting uncertainty, begins remotely to determine the point on which he must rest. He perceived that it was indispensable to the safety of his parents that they should, without delay, be extricated from the humiliating and perilous situation in which they then stood; and to the future claims of all, that they should be personally as well as jointly asserted in the country whence they were derived. It was not possible for the most decided mind immediately to ascertain the manner in which these treasures could be effected, but Conrad pledged himself to accomplish them in some way; and his mother, who had considered his long meditation as an inauspicious omen, felt, while he continued to speak, a sweet assurance that he would succeed. It was agreed that he should return an hour after the close of evening, to communicate the result of his own deliberations, was well as what passed in the interim at the palace; where, should any steps be taken that appeared alarming, he would be at hand to frustrate or oppose them.

At the moment of Conrad's departure, he was surprised by the entrance of the Hungarian, who, directed by a chance inquiry, had come hither in search of him. The latter had been assistant with himself in rescuing Stralenheim from the danger of the water, and had consequently partaken of his hospitality at M—; but as his manners did not bear decidedly the stamp of high birth like those of Conrad, he was far from being admitted familiarly to the confidence or society of the Baron. Josephine had at that moment no eye or ear for nice discrimination: conceiving her visiter to be the associate of her son, she did not, however, omit the civilities of life; but Conrad, who perceived it would be difficult to conceal the tender relation in which he stood to his mother, was impatient to depart; and hardly had he quitted the house when, shaking off his companion, whom the pre-occupied state of his mind rendered an encumbrance, he withdrew to revolve in solitude, and with deep consideration, those plans and feelings to which the singular events of the morning had given birth.

Josephine, previous to the departure of her son, had received from his hands a ring of very considerable price. Money he plainly learned from her detail could not safely be offered to Idenstein: yet some valuable that should secure the possessor from his insults might, nevertheless, should the pressure of circumstances demand it, be produced, perhaps, without danger; and he submitted it to her discretion, and that of her father, either to retain or dispose of

The Canterbury Tales

the jewel in question in any way they should deem most expedient. The Count was now in a frame of mind to listen to the event of his son's visit. The fever of his spirits had subsided: the softer and more delightful emotions by which he had been agitated at the first sight of Conrad had resumed their place in his bosom; and though he had not been able to resolve on voluntarily re-entering the room he had quitted, he yet listened to the parting steps of his son with anxious fondness and unavailing regret. Under this impression there was something peculiarly touching in the token of tender interest and concern which the ring offered: there was even more in it than the circumstance itself seemed to present.

Jewels, in the more remote periods of society, were considered as a sort of heir-loom, and rarely changed their fashion or their owners: that now before him the Count remembered to have frequently seen in common with many others, deemed the necessary and ceremonious appendages of a splendour which he had believed inseparable from his fate. He was at that period in the very dawn and first bloom of manhood! How strange had since been the alteration both in himself and in all around! The same jewel was now drawn from the hand of his son, and for the sole purpose of rescuing him from the bitterest poverty! – His youth was almost passed! – his self-importance annihilated! – the current of time had carried away half of those golden hopes with which life had been freighted, and his own indiscretion had made a wreck of the remainder!

Considerations like these were calculated to reduce the high tone of his imperious spirit, and bring him painfully down to the level of humanity and reason. They were, indeed, but too necessary to prepare him for what was to follow; for while he yet continued to muse over the ring he was surprised with the appearance of Idenstein. – The contemplations of the Count had insensibly devolved from the past to the future; and a plan which, though hazardous, did not appear unpromising, had presented itself to his imagination. Some person it was evident he must, to a certain degree, confide in, before it was possible he should free himself from the fetters that bound him to M—. His circle was too narrow to leave much scope for deliberation. Weilburg was merely a passive spy, with whom he had little communication: his mind revolted from the Intendant with that invincible disdain which low cunning and purse-proud habits ever engender: neither did he believe it possible, closely as the latter was connected with Stralenheim, to purchase either his silence or his acquiescence. In Idenstein, though there was much occasional insolence, there was something less habitually offensive; and had he not been needy he would probably have been only insignificant. The same temptation, therefore, and the same credulity that made him an instrument in the hands of one man, might, if duly acted upon, operate in favour of another: and though in the scale of society a being thus venal and trifling ranked, according to the estimation of the Count, among the lowest of the low, yet, by a sentiment not uncommon to proud minds, he felt it, therefore, the less difficult to descend, and treat with him on his own ground.

It would hardly be possible to conceive a state of more whimsical embarrassment than that which took place in the mind of Idenstein at the courteousness of his reception. He entered with a temper extremely sullen, and, as he believed, determined: his recollection of the rencounter that had taken place the evening before, though very imperfect, was, indeed, such as made him resolve to avoid all personal extremities with the Count: but, as he knew enough to be assured that Baron Stralenheim's measures with regard to the former were drawing to a crisis, he was willing to take his last chance for all possible share in the event of them; and to exort from some sudden gust of passion, which Josephine's presence would prevent from becoming dangerous, what it seemed no longer probable he should obtain by craft. But he was now to be encountered with his own weapons: for Siegendorf, who, despite of the perplexities of his situation, yet felt a confidence inspired by the late favourable circumstances and the certain support of his son, had resumed the command of his temper, and was no longer the imperious, unbending, and unobservant character he had hitherto appeared. Idenstein thus defeated, he hardly knew why or how, in his meditated attack, sank insensibly into a sort of silent and wondering listener while the Count continued to talk; till the latter, advancing slowly and obscurely towards his aim, made him at last remotely comprehend that it might be more for his advantage to betray, than to forward, the cause in which he had enlisted.

Throughout the whole circle of Idenstein's ideas this had never yet made one. The poverty of Kruitzner had been so obvious, that neither the delicate habits of Josephine, nor the air of distinction which even in his most humiliating moments eminently marked the Count, had removed the eyes of his associate from that formidable spectre: but when, in its place, phantoms of grandeur and affluence were presented to him, the whole prospect of the future underwent a sudden change.

He recollected, what was strictly true, that he had, in fact, little reason to be satisfied with the Intendant; who, whatever was the value of the service they were mutually to render Stralenheim, had suffered his coadjutor to discover too evidently that *he* would have little share in the reward. With Stralenheim himself he had even less cause to be pleased. He had seen him only once; but their meeting had served, nevertheless, to display those traits of cold and forbidding arrogance which at all times marked the character of the Baron; and which, as he was taught by the selfish cunning of the Intendant to suppose Idenstein of no consequence to his plans, he did not attempt to dissemble. Small as the consequence of the latter might seem in the eyes of others, in his own, however, it was pretty considerable; and his zeal was already cooled in a cause that neither promised him recompense nor thanks. While he continued, therefore, to pause with apparent complacency upon the arguments presented to him, the Count watched the critical moment; and, sensible that he had himself advanced too far now to recede, he produced the jewel. Idenstein started with astonishment! Chance, and some commercial connections, made him a judge of its value. He looked earnestly at it, and considered long. The Count had also considered well before he offered it: although to him it would have been known from amidst ten thousand others, it bore, as he believed, no family distinction, no appropriate mark, that could ever ascertain its original owner to an indifferent person: nor had he, in fact, an intention to part with it, except on such terms as should render all that might follow immaterial to him.

The hitherto wavering fidelity of Idenstein seemed at length on the point of being finally shaken: the Count pursued the advantage. With an equivocal and half confidence, he now observed, 'that he had himself important reasons for continuing his journey, wholly remote from any pursuit or project that Stralenheim might be engaged in – a pursuit of which it was by no means proved that he was the object, although the mere circumstance of being mistaken for such might very considerably embarrass him.' Siegendorf, though almost assured of success, was not, however, so unguarded as to betray either his name or condition: on the contrary, he still cautiously veiled both. But his air – his tone – an internal consciousness that he was nearly, though not wholly, speaking the truth, had the almost irresistible effect on his hearer, which truth rarely fails to produce. Idenstein was not indeed deceived into doubting whether or no Kruitzner would prove the person sought by the Baron; his conviction on that subject was even stronger than before, but his interest in believing it was less, in proportion as a more immediate and certain advantage than any yet held out to him now presented itself: he felt a secret persuasion that whatever were the temporary circumstances of the man before him, his pretensions in life were of no common kind; and gay, though undefined, visions of future fortune and patronage sparkled to his eyes. Siegendorf, who saw his purpose nearly accomplished, concluded his discourse by solemnly affirming the jewel to be a memorial of his family, which nothing but the last exigency could induce him to part with; and, valuable as it was in itself, he pledged his honour to redeem it at a future period with treble its price. That period, could either have looked into the future, they would have seen was never to arrive; but the argument was conclusive with his hearer: Idenstein acceded at once; and nothing remained but to discover in what manner his services could be rendered most efficient.

In the discussion of plans, however, much embarrassment still arose; as the secrecy necessary to the occasion was such as rendered it extremely difficult for the Count to quit M—, even with the connivance of Idenstein. How far the advice of Conrad might have been useful, or in what manner his parents could have been benefited by his interference, was also a subject of deep perplexity to the Count. It was necessary, however, so to arrange the plan with Idenstein, that the services of Conrad might not be essential in its execution, and to reserve the liberty of changing it, should a better occur; for Siegendorf had still too little faith in his new auxiliary to put his son in danger by an indiscreet discovery. He was moreover sensible that he could himself be but half in the power of Stralenheim, while Conrad remained unknown; and it was, therefore, of the first consequence to conceal the relationship between them. After much investigation, and many impracticable proposals, the Count and Idenstein at length simplified the plan of escape to so humble a one as seemed likely to defeat suspicion or vigilance. The latter engaged secretly to place a vehicle, of sufficient size to hold Kruitzner and his family, in a ruinous out-house that stood not far from the palace, and had once served as temporary stables. To this he was, at a proper season, to add an able horse, with such little accommodations as would prevent the hazard of sudden delay on their journey: he engaged, in the interim, to amuse the Intendant with fictitious accounts of the intentions of Kruitzner; to lull both him and Stralenheim into profound security; and, when the moment of discovery at length arrived, to baffle either inquiry or pursuit by every artifice that he could safely adopt. Such was the arrangement: yet, when made, it was difficult for the parties concerned, however fair the promises on both sides, to separate without a mutual distrust. The Count could not in common prudence recompense his ally till his share of the agreement was performed; and Idenstein was not without a secret surmise, that when it was performed the recompense might be either evaded or withheld. In this, however, they were equally unjust; for the one had too much to hazard by treachery, the other too little to gain. Although the favour of the Intendant might serve Idenstein, his resentment could in fact do him little injury; for he had nothing to lose but a character; and there were occasions on which he had himself been diffident enough to doubt if he had that. He knew to a certainty that he offended no law, since he had never been legally employed. Had it even been otherwise, all the little jurisprudence of M— was within his own hands; and, what was still better towards his security, the Intendant himself had strained the power so often, that his discretion would hardly admit of his entering the lists against an opponent likely to prove dangerous. All conclusions drawn, and all objections weighed, Idenstein was, therefore, sincere; and the communications he voluntarily made to the Count were of a nature at once to prove his sincerity, and to point out to the latter that precipice on which he had justly suspected himself of standing.

The inundation which had continued to increase, and which Siegendorf had at one time considered as the cruel finish to his ill fortune, he now learned, from the report of Idenstein, had been, in fact, the pledge of his safety. The latter could not, indeed, exactly ascertain all the particulars that had been canvassed between Stralenheim and the Intendant; but he knew that a messenger had that very day been despatched towards Frankfort, who had returned only from the impossibility of proceeding safely; and that the Baron waited, with the most anxious impatience, for his departure on the succeeding morning. The messenger had, in confidence, communicated to Idenstein, whom he knew to be trusted by his master, that his errand at Frankfort was to the commandant, and that he understood he was to return in company with a military guard! – All now then was at its climax! and four-and-twenty hours would decide the fate of Siegendorf: four-and-twenty hours would defeat the schemes of his enemy, place him for ever, perhaps, beyond the reach of the latter, and finally restore all that was great and desirable in life, or tear him from every thing dear there, and leave his son and wife to struggle as they could, in order to preserve for him that single, solitary blessing! – His mind was roused to the encounter. – A generous and justifiable indignation awakened his feelings, and strengthened his nerves. Tumult, irritation, and all the grosser particles of his character, subsided for the time and left a calm and steady surface, worthy of the son of Count Siegendorf and the husband of Josephine. To encounter his fate with vigour, and to bear it, whatever it might prove, with unshaken resolution, was the determined purpose of his soul. It is the wrong we commit against ourselves that corrodes and most bitterly envenoms the heart; that we receive from others sometimes displays its noblest faculties, either by the act of repelling or enduring the evil. Siegendorf owed half his faults, and almost all his miseries, to a secret tearing consciousness of error, which he never permitted to rise into reformation. In this case it was not so. – The inheritance was not the right of Stralenheim: the means he pursued to obtain it were not those of rectitude or candour: – the Count stood pledged to his family in an honourable cause, and he rose, with the dignity of an honourable feeling, to meet it.

The future now literally floated on the uncertain breath of a wind: for on the wind depended the continuance of the flood. It was during the course of the ensuing day that Idenstein had engaged to fulfil his promise: it could not be useful to do it sooner, and might be dangerous. Tedious hours were to intervene; and that fortitude the Count had so lately assumed was indeed necessary towards supporting them: yet even those hours were to present a solace long denied to his heart and his eyes: for he was once more to see Conrad – his eldest born: the first pledge of love: – the blooming young man whose features he had hardly yet had leisure to trace, and whose noble and susceptible heart he feared he had deeply outraged by the extravagant as well as indiscreet excesses of his own.

Under this impression it was hardly possible to present a countenance and demeanour more different from the morning than that with which the Count welcomed his son. He had even self-command enough to control his emotion, when he found his surmises confirmed, as he feared, by the reserve of Conrad; and, by a powerful effort, he obliged himself to respect in the latter the feelings of a virtuous indignation. Conrad, like his father, was indeed naturally haughty, and but little accustomed to the high tone of rebuke: nor had he yet recovered from the surprise of the morning, and the contemplation on the characters of both his parents to which it had given birth. That of his mother was plain, noble, tender: – a short observation had taught

The Canterbury Tales

him to comprehend and to respect it. It was far otherwise in what regarded his father: the first extravagant sally of the Count, and the singular avowal it contained, had presented to the imagination of his son the image of some bold and daring transgressor who stands aloof from society, and despises its obligation: – it was the leader of a banditti that seemed to start up before him under the name of a father, and every faculty of his soul had been roused to attention. Happily, as it proved for him, the fury of the Count had not allowed him to speak at a crisis when these sentiments would have betrayed themselves; and, in continuing to listen, they had gradually faded before the impression of wounded pride and embittered sensibility expressed in the accents of Siegendorf. But no distinct image was substituted for what which was effaced: – and though the words of the Count had sunk deep into the memory and heart of his hearer, they still left a strange uncertainty in both as to the character of that man, who, while he spoke with almost savage ferocity of destroying an enemy, could yet be worked up to agony by the eye of a son.

It was not, however, under the influence of a doubt, that Conrad could take his father to his bosom, or his confidence; and though he would willingly have suppressed what his features announced, it was easy to see that he came to scrutinize and to understand him. The Count was painfully sensible of this, and his mind strove proportionably to assert itself. It was long since Josephine had seen the sunshine of her husband's eyes, and the snatches with which it now illumined his countenance called forth all the brightness of hers. In the garb of poverty, under the roof of dependence, shrouded as it were in sorrow and suffering, the native dignity and charms of both prevailed. They had now also leisure to contemplate the manly beauty of their son; and mutually interchanged glances of applause and congratulation. The exterior of Conrad, though seen only by the imperfect light which the fire diffused through their spacious apartment, was yet grand, commanding, impressive beyond even what that of his father had been. His person, though tall, was vigorous and full: it seemed cast in the mould of a hero, and had nothing to do with the common and every-day race of men. The contour of his head and neck was singularly powerful and striking: it presented that bold outline sometimes formed in a moment of inspiration by the chisel of a master, and which the connoisseur or physiognomist alike seizes upon as exclusively his own: the strength of the features was, however, subdued by the soft glow and flexible muscles of youth. His mind and manners seemed in unison with this character of person, and had a tone of daringness and resolution that bespoke him formed for extraordinary enterprises. The Count gazed on him in silence; and a thousand bright visions of honourable distinction and happiness, for ever annihilated in his own person, insensibly revived in that of Conrad. The gloomy present faded before the perspective of the future; and, by the strange but natural magic of the affections, Siegendorf tasted a few moments of a felicity so exquisite, that nothing was wanting but the conviction that his son esteemed him to render it perfect.

The brow of Conrad, though he strove to clear it, was, nevertheless, evidently, clouded by disquietude. Those various feelings created by the circumstances in which he had so suddenly found himself placed, had been considerably augmented by the events which had passed at the palace during his absence from it. They were, he believed, of a nature once more to kindle the turbulent passions of his father; yet the communication neither admitted of hesitation nor delay: – the moments were precious to all, and the necessity of resolving most urgent.

That half resolution which prudence had induced Baron Stralenheim to form with respect to the robbery he had sustained, the habits of his character had not allowed him to fulfil: the time Conrad passed with his mother had unfortunately afforded leisure to the Intendant and the Baron for more open and familiar intercourse than they had hitherto entered into; and during this interval of mutual explanation, Stralenheim became satisfied that the man who called himself Kruitzner was in reality no other than Count Siegendorf. He felt little disposition, however, to communicate the importance of this discovery, or the advantage he meant to make of it. It would neither have been consistent with the discretion or the *hauteur* of his character, to elevate one of the Prince's domestics into the immediate confidant of his own projects or expectations in life: taking such measures as he believed would secure him the military assistance he desired from Frankfort, he left the Intendant, therefore, as much in the dark with respect to the grand secret as he had hitherto remained: but the subordinate one, as being more within the province of the latter, he resolved to communicate. Stralenheim was far from rich, and he loved money: the recital of his losses was not made, therefore, without some acrimony; and the jealous pride of the Intendant immediately took fire, as indeed the complainant had suspected it would do, at the bare idea of attaching disgrace to any of the household of the Prince. Something resembling altercation took place between them: each, however, believed it his interest not to quarrel with the other; and the disgust which seemed upon the point of arising on both sides was, therefore, according to their own ideas, happily subdued, by fixing on an intermediate person as the object of distrust. The appearance and manners of Conrad threw it, indeed, wholly at a distance; but nature had not been so liberal to the Hungarian, and they, therefore, kindly determined that fortune should be equally unjust: he had, besides, that dangerous and suspicious symptom – poverty; and though the Baron and the Intendant might probably differ in their estimate of wealth, they were nearly agreed on one point – that a poor man could seldom be deemed an honest one. On the Hungarian, therefore, they rested the whole weight of their suspicions; and though the nature of the loss did not admit of its being brought to proof, they treated him with an indignity that showed they did not wait for it. It was at the critical moment of his humiliation that Conrad, after a solitary walk, re-entered the palace. What his feelings were on the scene he there witnessed, it was not possible for him to recapitulate to his father. His own suspicions had, indeed, in the first instance, like theirs, fallen on the Hungarian; he had since learned their fallacy. So singularly, however, was he circumstanced, that it was not in his power to assert the innocence of the accused, though he knew it: – it was not in his power to quit the palace with him, and partake his fate, though he felt it to be unmerited: it was, unhappily, not even in his power to attest the general honour of his companion: for he had become such by accident – was little known to him – had shared his purse, because he appeared to want it; and had no other claim but that of seeming above his fortunes.

What those fortunes were, however, either the prudence or the resentment of the Hungarian induced him obstinately to conceal. He had retorted the indignities shown him with the determination of innocence, and the pride of a mind resolved to rest upon itself. Finally, he had, without hesitation, quitted the palace, though he knew not where else he could find shelter:– for the caution of Siegendorf's ancient host not forsaken him, and he had neither room for poverty nor for the rejected guest of the Intendant. Under these circumstances, Conrad had left the Hungarian a wanderer in the environs of the town; hemmed in by the waters from leaving it, yet resolved to encounter either peril or suffering rather than submit to further degradation. –

Such was the detail at length reluctantly given by Conrad, and such the feelings of which the avowal was extorted from him. What were those of the Count on hearing the recital? It seemed of late the peculiar misery of his fate to have the cup of comfort ever dashed from his lips at the moment he began to taste its sweetness. Humiliation – the bitterest regret – nay, even danger, appeared involved in this event. Again he was reduced to blush before hs son and wife; again he looked back upon the past with grief, and upon the future step it necessarily entailed upon him with apprehension. To receive the Hungarian under his own roof, at a period when every thing likely to pass there would be mysterious; – when his stay – his departure – his connections, – were of necessity such as he wished to bury in profound secrecy, was of all steps most hazardous; yet did it seem unavoidable; and there was even somewhat in the tone with which Conrad had uttered the narrative, as well as the penetrating observation of his eye, that seemed to show him alive to the necessity of making such a reparation for the injury inflicted on a stranger.

To counterbalance the many evils this unfortunate incident thus threatened, it was to be remembered that the very circumstance of the stranger's being suspected, proved the Intendant's total ignorance of the private doors of communication: that the Hungarian would be no less anxious to quit a spot which must be odious to his feelings, than the Count would be to dismiss him. Finally, and in itself an argument more conclusive than any other, all that Baron Stralenheim could know with respect to his vicinity to the Count, he probably did; all he could do, he unquestionably would. These reflections passed with the rapidity of lightning through the mind of Siegendorf; and almost at the moment of making them, he announced to his wife and son his intention of braving that danger to which he had himself exposed the Hungarian, by receiving him under his roof. Josephine and Conrad both paused over this: the former, nevertheless, felt, like her husband, that something was due to the innocence they had involuntarily wronged; and the opinion of Conrad, though not expressed, was not to be doubted.

The Count, on his part, now hastily related the arrangement made between himself and Idenstein. None more eligible, that could by any method be rendered secure, presented itself to the imagination of either party: and, as Siegendorf had calculated that he should not be many hours on his route before he crossed the borders, there was reasonable ground for supposing that they might then, without much risk, remedy the inconvenience that would attend their mode of travelling. For this purpose Conrad supplied his father with gold, and the Baths of Carlsbad were appointed as the spot where he should rejoin them.

Those sweet moments of repose in which all had indulged were now, as before, rapidly passing away; – they were even already past: and such had been the tumult and perplexities attendant on their meeting, that not one had been asked of those many interesting and important questions each so earnestly desired to hear answered. To pro-long the stay of Conrad was to direct suspicion to him; and perhaps, to involve him in that fate which, should it overtake the Count, he only could rescue him from. That he would do so, natural affection assured his parents; that he must do so, the mere tie of interest was sufficient to attest: for even the short explanation that had arisen, made it sufficiently clear, that without the personal appearance of the Count the legitimacy of his son would perhaps be ever contested. Yet his personal appearance, should the measures of Stralenheim prove successful, might, if not wholly prevented, be so long delayed as to give the latter that most dangerous of all rights, possession. To obviate this, however, every step had now been taken that caution could suggest; and the heart of Siegendorf, animated by the occasion, poured itself out with manly and inartificial magnanimity into the bosoms of his wife and son. Conrad listened with the deepest attention, and felt at length persuaded, by his own observation, that he had mistaken the character of his father; who, though the slave of passion, was not deliberately capable of those excesses it seemed to prompt. It was a doubt of the first importance to him to solve; and on which he had, in consequence, anxiously mediated.

Half an hour had hardly elapsed from the departure of Conrad when the Hungarian entered. He was not entirely unknown to Josephine, but she had noticed him little when they last met. To the Count he was wholly a stranger; and the latter, who knew not exactly the degree of confidence placed in him by Conrad with respect to the relative situations of all parties, though aware that it must be a limited one, prepared to receive him with kind but cautious hospitality. He was not impressed favourably, however, by his appearance. The Hungarian was, indeed, devoid of those exterior advantages by which his countrymen are generally distinguished: he was low in stature, and swarthy; his features were not plain, but their expression was disagreeable; and he had the air of a man who has seen and suffered much. His step and deportment, however, were military; and, together with his address, announced self-possession.

In the eyes of the Count and Josephine, which had so lately rested on the distinguished person of their son, that of their guest appeared to a particular disadvantage; nor could they avoid secretly feeling as if Stralenheim and the Intendant had not been altogether so wild in their conjectures as they had at first concluded. The stranger just touched upon the peculiarities of his situation, and the insults he had received, like one who felt them too resentfully to be diffuse; and he seemed, besides, somewhat restrained by a doubt whether his host had been made any party in the story. On his own side, he appeared to have received no further communication from Conrad than such as might lead him to suppose the family before him had once seen brighter days. He professed it to be his resolution to depart early the next morning at all hazards; and found an additional motive for desiring it: since, should the Hungarian effect the journey, it would afford a certainty that the roads would be practicable for himself and his family. Josephine now retired to rest, and Siegendorf and his guest soon after parted; but on the nerves or the imagination of the former an impression had been made not easily to be shaken off. He was haunted by a strange and vague suspicion that the Hungarian, despite of all appearances, would, in the end, prove some secret emissary of the Baron; and that both himself and his son were duped into receiving as a guest one who was, in fact, only a spy. Unwilling, therefore, to trust the general safety to a stranger, the Count continued to watch during the greater part of the night; sometimes traversing the room, at others mediating in profound silence, or attempting to read. Daylight at length surprised him; when softly advancing towards the chamber of his guest, he found him fast asleep. Ashamed of his own doubts, he at length threw himself on the bed and snatched a few hours of repose. It was, consequently, not early when he awaked; and Josephine, alarmed at his longwatching the night before, as well as the unusual season he had chosen for slumber, was anxiously near him: – to his great satisfaction he found that the Hungarian was gone.

The softness of the air and a bright sun, gave favourable promise for the day: before it was half over Idenstein made his appearance. He was in extreme good-humour with himself for having outwitted the Intendant; who, it was now clear, he thought, excluded him from the sight and confidence of Stralenheim. He announced to the Count the welcome intelligence that the inundation already began to subside;

that there could be no question but before the dawn of the ensuing day the country would be passable; and that the messenger despatched to Frankfort, angry at being again sent off on what he believed to be both a perilous and fruitless expedition, had, between his ill-humour and his haste, forgotten the bag of despatches; an oversight which Idenstein had taken care should not be discovered at the palace till it was too late to recall him; and which he, probably, would not discover himself till he had completed his journey. Idenstein laughed heartily at the success of his own schemes, and the lucky combination of circumstances that favoured them. Nor was he sparing of his expressions of satisfaction in thus balking the sulky Baron and his sagacious assistant.

Welcome as this intelligence was, in all its points, to the Count, he was, nevertheless, in no disposition to enjoy it. As the moment of his own departure approached, he was worked up to a pitch of impatience which he could hardly govern or endure. The period between the present hour and that of his journey was as a sort of 'phantasma, or a hideous dream:' and the only particular he was truly anxious to know was whether Idenstein meant to fulfil his promise faithfully with regard to the vehicle and the horse. This he engaged to do after the close of evening, and he was then to obtain his reward. It was from that moment, therefore, the fears, the tortures of the Count were to be doubled; for, the jewel once given, what should secure the fidelity of the receiver?

Previous to the last parting between Conrad and his parents, it had been settled on both sides that, to avoid all observation, he should appear under their roof no more. It was, nevertheless, his intention to remain within reach of the Baron, whether at M— or elsewhere, till Siegendorf might reasonably be supposed safe from pursuit. Nor would Conrad in this arrangement admit the possibility of hazard to himself, whatever the tender anxiety of those he spoke to might dispose them to make: and even the Count was obliged, after the storm of his passions had subsided, to acknowledge that no probable reason could be assigned that should lead Stralenheim to suspect the secret tie and relationship of Conrad. Prudence had induced the latter to point out to his father the advantage of their re-union before either entered Prague. The neighbourhood of the Baths of Carlsbad had been fixed upon as the most eligible spot for this purpose; and Siegendorf, while attending there the approach of his son, proposed to open a communication with the capital; to prepare the way for his own personal appearance, and to proceed forward immediately on the arrival of Conrad, with every circumstance of splendour and family concord that could give validity to their claims. Such at least was the intention announced by the Count: but his inmost soul did not confirm it: an ill-omened voice seemed incessantly to issue from thence, and to silence, with the force of presentiment, every hope he studiously cherished. It was not feebleness of mind; or, if feebleness, it was confined in its operation to a single idea: – for to all the accompanying ones he presented an undaunted, and almost heroic resolution: but he was secretly persuaded that he should never escape Stralenheim; and he was right: he never did escape him.

On the surface, however, every thing went well. The day continued fine: the flood obviously subsided; and soon after dark Idenstein fulfilled his promise: so disposing the horse and calèche, that should they, in the event, appear to have been left by him, he had reason to flatter himself that the Count's appropriation of them would rather wear the air of a fraudulent seizure, than a private convention of the parties. Siegendorf earnestly scrutinized the features of his ally before he parted with the ring. He saw much foolish exultation in them, but no insincerity: in fact, there was none to see. The most mature deliberation had not pointed out to Idenstein any motive of interest stronger than that he was now pursuing; and he, therefore, as heartily wished the Count gone, as the other wished himself. He failed not, however, to make him reiterate his promise of redeeming the pledge at a high price, whenever occasion allowed of his doing so, and of further rewarding the service now rendered. On his part, he swore solemnly to the faithful performance of all he had engaged for; and, having received his recompense, walked triumphantly home – never from that moment to know peace, safety or advantage, in its possession.

He must be a deep dissembler who evades all suspicion in a heart and eye keenly alive to it. The Count felt, at length, something like conviction that Idenstein was no such character. He had turned his steps, therefore, with a satisfied mind towards Josephine, when the steps of some one entering arrested his attention. He looked hastily round, and saw, not without a mingled sensation of surprise and displeasure, that it was the Hungarian. There was, however, nothing alarming attended the re-appearance of the latter, except in the circumstance of his re-appearing at all. He professed himself weary and exhausted; and the account he gave of his absence was such as, while simple, wore the air of truth. The flood, though hourly sinking, proved, upon trial, not to have sufficiently subsided to enable a stranger to ascertain the track. He had, nevertheless, made the experiment in different directions, and had in all encountered a degree of danger which had deterred him from proceeding; till being, at length, assured by the peasants that a very few hours would allow him to accomplish without hazard what it was evident would at that juncture be attended with much, he had given up the undertaking, and, putting his horse into one of the numerous out-stables of his Highness, had returned, again to claim the hospitality of his former host. He added, that he met Conrad not long before, who recommended to him the step he had now taken.

In the round of possible events there was hardly any from which the mind of Siegendorf, would have revolved more powerfully than from the simple one that thus presented itself. He had conceived an invincible disgust to the Hungarian from the very first moment he had seen him: – a disgust which he was conscious originated chiefly in that sense of humiliation the presence of the latter could not but inspire, by recalling to his memory the most disgraceful incident of his life. He had struggled vigorously against the injustice of his own suspicions, and it was only a few hours before that he had smiled at their fallacy: they now at once recurred in full force. The very consciousness that they did so, taught him to spurn a feeling which he conceived to be as unmanly and degrading as he supposed it ill-founded. It was not possible, indeed, for him to conceal from the Hungarian that his appearance was unexpected, and, it might be surmised, undesired: yet he controlled himself so far as to receive his guest with tokens of hospitality, and invited him to partake the frugal meal to which he was himself sitting down. The Hungarian, who stood in need of refreshment, accepted the offer. He was no talker: – but there was something clear and impressive in his language when he spoke; and his voice, equally full and sonorous, was of that sort which the ear when it has once received never forgets. His remarks, however, as well as the general character of his mind, had a hardness peculiarly offensive to that of the Count; and though it was easy to perceive that he had lived much in the world, and had observed closely upon it, the impression he made upon his host was not all more favourable than before. Busy imagination too still pointed out something particularly sinister and watchful in his eyes: yet the evil of admitting him, whatever its consequences, could neither be remedied nor further guarded against. His discourse betrayed that he was vindictive; and policy, therefore, no less than justice, extorted from the Count all the exterior office of courtesy. They at length parted. The Hungarian, as before, retired to rest; and Josephine, at the earnest entreaty and almost command of her husband, did the same.

But the power which Siegendorf had exerted over her, he could not extend to himself. He continued to walk the anteroom till the watching of the two preceeding nights at length stupified and overwhelmed him: when, throwing himself into a chair by her bedside, he gave way to what he believed to mere momentary drowsiness. Josephine watched likewise for a considerable time, till her own eyes, which had involuntarily shared the vigils of his the night before, though he had not imparted their true cause, became heavy: the profound tranquillity of all around, and the soft breathings of her child, who lay on a matress not far distant, united to lull her, as well as Siegendorf, to repose: her eyelids at length closed; and, in a few moments after, all three were buried in a deep sleep. That of the Count though apparently calm, was far from being really so. Confused images still continued to flit before him, with all the force of the mist frightful realities. Stralenheim, the Hungarian, and even Idenstein, alternately harassed his imagination: – the scene then changed; he lost sight of them; and, by a rapid transition, fancied himself within the limits of his own castle at Siegendorf. His father was alive there: but pale – meagre – hollow-eyed. On a sudden the figure ceased to be his father, and became a phantom. He would have avoided it – but it followed – it persecuted – it haunted him! – In the midst of these, and similar chimeras, the Count started and awoke. The watch-light, which was more than half consumed, announced the near approach of morning; and Josephine, whom his start had disturbed, awoke also; both instantly arose. Breathless with impatience, Siegendorf hastened to assure himself that the horse and vehicle were still under cover. All was precisely as he had left it the night before. He harnessed the horse with his own hands, and disposed their little baggage in the manner most commodious for travelling. Josephine meantime was preparing a scanty breakfast of pottage for Marcellin, when, at the moment that her husband re-entered the house, both recollected the Hungarian. The Count advanced towards his chamber door: it was slightly closed, but not fastened. He looked in, and perceived with some surprise that his guest was gone. A moment's reflection on the past told him that the lower door had been unbarred when he himself first descended; and a glance towards the future seemed to announce that the Hungarian was

189

somewhere stationed to detain him. There was no leisure, however, to pause over the mystery: life or death – liberty or destruction – seemed to hang upon the point of time before them; and whatever might be the schemes that baffled or opposed their departure, the die was cast – the effort must be made.

The moon in the interim had sunk, and it was yet dark; the Count, whose anxiety for those he was to guide, induced him to hesitate between the opposing dangers of precipitation or delay, once more quitted the house, to judge from the fading of the stars how near it was to sunrise. He had gazed earnestly on them for some moments, when, by their pale and uncertain light, he saw the branches move in a part of the garden nearest that of the palace: some loose stones fell from the wall, and a man at the same instant was seen to leap it. Siegendorf advanced hastily, but by the form and step perceived that the intruder could be no other than Conrad. Touched with this proof of filial anxiety the Count quickened his pace; but he was startled with the fierce demeanour and menacing gesture of his son.

'Stop!' said the latter, in an imperious, though smothered tone, and while they were yet at some paces distance.

'Before we approach each other, tell me whether I see my father or an assassin?' – Siegendorf paused in astonishment; but unable to understand him, again advanced near enough to perceive that he was extremely pale, and agitated beyond all common convulsions of the soul.

'Answer, as you value the life of either!' again exclaimed Conrad, motioning his father to a distance.

'Insolent young man! to what would you have me answer?'

'Are you, or are you not, the murderer of Baron Stralenheim?'

'I was never yet the murderer of any man.' replied the Count, fiercely; and starting in his turn some paces back:
– 'What is it you mean?'

'Did you not last night enter the secret gallery? – Did you not penetrate to the chamber of Stralenheim? – Did he' – and his voice suddenly faltered, – 'did he not die privately by your hand?'

The Count, who at length comprehended the horrible mystery included in his son's words, turned pale and aghast: while Conrad, bending distrustfully forward, gazed at him as though his very soul would have passed through his eyes, in order to ascertain the nature of the emotion which his father sustained. The wan and quivering countenance of the latter spoke a language not to be misunderstood.

'You are then innocent?' said Conrad, emphatically. – In terms fearfully solemn, the Count uttered an imprecation on himself, if his hand had ever executed, or his heart conceived, a project, of deliberate assassination.

'Baron Stralenheim is, however, dead,' continued Conrad, after a gloomy pause. 'It is past doubt that his chamber has been secretly entered this night. Yet no bar has been forced – no appearance of violence is to be discovered, save on his person. His household has been alarmed – the Intendant is stupified in a second debauch, and incapable of exertion. I, therefore, took upon myself the care of summoning the police: – nature and filial duty must plead my pardon if – ' he stopped in a tone of strong emotion. Siegendorf, who in its imperfect expression at once comprehended the terrible struggles that could not fail in a noble mind, agitated with the consciousness of his own degraded situation – the affecting contrast of his son's virtues – the danger – the disgrace – the infamy he saw prepared for them all, threw himself upon the neck of Conrad, and, for the first time in his life, wept bitterly. The language of truth carries with in an eloquence that is rarely doubted, and the Count read his acquittal in the eyes of his son.

'Yet you have no guests – no domestics – no visitors?' said Conrad, in a tone of rapid interrogation, as his mind seemed still eagerly to revolve all the possible chances of danger from the mysterious passage. Siegendorf suddenly struck his hands together, and repeated the name of the Hungarian.

'He is gone! – He went yesterday!'

'No! – he returned!'

'When? – At what time?'

'Last night!'

'And he slept—'

'In the only chamber I had to offer him – the last, and dangerous one!' – Conrad, without speaking, looked earnestly towards the house.

'It is too late,' said the Count, interpreting the glance, 'you will only terrify your mother! – the Hungarian is gone!'

A deep abstraction seemed for some moments to impose silence on both. Conrad did not break it, but the unhappy Siegendorf in agony of soul at length loudly cursed that indiscretion on his own part which had thus exposed them to danger; and traced, though too late, in the hard and vindictive character of his guest, all the portentous warnings of a bloody catastrophe. – That catastrophe, bloody as it had proved, was passed. – Stralenheim no longer lived either to suffer or to hope. It was Siegendorf who now stood a devoted victim: more surely so by the destruction of his enemy than by the bitterest rancour of his life! vainly did the removal of that enemy clear from his path the sole obstacle to honours and to fortune! Between him and all that he could claim, all that he could hope, a black and dreadful chasm had opened, impossible as it appeared to pass: – for where was he to find the Hungarian? How prove the crime upon him, or, when proved, exonerate himself from the charge of being at least an accessary?

Conrad, through whose imagination these and a thousand other difficulties and angers were tumultuously rushing, yet saw, and pointed out with that vigour which marked his character, the favourable chances that remained. Obscure and unknown as Kruitzner was, what individual at M— was to suspect in him the princely fortunes and hereditary distinctions of Count Siegendorf? Who could divine the connection between his fate and that of the Baron? Who was likely, for a time at least, to discover the possibility of Kruitzner's effecting the crime, or, when discovered, find a clue sufficiently unequivocal to guide him through that labyrinth in which the sullen pride and crooked policy of Stralenheim, together with the mysterious situation of his adversary, had placed them both? – No letters had yet reached Frankfort – none would probably ever reach it:– for how would Idenstein now venture to produce, what he had once so indiscreetly concealed? – At worst, the Count's name in the despatches was probably a borrowed one; and what testimony was to prove the identity of his person? – Who was even interested in doing it? Stralenheim was an individual of but common rank in his own country, in any other he was insignificant; on the spot where he had perished he was solitary. Law, palsied in its operations by the influence of circumstances, would do little: justice and promptitude might do every thing: they might teach the innocent man to rescue himself by a vigorous effort from that ambiguous situation to which he was in danger of falling a victim, and place him as far out of the reach of any present enemy as fate had now placed him out of the reach of a former one. Every moment, however, seemed invaluable! A dreadful responsibility might attach to Conrad, and make his stay fatal. Even at the period when he challenged his father as guilty, he had had the precaution not to expose him to suspicion by entering his door. The former stood fully acquitted in his eyes, and to guard him was consequently no less the duty of his justice than of his heart. The

Count it was obvious therefore must fly, and that without delay: the means seemed providentially prepared. It was equally clear to both that Conrad must remain; since, by becoming the companion of their flight, he would at once have exposed the connection between himself and his family, and doubled the danger of all: nor was he of a character to shrink from danger in any form; much less in that remote and doubtful one which attended his stay. The moment the secret doors of communication were discovered, as during the minute researches of the police they inevitably must be, Kruitzner and the Hungarian would alike become the decided objects of suspicion. The active character of Conrad might yet find means to trace out the retreat of the latter; and should his own relationship to the former remain unsuspected, as there was every reason to conclude it would do, he might without difficulty so misdirect pursuit, as materially to favour the flight of his father. With a sense of humiliation that could not but be painful, he himself pointed out this circumstance; and was reduced, with whatever reluctance, to sink the demands of a nice but savage honour in the tender and indispensable duties of a son.

Arrangements that have their foundation in necessity are almost intuitively understood: those for the Count's journey had been previously made. A very few moments served to decide all that remained; and hardly one was given to that embrace which each party painfully felt might be their last. Conrad a second time named the Baths of Carlsbad as the place of meeting, if they were indeed ever to meet again. – After which most earnestly recommending despatch and vigour to his father, he once more leaped the wall, and Siegendorf once more found himself alone. – Alone indeed! – or rather in a horrible gloom peopled with frightful and distorted images, which presented to him the spectres of a guilty mind even in the moment of innocence. A single quarter of an hour appeared to have changed the position of every existing object, of every relative feeling! – He looked around, and hardly believed the same heaven shone over his head, or that the ground was solid beneath his feet. – He looked within, and found it even more difficult to conceive that his enemy was annihilated: that all traces of him would soon be concealed from every human eye: that he lived only to his; and that, by an almost incredible transition, he himself obliged to lament his loss! He began to feel that he should now, indeed, never escape him; that a strange ordination entwined their fates with each other; and that the grave must close on both, ere it could map the mysterious link of memory.

Josephine, who had for some time anxiously waited the return of her husband, at length came to seek him. At sight of her he started from the wild and tumultuous contemplation in which he had been engaged, and her presence, like that of a spirit of light, seemed for a while to dispel all evil. Snatching Marcellin by the hand, he now eagerly, though silently, led both towards their little vehicle, and placed them in it where it stood in the road, sheltered by the extremity of the garden wall. – The growing light of the sun was just visible on the tops of the distant mountains: the early cocks began to crow: every eye and every shutter as yet seemed closed in the town, when Siegendorf, at length, drove rapidly from it, carrying away with him confused images of blood, robbery, assassination, and disgrace, which he had travelled many leagues before he could dissipate.

The low and marshy grounds of the neighbourhood were passed with a celerity that did not permit them to see the dangers to which they exposed themselves. In proportion as they receded from the vicinity of the Oder, the traces of inundation, which had chiefly been on the side towards Frankfort, disappeared; and the road became progressively firmer. They were before so close upon the frontier as quickly to find themselves beyond the boundaries of Silesia; and the Count was well aware that the incessant hostilities which had long prevailed throughout the whole range of country, though now suspended in consequence of an armistice that was believed to be the forerunner of a general peace, had so shaken the very foundations of civil society, that the intermediate links between each district were broken; and the police nowhere sufficiently connected to reclaim any fugitive beyond a limit so narrow, that it was in all probability passed. They already breathed the purer air of the highlands, and found the benefit of the increasing light. That sacred stillness with which nature in elevated regions seems to receive the new-born day, was calculated, in its constitutional effects, to silence the irritation of the nerves and the heart. By degrees the soft lines of the horizon strengthened and became embodied: light, shade, and colours, successively diffused themselves over the surrounding objects; and all was beauty and harmony, save in the restless imagination of the Count, and the anxious feelings of his wife. Josephine, who had ever at intervals continued to look back, on reaching the heights directed her eye as far as its power could extend, to the whole tract of country around: it presented one vast and tranquil solitude, disturbed only by the soft undulations that swept before the breeze. A faint blue vapour, which seemed to rise like smoke from the valley, and was just visible between broken hills, announced, however, to her imagination at least, the hateful spot where so much sorrow and suffering had been encountered; and, with an eternal adieu, she blended a sigh at the recollection that it still detained Conrad. Alas! how would her maternal heart have been wrung with apprehension, could she have divined the circumstances under which he remained!

Before the travellers lay the woods that bound Lusatia to the east, and stretch in long and blackening shadow southwards towards Bohemia. It was the intention of the Count to skirt these, and on entering Saxony slowly emerge from the debasement to which circumstances had subjected him. In the progress of his journey it was not, however, among the least of his sufferings that anxiety for the possible fate of Conrad would not allow him to confide to the tender feelings of Josephine that gloomy secret which engrossed so large a share of his own: or even strengthen the belief he himself entertained, that the danger of pursuit had, from the moment of their departure, been far less than she suspected: for what individual, in the tumult and horror of those scenes which must immediately have succeeded, was likely to turn his attention to a being apparently so insignificant as Kruitzner – *His* enemy was silenced! *His* pursuer slept in eternal forgetfulness of all he had so lately coveted – all he had confidently assured himself that morning's sun would secure to him! The Intendant, it was plain by the report of Conrad, was in no condition to take the directing power out of the hands of the latter: Idenstein had most probably shared his excesses; and, were it otherwise, had, by a conduct alike venal and worthless, inadvertently involved his own fate so deeply with that of Kruitzner as obviously to render it more his interest to withhold, than to forward, any cause of suspicion against the latter. There, nevertheless, yet existed one crafty and vindictive being Siegendorf believed he ought reasonably to fear, and whom, of all others, though to him his crime had been useful, he was most inclined to abhor: – it was the Hungarian; who, if yet lurking in the woods, might prove a dangerous enemy, because a desperate one. The Count was, however, not defenceless; for Conrad, previous to their last parting, had supplied him with arms.

The travellers at length entered upon the entanglements of the forest, and had no other guide than that the wheel tracks formed by the peasants supplied. But though at a distance all had appeared dark and sombre, nature, at their nearer approach, put on a more smiling aspect, and seemed to delight in contrasting that gloom with which the vices and miseries of man had disfigured her. The sun had long been above the horizon, and had dispersed a thousand fleecy though beautiful clouds that hitherto impeded his brightness. His rays sometimes checkered the ground, and were sometimes wholly excluded by clustered branches that were yet only covered with the light foliage of spring. A rich and dewy moisture lay on the underwood beneath; at intervals reposing on patches of turf, that thus assumed the appearance of velvet, or swelled into large drops, which, trembling from the points of the leaves, sparkled like so many diamonds. The air was perfumed with fragrance, and the thickets filled with numerous sportive, but timid animals, seldom visible to the eye, though they occasionally scudded before it: while the birds, more secure in their airy habitations, answered each other in that delightful language which is at once music to the heart and the ear. Josephine, who in the contemplation of nature experienced a sacred feeling, that, while it swells the soul with rapture, fills the eye with tears, laid her hand in silence on that of her husband, and gently checked the speed with which he was driving: –

> 'For, over all, she saw the form divine,
> The Uncreate, in the created shine,
> Bright as in drops of dew the sun's reflected beam!'

The Count, startled by the action, looked earnestly around for some cause of alarm, and then at her. He had mechanically, rather than from any effort of will, continued to urge the horse forward: he now loosed him, and gave him a short but necessary respite.

Although Siegendorf and his family could hardly be said to enjoy safety in the forest, they yet encountered no positive danger there. The simplicity and meanness of their appearance offered little temptation to the wealthy robber, and from petty plunderers the athletic form, and undaunted eye of the Count, was in itself a sufficient protection. As they approached the borders of Saxony, they frequently met light parties of troops who scoured the country: but though by these were casually reconnoitred, they were never detained, and they found themselves at length decidedly within the territories of the electorate. Siegendorf, who was now familiar with almost every spot through which he was to pass, judged no method so certain of confounding all personal identity as that of pursuing their road by way of Leipsic.

It was near the season of the fair, and a prodigious concourse of strangers were daily assembling from all arts of Germany of a rank and description precisely opposite to those with whom the Count had ever associated. There was little probability that he should be recognized by any one; and Josephine was totally unknown. They, therefore, entered the gates of the city, in company with many others, at a late hour, and, stationing themselves in an obscure quarter, enjoyed a short and salutary repose. From thence, slowly journeying forward through devious roads, they daily increased their comforts, till they approached Carlsbad; where, on arriving, all traces of the abject and impoverished Kruitzner were finally absorbed in the increasing splendour and princely titles of Count Siegendorf.

The Count had not proceeded thus far on his journey without having found leisure to weigh more maturely the danger that attended not completing it. He had now reached that spot where he had pledged himself to wait the arrival of Conrad: an event his heart eagerly panted for, but which his prudence suggested to be a subordinate consideration to that of entering Prague. Various reasons daily concurred to strengthen this opinion: yet perhaps amongst them that restless inquietude which ever agitates the human heart at the near approach of any interesting struggle, and disposes it at all hazards to rush on to certainty, was not the least. A communication which the Count succeeded in establishing with one of his father's friends, informed him, that no claimant to the family estates and honours had hitherto appeared. The total silence which had long prevailed with regard to himself had, however, led to a general conclusion that the was no more. There was, apparently, therefore, no reason to doubt but Conrad, if on the spot, would have been the admitted heir. But the Count's correspondent added that his son had disappeared several weeks before the death of his grandfather, and that public expectation was at a loss to decide, 'Whether, from some peculiar circumstances in which he was supposed to stand, the claims of the collateral branch might not be received in preference to his.'

Siegendorf, too well aware that these circumstances referred to the birth of Conrad, and alive at once to all the danger of leaving conjecture busy with the name of either, perceived that his personal appearance alone could silence it. The occasion was critical, and loudly forbad all delicacy or delay; yet could he not resolve on re-entering Prague without experiencing a sensation that shook his very soul. The ill-omened hour in which he quitted it returned to his imagination in vivid colours;

and a thousand painful as well as humiliating recollections of the past started forward, to blend with a sort of half-apprehension from the novelty and strangeness of the future. He had no longer a father – hardly a country – still less a friend! – expatriated as he had been, and shook as the nation itself was to its very foundations, he felt that he should at best be received by it without being known – allowed without being claimed. Under this impression, he entered the gates like a man who expects them every moment to be closed against him; till well-remembered and familiar spots once more saluting his eye, he at length began to breathe freely: to rouse from that state of agitation which for a while rendered all objects visionary; to feel that he was still the son of Count Siegendorf; and to assure himself that the sorrow or degradation of the past was to be ranked henceforward among those fearful chimeras conjured up by the indiscretion of youth, and which fade of themselves before the season of maturity. This was, unhappily, a disposition of mind the Count was ever too much disposed to indulge. He had a natural propensity towards classing every error into which he plunged among the chances of the moment; – an insignificant link in the great chain of human events, and well deserving, therefore, to be snapped from it. The materials with which man forges his own fetters are seldom, however, of so brittle a nature! – but grievously as his had eaten into his soul, they had not yet changed its character: and, indeed, judgment far more steady might have been shaken from its equilibrium by the sudden transition to a station so splendid as that which he was now entitled to resume.

Elevating and tumultuous as the secret feelings of Siegendorf became, the deep-rooted pride of his nature, nevertheless, enabled him to conceal them. His exterior presented a man chastened, not subdued: – self-governed, not humbled; – and who, in the resumption of his rank, felt nothing so strongly as his claims. The city was at that period rising from its own ashes. Repeated sieges and pillage had reduced the inhabitants to despair, when the treaty*, which was on the point of being ratified, once more awakened all to vigorous exertion. The states were solemnly assembling, and Siegendorf presented himself before them like one arisen from the grave. There was something in the incident peculiarly in unison with the whole condition of society. All that was great or illustrious had undergone a temporary eclipse, and the hearts of men leaned with indulgence to every thing that

---

* Of Prague, signed May, 1635

looked like the restoration of order. Of those nobles whom the Count formerly believed to be his enemies, many had disappeared, as he had prophetically deemed they would, amidst the political convulsions of the times: others, who retained only a confused recollection of the past, were struck with silent respect at his appearance and demeanour: while the larger body, by whom the name of Seigendorf was habitually honoured, acknowledged, after little hesitation, the family lineaments and claims: the Count was received as its genuine representative with a facility which he had no reason to expect: its estates were made over to him; and he took formal possession of all the privileges and rights of nobility.

The proudly cherished hope of his heart, so long deferred, was then at length completed! Neither his own errors, nor the resentment of his father, had defeated his fortune! Josephine, in defiance of all obstacles, was raised to that eminence on which he had so much desired to place her: Conrad only was impatiently looked for, to fill the void in his affections; and neither ambition nor avarice could covet any gift that did not present itself at the shrine of his pride.

Amid the reflections thus gratifying, the Count could not forget that two acts of self-humiliation yet remained to be fulfilled before he could so discharge the past from his mind as fully to enjoy the future. The gold of the miserable Stralenheim was cankering on his hands and in his heart. Both pride and sensibility imperiously demanded its immediate application to some pious purpose; and it was accepted with gratitude by the religious of a neighbouring convent. The person and character of the donor were not unknown there, and they believed that God was calling home to himself a penitent, whose licentious life extorted from him this atonement. The second act of duty, though not less indispensable, carried with it a blended feeling from which he would willingly have shrunk, had decorum permitted: the self-acquittal it seemed to promise, nevertheless, induced him to fulfil it; and with a lingering and reluctant heart, he turned his steps towards the grave of his father.

Count Siegendorf had been buried in the great church at Prague: nor could his son see without emotion the simple monument dedicated to his memory; the sole memorial of one, who, whatever his faults, had fondly loved him. A sense of compunction irresistibly obtruded as he remembered the paternal remonstrances so often made on one side, and the filial reparation so vainly promised on the other. – All was now over: his father slept in that quiet sanctuary where no reparation could reach him, and whence no voice, save that of conscience, ever yet issued to a son. The Count, after a confused and painful meditation of some moments, turned from the spot. He then ordered a magnificent piece of sculpture to be placed over it; and there elative ideas, if not expelled from his bosom, were at least blended with such as more immediately interested him, when, on his return to the palace, he found a billet from Conrad. It was forwarded from Carlsbad by the courier who had been despatched thither to receive either that or the writer, and announced the speedy approach of the latter; communicating at the same time, in mysterious terms, the important intelligence that all had gone well since they parted.

The Count, relieved thus from the deep anxiety he had hitherto experienced with respect to the situation of his son, now prepared to revisit his own patrimonial estates. Princely as they were, and defended by the vassals of the family, they had not wholly escaped devastation, though their vicinty to Prague had secured them from an evil more horrible than even war itself had inflicted. Arms were, indeed, no longer the sole employment of Bohemia; but unhappily that licentiousness which becomes the habit of a nation after any long and bloody struggle had not subsided there. For more than twenty years, all Germany had been a theatre of warfare and desolation; where numerous hordes of banditti, lurking in the fastnesses of mountains, or in the recesses of forests, were ready to pour down upon the weak and the unguarded. Mercenaries in the open field, it was not wonderful that in private scenes of action such men should become robbers and assassins. Yet, veiling the atrocity of their conduct under specious pretences, they frequently gave the name of justice to the most bloody revenge; and in default of those laws, to which, indeed, the circumstances of the times allowed little efficacy, they executed their own verdicts with the most unrelenting cruelty. Nor were these excesses confined to the base and the ignorant: – souls class *themselves*; and among the higher orders of the community some stood strongly suspected by the state of allying the animal nature too closely to the human and of wasting, in savage and ferocious pleasures, those gifts which were bestowed for the sacred purposes of protection and kindness. The enormities of such men had not even the common palliation of neccessity: riotous, on the contrary, with prosperity and youth, their faculties, like some kind of plants, seemed to have grown rank by the very richness and exuberance of the soil on which they fell. From invaders like these no spot had hitherto been secure: they came no one knew whence, vanished no one knew whither; and when they re-appeared, it was in such scenes of splendour or force as suspicion dared not invade: their partisans, as well as themselves, were invisible; and, like the cur who slaughters the sheep in the night, reposed sleek and quiet at their master's door in the morning.

The castle of Siegendorf, covering a territory in itself, and equally secured by its bulwarks, and neighbourhood to the capital, bore, however, no traces of a desolation from the contemplation of which the soft and voluptuous character of the Count induced him to revolt with peculiar horror. His return there, at a crisis so little expected, seemed to operate like a charm upon every individual within his estates. Crowds to whom he was personally unknown hastened to greet him. Nature herself seemed to welcome his approach, and to put forth the loveliest colours of her loveliest season. Joy, acclamation, and an enlivening spirit, pursued his footsteps: the young spoke with generous indignation of the reports transmitted by their elders; while the latter, to whom the excesses of his youthful days were known, saw, with delight and surprise, the alteration which time appeared to have effected. They admired the temperate dignity of his manner, the equanimity with which he entered again upon his former fortunes, and the sobriety of his domestic establishment: they were never weary of gazing on Josephine and her blooming boy: the castle was presently filled with innumerable retainers, together with all the pomp, civil or military, of a Magnate of the feudal times; and it was at the crisis of universal festivity that Conrad arrived to partake it.

The past, however, it quickly appeared, had not faded from the recollection of Conrad in the same degree which it seemed to have done from that of his father: and his presence, therefore, by an effect to others wholly inexplicable, first chilled the glow of exultation and felicity in the bosom of the latter. The events that yet remained to be related by Conrad were, indeed, of a nature again to darken the imagination of both: however favourable in themselves, they were, at best, but the winding up of a black and gloomy tragedy; and all the horrible suggestions that arise from blood yet unappeased insensibly presented themselves, and mingled with the detail. That reluctance the Count had ever felt to shock Josephine with it had been increased by his late habits of reserve, and became almost invincible, when he reflected on the security and happiness in which she now reposed. He himself learned with deep, though useless, and therefore silent regret, that the Hungarian had escaped all research. That the

Intendant, stunned by the danger which he apprehended from his own indiscretion, had, for the most part, confided in Conrad, or taken such feeble and undecided steps as were of little avail in the pursuit of the criminal. That Idenstein, equally selfish, had even tacitly assisted to baffle the measures he pretended to enforce, through fear of being involved in their consequences. Finally, that the wretched Stralenheim – unknown, unlamented – had been hurried to an obscure grave; and that vague depositions, lodged in the hands of magistrates little disposed to interest themselves in the fate of an alien, seemed all the reparation likely to attend his memory.

Selfish and proud as was the nature of the Count, there was constitutionally a sort of tender point in it, which the mode of his very pleasures and pursuits had contributed to increase. Mystery and blood were offensive to his imagination; yet had he so closely entwined both in his own fate, as to render it almost impossible to free his recollection from either. Nor was his pride less wounded than his sensibility, when he remembered that there existed a spot upon the globe, where, though he himself might indeed remain for ever unknown, his person was devoted to infamy; where the name he had borne would be deemed synonymous with robbery and murder; and where to be seen only, was to incur the penalty of the rack.

These were particulars Conrad could not conceal; nor did the character of the latter appear gifted with the refinement that might have taught him to think it necessary to do so. The past still seemed too strongly impressed upon his mind, to permit him to lose sight of it: and Siegendorf, who, in the tumultuous succession of feelings incident to his own change of fortune, had lost, for a time, the bitterness of retrospection so long the habit of his heart, yet knew well how to allow for it in that of his son. Conrad, nevertheless, felt for his mother; and strongly urged the Count to conceal from her a secret offensive to the sensibility of her sex, and which might encumber her with a thousand weak fears, or superfluous regrets, calculated to embitter the future lives of all. Seigendorf had discernment enough to trace in the tender consideration thus shown by his son a proud repugnance to the avowal of those degradations which the circumstances of his situation had obliged him to endure: but it was an allowable pride; it had yielded only to the safety of his father; nor could the latter resolve to extort a farther sacrifice: he, therefore, acceded to a reserve which he had never till lately practised towards Josephine; and, with a generous, though half sullen tenderness, strove to confine to himself feelings he yet found it would be impossible ever to silence; – the aching consciousness of a sullied mind – a sort of accessary guilt – and an indefinite remorse! Nor was this, alas! the only cankerous speck upon the apparent prosperity of Siegendorf! a sort of secret foreknowledge; which is, in fact, only a nice calculation made by the feelings, before we permit it to become an operation of the judgment, already corroded that distinguished lot fortune seemed to have prepared for him.

The employments of the Count had been hitherto so numerous, and his reflections so much engaged, as to have precluded the discharge of various duties imposed upon him by the nature of his situation. The rank he held in the state, together with the favour shown him by the Imperial court, bade him hope for the highest honours either could bestow: yet, alienated as he had been from his family, it was not possible for him to know what had been its views or connections during his absence, except by an examination of his father's papers. To the memory of that father the Count had not yet learned to be just. The habitual resentment he had permitted himself to cherish against him while living had even withered those sensibilities which so often wait to ripen over the grave: and though; in returning to his native domain, Siegendorf could not wholly divest himself of local and tender recollections, the circumstances succeeding his return had blunted their force: nor had he been desirous to conceal from himself, that he retrod, with exultation, spots whence he had at one time believed paternal authority for ever excluded him; and triumphed in the consciousness of having vindicated his own rights and judgment. Hours of reflection had succeeded these temporary transports; and had combined with some late observations to create a secretly agitating feeling, which impelled him to enter with the deepest interest upon the investigation: shutting himself up, therefore, alone in his chamber at a late hour he prepared to fulfil it.

In reviewing either the political or military transactions of his father, the Count found little interest, though some information. The party under which the former had acted was now wholly subdued; and the latter, from the early bias of his life, rather than any just mode of thinking, had ever cherished a decided preference for the Austrian cause, which the favour shown him by its leaders had considerably strengthened. Passing, therefore, rapidly forwards, he fell upon such papers as more immediately related to himself: they were of a nature to touch the most secret recesses of his soul; and never had the occurrences of his early life been presented in colours so vivid, or so touching, as in the affecting comments which solitude and affliction left his father leisure to make upon them. He pursued the examination with still increasing interest as the dates grew nearer and nearer to late events. At length he reached that which ascertained the exact period of Conrad's departure from the castle. The chain there snapped; but while the mutilated and imperfect fragment announced no reality, they left a field for conjecture respecting the conduct of the latter, at once singular and alarming. With conjecture, indeed, the Count had been before too busy; but never had his imagination extended to that fearful point which now indistinctly presented itself. A palpitation seized his heart: his head swam, his eyes were darkened: by a violent effort he again attempted to read, but all that followed seemed confusion and mystery. His father had survived many weeks – long enough, indeed, to be convinced that the defection of Conrad, which it was obvious he had in the first instance considered as an insidious violation of the compact between himself and his son, had, in reality, not originated in any seduction employed the latter. That Count Siegendorf had in consequence of this conviction again written to Humburgh to re-establish the correspondence and remittances there upon their former footing, was rendered sufficiently clear by many annexed memoranda. Unhappily the dates of these second letters proved them to have been despatched too late: they were among the last acts of his life, and reached not their destination till he for whose advantage they were intended had studiously escaped all research, and was on his way to Silesia. The remaining papers of the afflicted and venerable parent tended therefore only to discover a broken heart – a heart deeply lacerated by his son, and finally broken by some inexplicable misconduct on the part of Conrad. What an image to present to his eyes who was now in turn become a father, and who had already learned to fear that he might not prove a happy one!

Awful were the phantoms which midnight and deep contrition united to call up before the imagination of the Count; and it was at the very climax of his worldly prosperity that the sceptre, *conscience*, first appeared to him. He banished it, and strove by a more regular examination of the papers to detect some error that might at least dispel a part of his inquietude. His researches were fruitless: every succeeding memorandum but proved more incontestably that the fatal billet sent to Hamburgh, which consigned him to poverty – nay, in its effect, almost to madness – had been written immediately under the influence of a resentment excited in his father by the desertion of Conrad; and that he had himself consequently owed to the imprudence of the latter in quitting Bohemia the most afflicting calamity of his life. – Yet that imprudence, fatal as it proved, and sullied as it possibly had been by errors of a less venial nature, was, at worst, only the pardonable consequence of filial fondness and duty! at least thus officiously argued the heart of the Count. – Ay, indeed! Who testified this? – Conrad! and *Conrad only!* – but his subsequent conduct had confirmed it. – How? in what instance? – He had adopted the cause of his family: – was it not his own? – By an effort of painful and humiliating duplicity he had extricated his father from disgrace: – Could any thing but his father's personal appearance at Prague have saved him from that of illegitimacy? – He had restored the latter to his hereditary rights and honours: – not so! – he had indeed assisted in giving him liberty; or rather, he had lengthened his chain. He had bound him by a solemn promise, which nothing but the exigency of circumstances had induced the Count to violate, to attend his own arrival at Carlsbad. – When that promise *was* violated, when Conrad *did* arrive, not at Carlsbad, indeed, but at the castle of Siegendorf, and found his father invested by the state with unlimited possession, did his countenance announce *his* share in the general joy? – Did his voice rise with the general acclamation? – Alas, no! – It was precisely at that critical moment the Count had learned to doubt. Conrad, ever meditative and observing from the first hour he had presented himself to his parents, had on the second occasion, however different the circumstances, manifested the same reserve, the same abstraction, the same haughty distrust. He neither appeared to give, not take joy: every eye had sunk before his, and every voice had been hushed into silence. Neither his youth, the grandeur of his person, nor that lustre which attends the rights of an heir, had created any exultation at his presence. Even the most indulgent of his parents had discovered that he was not beloved; and the feelings of both had secretly assigned the reason – he was not capable of loving.

But although the exterior of Conrad dazzled not the eyes of dispassionate observers, the Count had now learned to suspect that it might too successfully have misled the hearts of Josephine and himself; or rather that those tender hearts had been duped by their own sensibility, and that the agitating moment of their son's appearance at M— had converted into an angel of light the being who shone upon them amidst such a gloom. It was even because he was not a hypocrite that he had, perhaps, best deceived them: the character of his mind accorded too well with every circumstance of time and place; and when to smile would have been to insult their feelings, was it necessary to disguise his own? Such were the reflections of Siegendorf; which like a stream swelled by many small and invisible springs, now suddenly acquired the force of a torrent, and rushed forward with irresistible rapidity. He still held the papers in his hand; but he read them not – he saw them not. Questions which even in the bosom of misery, and during their short meetings at M—, had not escaped him, now passed in tumultuous succession through his memory. If Conrad really sought his father, why was he found wandering so far from the track that should have led to him? By what accident was a being so detestable as the Hungarian his associate? and wherefore did he bury beneath an obscure appearance his own name and condition in life? During the short and anxious meetings that preceeded the Count's departure from Silesia, some cruelly impending evil had ever banished those interesting subjects on which the ear of affection delights to dwell. The details of Conrad had necessarily been then concise and imperfect: there was even a sort of anticipated pleasure in permitting them to be so. The narrative of the past was suspended to enrich the future – to fill up many an evening of social and domestic intercourse with than innocent but exquisite luxury which arises to tender hearts when they interchange their history and their feelings. Those hours of leisure were now come, but they had not brought the pleasure which should have gilded them. Conrad, after the first meeting between himself and his father, had been little at the castle of Siegendorf. His manners, when there, were forbidding; his communications cold and unsatisfactory: he sought no intercourse; he desired no confidence; he delighted only, as it appeared, in such sports or exercises as withdrew him from his parents; and behind the more prominent features of his character a discerning eye might perceive some, which thrown, as it were, into dark shadow, inspired an apprehension the more acute from their very indistinctness. – Alas! was such then in reality the darling son of Siegendorf; the promised comforter of his future life; the cherished being on whom he had gazed in childhood, and so ardently desired to elevate to that point where fortune in very malice had now placed him.

That Conrad was placed in a sphere far beyond his mother's influence, Josephine was also deeply sensible; but her affliction was little tinctured with surprise. The habits of her mind, unlike those of Siegendorf, ever leading her to discriminate the sensations and opinions of others, created that nice perception of character to which he was a stranger. – By an effect, therefore, less of judgement than of feeling, she quickly understood that of Conrad; and though sensible that there might have been hearts over which hers would have possessed an influence at almost any period of life, she perceived his was not of that description. This, with many other sorrows, alike impossible to remedy, she endeavoured to forget, or rather to confine to the sanctuary of her own bosom: for Josephine was no longer the creature of philosophy and solitude. Agitated incessantly by the turbulence of Siegendorf's character, yet thrown back upon herself, she had contemplated with an aching sensibility, and an observing judgment, that mass of passion, inconsistency, and suffering, by which life is disfigured. Successive conflicts had insensibly given to her own character a deeper, but a softer shade; and if it did not appear tinctured with sadness, it was because sadness itself took the colour of resignation. The first found love of a virtuous woman's heart is, nevertheless, a tenacious sentiment: hers, sanctified by every tie, had survived almost every disappointment. In ceasing therefore, to feel with her husband, she had not ceased to feel for him; and the affections ever in some degree reward themselves, by the animating principle they create throughout the bosoms in which they are deeply rooted.

Possessed as Josephine was with the belief that Siegendorf's wishes were at length amply gratified by the resumption of his patrimonial rights; that Stralenheim had withdrawn his pretensions from a conviction of their inutility; and that nothing stood between the Count and all he could desire of happiness but the disposition of his mind, and a shade of displeasure towards his son, she earnestly strove to correct the one, and to palliate the bitterness of the other. Magnificence, as far as it respected her own gratification, she had never yet coveted. The first sorrow that ever assailed her had been introduced by the remote prospect of it; but she believed it necessary to the felicity of her husband, and, therefore, had rejoiced in the acquisition. It was consequently with surprise, as well as regret, that she saw its effect upon their different characters; and felt, that, while it elevated one, it depressed the other. By multiplying her sympathies, and extending her benevolence, it indeed afforded her a new spring of existence; while in him it seemed gradually to increase the apathy of a joyless and exhausted heart.

Joyless, indeed, was the heart of Siegendorf! – nor could either the splendour of art, or the beauties of nature, fill up the void. To him

'The disenchanted earth lost all its lustre.'

He had embittered the paradise around, and found it impossible to banish ideas that were his torment. The Count had quitted Bohemia in the plenitude of health and vigour – every appetite and passion alike ripe for enjoyment, and impatient of restraint. Since those days of inebriation, half the circle of life had revolved, and its irresistible progress had placed him precisely in that sphere of existence which his father formerly occupied. Conrad now filled his. In all, save identity of persons, they were the same; – too much resembling in the tenor, though not in the features of their characters. But life no longer presented to Siegendorf those allurements which in early youth had rendered him indifferent to the value of the affections; and, from the moment he had regained Conrad, it had, therefore, been among the most passionate wishes of his heart to be beloved by him. This wish was, however, defeated by the very first meeting between himself and his son: for Conrad, it had been evident, from that period, neither loved nor esteemed his father: – the past, therefore, became a blank, and the future a field of anxious and fearful apprehension: – a melancholy, deep, silent, unconquerable, took possession of the mind of the Count, as he continued to meditate on both: a melancholy so nearly allied to remorse, as to find food for the latter even in what appeared only the common chance of circumstances; for he insensibly began to persuade himself that it communicated its influence to every thing within his circle: nor was the observation founded on chimera, whatever the application might be. His castle no longer wore the same aspect of cheerfulness with which it had greeted him: his native followers and retainers strangely diminished: their places were supplied by persons unknown to him, and by whom he had no appearance of being beloved. The crowds that had returned to his estates with alacrity, that had officiously sought his presence, and implored to be admitted under his protection, either fulfilled their duties with coldness, or silently abandoned them: the voice of joy was no longer heard, and industry no longer exerted itself: while even the domestic retinue passed silently through the apartments of the castle, and seemed mutually to distrust each other.

The mind and constitution of Siegendorf became shaken; and such was the irritable state of his nerves, that a thousand wild, chimerical, and even superstitious fears assailed him by turns. Was Slander busy with his name? Did any secret whisper from Idenstein or the Intendant remotely pursue his footsteps? – Was the Hungarian at hand to plan fresh scenes of blood? Or did the spirit of Stralenheim walk abroad to wither the prosperity of that man who had opened the door of murder upon him? – Every method taken to trace the evil to its source, for an evil it too obviously was, – proved alike unsuccessful. Superstition did not, even on the minutest investigation, appear to have peopled the castle within; no enemy threatened the person of the Count without; yet a secret and inexplicable curse seemed to hang over its walls, and the miserable Siegendorf was at length obliged to conclude that it was the malediction of a father.

Unable to control or endure these gloomy ideas, the Count at length quitted his own estates and fixed his temporary residence at Prague. He was received there by the ministers of the Imperial court with a distinction eminently flattering to his public character, and which, if it afforded no real solace to his feelings, at least diminished their acuteness, and forced him upon occupations that expelled the constant recollection of himself. He had now reached the maturity of life; and the intense thought that marked his features, insensibly impressed those around with the deference due to a superior mind. Apparently devoid of arrogance of ambition, yet rising gradually to every honour that could gratify either, he seemed to live, while yet in the world, like a man whose soul is already beyond it; and through an effect of that singular deception sometimes produced by invisible causes, those who penetrated not beyond the surface soon accustomed themselves to look upon Count Siegendorf as not only amidst the most prosperous, but the most meritorious of the favourites of fortune. All hearts but one seemed to welcome and applaud him: yet to that only one, the esteem of which he feared he had irrecoverably lost, his invariably turned with a tenacious fondness that was fated to be his misery.

But while sadness and desolation thus reigned within the immediate circle where the Count had hoped to find joy, she appeared to have taken up her residence where desolation had indeed long prevailed. The kingdom, torn by a series of fierce and bloody contests, prepared at length to enjoy the peace for which it ardently panted. The preliminaries, so long in agitation, had in the bare prospect awakened the spirit of the people; and the ratification, recently signed, communicated that transport peculiar to a suffering multitude. A day of festivity was appointed: solemn thanks, and every ceremony, religious or civil, was ordered to attend it; and man, recovering a blessing to which he so often voluntarily deprives himself, seemed to believe he could want no other.

The rank and indispensible duties of the Count called him early from his palace, though a fluctuating state of health, and a deep depression of spirits, little disposed him to share the activity he found abroad. At sunrise every window of the city had been decorated with flowers or streamers: frankincense from the censers perfumed the air; consecrated images were offered with devout awe from hand to hand; and processions of the various religious orders were seen passing in different directions. The attention of the multitude was, however, chiefly engaged by that of the States, which moved solemnly towards the great church, attended by the Imperial and national guards, and composed of all that was most splendid or illustrious in the kingdom. Spacious as was the building, it was immediately filled. The nobles, the populace, youth – age – an immense concourse, quickly hastened in: the doors were then closed, and the hum and press of the multitude insensibly subsided to a low murmur: – that ceased! – every knee was bowed – every head was devoutly inclined downwards; while the various military bands played some of those sacred and almost divine airs which supply language to the soul when she faints under the want of it. Happy for each individual had this sentiment of devotion, so grand and impressive in the exterior, conveyed its purifying influence to the heart! That of Siegendorf was deeply moved. No word, indeed, escaped his lips: but while the long here and hereafter passed through his imagination, the silent and secret aspiration they dictated was not unheard. From the posture in which he had mechanically continued, the Count was at length roused by the rush of the multitude around, and the grand burst of the *Te Deum*. He arose with the rest: when, casting his eye, from the elevated situation in which he stood, upon the long though distant line of human faces beneath, he suddenly fancied he saw that of the Hungarian amongst them. – A mist obscured the sight of Siegendorf, and a shock like that of electricity ran through his frame. So deep, indeed, had been the abstraction of his mind, that the revulsion of the senses was almost too mighty for his bodily strength. By a vigorous effort he recovered his powers of perception, and again eagerly looked forward. But the crowd had in the interim moved toward the gates. The sway and pressure caused every space to be immediately occupied by new-comers, nor could the most penetrating gaze ascertain the place or features of an individual.

Those turbulent passions, once so habitual in the character of the Count, now impatiently strove again to burst forth. Vainly, however, did he look above, around, below, for some sympathising bosom, some answering eye that could at once catch and comprehend all that his would have conveyed. Encumbered with pomp and empty distinction, he found it equally impossible to quit his own rank, or summon Conrad from the distant one in which he was stationed. The train meantime continued to move on, and the Count was reduced still to make a part of that pageantry to which both his senses and his soul were alike insensible. It at length reached the river. The broad expanse of the Muldau was covered with innumerable boats and vessels, which displayed their streamers to the sun, and with incessant motion dazzled the eye by their brightness and variety. On the centre of the bridge, itself a sublime and commanding spectacle, the elevated banners of the nation were seen to pass, escorted by the younger nobility; while the thunder of their music, which, with a more sprightly movement, swelled above the pitch of that sacred and imposing solemnity it had so lately assumed, was now distinctly heard, amid the trampling of the populace, and the confused shouts of a multitude who at every pause rent the air with joyful acclamations.

Siegendorf, after vainly continuing to strain his powers of sight in search of the Hungarian, rested them, at length, on the helmet of Conrad, distinguished by his superior stature, among the rest; and though to exchange a single glance was beyond all force of vision, the anxious father darted his eye forward, as if by a supernatural effort he could make the perturbed feelings of his own bosom known to that of his son.

The name of *Kruitzner*, articulated precisely at this moment, in that low, deep, and deliberate tone which makes itself heard even amid general clamour, suddenly arrested the attention of the Count. Without sufficient presence of mind to recollect the danger of recognising the name, Siegendorf turned hastily towards the speaker, and within the distance of a very few paces again beheld the features of the Hungarian. He was not to be mistaken. He wore the dress of his country, and fixed upon the Count a glance so worldly and alarming as caused the heart of the latter to start, as it were, from its place, and involuntarily to stand upon the defensive. Siegendorf perceiving him again about to escape among the multitude, stretched out his arm to detain him: but the strong emotion of his own mind caused him at the same moment to stagger; and as the accompanying change of countenance announced an indisposition that almost approached to swooning, the action was misconstrued. The zeal of those near made them press closely around; and before his powers of recollection returned he found himself dragged, not merely from the spot, but even from all probability of regaining it. The fact was, however, indubitable: the recognition had even been mutual: and the Count saw a horrible and indefinite evil impending over his head, by the uncertain apprehension of which, life, and every good it could bestow, must of necessity be blasted. Of earthly goods, his honour and his estimation in society were now become the dearest: yet it was exactly those, perhaps, indeed those only, of which the Hungarian might deprive him. The unsettled but painful sentiment that had so long harassed the bosom of Siegendorf, uniting with the tumultuous feelings of the moment, now rose to a point of almost desperate energy. He could not fly to Josephine for solace. She was happily ignorant of the dark and complicated history his recollections involved. The feelings of Conrad he had but too much reason to know rarely accorded with his. It was, nevertheless, to Conrad – and to Conrad only, he could venture to communicate them: yet even this relief was denied; for the latter, though summoned, was many hours before he appeared.

The Count, meantime, solitary in the midst of his palace, grew every succeeding moment more and more a prey to the irritability of his feelings; till nothing predominated by an unextinguishable desire to appease them by assuring himself at least of the person of the Hungarian. To accomplish, this, however, required a method and deliberation to which he was little equal: he chose out, nevertheless, such of his domestics as he could best confide in; and describing, with minuteness, the dress and figure of the man he sought, enjoined them to make such inquiries as might at least ascertain his pursuits and his residence. Their absence was long, and their researches fruitless. The return of Conrad in the interim, earnestly as it had been desired, afforded little relief to the agitated heart of his father; who found it impossible to make him enter into the feelings by which he was himself actuated; and who even felt that he had no right to expect that he should do so. Conrad, in remaining at M—, so long after the departure of the Count, had amply discharged all due to honour and to justice. It was Siegendorf alone who had shrunk from what either dictated. It was he who had deserted the defence of his own honour; who had left to his son a painful responsibility, for which, as it appeared, no gratitude could reward him: an odious tax of duplicity and meanness, that had debased the minds of both, and created a spirit of distrust and alienation which time itself seemed unable to remove. Was it then the part of Siefendorf to resent that his son could not sympathise with him? Ah! had he not much more reason to regret that he had not earlier sympathised with his son?

While the Count was thus secretly tortured by feelings which retrospection and inflamed sensibility had long since engendered, day insensibly began to close, and the events of the morning were almost driven from his thought by the deep and varied contemplations that engrossed them; when his domestics, in announcing the request of a stranger to see him, at once recalled the whole. The Count, struck with a sudden conviction that he was on the point of receiving some tidings of the man he sought, commanded, without hesitation, that the inquirer should be admitted: the doors were instantly thrown open by his attendants; and, to the utter astonishment of Siegendorf, the Hungarian himself appeared at the threshold. He advance a few steps, and then looked earnestly around, with the air of a man who receives a deep impression from the scene before him, though not exactly that of common or vulgar surprise. To him who recollected the circumstances under which parties present had before met, those of the moment were indeed calculated to create a sensation not easily conquered.

They stood in the inner but most magnificent hall of the palace. It was of Gothic architecture, grand, spacious, and gloomy. The last rays of a western sun shot obliquely between the massy pillars, and gilded the trophies and banners of the family of Siegendorf as they were suspended around. The Count himself was at the upper end. He was splendidly habited for the ceremony of the morning, and the insignia of various orders with which he had been invested sparkled at his bosom. Conrad, so lately entered, had not yet thrown aside the high military plume or the sabre by which the younger nobility had been universally distinguished; and the appearance of both was in singular contrast to the simple, though characteristic garb of the Hungarian, who stood in dark shadow below.

'*It is Kruitzner?*' again repeated the latter, in a tone of slow and deliberate interrogation. The Count, who scorned longer to dissemble, inclined his head with a token of acquiescence, While Conrad, in astonishment at the scene, folded his arms, and, drawing near, fixed a steady gaze on the inquirer. The Hungarian again looked around, as if, satisfied at length of the identity of the persons, he was comparing what he saw with what he recollected: then advancing, with no less

The Canterbury Tales

firmness than before, 'Your people', said he, 'I understand, have made inquiries concerning me: – I am here!'

There was a simplicity both in the speech, and the manner of delivering it, that staggered the Count. But he recovered his presence of mind; and, by a proud effort, strove to assume that self-possession which seemed to mark the Hungarian.

'It was by my command that you were sought,' said he: 'The monitor within will sufficiently explain my motive! – you stand suspected of an atrocious crime: – acquit yourself – or prepare to attend its consequences.'

'I come to meet them. Who are my accusers?' – Siegendorf hesitated.

'The general voice – mine in particular: the time, the place, and every probability that authorises either internal or presumptive evidence.'

'Did these attach suspicion to no other name than mine? Recollect well before you speak,'

'Prevaricator!' exclaimed the Count, roused to his accustomed pride and fierceness by the implied accusation.

'Of all existing beings,' pursued he, after an agitating pause, 'you best can attest the innocence of the man you allude to. But I hold no other conference with a murderer than that which an overwhelming sense of equity demands of me. Answer directly to my charge.'

'I deny the crime altogether!' 'Upon what ground?'

'Because I know the criminal.' 'Name him.' 'He stands beside you;' and he pointed to Conrad. The Count, who had roused his whole soul to dare the accusation in his own person, recoiled speechless and aghast; but perceiving Conrad start forward to aim a desperate vengeance at his accuser, he threw himself, without hesitation between them.

'Liar and defamer!' exclaimed Siegendorf. 'This,' he added, turning to his son, 'is indeed a calumny so monstrous that I was not prepared for it!' The lip of Conrad was pale: his eyes rolled with a singular expression; and there was that in his features which struck a chord within his father's bosom that never yet had vibrated. He saw them convulsed, as they had appeared by starlight in the Prince's garden at M—; and both the heart and countenance of Siegendorf for a moment fell.

'Count,' said the Hungarian, who attentively scrutinised the looks of the latter, 'I came hither with no light or fluctuating resolution; yet let me premise that I sought not this occasion, nor was it even possible for me so to do. When I knelt with the multitude in the great church, curiosity alone attracted me thither. By what extraordinary calculation, indeed, could I suspect that among senators and nobles I should behold the forlorn and destitute Kruitzner? By what calculation still more extraordinary could I guess that under such circumstances, he would ever again desire to behold me? He *has* desired it, and we have met. Before we proceed further, answer me at once, who profited by the murder of Baron Stralenheim? Was it the man, think ye, who became immediately after an outcast and a beggar? The Baron, *on that occasion*, lost neither gold nor jewels: it was his life only the assassin sought; and that life was the sole bar to a rich and contested inheritance.'

'These, said the Count, again fired by interrogations which he felt to be equally fallacious and inconclusive, 'are surmises that attach no less to myself than to my son.'

'Be it so. Let the issue light on him amongst us whose soul secretly acknowledges the crime! It is to you only, Count Siegendorf, I now speak. You are my accuser and self-created judge. Beware, therefore, how you incur the penalty of collusive guilt! I have submitted voluntarily to your tribunal; and, remember, I demand justice from you, as you expect it either here or hereafter! My narrative,' continued he, perceiving the Count had no words to interrupt him, 'will be long: it will include a period to the events of which you are probably a stranger, and an accusation no less deadly to your peace than that you have already heard. *Dare* you protect me? *dare* you enjoin me to proceed?'

Siegendorf would have spoken, but his lips refused their office. He once more motioned with his head, however, in acquiescence; yet was there something savage, and alarming in the tone of the Hungarian, at which his soul indignantly, though apprehensively, revolted. Conrad, whom it seemed to have roused, awakened to curiosity by the whole of this extraordinary exordium, leaned with an undaunted and contemptuous air against the pillar near which he stood. He had detached his sabre from his side, and occupied himself in forming fantastic lines with it on the marble below: now and then he half unsheathed it, and seemed curiously to examine its polish.

'I am unarmed, Count,' said the Hungarian, who kept a watchful and steady eye upon him. 'Command your son to lay aside his weapon.' Conrad smiled disdainfully; and, returning the sabre to its scabbard, threw it some paces from him.

'Proceed safely,' said he: 'the tale will, now doubt, be worthy of the relater; but is it worthy of my father to listen to it?'

215

The Count, who had recovered from the first shock of an over-anxious mind, and more deliberately weighed the dark and suspicious character of the man before him, penetrated by this indirect reproach, extended his hand fondly towards his son, in token of unshaken confidence and love. The brow of the Hungarian changed: it seemed to be among his peculiar characteristics to analyse exactly every transition of sentiment in the bosoms of those around him; and, by an instantaneous impression, he felt that he stood on different ground both with father and son from that he had occupied a few moments before. His own purpose seemed shaken, and he paused for a considerable time before he proceeded further.

'It will be unnecessary,' said he at length, 'to enter into any detail that respects only myself. I was thrown early upon the world, and *am* what it has made me. Circumstances induced me to spend the winter that preceded your arrival M— at Frankfort on the Oder. I lived obscurely; but I occasionally frequented the coffee-houses and other public meetings; and I generally, therefore, knew something of what was passing in the city. Towards the middle of the month of February, a singular occurrence engaged attention, and formed the common topic of discourse there. A military party had secured, upon the borders of Lusatia, a desperate band of men, who were conjectured to be marauders from the Austrian camps. It proved otherwise, however; for further investigation left little room to doubt that they were part of a more wanton and lawless association which infested the forests of Bohemia, and whom either accident or savage audacity had carried beyond their accustomed haunts. Some among them were reported to be of distinguished rank; and military vengeance had been, therefore, suspended: they were escorted through different outposts, and placed at length within the jurisdiction of the civil magistrates at Frankfort. Of *their* fate I know nothing.' Siegendorf breathed; but it was only to be doubly roused by what followed. 'The curiosity it had excited seemed suddenly to die away, or to be authoritatively silenced; and there was only a certain limit within which rumour still dared to whisper tidings concerning it, or rather to condense all in the wonderful report she gave of one man amongst them. His birth and fortune were said to be princely; miraculous stories were related both of his natural and acquired advantages; his person was exaggerated to something super-human, both as to strength and to beauty; his prowess was deemed unrivalled; and his influence, not only over his associates, but even with those who should have been his judges, was represented to be almost that of witchcraft. I had no faith in the influence of any advantage where the latter were concerned, but that of wealth; and I therefore concluded he was rich. My curiosity, as well as some other feelings, were excited; and I made it my employment to seek out this extraordinary and mysterious being. Such, however, was the awe he inspired, through the protection afforded him by the police, that though I suspected many within my circle of knowing his person, none dared to identify it to me. I was left to the burnings of my own impatience, when by accident, and in the public square, I encountered your son. It was a popular affray that drew us together; but it happened to be one of those singular occasions when the human mind breaks loose from the fetters of habit and society, and betrays its character upon the countenance. My eye no sooner fell upon his, than I said to myself, "This is the man!" He was then, as since, with the nobles of the city; but I, nevertheless, felt that I was not mistaken. I watched him long and closely; I compared what I had been told with what I then observed; I examined his person, his gesture, the varying expression of his features; I noted down in my memory all those minute characteristics which pass unobserved by common perception; and, amid every distinction of nature or of fortune, I believed I discerned the feelings of a gladiator and the eye of an assassin.'

Siegendorf, who had 'drank poisons' as the Hungarian continued to speak, started from his seat at the concluding sentence with a desperation almost approaching to frenzy. – Not so, Conrad, who, collected within himself, motioned to his father to be silent; and, turning full towards the Hungarian, prepared with steady, but intense curiosity, to hear the rest.

'I now believed I had found the sort of man I so long sought; and having, by indefatigable perseverance, at length gained circumstantial information on this point, I waited my opportunity, and introduced myself to his notice. It was not difficult,' added he, with a malicious smile, 'to perceive that my attentions were undesired, but I was not to be repelled: the more he strove to disencumber himself of me, the more I felt persuaded of the truth of my own calculations. It was upon men like him that I had seen the less lucky or less daring of their fellow beings fated to depend; and I felt an ill-founded assurance, as it afterwards proved, that I had discovered my point of fortune. – The nameless and inexplicable shadow that thus haunted the footsteps of your son soon became, as I believed it would do, a scourge and an oppression to him: but I grew at length familiar

The Canterbury Tales

to his eye, and he seemed to understand my meaning. He was on the point of secretly withdrawing from Frankfort. I discovered this, and he knew I did; our intercourse increased; my hopes increased with it: and though I could not fathom the motives of his irregular conduct, I learned enough from his habits and education to doubt my own sagacity with regard to his real condition in life. Be that what it might, it was such as could not but be advantageous to mine; and acting under this conviction, I made myself, less I must confess by his choice than sufferance, the companion of his journey to Silesia. You are no stranger, Count, to the event that rendered us mutually serviceable to Baron Stralenheim on the banks of the Oder; nor to the indiscreet gratitude of the latter, through which we became inmates of the Prince's house at M—. How extraordinary! how memorable to all were the scenes that passed there!'

The Hungarian made a solemn pause, as if revolving within himself the manner in which he should proceed. Conrad, with stern, but breathless impatience, seemed to attend the result; while Siegendorf, who in the frightful story of the past perceived an alarming connection with the hints afforded by his father's papers, had hardly vigour enough left to rouse himself to the last deciding testimony: – yet his heart still beat fondly towards his son, and revolted from a being who, despicable even by his own confession, was stained with every evidence of circumstantial guilt.

'Your story is excellent,' said Conrad, at length. 'Proceed!'

'It will improve,' replied the Hungarian, bitterly. – 'Miserable young man! You do not yet then see – you do not even yet then conjecture the invisible eye that was open upon your actions? I was your dupe, indeed, at M—, for I began at length to believe you my friend. You introduced me to your father; he was insignificant – miserable – degraded! – soiled with all the exterior debasements of poverty: but I knew enough of life to see in him an extraordinary man. Through your means, or his, I became the victim of a disgraceful calumny! Woe to the worthless heart that inflicts on another the penalty of its own crimes! Most heavily will yours rebound upon you both!'

As if roused by the acute recollection of personal indignity, the Hungarian poured out this denunciation in a tone so forcible as struck to the inmost souls of his hearers.

'Such,' continued he, after a momentary pause, 'was the apparent disparity of circumstances between Kruitzner and yourself, as left it impossible for me to guess the nature of your connection with him:

but I quickly perceived there was some. I weighed – I calculated – I conjectured! – I knew too well the ground I stood upon with you, to suspect you of real kindness or generosity: wherefore then did you protect me from Stralenheim and the Intendant? Some unfathomable project – some dear and highwrought interest was at stake: but it was evidently one in which I was to have no share. I quitted the house to give you leisure to construct it. I re-entered to mark its progress. The momentary prattle of a baby gave me to understand that his father had once been concealed in the chamber where I slept. The secret then lay *there*! Do you start?' said he to Conrad, who did indeed betray some emotion. 'Now mark the end! I returned to your father – obviously a most unwelcome guest; though I was yet at a loss to conjecture wherefore. I met you on my way, and you advised me to remain under his roof another night. My soul half acquitted you of a share in the mystery upon this evidence of apparent frankness. I was yet to learn that you were the very master-dæmon, and moving-spring of all; and that while you courted, it was for the purpose of plunging me into perdition. Midnight came: I arose, and examining my chamber, perceived that I had divined the truth. My course of life had made me acquainted with the courts of princes, and the mysteries of intrigue. Pressing the spring of the secret door, I found myself in the gallery adjoining to it. Recollection of the Baron's losses, and the poverty of Kruitzner, then directed all my suspicions towards him; and I was credulous enough to acquit you I had no light, but an irresistible curiosity impelled me forwards. Suddenly I heard a noise: it resembled a groan; low-murmured, but distinct. I stopped – listened – turned every way to ascertain whence the sound issued: – but it was not repeated. In the attitude of listening I lost my recollection, and knew not whether I had advanced, or was retreating: – yet my hand touched the panel of a door, and it was necessary to determine whither it led. My risk was however evident. I drew back, therefore, only as much of the partition as formed a crevice; but my hair stood erect on my head, and my blood froze in my veins, when through it I saw the yet bleeding body of Stralenheim!'

'But you saw not the murderer!' exclaimed the Count, in a tone of supernatural vehemence.

'He was not, at that moment, in the room: but the locks of the Baron's apartment had been changed chiefly under his inspection the day before, and he had doubtless possessed himself of master-key, for the door of the anteroom was ajar. I saw a man bathing his hands in water; their colour bore horrible testimony against him: at intervals he raised his head, and looked steadily towards Stralenheim: – a lamp stood on the marble table close by, and its pale but steady light then showed me distinctly the features of your son. – Have I said enough?' continued he, directing a penetrating glance towards Conrad; 'or does a father's eye and heart want further confirmation? – Yet hear me to the end,' he added, abruptly arresting the attention of both, which he perceived was on the point of utterly failing. 'Something, Count Siegendorf, is yet due to you! – you, who, in the first tumult and agitation of my soul, I doubted not to be an accomplice in the crime. – I saw myself at once its victim. I saw at once why I had been by him persuaded to return; and I concluded that I had been purposely stationed by you in the suspicious chamber. For a moment I hesitated upon my conduct; but I was unarmed, and no match at any time for your son in personal address or strength. He too had rendered himself the trusted friend of the Baron; I, at the best, had entered his apartment by subtlety and stealth. – It would be impossible to describe the feelings with which I returned to my own. Josephine and her babe were yet within my power. I provided myself with the dagger which I wore commonly at my girdle; and had Kruitzner, by being absent, confirmed my suspicions, I know not what the bloody vengeance and despair that then possessed my soul would have dictated. But when I passed through his chamber, and saw the watch-light dimly burning, while the family group was buried in a tranquil slumber, I exclaimed to myself – "Peace be with you, miserable innocents! – Ye know not what the morning will awaken you to!"

'Self-preservation now called loudly upon me; and hastening from scenes in which I should infallibly have fallen a sacrifice, I concealed myself in the hollows of the mountains of Bohemia. I there learned enough to ascertain that all power was in the hands of the murdered: and, though by some act of, to me, inscrutable foresight, Kruitzner and his family had, indeed, escaped every thing but infamy I could gain no further tidings concerning them. I concluded, therefore, that they had buried both their miseries and their poverty in some far distant country. Their danger, and my own experience, sufficiently warned me of the merciless character of the man we had to do with, and I finally withdrew from the neighbourhood. I lost sight of him altogether. *Him*, indeed, I never more desired to see: – yet my eye sometimes explored the habitations of sorrow and penury in search of Kruitzner. What then were my emotions, when I lifted it suddenly upon him in the person of Count Siegendorf! – what my conclusions, when a more minute inquiry gave me to understand the relation between him and Baron Stralenheim! Yet my soul acquits *you*, Count, of the crime. – Guilt sleeps not as you did, the night on which it was committed; and it is upon the faith of that acquittal I ventured hither. – You now know the extent of the secret I am possessed of! – *Consider its value well before you dismiss me.*'

Siegendorf, to whose jarred and perturbed faculties the latter part of the Hungarian's discourse had been nearly lost, started with confused recollections, when the voice ceased to sound in his ear. Alas! of what importance to the Count did his own guilt or innocence appear! – Conrad, a savage and a murderer! – Conrad, his soul fraught with horrors, and his hands dipped in blood, had been the only distinct image that for a time swam before the eyes of the suffering father! – Suspicion or acquittal – wealth – honours – life even, with all its various and fluctuating scenes, had given place to this horrible one. Absorbed in the contemplation of it, the Count had, for a considerable period, lost all sense of identity, all power of judging or comparing. He was like a man in whom little more than animal existence remains, but who starts at intervals under the lash of torture, and awakens to a frightful consciousness, from which he again willingly relapses to stupefaction.

From this state of mental exhaustion he was unexpectedly roused by the concluding address of the Hungarian. The few words in which it was couched presented a hope that seemed in itself the renovation of existence. If the accuser of Conrad were thus venal, Conrad himself was doubtless innocent! – Plausible as was the tale, circumstantially as it had been related, and deep as was its impression, it rested at last on the testimony but of one man; and that one among the most worthless of his species. Leaving behind every adventitious circumstance calculated to confirm his fears, the Count passed with the rapidity of lightning to all that could dissipate them. The first hateful impression he had conceived of the Hungarian – the subsequent dissimulation of the latter – the implied baseness of his past life, the avowed meanness of his present, were all so many evidences against him. The last sordid appeal was in itself conclusive; he who was to be bought was surely not to be believed! Believed, too, against whom? – a darling, an almost adored son, who, had he been even guilty, the miserable Count felt too closely entwined with every fibre of his heart to be torn from it without agony.

Siegendorf, with that vehemence of feeling which sees no medium between desperation and security, at once clung to the latter. Yet while thus, by a violent effort repelling the worst of his fears, a numerous train, sufficiently alarming, though subordinate, started up to supply their place. In proportion to the villany of the Hungarian, the magnitude of those evils which surrounded the future fate of Conrad and himself would inevitably increase! – Both were in the power of an enemy, who could torture if he could not crush; – who might so speciously blend truth and falsehood, as to defeat the clearest judgment, and the most impartial heart; – who beheld, for the first time, in the splendid fortunes of the family of Siegendorf, an allurement to plunder, of which he had hitherto been ignorant; and who, like the beast that scents blood, would too probably be satisfied only when he has glutted. The imagination which had before swallowed up all the faculties of his soul, saw, in the clearest and most extended point of view, how much was to be considered – how much to be guarded against! He threw an anxious and inquiring gaze upon Conrad; but the latter, buried, as it appeared, in a resentful and proud silence at the hitherto tame acquiescence of his father, seemed willing to leave everything to the hazard of the moment. Only now and then he measured the Hungarian with his eyes, as an enemy too daring not to excite astonishment. The extraordinary pause that had succeeded the narrative of the latter was at length interrupted by himself.

'Is it vengeance, Count, or justice, on which you meditate so deeply,' said he, with some surprise. 'Neither,' returned Siegendorf. 'I am weighing,' he added emphatically, 'the *nature*' and the *value* of your communication.' 'The first needs no comment! I will speak to the last with the same frankness I have hitherto used. My life is a life of hardship and necessity – it is in your power to make it otherwise! You are affluent, and rank high in the state.' 'I understand you!' 'Not wholly, if I judge by your countenance. You believe me venal, and are not quite convinced I am sincere. It is nevertheless true that circumstances have rendered me both. Again I repeat – Consider well before you answer me!' 'Dare you attend the event of my deliberation?'

The Hungarian hesitated, and cast his eyes distrustfully on Conrad, who was walking to and fro between the pillars. The latter raised his in return; but, disdainfully withdrawing them again, passed on in silence.

'I pledge my life – my honour – my salvation for your safety within my walls,' exclaimed the impatient Count.

'I have yet an additional security,' replied the Hungarian, after a moment's meditation. 'I did not enter Prague a solitary individual; and there are tongues without that will speak for me, although I should even share the fate of Stralenheim! Let your deliberation, Count, be short,' he added, again glancing towards Conrad: 'and be the future at your peril no less than mine! Where shall I remain?'

Siegendorf opened a door that admitted to one turret of the castle, of which he knew all other egress was barred: the Hungarian started, and his presence of mind evidently failed him. He looked around with the air of a man who is conscious that, relying on a sanguine hope, he has ventured too far, and neither knows how to stand his ground nor to recede; yet he read truth and security in the countenance of Siegendorf, although not unmingled with contempt. By an excessive effort of dissimulation he, therefore, recovered his equanimity, and made a step towards the spot pointed out to him.

'My promise is solemn – sacred – irrevocable,' said Siegendorf, seeing him pause again upon the threshold: 'it extends not, however, beyond my own walls.'

'I accept the conditions,' replied the other. His eye, while speaking, fell on the sabre of Conrad; and the Count, who perceived it did so, invited him by a look to possess himself of it: he then closed the door of the turret upon him, and advanced hastily towards his son.

'You have done well,' said the latter, raising his head at the near approach of his father, 'to listen to this man's story. The evil we cannot measure, we cannot guard against: – but it would be fruitless to temporise further – He must be silenced more effectually.' The Count started. 'With you,' pursued Conrad, drawing nearer and dropping his voice, 'it would be unwise longer to dissemble – his *narration is true*. Are you so credulous as never to have guessed this?' added he, on perceiving the speechless agony of his father – 'or so weak as to tremble at the acknowledgment? Could it escape you, that, at the hour we met in the garden at M—, nothing short of a discovery during the very act could have made the death of Baron Stralenheim known to any but him who inflicted it? Did it appear probable,' continued he, with the tone of a man who is secretly roused to fury by a consciousness of the horror he inspired, 'that if the Prince's household had really been alarmed, the care of summoning the police should devolve on one who hardly knew an avenue of the town? Or was it credible that such a one should, unsuspected, have loitered on the way? Least of all could it be even possible that Kruitzner, already marked out and watched, could have escaped unpursued, had he not had many hours the start of suspicion! I sounded – I fathomed your soul both before and at the moment: I doubted whether it was feeble or artificial: I discovered it to be the former, or I should have trusted you. Yet such has been the excess of your apparent credulity, that I have ever at intervals disbelieved its existence!'

'Monster!' exclaimed Siegendorf, frantic with emotion, 'what action of my life, what sentiment of my soul, ever authorised you to suspect that I would ever abet a deed thus atrocious? Yet did you basely dare to impute the crime itself to *me!* Dare to appal my imagination with the horror of its indelible disgrace!'

'Would any fear less appalling have induced you to fly? And what but instant flight could guard the dangerous secret of your name? Father, father,' continued Conrad abruptly, and his form seemed to dilate before the astonished eyes of the Count, 'beware how you rouse a devil between us that neither may be able to control! We are in no temper nor season for domestic discussion. Do you suppose that while your soul has been convulsed, mine has been unmoved; or that I have really listened to this man's story with indifference? I too can feel for myself; for what being besides did your example ever teach me to feel? Listen to me,' he added, silencing the Count with a wild and alarming tone: 'if your present condemnation of me be just, I have listened to you at least once too often. Remember *who* told me, when at M—, that there were crimes rendered venial by the occasion; *who* painted the excesses of passion as the trespasses of humanity; *who* held the balance suspended before my eyes between the goods of fortune and those of honour; *who* aided the mischief-stirring spirit within me, by showing me a specious probity, secured only by an infirmity of nerves. Had not your own conduct, by stamping you with disgrace, and your son with illegitimacy, deprived me of all power openly to defy Stralenheim? And were you so little skilled in human nature as not to know that the man who is at once intemperate and feeble engenders the crimes he does not commit? Is it wonderful, then, that *I* should dare to act what *you* dared to meditate? I have, nothing now to do with its guilt or its innocence. It is *our* mutual interest to avert its consequences. We stood on a precipice, down which one of three must inevitably have plunged; for I knew my own situation with the state to be as critical as yours. I therefore precipitated Stralenheim! *You* held the torch – *you* pointed out the path! Show me now that of safety, – or let me show it you.'

The Canterbury Tales

Siegendorf, past all power of replying, motioned to his son to leave him. But although the unhappy Count spoke not, that active faculty which, defying time, space, debility, and every thing but death, combines, arranges, and tortures at the same moment, was busy within. The extravagance of his indiscretion, the excess indeed of his credulity, the blindness of his self-love, all seemed at once to rise in terrible array before him. Ever palliating, or fiercely vindicating, his own errors, - ever shutting his eyes on the griefs or the temptations to which alternately they exposed others, – he perceived, too late, the multiplied calamities created by such a character, and the maze of inextricable misery in which it had involved himself.

'Let us have done with retrospection,' said Conrad, lowering his tone, as not wholly insensible to the effect his words had produced on his father. 'We have nothing more either to learn or to conceal from each other. I have courage and partisans: they are even within the walls, though you do not know them.'

'Siegendorf shuddered. Alas! these, then, had been the substitutes for those affectionate and innocent hearts whose welcome had rendered his return to his native domain in the first instance so delightful: these were the baleful spirits before whose influence virtue and industry alike had withered.

'You are favoured by the state,' pursued Conrad; 'and it will therefore take little cognisance of what passes within your jurisdiction: it is for me to guard against danger beyond it. Preserve un unchanged countenance. Keep your own secret,' he added, glancing emphatically towards the turret; 'and, without your further interference, I will for ever secure you from the indiscretion of a third person.' So saying he left the hall.

Siegendorf, wise too late for happiness, yet felt the necessity of living yet a little longer to honour. Solemnly and sacredly had he pledged his for the safety of the Hungarian, yet he could hardly doubt but the bloody purpose of his son was to destroy him. Nor was this difficult: Conrad, as well as his father, was furnished with keys that would afford an immediate access to the opposite side of the turret; and circumstanced as the Count now found himself, even within his own palace walls, no certainty remained of saving the Hungarian but that of instantly liberating him.

Siegendorf, actuated by an impulse of honourable desperation, not wholly unmingled, however, with an indistinct hope of silencing the accuser, hastily tore the jewels from his bosom and hat, and mounted the steps. The danger that could thus alarm *him* was manifestly too imminent, the prize he offered too valuable, to leave the Hungarian room for hesitation. The few but gloomy moments the latter had already passed in solitude afforded him leisure to weigh all the hazards of an enterprise from which, in the temporary exultation of sudden hope and astonishment created at sight of Siegendorf, he had promised himself every thing. The acuteness of his penetration had indeed enabled him to calculate very accurately the character of the Count in some particulars; but the excess of paternal fondness had not been included in that calculation, and he saw with surprise its operation upon his judgment. He began even to suspect that it might in the end prove powerful enough to make him abet what his genuine feelings revolted from, and render him an instrument in the hands of his son to perpetrate that vengeance he had himself thus rashly put within the reach of either. Under these circumstances, the Count's admonition to escape was too perfect a demonstration of the necessity for doing so not to be immediately complied with. The mind of the latter was wrought to a pitch that allowed him not sufficient recollection to enter into compromise or engagement. Blood alone was before his eyes; and from blood only he desired to avert them, though at the expense of every future good in life.

The unhappy Siegendorf was found by his attendants, not long after the departure of the Hungarian, alone in the turret, stripped of his jewels, speechless and insensible. As it was not doubted but the stranger had plundered him, a strict search was immediately instituted after the latter. It proved vain; for the Hungarian, satisfied with his spoils, or suspecting that by an unwary acceptance of the jewels he had fallen into a snare purposely laid for him, was heard of no more. It was not true, however, that he had either injured or attacked the Count, whose frame had in reality sunk under the struggle of a violent convulsion; but Siegendorf was at no pains to confute an opinion, the probability of which spared him all further explanation; and Conrad, who alone surmised its fallacy, had, on discovering the flight of the Hungarian, immediately quitted the castle.

The internal anguish of Siegendorf, his smothered groans, his deep despair, together with the extraordinary absence of his son, quickly betrayed to Josephine the source, though not the extent, of their mutual calamity. For the Count, happily as far as respected her, had learned to control his words; or rather the gloomy despondency with which he was oppressed, hopeless of relief, bade him abhor all sympathy. But the grief that thus struck inward soon announced itself to be mortal: his exterior visibly changed under the conflict; his eyes sunk; his countenance became hollow: the never-dying worm seemed to have seized upon his heart. With health vanished the pleasures of sense, and with peace those of intellect. The voice of his wife was no longer music to his ear; and the sacred hope it yet strove to cherish was lost to him. His bosom, like a sullied mirror reflecting every image with its own stain, saw even in the form of the blooming Marcellin only the germ of depravity.

It was otherwise with the deeply afflicted but still magnanimous mother: she felt the reality of unblemished rectitude in her own heart, and looked forward therefore with heroic confidence to the probability of its being perpetuated in that of her infant son. Her imagination showed Marcellin imbued with qualities capable of rendering him an instrument in the hands of a beneficent God, to correct the vices, or to alleviate the miseries of his fellow-creatures. She expected not indeed that, whatever his claims, he would find the world a state of elysium. She felt that, in his progress through it, he must often sympathise with the unwise, and suffer from the unworthy; but she knew how to calculate his resources as well as his trials in this life; and cherished that pious confidence in another, which alone enables the scale of happiness to preponderate.

Whether Conrad and his father ever met again, the spirits that have long since plunged into eternity alone can tell: on this side of it they saw each other no more. A considerable period elapsed without realising the hopes or fears of the Count. Continuing throughout that time to meditate on the character of his son, it seemed, like some hideous shadow, to grow blacker and more gigantic as he gazed at it. Having combined every particular related by the Hungarian with those which his father's papers had confusedly announced, and his own observation more perfectly assured him of, they formed an image, alike frightful to his imagination and repulsive to his heart. Still linked, however, to this savage by the mysterious tie of nature, by the indissoluble regulations of society, by the no less forcible though less tender bonds of family interest and honour, all of life that yet lingered in the pulses of Siegendorf seemed to draw its nourishment from endless inquiries or conjectures respecting the fate of his son. They had hitherto proved fruitless, when his duty as a senator suddenly made that terrible demand upon his fortitude which the heart of the miserable father had already deprecated. A strong military force, acting under the orders of the state, was deputed to extirpate a banditti that harassed the country on the side next Franconia. The Count, ere the fatal mandate was signed by himself, made every possible effort, even of the most dangerous kind, to ascertain their number and their leaders: – unhappily he learned both too late: – Conrad, whose savage and ferocious pleasures had led him again to join his former associates, had been cut down in a skirmish, together with many others, amidst the recesses of the forest, by the sabre of an Austrian hussar. He fell indeed undistinguished: but living or dead there was no form like his, and it was recognized, as soon as seen by the commanding officer.

The final blow was at length struck, and Siegendorf touched the extreme point alike of suffering and of existence. A rapid decay had already enfeebled a frame that seemed formed for duration. In proportion as his passions had once been stormy so had they now sunk into profound stillness. Nor had his constitution vigour to cherish their habitual irritability: the arrow had gone deep into his heart, and the mortified wound ceased to be painful.

Consideration for the rank of Conrad, as well as for the affliction of his family, induced the state to consign the trespasses of the former to oblivion: it was, therefore, permitted that he should be privately interred. The grave of his grandfather was opened, and the Count, despite of all remonstrance, attended in person to see the hitherto discordant ashes finally blended. After contemplating the scene with the gaze of one who strives to look through it into eternity, he seemed to feel that all was painfully expiated, and was conveyed from the spot – never more to revisit it while vital consciousness remained.

The disposition of Siegendorf's worldly fortune secured his wife and Marcellin those honours to which the past life of the one, and the succeeding career of the other, well entitled them. But never did wealth or honours efface from the memory of Josephine the husband of her heart – its first fond choice – the dear and invariable object of all those tender illusions which santified the period of youth and love! The emaciated form which hardly any other eye had recognized became, even when laid in dust, most precious to her recollection! The lowest whisper of a voice inaudible to every other ear was yet distinct to hers, as long as breath and pulsation allowed it to articulate a sound. Breath and pulsation at length failed; the tranquillised spirit of Siegendorf was exhaled upon the bosom of his better angel; and though sent too late to teach him how to live, she succeeded in preparing him to die.

The Count expired in the forty-eighth year of his age, and amidst the plenitude of all those enjoyments in which he had at once sought felicity: yet, through a singular chance, doubtless aided by afflicting recollections, precisely six-and-twenty years from the day on which he first quitted Bohemia. He was buried in the same vault with his father and Conrad. – If the measure of his misfortunes should appear to exceed that of his errors, let it be remembered how easily both might have been avoided: since an adherence to his duties at almost any one period of his life would have spared him more than half its sufferings.

THE SCOTSMAN'S TALE

CLAUDINE

> So shall I court thy dearest truth,
> When beauty can no more engage:
> So, thinking of thy charming youth,
> I'll love it o'er again in age.
>
> *Prior*

A man may travel a good many miles without meeting with an adventure. Nay, if he be a man of business, the chances are ten to one that he may never meet with such a thing at all; except, indeed, it be a bankruptcy or a broken bone. The latter was near falling to my lot as I was travelling at my ease, at the pleasant pace of about three miles an hour, in a commodious carriage; composed, I apprehend, of a certain number of planks, clumsily put together by some clumsy joiner, and supported by two crazy wheels. This post-waggon, as it was termed, drawn by horses, one of which was blind and the other lame, seemed, at the rate we drove, to require some ingenuity to overset it. That business, however, was accomplished. I was picked up in no condition to thank my benefactors, as the blood flowed plentifully from a wound in my head, which, though it did not dispossess my brains, threw them at least into such a state of disorder, as required some hours of repose to set them right. There are, indeed, certain of my acquaintance who affirm that they never have been right from that time: but these are mere calumniators. My disorder since has lain in my heart; and is, therefore, of a nature which only the infected can judge of.

The moment I thoroughly recovered my senses, I began to reconnoitre my situation. It was no bad one for a man who had been jumbled in such a conveyance as that I had quitted, could the exchange have been effected with less hazard to my bones. I found myself in a neat bed, furnished with white curtains. It is to be observed that I always had a particular predilection for white curtains; especially in foreign countries, for reasons unnecessary to detail. My chief attendant was a respectable middle-aged woman, who seemed most kindly officious in assisting my recovery: – but truth must be told; my gratitude was not sufficiently just to direct itself principally to her, for I saw at different times several other females pass and repass my chamber, some of whom were almost children, and the eldest of them not apparently above eighteen. They were all slight, blooming, and generally distinguished by the bright polished skin and fair locks, approaching the golden, by which the lasses of the northern hemisphere are mostly to be known.

As a Scotsman I ought to have admired this complexion beyond all others; but Scotsmen can sometimes be perverse: nay, though I know that the contrary has been maliciously asserted, they can even fail to be national. Among these pretty girls there was one then who appeared to me no less remarkable for the superiority of her charms than for the different character of her countenance. She had dark eyes, and curls of shining black hair fell almost into them over her forehead; while the longer locks were twisted up in a sort of tress infinitely graceful. Her features, I am told, were not altogether perfect: but for my life I never could get further in the scrutiny than her eyes: yet they were ungrateful eyes too! for they rarely, indeed hardly ever, would meet mine. But when they did – oh then –

> 'The large black orbs, fill'd with a sprightly light,
> Shot forth a lively and illustrious night!'*

From being over head and ears in the mire, I was almost as quickly over head and ears in love. Yet not wholly with a face either; for my fair Swede, who by the by turned out to be no Swede at all, spoke French; so luckily did I; and during the days of my convalescence, the hospitable family, without distrust or guile, gave me frequent opportunities to hold conversation with any of the young women by turns. I must have been a monster had I abused the confidence shown me. Not I mean by any decided act of libertinism; for I found them sufficiently well educated and decorous in their habits to put that out of the question; but even by sullying the genuine purity of their minds with gross flattery or worldly address.

* Cowley.

My eyes and my heart, nevertheless, turned towards Claudine, with that decided preference which makes itself alike understood either in simple or polished life.

Thus agreeably circumstanced, I took care not to recover the effects of my accident too hastily: nay, it is not at all clear to me when that recovery would have been perfected, had not an anxious letter from my father, who was equally alarmed for the health of his son, and for some particular commercial concerns, roused me from my dream of idleness and felicity. I well knew, in fact, that I had no business in Sweden at all. I had been sent to St. Petersburgh on an affair of consequence to my family, and nothing but the levity and busy curiosity of two-and-twenty had led me out of my way, to explore copper-mines and herbalise upon mountains.

The man who turns from his road at all stands a chance of going much further than he calculates: such was my case in every particular; and how to get into it again, in truth, I hardly knew. My letters had been forwarded to me from Russia: should I say I had remained there, or should I acknowledge my wanderings? I chose to dissemble, and experience showed me I chose wrong. I sent to my correspondent at St. Petersburgh such letters as I wished transmitted to England: I enjoined him faithfully to conceal my real abode, and I prepared to stay awhile longer with my host and his charming family. To this arrangement, however, I had, as it appeared, nobody's consent but my own: for the good man, who was a Lutheran priest, – frank, well instructed, and a more strict observer than I supposed him to be of the characters and feelings of those around, – no sooner discovered, by my despatching letters to St. Petersburgh, that I did not intend yet to go thither, than the tone of my reception entirely changed. I shut my eyes, nevertheless, to this for several days, at the expiration of which time my host invited me to walk after breakfast with him one morning in his garden. I had an ugly presentiment of what was to be the subject of our conversation, and I would, therefore, very willingly have declined it; but the thing was impossible.

It was a fine sunshiny day. Nothing could be more delightful than the scene. A balmy air just stirred the leaves of the flowers that were distributed around us; and the dew, not being yet exhaled, caused them to send forth that pure and exquisite fragrance, which seems the immediate breath of Heaven. The cottage of the pastor was situated in a wild and almost savage country, the rough features of which, softening as they approached, presented within its immediate precincts an image of tranquillity that every thing seemed to realise. The sea, like a broad blue belt, skirted the distances; and a good eye might even occasionally catch the outline of the larger vessels as they steered through the Gulf of Bothnia.

With all this flowery description, however, which my recollection has since obtruded upon me, nobody could be further from relishing the beauties of nature than I was at that moment; at least such as then presented themselves to my eyes. To hear me, nevertheless, you would have concluded me to be an enthusiast. It was impossible to speak more fluently, or with more eloquence, than I did upon them: I remember I was particularly inspired upon the subject of bees, of which my host had a large provision in his hives; and it was true that their soft, but busy murmur, really contributed in no small degree to the species of rustic voluptuousness which his garden otherwise afforded. I was even entering into an exact inquiry concerning their domestic economy and regulations, when my companion interrupted me.

'My good young Englishman,' said he, – which, by the by, was a mismoner, for I was a North Briton, – 'I perceive you are very ingenious in evading the question on which I wished to speak with you. But, with your leave, I must be permitted to obtrude it. It is evident that you are not disposed to quit us; and I may tell you, without flattery, that I shall be no less sorry on my side to part with you. There is something of simplicity and nature in your character that pleases me. Unhappily, indeed, it is too natural; for you have stumbled upon an old-fashioned error which the combinations of society have almost exploded. You are fallen in love, as it is termed; that is, you have seen a pretty girl for whom you have a tender preference, and who indeed justifies it, as I believe her mind to be no less innocent and charming than her person. But have you considered what you are about? You are apparently a very young man, – dependent, if I understand you rightly, on your father: your country is at war with that of Claudine; and, were it even otherwise, it is extremely improbable that your parents should sanction your attachment to a young French emigrée, who has neither family nor establishment on which she can rely. I know the English are a generous nation: but I also know human nature to be, under various modifications, the same every where; and I cannot, therefore, be of opinion that your choice will obtain the sanction of your friends.'

The discourse of the good man opened a new light upon me. I spoke French fluently, it must be owned; so too did all his family; but

I had a true British accent, and my ear had not been nice enough, or my eyes had monopolised the power of my other senses, to discover that Claudine was a native French woman. To my worthy friend's harangue, I could only observe in answer, 'That young men seldom did consider what they were about when they fell in love, or they would possibly never do so at all. That I had, besides, been taken at an unfair advantage, since my senses were not my own at the time; and that I verily believed they never would be so again, unless I were happy enough to possess Claudine. That he was perfectly right with regard to my dependence on my father; but that I was blessed with the most affectionate parents in the world, who would not, I was persuaded, be tempted by any consideration to destroy the happiness of their son; and that, with respect to my future steps, it had been my intention maturely to consider before I ventured upon them.'

I did not pronounce the latter part of my discourse so emphatically, or with half so good a grace as the first: for my conscience told me that, to say the very best, it was but half true. Not, certainly, that I suspected my parents of being willing to destroy my happiness; but till fathers and sons agree more exactly in what happiness consists, I am afraid the expression will always be a little equivocal between them. My sincerity was even more questionable in the concluding sentence; since, far from having resolved maturely to weigh my future steps, I had never looked into the future at all. My love was yet in its infancy; or rather in that progressive state of the passion when the present is all-sufficient to happiness; when the new and delightful sentiment is just awakened in the bosom, and has not yet given one single jog to that long train of doubts, jealousies, and disquietudes, which render it ever afterwards so troublesome. My host, however, had done this business completely for me. From the very hour he and I talked together, I found that love was no such sport of the fancy as I had hitherto imagined, and I began, indeed, to look to the future with an anxious eye.

I presently discovered that the birth of Claudine was noble: this I was sorry for, because mine was not. Her story was simple, and, in fact, the history of thousands. She had lost her father, who had fallen a sacrifice to his political opinions, at a very early period of the French revolution. Her mother, in escaping from France, had been shipwrecked in her voyage to St. Petersburgh; and, from the consequences of fatigue and suffering, had soon after left Claudine an unprotected and impoverished orphan. For this I was no less sorry than for the circumstances of her birth: for I suspected that it would be my lot to be too opulent; and I began, like my good host, to doubt the concurrence of my family in the step I was meditating. My calculations on this head have proved erroneous however. It has not yet been my lot to be very rich, and it probably never will; but my mind is made to my fortune, and I do not envy those who boast a more splendid one.

My first effort at thinking was not at all successful. I saw no point on which I could reasonably build; and I therefore grew fretful, – consequently fancied myself indisposed. I was indeed really ill for two or three days. My host perceived it, and insensibly relaxed the rigidity of his muscles. What was much better, Claudine perceived it too; and I had the exquisite happiness of believing that I was not indifferent to her. Sweet though transitory moments that enliven existence, how precious is your recollection to a tender mind!

The first use I made of my returning health was to impart to Claudine the sentiments with which she inspired me; and I received from that grateful and generous girl such a hearing as made an indelible impression upon my heart. Claudine, however, was so entirely the child of nature, and so wholly unskilled in the ways of the world, that to have consulted her upon those difficulties and probable inconveniences which her reverend guardian had conjured up to my imagination, would only have doubled them. She was, besides, not much more than seventeen, and had seen little beyond her mother's house and the walls of a convent. I was, therefore, thrown entirely upon my own fund of sagacity and prudence; and, to say truth, when I consider with how small a principal I set out, I must confess myself, in the commercial phrase, to have made no bad speculation.

I learned from Claudine that she had a brother who served in the army of the French princes, and whom her mother hoped to have joined at St. Petersburgh. She had herself reason to suppose she might learn tidings of him at the court of the empress, although the obscure condition of the family with which she resided, and their distance from St. Petersburgh had rendered the vague inquiries they had hitherto been able to make totally fruitless. The opportunity it must be owed was most tempting to a lover – a poor fellow who saw himself constrained to depart with a heart half broken, and a head not quite healed. I weighed secretly with Claudine the possibility of prevailing on her reverend protector to suffer her to depart with me in search of her brother: it was plain that we were novices in the ways

The Canterbury Tales

of the world, or such a plan could not possibly have entered the head of either; but among the few peculiarities that marked the dear girl's character, and she had none that were not graceful and becoming, was an anxious desire to be restored to her family, and an opinion that she had no right to dispose of herself without the consent of this brother; who, being by many years the elder, she had been taught by her mother to look up to as the arbiter of her fate. She had, besides, long felt that her continued residence in Sweden was a burden on her benefactor, whose scanty income ill allowed him to exercise the generous feelings of his heart; and Claudine, brought up in affluence, had not yet been able to image such a genuine picture of poverty as should incapacitate her brother from receiving or maintaining her. Alas, she little knew the condition of many of her countrymen! I was not myself much better informed on the subject; and, to say truth, had I even been so, I fear I should have preferred the delightful idea of having Claudine my companion at St. Petersburgh to all the sober objections that reason could possibly have presented to me.

We were not gone so far, however, in love or Areadian simplicity as to conceive the idea of her accompanying me alone. Chance presented her a suitable protection in the society of a Swedish merchant and his family, to whom she was known, and who were to embark in the same vessel with myself. After much hesitation, then, I ventured to communicate our mutual wishes to my kind host. He looked extremely grave on the project, although I had dressed it up in colours as soberly simple as fancy and love would permit me. I found an auxiliary, however, where I did not except one – in the person of his wife; who, being a good economist, and a woman of no great expansion of mind in other particulars, was not, I believe, sorry to seize the opportunity of freeing herself from a person whom she conceived to be an encumbrance in her domestic arrangements.

To be short, the lovely Claudine was committed to my protection, – but under the superintending eyes of a female Argus, who promised to watch carefully over her. On my part I faithfully swore either to place her in the care of her brother, or to make her my wife, at every hazard of circumstances, should she consent to become such without waiting his concurrence. In the interim I engaged to lodge her in the house of my own correspondent at Petersburgh, a respectable merchant, the regularity of whose family left nothing in the arrangement liable to objection, and where I was not to become an inmate myself. I was so truly in earnest in all my declarations and plans, that I believe I left no doubt of my sincerity in the mind of my hearer. Yet the good man was not quite sure he was doing right in consenting to our scheme, and I saw tears in his eyes as he embraced us previous to our departure. Claudine also wept; nor could I forbear shedding tears of sympathy myself: though such was to me the joyful sorrow of the moment, that I will not swear they did not spring from a least a blended emotion.

The clear beauties of a northern hemisphere in summer are only to be known by those who have witnessed them. The sun, hardly setting, left throughout the whole night a gentle twilight; which, illuminated by the aurora borealis, presented new and innumerable charms both in the heavens and the ocean. The merchant's family, Claudine, and myself, often sat upon the deck during the greater part of these nights; and her sweet voice, in unison with the voices of some other female passengers, frequently chanted a sort of national and simple music, so perfectly harmonising with the scene before us, as to fill the senses of every hearer with nearly equal delight. Never did the charming features of Claudine appear to more advantage than when seen by this soft and shadowy light. For my part I almost wished my whole life was to be a voyage; and felt truly sorry when we cast anchor in the harbour of Cronstadt. Here all was in contrast to the tranquility we had been witnessing; and the bustle of trade and shipping would have driven away almost any sentiment less vigorous than love before the potent genius of gain.

Our plans at St. Petersburgh were, I quickly discovered, in no immediate way to be realised. The traces Claudine had of her brother were so very imperfect, and so many changes had taken place in the distribution of the French regiments there, that it was extremely difficult to pursue our inquiries concerning him. I continued to make some, however; and, during the interim, had the double satisfaction of keeping in view the business my father had intrusted to me, and of enjoying daily the society of the woman I adored. Claudine, on her side, was anxiously employed in acquiring the English language and accent; and such was the delicacy of her organs, or her ear, perhaps sided by the inspiring influence of her tutor, that I have never since heard it spoken by any foreigner with equal purity. Although I had fulfilled with the strictest fidelity every engagement into which I had entered concerning her, she was yet by no means satisfied with her situation. Not that it was any way objectionable on the score of propriety; for she had every protection and accommodation that could be demanded. She was besides embosomed in an affluent family, and had dress, pleasures, in short all the advantages that affluence itself could bestow: but it was to me that she owed them, and the delicacy of her mind taught her daily to revolt more and more from the nature of the obligation. Vainly did I represent to her that she had received the same, at least in the proportion of worldly circumstances, from her former protectors; that she was, in fact, my affianced wife, and that all I could offer her would be only what she had a claim to. Young as she was, she felt the difference of the relative situations; and such was the soft and retiring propriety which this consideration gave to her manners, that though I complained, I could not but love her the better for it.

But although Claudine was, on the whole, self-denying and discreet in the extreme, she was too gentle, young, and lovely, to be always proof against solicitation. I delighted in showing her beauty, and I therefore, took every opportunity of leading her into such scenes of elegance as might display it to advantage. The approach of winter in the northern courts is the signal for a species of festivity unknown in milder climates; and the amusement of driving *en traîneau* is practised with a luxury and splendour that to a stranger is singularly dazzling. I was myself an expert performer that way, and, therefore, extremely ambitious of exhibiting at once my own talents and the charms of Claudine. She was, for a long time, averse to this proposal: I nevertheless extorted her consent, and I provided an elegant *traîneau*, in which I placed my fair charge. Nothing can exceed the brilliance and gaiety of this kind of diversion. Numberless carriages, fancifully ornamented, all in motion at once, and flying with the velocity of fairy cars, carrying their beautiful enchantresses along with them, form a *coup d'oeil* altogether delightful. Claudine was in high spirits; nor was I less elevated, though I cannot impute even to the giddiness of my pleasure any blame as to the accident that followed.

We had already made our course, and were on the point of returning home, when a more numerous succession of carriages than before caused some slight apprehension from probable entanglements or embarrassment. Among the *tráineaux* that lately entered was one guided by an officer: the lady who sat in it seemed, by the splendour of her appearance, and the rich furs in which she was wrapped, to be of very considerable rank; and her conductor, with more zeal than skill, threatened destruction to every carriage that came within his vortex. Unfortunately mine happened to be of the number. I remembered my last accident, and I was not willing to try the thickness of my head a second time. I was besides anxious for Claudine's safety, and I therefore exerted my jockeyship in making over the danger to my antagonist. I was but too successful. We had a rude shock that threw us both into confusion. On his part the danger was imminent; and it was the chance of a moment that both he and the lady with him did not suffer material injury. His resentment burst out into an intemperance of language I was not at all disposed to endure. Our contention, therefore, soon amounted to little short of defiance on both sides. A general disorder ensued; and, such was the overbearing insolence of my adversary, that it would have been difficult to have foreseen the event between us, had not a party of guards interposed, and put an end to the tumult. We were separated; and I was, by authority, enjoined to return home.

Claudine, who had during this scene been ready to faint with fear, now drew great consolation from a circumstance which certainly afforded me none – that of my being put under arrest within the house for several days. Her apprehensions for my personal safety left her no sympathy for the indignity to which I thought myself subjected. I was not so calm, though I found it necessary to seem so; and the first care of both, though for different reasons, was to inform ourselves of the name and rank of my antagonist. He was called, it appeared, the Count St. Victoire. Nothing more was necessary to assure Claudine that it was her brother. – St. Victoire had quitted his country before the death of his father: he was, indeed, among the first of that ill-informed or ill-judging part of the nobility who sought safety or revenge in a foreign one. His sister was at that time a child, and immured within the walls of a convent. The duties of the service into which he had entered, as most of the young nobility of France were accustomed to do at a very early age, had not permitted him to be much at Paris; and she had, therefore, seen him so rarely, that it was not at all surprising she did not recognise him, clothed as he was in furs too for the occasion, and under the circumstances of terror and agitation on her part in which they at length met.

The alarm I experienced on this discovery was little short of that felt by Claudine herself. Of all men living her brother was, perhaps, the one I would most have wished to serve: he was certainly the last I would willingly have offended. Yet I felt that, after what had passed, it would be difficult, to say the least, for either to conciliate the good will of the other. There was something in the manners of St. Victoire that announced him at first sight to be what he really proved; and I conceived from that moment an evil presentiment concerning him. I left Claudine to take her own measures in making herself known to her brother, and I waited impatiently to see what would be the event of our quarrel, as soon as it should be ascertained that my temporary restraint was at an end. This happened sooner than I expected. On the second day my arrest was taken off; but an express order from court forbade either of us to testify further resentment against each other; and enjoined, what it was not in the power of any court to enforce, a total forgetfulness of the past. On my side I was obliged to enter into a sort of recognizance that should secure my obedience; which I was contented to do, as I found St. Victoire lay under a restriction from his commanding officer little inferior to mine. I had afterwards reason to know that the argument made use of to induce his easier compliance with what was required of him was the disproportion of rank between himself and his antagonist. I was far from suspecting this at the time; otherwise I am not sure my Caledonian blood would patiently have tolerated it.

While peace was thus apparently restored between us Claudine had not been wanting in any effort on her part that might render it either permanent or sincere. St. Victoire was at first greatly surprised at discovering his sister, and much struck with her beauty, as well as with the native charms of her character. The dear girl I doubt not spared no eloquence to make him a convert to mine: but she was not so successful as, I will venture proudly to say, she deserved to be. St. Victoire could not indeed deny that I appeared to have acted both generously and delicately towards his sister; but he took care to invalidate the merit of my conduct by representing the probability of its proving, in the end, to be either uncertain or insidious. I burned with resentment, but I had no resource. I could not again embroil myself with the brother of Claudine; and had I done so, I should not have remedied my misfortune: for, although she lamented his injustice as much as I did, she could not be prevailed upon absolutely to revolt from his authority. She was, besides, much under age, and had no power, either according to the regulations of her own country, or of those in which she resided, to set him at defiance. – And now I believe we both bitterly regretted Sweden, our good old friend there, and the tranquil happiness we had enjoyed under his roof. St. Victoire, however, after some days of deliberation, constrained himself to render me personal thanks for the protection I had afforded his sister. He did it so proudly as to convince me that he meant to discharge both himself and her from the obligation: but I had not much leisure to ruminate upon his intentions; for he presently announced to me, 'that Claudine was now become his care: that it was his purpose immediately to remove her from the *very respectable* hands in which I had placed her, to a situation more suitable to her country and her condition in life: that he should be very happy to acknowledge my civilities in every mode that lay in his power; and he hinted at any pecuniary demands which I might be entitled to make.' This put me out of all patience. I knew him to be poor; and I believed myself to be rich enough to have bought half his regiment: but it was not the question of poverty or riches that lay between us: honour, sensibility, and every thing dear to a noble mind, was included in it.

I told him plainly, and at once, the mutual engagements that subsisted between myself and Claudine. I professed before Heaven there was no affluence I could have offered that deserving and lovely girl which I should have thought equal to her merits; but I could not conquer myself so far as to forbear advertising with disdain to the pecuniary indemnification hinted at in his speech, whether I considered the offer only, or the resources of him who offered it. – I concluded with a protestation that nothing should tear Claudine from me; and I referred him to herself, to know whether she would be prevailed upon to give me up.

I had now made things a thousand times worse than they were before. St. Victoire commanded his pride, indeed, so far as to answer me in terms of decent civility; but I could easily perceive that I had exasperated and nettled him to the very soul. He made extremely light of my reference to his sister; affecting to consider her as a child who was incompetent to judge of her own wishes. He gave me very clearly to understand that he had influence enough at court to defeat any I might flatter myself with possessing; and very civilly insinuated that the son of a merchant could never, under any circumstances either of wealth or poverty, be a match for the sister of the Count St. Victoire. – Nothing more could be made of our conference, unless it had come to a serious and hostile appeal; which, for various reasons, each was unwilling it should do. We parted mutually out of humour, and mutually resolved to carry the future our own way.

Claudine was overwhelmed with grief when she learned the event of our conversation. Both she and I had been so deficient in knowledge of the world, and so little used to calculate the various points of view which circumstances appear to various characters, that it had never at any moment occurred to either of us to doubt our reception from her brother, or his approbation of the measures we had pursued. How great then was our disappointment to find that the event we had so much desired now threatened to prove an insuperable obstacle to our union. I had even cause for additional chagrin, on reflecting that my own indiscreet wish of exhibiting my fair charge had exposed us mutually to this unforeseen mortification. I had, nevertheless, entertained hitherto so clear a conviction that the sentiments I cherished for Claudine were such, as while they contributed to her happiness, would also place her out of the reach of those worldly sorrows and carking cares which corrode the sweetest buds of youth, that I experienced something like astonishment at the new light which St. Victoire's opinions had thrown upon the whole business. They were not altogether so irrational, however, as my situation naturally inclined me to believe them. I even felt they were not so; though I was unwilling to acknowledge it even to my own heart. In spite of that air of levity and nonchalance with which he affected to speak of his sister, it was evident to me that he was much struck with her beauty, and built secretly upon it, as a certain means of procuring her a brilliant establishment. To say truth, I was not without an internal conviction of the same nature; and it was this which was my torment. Perhaps we were both blinded by our partiality towards her; – so however it was.

Claudine entertained no such views or feelings. She conceived herself bound to me by every tie of gratitude or love, and she vindicated both my behaviour and intentions with the dignity of a mind that feels itself above misconstruction. She did not indeed think herself entitled either by years or experience to determine her own conduct; but though she submitted that to the temporary authority of St. Victoire, she did not fail to tell him that nothing short of the conviction of demerit on my part would ever induce her to violate the engagement between us: and she peremptorily refused to shock or exasperate me by returning any of the gifts I had lavished on her. 'Nothing fortune could bestow.' she tenderly declared, 'would be in her eyes so dear or so honourable as those lasting memorials of poverty on her side, and of the most unalloyed generosity on mine.' – These were refinements quite out of the way of St. Victoire. He had concluded it to be a matter of justice that, in taking away his sister, he should guard against my suffering any other loss. Alas! he had no conception of those feelings which, in certain cases, render acquittal an insult, and degrade us in our own eyes, by forcing us to discover that our best actions have been deemed venal and selfish! – 'Oh! consent to be obliged to me!' have I been ready on other occasions to exclaim, when I have seen the proud and too susceptible heart shrink distrustfully from the tender offices of a kindness it could not hope to return. 'Prove that you esteem me enough to believe that I am rewarded in the action of serving you!'

St. Victoire, in fine, like a true man of the world, concluded that his sister loved the baubles I had presented her with. He, therefore, gave up the contest; satisfied to gain his chief point her way, since he could not gain it his own; and he removed her that very night from the house in which she had hitherto resided, to that of the Marchioness de S—, a young Frenchwoman of considerable rank, whose husband had emigrated some time after St. Victoire, and was in the same regiment with the latter. The finances of the Marquis de S— were said to be in better order than those of his friend: but he lived expensively, made a great figure, and indulged his wife in the same habits of dissipation and high play which they had both formerly pursued at Paris. St. Victoire was by no means behind hand in extravagance. Through that mist of disappointment and chagrin which clouded my present prospects, I was not, therefore, without a ray of hope that the whole establishment of these high-toned noblesse was upon so uncertain a base as might bring Claudine once more within my reach, without any violent struggle on my part. How sweet was to me the idea that *she* would neither feel humbled nor degraded by such a circumstance, but would do me the justice to understand me. I had an interview with the dear girl on the evening before she left the house of our mutual friend. Her tears, her endearments, her protestations of unshaken constancy, calmed the burning indignation of my heart. I could deny nothing to her solicitation, and I, therefore, promised to attend the future with a degree of moderation that I was not at first disposed to show.

The house in which Claudine now resided was one where I, of course, had no access; and, in spite of my promises, a few days rendered this constraint insupportable to me. I weighed maturely every possible motive of interest, kindness, or even hostility, by which I might hope to act upon St. Victoire; but in vain. He was a man so entirely out of my sphere both as to character and connections, so wrong headed, and cold-hearted, that I found no medium through which I could reach him. I was a thousand times tempted to have recourse to the most desperate; but to what purpose? – We were both, in the first place, under the immediate cognisance of authority: an attempt to defy it might occasion the most serious ill consequences, not only to ourselves, but to our countrymen. St. Victoire was, besides, unquestionably brave; and we could, therefore, at best meet only on a footing of equality. How, if fortune gave me the advantage, should I be benefited by it? In truth, the only benefit it appeared to me I could possibly derive from such a rencontre, was that of dying. – I had a little of the Anglo-mania in me; and there were moments of impotent rage and grief when I was inclined to think that no despicable resource.

A man, however, must take more than one bitter dose of disappointment, I believe, before he really comes to such an extremity: at least that was my case. I now endeavoured, under the auspices of my correspondent at St. Petersburgh, to apply myself more assiduously to business, in order to lighten my cares. – I had soon reason to suspect that it would, in fact, only increase them. I was seized with alarm at some critical circumstances that occurred, and censured myself for a remissness which yet, I believe, had no material influence over my father's concerns; though in the moment of surprise I was disposed to think otherwise. My friend now also communicated to me some particulars relative to our affairs in England, which my correspondents there had, through kindness, forborne minutely to relate; and I perceived that while I had been solely occupied in lamenting griefs, some real, some chimerical, but all of them wholly selfish, an evil of the most serious nature impended over my family, and threatened to bring my own mortifications to their climax. I now exerted myself to retrieve lost time, and to recover certain debts, the amount of which had not hitherto appeared so material in my eyes as I found it ought to have done. My zeal, however, was too late: it could not have saved us, had it been earlier awakened; but it would have acquitted me to my own heart, which ever painfully throbs at the recollection; and I should have been better prepared to encounter what followed: – the first ships that arrived from England told me that my father had been declared a bankrupt.

I cannot even yet think of the circumstance, without a renewal of those afflicting sensations by which I was at the moment stunned and overwhelmed. Here then was an end of my towering hopes, my high-spirited affluence and independence. Here was such a termination of every claim with respect to Claudine, as it would not be in her power even to counteract. For though she had been willing to bestow herself upon me, could I accept her? It seemed, on the contrary, that honour and justice commanded me to free her from her engagements, and thus give her those chances in life, on the event of which her brother had been so sanguine. From his my heart now revolted more entirely than before. I could not endure the triumph I believed he would have over me, or the opportunity he would take to exult to his sister in the superiority of his own judgment and prudence. I made no doubt that he would be little-minded enough to conclude that I had foreseen the misfortune that was likely to fall upon my family, and that I was aware I should make no sacrifice whatever in securing the possession of Claudine. Nay, it was not even clear to me that, in the excess of his vanity and self-love, he would not suppose I had built something upon the advantages of such a connection. These, and similar reflections, together with various additional chagrins resulting from my situation, made me now in reality almost weary of existence. But I owed the care of mine to those dear relatives who were suffering with me, and who had not, like myself, youth and health to combat with difficulties.

It became highly necessary that I should return to England: but although I meditated so doing without taking leave of Claudine, my resolution, nevertheless, failed me as the time drew near. I will own, however, that, among my objections to seeing her, the situation in which I now stood was one. My mind, unlike hers, was not sufficiently self-poised to avoid finding a humiliation in poverty; or possibly the recollection of her brother was blended too intimately with that even of herself, (and how different were they in their natures!) to admit of my being governed by a genuine and unmixed feeling. – The cruel hour of separation at length arrived. Claudine and I parted as most lovers part, with many tears, many protestations, and some caresses. She was never very lavish of those: yet I know not how it was, but she had the art of convincing me that no want of love occasioned her reserve. She had little reason I found to be satisfied with the situation in which her brother had placed her. It obliged her daily to see a number of giddy young officers, none of them in circumstances to realise the sanguine expectations of St. Victoire, though sufficiently susceptible or gallant to be troublesome to his sister. Nevertheless, so great a blemish does the want of fortune cast on beauty, that I did not learn Claudine had any decided admirer of rank or affluence enough to expose her to persecution. In fact I gathered nothing of all this from herself; for of herself, except when the question of duties or affections arose, she seldom or never spoke. But my good friend the merchant's wife, with whom she had resided, reserved for me constantly all the information it was possible to collect; and when that proved insufficient to fill up our conversations on the subject, we had a supplementary fund of conjecture that was never exhausted.

I did not fail to relate faithfully to Claudine, before we parted, the misfortunes in which I found myself involved, and those future ones I apprehended. Claudine, however, I quickly perceived, had not yet attained any distinct idea of poverty. She, indeed, conceived very clearly what it was to lose the luxuries of a hired carriage at command, and to be restricted by prudence in the purchase of a trinket. All this she had felt; therefore she understood it: at her age, we rarely look deeper. But such was the character of her mind, both for genuine simplicity and rational pleasures, that she was not able to make herself any griefs out of these and similar losses. Her humblest ideas of indigence extended to a plain, and sometimes scanty meal, like that of our good pastor; a cottage, too, like his, more calculated for utility than ornament; and certain humble domestic occupations which the narrowness of his circumstances necessarily imposed on his wife and daughters. How many people picture poverty in the way Claudine did! Ah! should such be carried into the miserable hovels where real indigence resides! Should they there see their fellow-creature, possibly their equal, stretched out in sickness and hopeless misery! – should they see, not privation, but famine; not disappointment, but despair; babyhood without playfulness, manhood without vigour, and age without nourishment, – how would their erring, but tender and humane hearts, suffer under the spectacle. Let us not deceive ourselves. Extreme and abject poverty is, vice excepted, the most deplorable condition of human nature. It carries not, as the more acute sufferings of body or of mind do, a balm or a termination in itself. No; it is like water poured drop by drop upon the brain of a criminal, till the whole man groans under excruciating torture. Should I expose the dear girl I loved, even remotely, to the experience of so cruel an evil? My whole soul revolted from the idea.

'Listen to me, my dear Claudine!' said I, as we were parting. 'When I offered you my hand and my heart, I believed that I could add to them the blessings of independence at least: it has proved otherwise; and your brother was more correct in his calculation of the chances of life than we supposed him to be. I will never rob the sister of the Count St. Victoire, or rather I will never rob my own Claudine, of such real advantages in it as she has a right, from her merit or charms, to expect; though I would, without scruple, have permitted her to sacrifice to our mutual attachment those ideal goods, those factitious substitutes for all that is really valuable and honourable in human nature, to which common minds bow down with so implicit a reverence. While you love me, however, dearest Claudine! you are and can be only mine; but should you cease to do so, the bond between us is from that moment broken; or shall an injurious thought, much less a reproach, pursue you on my part.' These were high-sounding words; but I have, on reflection, believed them not so sincere as they then appeared to be. There was certainly a little of the chicanery of love in them. I softened her soul by the idea of my approaching departure; I won over every tender and grateful feeling of her mind by the recollection of the past: finally, I subdued her sensibility by the extravagance of my own; and when her enthusiasm was at its highest, I then said to her, 'Claudine, if you can prefer any other man, renounce me.' All this was, perhaps, at last only an ingenious artifice of self-love; but when a man does not know he is artificial, I think he may be pardoned. Nevertheless, if it was really my intention to extort fresh protestations of constancy from Claudine, I was disappointed; for she made none: she wept bitterly, however; and her expressive eyes, while she listened to me, rendered language unnecessary. I embraced her once more, and immediately after embarked for England.

This voyage was not like the last. I no longer found any charms either in the heavens or the ocean; and my thought wandered incessantly over the past and the future with the most painful anxiety. We had not been long at sea before a heavy gale arose that rendered our navigation even less pleasant than before. When I heard the sailors talk of the danger of the breakers, and saw, though at a distance, the horrible prospect they presented, I thought of Claudine and her unfortunate mother, flying, like many others of their countrywomen, from their native land, from all that was dear or familiar, to contend with elements no less inhospitable to them than the human race. After beating about some days, we ran at length for security into a small Swedish port. I was tempted to land, in order to set my foot in the country where I had first seen Claudine, and to make a sort of love-pilgrimage towards the very spot. However, I resisted this impulse of romance; and it was lucky I did so: I should otherwise have lost my passage; for the wind became fair a few hours after, and it was not long before I landed in England.

I found my father's situation there even more perplexing than I had expected it to be. His concerns had been so multiplied and so various, that it required the most perserving assiduity to disentangle them, or reduce the chaos to order. This was, in a great measure, my employment: my days were necessarily devoted to it; and, after immense application, I returned home spiritless and exhausted of an evening, to rise the ensuing morning to the same painful occupations. People to whom life is a plaything know nothing of such cares as fill up the hours of one half of the community, and too often unfit them not merely for its frivolous, but even its social intercourse; yet these apparent favourites of fortune, like spoiled children, often become weary of their toy; while those in whose hands it is an engine of either private or public utility have always within themselves a source of honourable satisfaction; and such, in the midst of my vexations, was mine.

My father was a man of strict probity and deep intellect; but his manners were not ingratiating, and his understanding was of that biting and repulsive kind which makes few friends. He had a decided love of scheming; and his plans had, for the most part, been both sagacious and successful: a concurrence of circumstances had now rendered them far otherwise. The consequence was that he became bitterly censured, and even indirectly calumniated. He was too proud to endure this, and too helpless to remedy it. His constitution sunk under the conflict; and I found him, on my arrival in England, far gone in a malady that had every appearance of proving mortal. It is in the hour of sorrow, sickness, or poverty, that we learn how to estimate our natural affinities. Placed on the pinnacle of health and prosperity, man stands a sort of independent and self-possessed being, whom the ties and affections only touch at certain points: reduce him from this station in society, and he will at once become sensible of his own insufficiency. It is then he will, perhaps, best learn the value of those friends with whom nature has providently furnished him, and whose habits, tastes, affections, nay even weaknesses, most in sympathy with his own, calculate them to take place of all others. Never were my parents and myself so much attached as at this juncture: yet it was a sorrowful one; and I still cannot remember without a pang the hour when I lost my father. In addition to this heavy calamity, my mother had the grief of seeing her only brother alienated from us some months before, by the circumstances in which our late bankruptcy had involved him. He was a man of considerable property, and therefore stood the shock; but he did not easily forgive the person who exposed him to the hazard, and all intercourse between him and my father had been consequently broken off. On the death of the latter he came to visit my mother; but he expressed no desire to see me, and I was too proud to obtrude myself upon him.

I had now neither hope nor dependence in life. The narrow income my mother's settlement enabled her to rescue from the wreck of our affairs was barely equal to her support. I had myself received too many indignities, or at least what I conceived to be such, from the few who called themselves my father's friends, during the progress of our misfortune, to place the smallest reliance upon them; and I was torn to pieces between nature and love. Claudine was ever first and last in my thoughts, amid all my cares and torments; but I saw no chance of calling her mine. I could even hear from her but seldom; and although her own letters, when they reached me, breathed the most unchanged affection, my friend the merchant's wife failed not to supply her husband with little reports, which, if they did not absolutely excite my distrust, yet created something in my bosom so nearly allied to jealousy as severely to increase my incidental chagrins. His manner of relating them was, besides, so cold and laconic, that I hardly knew what to conclude or gather from his hints: to say truth, I have since had reason to believe that the chief object of both these well-meaning, though misjudging people, was in unison with what they believed would be the wish of my friends, – to break an engagement that threatened only ruin to either of the parties concerned. I, like Claudine, was not without some natural or acquired advantages; and the worthy man at St. Petersburgh, therefore, concluded that, if detached from her, I should most probably settle with some commercial family in England; marry, as he had done, one of the daughters, and step in for as large a portion of the goods of this world along with her as I honestly could contrive to do.

This might, perhaps, have happened; and, indeed, my affairs went on in a train that seemed not to make it unlikely: but I had no taste for the project. I revolved many, although that was not among the number, without being able to fix on one. I had secretly a strong desire to plunge into some adventurous scheme abroad; but I was fettered by two opposing sentiments, which were fated by turns to engross my life and my heart. My mother's health was daily declining: she had neither support nor consolation in the world but me, and the period of her existing there seemed likely to be so short that I could not resolve to abbreviate it. I, like Gray, had found out that 'a man can never have more than one mother;' and mine had, from very childhood, retained a strong interest in my affections. I never in my life saw a creature so perfectly feminine, without being insipid or weak; yet she had neither a very lovely person, nor a highly cultivated understanding; but she was so gentle, so indulgent, so truly conjugal and maternal, so admirably calculated to soothe the bitter moments of life, and to enjoy without intoxication its modest and genuine pleasures, that my heart, even in manhood, was almost as much hers as though she had been amongst the most dazzling of her sex.

While I was in this anxious state of indigence and indecision, a proposal was made me from a house with which my father had had some commercial connections that promised to be in the end sufficiently advantageous to merit consideration at least. My mother was urgent with me to accept the overture. She did not at the moment confide to me all her reasons, because she feared they might prove visionary; but I could easily see she had the matter deeply at heart. The situation was not such as I should myself have desired; but I knew that I had the reputation of indulging a proud, and almost a rebellious spirit, as far as the world was concerned, the energy of which had been increased by my education and habits. I took, therefore, a sort of malicious pleasure in disappointing the plodding calculators of my father's acquaintance, who had affirmed I had no useful abilities; and I half resolved to prove to them that what I could resolve to undertake I could execute, with talents far beyond their methodical dulness. This was again the project of a young man; but I never could feel a half interest in any thing. My pride, as well as my future advantage, was deeply staked upon that before me; and I consequently turned my attention towards it, with a zeal that not only astonished others, but, to say truth, surprised even myself.

Behold me, then, doomed for my offences, whatever those were, – and my own conscience did not reproach me with many, – to spend the greater part of the day on a high stool, and go through all the drudgery of a counting-house, busy with invoices, &c. &c.; and at intervals execrating French aristocracy, Russian *traîneaux*, and English speculation. I saw my mother only of an evening; but I saw her countenance lighted up at those meetings with an unusual degree of complacency and softness: even her health seemed to amend; and if I was at some moments disposed to break my chain, I never visited her without finding fresh motives for enduring it. Our meals were necessarily frugal, and our indulgences few; yet my income, though narrow, was a considerable addition to hers. I therefore daily perceived the impossibility of alienating it. On feeling the lightness of my purse, my conduct towards St. Victoire nevertheless sometimes came home to me. I remembered the half-disdainful hints I had thrown out on his poverty; and although they were certainly extorted by no small degree of insolence on his side, I became sensible that I had degraded my own character by returning it. It was now my part to be indigent. I did not feel myself at all the less proud on that account, and I therefore learned to make allowances for him: yet I saw, with half despair, that I was further removed than I had been at that period from all chance of conciliating his regard, since it was not even a concession like that I made to my own heart that would have done it; and it was very clear that the man who had despised a rich merchant would, at all times, utterly shut his door against a poor one. Claudine and myself were, however, both growing older in the interim; and I concluded that if we could but contrive to grow richer too, we might at length reasonably set his authority at defiance.

In spite of the mystery my mother had thought it prudent to observe, it was not long before I penetrated into the motives of her conduct. When chance sent me home to her lodgings at an unexpected hour, I more than once encountered my uncle coming from them. Our meeting appeared at first to disconcert him: by degrees he seemed to accustom himself to it, and at length bestowed on me a half-gracious salutation. I returned the civility, but made no overtures towards improving it. I learned, however, from third persons, that his visits were pretty frequent; and had I not done so, I should have known by a certain number of additional comforts and conveniences I observed my mother to possess lately, and which I knew our limited means would not have allowed her to indulge in, that some more certain resources than our own were concerned in them. This was every way balm to my heart; not from its flattering any views that immediately respected myself, but as I knew that the returning kindness of her brother was, of all possible events, the most grateful to hers, and could not fail to be in worldly circumstances infinitely advantageous. In law I was eventually my uncle's heir; but he had cut off both my mother and myself, by a will made several months before the death of my father; and as his fortune was his own to bestow, we could, under these circumstances, claim nothing but the little stipend which his fraternal regard had induced him to allot his sister. A reconciliation might still, indeed, incline him to change the disposition of his worldly concerns; but I now knew too much of life to have any great reliance upon this hope, and too much of the dilatory nature of most men not to doubt whether mere indolence might not defeat his purpose, should it even be favourable towards me. I made no doubt, however, but my mother formed a thousand chimerical projects, the first step towards the accomplishing of which would be to associate me in my uncle's commercial undertakings; and as she was most sanguine in her opinion of my personal influence and abilities, to whatever point they were directed, I was sure she secretly persuaded herself that I should in time prove the sole manager, and, finally, the heir of his wealth.

My plan was far different; but I seemed to shut my eyes to what was passing, and permitted her to follow her own in the manner she deemed most judicious. In fact, I earnestly wished her to acquire such a share, both in the heart and domestic concerns of her brother, as would make her accede with less reluctance to any bolder project I might adopt towards my own establishment in life; for in spite of the external show I continued to make of content and application, my very soul was secretly weary of the uniform and mechanical existence I now endured; or, perhaps, it was the restless spirit of love that thus undermined my quiet, and rendered me at heart thoroughly averse from a sort of occupation, which, had I possessed a disengaged mind, my early acquirements and habits ought to have fitted for me. What led me to suspect this was, that my plans, begin at what point of the compass they would, always in the end pointed towards St. Petersburgh; and though, reasonably speaking, it was of all places on the globe the last where I could have submitted to appear in any subordinate situation, something relative to it was ever uppermost in my fancy. Even while meditating a voyage to India, I detected myself thinking of the snows of the north; and winter, 'all unlovely as it was,' proved, from the association of ideas, to me a season of enjoyment.

Whatever was to be the event of *my* plans, my mother's, at least, seemed in a way to be slowly successful. My uncle invited me several times to dine with her at his house; and although I had no great cause to be flattered by my reception there, for he still continued to show me very little distinction or regard, I was, on the whole, better pleased with this sort of conduct, than if he had conceived a strong personal liking for me. I did not, in fact, believe he had any; though his indulgence towards his sister induced him to put a constraint on himself: but I was, nevertheless, a little staggered when I learned, from a mutual friend on whose veracity I could rely, that, however cold his manners were to me when present, he had spoken of me, when absent, in such terms as hardly any but a father would have used. I began myself to suspect that a gleam of sunshine was likely to burst remotely upon my path; and though I could not altogether shape my expectations into any form wholly gratifying, I felt the burden I had imposed upon myself become daily less heavy.

Mine, grievous as it seemed to me, was, nevertheless, far short of what I continually saw fall on others. Among those whom the concerns of business threw in my way, was a young Frenchman of the name of Vaudreuil. He had been recommended by an eminent house at Rouen, and was engaged for the foreign department in ours. His talents for business seemed to be moderate, but his industry and application were unequalled; so was his temperance. He lived on air: never tasted wine, nor shared in any conviviality whatever. Contrary to the general character of his countrymen, he was serious in the extreme. His manners were thought proud; and as he was known to be poor, he was of consequence little liked by those with whom he was, in some degree, obliged to associate. I had, for Claudine's sake, a slight partiality for those of her country; and I occasionally manifested it towards him. It was increased when I found he had been despatched from Rouen to St. Petersburgh, before he was sent over to England, and had seen Claudine herself. It was not at all probable that his condition in life should have allowed him to mingle in her circle; but I, nevertheless, took pleasure in talking with one who had even seen her. I found him extremely agreeable when I came to converse with him; and I suspected that he had not been always a man of business. This, however, was a confession I never could extort from him; and his reserve naturally created the same sentiment on my part. Once the extreme narrowness of his circumstances obliged him to have recourse to me for a pecuniary assistance; and I could see the excessive pride of his soul by the tears it forced into his eyes. As this event, however, did not seem to increase his confidence in me, it naturally threw a still greater check upon every attempt I might have been inclined to make towards acquiring it. I think we esteemed each other more than before; yet a sort of coldness grew up between us – the natural consequence of a feeling which, by some opposing principle, is not permitted to act with the force it demands. One more powerful, and even torturing, was awakened in my bosom by a very simple accident, and it related to Vaudreuil.

We had engaged to go into the country together on a particular day, as much to satisfy ourselves on a point of curiosity as pleasure.

I had promised to call upon him. He was not quite dressed, and I went into his room. While conversing with him there, I happened to cast my eyes upon a black riband which was at his bosom: – it seemed to me as if a picture ought to depend from it, and I was seized with a singular fit of curiosity to ascertain whether there was one or not. I kept my attention earnestly directed towards the riband, and at length was gratified. I saw it was, indeed, a picture, but my heart suddenly bounded, and my pulse throbbed, for I believed it to be that of Claudine. I had now the eye of an Argus, and I had more than one accidental opportunity of reconnoitering the portrait. It was, beyond doubt, either that of Claudine, or of some person strongly resembling her. In a broken and irresolute tone I strove to rally Vaudreuil on the subject. He made no answer, but he sighed deeply, thrust the picture into his bosom, and buttoned it up there. I had now room for meditation more gloomy than any I had ever yet indulged. I recollected all the hazards that attended my engagement with Claudine, and the indirect release I had proffered her when we parted. How could I be assured that she had not availed herself of it? Vaudreuil might be nobly born and highly bred. I saw nothing against this supposition. He had been to Petersburgh. He might, for ought I knew, be the most intimate friend of St. Victoire, and in his eyes, therefore, however poor, not exceptionable, as the husband of his sister. Claudine's country, her habits of thinking, time, distance, and the influence of her brother, might have wrought a change in her affections; and while I was waiting the slow aid of the future to assure my happiness, the past might already have undermined it. While I think of the tragical moments I endured in consequence of all these conjectures, I cannot help admiring how ingenious man is in tormenting himself, and how much a little common sense would on certain occasions befriend him.

As our party was composed of several persons, it was not possible for me, throughout any part of that day, to bring Vaudreuil to such conversation as might enlighten my doubts. I passed, therefore, the most anxious and miserable of nights, one half of which was spent in writing to St. Petersburgh; and I arose almost with the dawn, determined to satisfy myself on the subject which agitated me. Alert as I was, Vaudreuil seemed no less so; for at a very early hour in the morning I received a note from him, expressed singularly well, but with a tone of depression, that, in spite of the suspicions which haunted me, excited the deepest interest in his fate. It contained a request for a small sum of money, and an urgent entreaty that it might, if possible, be sent by the bearer. Vaudreuil had acquitted himself of his former obligation to me in a manner highly honourable to his feelings, though in reality grievous to mine: for I was sure that nothing but the most painfully rigid economy could have enabled him to do so. Yet what he would not acknowledge, delicacy forbade me to wring from him; and I had, therefore, contented myself with obliging him by every indirect method I could possibly devise. Though he did not notice this, I had seen, on many occasions, that it sunk deeply into his soul, and I believed it had rendered him even more reluctant to demand any service from me. I had no doubt that something critical had occurred that induced this application, and I, therefore, without inquiry or hesitation, sent him a larger sum than that he requested, reserving my explanation with him to a late hour of the day, when I hoped the exigency that had thus suddenly occurred would be settled.

I found the time insupportably long in the interim. It did not at all surprise me that Vaudreuil failed to appear to execute his usual daily employment; but I was thunderstruck on being informed that he had thrown it up. This, however, was not altogether true. He had, indeed, stated to his employers that it would not be possible for him to attend during a period, the extent of which he could not decide; but it was by no means clear, from the tenor of his letter, that he would return to it no more. I flew to his lodgings; but I there learned only a confirmation of my chagrin; for he had discharged them the moment he received the money from me; and the persons of the house could give me no other account of him than that he walked towards the city to find out some public conveyance by which he might leave London.

Had I been sure Claudine was his companion, I think I could hardly have been more enraged. In the first transports of my surprise and indignation I at once concluded that he had seen me notice the picture; that he was perfectly aware of the interest I took in the original; and that he had basely practised upon my credulity, by making the supply I had sent him the means of extricating either her or himself, or both, from my resentment. Nothing, however, was less likely than any of these suppositions. Vaudreuil did not seem the man who would shrink from any person's resentment; much less take advantage either of generosity or credulity. It was improbable in the extreme that Claudine should be in England; and it was perfectly absurd to suppose that he had shipped himself off, at an hour's notice, for Petersburgh. – I was not without an inclination to ship myself off, nevertheless; but I grew cooler as I continued to reflect. The picture, after all, might not be that of Claudine. Vandreuil might have concerns that called him thus suddenly away, without any reference to love; and, above every thing, there was internal evidence in the style of his letter, and my knowledge of his character, that he would, under any circumstances, return.

My reason was tolerably satisfied; but the aching demand of my heart was not appeased. More events, however, are sometimes comprised within a few hours than at others pass in years. While I was thus racking my imagination on the subject of Claudine and Vaudreuil, my mother's patience, and her messenger's, had been wearied in seeking me. I was found at last; and I learned, not without a strong emotion of anxiety and surprise, that I had been sent for to my uncle, who was taken with an apoplectic fit. I hastened immediately to his house, where I found my mother, by whom I was informed that every effort to recover him had been fruitless. – As he had never been sensible from the moment she saw him, she had had no opportunity of strengthening his good will towards me; or of influencing him in the disposal of his worldly affairs by the sight of her own tenderness and grief. All her highly cherished hopes, therefore, were suddenly blighted; and, in addition to a very afflicting calamity, she had a disappointment to encounter for which she was wholly unprepared. – That I felt was very small. – I had never relied on my uncle, and had been, in fact, more afraid of his entangling me by some half kindness that would have rendered him the arbiter of my actions, than sanguine in my expectations from his generosity. My mother knew, however, that she should in some degree benefit by his will (though resentment towards my father had excluded me from so doing); and we were accordingly present when it was opened.

The first thing that excited our attention and surprise was the date, which was more recent than we expected. Being a bachelor, he had no immediate relatives, ourselves excepted, on whom to bestow his wealth. He gave a considerable number of legacies, however, to many of his friends; he settled a large portion of his personal fortune on my mother: – both both she and I looked at each other with astonishment, when we found the residue was allotted to me. This residue included a commercial property to some extent, together with an estate which he had purchased in his native country, Lanarkshire. Never shall I forget the look my mother gave me: – it was so sweet an approbation of the sacrifices she believed I had made to moderation and to her tranquillity: – it conveyed to my soul so tender an assurance, that she was persuaded I owed to my own self-government the good fortune I had thus unexpectedly encountered, that it was more flattering to me than if I had received the wealth of the world. On her side, I believe the acquisition of half of it would have been less delightful than that of her 'simple native vale.' – The romantic falls of the Clyde had been the scene of her earliest and tenderest recollections: it was in that neighbourhood, too, I was born; and the spot was endeared by a variety of nameless local charms, congenial to the most insensible bosom, and particularly so to those of my country. *I* also was not without my little hoard of hopes and recollections; but they were somewhat damped by the vague doubt I had something struggling in my mind beyond even those emotions naturally excited by the occasion. – She had long entertained a surmise that I had some attachment; but she naturally concluded that it was subdued by prudence, and therefore waited tranquilly till the impulse of my own heart should induce me to confide it to her. This was not the moment to do so. I could not prevail on myself to let her see that I doubted the fidelity of Claudine; and, in truth, the circumstance on which I founded my doubt, however perplexing to the imagination of a lover, was in itself so puerile and uncertain, that I knew not how to reveal it.

I waited impatiently the return of Vaudreuil; for I was persuaded that he would return, or that I should at least hear from him, though it were only in discharge of the pecuniary obligation between us; and I was necessarily obliged to employ myself, in the interim, in the regulation of my uncle's concerns. I did this with the more alacrity, as it was my intention, the moment they were in any safe train, to embark for Petersburgh, bear the news of my own change of fortune to Claudine, decide by her looks and her reception of me upon the interest I still held in her heart, and, if I found that unchanged, prevail with her to withdraw, either openly or in secret, from the authority of St. Victoire, and accompany me to England as my wife. – A long and cruel fortnight passed, however, without any tidings of Vaudreuil. During that period I could hardly forbear smiling, at intervals, to see those who now called themselves my friends imputing the indifference and half melancholy which hung about me to a hypocritical sorrow for my uncle's death. I believe I was looked upon by these men of the world as a complete dissembler; and so far were they from calculating what passed in my heart, that I have no doubt they thought me secretly overwhelmed with exultation and joy.

I had been so indefatigable in my exertions, as soon to prepare every thing for my approaching departure. I meditated in what manner I should, without saying too much, communicate to my mother the nature of the business that carried me abroad; and I was walking, deeply engrossed with my own reflections, along the Strand, when, happening to cast my eyes upon a hackney-coach that passed me, I saw Vaudreuil in it. The coach was going very fast; and was beyond my reach before I had recollection to stop it. – I could entertain no doubt, however, that it was he, for he bowed to me smilingly. His countenance was more lighted up; and, from the glance I caught of him, I thought he seemed better dressed than usual.

This was a mystery, the unravelling of which at once engaged all my attention. That Vaudreuil should be in London, should know himself to be my debtor, yet neither write nor call upon me; should be aware that he stood exposed to the most degrading suspicion, yet coolly bow to me from a hackney-coach, seemed almost beyond belief. I went to his former lodgings; but he had not been heard of there. I then hastened to the counting-house where he had been used to attend, but no tidings of his return had reached any of the clerks. A letter, however, was put into my charge, addressed to him that had been sent thither by the people with whom he had lived. I knew it instantly to be the hand-writing of Claudine, and I could, therefore, no longer doubt it to be her picture which he wore. – All my suspicions again recurred. I was on the point of tearing open the letter in order to satisfy them: – but I remembered that I had no claim over Vaudreuil, but one I should have blushed to assert; and that, if he had even robbed me of Claudine's affections, it was sufficiently probable that he never knew I had engaged them. No other acquittal but that of the petty money concern between us was, in the apparent state of the business, necessary on his part; and such was the confidence inspired by the kind of character I had observed in him, that I was still persuaded, if there was any thing treacherous in his conduct, he would at length appear to answer it. The letter had no shipmark: I examined that of the post; it was from Hull. – My voyage to Petersburgh would then be fruitless. – Claudine was evidently not there. – The appearance of Vaudreuil would be, perhaps, alike useless to me. She would probably have bestowed herself upon him before we met; – for, if there was no deceitful motive in her voyage, why did she not write to me? I had not even heard from her for a considerable time before. But this circumstance I had hitherto imputed to some accidental failure of her

The Canterbury Tales

letters: that before me announced a different reason for her silence; and I had the torture of supposing she was at that very moment in London, yet as far out of the reach of my penetration as if in the wilds of Siberia. I returned home extremely melancholy; and, to my great surprise, found waiting for me there the very person I had been over half the town in search of – in other words, Vaudreuil himself. In my hand I held Claudine's letter, which I had taken possession of, leaving word where it was to be found; and I advanced towards him with a turbulence and impatience of which he did not seem at all sensible. His countenance was, indeed, as it had appeared to me in the coach, animated and cheerful: in a word, he looked happy, and that was enough to make me miserable.

'I come,' said he, stepping towards me, 'to demand your congratulations, and to announce a fortunate event in which you will sympathise with me.'

'Spare yourself the relation,' said I sullenly – 'I know the good fortune that has befallen you without its being told. You are married – or on the point of being so. And, to show you that I am better informed of your affairs than you suppose, I can even name the faithless woman who has bestowed herself upon you.'

'When I do marry,' said Vaudreuil, laughing, 'I hope it will not be a faithless woman, at least. You are, in truth, a most ingenious guesser: and after you have pointed out the fair one who means to do me the favour of bestowing herself upon me, I shall know what portion of gratitude is due both to you and to her. In the interim, however, assure yourself that it is not matrimony, but that which has of late engrossed a much greater share of the thoughts of mankind, politics – which is in question with me. I have received undoubted information that the new government in France will allow me to recover at least a considerable portion of my family claims and property there. I have never borne arms against my country; and should I prove successful in my application, I shall be enabled to serve a brother who is less fortunately circumstanced, and a sister inexpressibly dear to me.'

'You have a sister!' exclaimed I.

'Undoubtedly I have,' returned Vaudreuil, smiling archly.

'And you wear her picture – '

'At my bosom!' and he drew it from thence.

'Ah, it is Claudine! – *my* Claudine – my *own* Claudine,' cried I, snatching ad kissing it rapturously a thousand times. Vaudreuil could

The Canterbury Tales

not forbear smiling at an *étourderie* so foreign to all he had yet seen of my character.

'I am ignorant how soon she is to be your Claudine,' said he at length, gently disengaging the portrait; 'but I know she is at at present mine; and I am not quite assured that she will permit me to authorise such violent caresses. Let us be seated, my kind friend,' he added, recovering his usual interesting gravity of tone and manner; 'and if you can command these transports of yours, – so little in unison with our ideas of English phlegm, – I will tell you, what I am sure you will have real pleasure in hearing – I will tell you that your generous interposition rescued Claudine and both her brothers from a state of despondency; that your pecuniary kindness supplied with necessaries and comforts the proud spirit and suffering frame of St. Victoire; – finally, that it has afforded Claudine herself the means of coming up to London, and of thanking you in person. These, believe me, are not dreams,' said he, perceiving me stare with astonishment: 'it is but very lately that I have known the history of my own family: such as it is I will relate it to you. I need not tell you that I am much younger than St. Victoire - there is, in fact, only the difference of two years between Claudine and myself: – but I look older – for I have suffered,' – he added, sighing. 'From the time I had any use of reason, it unfortunately happened that my political opinions did not accord with those of my family – I was, therefore, an early outcast from it, and remained in France, when my relations quitted it, without their deigning to take the smallest interest in my after fate. My name was prohibited to Claudine's lips, as attaching disgrace to her own; and it was the constant habit of suppressing it that probably prevented its reaching your ears. I was not much more fortunate, however, in my public career than my father and my brother had been. The fickle and too enthusiastic nation, of which I was an individual, became sanguinary, and disgraced the noblest cause of humanity. I was near falling a victim to the guillotine; but a friendly banker at Paris concealed me, and by his assistance I passed in safety to Rouen. I was not without abilities, and am among those of my countrymen who think it no disgrace to use them. I applied myself under a borrowed name to business: but I did not find that I was wholly safe from persecution, and was, therefore, advised to quit France. My heart fondly turned towards St. Petersburgh, where I believed I should find my mother, my brother, and my sister. As I was now rather more unfortunate than themselves, I conceived that my offences would be expiated in their eyes; and I accordingly embarked. I soon found that I had had the misfortune to lose one of the three, without being happy enough to recover the other two; for my reception from St. Victoire was neither brotherly nor generous. It was indeed such as determined me to meet him no more; for I was not without some share of the family pride when it was roused. I saw Claudine accidentally for a quarter of an hour, but he would not permit me to converse with her freely. I wrote to her, however; and I requested from her my mother's picture, as a memorial of my family. She did not possess it; but she sent me her own, together with an earnest entreaty to see me again. No doubt she thought me very unkind; for I was so circumstanced that I could not enter the lists with St. Victoire on that subject, and he eluded my address when I attempted to send her another letter. I, therefore, quitted St. Petersburgh without having an opportunity of vindicating my sentiments to her, and came over to England; where, by the continued assistance of my worthy friends at Rouen, I obtained the employment in the course of which I was fortunate enough to meet with you. Ah! your generous heart, my dear friend,' said he, pressing my hand, 'has sympathised with mine during his narration! May it be thus that good actions ever come home to the bosom of him who performs them! You respected the innocent tenderness of Claudine, and that tenderness will, I hope, henceforward be unremittingly exercised to reward you! You extended your philanthropy and good offices to a foreigner whom your countrymen did not always treat with the indulgence due to the unfortunate: – you have gained by it a friend, who will, to the latest hour of his life, be the friend of Englishmen, and the protector of those of any country to whom protection is necessary.'

Vaudreuil spoke this with an energy and seriousness that was extremely affecting; or else its being my own panegyric caused it extremely to affect me. He spoke English tolerably; but on this occasion he expressed himself throughout in French: and I know not how it happens but my translation seems to have lost all the fire and spirit of the original. Nothing now appeared necessary towards my felicity but to see Claudine. I told him as much; and at the same moment, recollecting the letter of hers I still possessed, I offered it to him. 'I have conversed with her since it was written,' said he, putting it in his pocket; 'and, therefore, know its contents. St. Victoire is at this moment extremely fatigued, and in no condition to receive you. Claudine, who had not been many hours in town after a most rapid journey, will herself be the better for a short repose; and as she cannot calculate that I should meet with you so soon, she will probably find it. You do not yet know by what means I became possessed of your secret. Have you no curiosity? – or are you so inhospitable that you are already solicitous to get rid of me?'

Vaudreuil was not wrong in his surmise. I could with great pleasure have taken him by the arm, and led him out of my house towards that in which I should find his sister. I had not the least curiosity to know how he became acquainted with my *secret*, as he called it. It appeared to me that the story would have done equally well at any time: and, in plain terms, that he could not have found one more *mal-à-propos* for telling it than the present; but I had my measures to keep. Vaudreuil had generously humbled both himself and his family too much before me, to allow me any liberty of action where they were concerned. I had, therefore, nothing for it but patience; and I endeavoured to collect myself to a decent attention. I was restless, however, at first: but the subject was still Claudine and her brothers; – it therefore again insensibly interested and tranquillised me.

'I had not been long in England,' said Vandreuil, 'before I wrote to St. Victoire. We had parted from each other in high displeasure: but when I recollected that it might perhaps be for the last time, I could not resolve to leave him and Claudine without any trace of me; or myself without a place in the remembrance of either. I thought it vain, however, to write to her; as he would, doubtless, again suppress my letter. Without being circumstantial, I gave him to understand that, on my arrival in England, I had fallen upon a plan by which I might secure myself from the horrors of penury. To say truth, I was afraid of explaining the nature of my employment, lest I should irreparably offend his aristocratical ideas; but I made it plain that I solicited nothing from him but brotherly good wishes and regard. I exhorted him to allow Claudine at least sometimes to write to me, and gave him my address for that purpose. I received no answer to this letter: as indeed I hardly expected I should.

'A considerable time passed away, every hour of which added to my melancholy, as I began to believe that I was fated to be always an alien from my family connections; when, on the evening, or rather night, of that day on which you and I had been in the country together, I returned late to my lodgings, and, to my surprise, found a letter lying there for me, directed in a female hand. It was from Claudine, who wrote, at the desire of St. Victoire, to request my protection and assistance. They had landed together from a Russian merchantman at the port of Hull; driven abruptly from Petersburgh by the indiscretion of St. Victoire. Claudine will give you the particulars of his quarrel with a Russian officer of distinction. They had a meeting in consequence of it, when both were wounded, the Russian, severely. My brother, notwithstanding his own suffering, was put under confinement; and death or exile to Siberia seemed the punishment that awaited him. The recovery of his antagonist, however, and an interest he had the address to create for himself in the heart of a female favourite, mitigated his sentence. He was commanded to quit the Russian territories within a limited time, and to return thither no more under pain of death. The period allowed him to prepare for his departure was extremely short: his sickness, together with his extravagance, had left him totally unprovided with money, nor could his friend the Marquis de S— assist him; for he had been himself obliged to withdraw from St. Petersburgh some little time before; and his wife, from distress of circumstances, and retired to her father, the Duc de C—.

'In this exigency, without assistants, advisers, or friends, St. Victoire and Claudine could think of no better plan than that of coming over to England, and throwing themselves upon me! – Me! – whose miserable and impoverished state you are so well acquainted with! – The calculation they formed of it was, however, very different from the truth. In writing to St. Victoire, I had forborne to draw it in its worst colours, both for the reasons I have before given you, and the fear lest he should suspect me of wanting any pecuniary service from him. This delicacy on my part was the source of their error: they embarked full of chimerical hopes. Claudine has since told me, that although she dared not hint as much to St. Victoire, there was yet another heart in your island on which she relied even more entirely than on mine – how justly, I have since had ample occasion to prove! – Their passage was rough. My brother's wound, which had been too hastily closed, opened again; but for Claudine's knowledge of English they would have been totally helpless; and such was altogether their situation soon after they landed, that no resource remained but to write to me, and exhort me to come and extricate them from it.

'Alas! I had no means to do so; and Claudine's letter was, therefore, a stab to my heart. At the moment I received it I neither possessed a single guinea, nor the means of raising one. You were the only human being to whom I had ever applied on a similar occasion, and I now ventured to throw myself a second time upon you. By an effort better suited to the liberality of your mind than to your circumstances, you sent me a more considerable sum than I had requested. I travelled night and day to reach Hull, and fortunately arrived there sooner than I had been expected; when I immediately called in proper assistance to St. Victoire, who was sufficiently altered both in constitution and manners to excite my tenderest sympathy. As to dear Claudine, she and I had soon cause to regret that we had not earlier understood each other's heart. Nothing could be more delightful than this first intercourse between two beings so nearly allied in blood, yet hitherto strangers. Your conversation and habits of thinking had enlightened her mind too much to allow of her cherishing the prejudices which had originally disunited me from my family; and I was no less delighted with the cultivation of her judgment than with the charms of her person. I told her exactly my own situation; and, without precisely naming you, described the generous friend whose assistance had enabled me to undertake my journey. Claudine, on her part, was not less frank. She related to me all the secrets of her heart, and bespoke an interest in mine for the man she loved. Imagine our mutual surprise – our lively and exquisite pleasure, when we found that we had in reality been talking of one and the same person! – There was nothing after this discovery so much the wish of either as to reach London with all possible despatch.

'Claudine had already written a long letter to you, in order to account, by a relation of the late events that had befallen St. Victoire, for a silence that had exceeded her usual limits. At my desire she suppressed this letter. I hardly entertained a doubt but on the receipt of it you would have come to us at the hazard probably of great inconvenience to yourself; and, to speak frankly, I also promised my own heart an indescribable satisfaction in being the first to announce to you those delightful sensations in which I was certain you would sympathise. Claudine did not, I assure you, make the sacrifice I demanded of her without some regret: but she did make it: and the rather, as we had reason to suppose St. Victoire's health would amend rapidly enough to allow of our setting off without much delay. In fact you will perceive by the time of my absence that we made all possible speed. Our circumstances, nevertheless, did not allow us to choose the most commodious method of travelling, and my brother is of consequence ill and exhausted. My first business was, indeed by Claudine's express desire, to seek you: nor was there more than one interest in the world that could have detained me in the pursuit of you. It was precisely that, however, which happened to occur. I

met on the way one of my countrymen, from whom I learned some
particulars relative to France which I had long most anxiously waited
to hear. He referred me for further authentic details to another mutual
friend, who was that very morning to set out on his return thither. Not
a single moment was to be lost. I drove with all the rapidity I could
command to the lodgings of the latter, and was fortunate enough to
meet with him. As the situation of our affairs was in all respects alike,
the account he gave me of his, left me no reason to doubt the event
of my own representations at Paris. I intrusted to him a memorial and
other papers I had long since prepared against a similar occasion;
and I rely so much both on his zeal, and the justice of my cause, as
to assure myself that I shall quickly obtain the proper passports and
security. If, in addition to this, I should be happy enough to recover
my family property, how joyfully shall I share my affluence with the
man who was the friend of my poverty!'

Vaudreuil had spoken so long, that I really began to apprehend
he never intended to conclude. He was no talker in general, and
therefore I wondered the more at him. But his heart was full of his
subject, as I could see in his eyes, and I believe he felt an absolute
necessity for thus pouring it out. In spite of my impatience I had not
failed, however, at intervals, to be both flattered and touched by his
recital; and under any circumstances not gratification would have been
greater perhaps than that of listening to it. I had just then, however,
a much greater in view, and I, therefore, hurried him away. I had
gathered from the conclusion of his discourse that he was yet ignorant
of my uncle's death, and the change it had occasioned in my worldly
concerns. This was not surprising; since that I should have become,
during his absence, either a guest or even a constant resident in my
uncle's house, was among the occurrences of life that might naturally
happen. It was now time to explain my situation to him. I could see that
he was much struck with it, and felt as though Claudine and himself
were suddenly rendered bankrupts both in fortune and in love. But
the native dignity and candour of his mind made him quickly recover
from the surprise, and he rejoiced in my prosperity.

'Poor St. Victoire!' said he, smiling, as we entered his lodgings: 'his
pride will not even have the consolation of believing that he is going to
take an impoverished man to his bosom!' – I was far from being assured
that St. Victoire's pride was of so generous a nature: on the contrary, I
was strongly inclined to suspect that my affluence would be the only
consoling circumstance to him under the mortification of having me

The Canterbury Tales

for a brother-in-law. I made no comment, however, on Vaudreuil's speech; nor indeed had I time. Claudine was before my eyes – she was in my arms: more lovely, as it appeared to me, than ever: for that pure pleasure which springs immediately from the heart embellished her features; her person was in reality improved. She was grown taller: – her figure, without losing its slightness, was more formed; and she had a decided character of countenance. A scene of the most unalloyed transport succeeded, and it was not immediately that I could recollect myself enough to think at all of St. Victoire. When I did, I was not unnmoved by his paleness and apparent depression. His arm was still in bandages, and the loss of blood which he had sustained had altered him very considerably. The ground between us had been rendered perfectly smooth by the kind offices of his brother and sister. We therefore saluted each other with some degree of cordiality; and both studiously avoided all reference to the past. As the house I had lately come into possession of was spacious. I earnestly entreated the whole family to take up their abode there: and this was the more necessary, as the situation of the invalid demanded comfort and an attention he could not so well receive elsewhere.

'It seems only a question whether we shall live with you, or on you my good friend,' said Vaudreuil, perceiving my proposal had given birth to some scruples: – 'for my part I think it is very clear which we ought, for our own gratification, to choose.' To this decision Claudine and St. Victoire, without much difficulty, acceded. I stayed several hours with them, and then returned home, to give my mother notice of the visiters she was so soon to receive. Her surprise was at first very great. She questioned me abundantly concerning Claudine; and I could easily discover that she secretly regretted my not having chosen an English woman: though, even in that case, I felt that one of her own country would have been still preferable in her eyes; but she was too indulgent and too deeply interested in my happiness to raise any obstacles to my present plans; and on my part I was persuaded that she had only to see the woman I had chosen in order to be convinced no other was so well worthy to be my choice.

Before evening every thing was in readiness to receive our guests. My mother herself accompanied me at a very early hour to fetch the lovely Claudine to that home, of which she was soon to become the mistress. My uncles's carriage, as he had been old and infirm, was a conveyance perfectly convenient to St. Victoire, and he arrived at my door without much fatigue.

'It is the fate of our family to be overwhelmed with your bounties, Monsieur,' said he, as I gave him my arm to mount the stairs, – I thought it was said proudly too. He was sufficiently a man of the world, however, not to overlook that portion of its goods with which I was surrounded. I saw him eye the apartment we sat in, which had been indeed somewhat expensively furnished by my uncle, and I could fancy I heard him say to himself – 'Humph! This then is the house of an English merchant!' - Vaudreuil and Claudine, on the contrary, saw not a mirror or a carpet it contained. That dear girl's spirits soon rose in sympathy with mine, and we became a pair of the most giddy, laughing lovers, that can easily be imagined. To look at us indeed, any body would have supposed we had never known a sorrow or a care; and Vaudreuil, who had hitherto seen nothing in his sister but a pretty pensive young woman, or in me but a sombre man of business, was perfectly astonished at the metamorphosis in both. We quickly seduced him, in spite of his habitual seriousness, into a participation of our mirth. And St. Victoire himself, though a little starched at first, forgot, before the evening closed, his indispositions, his pride, and his prejudices, and condescended to have more than one hearty laugh along with us. I was very sorry when the hour of parting and repose came. Nevertheless I slept soundly, for I was certain of seeing Claudine again in the morning; and, in return, she has since assured me she never had a more delightful slumber than that she enjoyed under the protection of my roof.

I had judged rightly with respect to my mother: she felt herself the happiest of creatures on being thus suddenly embosomed in a youthful circle, each individual of which looked up for her approving smile to sanction their own. The ingenuousness, the youthful gaiety, the sweet playfulness of Claudine's character and manners completely won her affections, and she soon lived in her sight nearly as much as I did: nor did the former fail to cultivate this tender regard by every office of duty and attention on her part.

Our first business was to make a little establishment for St. Victoire, that should ensure the recovery of his health, and then to forward those measures that promised to be favourable for Vaudreuil. We were successful in both instances. The applications made by the latter were approved by the men in power of his own country, and he had very soon the satisfaction of learning that he might return thither without danger – to say the least: but, in fact, he had every reason to believe that he should be reinstated in great part of his rights. This was certainly no music to the ears of St. Victoire: nevertheless, it was better than that the whole family should be proscribed; and the generous character of his brother left the Count no cause to doubt but he would derive his share of advantage from the return of the former to France. Nice as this business was to settle, Vaudreuil and I contrived to arrange it between us. For, in spite of his political opinions, he was not without a delicate but strong repugnance to the dispossessing an elder branch of the family of his rights in life. As to Claudine, she was out of the question. I was rich enough for both, and I, therefore, lent no ear to any thing that could be said on that subject. She was now, alas! not so ignorant of the real sufferings of poverty as she had been; and this knowledge, which I had at one time so deprecated and earnestly endeavoured to shield her from, became in the end an affecting monitor that taught her to feel for others when she ceased to have anything to feel or fear on that head for herself.

My mourning for my uncle obliged me to postpone my marriage for a short time: it would indeed have been postponed still longer but for the necessity of Vaudreuil's return to France. Both Claudine and myself were solicitous that our union should be sanctioned by the presence of that tender and amiable brother whom we were so soon to lose. How sincerely did we all lament that the tide of human affairs should separate beings united by every principle of affection or intellect! – How gloomy was the consideration that the human race at large, accustomed to blood, should forget in mutual animosity that sacred tie common to all! – Surely it is for the liberal-minded and humane of every nation to counteract the destructive influence of general prejudice, by extending and strengthening, in their private habits, those social feelings which bid man acknowledge his fellow-creature in every quarter of the globe.

On the day preceeding that fixed for Vaudreuil's departure, Claudine and I were united. St. Victoire himself bestowed her upon me. I should have been better pleased to have owed the gift, dear as it was, to his brother: but Vaudreuil and I understood each other, and that was enough. A most sorrowful parting succeeded: but it has been the only real chagrin that has clouded my life since my marriage. There are heretics who will smile at this sentence. To such I answer, that I have not yet been married many years; and even if I had – but they will smile again! – There is no curing these sort of people!

My mother, good woman, often looks at us, and observes, 'that marriages are (according to the old proverb) certainly made in heaven.' So also say I! but she, in the simplicity of her heart, draws her conclusions from the extraordinary circumstance that occasioned our meeting; I, mine, from the still more extraordinary one of our desiring never to part!

St. Victoire has entirely recovered the ill consequences of his wound, and lives at no great distance from us on a pension remitted him by his brother, who has retrieved great part of the family fortune. The former has not yet, however, forgotten his passion for noblesse, and is a little inclined to drop my acquaintance if we happen suddenly to encounter each other in Bond Street or Pall Mall. I forgive him: for he keeps the first company, and is a fine man. Vaudreuil's circle is smaller, and he, I am assured, is a very happy one. His happiness, indeed, as well as mine is of that tranquil nature at which men of the world will wonder. Be it so! I neither envy them their inflamed passions nor sophisticated tastes.

As leisure has served, Claudine and myself, in company with my mother, have more than once visited our little native spot on the banks of the Clyde; when, in the enjoyment of rural beauty, we do not fail to commemorate the worthy pastor, our kind and first friend; we talk of his flowers – his bees – and *his sun*. We mutually agree that none ever shone so brightly to our eyes before. We have long since established a correspondence with the good old man, continued by small but grateful offerings on our part; and we sometimes even amuse ourselves with chimerical projects, of presenting to his eyes those fragile but interesting human blossoms, which alone could to us embellish his garden, as they form the chief charm of our own.

THE LANDLADY'S TALE
INTRODUCTION

> Youth of the quick uncheated sight,
> Thy walks, Observance, most delight.
>
> *Collins*

'Did you please to look for a lodging, sir?' said a respectable women, to an elderly gentleman, whom she had observed loitering for some time in the neighbourhood of the Esplanade at Weymouth. 'What *there*, do you mean?' replied the stranger, drily, and pointing to the sea, on which, indeed, he had been most intently gazing at the moment she addressed him. 'I beg pardon, sir,' rejoined the first speaker, somewhat out of countenance at what she conceived to be a rebuke; 'but as the day is so *uncommon* hot, and you seem to be a stranger, it struck me' – 'That one might be perfectly cool in such a spot as that? – truly many a brave fellow has been cool enough there.' – 'To be sure they have, sir: but it is not the custom to bathe at this hour of the day.' 'Bathe, my good woman! – bathe! – Why, would any body in their senses think of bathing in such a sea as that?'

Confounded at this question, the good woman, as he took the liberty of calling her, first looked earnestly at the sea, and then as earnestly on her new acquaintance: there was nothing in his countenance that appeared like banter: nor in truth any thing in either prospect that struck her to be at all remarkable.

'Don't you perceive,' added he, with evident surprise, 'how tremendously rough the water is? – 'Rough! dear heart, sir! – and half-suppressing a smile, she again looked towards the sea. The tide came rolling in with a full wave, the force of which was increased, as well by the season of the year, as by a most refreshing breeze: while the sun played over a vast expanse of green, dazzling the eye with its lustre, and brightening the spray, which dashed high as it approached the shore; the whole scene conveying to those that were accustomed to sea-views the most lively sensation of spirit and gaiety.

'Rough, sir, did you say?' again exclaimed the last speaker, with fresh surprise once more surveying the prospect. 'What a terrible situation! That boat will certainly be lost!' – 'Bless you, sir! that boat's only a pleasuring. I know the gentry in it extremely well.' –

'Their pleasure will then be very short, for I am convinced that we shall have a dreadful storm as soon as the sun goes in.'

This last proof of nautical judgment settled the opinion of the good woman with regard to the person who uttered it; and having reconnoitered him from head to foot with even, if possible, more accuracy than she had done before her first salutation, she made up her mind, that he was no other than a Londoner, and had never seen salt water till then: – a conclusion more charitable than she had at first been inclined to draw; inasmuch as it left him the possession of his right senses, however small the purposes which they appeared to answer.

One of those light showers that so often sweep across the sky at the rising of the tide, and give to the whole view indescribable variety and beauty, now began to 'shed prelusive drops' from a dark cloud, little larger in its apparent dimensions than a pocket-handkerchief; when the stranger, hastily unfurling a prodigious umbrella, which, in defiance of the heat, he had carried under his arm, good-naturedly called to his companion to take shelter beneath its circumference; and appealing very forcibly to the truth of his own predictions with regard to the approaching *tempest*, hinted to her, that the opportunity was a favourable one for looking at the lodgings which she was disposed to recommend to him.

'Would the family like a house, or only a set of apartments, sir?' said the female speaker, in the most insinuating tone, as, to the great annoyance of other walkers, they pressed forward under their formidable umbrella.

'I have no family,' replied the gentleman, laconically. The countenance of his companion fell: and indeed, simple as the sentence was, it conveyed a great deal: for, instead of the prospect in which she had indulged her imagination, of letting a large expensive house, 'with all appurtenance and means to boot,' the view suddenly contracted to a single gentleman, a parlour floor, and all the minute economy attendant upon such establishments, where youth and carelessness have no share in making out the account. A long observation upon life, and certain studies peculiar to her employment, though they had not rendered Mrs. Adams a philosopher or a physiongnomist, had bestowed a portion of knowledge perhaps upon the whole less fallible than theirs; for while they, with infinite labour and research, endeavour to describe man such as God originally made him, or as his passions cause him to make himself, she, with more summary decision, judged him simply by his habits; whether they were of person or of mind: in other words, she saw him such as his tailor makes the one, and his employments the other: inferring, that both together made the man. Nor was she often deceived: half the world have no genuine characteristics left, and are to be tried by some standard not very different from that employed by Mrs. Adams. It was by such kind of calculation that the good lady had concluded her companion to be either the butler or steward of some family of fashion, and made her advances accordingly. In this conjecture she now began to suspect that she had been wrong: he might be rich, however: nothing in his exterior announced the contrary: and though unprovided with a wife and family, either of his own or other people's, the chances were evidently in favour of his finding one, or possible both, during his stay at Weymouth, if he were so disposed, and made a proper appearance. With all due attention, therefore, to his future comfort, she persisted in showing him this house and that house: assured him that many single gentlemen chose to be handsomely accommodated, in order that they might be able to give entertainments to the ladies; and threw in occasional descriptions of balls, and pretty girls, whose mothers did not disapprove of their forming such parties when properly countenanced. Her hearer listened meantime with some complacency; inquired much, answered little, and finally, almost tired the patience of his would-be landlady, by an irresolution that seemed to have no end. 'That house was too large: those apartments were too small: the view on one side was confined; and on the other, it is so melancholy,' said he, 'looking, as it does, only on the sea.'

'That's an odd fault to find at a watering-place, sir,' said Mrs. Adams, whose complaisance began insensibly to diminish. 'My last lodger was not of your mind. Heaven help him, poor gentleman! to think of the hours that he used to spend in rambling by himself on the sands! you should contemplate the moon, sir, as he did, when she rises from the very bosom, as I may say, of the bay, and throws a long stream of light down to your very door, before you call the apartments melancholy.' Mrs. Adams had now touched a theme, though it was not that of the moon, which by an odd chance excited the curiosity of her hearer: she was pleased to observe that he was pleased, and conversation began once more to flourish.

'I can't say as to his fortune, Sir,' said Mrs. Adams, in answer to a question on the subject; 'but he was a gentleman, I am sure; and while he was in my house he paid like a gentleman: but his great delight was the moon. "Mrs. Adams," says he to me one night when I went to settle a little cash account with him, and found him sitting without candles in the room, "it is impossible to wish for any other light than from that beautiful planet: do you observe the single bright star that seems to follow her track through the heavens? Methinks they resemble a mother and her child." On saying this, he did so sigh, sir!' – 'And pray what became of this gentleman when he left Weymouth?' said her hearer, impatiently, and indeed somewhat fatigued with the episode of the moon. – 'I can't say that I know whether he *has* left it, sir,' returned Mrs. Adams. 'The poor gentleman, I believe, rather fell into misfortunes; and my lodgings did not suit him any longer; indeed, they can't be expected to suit those that have not wherewithal to pay handsomely: so we parted mighty good friends – ' Mrs. Adams made a sudden, but very marked pause; for she perceived that her hearer had picked up a slip of writing-paper from the floor, on which he was looking with an air of curiosity that instantly excited hers. The paper, however, for he put it into her hands a few moments afterwards, contained nothing interesting. It seemed to be only a miscellaneous catalogue of books, which the writer either possessed, or wished to possess: but the handwriting conveyed to him who saw it, more than Mrs. Adams could possibly guess, and more, in fact, than he expected to learn; for it convinced him that he was in the right track, and that her ci-devant lodger was no other than the man in search of whom he had travelled to Weymouth. This was, in the language of the world, a lucky hit: for, by a singular chance, it happened that their personal meeting would have been of no avail: the handwriting being the only particular by which the seeker could with any certainty have recognised the person sought: so long was it since they had seen each other.

The stranger now returned to his inn, and Mrs. Adams to her own apartment and her bit of mutton: convinced, to use her own language, 'that she had taken all this trouble for some quizzy old bachelor, who intended to establish himself in a two pair of stairs room.'

The good lady was not altogether deceived. Mr. Atkinson was certainly a bachelor: his face showed that he was not young; and

The Canterbury Tales

his coat intimated him to be a quiz. But under this face and coat lay a store of good sense, integrity, and kindness of heart, somewhat disfigured by whimsical peculiarities of manner indeed, but ever active, as at that moment, in the cause of misfortune. He had been originally designed for the law, and brought up, though in a very humble line, accordingly. Circumstances rendered him afterwards the agent, and indeed factotum to a family of very considerable opulence: where, after spending his youth in dutiful service, and his mature life in domestic, though respectful intercourse; after directing the juvenile sports of several fine lads, the beloved sons of his benefactor, and sharing in all those hopes which their promising outset announced; he had had the pain of beholding this bright prospect clouded by storms the most unforeseen:

——'The houses, lands,
And once fair-spreading family dissolved,'

or, after a succession of different events, centred in an heir of whose existence he could not assure himself, except by such steps as necessity and long-rooted attachment now induced him to take.

The chase proved tedious. For it was not in palaces, nor in assemblies; neither among the gay nor the happy, that Mr. Atkinson could hope to find this heir of five thousand a year. He was to be looked for in the habitations of indigence and obscurity: where inquiry was baffled by the apprehensions of him who alone could satisfy it; and the person sought was ever flying from the benignant friend that was seeking him. Under these circumstances, all the sufferings of poverty, and all the evils of indiscretion, had alternately been exposed to view: and Mr. Atkinson had seen more of man, erring, inconsistent, prodigal, yet miserable and much-enduring man, within the last two months, than the whole tenor of his life, till that period, had ever displayed to him. Mrs. Adams, however, had not been quite wrong in her conjecture: amongst all the sights that had presented themselves, Atkinson had *not* seen the sea: not in truth any larger body of water than that which his benefactor's grounds afforded; or the small river which ran through his own native town. He had indeed peeped at the Thames, during the time which necessity obliged him to employ in visiting London; but not the majestic Thames that bears navies on her bosom, or conveys to an overgrown metropolis the luxuries of two opposite hemispheres; nor that more beautiful Thames which flows

The Canterbury Tales

between the consecrated banks of Twickenham and Richmond, ever dear to poetical imaginations: no! – willing to satisfy his curiosity with two superb views at once, and to make the most of the little time he could spare, it was at Billingsgate, during the intervals of admiration excited by that famous market that he had taken his chief survey of the famous river. What wonder, then, that, beholding the vast bosom of the ocean, he shuddered at the temerity of people who venture upon it in boats that seemed to him only larger than cockle-shells! or that those bright waves, whose lightly-silvered points convey to some constitutions the gayest and most exhilarating feelings, appeared to his alarmed imagination hardly less than mountainous billows! Taste he had none: reading he had little: of the world he knew nothing. To do all the good he could in it, partake a temperate meal with a temperate friend, keep his heart and his coat equally unsoiled; tuck his umbrella under his arm, and shelter his eyes with a beaver of most primitive shape and dimensions, was with him the summum bonum of life. Such was Mr. Abraham Atkinson.

Now, Mr. Abraham Atkinson had a female counterpart on this earthly globe, although he did not yet know it; by name Mrs. Dixon: an obscure personage, whose chief business was, like Mrs. Adams, to let ready furnished apartments. Mrs. Dixon however resembled her compeer in no one thing except that by which she lived. For, whereas the latter was tall, thin, had a sharp eye, a shrewd mind, and a most accommodating cast of countenance, in which nothing of the original character could be discerned but its leading feature – self-interest; Mrs. Dixon, on the contrary, was fat, good-humoured, liberal, credulous, and so willing to do what was kind by every body, that there was only one person in the whole circle of the neighbourhood whom she neglected. But that one never complained; never knew what it was to be discontented; buffeted ill-fortune with a magnanimity that would have immortalised her, had it been the gift of intellect and not the mere result of a happy temperament; enjoyed all the little good that fell to her lot, and never repined though Benjamin's portion went to those who less deserved it. In a word, this neglected individual was Mrs. Dixon herself; but the error which she was not conscious of, she never strove to amend: and thus remained stationary till forty, in the self-same town, street, house, and employment, in which she had found herself at five-and-twenty.

It happened that these counterparts, as is frequently the case with the counterparts of this world, were far from suspecting each other to be such: and it was the exactness of the resemblance that prevented their seeing it: for both, without a spark of what is decidedly to be called vanity, had a certain habitual blindness to their own exterior, which did not extend one degree further; so that while Mrs. Dixon secretly congratulated herself that she was not such a prim, upright, particular-looking figure as Mr. Atkinson, the gentleman, on the contrary, thought himself fortunate in having passed the meridian of the life without attaining the plump insignificance of Mrs. Dixon. As yet, however, these two good creatures were unknown to each other: but their guardian angels, if guardian angels are ever allowed to persons not handsome, and past five-and-twenty, or rather the guardian angels of those they were to serve, were at work to bring them together; and this was facilitated by means of a terrestrial deputy, who certainly had nothing of the angelic either in her form or her mind: it was Mrs. Adams.

A conversation between this lady and Mr. Atkinson, not necessary to be detailed at length, as it is probable enough of it has already been set down, had, before they parted, pretty nearly convinced the latter, that the gentleman whom he sought, after quitting her house from not having, as she elegantly phrased it, 'wherewithal to pay,' had certainly taken up his abode in the neighbourhood with some person less rigid in that particular; and a very little address had brought out Mrs. Dixon's name: it was immediately subsequent to this discovery that Atkinson returned to the Red Lion and a solitary dinner; where, after drinking his usual small allowance of port, he fell into a fit of meditation, which terminated, as meditations after dinner rather frequently do, in a gentle nap. On awaking, he found the heat of the day considerably abated: the sea, which most impertinently seemed to lie in his way, whichever road he took, had sunk into profound tranquillity, and the soft murmur of an ebbing tide alone rendered it distinguishable to the ear. The sun was setting behind the town, which already began to cast its shade over the beach and nearer view; while the barren hills of Portland, with the small vessels sheltered beneath, still lying under the reflection of the distant brightness, presented an amusing spectacle to the eye.

As Mrs. Dixon's window held out an invitation that made it no intrusion to knock at her door, the business of introduction was accomplished without any difficulty: yet, by an ill-luck perhaps to be accounted for in the want of those exterior graces of which nature had not been liberal to either party, these two worthy people did not immediately make the favourable impression on each other which they were mutually entitled to do. Mr. Atkinson had taken it into his head that some portion of ingenuity would be necessary in order to effect the discovery he wished: his exordium therefore was by no means prepossessing, for the simple reason, that it was studied: trusting to nature the chances had been fifty to one in his favour, but he was a mere bungler at finesse; and the consequence of his attempting it was, that Mrs. Dixon, struck with the quaintness and peculiarity of his manner, became in her turn no less ingeniously mysterious than her visitor; so that the chief purport of the visit, which was to learn some tidings of her last lodger, was as little in a way to be accomplished as though they had never met. But if the negotiation did not promise to be very successful as to its principal aim, there were some subordinate considerations not totally to be neglected by either party. Mrs. Dixon's apartments had been empty for a considerable time past: the stranger was evidently not provided with any: his appearance was quiet; respectable: denoting ease, if not affluence; and, but for some suspicious circumstances attending his supposed employment, rendered him precisely the sort of person whom she would approve as an inmate. Atkinson, meantime, was not without his prudential observations; and they were exactly in character with the tone of his mind. In the landlady he saw, indeed, very little to like, but a great deal in the house: its neat window-curtains, pretty-patterned sofa, and unsoiled carpet, with a well-washed bed lately fitted up, and a snug chamber that did *not* look towards the sea, an element to which he had taken a most decided aversion, possessed irresistible attraction. The intimations he had previously received, his recent discovery, and a confused suspicion, which, in spite of Mrs. Dixon's equivocal answers, he could not help cherishing, that he should learn from her something more as to the object of his journey, than she at that juncture chose to impart, made her house, of all in Weymouth, appear most desirable as a residence; and, not being among those easy or isolated mortals who find themselves most at home in an inn, he was as impatient as the tranquillity of his nature allowed him to be, to quit that in which he was stationed.

The agreement was soon made. The tabby cat was licensed to hold her place; hot rolls for breakfast, a comfortable dinner, never later than three o'clock, and a dish of tea when it suited him to take it, were the preliminary articles: after which the two counterparts prepared themselves on both sides to dismiss from their recollection whatever had not pleased them on either, and to make their little home, what home ought always to be, a scene of tranquil enjoyment.

'You are a great reader of the Bible, I see, Mrs. Dixon,' said her guest, as he entered her parlour from his walk on the following evening, and found her still poring over a large book, on which he had left her engaged two hours before.

'Heaven forbid that I should not be so, sir,' said she, taking off her spectacles, and laying them on the table, 'but this, to my shame be it spoken, is not the Bible. You, perhaps, never saw so curious a book as this, sir; for, thick as it seems, it is nothing all through but writing: and, to be sure, the beautifullest hand one shall see.' Atkinson looked over her shoulder as she spoke, and recognized it well.

'The handwriting of your lodger,' said he, dissembling his surprise. – 'My lodger as *was*, sir.' – 'And where is he now? I may have particular reasons for asking.' – 'And I might have particular reasons for not telling, sir, even if I knew: but, wherever he is, he is a sweet young gentleman.' – 'Is he so very young then?' – 'Why, not so *very* young neither: a matter of three or four and twenty.' – Not so much as that,' muttered Atkinson to himself. 'What person of a man?' – 'Very handsome, if he was not so pale.' – 'He was not pale when *I* knew him,' again murmured Atkinson, shaking his head: there are tones and gestures liable to misinterpretation; Mrs. Dixon, who could only catch those, without being able to understand the accompanying words, did certainly, on this occasion, interpret very erroneously.

'That person must have a heart of iron,' she continued, with no small indignation, 'who could think of injuring such a charming gentleman.' – 'But if this gentleman, by some unfortunate prejudice, injuries himself, Mrs. Dixon.' – 'Why, then let him punish himself! you and I need have nothing more to do with him.' – 'Yet you value his book?' – 'That I do, as I would my life! and read it too whenever I can find an opportunity. 'Tis the history of my house.' – 'That must be a curious history indeed,' said Atkinson, relaxing his features to a smile. – 'So I said, sir,' returned Mrs. Dixon, smiling in her turn. '"The history of a lodging-house!" says I. – "Ay, Mrs. Dixon," says he; "do you not believe that the history of a lodging-house would afford many an interesting tale? I could tell you one, perhaps" – and there he stopped, sir. "Let me see," he added, after a pause; "you have four sets of apartments for instance: the kitchen, the parlour, the drawing-room, the attic: – I think we may call it five, if we add the *poetical* floor: and that is privileged time immemorial: any flight of imagination will do for it." I could not guess what floor he meant, sir, but it seems it was the garret. "Well," continued he, 'for the attic I think I need not go farther than myself. Then for the drawing-room ———" – "Which Mr. Seymour and his family have just quitted, you know, sir." – "Mr. Seymour's family!' repeated he, sighing: he was a great sigher, sir; and then there was a long pause between us. "We may pass that floor securely, Mrs. Dixon – I know too much of what relates to that; and a little – a very little imagination will supply the rest. For the parlours I must, of course, refer myself to you." – "Me, sir! Heaven help us! I have no story belonging to me. Pray skip that over, I desire. I am as it were a mere nobody – between the highest and the lowest." – "Right; the middle rank: too humble for the vices of luxury, too well taught for those of grossness. That is indeed the rank of which there is little to say on earth, though it has much to expect in heaven. Now to descend to an humbler scene – the kitchen." – "I think I may venture to defy you there," said I. – "To convict you of being in the wrong, I need only repeat a story which you have yourself related to me, though by snatches indeed, twenty times." – "Dear sir, all the stories I ever related in my whole life would not make a book." – "Wrong again there to a certainty," said he, archly: for when he was not so melancholy, sir, he could be arch: – and on those occasions he had such a taking smile! – "What think you, for instance," continued he, "of the history of your former servant?" – "Not old Mary, to be sure!" – "She was not always old!" – "No truly – nor always crazed – nay, for the matter of that, she is not so old now! – but, poor thing, she has had enough to craze her!" – As you're alive, sir, while we were speaking the words, who should put her head in at the parlour window but Mary herself. – You saw her the other day as you and I walked down street together.' Atkinson nodded assent. 'A melancholy looking body!' – Atkinson nodded again. 'Well, as I was saying, in she puts her head. I declare she made me start downright. "Good day, Mary," said I, trying to recover myself. – "They will sail to-morrow," returned she, in her hurrying way, and without noticing my salutation. – "Who will sail?" – "Why, the Captain and the Admiral. The King will go on board his frigate, and Bob will be there. – The sun will shine *so* brightly! – and the Princesses have promised to lend me fine clothes, that I may see the sight." – "Alas, poor Mary!" said the sweet gentleman, as he saw her go smiling away: "if this is to be mad, why should men like me wish to keep their senses!" – I was quite downcast to hear him make this sorrowful reflection. So I thought I'd

The Canterbury Tales

talk to him a bit about his book; for, between ourselves, sir, I rather believed he was in earnest to write it. He had no other amusement, and so he would write, write, all day. Mostly verses indeed; and I knew that he had touched up some pretty melancholy love songs and sonneteerings.

"'Well, sir," says I, "you have travelled on nearly to the end of your journey." – "You think then, that poor Mary will do," replied he, half-musing, half-smiling. – "Bless me, no! Who would dream of writing such an old story as that?" – "I will." – "Dear sir, there are a hundred such in the world. Take my word for it, it will pass for a mere Canterbury Tale." – "With all my heart! I have not the least objection. I shall not attempt to decorate the one in question, Mrs. Dixon: it shall remain your own story, told, as nearly as I can recollect, in your own words," – and to be sure so it is, sir! and that, so doubt, makes me so fond of reading it. – Only look at the line he has written at top; it is quite one of the best parts of the book.' – Whether Mr. Atkinson took the trouble to read all that followed that line, may be problematical: but he turned immediately to the first leaf, and saw written in large, but familiar characters, –

THE LANDLADY'S TALE

MARY LAWSON

That holy shame, which ne'er forgets
What clear renown it used to wear;
Whose blush remains, when virtue sets,
To show her sunshine *has* been there.

Moore

Mary Lawson, sir, however crazed and altered you now see her, was, within my memory, one of the best-looking girls in Weymouth. Not but there were different opinions concerning her. Many of our lodgers used to say, that she would be pretty enough if she would open her eyes: but to my thinking there was something soft and sorrowful in them when half closed, as they generally were, that was quite out of the common way. Mary was born in a village upon the banks of the Dee, not very far from the neighbourhood of Wrexham. Her father, though he held only a small farm, lived in a very reputable way, and Mary's education was therefore not neglected. She could read and write; and to be sure it is not saying any great things to add, that she had a better head than mine ever was for accounts; and as to her needle, she was a perfect mistress of it. Many a beautiful piece of patchwork have we contrived together! but all that will come in its place.

At fourteen Mary lost her mother; nor was that the greatest of her misfortunes: for her father soon married again, and as his second wife was a careless idling sort of body, the charge of a young family, which quickly came on, was left almost entirely to his eldest daughter. 'I did not at that time love children,' said Mary afterwards to me, 'I thought them all noisy and troublesome alike; and often wondered at my mother-in-law, who, although she did no one useful thing for them, cried them up as patterns of perfection. Oh, Mrs. Dixon, who could have persuaded me, young and giddy as I then was, that to sit by the cradle of a sick baby, to listen to its little moans, and to give it the bread that I wanted myself, would be a more precious employment to me than all the pleasures of the whole world besides! But I then thought there were a great many people and things to love in the world; and perhaps to fine folks there may be: *my* lot was different; but my sins began with children, and so did my punishment.'

This was only the poor girl's talk, sir, for I could never gather that she did any harm at that time, only, I suppose, was a little heedless, like those of her age. However her mother-in-law and she did not agree; and it would have been wonderful if they had, considering the way that things were managed. So the father bethought himself of an expedient that pleased both parties, though Mary acknowledged to me that she was best pleased of the two. An aunt of hers was settled at Bristol in the haberdashery line. Her shop drove no mighty trade; but she was an infirm single woman, and therefore not unwilling to take her niece in, as an assistant. Mary was accordingly fitted out with two new gowns, great doings, as she said, for those days, and I know not how many different ribands; which to be sure was a very idle expense; however they were mostly tokens of good-will, presented by the neighbours, and she kept them as such till a long, long time after; for she had a tender heart, as was proved to her sorrow.

Well sir, those who live in large towns, such as Weymouth, and see a great deal of the world, as you and I have done, can have no guess at Mary's surprise when she arrived at Bristol. For a short time she thought it the finest and happiest place in the whole globe. Her aunt was not unkind to her; she herself was naturally of a gay and cheerful character, and all the new scenes around made her gayer still. But by-and-by this novelty began to fade a little; and after being familiar with busy streets, and close-packed houses, she could not help calling to mind the green lanes and clear river of her native place. Her greatest delight was to walk on a fine Sunday to a village not far distant called Clifton, and to sit on the brow of the rocks. A large river runs there, sir, I understand; but whether it be the Thames or not, is more than I can tell you.

These walks, however, proved very unlucky for Mary. A regiment was at that time quartered at Bristol and some of the officers (which to be sure proves their want of taste) were fonder of being at Clifton than in that great city. One of these took particular notice of Mary: there are strawberry-gardens, it seems, in that neighbourhood sir, where common folks, and sometimes gentry, go to eat fruit. It was at one of these that Captain Mandeville contrived to make a sort of acquaintance with the poor girl. He was at that time about eight-and-twenty; a very fine-looking man, and I understand (for Heaven knows he was strangely altered when I saw him), and had all the dashing air that gentlemen of the army affect. Mary's eyes were treacherous ones, for they played her heart false, and showed her this gay young officer in his best colours. He was not wanting to himself: it was very easy to find out where she resided; and Captain Mandeville soon became a great customer for ribands and feathers, which he pretended were bestowed upon recruits. Never did man enlist so many in so short a time; for by-and-by there was hardly a yard of riband left in the shop. In the mean while, vows, promises, letters, and presents were lavished upon Mary, though in an underhand way you may be sure. The poor girl loved him, and he had discernment enough to perceive it; nevertheless she was innocent and well-disposed. – I do not want to excuse her fault, sir, – it was a great one: – the greater, as she herself in bitterness of heart acknowledged, because she had not been brought up in ignorance of her duty. But what is to be said to this man, sir, who saw she was no bold, nor forward creature, really to throw herself in his way: for she has affirmed to me, and I will pledge my life she spoke truly, that she has many times shut herself up in the back shop, and avoided her accustomed walks in order to strugggle with her own weak heart, and endeavour to forget him. What is to be said to him, I ask? Only what he has been obliged since to say to himself: you will hear it, sir. – All Mary's efforts, however, would not do. The Captain had an emissary, his serjeant, I believe it was, no less active than his employer in watching and persecuting her. To be short, sir, it was *his* day of triumph, and the poor girl became his victim.

Melancholy was the change that succeeded. Captain Mandeville must have been a hard man, though Mary's partiality made her think otherwise. His heart, his pleasures, his fortune, except when he had some great objection view, were all for himself. He had no care for others; nor, for aught I could learn, had he really any for her, when his first passion had subsided. He was one of those rattling sparks, sir, who dash on in life without looking to the right or the left, through a long lane of the maimed and the blind, whom they have made so; till, being come to their journey's end, they are obliged to cast their eyes back, and see the sad spectacle of human misery. But Captain Mandeville was then a young man, full of health and spirits: things have changed with him since that time.

All seemed now at the worst with Mary. She was ruined, neglected, and had reason to suppose herself in a situation that would soon render her disgrace apparent. Sometimes, as she told me, she thought with horror of being a mother. At others, the recollection of the infantine caresses of her little brothers and sisters, and of the pleasure their parents used to take in them, came to her heart; till, between that, and conscience, which began every way to afflict her, it nearly burst. To expiate the sin of having wished to leave her family, and to be sure that was but a fancied sin, she had almost resolved to make a voluntary sacrifice of herself, and carry back her shame and her penitence to her father's house, quitting for ever all sight of the man who had wronged her; when another idea more flattering to her passion suddenly came across her mind; for poor Mary's remorse was, I fear, as you will see, sir, only love in disguise.

Captain Mandeville had a very fine estate and house in Northumberland. It was a family mansion, and his mother, as the serjeant, from whom alone Mary got any information concerning him, had told her, resided in it. The wild project of fixing herself somewhere in the neighbourhood of Mandeville Park, occurred to the poor girl. If she lived, she doubted not to get an honest maintenance by labour and ingenuity: but, like most young women in her situation, she was persuaded that she should die; and it was her determination, in that case, to leave such information, together with her child, for the old lady, as would, she thought, secure its being brought up in a creditable way, if only for the sake of its father. Ah, sir, what sort of a father must that have been whom Mary dared not, even under such circumstances, trust with his own child! It was at this period of fear and irresolution that the old aunt died. She had long been infirm; yet her death was somewhat sudden. Her stock in trade was sold according to her own desire, and the little produce fell to the share of her niece. Rich Mary! Poor Mary! for she was comparatively both. Never had it been her lot hitherto to possess so many of the goods of this world, never did they appear so worthless in her eyes, nor she in her own. Providence, however, seemed to have furthered the scheme which was agitating her mind, by thus unexpectedly supplying her with means to accomplish it. Yet the great effort still remained to be made: which was to resolve on separating herself for ever from the only man on earth whom she loved; and to convince him, by so doing, that though she had been frail, she was not vicious, nor would consent to continue the disgraceful correspondence, which, more from habitual libertinism than any particular fondness, he still would have preserved.

During the hours of grief and apprehension, which Mary had occasionally passed with Mr. Mandeville, she had more than once talked of returning to her father's house: and as I suppose there were times when the Captain was sufficiently inclined to get rid of her, he had suggested an expedient to conceal the disgrace of her situation, by offering her a paper, signifying that she was the widow of a soldier who had served in his regiment. With this deceitful paper, easily obtained from a careless, licentious young man, who thought nothing of its consequences either to himself or others, a breaking heart – a blasted character – and the little portion of money that her aunt had left her – for she scorned to take any thing from her seducer, Mary one night secretly departed from her usual residence, and turning her back for ever upon Bristol, took the road towards Northumberland.

It was a long journey to Newcastle, in the neighbourhood of which lay Mandeville Park. When the poor unhappy girl first saw its outward paling, her heart, she often declared to me, died within her, as though she had at the same moment foreseen all the guilt and the sorrow that was to arise from thence.

At last she came within view of the house: and, 'Oh,' said she, 'how great did *he* seem, and how little did I!'

'What, Mary,' said I, 'were you not yet cured then of judging by appearance? – Was it because he was gay and handsome, and had magnificent houses, and large parks, that he was in reality better than you? or how were you sure that in the end he would be happier?'

'Most true,' she replied; 'but I had sinned against my conscience, and every living being seemed greater and happier than I was at that time.'

No wonder Mary was dazzled, however, sir, for I have been told since that it is a very fine house. The hall had grand marble statues in it: there was a shrubbery of I can't tell you how many acres extent, and grounds without end. A stately lawn was in front, and vast quantities of deer feeding under the trees. Then there was a library, worth I know not how much money, with painted glass windows, and curious busts. What a pity, sir, that these rich gentlemen who set up the heads of so many good and wise folks, can't get a little of their hearts! For my share I never saw the Captain, and heard talk of his fine seats, without calling to mind the parable of Nathan and the lamb. How can it be that those who are able to command so many pleasures, can, for a temporary gratification, deprive another of their only comfort!

Under pretence of indisposition, though indeed it could hardly be called a pretence, Mary was set down at a decent public house, in the neighbourhood of the great estate. And here, what with agitation of mind and fatigue of body, she found herself really so ill as to be obliged to go to bed. Sleep, however, she could not. So after a restless night full of melancholy reflections she was up with the lark, and once more on foot. I need not tell you, sir, which way she turned her steps. It was a clear fresh morning. The dew lay on the grass: birds were singing in every tree, and at a little distance was a fine piece of water, with a hanging wood on one side of it, that dipped its branches in the stream. The village where she was born, and all her girlish days, came at once to the recollection of poor Mary: so leaning her head on one of the outer green gates, she relieved her over-charged heart with a flood of tears. In this situation she was seen by a young woman, who observing her, I suppose, to make a respectable appearance, for she was in mourning for her aunt, and interested, perhaps, by her condition, very good-naturedly invited her to rest herself in a house hard by. This woman was the park-keeper's wife, and the house to which she invited her was that in which they lived. A pretty place, with a fine honeysuckle curling all over the windows on one side, and clusters of grapes ripening on the other: but no comfort did the sight of it give to Mary, though it was as neat as a palace. There was a baby in a cradle, and a breakfast set for the husband, who was just returning home: they were young people, sir, and had not been married above a twelvemonth, which no doubt made them so fond of each other: and to be sure the father did so caress and dandle the child! Mary's heart was ready to burst. Every thing she saw put her in mind of some happiness that was past, or which she could never hope to enjoy; and she began to cry more bitterly than before.

Well! with much ado she made out, between whiles, the story of her soldier husband, and supposed widowhood; blushing and trembling all the time with the consciousness of deceit. But the good folks took it all for gospel. So they comforted her in their way, and pressed her to swallow something that she might keep up her strength and spirits: when lo, just as they were themselves sitting down to breakfast, a little boy that worked hard by, pops in his head, calling out that Mrs. Mandeville was coming; and sure enough, the words were scarcely out of his mouth before an elderly lady came to the door. She had a sharp shrewish-looking face, though she was not a small women, and was followed by a young lady, who appeared to be her daughter. The latter had a consumptive air, and was bundled up, as I may say, in a large muslin wrapper. They both walked in, without any ceremony. The young one sat down, like a person who was tired; but the other kept standing, and asking abundance of questions. To be sure all those present stood too, out of respect; and Mary among the rest; though her legs trembled so it was as much as she could do to make them support her: the old lady glanced at her from time to time, but deuce a bit did she desire her to sit down, ill as she could not but see she was. The young one hardly looked at her at all; but amused herself with some very choice flowers which she held in her hand; only once she said to her little dog, who had been all the time snarling and barking at Mary, 'Flo' let the young woman alone.' This drew the attention of the other lady. – 'You have a stranger here, Mrs. Such-a-one,' said she, calling the park-keepers's wife by her name, which what it was I have forgotten. – 'A poor body, madam, that is in great affliction,' replied the woman, in a kinder and softer tone than that of the person who questioned her. 'She has lost her husband but lately: he was a soldier in his honour's regiment.' – Oh, sir, would you believe it? one kind pitiful look from either the old or the young lady, Mary declared would have made her fall at their feet, and tell them the whole truth at that very moment. She felt so ashamed of lying, so afraid of being discovered, and so conscience-struck altogether, that a little, the very least indulgence or sympathy in the looks of those great ladies would have reclaimed her from all her deceits: and what a world of grief would then have been spared! but they only stared at her, although she was ready to sink into the earth. Yet it was not as if they suspected any thing wrong; but with a sort of careless, inquisitive air, such as rich people, who have no thought for the feelings of others, often show to their inferiors. – Have you a certificate, young woman?' said the elderly lady at last, in a drawling tone. Mary took the paper from her bosom, but not a syllable could she say. – 'It is Mr. Mandeville's own hand, I see,' said the old lady, giving it to her daughter, after she had read it. The latter only cast her eyes over the writing, and returned it without any remark.

This was all the notice they took at that time. However, when they were going away, which was not till they had tired themselves, and spoiled the good people's breakfast, the elder lady turned to Mary, and said, – 'If you stay any time in this country, young woman,

The Canterbury Tales

Such-a-one.' naming the park-keeper's wife, 'will be willing, I dare say, to do you any kind office in her power.'

And here, sir, was an end at once to all the hopes that Mary had entertained from the fortune, the fine education, and the tender heart of a great lady! – 'I did flatter myself,' said she, 'that seeing me look sorrowful and sick, and having nothing to do but to comfort the sick and the sorrowful, she would haved taken some little compassion upon me. I was a young creature then: she had no reason to think that I was a wicked one, and I was in circumstances when a women ought to feel for a woman: yet, like the Priest and the Levite, she passed over to the other side, and left me to the poor Samaritan: and this was done both by the elder and the younger lady: yet they gave a great deal of money, I am told, to different charities at Newcastle; but they would neither tax their time nor their feelings.' – 'To my thinking Mrs. Mandeville looks very sick,' said the woman to her husband, when they were gone. – 'Much as usual,' replied he; 'she was always so pale since my knowledge.' – 'She has Madam Selborne's own complexion,' returned the other. – 'And who is Madam Selborne?' said Mary, who had concluded the stranger to be Mr. Mandeville's sister. – 'Why my lady's own mother. Bless you, you did not take the *elderly* gentlewoman for his honour's wife, to be sure: – the *young* one is Mrs. Mandeville.'

The good folks were sitting at their breakfast, and did not look at Mary as they spoke, for she was standing behind them, near the cradle. Lucky it was that things were so disposed; for she had time to lean her head down, and recover herself from this last stroke; which, although her presumptuous heart had never whispered to her would be any new affliction, yet seemed to double all that she had before felt. She now perceived the extent of Captain Mandeville's art, and that of his emissary; both of whom had carefully kept from her the knowledge of his being a married man: a knowledge which they rightly conjectured would have been an additional motive with her to guard her affections against him. For it was plain to be seen, that Mary might be sooner persuaded to wrong herself than any one else. Who can tell, sir, besides, what vain thoughts enter into the heart and head of a young woman in love; or how far they might, on her first acquaintance with the Captain, have assisted to lead her astray? Many a man knows how to raise hopes, where he is too artful to give promises; and belies his own conscience when he disclaims having done so. The self-command which Mary assumed on hearing this news was for a time of service to her, as far as in concealing the interest she took in it. Her spirits, however, could not hold out long, and she fell into convulsion-fits, which, though they did not directly destroy the poor baby, as surely caused its death as if it had been killed that moment.

And now, sir, she was to choose where she would go. Home she could not: her story and certificate would never have passed current with her father: much less with her mother-in-law: there was not a person nor a place in the whole world that was dear to her; and so she lingered in the neighbourhood of Mandeville Park, uncertain what was to be her future destination, or that of her baby; and only hoping and believing that the same moment would end both.

Mrs. Selborne and Mrs. Mandeville were not much beloved in the country: the old lady was one of those fretful, droning, discontented people, that are always busying themselves about little things; and talk a great deal, without saying any thing to the purpose. Not a pale fell by any accident in the park, nor a plant withered in the greenhouse, but she was *sure* that it was owing to the neglect of some of the servants; and it furnished her with subject of conversation – that is, of complaint – for two or three days; till a new disaster of no greater consequence fell out: and so, without looking about upon all the beauties of nature, or art, with which she was surrounded, these little cross incidents did so ruffle her temper that nothing was to be heard but reproaches and grievances. Her daughter was somewhat of the same character with herself; or rather, of no character at all: for as the only subjects she ever thought about were of the like trifling kind, her mother left her nothing to say upon them; so she passed her life in a sort of dawdling, negligent way, without seeming to care much for any thing; neither receiving, nor communicating, the least spirit of enjoyment. She had had a great fortune, and a fine education, however; but her pianoforte was always out of tune; and as to drawing and reading she had no taste for either. Her learning, in short, had been so much time and money thrown away. All rich people are not I know of this description: but I have seen a great many who are; and it is a consideration that may reconcile common folks to their lot. 'The world is divided into classes, Mrs. Dixon,' said a gentleman to me one day, when we were talking together about poverty and wealth. 'There are those in it who have an appetite, and no dinner, and those who have a dinner, and no appetite: your rich folks are in the second class; and I doubt whether they are better off than the other.' I could not quite agree with him as to that point, sir; nevertheless it is certainly a great drawback, to sit down, like Mrs. Selborne and her daughter, to the banquet of nature, without having the smallest relish for the feast.

Mrs. Mandeville was with child, and near her time. On the first occasion she had gone up to London; but not having done well there, and losing the child, she was persuaded that the journey did not agree with her. She therefore resolved to go through her second confinement at Mandeville Park: it was for this reason her mother staid with her. As to the Captain, either business or pleasure detained him elsewhere.

Near the limits of this Park, poor Mary still loitered. The very little which Mrs. Selborne had said in her favour was yet something with all the tenants: especially as it had been reported by her first acquaintance, the park-keeper's wife, in the most advantageous manner. She therefore hired two small rooms, in a cottage which was inhabited by a good motherly kind of woman; and, as a little money went a great way in that part of the country, she saw that she had means to make herself welcome.

Rowing upon the water was among the few amusements which Mrs. Mandeville had a taste for. She used to go out almost every sunset in a small pleasure boat, built on purpose; and Mary, who during these excursions was sure of not meeting her, a circumstance she always dreaded, lest it should involve her in new and more deliberate falsehoods, used to take the opportunity of walking about the grounds. She was on the brow of the little wood one evening, from whence she discerned the boat, with its gay flag and decorations, moving backwards and forwards on the water: Mrs. Mandeville and Mrs. Selborne both were in it; and the latter seemed, by the motion of her hand, to direct the men to approach a small woody ait, where swans were kept. They accordingly did so: but the water was very low, from the dryness of the season, and the bottom reedy. It was plain that they were soon aground, and were making efforts to free themselves. There was, however, no probability of danger, till one of the men, in pushing off from the shore, suffered himself to incline too much, and in consequence fell overboard. Both ladies started up at once; and by running hastily to the edge of the board, overset it. Mary waited not to see the event, but shrieking with apprehension, ran to the house for assistance. All was soon well with Mrs. Mandeville and her mother: for the water was so shallow that the boatmen rescued them almost before they were thoroughly wet: but the fright and exertion were too much for her who had witnessed the scene; and while the servants were carefully conveying the two ladies into the house, Mary, whom no one noticed, found herself so ill, that it was with great difficulty she reached her own humble home.

'Oh, Mrs. Dixon,' said she to me, 'imagine what my sufferings were, when, after a long and painful trial, the first thing I distinctly saw was my own dear baby dead: the first feelings that entered my heart were those of a mother, and of a mother without a child! to have been lodged in the cold grave, where I imagined Mrs. Mandeville, would have been happiness to what I endured.'

I am afraid poor Mary never knew what she did endure. Her child did not come dead into the world, however; but it went off, almost immediately, in convulsions. She had nevertheless an excellent constitution: and God, sir, could never intend that women should die, just when it is most necessary that they should live. Not but poor Mary might have been released: for, alas, she had no infant to take care of! however, it pleased Providence to save her; and, contrary to all probability, she began to recover her strength. She was sitting up on morning, disconsolate and alone, when the woman of the house came in; a good creature, but a very ignorant one, as you will see, sir.

'Well,' said she, on entering, 'God Almighty don't send burdens to common folk alone! there's the young Squire, as the servants says, wont live neither. His mother won't suckle him; and the dry-nurse, as come from Durham, can't manage to make him keep life and soul together, with all her fine silver boats and new-fashioned ways. Old Madam Selborne says, that for self-willedness he is his father's own son, for nothing will he swallow: so you may comfort yourself that you are not the only poor soul as loses a child.' – 'Oh that I could save one!' said Mary, and a thought glanced across her mind. 'Will he live if he is suckled, do you say,' added she, impatiently. 'Is it Captain Mandeville's child of which you speak? Is *he* born?" – and then the recollection of her own words, is it *Captain Mandeville's child*, as though no other than the heir could be his, put her into a second agony of tears. The child had indeed been born several days before, but it was in no way to live. It was a sickly little thing. The mother never intended to nurse it herself: and if she had had the will, the doctors said she would not have the power; so the poor babe, as they could not rear him with dry-nursing, which they had all along intended to do, was like not to be reared at all.

Well, sir, it does not signify going round about the bush: by the recommendation of the park-keeper's wife, the babe was put to

Mary's bosom. With many a bitter heartach, and many a tear, did she receive it. The poor little thing began from that day to get strength, and its first smiles, its first looks, were Mary's. His mother saw him not, or very rarely. She and Madam Selborne were shut up together, grumbling and scolding at every thing and every body. The old lady insisted upon it that her daughter could nurse the child; that it was the custom of her day, and that the new-fangled notions were all mere nonsense. The daughter, on the contrary, would neither spoil her shape nor endanger her health by any attempt of the kind. 'She saw no benefit arise,' she said, 'from having been suckled by her mother herself; and that all customs were good for nothing but to contract people's ideas, and make their lives uncomfortable.' Whether comfortable or otherwise, it was soon seen, when Mrs. Mandeville came abroad, that she was not long for this world. All her family had been consumptive, except her mother; she herself had shown symptoms of being so, before she was confined, and she brought out of her chamber all the appearance of a rapid decline. This she imputed, however, only to delicacy of constitution; for she was very fond of being thought delicate: so nobody ventured to tell her the truth. It told itself at last: but too late to be remedied. Captain Mandeville was therefore sent for in all haste: however, he made none in coming: and before he arrived another express was despatched to inform him that his wife was dead. He stopped short at York, and wrote from thence to Mrs. Selborne, requesting that she would undertake to order every thing that was suitable on the occasion, and informing her that he would be at Mandeville Park within a certain time.

This was a dreadful interval for Mary. She could not resolve to stay; much less could she resolve to depart. The baby's very life seemed to depend upon her care: neither night nor day had she ceased to watch it; and if there was a moment when she remembered with sorrow that it was not her own, she at the same time called to mind that it was Captain Mandeville's. None but a women, sir, can tell how closely the infant creeps into your heart that lies at your bosom; and, if in common cases this is daily proved, what wonder that Mary's fondness exceeded all common measure! It had even no longer a mother to excite her jealousy, or share her attentions: and the early loss which it had sustained seemed to point out a particular providence in the manner by which that loss was supplied. In short, sir, love, *maternal* love, I think we may call it, conquered fear, shame, and every other feeling. Mary, therefore, at length resolved to stay, and encounter the man, whom, in any other circumstances, she had determined to fly to the world's end to avoid.

Captain Mandeville arrived within the time appointed, just after evening had closed. Mary heard the clattering of the horse's feet, and soon after his well-known voice and step. The many – many occasions when she had listened to them with a beating heart, interesting as they had been, were all, she thought, nothing to this. He staid some little time below with Mrs. Selborne, and then the feet of both were to be heard on the staircase.

'Now,' exclaimed Mary, with a palpitating heart, 'now comes the trial!' – and she turned to the infant that was sleeping sweetly in its cradle. – 'Oh, if it were *my* child that he was coming to look at,' she softly whispered – 'but mine sleeps sounder still!'

Mr. Mandeville came in: he neither cast his eyes to the right nor the left: but, with a candle in his hand, walked strait to the cradle, and stooping down to see the baby, kissed its little hand.

'Will he wake, do you think?' said he to Mrs. Selborne, motioning to kiss its cheek. – 'Oh, no, no, no,' murmured Mary, pursuing, in the anguish of her heart, nothing but her own recollections, 'mine will never wake again.' Mr. Mandeville started at the voice, indistinctly as it reached him, and turned towards the speaker; but she was at a remote end of the room, and the single candle which he held did not enable him to discern her features. 'Who is that person,' exclaimed he hastily, to Mrs. Selborne, 'and what is she saying?' – 'She says that you will not disturb the child: it never wakes, I believe, at this hour.' They then talked together in a low voice, of its health, its age, and its mother. 'You will probably recollect the young woman who nurses him,' concluded Mrs. Selborne, after saying something which Mary did not distinctly hear. 'She is the widow of a private who served under you; she owes the place to your recommendation.' The abashed and unfortunate girl leaned against the chimney; her eyes, which she raised only for a single moment, swimming in tears. How Mr. Mandeville looked she had no opportunity to observe, but not a word had he presence of mind enough to utter. Mrs. Selborne, meantime, was settling the cradle-clothes, and thought of nothing less than of watching either of them. She at length broke the silence by finding a hundred faults; after which, without waiting to see one remedied, she took the candle, and, followed by Mr. Mandeville, walked down stairs. And thus, without the interchange of a single syllable – nay, even of a look, parted Mary, and the man who had so often sworn that he lived only in her eyes.

Mr. Mandeville staid but two days longer at the Park, during which time Mary, by substituting in her own place, at certain hours, a girl who was sometimes employed as under nursery-maid, contrived that they should meet no more. She learned, however, that by means of this girl Mr. Mandeville had satisfied himself that her child was dead; and she had reason to hope that he had gathered enough information as to what related to her, to be assured that she must on this occasion have purposely shunned him.

And now, after Mary had been so heavily beaten by the storm, an interval of tranquillity seemed to succeed in her life. As Mrs. Selborne's house at Durham was repairing and painting, it was settled that she should continue to reside at Mandeville Park till the autumn; after that time, the child, the maid, and all that belonged to the nursery, were to remove with her, and to remain under her charge till the boy was of an age to be put into that of his father. The old lady took care to secure herself a handsome allowance for all this trouble; though even when that was done, she did nothing but lament and complain that she should be so unfortunate as to have such a tax laid upon her at her time of life! Her poor dear daughter, with whom she never could agree when alive, was now talked of as a miracle of perfection. The finest boy in the kingdom, she declared, would have been too dearly purchased by her loss: 'and for that poor little puny thing, I am afraid,' she used to add, 'that, with all our trouble, he will never live to be a man; which would be a great pity, considering what a fine estate he is heir to!'

Mary hoped better things. The infant was not robust, but it daily grew stronger, and to her daily more precious. It was her care, her pleasure, her employment: it engrossed her whole soul, and, by degrees, filled up all those fond affections of her heart which had no other object they could venture to swell upon. The very circumstance of not being a strong child made it only the dearer, by furnishing a perpetual succession of hopes and fears: both were already in some sort rewarded. He began to distinguish her; would crow when she appeared; 'and stretch its little arms as it would fly,' when hers opened to receive him. The range of Mandeville House, with the beautiful grounds, pleasure-garden, and country adjoining, were in themselves sources both of health and delight. She enjoyed almost undisturbed possession of the whole. 'What more could I gain, had I been born in a rank to have become its mistress,' would she sometimes say to herself, 'except an ungrateful man!' Tears then would fill her eyes:

'but this baby would indeed have been mine. – Well – and could I have loved him better?' The recollection that had she been his mother she need never have feared parting with him, would again agitate her heart, and unsettle her spirits. 'But I will never part with him,' thought she, 'even as it is, till he be a man grown – and then his very mother must have done so had she lived. Mrs. Selborne, when I am no longer wanted in one capacity, will be sure to let me stay with her in another! – I will make myself so useful! – Nobody will bear her humours so well, for nobody will have so strong a temptation to do it: so that it will be a great many years before I lose sight of my little boy, and I warrant I will teach him to love me before that time!' She *did* teach him to love her, sir; he must have been an unapt scholar, indeed, that had not learned.

I would not have you believe, however, that these quiet days were without their alloy. Mrs. Selborne was not a women to let any body in her circle enjoy themselves too much: every now and then she was seized with a fidgeting humour that was the torment of all around, and of Mary in particular; nothing then went right; nothing pleased her. This fit held just long enough to make her find fault with every thing, but never induced her to take the trouble of setting it to rights; so that she constantly left off where she began; only with an idle waste of time and spirits to all the parties concerned. This was far from being her only employment, however; she was a very stately dame, and fond of visiting; so that every other day her old-fashioned face was to be dressed, and the chariot and best liveries to be brought out, that she might dine or drink tea with Sir Thomas's family, or Lady Dowager Such-a-one, for she did not condescend any lower; and it was not seldom that she gave fine dinners at the Park: the servants said, because it was not at her own expence. Then young Master Mandeville was brought in, to be shown, during the dessert; and *her* cares – *her* anxiety – *her* fondness, as pompously detailed, as though she had spent her whole time in watching him. But these, and other things of the like nature, were nothing in Mary's calculation; all went as well with her as after her sorrowful outset could be expected: so well, that she ventured to write home, in order to inquire after her father and friends; though she did not tell them any thing that related to herself, except that she was in the service of a very great family.

Just in the beginning of autumn, when every thing looked full of happiness and beauty, and Mary's heart was daily more light on seeing her nursling prosper in the way he did, – dear sir, would you believe it? – One night Mr. Mandeville alighted at his own door! his coming was quite unexpected on all hands. The old lady was at cards with some of her grand neighbours, and not much better pleased at the surprise than Mary was; but *she* was not afflicted. It seems that there were some races in the neighbourhood, which he purposed to visit; so not thinking it necessary to give notice of his intention, while his household was kept up, he came thus, all at once, upon them. He only showed himself, as I may say, in the drawing-room; and then, observing that his boots made him not fit company for ladies (I suppose those present were none of the youngest), he walked at once to the nursery. Mary had summoned all her courage to meet him; but as she trembled so that it was difficult for her to hold the child, she called up the young woman I mentioned before, to her assistance. When he came in there were two of them, which he did not seem to expect. However, he took no particular notice, but kissed and tossed the child about, bidding Mary catch it; and all this with an easy familiar, careless air, which, together with his rough play to the infant, so overpowered her that she was near fainting. I suppose he drew his own conclusions from her agitation, but he said nothing at the time; only, on going down stairs, he took out five guineas and gave them to her, as he said, for her care of the child; offering something at the same time to the other girl, who most thankfully accepted it.

Mary's happy days were now at an end. The woman that does wrong must, I fear, remember, sir, that she will be always exposed to suspicion. Captain Mandeville, it was plain, had no faith in after-virtue, when he had found it failing in the first instance; and although a decent respect for circumstances, or accidental indifference, had induced him to take no notice of her during his first visit to the Park, these motives had ceased to operate, and she even perceived that he suspected her of placing herself voluntarily within his reach. Humbled by this opinion, which she was unable to remove; finding all remonstrances vain, and all efforts to avoid him useless, her life now became as miserable as it had before been tranquil. To complete her affliction, Mrs. Selborne soon suspected that some particular pursuit detained her son-in-law at Mandeville Park, and she quickly guessed its object. How Mary passed her days in consequence of all this, you may judge, sir. Her greatest fear, nevertheless, was that of being dismissed, which she was in hourly expectation would be the case; and her only hope, that Mrs. Selborne, not having authority to do that, or to control Mr. Mandeville, would hasten her departure to her own house. No such fortunate circumstance, however, happened. Mr. Mandeville, finding solicitation and allurement vain, grew insolent and troublesome; the servants sneered; the park-keeper's wife avoided her; there was no security from persecution, either in the house or the grounds; and, in short, of all that had soothed or comforted her poor heart, nothing remained the same but the baby.

Mary's mind began, I fear to undergo a strange revolution about this time. She grew desperate, as it were; and has acknowledged to me, that she sometimes debated with herself whether she should not accept his fine offers; for, rather than be crossed in his inclination, he did offer her liberally, sir; at others, she determined to tell the whole story to Mrs. Selborne, and throw herself upon her mercy; but against one temptation there was remorse, and a thousand other painful feelings, resulting from her experience of the selfishness and cruelty of the man: against the other, stood the severe temper and unfeeling character of the woman. Shame, too, at the thought of being exposed and degraded in the eyes of the neighbourhood, for she feared they would judge hardly of her, made her resolve, whatever might be the consequence, to keep her own secret. No third project then remained, but that of quitting the family altogether; and this she so nearly determined upon, as to collect all her little savings; so that if driven to extremities, either by the persecution of Mr. Mandeville or Mrs. Selborne, she might be able to leave the house at a moment's warning: but how was she to leave the child? – The thought of doing so was little less than a death-stroke.

I am afraid, sir, that when temptation of any kind fails even as to its main object, it often brings with it a great many evils not included in the views, nor present to the mind of the tempter. In the first place, it encourages a certain daringness of spirit, not favourable to modest virtue; it teaches us to weigh the right and the wrong of things that have been hitherto sacred in our imagination; and that not fairly either: for it puts the weight into the wrong scale, by showing us how much may be justified by sophistry, and how much may be palliated by example. In a word, it carries us out of our own bosoms for a rule of action, and bids us whiten by a comparison with the imperfections of others. I speak, sir, of common understandings and characters, such as have no great head for deep thinking, like Mary and myself. Some transition of this kind must have happened in her; for the whole frame of her mind seems to me to have changed during this period of perplexity and self-contention. She began to believe all the world wicked or foolish;

and it was not till after she had lived a good while with me that she was persuaded of the contrary.

Well, things continued in this way till near the time when Mrs. Selborne and her part of the family were to quit the Park: the day was anxiously expected by Mary. On the last but one preceding it, she had the ill-fortune to encounter Mr. Mandeville as she was returning to the nursery from her dinner. He insisted on talking with her; which she positively refused: but finding that he prepared to follow her up stairs, she thought it better to listen to him where she was: Mrs. Selbourne was abroad. All that Mr. Mandeville could offer, or say, on such an occasion, for it was his purpose to engage her to remain at the Park with him, may, as one should think, be easily imagined; but you would *not* easily imagine, sir, that, finding all other efforts fail, he should, before the parted, strive to alarm the fears of the poor girl, by indirectly threatening to publish her former misconduct. I cannot think so ill of him, or of any man, as to believe that he was in earnest: but Mary's agitated heart, and distempered fancy, gave credit to the worst. With what little eloquence she was mistress of, she endeavoured, it seems, to represent to him the great disadvantage her loss would prove to his child; an argument which, she flattered herself, would certainly prevail, when all others failed: but he treated it as a matter of no consequence. 'The infant was nearly weaned, and any old woman in the parish might nurse it,' he said. Driven to the last extremity, she then positively declared her resolution to quit the country, and find a situation elsewhere.

'And where will you find a character?' said Mr. Mandeville, with a sneer: he had little time for more, as the old lady's chariot drove up at that moment to the door. 'Remember, Mary, what I say to you,' repeated he, emphatically, as he opened that of the parlour to let her out: 'a hint from me to Mrs. Selborne dismisses you with disgrace from the house: – where, I say, will you then find a character?'

It was not necessary to bid her remember the words; they were engraven in letters of fire, as it seemed to Mary, both on her heart and her brain.

'Where, Mary, will you find a character?' exclaimed she, as she ran up into the nursery, and mechanically took the child in her arms: for it was her hour for walking with him round the grounds. 'Where will you find a character?' she continued repeating to herself, as she hurried on, without exactly knowing whither; tears, caresses, and every thing that was afflicting succeeded this tumult of resentment. – I cannot give you an exact account of what followed, sir; she could never give me one herself: but certain it is, that she continued to walk till she reached the mouth of the river; and there, meeting by ill-fortune with a small vessel bound for London, and in the very act of sailing, she got directly on board, and still carrying with her the precious child, was in a few hours many leagues out at sea. – Now comes the fearful part of Mary's life! now comes the time when *she* strove to whiten by comparison: to use her little knowledge and experience in justifying a wicked action, and to say to herself, 'Why should I alone be upright in a worthless and cruel world!' Mr. Mandeville, sir, could no longer tempt, but his influence had corrupted her, and left her exposed to the temptation within.

She was a total stranger in the vessel where she had taken a passage: indeed, neither the child nor herself had ever been seen in the neighbourhood, nor was it probable that any living creature could know or give an account of them: the baby was in its night-clothes, for they dined late at Mandeville Park; consequently was no way remarkable by the fineness of its dress. She did not believe that Mr. Mandeville, after what had passed, would venture to seek her that evening in the nursery; and unless it was noticed that she did not return from her walk, the chances were that no inquiry would be made till the ensuing morning: for such had been her unremitting attention to the child, that it was very customary with her never to leave his apartment for a moment when once she had put him to bed.

All these, and a thousand thoughts besides, passed through her mind; but her whole care was for the baby: the very few minutes, as I may say, that preceded her embarkation had been employed in providing for its comfort; and as, for security's sake, she had secreted her little wealth about her, in order to convey it to Durham, or elsewhere, there was no difficulty in securing the very best accommodation.

What passed at Mandeville Park, when the loss of the child was discovered, or in what manner or time the discovery was made, I never learned: no doubt every effort was used, by advertisement and inquiry, to regain the infant, but none could reach the ship's crew while they were at sea, and before either could come to their knowledge on land, things had so fallen out that no indications remained to guide the search. It was long before Mary knew any thing farther of Mr. Mandeville, and sorrowful was the day when she did.

The voyage was very rough, and Mary herself extremely ill: but the child did not appear to suffer in the least: they were driven by stress of weather into a little port not very far from London, where she made it her choice to land: a public carriage, which was stopped by mere accident, conveyed her to town; and thus, almost without premeditation on her side, was every clue lost to those who might have sought for her. What Mary's feelings or thoughts were during the period that succeeded, it would be difficult precisely to ascertain. She was not without money; but she had neither friends nor connection. Industry, sir, is nevertheless a trusty auxiliary, and either finds, or makes its way. By giving security, which her stock of money enabled her to do, she contrived to get employment in a small but creditable shop, not unlike that in which she had lived with her aunt: her readiness and good qualities rendered her valuable wherever she had an opportunity of making them known, as she very quickly did. Her wants were few: she had neither vanity nor pleasure but in the child; and he, little fellow, grew and did well; while her excessive fondness for him made it impossible for any one to suspect that she was not its mother. He was no longer, indeed, at Mandeville Park, the heir of a fine estate, and waited upon by a numerous train of servants: but he had still one servant more anxious, more devoted than any he had left there: he had also the best of every thing, however plain: all her leisure was employed, as he grew older, in teaching him the little she knew either of writing, reading, or accounts: his health was still tender and uncertain: she watched him with the care of a mother, and the fatigue of a nurse. No thought like self-reproach, I believe ever crossed her mind with respect to his father: her heart was quite hardened towards Mr. Mandeville; and she was persuaded that Mrs. Selborne would grieve but little for the child when it was once out of her sight. She shut her eyes deliberately to the past and the future, and determined to think only of the present day.

Such was her own account of her life in London; and I never had reason to doubt its truth. There are those that would have done so: but from the circumstances she stood in, when she gave me the relation, I believe it as firmly as that I now exist. It was a strange life for a young woman, and a pretty woman, for she was still pretty: placed, too, in the very heart of a city so famous for its vices and profligacy: but I have heard Mary say, and indeed I believe her, that many and many a poor creature earns her bread in London by the sweat of her brow, and during her laborious and daily employment knows no more of its vices or its luxuries than if she were living a thousand miles off it.

I saw Mary for the first time about eighteen years ago: she was then nine-and-twenty: it was in the beginning of summer, and a very sultry day. I was sitting, during the forenoon, at work, with my parlour windows open, when a young woman, holding a little boy by the hand, walked past the house and returned. She did this more than once without my taking any particular notice of her, though she, as I afterwards found, took a great deal of me: at last she made a little stop close by the window.

'Did you want an industrious person to assist you in needle-work, madam?' said she.

I looked up, supposing that I should know her, but her face was quite new to me: so I went to my stitching again, only carelessly answering, 'that I never employed strangers.'

'I am sorry for it,' said she, and sighed softly: there is not telling you how winning her manner was: I could not help looking after her; she saw I did, and returned; but a little irresolutely.

'It is true that I am a stranger here, madam,' said she; 'but if I were known to you, perhaps you would not object to employing me.'

I can't say that I should,' returned I; and to own the truth sir, I should have been very glad of assistance; for the season was drawing on: I was making up those very window curtains which you now see in the parlour; they were then drawing-room furniture. I had my hands full of business besides; so I looked more steadily at her, to judge what sort of a person she might be; and then I looked at her companion; both were plainly, but very neatly dressed; he was rather a delicate child, but he had lively intelligent eyes: his complexion, however, did not announce health.

'Your little boy,' said I, 'seems sickly:' tears flowed down her cheeks in a moment. – 'He has had a fever,' she replied, 'but thank God he is now likely to do well: the doctor tells me that bathing in the sea will recruit his strength, and I have therefore brought him here for that purpose.' I know not what there was so taking in her and the child, but for my life I could not turn them from the door.

'Well, come into the parlour,' said I, 'and let us talk together: perhaps you may be able to refer me to some one that knows you.' *That* she could not do: but she made me the same proposal which she had found successful in London, of taking work home with her, and leaving a deposit to its value, till it was returned. This looked honest and open; so we began to talk of what she could do. Meantime I had a favourite bird in the room, and the little boy and the bird were grown very intimate. – 'I will teach you to sing,' said the child; and in truth I thought he might well say so, for so musical a voice as his was in speaking I had never heard. Sing, however, neither bird nor child would, when desired; but I was mightily pleased with my new acquaintance; and, to be short, it was settled that she should come the next morning and work with me for a certain number of hours. She required nothing, she said, but her day-board for herself and her child, till I could judge of what she was capable.

It was now all plain sailing, sir, and she knew it; for I presently discovered that my industry and usefulness, on which I valued myself, were nothing to her ingenuity. She did *so* cut out and contrive! 'And this, Mrs. Dixon,' said she, 'is just the right pattern for such a thing; and that will do for another.' She was like a good fairy: my whole house presently seemed furnished by her skill and industry. I could not doubt but a woman who was so clever must be honest, so I fitted out a little decent back room up stairs, and took both her and the boy as inmates. I can't maintain that this was a discreet step, sir, considering how very little I knew of my guest. I heard enough talk of its folly from all my neighbours: but I know not how it is, I have seen people wait so long before they could resolve upon a kind action, to know if it was a wise one too, that they never found the opportunity for doing any such in their whole lives.

Mary was now, as I may say, my factotum; and nothing was performed cleverly that she had not a concern in. We had no regular agreement together: I paid her as well as I could afford to do for her services, and in truth there was no service, however humble, that she was not willing to render me. But, although in this particular she never changed, we had not lived many months together before I saw something remarkable in her general disposition. She had an ill opinion of others, and believed every one selfish and hard-hearted. So that her own good conduct seemed rather to spring from some feeling that was natural to her, than any principle or necessity she saw for it. To hear her speak of a fault, or even of a misfortune in a neighbour, you would have thought her to be almost without any sensibility: but let her witness the smallest affliction, her heart would overflow with kindness, and her eyes with tears. In her general habits she was zealous, active, and obliging: yet there were times when her whole appearance and manners changed. It was then impossible to make any thing of her; for she was absent and negligent: would sigh as if her heart were breaking, and had a nervous, agitated, irresolute air, that sometimes alarmed me for her head. These fits, however, returned less frequently after the first twelvemonth of her residence with me than they had formerly done; and for several years after, her active employments, together with my company, who am not, as you see, of a very melancholy character, drove off the evil day. But conscience, as the rector told us from the pulpit two or three Sundays ago, is a sleeping giant: we may lull him into a longer or a shorter slumber: but his starts are frightful, and terrible is the hour when he awakes. I thought of Mary as he spoke the words.

Her fondness for the little boy, sir, was downright folly: but I had seen enough of mothers not to be surprised at that: he was always dressed above his apparent condition: she could deny him nothing; and indeed he was an engaging little creature. When she brought him to Weymouth he was about eight years of age: the sea air agreed with him wonderfully, and he was never sickly from that time; but grew so sprightly, so arch, so diverting, that *little Bob* was the universal favourite. He was, withal, very proud; although nobody could tell of what: it could not be of his birth, or his great estate, poor child! for, alas, he knew nothing of either! but in spite of his humble situation, Bob was a great *hoper*, and was always talking of the mighty things he would do when he should grow to be a man: – I beg your pardon, sir – my eyes *will* fill with tears at the recollection: his mother encouraged this folly in him.

'Mary,' said I to her one day, 'you will totally ruin that boy.'

'Oh, no, no,' returned she, impatiently.

'You will make his mind a great deal too high.'

'*I* do not make it,' said she; – 'it makes itself.'

'But ought it to make itself? Consider he is growing a great lad.'

'Don't talk to me, Mrs. Dixon. I cannot control his spirit. – If you knew how dearly I bought him ——'

'At what price *did* you buy him?' returned I. She started, and looked at me very earnestly for a moment, but said nothing. I cannot but own that I had my private thoughts. Mary had told me that the boy's father was a soldier; and so indeed he was, sir: but she had never been circumstantial as to the time of his death, nor any particulars relative to him. I had my suspicions, therefore; though, God knows, they were far from the whole truth; and she was so guarded, so discreet in her conduct, and seemed to have so deep a sorrow at heart for the past, that I had not the courage to add to it by what I thought idle inquiries. It would be very hard, said I to myself, if a woman should not be able

303

to recover one false step! and – I do not know – I may be wrong, but it seemed to me, that being obliged to acknowledge and talk of it, inflicts useless suffering, if the person be indeed penitent; and if the contrary, perhaps puts perverse arguments and thoughts into the mind that are better laid aside. For the more frequently a woman blushes, sir, the less painful it becomes to her: this was my way of reasoning. I have but a poor head, however, it must be owned, for these points; so I do not reckon much upon it, but mostly question my heart: *that* always tells me how I would have others do unto me, if I were in affliction, and therefore I go no further.

Weymouth is a gay place however in the season, as you know, sir. I was aware of this; and, at our early acquaintance, I watched Mary very narrowly. We have abundance of fine gentlemen walking about, but none did I ever see her so much as look at: and if, by any accident, their eyes were directed to her, and that was an accident that would have happened pretty frequently if she had encouraged it, she was never to be seen a second time. I used to observe, at first, indeed, that she was somewhat curious to know what regiments were coming and going: but that seemed natural enough, as her husband had been a soldier; and long before I learned to doubt the story of her having been married, I knew that I could trust Mary.

Bob was now twelve years old. No longer a delicate, small-limbed child, but a fine, well-grown boy; with a manly and open countenance, a forward and proud spirit; full of frolic, but without any mischief. He had beaten a neighbour's son, much bigger than himself, who persisted in calling him *little Bob*; so he was now Robert; and it was laughable to see the vehemence with which he insisted upon this claim. All our acquaintance blamed us for keeping such a great boy at home, without any occupation, and I began secretly to be a little ashamed of the weakness myself: for, to say truth, sir, I was nearly as weak as Mary on that subject. The child was never idle either, nor was it in his nature to be so: he made himself useful ten thousand ways. There was nothing so low that he disdained to do for those he loved: he has cleaned knives, and gone on errands. Good God, little did I think who it was that was so employed! It was not with Mary's approbation, however, that he did this: but she could not prevent him; he undertook it all as if it were sport: 'all for his dear little granny Dixon,' as he used to call me. Think of his making me his grandmother, sir! – I was then a young woman; but it was his playful way. The fact was, that he had an inexhaustible stock of health and spirits to spare, and having neither companion nor employment, was fain to spend both as he could. Every one, however, that came to the house noticed and spoiled him. – 'Gads my life, Mrs. Dixon,' said one of our actor gentlemen, who was drinking tea with me, while Bob, in tip-top spirits, handed us the tea-kettle, 'this is a fellow of whom the world may say that "he will ride a bay trotting horse over a four-inched bridge, and course his own shadow for a traitor."'* – To be sure, sir, Bob was too fond of riding strange horses; but how the child's foible came to be so generally known was what I never could guess.

Bob's own mind was quite made up as to his future destination. 'He would be a soldier,' he said, 'like his father.' *Like his father!* said Mary, and tears came into her eyes. The boy was present, so I could not make any comments upon her speech. We taught him, and had him taught by others, all the little learning we could. I must own that he was not very fond of it, yet he was no blockhead neither; only sprightly and heedless: but in proportion as he grew older his pride made him set more value upon these sort of things, for he could never endure to be wanting in any point that others knew: and though for the heir of Mr. Mandeville he would have made perhaps a poor figure, he was not ignorant for one in his station. The soldiers took to him mightily. The master, seeing how fond he was of horses, taught him to ride; which Mary did not object to. They looked upon him as one of themselves, and acted very kindly by him. But still they were men, and he was only a boy; so that, without meaning it, they made him forward and presuming. The neighbours and people around told ill-natured stories of his pride and extravagance; but they were so exaggerated that we hardly gave them any credit. Time slipped away, and he was getting on some months past fourteen. Mary's disquietude visibly increased. She made him solemnly promise that he would not enlist for a soldier without her consent; and as he believed that she would not withhold it in due season, he very readily gave his word. We thought him too proud to break it; and, to do him only justice, too kind-hearted; for he well knew the grief it would cost us.

The interval between this time and his fifteenth birthday was the most melancholy we had ever passed since we lived together. He was almost beyond our control; yet we knew no harm of him; but he kept growing very handsome and very tall: every day, therefore, told us that something must be done with him. A dreadful gloom came over Mary.

P711.50* Shakespeargned May, 1635

She was no longer the same creature she had been. No sleep did she get at night; no quiet in the day. All was continual restlessness. Her very temper changed; so that at last we hardly cared to speak with her. Perceiving that she was so very miserable, I concluded that her fear of his going to sea, if not in the army, was the cause of her disquiet; and I therefore proposed to her to try to get him into some respectable gentleman's service. With all his wildness he was so docile to us, that I think we could have persuaded him to this. She changed colour at my proposal, and looked at me with an expression I never saw in her countenance before. – 'No, Mrs. Dixon,' said she, very emphatically, when I had done speaking, '*that* shall never be.' – 'And why not? He has acted as my servant, you know' – 'And well he might: he cannot do too much for you. There is no disgrace in the service of the heart: – but Bob shall never take hire!' I did not venture to afflict her further, and we went on as before. About this time a family came to lodge at next door, who brought with them a young woman that was born in Mary's native village: she had not been long from thence, and could give an account of all that had passed there. Mary learned that her father was alive, though in a very infirm state of health. He had lost several children, but her mother-in-law had still a large family remaining. The old man, she understood, had been anxious to see her once more before he died; but having no direction to her, had not been able to make this wish known. He was certainly not dead, however, at that time.

This intelligence seemed at last to make up Mary's mind. The terrible necessity she felt at parting with the boy, had been a canker that had been eating into her very heart; for part with him some way it was evident she must; since neither his age nor his character would allow him to stay any longer with her; and to whom could she give him up, but to his own father? In what manner exactly she meant to effect this I know not. Amid the despair that preyed secretly upon her at the prospect of losing him, after turning her thoughts a thousand different ways in search of comfort, she found no gleam of it but in the idea of going back to her own village. She had been innocent – she had been comparatively happy there. She believed she should find something to love, and Mary could not live without loving something. I believe she soothed her conscience with the hope of attending her father's age, and watching his death-bed. In short, she found it absolutely necessary to hope, if she meant to live; and this was all she *could* hope.

I tell you merely my own conjectures; for her restlessness, her total loss of appetite, and the long fits of absence that now grew very remarkable in her, were the only symptoms by which I could guess that she was privately forming some resolution. I had no clue at that time to her inmost thoughts; but by after events and confidence I could trace them. Her health suffered too much to permit me to ask any questions, for I really could not guess what their effect upon her might prove. At length she fixed her determination: but, like a drowning person catching at straws, she could not prevail on herself to take the great step till she had settled every thing that concerned her besides. And so, sir, this new delay in entering upon the path of justice and uprightness was the cause of all the melancholy story that followed.

I was not much surprised when she told me that she meant to take a journey home: but when I found the boy was not to accompany her, I was then sure how things stood between her and her family; and that he was no lawful son of hers, however fond she might be of him. I must own to you that I had my doubts as to the object of her journey altogether. It is natural to suspect deceit where we meet with it in one instance; and being now convinced in my own mind that the child was base-born, I assured myself that his father was alive; I concluded that he was some great man, and that Mary, far from turning her steps towards home, was only going to solicit him in favour of his son. I could not misunderstand her intention in other particulars. She was too reluctant to go, to leave me any fear on that subject: and whether the child were base-born or no, I must own that I thought the father had a right to be consulted as to its future destination.

'Well, Mary,' said I, 'you leave me a great charge, and yet you don't tell me your secrets.' – 'They are sad ones,' replied she mournfully: 'but when I return I will tell you all.' – 'I am afraid I can guess one already,' said I, in a very significant tone. She shook her head, and looked the image of despair. – 'I cannot prevail upon myself to reveal it now. I have tried, but my lips will not move to do it. When it is told, you shall give me your advice how to proceed, and I faithfully promise to follow it.' – I believe she spoke truth, sir: I had seen her lips tremble several times when she opened them to speak to me; and I greatly suspect that half her reason, though she did not know it herself, for resolving to live from me, when once I had heard her story, was, that she felt it impossible to endure the eyes of any one who knew it.

On the eighth of July, sir, eleven years ago, Mary left me. She looked very pale as she stepped into the stagecoach; but she reckoned that her absence would not much exceed three weeks; which, considering the long journey she had before her, was the least time possible. Bob, who at his age thought that period a mere nothing, presently recovered his spirits, for he had been much affected at parting and began to tell me what we should both do during her absence. His account of my occupations would have made any one smile, the picture was so like me! he did not tell me all his own, you may be sure, but we made out the evening together between mirth and sorrow; nor did he, throughout it, show any impatience at passing so many hours with a talkative woman, old enough to be his mother; for he knew that I should have felt lonesome had he left me. Two or three days passed thus very pleasantly: the boy was not constantly in the house, but he was continually coming backwards and forwards, and asking good-naturedly whether he should do this thing for me, and the other. What a charm is there in youth, sir! I, that was not his mother, nor even related to him, could not help fancying that any father on earth must be vain of such a son; and most heartily did I wish I had known his, that I might have recommended him to his favour.

On the evening of the fourth day, as well as I can recollect, a message came to me from the people at the hotel, to inquire if my house was let. The season was likely to prove very full, and I had at that time more than one treaty on foot, but the families were undecided, and nothing had passed by which I conceived myself to be bound. I found that the person for whom the inquiry was made was a single gentleman, and a member of parliament. It was plain, indeed, that he was a man of condition, for he would have nothing less than the whole house: I mean those apartments excepted which I always kept for my own use. I did not hesitate to conclude an agreement that promised to be very advantageous; and as the gentleman, being an invalid, was impatient to settle himself, I did my best to make every thing ready for him that very night. My apartments were always aired, and there was therefore nothing to hinder his taking immediate possession. When his servants, however, began to dispose of themselves, I was sadly grieved to find that he had so numerous a train as made it impossible for me conveniently to lodge them. There was Mary's room, with a little closet within it, where Bob slept. I found I should be obliged to take one of these for the groom. The butler told me that he was a civil, well-behaved young man, and he was smart enough, nay, even genteel to look at: but I did not like to throw Bob thus into the familiar society of servants, and strangers too: there was no remedy, however; so the thing was ordered as well as it could be, and the two lads were lodged together. I understood that the groom was a very great favourite with his master; therefore, much against my inclination. I was obliged to give him the best room of the two. In the evening his master came: – oh, sir, would you believe it? – it was no other than Mr. Mandeville!

Yes – it was Mr. Mandeville himself! but not that Mr. Mandeville who had robbed Mary of her heart, in all the bloom and fire of eight-and-twenty; free-living, and the years that had passed over his head, had left strong traces on his features. He had a fixed redness in his face, and had lost the slightness of his person. One might indeed see that he had been handsome, for he had a manly character of countenance; and I could afterwards recollect that his son greatly resembled him in this: but such was then the wide difference in their age and appearance, that nothing of the sort occurred to me. How indeed should it?

Mr. Mandeville was well enough pleased with his accommodation; and had he been otherwise, he had very little choice besides: but the satisfaction was by no means mutual. I soon perceived my mistake in believing that I had secured a quiet invalid for my lodger, who proposed nothing to himself but health and comfort: these were the last things thought of by any of the family. Such a scene of confusion as now presented itself, I had rarely ever before witnessed! eating, drinking, and rattling the dice-box were the sole employments of the day. Mr. Mandeville went little abroad; but two or three gentlemen, at least, were constantly of his dinner party; and it was seldom that all of them went away sober. These modes of life did not agree with him. He was frequently very ill, and on such occasions I often went to see and attend him. I could not help one day representing to him that he had but little chance of recovering his health, while he continued the very habits that had injured it. He was in good humour, and heard me out with much patience; only he laughed heartily when I had ended, and said, 'You talk like an oracle, Mrs. Dixon; but I fear I am too old to mend.'

'Nay, sir,' said I, 'age will not hinder your amendment. You cannot have seen fifty, I am sure.' – Between ourselves I thought I spoke within compass when I said this: he laughed again.

'What, is that your standard age?' said he. 'I have six years good then: though I see you think me an older fellow than I am. However,

The Canterbury Tales

spare your preaching: for I believe, Mrs. Dixon, that I shall die as I have lived. My faults injure nobody so much as they do myself.' I had not the boldness to contradict him, but this was not true, sir; nor could Mr. Mandeville seriously believe it to be so. I know not whether it can be safely affirmed of any man, but I am sure that it cannot of a rich one; and to convince myself of this, I had only to look at the instance before me. Mr. Mandeville's profusion and vices were imitated by every servant he had; and if they strove a little to conceal this from him, they only added hypocrisy to every other fault: but they did not endeavour to conceal it, sir; or in a very trifling degree. His own man openly professed to follow his master's example in all things. The butler was several years older, but he was insolent, unfeeling, and extravagant. The other servants did not fall short of these models: but, oh sir! a worse grief than all remained behind, though I did not immediately know its extent: the groom whom I had been obliged to place with my poor innocent boy, was a very ill-disposed lad; and the bad effects of his society were too soon visible in the latter, though sooner to others than to me.

The loss of Mary's assistance threw a vast load upon my spirits and time. In truth, where servants were so disorderly and ill-managed, I had hardly a moment to spare from my domestic concerns, or to call my own. Occupied as I was, however, I observed that some alteration had taken place in Bob. He affected to be the man more than I thought became him; and began to be very nice in his linen and appearance. He had been hitherto a fine rough boy, ten thousand times more manly than the groom that he admired; yet the latter was a personable lad too; but there was something of native fire and character about Bob, or I fancied so, that was much above his degree: it could not be fancy either, for every body that saw him used to say the same thing.

Mr. Mandeville was more partial to his groom than to any one of his servants. He was of light weight, active, clever, knowing in horses, and had rode several matches for his master; nor did he ever fail to win: so that for me to pretend to find any fault with Thomas was quite out of the question. Not but Mr. Mandeville was himself sufficiently severe with him sometimes, when any thing put him out of temper; and he was not good-tempered in general: but as to the lad's private conduct or character, 'he had no business with that,' he said: 'he supposed he was just like the rest.' People are men, however, as well as servants, sir; and by this doctrine may do more harm in one capacity than they ever do good in another.

It was with very great vexation, and some alarm, that I heard of the increasing intimacy between Bob and this young man. I could not greatly blame the boy: he had no other companion; had had one. He saw the groom caressed and praised by his master; noticed by all the gentlemen that visited at the house; encouraged to be saucy; ruling in the stable, where, unfortunately, *Robert* would have loved to rule too; for he was passionately fond of riding: and how was a boy of his age to make a distinction between right and wrong, when so many of his superiors made none? Yet he had no mind to be a groom either; for, to try him, I asked him the question. 'No,' he said, and coloured, 'I will be a soldier.' For several days after this I observed that he was thoughtful, and staid more at home than before. At last he inquired of me whether Mr. Mandeville was not in the army. I told him that I believed he was, from the number of military gentlemen that visited him. I fancy, poor lad, the project entered his head of recommending himself to his notice, for he took two or three opportunities afterwards of falling in his way. Once, in particular, he was standing at the door when Mr. Mandeville came down to ride. Thomas, by some accident or other, was not close at hand, and Bob officiously started forward to supply his place. Mr. Mandeville looked at him, indeed, but called at the same moment to the groom before he put his foot in the stirrup, and Bob hastily retired, blushing up to the very ears at the repulse. This I believe, sir, was the only time that Mr. Mandeville ever cast his eyes upon his son so as to notice him. Nothing, however, came of it, nor did the boy from that day make any further effort.

Three weeks and more had passed, yet Mary did not return. She had promised to write if any thing detained her. I knew not what to make of her silence, and grew uneasy, both on her account and that of her son. My warnings to him to break off the intimacy which he had so lately formed were not attended to, and I had no power to enforce them. Nor could I send either lad out of my house. They were constantly together. They rode matches on the sands, or elsewhere. Their companions betted upon them: they betted themselves; and I was convinced that Bob lost. I taxed him with it. Nothing spoils the temper, sir, like the consciousness of doing wrong. This boy, this child as I may call him, formerly so complying and open, was capable of being rude and sullen: quite at a loss what to do, I desired him to write to his mother, and hasten her return. He obeyed me, though not with a good grace: but she came not, nor did we receive any answer, and I repented that I had not written myself; but I was not a ready pen-women, and had much occupation. – I thought that I was now quite miserable! – I did not know how much more miserable I was to be. Every possible way did I turn over in my mind to remedy the mischief I had so innocently caused: but the mischief was doing, sir, past all remedy: – it was done, as I may say, even while I was considering.

Of what nature the extravagance might be of these two boys I cannot tell, but they had been very extravagant. Bob's means were scanty indeed; the other threw money about like dirt; but I have much reason to believe that he was as ready to take as to part with it. At last neither of them had any left, and both grievously wanted it. My boy would have stopped short; but the wicked one with whom he associated had other ways of proceeding. The old butler was, in private, his constant theme of aversion and ridicule: and more, as he made it appear, in sport than in wickedness; but it *was* wickedness, I am persuaded: he now proposed to secrete several valuable articles that were in this man's possession, on which, he assured Bob, he could raise money, and return them without difficulty in the course of two days; declaring, that should it in the interim be discovered they were missing, *he* would easily face it out for a joke. Robert was, as he confessed, in debt: he had besides contracted a thousand wants, and a thousand wishes, during his intercourse with the worthless crew around him; and too proud to own to any but his immediate companion that he had no resources, he fell into the snare which folly, vice, and ill-fortune prepared for him. The butler, however, was either more subtle, or more watchful, than they had believed him to be. He discovered the fact a very few hours after it was committed; nor did he fail to guess at the culprits. Thomas was first secured, and his evidence incriminated Bob. The latter was with me when they came to fetch him. Never to the latest moment of my life, sir, shall I forget *that!* There was no need of accusation nor proof; his countenance told all, and both lads were thrown into prison. The groom, however, was too cunning, and, I am afraid, too well practised in secrets of this kind, not to know all the advantage he had over his companion; and in order to avail himself of it, he immediately applied to Mr. Mandeville. The fact was too well established to allow the butler to recede from his first testimony; but he presently comprehended which was to be the victim, provided either must be so, and a lawyer was accordingly employed, who ascertained it.

If there was any faith to be placed in one, who till the last two luckless months never was found guilty of a lie, Bob was no otherwise concerned, than in being privy to the villanous secret. He neither plotted, weighed, nor executed it: but, with the incomprehensible inconsideration of youth, ran headlong on, without adverting either to its criminality or its danger: but of what avail was this testimony, sir, to any head but that in my bosom? It was close upon the time of the Dorchester assizes: the two lads were conveyed to the gaol there, and Mr. Mandeville's lawyer continued to be employed in the cause.

At this crisis, I at length received a letter from Mary. It was in answer to one I had written her ten days before. Another from me had followed close upon it; for though I was but a poor scribe, I had taken the trouble to send her a second letter, because I had not been sufficiently pressing about her return in my first: that second, however, was still on the road. What a story had I now to add to it! Her father, she informed me, was dead before she arrived. She had found her mother-in-law extremely ill of a fever, which, it was plain, was infectious throughout the neighbourhood. It had carried off one little girl of the family, and another was sick: her home, therefore, had been a sorrowful scene from the day that she reached it. 'And yet, could you suppose it, Mrs. Dixon,' said Mary, 'I have experienced more tranquillity of mind, on finding myself useful to my friends, and kindly treated by my old companions, than I have done for fifteen years past. I will make many hearts happy when I return to you, and then there will be some chance for my own. I should tell you,' she added, 'that I have had the fever so badly as to be quite unable to use the pen, which must plead my excuse for my silence. I have got out to-day for the first time, though still very weak, and have crept down to one of my old haunts near the river. I remember when I used to sit in its stony bed where the channel was dry, while the low branches that shoot out of the bank sheltered me from the heat, and envy the water that flowed through so many new places. Now I have been there on purpose to see the sun set; and you will hardly guess why. I pleased myself with thinking that Bob and you might be walking on the sands together, and looking at it, at the same moment.' – Alas, sir, Bob saw no sun! he was shut up in a cell, where it was plain that neither sun nor air ever visited him, for in a few days all his freshness was quite gone.

I cannot tell you how many times I applied to Mr. Mandeville; but he was all on the wrong side of the question; so he shuffled me off, and told me that the lawyers must decide, and I know not what stuff beside. The lawyers did decide, sir, for it could not be the law. The vile groom was, with difficulty enough, acquitted; and the innocent child sentenced to Botany Bay. There is no telling you the falsehoods the groom asserted to save himself: it was a scene of wickedness that no judge less than God Almighty could have set right. I do not say that any body meant to persecute, or that Mr. Mandeville's lawyer did more than he might think fair: but some one was to suffer, and every thing may be seen, where minds are not habitually upright, through the medium of prejudice and opinion. There were, besides, a thousand lies circulated and believed in the town: lies of idleness, lies of ignorance: – for aught I know, of malice. And poor Bob, who never, I supposed, made an enemy in his life, had every little fault magnified into a vice. – But when it was all over, and they could do no more, many a one dropped a tear, that had carelessly accredited a falsehood; and few were hard-hearted enough not to pity so young an offender.

I had now no hope but in Mr. Mandeville's compassion. I flattered myself that his interest, if he could be prevailed upon to use it, would obtain a pardon at least, and I sent a most pressing entreaty to be admitted to him.

'You have a face full of care, Mrs. Dixon,' said he when he saw me: – 'out with it!'

'Oh, sir!' said I, bursting into tears, 'I come upon the old errand – Robert Innis.'

'Do not talk to me of Robert Innis,' said he: 'he has cost me money and trouble enough already. I shall after all, be obliged, on his account, to part with the best lad I ever had.'

'I am afraid you are mistaken, sir,' replied I.

'No, no, I tell you,' said he passionately; 'there is not his fellow left in the stable. – 'I would rather,' and he swore a great oath, 'that he had robbed me every day in the year than have lost him. He was a good lad enough till he knew your 'scape-grace.'

'If you would take the trouble to examine into the rights of the case, sir' returned I.

'A man cannot spend his life in examining your rights and your wrongs, Mrs. Dixon.'

'I beg your pardon, sir,' said I; 'I thought that members of parliament, and rich gentlemen, *did* spend their lives in such examinations.' – I cannot affirm that this was uttered without some malice, for my heart was over-fraught, and I was quite desperate: but I did not suppose that it would ruffle him so greatly as it seemed to do. He was too proud to say all he thought, but he *looked* at me!

'You take great liberties,' said he at length: 'great liberties indeed, and know nothing of what you are talking about. I desire that I may never hear another syllable upon this business. Justice must take its course. *I* have no concern in it whatever. Justice,' he sternly added, as he went down stairs to his carriage. '*must*, and *will* be executed.' – Justice *was* executing at that very time, sir, upon the prime offender; but he knew it not.

I spent the night in tears, and without going to bed: often wishing the day would never dawn; for I had promised to go to Dorchester, and inform my poor boy of the event of my application. Would you suppose it? I found him fast asleep. He had not slept for a long time before. But youth and nature had at last prevailed, and he was in the sweetest, soundest slumber I ever saw. What a thing it was, to wake and hear the tidings I had to tell! But affliction makes people old before their time. This boy, who had been hitherto so sprightly, and so thoughtless, listened to me with all the silence and self-government of a man. He spoke but very little afterwards indeed: nor would he trust himself to read Mary's letter while I stood by; but earnestly requested me to write to her. I almost overset him by desiring that he would do so. But on looking in his face, and not being able to endure the sight of what was painted there, I promised to do it myself; and then, at his particular desire, I went away. I *did* write to Mary, and it was, as you may guess, sir, a letter that I feared would break her heart when she received it.

What signifies describing all the sorrowful hours that succeeded! but never – no, never shall I forget the last time I saw the poor lad, which was the night before he was sent from Dorchester to be put, in with other convicts, on board the vessel. He was sadly downcast when I came into the cell; and his once healthy countenance was as pale as ashes, except for the red marks that tears had left upon it; for he was too proud to shed any before me, though his breast swelled and heaved as if it would have burst. To be sure it was a dismal sight! so promising a boy! – and not yet sixteen! Ah, sir, was this, as I afterwards thought, the little fellow that had been fondled and caressed at Mandeville Park, and for whom so much had been expected! – But is not every infant fondled and caressed? – The poorest outcast that ever went in irons to finish his miserable life, as Bob did, in a distant country, has been pressed to some maternal heart, more tenderly perhaps than ever he was.

'I have been considering, Mrs. Dixon,' said the dear fellow, 'how it happens that all this evil and wickedness have fallen upon me; and

I think I have found out the cause,' – 'And what is that, my dear Bob?' said I, for I was still accustomed to call him so, and he never took it ill of me, though he would not suffer any body else to do it: it was the name I used to him when he was a bit of a child on my knee, and I loved it for that reason. 'What is that, my dear Bob?' said I. – 'Why it comes from my having no father. My mother, to be sure, was very good; but then she was only my mother: and you were very good too; but I was a boy, and I often thought to myself that boys should not be governed by women; and her hand was as gentle as her heart: so I grew up without any other guide than my own proud thoughts, and easily fell a prey to the wicked suggestions of others. – Now, if I had had a father, Mrs. Dixon, you see I should have been saved from all this; for if he had been a rich man I should not have fallen into the way of temptation; and if he had been poor and industrious, I should have early learned not to be ashamed of poverty, and his example might have made me industrious too: for indeed I was not naturally wicked; but God,' added he, laying his finger on the Testament, which the chaplain had left with him, 'as this book assures me, will be a father to the fatherless; and although I have none to apply to in this world, I will put my trust in Him.' – I thought my heart must have broken: for, with his finger between the leaves of the book, he dropped on his knees, and hid his face over it; and when he raised it again, on hearing my sobs, there was something so sweet in his eyes that mine were quite blind with tears. Oh, what, have I since thought, had not Mary to answer for! Dreadfully, sir, *did* she answer for it! Yet, had Bob been Mr. Mandeville's son by her, would not his fate have been the same! for where, even in that case, would he have found a father?

'Be comforted, my good friend,' said he, taking hold of my hand, and forcing a smile as he saw my bitter distress; 'I am not going away, you know, for ever: and as to the place – one should not mind that at my age; one may be honest, even among rogues and thieves. I have a proud heart: my pride made me do a bad action: I will teach it to make me do good ones. No doubt there will be people among those I am going to, that will know how to distinguish between a single transgression and hardened sin: and when I have gained their good word, which I will be sure to do, and have served out the appointed time, who knows but I may be taken notice of, and return a great rich man, to you and my mother! – Yet then, perhaps,' – here his voice suddenly faltered, and his heart seemed to beat so quick that I thought it would have bounded from his bosom, – 'perhaps, after all this sad disgrace, *you* will be ashamed to acknowledge me, – and my mother, – oh, she will, I am sure, be gone to that world where neither the shame nor the sorrow of her poor son will ever reach her.'

This, sir, was the only time, for some days past, that he had ventured to speak of his mother. And I saw that all his courage and pride was quite overcome when he mentioned her name; so we wept for a long time together: – and at his desire, I solemnly blessed him for her, and did all I could to persuade him that she would outlive this sad grievance; though, God knows, I had no faith in my own words: he *had*, however: and when his grief had taken its course, he began to recollect himself, and to resume his natural character. Though in years little more than a child, he had the spirit of a man in him; and his mind seemed so full of youth, and hope, and life, that in spite of his sad situation it boiled over: and he talked to me with so much eagerness of the future; and of all the plans he had laid, and all the resolutions he had formed! – Poor lad! he little thought that there was no future for him.

In short, sir, we parted: I, blind with tears, and half dead with fatigue. From that time I staid constantly in my own little parlour, as though *I* had been a convict in a cell: for I could not endure to see any of Mr. Mandeville's servants, nor himself. My whole prayer was to get rid of them all: and so I remained the most solitary creature alive: for there was no Bob now to come smiling and rattling in, to amuse my long evenings. I reflected, and conjectured, and considered, as much as though I had had the power to bring him back: and it seemed as if I still felt some hope while he had not quitted England: but whether he had done so or not, it was impossible for me to ascertain: I waited, therefore, most anxiously for Mary's return, who, having more sense than myself, I thought might afford us some counsel or information.

I was sitting very sorrowfully alone one evening with the newspaper in my hand, waiting for the tea-kettle to boil, and examining, as I constantly did, whether I could find any tidings about the vessel that was to carry away poor Bob, when suddenly a voice that was more like the shriek of a ghost than any human tongue, called me by my name. I looked up, and standing in the doorway beheld Mary. It was horrible to see her. She was not merely white, but livid. Her figure, which was slight, and generally somewhat drooping, was unnaturally stiff and erect. Her eyes were wider open than usual, and seemed quite glassy: in a word, she looked exactly like an untended corpse placed upright.

'Lord have mercy on us, Mary!' said I, starting and dropping my spectacles, 'when did you arrive?'

'Where is Mr. Mandeville?' said she, in the same hurried and frightful tone as before, without taking her eyes off me, or the smallest notice of my question.

'Why, what signifies where he is?' replied I, much alarmed, though I did not exactly know at what.

'Where is Mr. Mandeville?' again repeated she with great violence, and with a gesture as though she would have seized hold of me.

'I do not know – I cannot tell,' cried I, holding back in prodigious perturbation. – 'William, where is your master?' I added, to a servant who was passing the door.

'In the drawing-room, madam, playing with the Major.'

'Tell him, Mary Lawson must see him this moment,' said she, addressing herself to the man in the same extraordinary tone. What he thought of her, I know not; but he semed startled: so without farther delay he ran up stairs, and opened the drawing-room door. Sure enough we heard the rattle of the dice, and the two gentlemen laughing: Mr. Mandeville in particular; for he had a loud and noisy laugh that one could not mistake: it was his last, however, for many a long day! – I suppose the man delivered his message exactly, for the laughter ceased as it were all at once.

'*Mary Lawson!*' exclaimed Mr. Mandeville with great vehemence, 'and where the devil does she come from?'

He had no time to say a word more: for Mary, who had run like a wild thing up stairs, in spite of all my efforts to prevent her, heard his voice, and burst into the room.

'Your child – your own child, Mr. Mandeville, save your child!' was all she could say.

He shook her off roughly, for she had snatched hold of the sleeve of his coat: but he changed colour, and looked very earnestly in her face.

'I call God to witness,' said she, in a faltering, but very distinct voice, 'that Robert Innis is your own lawful son. He is *Robert Mandeville.*' A pistol bullet could not have taken a more sudden effect than these few words; it was a frightful sight, sir, to see this great strong man drop dead like a stone at her feet: it was because he was so strong that the surprise thus acted upon him.

A surgeon was sent for, and Mr. Mandeville was immediately bled; his friend the Major staying by. They were then shut up in the room together for some little time; after which, down comes the Major into my parlour, with a face full of importance and care.

'Mrs. Dixon,' says he, 'where is the woman that spoke to Mr. Mandeville just now? I must find out the meaning of her address to him.'

'Truly, sir,' replied I, 'I believe you must find her senses first; for seems to be quite bereft of them.'

I wish she may,' returned he. I did not altogether understand him at the time, though I did upon reflection. Mary, in the meanwhile, was lying on the bed in the back room. She had been in strong fits, and being at last quite exhausted and half insensible, (she had travelled, sir, without stopping, two nights and two days,) I had placed her there, hoping she might sleep; but she heard a man's voice, and was in the room in a moment. Her appearance, however, was quite altered from what it had been half an hour before; and she was so feeble as to be obliged to support herself by whatever was nearest. The major looked at her most intently. Mary had a sweet face when she was a young woman, sir; it was a sweet face even at that crisis: for I know not how, but she always looked prettiest when she was very, very pale. Her deep-set dark eyes and long black lashes then gave her an air as if something from another world were looking out upon us: you never saw such lashes as she had.

The Major, I say, surveyed her very earnestly; and although his countenance had been extremely stern when she entered, it relaxed a little. He had no need to question her, poor soul! as to what she had before affirmed; for out came the whole of her melancholy tale at once, without farther preamble or delay. He seemed much disturbed at it.

'Woman,' said he, resentfully, when she had finished, 'you have ruined Mr. Mandeville!' – Mary looked up at him, but not a word did she utter.

You have robbed him of what was as dear to him as his life!' – Mary looked again; to my thinking they were speaking looks, but not a syllable did she say. I thought the Major seemed embarrassed by them, however.

'This cursed connection,' continued he, turning half to me, only, I really believe, to avoid looking at her again, 'will cost him both his credit and his happiness.'

'It cost me both,' said Mary.

'Circumstances were very different,' replied he, angrily.

'Very! – for *I* had nothing else to lose!'

I am sure he was moved, for he was a good-natured man, sir; but he did not care to show it. – 'The boy – the poor unfortunate boy,' said he to himself. 'What has become of him!' – This was touching the tender string with Mary; and off she went again, into something between madness and hysterics: so that finding he had obtained all the information that he could, he charged me to keep the girl close from observation, and returned to his wicked companion.

And now, sir, if a ship freighted with gold could have redeemed the poor lad, his father would have thought it too little. Letter after letter was despatched to all the great lords in town, and to all commissioners, at every port where it was supposed to be barely possible the vessel might touch. As to his Majesty's free pardon, that was the very first thing secured. Then there was such hoping, and such expecting, that *here* he might be stopped – and *there* he might be stopped! and such precautions taken to supply him with money, and necessaries, and protection of every kind, that he might appear like a gentleman when he should be landed! – Poor fellow, little did he think how many great folks, such as once would not have deigned to look upon him, were not daily employed in his service. But, alas! time passed away, and wherever the ship put in, it was at no place where any tidings of comfort reached him: he was on his dreary voyage, while Mr. Mandeville, racked between hope and fear, was counting the days and the hours. To increase his chagrin, the business could not be kept so quiet but that all his own friends, and great numbers besides, talked of it openly; and various falsehoods were circulated, of the early wickedness and bad disposition of the boy; so that it seemed as if that cruel speech of Mr. Mandeville's, which drove Mary to desperation, 'Where will you find a character?' was now to be verified in the person of his more innocent, and no less friendless child.

All hope of rescuing poor Bob, till he should arrive at the place of his destination, seemed at length over: but orders were forwarded to expedite him from thence by the very first possible opportunity; and during his stay he was to be treated as the Governor's own son, and I know not what fine things were to be done for him. But, in the interim, that better Father, in whom he trusted, called him to his last home: for, what with mortification, and grief, and hard treatment, as we suppose, the poor lad died just in crossing the line;

and the end of all this mighty bustle and preparation was to hear that, after tedious sickness, he was committed to a watery grave. Mr. Mandeville continued to flatter himself that there was some error in this intelligence, till proofs were received, so authentic, as left him no possibility of doubting.

From the very hour that Mary was convinced that the ship had left the Channel, her head had never been right. It would have broken any body's heart, sir, to hear her talk continually of her boy, and of going to Newcastle to find him; for in her rambling fits she confounded her own first unhappy voyage and his last together, and nothing could persuade her that he was not there. Possessed with this wild project, she escaped from those who had the care of her, to undertake the journey on foot. No Robert, as we well knew, could she find; but, to the great surprise of the household, who were now all strangers to her, she re-trod, in this fruitless search, a hundred, and a hundred times, the walks, the gardens, and the fields where she had carried him, when a baby, in her arms. At last, knowing every avenue to the house, she stole by some means into the nursery: where, after remaining, as it is supposed, nearly two days alone, she was found watching an empty cradle, and dismissed by the servants. My story would have no end were I to recount all the hardships she must have sustained in her fatiguing and perilous journeys. To be short, after wandering. Heaven knows whither, she returned to me, so emaciated and altered that I hardly knew her. I comforted her to the best of my power; when, by some good luck, she suddenly took up the idea that one of those great Lords of the Admiralty, who had been applied to for the boy's release, had secreted him from her, and intended to keep him under his own protection. Since that time she has been perfectly harmless and quiet; talking only to herself or to me, and in terms so obscure, that only those who know her story can understand her.

As to Mr. Mandeville, he lives on in a miserable way; infirm of body, and very sick, I believe, in mind. The tide of public opinion had changed before he left Weymouth; and I am told that, great and rich as he is, he too, in advanced life, knows what it is to want a character – for respectability at least. Common report has now laid all the blame on him. He has been at one time accused of wilfully persecuting his own child; at another the groom was said to be his, and the stranger boy to be the victim. Among so many tales, few people have known which to credit, but all of them tended to the disadvantage of Mr. Mandeville. He has been wounded by cold looks and private whispers; nor, while suffering under the double penalty inflicted by a reproaching world and a reproaching conscience, has he even the same poor consolation which Mary finds, when she fancies, in her rambling fits, that Bob is a great man, and lives in a palace. Alas! poor Mary!

THE FRIEND'S TALE

STANHOPE

> Through these soft shades delighted let me stray,
> While o'er my head forgotten suns descend;
> Through these dear valleys bend my casual way,
> Till setting life a total shade extend.
>
> *Shenstone*

'This day Colonel R—, his lady and friends, left my house, and set off at nine o'clock in the morning for London.'

Thus far says good Mrs. Dixon's memorandum book: but what does the *poetical* register add to this scanty allowance of facts? It tells us, that nearly on the same day of the month in the preceeding year, and Englishman of rank in the service, stopped with his bride, the young and charming Countess de T—, at the warm baths of Leuk. A three months' tour through some of the most romantic spots of Switzerland, after satiating their minds with the bold, the sublime, and the terrible, had at length brought them down to that point, when the human face, even though it may bear but little resemblance to the divine, becomes one of the most interesting of all spectacles. The country, into which they had entered during the full glow of summer, already began to assume a new aspect: rich shades of brown, or crimson, mingling with bright and delicate purples, had taken place of the green; and the soft vicissitude of seasons, imperceptibly extending its influence to the heart, seemed, by a wise ordination, to render society delightful, at the very period when the multiplying wants of man make it necessary.

Never were two beings more calculated to enjoy this social system than the travellers. Recently united by the tenderest of all ties, they viewed the world, as they viewed each other, with a disposition to be pleased; a disposition which the spot they now visited was

The Canterbury Tales

peculiarly calculated to cherish: for it was that on which they first met; and where the casual civilities of acquaintance had ripened into an attachment that decided their fate. Love, however, that tempted them to the union, took care to confine the reward almost wholly to itself: for the chief inheritance of the young Countess, whose father had been a German, was an illustrious name, and a genealogical tree large enough, unhappily, almost to have shaded his whole domains. It might indeed have passed for the sibyl's bough, as far as gilded coronets could make it such; but of that more substantial and common fruit which modern times demand, it was nearly barren. English, however, as Madame de T— was on the mother's side, and brought up at the court of an English princess, her tastes, her affections, her habits, and, finally, her husband, all were English: perhaps too absolutely so. For Lieutenant-Colonel Raymond, hardly in the meridian of life, handsome and agreeable, presumptive heir to a good estate (the actual possessor of which had wintered at Florence on account of a languishing state of health), was diffident enough to meditate a thousand extravagant projects to conquer his passion before he ventured upon the more simple expedient of making it known to the object. Nothing could be more unseasonable than this delicacy, nothing more perversely captivating: in a moment of tender enthusiasm it was nevertheless forgotten; and Madame de T—, after hoping and fearing six whole ages in lover's calendar, six months in the vulgar one, had, at length, the unexpected satisfaction of seeing the man she loved at her feet, and of receiving from him a sweet assurance that he had been so long withheld only by a generous doubt with regard to his pretensions. The young Countess could hardly conceal either her joy, or her surprise, at this avowal. It was so strange, so strange, so extraordinary a prejudice! – Where could be the disparity between them? He was well born – so was she: he was not rich, neither, alas, was she! but he had ten thousand natural advantages, while she – deceitful power of love, how dost thou render the proud humble, and the vain modest! level the various fantastic distinctions of life; and rub off, through the influence of the favoured individual, all the rough edges of character with which we boldly incommode society at large!

The joyful surprise of the Countess had hardly subsided, when a surprise of a very contrary nature seized upon all her friends, or those who called themselves such.

'How! the favourite of her Serene Highness the Princess of * * * *! the heiress to the most illustrious branch of * * *, the lovely and admired

Countess de T—, espouse an indigent Englishman, only because he had fine eyes and a good set of teeth!'

'Ah, his teeth are indeed very fine,' said the Countess, with the most tender and naive tone imaginable; 'but it was not for that reason! – it was his understanding, – his heart!'

'His heart! – My dear Countess, how you talk! Has he rank – has he fortune?'

'He has rank in the army: he has an estate in reversion.'

'That indeed qualifies the mischief, – but if he should chance to die before it falls to him – '

'If he dies,' murmured the fair pleader, with a voice subdued by sensibility, 'of what consequence will it be how I live?'

By arguments thus incontrovertible, our young orphan, for such she was, at length silenced all opposition; and while she hung delighted upon the arm of her husband, as they bent together over the brow of a romantic precipice, or guided him, in her turn, to some simple picture of domestic felicity in those rustic cots which embellish solitude, her defection was lamented by her rouged and titled friends, at the court of * * * *, as pathetically as if the world had been coming to an end.

But although woods, mountains, and glaciers, are fine things, yet society, that labyrinth into which the adventurous delight to plunge in search of pleasure, and from which the timid shrink only through the fear of encountering pain, is still the point that every human heart more or less inclines to seek. The love of this, and the same delicate state of health that before brought Madame de T— to Leuk, now induced her to try the salutary influence of its springs, previous to her visiting England. Yet the spot, though embellished with the smiles of love, was not a scene of gaiety. The beginning and concluding seasons of a watering-place often present to the view only those whom necessity confines there; a group of melancholy invalids, anxious still to bask in that sunshine which they appear never again likely to behold.

Madame de T— became but too sensible of sufferings which she daily witnessed. She had at first chosen a situation as near the springs as she conveniently could: but the attentive fondness of the Colonel quickly removed her from thence, to one of those beautiful though rustic habitations peculiar to Switzerland, where the household, presenting a minature of the patriarchal days, becomes no longer an establishment, but a family: in this sweet retreat she devoted herself to her music, her books, and above all, to her husband.

'Yet, my friend,' said she to the latter, 'let us not be wholly selfish! Sorrow and sickness are around. Shall we fly from them because we are happy? I remember well my first visit here. I accompanied my mother, who was suffering under that malady of which she afterwards died: but I was very young, and as I saw many persons look much more indisposed than herself, I though her complaints half imaginary: and the greater part of her acquaintance declared them to be so. I am ashamed to remember how easily I was induced to rely on this opinion. How reluctantly I broke from my gay companions to mingle with the infirm and the dispirited. "Child," said she to me one day, when I had been somewhat impatiently looking out for favourable weather, which I was inclined to persuade myself would remove all her sufferings, "let us not murmur against what we cannot command: let us make the best use of what we can: healthful days are the gift of God only; but, trust me, that to an invalid there is no sunshine like the smile of cheerfulness; nor any breeze so reviving as the breath of love!" Do you think I did not weep?'

Colonel Raymond entertained the greatest respect in the world for his wife's mother, although he had never had the honour of seeing her: he would have extended the regard to her grandmother had she insisted upon it, but he had no taste for weeping parties.

'We will have a little music this evening,' said he, as he tenderly dried her tears. 'The Syndic will bring his violoncello: he is impatient to hear you sing, before he departs from hence: so are Rivaz and his wife: it was only yesterday that they importuned me to remind you of your promise.'

'They have a visiter at present.'

'Yes: an Englishman. He has been a military man, I think.'

'He has been a very handsome one.' Nothing, perhaps, could be more true than both these remarks: yet it happened that the Colonel was as much out of the secret of the stranger's features, as his wife was of his profession. So certain is it that our habits of thinking decide the measure of our observations: the reason why some people make none, and others, such an abundance of frivolous ones. That the stranger was not in health had, however, been obvious to both: it was therefore agreed, that to amuse him he should be added to the party; but he proved ungrateful, and would not be amused; on the contrary, he charged his host with his thanks and apologies. He was evidently wrong; for the party was delightful. Among those who embellished it, Angelique, the fair daughter of Rivaz, was not the least admired. Just turned of one-and-twenty, tall, graceful, with one of the sweetest voices in the world, breaking into natural trills and graces, it was only when she sang that one discovered she could be beautiful; but who then could be so beautiful?

Madam de T—, no longer encumbered with a stiff coiffure, and all the troublesome formality of a court-dress, was herself very captivating. To the sprightly graces she united that delicate taste, which, by a charm incomprehensible to those who do not possess it, is communicated to every thing it approaches. Within her precincts all was fairy-land: without, the eye commanded a bold and romantic scenery, the features of which insensibly harmonised towards the fore-ground, into an image of tranquillity, that made the little spot which she consecrated seem its centre.

> Each sound too, here to languishment inclin'd,
> Lull'd the charm'd bosom, and induced ease:
> Aerial music in the warbling wind,
> At distance rising oft, by slow degrees
> Nearer and nearer drew: till o'er the trees
> It hung!—

'Is not that your guest, who stands at this moment on the brow of the hill?' said Colonel Raymond, taking the flute from his lips, and pointing towards the spot.

'I think it is: but he is not, properly speaking, our guest, he is our lodger,' returned Monsieur Rivaz, with the frankness of an honourable poverty. 'We are not rich enough to entertain guests.'

'He must be very unsociable,' said the lady of the house, 'since he refused to join our party.'

'Parties are his aversion; and, I believe, he does not love music.'

'Then he has no sensibility.'

'I doubt the conclusion,' rejoined Rivaz, with a shrug. The stranger, who considering that he did not love music, seemed oddly fixed to a spot where the distant strains could just reach him, now appeared to suspect that he was observed, and slowly withdrew; but he withdrew only, as it proved, to show himself again with more propriety; for the Colonel and his lady were yet loitering over a late breakfast the next day, when, in acknowledgment of the invitation of the preceding one, Mr. Stanhope was announced. Mr. Stanhope was a man of about five-and-thirty; tall, and gentlemanly; with eyes that announced more of mind than all Lavater's noses and chins ever promised. His dress was an English blue coat, and he wore his left arm in a sling. In his manner there was a tincture – a very little tincture – of singularity; a sort of proud indifference, that seemed at once to assert its level: in a word, the influence of a decided character, acting upon an habitual politeness. Madame de T— had not forgotten her old good eyes and teeth. Now it happened that Mr. Stanhope's smile, though rarely to be seen, was by far the most pleasing expression of his countenance. He did smile, however, very agreeably, on being rallied by her on his aversion to music.

'The report of Monsieur Rivaz,' replied he, 'is not quite exact: it is only good music that I shun, I have no objection to the mediocre.'

'Surely one objection is rather more unaccountable than the other.'

'Indeed! – I hope you will always think so, madam,' replied Mr. Stanhope.

'Ah, the chords of that heart have, I fear, been strained into discord,' said Madame de T— to herself, as she looked at him; for his smile vanished as he uttered the last sentence.

'What say you, Augusta, to Mr. Stanhope's exception?' cried Colonel Raymond: 'may he venture within our circle?'

'By all means: his exception is exactly what some of us ought to desire. We may, perhaps, convince him that his feelings are in no danger from our harmony.'

'I am a bad visitor,' returned Mr. Stanhope, whose countenance had insensibly resumed its serious cast. 'My tastes, my habits, have long been unsocial; – and my stay here will be so uncertain! – In the interim I visit the springs every day for the benefit of my health; see I know not how many strange faces, and speak to I know not how many strange people: if you knew what a solitary mountaineer I am, when at home, you would calculate the trouble it costs me to prepare both my mind and my person for such an exhibition. I cannot resolve to mingle in general society; and how shall a stranger dare venture to propose intruding on your domestic retirement? I shall not, however, acquire a character for diffidence,' he added, after a pause, and half smiling, 'when I add, that it was nevertheless with this hope that I presumed thus to present myself to you.'

'Choose your own mode of visiting,' replied Madame de T—: 'our plan is, indeed, retirement, but not seclusion; and those who can embellish it will always be welcome.' So gracious a reception seemed to encourage and attract their new acquaintance. His visit was of some length, and he took his leave with reluctance.

There was that in Mr. Stanhope's conversation and manners which greatly pleased the Colonel: there was that in his countenance which as greatly pleased the lady; and, while listening to a discourse between him and her husband, is which she had taken little share, she had revolved in her imagination every probable circumstance that could give to such a countenance an air of spleen and depression, that did not seem natural to it. In the midst of these contemplations she cast her eyes – it may be by chance, or by the habit of her sex, upon his coat: it was a well-cut coat, – but it seemed to have done hard duty, – in truth, it was somewhat shabby. One secret at least was discovered, therefore – Mr. Stanhope was poor. She now surveyed him again, and thought him rather more prepossessing than before. Whatever in his address had struck her to be pride, rose into dignity: negligence was graceful self-estimation: in short, having looked away all of her heart which she had to bestow, she was not dilatory in communicating its impulse to her husband. They walked the next day to the spring, and while discussing the subject, encountered him who had given rise to it: but he was in one of his unsocial moods, for he only bowed and passed on: yet, as at a certain distance he turned his head, Madame de T— noticed something anxious, and even singular, in the earnest look which he directed after them; a curiosity almost amounting to interest at once took possession both of husband and wife, nor was it very soon either gratified or subdued; for Mr. Stanhope, though he neglected not to avail himself of their invitation, remained perfectly silent on all that respected him individually; leaving it to his general conversation and habits to create internal conviction that he was at least well-educated, and, most probably, well born.

'Our new acquaintance, Stanhope, has, I suspect, been in the army,' said the Colonel to Rivaz, protracting a morning visit, in order to sound him on the subject of his guest. 'You, probably, have known him long, and can tell me something of his profession and connections.' Rivaz knew nothing of either: he was a quiet downright Swiss, who, having served his country in a civil capacity, and lost an only son in the military one, had for many years retired from public affairs, and devoted himself wholly to agriculture; nor had he the smallest curiosity as to the business or concerns of any one with whom he associated.

'Of Mr. Stanhope's English connections,' said he, 'I know nothing. He resides at present in that part of Switzerland which borders the

Valais; where the hills of St. Gothard, intersected by another chain, form a wild and savage country, inhabited by some of our poorest mountaineers. There are, I have been told, spots of singular beauty to be found there, by those who have personal strength and agility to explore them. Mr. Stanhope seems hardly to rank among that number; but he has an undaunted spirit and perseverance in everything he undertakes. He is known to some of the most respectable persons in Berne; and when he first visited this spot, which was about two years ago, his interesting manners, and a resemblance which my wife fancied she saw in him to her son, induced me, on the authority of one of those persons, to admit him as an inmate. He was then suffering very severely from a bullet lodged in his arm, the consequence, I fear, of a duel; and which, as no operation has yet been able wholly to relieve him from, occasionally enfeebles it. But I have never repented my hospitality. He is intelligent, brave, and humane. He was a brother to my poor boy, when he returned wounded from the army; and on his death Mr. Stanhope forgot all his austerity and reserve in order to console us.'

'Austerity and reserve! Are those, then, features of his character?'

'To me they appear the marking ones.'

'I should not have judged so.'

'Then you have seen him in a very favourable point of view. In truth, I rather think you have. For what purpose he has relaxed from his usual habits I know not; but I was certainly surprised to find that he had the other day volunteered a visit to you: it is a circumstance that I have never known occur in the case of any person besides; for he uniformly and decidedly shuns society.'

'Why, then, does he come here at this season?'

'I know not; something unusual disturbs him. I remember he said that he wished to find a friend.'

'And he has sought only me,' said the Colonel, musing. 'There is, indeed, no other Englishman here. But his reliance ought not to be thrown away.'

'I hope that it will not.'

'I am sure that it shall not, provided I have the power to be useful to him.'

'Dear Colonel!' said Rivaz, whose eyes and countenance brightened as he spoke, 'you are then the friend he wished to find. I suspected as much. It is so rare a thing for Mr. Stanhope to be interested in any person, that when he broke silence the other evening to speak with such high panegyric of you and your charming countess, I own it appeared to me somewhat extraordinary; but why, then, does he profess never hitherto to have known you?'

'For the best of all reasons, my good sir, – because he never hitherto did. You have misconceived me. Mr. Stanhope's acquaintance and mine is of very late date. I must cement it by serving him.'

'Ah, Colonel! you come from a happy country, where every body is rich enough to be able to oblige.'

'I am unfortunately, an exception to the general rule, then,' returned the Colonel, laughing; 'as far, as least, as wealth is concerned. But I have influence and credit: let Mr. Stanhope, therefore, convince me, by his frankness, that he deserves I should employ them, and I may really turn out to be such a friend as he came in search of.'

'Let *me* speak to his desert,' replied Rivaz, with unusual enthusiasm. 'I will pledge my life that there is not a better man existing. My wife quite adores him for his goodness to our family; she often says, that if he were not so much of a philosopher, he would be an angel.' The philosopher entered the room at that moment; but his appearance had somewhat more of the angel in it than a mortal wellwisher would have desired to see. A faint and hectic glow upon his cheek, languid eyes, and an exhausted air, were all symptoms of suffering. The Colonel eyed his features steadfastly, – by stealth, too, he eyed his coat. Madame de T— was right: symptoms of suffering *there* also. 'He has, perhaps, been soliciting a favour,' thought Raymond; 'has been refused, disappointed, treated possibly with insolence by some proud German: a man of talents, and an Englishman too. I cannot suffer the occasion to pass.'

The testimony borne by Rivaz to the merit of Mr. Stanhope had not been precisely of the nature desired by the Colonel, as it had no reference to the past life or conduct of the former. But it was warm, – it was unequivocal; calculated to enlist every generous feeling in the service of the person whom he praised; it *had* done so. Colonel Raymond found himself disposed, indeed, to an unusual degree of active liberality; for it happened to be one of those bright days in his life when his power to be generous seemed to extend with his will, the mail of the morning having brought him letters from England that announced a considerable addition to his fortune. Buoyed up, therefore, by that happiest of all sensations, – the hope of making happy, – he drew Stanhope into the garden; and, forgetting in his zeal that he had presupposed almost every circumstance that could excite it, made him, after very little preface, an indirect and delicate offer either of his services or his purse.

Nothing could equal the surprise of his companion at this unlooked-for overture, except, as it appeared, his pleasure. The latter, indeed, soon announced itself, by the change in his countenance, to be so genuine and unalloyed as quickly to take place of every other feeling.

'I could almost wish,' replied he, 'to be indeed in the circumstances your offer supposes, that you might, by the exercise of your philanthropy, feel a glow like that you have excited. Sensations so pleasurable are not familiar guests here.' – and he laid his hand on his heart; 'nor can I, at this moment, tell you their source. In truth, however, dear Colonel, I have no suffering but of mind. The appearance that has awakened your concern for my health is now, I believe, merely caused by the fatigue of those long rambles I am apt to indulge in, and which, perhaps, accord better with my inclinations than with my strength. So much for one point. With regard to the other, – on what circumstance you can possibly have founded your suspicion of my poverty, I own I am curious to know.'

'The inquiry will not lead us far,' said the Colonel, laying his hand, with a most speaking glance, on the sleeve of his companion's coat. Mr. Stanhope's gravity was not proof against this acknowledgment.

'Alas, poor Yorick!' said he, laughing, 'is it even so? I knew that I was negligent; but I must confess that I did not suspect I had so far forgotten the habits of a gentleman as to be remarkable. I find myself, nevertheless, more indebted to a shabby coat than I ever was to a good one. So, having tried your kindness, I will endeavour, for the future, not to disgrace it.' The Colonel now felt a little embarrassed, and attempted to apologise.

'I see that you are singular in more instances than one,' said Stanhope: 'you thought better of me when you believed me to be indigent, than since you have been undeceived. The world at large decides very differently upon these points. Allow me so far to profit by my knowledge of your character as to wave, for the future, all the ceremonies of new acquaintance. You took the nearest road to my heart, when you permitted your own to expand. It is an obligation which I shall never forget; and when I am able to conquer a reserve now imposed upon me by circumstances, I will acknowledge it more fully.'

The Colonel was too generous to press, exactly at that juncture, into a confidence which he doubted not would soon be freely offered.

Intimacy was therefore at once established between them, and every day rendered it equally amusing to both parties; yet two men could hardly be found who, while in essential points they resembled, differed so widely in the minuter ones of opinion. Stanhope's character of mind, like that of his countenance in its habitual expression, was reserved and severe; but the sunshine of either was irresistibly prepossessing. Colonel Raymond – seen, indeed, in happier circumstances than his friend – was more consistent, generous, and rational. His temper was open, and liberal even to the extreme; and his frank and inartificial manners were at once the result of his feelings, and of the habits of his profession. The Colonel's connections were of the higher class; but, in his progress through life, he had had occasion to look below as well as above him; and, either from prejudice or judgment, was decidedly of opinion that the best qualities of the heart are more likely to be vitiated by ignorance than by refinement: in other words, that a certain degree of intellectual improvement is necessary to both sexes, in order to render the virtues permanent, and a certain degree of polish to render them valued.

This doctrine of intellectual improvement and external polish was a terrible heresy, according to the opinions of Mr. Stanhope. In *his* view of life, nothing was admirable that was not the fruit of unsophisticated nature. What unsophisticated nature might be, was a question that necessarily obtruded itself, and which they found it impossible to settle. They reasoned, they quoted, they wrangled; they brought authorities on both sides. To listen to the two disputants, one should alternately have believed that men, in their natural state, were to creep upon the earth like brutes, or to exalt themselves to the rank of demigods. They canvassed the point in all manner of ways. They were sometimes pleasant, sometimes serious; and sometimes, as is too often the case with disputants upon every subject, secretly more irritable than either chose to avow. Nor did they fail still to go hand in hand with other disputants in bringing home one conviction at least to the minds of by-standers, that the most common effect of argument is to confirm each party more strongly than before in his own opinion. All this time, however, confidence did not increase. They liked each other better every day, and understood each other less. Colonel Raymond was found undeniably guilty, according to the persuasion of his new friend, of tolerating frivolity and vice in a degree that could hardly be pardoned. Mr. Stanhope, on the contrary, surveyed every thing allied to cultivation or elegance with a suspicious eye. Polished society presented to his imagination nothing but men who deceive or are deceived, whose hatred or love is equally selfish, and who have wandered so very wide from the natural standard of morals and feeling as not even to know how to value that which is most valuable in each other. Of women he thought still worse. The sex is indeed one of those unlucky topics that generally distances a man's head or his heart; for where is the phoenix that calls both into the council when he speaks of it? Mr. Stanhope, at least, was not such; and his philippic would probably have run to some length, had he not been interrupted.

'By your leave, we will stop at one half of the creation for the present,' said the Colonel; 'and having, under the name of argument, nearly exhausted invective, suppose, my good friend, we turn to facts. Your experience, it should seem, has shown you the worst side of the world. I will reverse the picture; yet go no further for the example than my own situation. I have told you that it is not very affluent, and that my hopes of the future are involved in uncertainty. I marry a charming woman, who could have no other motive—'

'Pause there, if you please,' interrupted Stanhope, in his turn. 'I admit no panegyrics as facts, from a man who has been married only four months.'

'Neither Turk nor Tartar was ever more iron-hearted, I see, to the sex,' said Raymond, laughing; 'to spare your feelings, however, on the subject, give me leave to observe, that my panegyric there was merely thrown in *en passant*. In the argument of disinterested regard, I give you permission, if you demand it, to except both matrimony and love. Mine will still be drawn from my experience; as, to say truth, I suspect your more splenetic ones may be traced to the same source. I have the prospect of a fine estate in reversion: the person who holds it is a valetudinarian, and not indeed a marrying man; but on the subject most men are fickle. I have no present claims on his fortune, never obliged, never served him; and should he, by any caprice, marry and have an heir, he cuts me off at once, both now, and, if he so pleases, eventually. Yet this very man, on hearing that the connection I had entered into afforded a very inadequate provision, has, without solicitation, made over to me a considerable property. I received legal information of this business on the very day when I made certain unnecessary offers to you; and I will not deny that the occurrence influenced both my feelings and my conduct. What answer have you for this?'

'That *I*, at least, was very much obliged to him.'

'And am not I also?'

'Of that I cannot speak, unless I knew *his* motives of action: yours I am able to decide upon.'

'What other than a liberal and disinterested spirit could possibly actuate him?'

'As if one could judge of a man's motives whose character is wholly unknown. Ostentation, caprice, a thousand peculiarities occasion such strokes as this. Perhaps he wanted to purchase a friend.' Colonel Raymond looked offended. 'Pardon me,' said Stanhope, extending his hand towards him, 'it does not necessarily follow that friends are to be purchased, because weak men go to the market in search of them.'

The Colonel did not refuse his hand, but he was secretly displeased. The more easily so, as he had spoken unreservedly of his own concerns, in order to encourage a confidence that yet did not promise to be mutual. He communicated his feelings to his wife; but the character of Madame de T— was formed of still more indulgent materials than that of her husband.

'We must have patience,' said she, gaily. 'Mr. Stanhope, it is evident, is a disappointed man. He appears therefore severe, acrimonious, unbending. These are the marking features of his understanding, and it is by that you have judged him. My calculations of his character are drawn from his heart; *which* most contributes to decide the fate of the individual I leave the sages of the world to determine. For my own part, my opinion is fixed. Our new acquaintance, like an animal shut up in an exhausted receiver, has panted and gasped almost to death: but do not despair, for he is not quite gone! let us supply him an atmosphere, and the creature will live. I think, too, I know the atmosphere that will revive him. Nature is in her beauty: – we will try her influence to-morrow.'

It was the season of harvest. Angelique, adorned with garlands of wild flowers, thrown over her by the rustics, and crowned like a youthful Ceres, presided at the rural festival that closed it. She mingled with the dancers, while the elder peasants of the neighbourhood, and those more immediately employed by Rivaz, assembled in crowds round the kind-hearted old man, and his respectable wife. A thousand demonstrations of regard were interchanged in the circle, and the air was filled with the soft murmur of happy and social life. Stanhope was deeply sensible of its influence.

'Ah, this is indeed genuine cordiality and attachment!' exclaimed he, as with Madame de T— and her husband he stood a distant spectator of the joyous scene. 'I too may flatter myself that I have many such friends at home!' The Colonel could not help smiling: for while this burst of general philanthropy escaped from his lips, his looks were fixed solely upon the lovely girl who presided at the festival; and that with an expression that could not be misunderstood.

'Do you then keep a harem?' said he, very gravely. 'Nay, never start, my dear Stanhope! your eyes could not be better directed than towards Angelique.'

'Angelique did not engross my thoughts.'

'I spoke only of your eyes: but pray of which sex are the friends capable of extorting that title from such a stoic as yourself?'

'Come with me, and judge whether or no they deserve it. I must return home within a very few days: an indispensable duty calls me thither. *Duty*, did I say?' – and he paused, – 'Let me term it inclination: be my companion, and I shall quickly convince you that I am no stoic.'

'I am perfectly convinced of that, without stirring a single step from hence, my good friend: but let us strike a balance of pleasure; you are obliged to return home; the journey, from your account of it, promises me a view of some parts of the country too wild and dangerous to be explored with a female companion. I will be your fellow-traveller, if you will engage that your stay shall not exceed a limited time: I may afterwards call upon you to be mine.'

The arrangement was made in a very few days. Colonel Raymond had not seen the glaciers, and, as his residence at Leuk was now drawing to a close, he was willing to complete his view of Switzerland. It was his intention to pass from thence to Florence, in order to visit the relation and benefactor to whose liberality of spirit he stood so much indebted: after which his professional duties recalled him to England. To England, Mr. Stanhope also declared his intention of going: but whether the intimacy now subsisting between them was to be prolonged beyond the usual date of accidental acquaintance, it remained with circumstances to decide; or rather, it remained with Mr. Stanhope himself; who could not reasonably expect its duration, if he continued to preserve that mysterious silence which left his past conduct and character in total obscurity. In proportion, however, as the day fixed for his departure approached, he grew more thoughtful. It seemed as if the charms of that home of which he boasted were hourly less attractive. He courted the regard of Madame de T— with an assiduity which he had never before shown, and for which she could not account. How indeed was it possible she could calculate the aim he proposed to himself in thus deviating from the habits of his character! he did *not* court Angelique; but there was an eloquence in his silence, even in his reserve, where she was concerned, no less moving or convincing than words would have been.

'We shall civilise him, I perceive,' said Madame de T—, 'but it will be a work of time. In the interim, he is throwing his own happiness to a distance, and wounding a tender bosom. Angelique, I am persuaded, is afflicted at his approaching departure. She sheds tears in private. If I believed him capable of reading her heart, and of trifling with it, I should hate him.'

'Of such a trespass he may safely be acquitted. A heart like Angelique's is of all others that which he is least likely to understand. Extravagant passions, and corrupt tastes, if not principles, for, to him, the picture of the human race. He is yet to learn the softer shades of the mind; and to see how duties, affections, and decorum, blend together in the habits of what he calls sophisticated life; and though they take something from the force of the character, bestow at least an equivalent in preserving its equilibrium. Angelique will never display the best qualities of hers, much less its tenderness, unless both are called forth by unlooked-for scenes. Her manners are tranquil and unpretending, and her character is only to be found in her heart. I am not convinced that he will have judgment enough to seek it there. But the ancients raised altars to good fortune, and your charming friend must, I fear, do the same thing, if *she* hopes to make him a proselyte to the sincerity of love, or we to that of friendship: but let us first be convinced that he is worth the trouble of converting.'

On this subject the Colonel began secretly to entertain doubts. The continued reserve of his new friend surprised and offended him. He had himself gone great lengths to invite confidence, and to see it thus obstinately withheld induced suspicions with regard to the life and connections of Mr. Stanhope, which it was absolutely necessary should be removed, before intimacy could be carried further between them. It had begun in favourable circumstances; it had been assiduously cultivated by a man who evidently shunned society at large: from what motives he sought it in this particular instance remained therefore to be discovered. Not mercenary ones, it was plain: yet on this single testimony rested all that the Colonel could ascertain to be truly estimable in his character. It was no little argument in favour of its agreeableness, that, under such disadvantages, he should have conciliated a portion or regard from every individual of the circle in which he lived. But there was a grace in the negligence of his manner, a charm even in the faults of his understanding, which it was impossible wholly to define or resist: somewhat that awakened all the higher tones of mind in those around, and gave an interest to common events and topics that is very rarely created by them. Colonel Raymond, however, was not to learn that advantages of this kind are often found to be, of all others, most deceitful; – and he would have been inexcusable to himself; had he carried to any unusual length his interest for a man whose habits of thinking were so likely to have tainted his heart. In the persuasion of obtaining every necessary information that should justify intimacy, the Colonel had not long before mentioned the plan of his intended journey to Florence; as well as the particulars of his subsequent route to England; and indirectly placed it within Mr. Stanhope's choice to accompany him to both, or either place.

'And wherefore,' said the latter, who did not by any means approve of the delay, 'should your journey to England be thus retarded? will not the friend you are going to see at Florence be more surely your friend when at a distance from you? and why should you place yourself in the power of a benefactor? benefactors are dangerous people. Are you certain that he will not in some way shackle you my means of the obligations which you conceive him to have conferred? Be assured that this is a work of supererogation of your part which will answer no good purpose. Men are best situated when they know not each other intimately.'

'That is, when they can deceive, without giving us a right to reproach them: for such is the common privilege of superficial acquaintance. A qualifying doctrine for cold hearts! – was yours of that number when your countenance kindled at a mere intentional kindness on my part?'

'I was taken by surprise,' replied Stanhope, with embarrassment.

'It is necessary then to surprise you into your best feelings: but let us have done reasoning each other out of them. I can sympathise with disappointment, my dear Stanhope; it is a blight: but beware of a canker! eternal distrust is neither manly nor honourable.' Other company intervened, and the conversation concluded. Subsequent recollection was not calculated, however, to produce reliance on him who supported it; and it was under a mingled impression of doubt and curiosity that the Colonel had consented to the expedition, which the two gentlemen were on the point of undertaking together: but

Stanhope had spoken of *claims* that called him home. A word often contains a volume: and a single monosyllable, dropped by accident had informed Colonel Raymond that a female was concerned in those claims. He did not communicate his surmises to his wife: it was enough that he would soon have the opportunity of ascertaining their truth; and on the particulars which this opportunity should elicit rested all his future determinations with respect to Mr. Stanhope.

Chance sometimes produces more than is effected by our deepest laid plans. The Colonel had occasion to go to Sion. He resolved on this late in the evening, set out at daybreak, and was not many hours absent; yet, by a singular concurrence of circumstances, he became apprised in that short space of time of all that related to Stanhope: – his disappointments, his connections, his probable views: every thing, in short, that was necessary to be known in order to decide his own conduct respecting him; nor had he the smallest scruple left in becoming for the future his most intimate associate and friend. Plans still more liberal and enlarged passed through his imagination, but they yet rested there. The secret of the female companion was the only one he now had to learn, and till that could be explained he judged it most prudent to confine to his own bosom the knowledge which he had so lately acquired. He was therefore impatient to depart; and although it was evident that his friend, whatever the claims that called him away, was still disposed to loiter, they set out within four days from that period.

It was the first time that Madame de T— had parted with her husband from the hour he became such; and, in truth, she secretly prayed that it might be the last.

'This, my dear Angelique, is a terrible experiment,' said she, in a half whisper, 'but it must be gone through with. The hearts of men differ strangely from ours! I could live in his eyes; but his I perceive must wander over other objects if I would have them always meet mine with delight.'

'Yet you resolved unreluctantly.'

'Oh, no – not unreluctantly! – a tender woman must suffer when she misses the society of her husband – but a wise one, methinks, would desire that he should sometimes miss hers. – Go then' she added, turning to the Colonel and gaily raising her voice, 'go and reconnoiter the manner in which our philosopher lives, not wholly unlike that of Robinson Crusoe, if I may judge by his hints. Gun – fur cap and all! – follow him, then, honest Friday! I think your brother savages in that part of the world will not eat *you*, and we have only to hope that a hard frost will not lock you up, and oblige you to eat them.'

The evening of the first day lodged the travellers at the small village of M—, within the canton of Berne: where they were received by a respectable ecclesiastic with characteristic hospitality. He was a man of a dignified and interesting appearance, intelligent and well educated: who, after spending several years as tutor in a family whose château extended its domains as far as to his own small habitation, had retired to the latter in order to finish his career. The second day's journey presented a wilder scene. At a certain station they met peasants previously appointed by Mr. Stanhope, who brought several necessary articles of provision, besides garments lined with warm furs; together with crampons and poles for passing over the smooth ice, or leaping the chasms.

'If you are an adventurous traveller,' said Stanhope, 'these will be useful. We will, in that case, dismiss our horses and trust only to ourselves. If otherwise, I can lead you by a road, less wild indeed, yet rich in natural beauties; where from different points you may safely see much of what the other would present you.' It is needless to say which path the Colonel preferred; but it may be charitable to suppose that he did not repent it, even when he saw his companion tottering on the brink of a precipice, or, by personal agility, passing clefts, where the smallest failure would have been certain destruction. While the river (the devious course of which they frequently pursued) sometimes rushed in cataracts that half stunned them; and sweeping away every thing that approached to vegetation, presented a wild chaos of rock and water. At others, overshadowed by forests of pine, it was visible only from the foam that dashed through their dark branches. Alps piled on alps apparently bounded their course as they proceeded; till, silently reposing in the bosom of solitude and winter, immense glaciers seemed to form the central station of both.

The shadows of the third day were lengthening, when, in consequence of a new direction which they had taken, the country insensibly became less savage. Cottages were occasionally sprinkled in the hollows of the mountains; and the faint tinkle of bells from the cattle announced civilization. Mr. Stanhope quickened his pace as he approached a spot, where, at the opening of a valley, he cast his eyes eagerly forward. Those of Colonel Raymond followed them, and rested upon a low but spacious building, which, fenced by its situation from the keener blasts of winter, yet, by its well-defended roof and solid sides, denoted the necessity of providing against them. A whistle from Mr. Stanhope brought out at the same moment a very fine dog, which, springing towards him, announced by the most extravagant caresses the joy that his master's return had created. The Colonel entered his friend's habitation with curiosity and surprise. The light was still strong upon the mountains, but mists were creeping over the valley; and the blaze of a large wood-fire, that spread its social light through a well-furnished apartment, inspired that exquisite sense of comfort which is only known in winter. For winter the feelings of both parties determined it to be, in spite of the calendar. Stanhope quitted his guest for a moment; but presently returning, –

'I am too soon,' said he, 'my household is not yet assembled.' While he was speaking, the low note of a shepherd's pipe was heard from the mountains. – 'They are approaching,' he added; 'come and see my family.'

The Colonel instantly followed to the kitchen, where, at the further end, near the fire, sat a young woman peeling hemp. She wore a scarlet corset laced with blue, the short waist and petticoats of her country, and her hair twisted up with a silver bodkin. On a sort of rug, not far distant, lay two little sturdy mountaineers; one, to appearance, about four, the other, perhaps, five years of age. Whose ruddy cheeks and curling locks were half hid, as, weary with the sports of the day, they lay twined in each other's arms. While across them, not less weary with his joy, the dog stretched his nose with social familiarity.

'Are these *all* yours?' said the Colonel, pointing with a smile to the group.

'Arlette will tell you,' replied Stanhope; – 'Arlette understands a little English.' The Colonel felt reproved; for he had spoken in that tongue on the supposition that she would not comprehend it: but Arlette either did not hear, or did not attend to him; for with eyes earnestly fixed upon her benefactor, as on a superior being, she seemed sensible of nothing but the delight of seeing him again. The strain of music, which in the interim had grown stronger, now suddenly ceased: and into a spacious and low apartment beyond the kitchen, where long tables were spread, and the hearths heaped up with fuel, poured a promiscuous train of peasants to their evening meal. Stanhope suddenly advanced amongst them: when, as if touched with electricity, the whole group burst at once into a hum of joy and congratulation. The children familiarly advanced to kiss his hand and

The Canterbury Tales

stroke his coat. A more respectful sense of pleasure was announced in the countenances of the young men; while still stronger tokens of it flowed down the furrowed and silvery cheeks of the old. Age seldom weeps for sorrow; it is the stranger, joy that calls forth its tears.

'You have indeed friends, and I perceive that you deserve to have them,' said the Colonel, moved by the scene before him. 'Why, dear Stanhope, do you quarrel with a world which owes you so much?' Unwilling to appear an obtrusive observer, he then passed to the inner apartment; where, after considering with deeper interest than he had before felt the character and conduct of his companion, curiosity once more revived on the subject of the female inmate whom he yet was to see. None such had been hitherto visible, except Arlette. Although young, she was not remarkably handsome, and the manners of Stanhope towards her produced internal conviction that she was no way particularly interesting to him. Her husband, a sun-burnt, but well-looking peasant, had also formed one of the group: Arlette could not, therefore, be the mysterious fair one that had attached a man of Mr. Stanhope's education and fastidious habits. While he was yet agitating the point with himself, Stanhope appeared.

'Are you converted?' said he, with a smile, as he entered. 'Do you not approve of the exchange I have made from more elegant society to that of rustics, whose attachment to me is at once genuine and warm; whose manners bespeak the uprightness and candour of their lives, and on whom I may safely rely at every period of mine?'

'I see much to approve, and much even to admire,' replied the Colonel, who did not at that juncture feel himself disposed to enter more deeply into the subject; 'but I am mistaken, or you have not yet shown me *all* that is admirable here.'

'No! – but you shall see her immediately.' – He then took a light and passed on to another end of the house, where stopping at an outward apartment, he laid his finger on his lips in token of silence, and invited the Colonel softly to advance. The latter impatiently looked into the adjoining room, which was spacious and neat. In a canopied recess stood a small bed with white fringe and furniture, and in it lay, fast asleep, a lovely child of about six years of age. One ivory shoulder was almost bare, as the arm that belonged to it had been negligently stretched over the counterpane; the other arm, which was under her head, by communicating an unusual degree of warmth, had called up the richest and most lively carnation into the cheek that reposed on it.

'This is a fairy Venus indeed!' exclaimed Raymond, with admiration and surprise; and looking nearer, he saw the miniature features of his friend. – 'What,' he added, 'can possibly induce you to keep her here?'

'I can keep her here no longer. Yet for many months, she has been my chief companion, and my only felicity. But I dare not expose a frame like hers to the piercing blasts of such a winter as we have to encounter. Nothing, however, can be more vigorous and sprightly than she has hitherto been. Here are roses!' – Stooping, he gently kissed her cheek, and as gently covered up the beautiful little shoulder. –' Arlette,' he added, as they quitted the room together, 'is the best creature in the world. She is also a mother – and her care has been unremitting: – but her care alone will no longer suffice.'

'Bring the sweet child away with you by all means.'

'Whither? – to whom?' replied Stanhope, with some asperity.

'To my wife – to Angelique.'

'Madame de T— will have other cares to engage her – and Angelique' – he faintly coloured as he pronounced the name – 'Angelique cannot be a mother to her.'

'I am not sure of that, unless you are determined to the contrary.'

'No, no: Angelique has no tenderness: she does not know how to love.'

'Oh, you are further gone yourself than I suspected, if you have already arraigned for her that crime, Come, do not be affected, dear Stanhope! leave that sort of stuff for the world you have fallen out with. You cannot be ignorant that Angelique only waits to know that she is beloved, in order to bestow her heart.'

'Waits to know that she is beloved!' repeated Mr. Stanhope, acrimoniously. 'It is thus that hearts are bestowed?'

'Yes, my good friend, it is thus that the heart of an amiable and well educated young women is – nay, *entre nous* – I think, *ought* to be bestowed. You have accustomed yourself to think otherwise. You have possibly, at your outset in life, encountered some Heloïse, who has broken a thousand obstacles to throw herself into your arms; and, ten to one, as many more to free herself from them. You have believed that the world has seduced her; and you have not seen, that she did not know how, in any instance, to contend with herself. If you are resolved to persist in this dream of the imagination and the senses, I have nothing more to say: but if you are in search of permanent happiness, you will find it associated with gentleness, with modesty, with self-denial; in a word, with that sort of character which the high-fliers of romance, as well as those of ton, who often mean nearly the same thing under a different name, will perhaps choose to depreciate by the term mediocrity. Angelique's,' he carelessly added, 'is, I rather believe, of this description. It may be best therefore to think of her no more.'

'I see nothing that should prevent my continuing to do so, in what you have announced,' returned Stanhope, a little peevishly, and without perceiving the good-natured malice that had dictated the last sentence.

'Guilty, decidedly, my dear friend, by your own confession,' said the Colonel, laughing: 'and since that is the case, *continue* to think of her in any way you like, – it will come to the same thing in the end.'

'I had very different plans when I left – that is, when I returned this second time to Leuk,' said Stanhope. 'I had banished all ideas of the kind, and had resolved never to marry.'

'Then no man living is so well entitled as myself to tell you that you made a very foolish resolution.'

'I might perhaps convince *you*, sooner than any other man living, to the contrary, were I to try.'

'Then pray forbear the experiment! my wife will not thank you for it: besides, we have not the knack of convincing one another; it would therefore be so much time lost. Make your determination at once. Return to Leuk: take your little girl with you; and if your heart is so inclined, try whether Angelique can be taught how to love. Remember that it is I who advise this, and who am willing to stand by all the ill consequences that may arise from it.'

'I *shall* remember,' said Stanhope, musing: 'but I am grown so savage – so unaccommodating – so little likely now to inspire affection.'

'You want me to say that the girl is in love with you.' Mr. Stanhope defended himself very gravely from this accusation. His friend laughed at his earnestness, and denied love altogether on the part of Angelique: but he could hardly forbear a smile on penetrating into the secret pleasure which Stanhope felt in disbelieving him. The conversation ran into length, till the Colonel was finally obliged to break if off.

'My dear friend,' said he, 'it is very plain that you *are* in love, and that I am not; for I am terribly sleepy. Remember how many miles we have travelled to-day: and *what* miles; give me a candle, therefore, and show me my chamber, if you do not mean that I should disgrace myself.' Never did Colonel Raymond enjoy better rest than on that night. A sense of self-approbation, which he was well entitled to indulge, united with real fatigue to lull both body and mind into the most refreshing sleep. He opened his eyes upon a bright sun, which fell in strong lights and shades over a country of various and exquisite beauty. Stanhope was already abroad, and his friend sallied forth in search of him; but, being wholly unacquainted with his haunts, their meeting was not very probable: nor was the Colonel impatient that it should take place. He had some points to consider, in order that he might perform to his own satisfaction the part he had undertaken in the little romance of the day. It was one which, however accordant with his character, required caution and address: nor was it therefore without previous thought, although veiled under the appearance of gaiety, that he endeavoured to contrast the passion which he well knew had marked the early part of Mr. Stanhope's life, with that which there was reason to believe would fill up the remainder of it.

The particulars of that life the Colonel was lately become sufficiently acquainted with, though a long and professional absence from England had prevented his observations from being personal: it was indeed the common history of thousands of men, born, like Mr. Stanhope, with advantages that enable them to choose their own fate. Deceived by a mistress – betrayed by a friend – duped alternately by violent passions and refined tastes, – he had run a tumultuous career, in which nothing indeed had been dishonourable, but all had been vapid and disappointing. He had revenged himself, as men of honour too often do, upon those who have none; and after wounding his antagonist so dangerously as to be himself obliged to quit his country, and find temporary obscurity in another, he had resolved, in a fit of spleen, to return thither no more. The fact was, that Mr. Stanhope had attained that period of life at which man first begins to discover the limit of his own views and his own powers. A period when minds of strong imagination, and sanguine hopes, as often quarrel with themselves as with the world; and he had quarrelled with both, merely because he knew not how to circumscribe his expectations from either. In quitting it, he carried away with him no approving reflections: for the child, whom he doated upon, he could not legitimate; nor did he know where to find a female protector or friend, that should shelter her from dangers, which his own dear-bought knowledge of the world taught him to calculate, with even exaggerated apprehension. A plan had indeed occurred once to him with regard to Madame de T—; which he now was no longer eager to realise. All that related to

Angelique, even when his own election was made, it still remained with her to decide upon; and the distrust he had long cherished, both of himself and of others, caused the interval to be filled with a thousand disquieting and impatient feelings. Having lived in the land of shadows, he had learned to suspect that friendship and love were nothing else; and he felt that were he to grasp at them a second time, and find them only such the disappointment would be irremediable.

Colonel Raymond had, however, by no means calculated the extent of his friend's partiality for Angelique. That was now so completely ascertained, by the conversation of the preceding evening, as to leave little more room for discovery. The engines then were in his hands, that might bring back a valuable heart to society; and the generosity of his own induced him to resolve upon using them. Stanhope, when *tête-à-tête* with a man whom, spite of prejudice, he began greatly to esteem, was a very different being from that which he appeared to superficial observers, and infinitely more amiable. He was passionately fond of his little girl, and the wish he felt that she should create fondness in the hearts of those to whom he was about to present her, was as sufficient attestation of the interest he took in both parties. It seemed difficult to arrange in what manner she could be made their fellow-traveller; but Stanhope was perfectly familiar with every mode of conveyance; and his little mountaineer, as he called her, was active and adventurous. Never could heroine of any age or country boast two more vigilant knights to protect her, and never did heroine reward her protectors by more playful and fascinating gaiety. The parting with Arlette, and the little boys, was nevertheless a sorrowful scene, – nor was the dog forgotten. She kissed them all affectionately by turns; and it would have been difficult to say which of the three had most of her fondness or caresses. To Arlette, and her husband, together with the parents of the former, was consigned the numerous family to whom Stanhope was in the habit of extending his care. It was not without emotion that he recollected the indefinite time for which he now left them, or weighed how far his new pursuits might estrange him from that mode of life, which he had endeavoured to persuade himself alone was rationally desirable. But his child, and yet another object, almost, he thought, was dear as his child, for he was far from granting, even to his own heart, that Angelique could possibly divide it with the latter, called him to other scenes.

They now passed through a circuitous road, less gratifying indeed to the imagination than that savage one they had before travelled, but infinitely more delightful to the heart. Innocent and happy nature seemed to present herself to their valley, and in every cottage; nor did Stanhope fail to comment with enthusiasm upon it. As they approached that limit lay within the jurisdiction of Berne, the appearance of things nevertheless seemed insensibly to change. They met several peasants, chiefly women, who had all of them an air of hurry and apprehension for which the travellers could not immediately account. But, in proportion as they advanced, they gathered intelligence, that within different quarters of the canton various petty tumults had arisen, in consequence, as it was supposed, of the intrigues of French emissaries; that some hamlets had been burned by the opposite factions that inhabited them; and several individuals had been obliged to hide themselves from popular fury. Intelligence of this nature could not but excite emotion in bosoms that glowed with the love of liberty, of nature, and of virtue. It as so delightful to every generous mind, to believe that there existed a spot on the globe where those blessings remained inviolate, that, had the persuasion been simply a dream of the imagination it would have been impossible to awake from it without reluctance and resentment.

Consideration for their young companion rendered both gentlemen impatient to reach a destination that should secure them from alarm. How greatly were they grieved and surprised to find that they rather seemed to have penetrated into the chief scene of the commotion, when they reached the village of M—, which had been their first night's station after leaving Leuk. All was indeed now tranquillised; but the stillness that had succeeded was of that frightful kind, which both in individuals and in societies seems the consequence of crime, and bespeaks the consciousness of it. The inhabitants that remained upon the spot kept within their doors; but many had quitted it; and among the houses that were deserted was that of their former kind host. A respectable woman who lived in the cottage adjoining answered however to their interrogatories concerning him; and they gathered from her account, that if he had escaped in safety, a circumstance which appeared extremely doubtful, he had been obliged to purchase security by abandoning every thing else. His home had been nearly demolished: his books which were almost his sole wealth, lay scattered over the desolate apartments; and the furniture had been pillaged or destroyed.

'He was, no doubt, particularly odious in the neighbourhood,' said Stanhope.

The Canterbury Tales

'No, not he, sir, but he was suspected to be of the same party with the great family *there*;' and she pointed to the château: 'they were not on the spot to guard their own property, and he endeavoured to dissuade the peasants from destroying it. But all would not do, – for they only committed more mischief.'

'But was he not severe? – Aristocratical? unkind to them?'

'Never that I heard of. I have seen him with my own eyes making pottage and soups for them, when times were hard; and he would visit the poorest man in the district that sent to him. He could not be bountiful, for he was not rich; – but he had such a good heart, sir!' – and tears filled her eyes.

'Hateful villains!' exclaimed Stanhope, with an indignation which he could not control.

'No, indeed, sir, they were no villains either,' returned the woman, with the same warmth on her side; 'they were the most honest people alive, and till this unlucky fray they were the most kind-hearted. But they were ignorant; – and when people are very ignorant, it is easy for wicked men to persuade them that the wrong is the right. There is but little reliance, I am afraid, to be placed on those who do not understand their duties. It is all right with such folks till it is all wrong; and then they are as zealous in the bad cause as in the good.' Colonel Raymond looked at his friend, who on his part evidently made his own applications, but no comment.

As it was impossible to proceed to Leuk the same night, they were obliged to put up with such accommodation as the village afforded; and on the evening of the ensuring day they found themselves within view of the Colonel's habitation. It had been agreed between the two friends, that the little girl and Mr. Stanhope should for a short time become the guests of Madame de T—; there seemed an impropriety in introducing the child at once, and without explanation, into the family of Monsieur Rivaz; and something too marked in separating her from her father, even if that could have been done without afflicting her, which did not seem probable, for she loved him most fondly.

'You had better not venture into the house, I think,' said the Colonel, turning with a smile to Stanhope as they approached the garden gate. 'Do you not hear music?'

'It was once like the memory of joys that were past,' returned the other. 'I am now disposed to look only to the future.' Whatever might be the disposition of Mr. Stanhope's mind, he certainly nevertheless felt a little embarrassed, though too proud to show that he did so. He was going to appear in two characters equally new to him, those of a lover and a father: he knew not what persons composed the audience that was to witness this unexpected exhibition; but he felt as if there was but one pair of eyes in the world that he would willingly at that crisis have encountered. Fortunately, the saloon was shaded to a most convenient obscurity; and though several people were there, it was not easy to distinguish them individually. His ear however, had informed him, when yet afar off, that Angelique was one of the number, for she had been singing; and, obscure as the light was, he contrived to see her as quickly as though they had met in the brightest sunshine.

'I bring you back, my dear Augusta,' said the Colonel, as he tenderly embraced his wife, 'two guests – this sweet child, and her father.' And he held up the former to her arms, giving at the same time her hand to Stanhope, who, kissing it, uttered some confused, half inarticulate sentence on the subject of his child. Whatever part of the company rejoiced at that moment in the obscurity, Madame de T— assuredly was not of the number. Her sprightly and inquiring eyes, which were turned with astonishment upon the trio, seemed to ask a thousand questions, and make a thousand observations: but her native delicacy as instantly conquered the impulse, and she suffered the various salutations and greetings attending the occasion to be entirely over, before she called for lights. Mr. Stanhope in the interim recovered his presence of mind, which the Colonel's sudden and unequivocal explanation had somewhat disturbed. Angelique too found her voice; and both of them had proceeded so far in conversation as to interchange civil inquiries concerning each other. The rest of the company, which was composed of Rivaz, his wife, and a very handsome young man who was lately come from Berne, talked with interest of the frightful political occurrences that had lately taken place there, and the probability of its being entered by the troops of France. Madame de T— meantime was employed in caressing and examining the features of the child, who on her part was no less busy in examining those of the company. Children are always decided on the article of physiognomy; and Stanhope's little girl seemed to have a very sympathetic taste with that of her father, for she presently made her decision in favour of Angelique, whose soft and persuasive glances won her over from the sprightly graces of the Countess. It was in Angelique's arms that she chose to sit; and twining her own little snowy ones round the neck of the latter, she whispered a thousand confidential and important nothings; pressing her hand upon the lips of Mademoiselle Rivaz, and stopping her mouth if she attempted to repeat them.

'How indulgent you are to a motherless child,' said Mr. Stanhope, drawing near to both. Angelique half raised her eyes, and a soft flush came over her cheek, which seemed to announce that the indirect information which the sentence was meant to convey was not wholly uninteresting; but neither of them spoke further. Mr. Stanhope only gently released her, after a time, from the child, who he feared was become troublesome; and taking the latter in his own arms kept her there for the remainder of the evening.

Yet this evening of long anticipated pleasure did not pass without alloy. The visiter, who during the absence of the two friends had been introduced into the domestic circle, seemed to receive a very particular sort of attention from Rivaz and his wife; nor was Angelique remiss in hers. She listened to him whenever he spoke with a degree of complacency, which thought it might be meant to convey nothing but friendship, yet gave Mr. Stanhope a new and very disagreeable sensation. The young man, on his part, was full of respect and devotion to the family. He was musical; could sing well, and was privileged by that talent to exercise a thousand little gallantries. He filled up the measure of his offences by officiously placing himself, like one who was accustomed so to do, next Mademoiselle Rivas at the supper table; and when her father, on taking leave, drew the arm of his wife under his own, and thus committed his daughter to the care of the stranger, Mr. Stanhope fairly wished himself again in his cottage and his solitude.

The party had hardly dispersed, and Stanhope, too much spleened for conversation, withdrawn, when the Colonel, whose observations had also been alive, began to interrogate his wife concerning her new acquaintance.

'I hardly know any thing of him,' replied she, 'except his name: but his manners, though a little Swiss, are lively and agreeable. He seemed to drop from the clouds within a day or two after your departure. The whole family of Rivaz are extremely confidential with him, and since the time of his arrival have been much less domesticated with me than they were before accustomed to be. If I did not rely on the heart of Angelique I should certainly suspect that some treaty is negotiating in which she is concerned.'

'Would it not be possible to question her?'

'Very possible – but that I have done it already to no purpose. It is a secret,' was her answer.

'Then I will question Rivaz. He is plain and straightforward. We shall therefore easily come at the truth. Stanhope is of a character either to control himself entirely, or not at all. If he suspects either indifference or finesse he will fly off in a tangent, and we may hear of him next from the North Cape. I can see that he is already anxious – irresolute – distrustful.'

'Bad characteristics!'

'Unlucky ones, I confess: though common enough with a certain inconsiderate race of men, who have purchased, at the expense of fortune and time, a power to taint their own happiness. But our friend has valuable qualities, and I owe it to myself to serve him.'

The Colonel's intended application to Rivaz was judicious enough, but unfortunately made too late; for the latter had risen with the sun the next morning, and set off for Berne upon business. His young acquaintance seemed also to have absented himself for the day; and Angelique, with her mother, remained at home. Stanhope and his little girl passed the greater part of the morning in their society. Contrary to the usual habits of all, he alone was animated and unembarrassed, – was even pointed in his attentions. The disappearance of the stranger had revived his spirits as well as his hopes; and he strove by a thousand indirect marks of tenderness, by the softest words and blandishments, to establish, through the medium of the child, a sort of intercourse between himself and Angelique. No man knew how to do this more gracefully; nor was it the first time that an infant messenger had been the interpreter of love.

Madame Rivaz seemed, during this scene, to be restless and out of humour. She spoke frequently to her daughter with a certain abruptness which denoted secret displeasure, and even made allusions, the tendency of which Stanhope could not comprehend. But Angelique, as if awakened to sudden recollection by them, quitted the room more than once, in order, as it appeared, to attend to some domestic occupation. She frequently returned, however, and Stanhope believed he could discern, that whatever was the mystery which called her away, it was her heart that as constantly brought her back. 'But that heart is so cold, so tame! – its whispers are so *very* gentle,' said he to himself, 'that how can I be sure they will be heard?' During the intervals of her absence, he was half tempted to be explicit with Madame Rivaz; but the good lady's countenance did not encourage him. He knew her character to be warm, and her partialities or prejudices equally invincible. He had once enjoyed the first in all its extent; but she was a rigid observer of propriety, and he fancied that she did not survey his child with indulgence. A consciousness that he was not willing to investigate taught him at least to distrust her.

'I have tired you,' said he, rising at length to be gone. 'My visit has been unreasonably long; but this house seems my natural residence,' – and he looked at Madame Rivaz. No invitation, however, succeeded the hint. 'It is the only place in which my heart finds its home.' He particularly directed the second sentence to Angelique, but no notice was taken of it. 'We see you this evening,' he added, still addressing himself to the latter.

'I fear not,' returned she, blushing and faltering. 'I have an engagement, – I am indispensably obliged to be at home.'

'And may I be permitted to join the family party for half an hour?'

'Not to-night.'

'To-morrow, then – to-morrow morning,' returned he, thrown wholly off his reserves by surprise and vexation.

'My husband is gone to settle some particular business at Berne,' said Madame Rivaz. 'When he returns every thing relative to it will be arranged, and we shall be at leisure to receive our friends.' Petrified with astonishment at this dismission, so unexpected and so new to him, Stanhope took his leave. 'No, Angelique,' said he to himself, as he walked home: 'it must be to-night that we meet – to-night that our mutual destiny, as far as that of either depends on the other, must be decided. *Every thing will be arranged.* What detestable words, and uttered with so much *sang-froid!* And I am dismissed as an intruder before this arrangement takes place! Some mysterious negotiation is evidently on foot which Angelique's heart does not sanction, whatever may be the dictates of duty: if I do not, therefore, explain myself to-night, tomorrow will perhaps be too late.'

He returned to Madame de T—, absent and thoughtful, but too resolute in his own purpose to desire any counsel from others. The change in his appearance was observed both by the Colonel and herself.

'Heaven grant that Angelique's passion may not prove of this dolorous kind!' continued the Countess, when he had vanished: 'far from improving, it has totally spoiled him. What a splenetic husband shall we have, if the lover is thus gloomy!' The gloom of this lover was nevertheless insensibly subsiding. He had, in a great degree, conquered the alarm and disappointment which for a moment had obscured his fairest hopes; and the persuasion he secretly cherished that Mademoiselle Rivaz was not indifferent to him induced reveries of a pleasanter nature. It was the sweetest evening in the world when he directed his solitary walk towards the habitation of Rivaz. The moon in full beauty checkered a close pathway, half covered with falling leaves, which were softly moved by a breeze that partook rather of summer than of autumn; while her more resplendent light struck at intervals through the branches, thus relieved from their exuberant foliage; and the whole landscape, as well as the air, was full of a divine tranquillity.

The lower windows of the house were thrown open, and the moonlight showed him Angelique's work, together with various trifles belonging to her, on a small table in the room where they were accustomed to sit; but neither she nor her mother were there. Hardly doubting that they had walked out, as they frequently did, to enjoy the freshness of evening, he directed his steps down a shrubbery which was divided by a paling from the orchard; the door of communication at the further end was open, and he had advanced within two hundred paces of it, when a soft and musical voice struck his ear from the other side of the enclosure. His heart immediately acknowledged the sound; and he was quickening his steps, when they were arrested by another and far different tone. It was evidently that of a man; and although the words which he uttered were indistinctly heard, it was plain that he spoke in answer to her. It was equally plain that he spoke low and familiarly. Stanhope checked his own feelings. It might be her father. Even if he were not returned, and the young stranger from Berne her companion, her mother was probably with her. That supposition was at once proved erroneous; for two persons only appeared at the door of communication: they were arm in arm, and one of them was certainly Angelique; the other was not Rivaz, but a man of better stature and appearance, though his features and figure were too indistinctly seen to be ascertained. While Stanhope stood still to contemplate them both, Angelique, on seeing or guessing at him, appeared to be startled. She hastily withdrew her arm; motioned to her companion to retire into the orchard, which was thickly tufted with trees; and locking the door upon him, advanced up the walk, where Stanhope remained, by this time a statue of surprise and indignation.

'I have intruded,' cried he, hardly knowing what he said. Angelique seemed little less confounded than himself.

'Did you not meet my mother?' returned she, as if desirous to evade his observation. 'I parted with her a very short time ago.'

The Canterbury Tales

'You have parted since with another companion. Tell me, Angelique,' and he eagerly seized her hands, ' what man was that who quitted you this moment?'

'Ask – my father,' replied she, abashed by an address at once so abrupt and unequivocal.

'Your father is not here; and even if he were, I should be little disposed to question him. It is you, dear Angelique! and your feelings only, that must decide my fate. Speak – tell me: if those do not induce confidence, I shall never seek it elsewhere.'

'Be assured that my actions,' said Mademoiselle Rivaz, still abashed and trembling, ' have the concurrence of my father; nay, more, are the consequence of his commands. Why, then, should you question their propriety?'

'I am answered. The concurrence of your father is, then, enough for your happiness: you feel no regret at destroying mine. You part with me, and for ever; for I cannot part twice with any being that I love as I love you, Angelique. You dismiss me without explanation or indulgence, simply because your conduct is sanctioned by your father.' Angelique, insensible to what she did, detained him as he attempted to leave her.

'What would you yourself say,' cried she, 'to a woman who should violate a serious engagement merely to indulge – ' She stopped, overwhelmed with the consciousness of her own meaning.

'That I loved, that I adored her, – that my life and my fortune were at her feet! and he threw himself there.

'Will nothing less than an immediate and unreserved explanation satisfy you?' replied she, in tremor and evident irresolution.

'Nothing less will, dear Angelique! nothing less can,' he replied, with the eagerness of invigorated hope. 'I should then owe it to your heart, and *only* to that: it is to that only I ever *will* owe it.

'Then relinquish the expectation of being satisfied,' said Angelique, after a pause, but with a voice that showed she was in tears; 'for my heart cannot resolve on the compliance you exact: it cannot sacrifice its duties even to – its feelings.' And disengaging her hands, she broke from him in the greatest confusion, and passed into the house. Agitated, but not satisfied, he followed her. She had retired, however, to her own apartment; and he threw himself into a chair near the work-table. 'She will then be bestowed upon another!' he exclaimed; 'and it is plain that she is willing to be so bestowed, rather than sacrifice some insignificant duty to the immediate dictates of her heart. But

Rivaz has more judgment. Rivaz—' While he spoke, his hand rested on somewhat which lay upon the table; and he perceived that it was the case of a picture. 'No! it is her heart that disposes of her,' he resentfully added, on opening the miniature; and discovering a likeness of the young man he had seen with her the evening before – 'and mine is the dupe, as it has been throughout my life, of its own sensibilities, its own ridiculous and ill-supported confidence in others.'

It was long before he thought of returning to the house of his friend. A thousand confused schemes agitated his impetuous temper in the interim. Solitude, – seclusion, – that hill which had 'lifted him to the storms' of heaven, indeed, but which seemed to have sheltered him from those of the world, again recurred to his recollection. But even seclusion had lost half its charms: he had seen that cruelty and ingratitude were to be met with in rustic as well as polished life: error crept in wherever man was to be found; and the only choice lay between the evils of grossness and refinement.

'Are you performing the part of Werter?' said Colonel Raymond, who, after long search, found him leaning, in a most pastoral attitude, under a spreading chestnut-tree that stood half-way between the two habitations. 'What evil spirit possesses you now?'

'The worst of all evil spirits – jealousy and resentment. Why did you persuade me to prove myself a fool?'

'First tell me by which of your foolish actions the proof is established, before I stand condemned as an accessary.' Stanhope, in few words, and not very distinctly, related what had passed between himself and Angelique.

'This has been almost heroic scene, indeed,' replied the Colonel, 'and the probable *dénouement* puts me in mind of some French riddles I have read; where, after imagination has travelled up to the seventh heaven, and down as low in proportion, in search of the marvellous, *le mot de l'enigme* turns out to be a conjurer or a rope-dancer. My dear Stanhope, do you know that you have made yourself mighty ridiculous? – Go, and ask pardon of Angelique as fast as you can.'

'For what offence?'

'That of having quarrelled with her because she was not romantic enough to give up a secret confided by her father, and betray the rites of hospitality, in order to indulge your freak of owing every thing to her affections. Be content, my good friend, for the future, to owe something to a woman's reason and her duties; or at least allow her to owe something to them herself; and, trust me, you will be a gainer in the end by the exchange. – Hearts are fickle, and apt sometimes to turn deserters: but there is a sort of supplementary militia of minor virtues, which the best soldier amongst us will grant may be trained into use.'

'I do not understand any thing you are saying.'

'Then understand it now. This rival, found guilty of being shut up in the house of Rivaz, – nay, worse, – shut up in his orchard, – with, or without Angelique, – no matter which, – is no less a person than our ci-devant host, whose habitation was burnt at the village of M—. The young stranger *was* his pupil, and is his most grateful and devoted protector. It is here that the good ecclesiastic sought a secret and temporary asylum from popular fury. It is here that the young man came to seek and advise with him; and, finally, it is from hence that Rivaz is now empowered by the council of Berne to dismiss him safely acquitted of all misdemeanors; and the portrait, had, you used your eyes a minute longer, you would have seen to be only one of many, – the labours of an artist whose talents were under discussion. Are you satisfied? – If not, refer you to Rivaz, who is just returned home, and has published the secret of his journey; or what think you of applying to the pastor himself? He will doubtless be much flattered by your jealousy; and the least he can do to remove it is to propose marrying you to Angelique, before she has time to discover more of your faults.'

While the Colonel was speaking, a variety of interesting recollections passed through the mind of his bearer. Mademoiselle Rivaz had not indeed given him the testimony of love which he solicited; but even while denying it, she had been betrayed into indirect but tender acknowledgments, that left him no longer any possibility of doubting his power over her affections.

'Yet, by what plea,' said he, 'shall I induce her to listen to me again, till I have had the sanction of that respectable father to whose authority she herself has referred me! How insupportably tedious is the delay. It includes, too, explanations without end!'

'One of which, – perhaps the *most* tedious, – I will spare you. My dear Stanhope (if it is still your pleasure to be so called), prepare for a surprise. – I am well informed that I now take by the hand my generous relation and my best friend. I know that you quitted Florence some months ago, and that you saved me the trouble of seeking *you* either there, or elsewhere, by seeking *me* here. I have gathered from your own broken sentences sufficient information concerning your plans to guess that you adopted this last with a view to the future protection of your child; and that unwilling to tax me by avowing yourself in the character of a benefactor, you were desirous to try me in that of a friend. You *have* tried me more deeply than you suspected; and I hope, that by adopting the views most favourable to your happiness, I have proved myself both honourable and disinterested.'

'Do you deal in magic?' said Stanhope, smiling in spite of his chagrin; 'how long since, and by what means, did you obtain this information?'

'Exactly four days before we set out for your habitation in the mountains. I had business at Sion which I thought it more convenient to settle in person than by writing. It happened that the banker with whom I transacted it had been employed by you on your first journey here; and though cautioned with respect to your temporary change of name, yet imputing it solely to the account of the duel, he entertained not the least doubt that your real one was well known to me, your nearest relation. I had presence of mind enough to conceal from him that he had made any discovery, nor does he to this moment suspect his error. Admire my indulgence, for I also left you in full possession of yours, till the object of our journey was completed. On my own part, as personal acquaintance was all that was wanting between us, in learning your name I had nothing more to learn. What say you now to my counterplot?' Stanhope smiled, and nodded approbation.

'Yet as it would be rather too much in the tone of romance,' continued the Colonel, 'to make this explanation to strangers, Rivaz may be suffered to suppose, for the present at least, that our knowledge of each other has always been mutual. Come and see my wife. She is now acquainted with the secret, which I only guarded long enough to satisfy myself that there was no hidden fair one, "no mistress in the wood," likely to chill your reception.' The lights of the Colonel's habitation, to which they had insensibly advanced, now glimmered through the trees. 'Show yourself,' he added, 'but tell your own story at your own season; you will find Rivaz and his friends with Madame de T——. Angelique, too, is most probably of the party. And although the little girl may not be present, to bring you together so conveniently as she did yesterday evening, you may nevertheless find an opportunity of making your peace.'

Stanhope impatiently entered the saloon, but Mademoiselle Rivaz was not there, and the apology her mother made for her deprived him of all hope that she would appear. In one of the guests he, with pleasure, recognized his kind host at M—, nor did the young stranger, who, with filial respect accompanied the latter, now strike him in the same disadvantageous point of view he had hitherto done. But it was Angelique only that occupied his thoughts; and hardly had he sufficient self-command to stay a few moments, in order to offer those congratulations which the occasion demanded. The Colonel was not surprised to observe that he disappeared immediately afterwards; or to learn, on his return to the company, that Angelique, who entertained not the smallest suspicion of seeing him so suddenly again, had once more been found alone: that he had pleased his cause with no less earnestness and better success than before, and obtained a full and kind pardon.

Stanhope found opportunity, in the course of the evening, to communicate to Monsieur Ravaz, in few words, the purport of a conversation which he requested might be granted him on the following day. The cheeks of the good man were suffused, and his eyes glistened with pleasure: he affectionately pressed the hand of his future son-in-law, and, in so doing, left little more to explain between them.

'But my former kind friend, Madame Rivaz, has looked coldly on me,' said Stanhope, returning with interest the friendly pressure – 'how am I to conciliate her favour?'

'My good, sir, you have never lost it. Angelique and I have been the culprits: on her part, poor girl, very innocently so; for she only obeyed my commands in guarding our secret. I found her, however, in tears on my return, so guessed that all had not gone well at home. My wife,' he added, in a whisper, 'is a little of a politician; and studies the best part of politics – safety. She conceived mine to be in some danger from the shelter I afforded our friends. Forgive a woman who loves her husband more than she does anything else in the world.'

Stanhope was never better disposed to pardon that sort of offence; and either the plea itself, or the consciousness that Madame Rivaz might be fairly acquitted of having caused the tears of her daughter, put him into so very good a humour that the former must have been hard-hearted indeed to have resisted his attentions. Nor was her heart composed of any stubborn materials whatever, where he was concerned; in fact he possessed, in a very uncommon degree, the art of rendering himself agreeable to both sexes; and especially to women, when he chose to exert it.

A period not remote was fixed for the celebration of the marriage; but the contract, and the rural fête that accompanied the latter, were announced two days after. These ceremonies were customs of the country, and therefore willingly complied with, though not essential. The peasants of the district were invited to share the conviviality and joy of the occasion, nor were those of the mountains forgotten in the order issued by Stanhope. Angelique, at his request, appeared in the same rustic garb which she had worn at the harvest-home, and never before looked so charming, for she had never been so happy. The whole scene was like one of those delightful visions of Arcadian felicity so rarely found any where but in romance.

'And now,' said Madame de T——, addressing herself gaily to the little group around her, but particularly to Stanhope, 'having each played our parts, to our own satisfaction at least, and wound up our little *proverbe*, with the old-fashioned *dénouement* of a wedding, suppose, my dear friends, that I undertake to deliver the finale of the piece. Rochefoucault, I am afraid, has said before me, that mankind are neither so good nor so bad as we fancy them to be. Ignorance brutalises, and refinement corrupts. Let us hope, however, that wise heads and generous hearts are still to be met with in every class of society: but while wandering in search of both, through the very odd mazes of this very odd world, it will be reasonable to recollect that we have no right to murmur at our disappointment, if we find that we cannot gather such flowers as the paths we have chosen never yet afforded.

THE WIFE'S TALE

JULIA

A creature, 'kind and generous,' fair and vain,
The creature, woman, rises now to reign.

Parnell

'I have certainly taken a very judicious step this morning,' said Mr. Seymour to himself, as he drove with a superb *cortège* from St. George's Church, Hanover Square. 'Every thing that respects my worldly concerns is now exactly settled to my satisfaction; and, properly speaking, I may call this period the beginning of my life!' – So pleasant a train of reasoning could not fail to put him in good humour. The conclusion drawn was not perhaps altogether correct; for as Mr. Seymour was near fifty, there might be people in the world ill-natured enough to think that life was somewhat nearer its sunset than its dawn; but who, in calculations of this kind, ever is correct? And what person would think of setting a man right that was so happy in his error, and so disposed to make his friends happy? For Mr. Seymour was philanthropic enough to comprehend, under that title, a numerous circle composed of both sexes, to whom he gave the best dinners, the gayest balls, and the prettiest rural fêtes of any man in London.

He was yet engrossed by the agreeable contemplations we have mentioned, when the carriage stopped at the door of an elegant house in the neighbourhood of Grosvenor Square. Curtains, and sofas of the rarest and most fashionable texture, were disposed with all then taste of modern improvement: a treillage enclosing the finest flowers perfumed the air from the windows, at one end; while virandas shaded the other, and only permitted the vulgar gazers of the street to peep at the rich tassels and fringes that decorated the apartments within. A *déjeûné* was displayed in the very first style, and of the most magnificent china; while the plants from the conservatory made a little Eden of the spot. Mr. Seymour was every where, and the life of the company. He wore his best Brutus wig, which was curled in the last new taste. His coat was made to a charm. He had a tolerable leg, and it was not neglected. His teeth were hardly so good as they had been, but he had supplied himself with a couple of new ones the week before, which enabled him to laugh with perfect security. He was therefore disposed to be entertaining in a high degree. In fact he was altogether in very good humour with himself, for he had that morning made a purchase that pleased him extremely: – he had bought a wife.

Presiding, under the auspices of her mother at this *déjeûné*, sat a young creature just turned of seventeen; lovely as one of the graces, and almost as slightly clothed. Her polished throat and beautiful arms, her lace and satin drapery, the ingenuous sweetness of her eyes, and the rich bloom of her cheek, which every moment as it passed tinted with a vermilion still richer, formed in themselves a picture so irresistible as to need no decoration. Yet it cannot be denied that there was somewhat in the general *coup d'oeil*, which made her, 'though far the fairest flower,' derive new grace and enchantment from those that bloomed around. What a delicious thing would life be in London, if balls, fêtes, and flattery, could make it so! but people do grow old, and sick at last, even in London; and when confined to a half-deserted apartment, they are obliged to meditate upon that solitary one which is perhaps shortly to hold them. It must be acknowledged that the contrast does not show the latter to advantage.

Having found Mr. Seymour at the very summit of human felicity, it may be proper to relate the degrees by which he attained it. Springing remotely from a family of opulence and great consideration, it had been his ill-fortune to find the path of life too smooth before him. At nine years of age he had good nature; at eighteen he had good sense; at one-and-twenty he had a good estate; at thirty he had lost almost all that was good besides; and at forty he was without any of these recommendations. It was convenient therefore to change his residence for one in another country, and he went to India in a civil capacity; but he carried with him indolent habits and moderate abilities. His fortune did not of course improve rapidly; but after a period of some years had elapsed, circumstances did for him what he did not seem very likely to do for himself; and he had realised a property, not splendid indeed, but considerable, when intelligence that the family estate, which ten times exceeded the patrimony he had spent, was likely to devolve to him by the deaths of several intermediate parties, determined him to sail immediately for England. He accordingly reached it in the beginning of spring. The business of securing possession detained him in town till the summer months; when, after having enjoyed, in their fullest extent, the pleasures of temporary celebrity, he retired to a villa which he had engaged for the season, on the Devonshire coast, in order to repair constitution somewhat shattered by his residence abroad, and to consider in what manner he could make his *début* with most effect in London the succeeding winter.

Within the neighbourhood of Mr. Seymour's superb residence was a manor-house, which had formerly been superb also; but time had committed such irreparable devastations there, as left the family who tenanted it little more real accommodation than they could have found in any thatched cottage of the adjoining village. Its size and appearance, however, the two particulars which alone recommended it to the favour of its inhabitants, attracted Mr. Seymour's attention; and a little inquiry informed him that he was no stranger to the person who dwelt there. He might, indeed, without any extraordinary effort of memory, have recollected, that he had been in fact very intimately acquainted with the gentleman in question; and that at a time when the latter was a much greater, and Mr. Seymour a much less man, than either of them now appeared to be. The Honourable Edward Cleveland was the younger branch of a family of rank, and had owed his acceptation in society chiefly to that circumstance. He had passed through all the gradations common to persona who have no original character of mind, and are merely what the world makes them. He had been successively a beau and a rake. Having undergone these transformations, and not exactly knowing what shape to take next, he married *pour se désennuyer*, and sank into a sloven. The happy pair continued to live in the gay world, till they had hardly the means to live at all; and then retired, with two girls whom the mother was obliged to educate as she could, to the petty grandeur of solitude, idleness, and the country.

In spite of the many dissimilar circumstances of character or situation that intervened to keep Mr. Seymour and his neighbour at a distance, there still was one that promised to bring them in contact; both gentlemen were terribly in want of amusement, or, as they would have phrased it, – occupation. Mr. Cleveland had evidently had the ill-fortune to leave the only one in which he ever truly delighted, behind him in London, – his taste for dress: nor did he carry any into the country that could supply its place. The situation of his pecuniary concerns allowed him not the pleasures of riding or driving; and how, as he often emphatically, and with some pathos observed, 'could a gentleman employ himself such resources!' Ladies it should seem have the advantage on these occasions over the male part of the world. Mrs. Cleveland, though, like her husband, born and educated in the circle of fashion, and no way superior to him in abilities, had the good luck, on being first driven into retirement, to fall in with two or three active and notable housewives, who gave her some hints with regard to domestic economy, without which indeed she perceived that her family were in danger of not having a dinner to eat, or a servant to prepare it. It was not that she had naturally any taste for these humble occupations; but she was of that fortunate sex which can sink to trifles without losing its dignity; while lordly man, once thrown, as he supposes, out of his place in society, often remains suspended, like Mahomet's coffin, a mere log – belonging neither to heaven, nor to earth. Mrs. Cleveland's good qualities were nevertheless, it must be acknowledged, the mere effect of accident and situation: necessity made her occasionally associate with her neighbours, but she always despised them; and had no other consolation, under the grievance, than that of seeing them gratefully look up to her in all matters of fashion and taste, whenever she condescended to avail herself of that more vulgar information which they could communicate.

Julia, the eldest daughter, was her mother's companion and favourite: all the soft and timid graces of early youth lived in the eye and on the cheek of this charming girl; but her form was finished and womanly beyond her years, and was, indeed, such as would have embellished any features. Was Julia herself aware of this? Perhaps no girl of sixteen is quite out of the secret, and she certainly had not quarrelled with the figure which her glass daily presented to her: but it is less the consciousness of possessing any advantage, than the degree of estimation which we attach to it, that renders it dangerous; and beauty was neither all-powerful nor all-sufficient in the eyes of Miss Cleveland. She was yet, indeed, but little in the habit of considering it; solicitous to free her mother from cares that were evidently irksome, she devoted herself almost solely to domestic occupations. Her tastes were simple, her enjoyments lively: a happy frame of mind, resulting both from nature and circumstances, accustomed

The Canterbury Tales

her to find her pleasures in her duties, or to make them there. Her understanding was stronger than it appeared to be; but it had hitherto been employed only in tranquillising her heart or her temper, if any little grievance ruffled either. The day was yet distant when it was to sharpen the arrow of affliction, and to show her, with more acute and extended perception, the evils of painful pre-eminence. Matilda was not yet eleven years old, but in person as well as mind she strongly resembled her sister. In spite of the difference of their age, the same tastes and employments often engrossed both; and the first delight their hearts had ever known, was one which they still continued to enjoy in common, – that of surprising Mr. and Mrs. Cleveland with some little proof of ingenuity or affection, calculated to lighten those hours which even their children had discernment enough to see hung most heavily upon them.

The arrival of so dashing an equipage as Mr. Seymour's was an event in the neighbourhood. Mr. Cleveland had not seen it, and those who had, knew too little of heraldry to give him any information as to the family honours of the owner. He had seen the horses, however, led out to air; had reconnoitered their size and their colour, had talked with the grooms on all other particulars relative to them; and after asking a few cursory questions, such as a well-bred man allows himself to put to servants concerning their master, he thought, with a sigh, of Hyde Park and Bond Street; and without recognizing his old acquaintance Seymour, under the importance of his new character, turned his steps slowly homewards.

'What can we reason but from what we know?' What is a man to talk of, but the only subject he is acquainted with? – Bond Street and Hyde Park would not quit the imaginations of Mr. Cleveland and his wife throughout the remainder of the evening; and they passed it so agreeably in discussing their mutual recollections, that to their very great astonishment the village clock struck ten before either of them yawned. Matilda had long been buried in a sweet slumber: but Julia was permitted to be a silent though much amused auditor during this unusual vigil, on the part of her parents. The conversation was not lost upon her: she in turn became troubled with a little curiosity to see this fine gentleman, and his fine equipage; nor was it long before she was gratified; for the owner, weary of solitary grandeur, at length condescended to acknowledge his old acquaintance, by stopping at her father's door; and poor Julia, without any premeditated mischief on her own part, soon after found herself in Cæsar's situation, for she came, saw, and overcame: in a word, Mr. Seymour fell, as he believed, desperately in love. His love, however, though decided, was not unmixed with other considerations and feelings than those of mere passion. It had no little reference to the figure she would make in the world, to the rank of her connections, the *éclat* that would attend himself on having such a wife to show, and the pleasure that must result from exciting the envy and admiration of all his acquaintance. His whole business in retirement had been to consider how he should emerge with due splendour; and splendour; and fortune on this occasion seemed, he thought, to enlist on his side.

The fair object of Mr. Seymour's choice was in the interim not a little surprised to find herself thus suddenly become such. The gratification which this unlooked for event seemed to afford her parents, operated upon her grateful and affectionate heart, with a force she was perfectly unconscious of. She listened to the decision, therefore, in favour of Mr. Seymour as to a fiat from which she neither wished nor knew how to appeal; and when they with one voice declared, that she must be the most ungrateful creature living, were she insensible of his good qualities, she most implicitly took those good qualities upon trust, and felt ashamed to acknowledge even to her own heart that she was deficient in the virtue expected from her. The first stroke was struck; for her feelings were silenced or deceived, and nothing remained but to kindle her vanity; nor was the undertaking in either case a difficult task. Matrimony and love had never for a moment engrossed her thoughts. No creature had moved within her circle calculated to excite the latter, and her youth and retired modes of life made it little probable that the former should occur to her imagination. Nor were either permitted even now to take their place there. Her parents, and Mr. Seymour himself, though little skilled in the intricacies of the human heart, were yet sufficiently aware of the sensibility that might secretly ferment in hers were she permitted to think; and in consequence of this persuasion, they, like practised jugglers, so dexterously shuffled the conjuring cards, that diamonds was the only suit presented to her eyes.

The acquiescence of Julia was all that had been expected by her parents or her lover. Yet the unswerving filial affection with which it was granted now betrayed poor Mrs. Cleveland, of whom it could not properly be said that her understanding was corrected, but simply that her modes of thinking were changed, into a warm panegyric upon the sweetness of temper, and retired habits, and *domestic* good qualities of her daughter. The subject was Julia, and therefore Mr. Seymour had the complaisance to listen to it. But he continued to amuse himself with his toothpick while she talked, and to examine at intervals the medallion which enriched a beautiful case that lay by him.

'I am mighty easy on all the particulars you speak of, my dear madam,' said he, when she had finished. 'My establishment, as you may suppose, will be upon a very extensive scale, and I mean to keep the best company. – Provided, therefore, that my wife be attentive and devoted to me, I shall readily dispense with *domestic* good qualities.' – Mr. Seymour did not recollect that the virtues are rarely solitary; and that he who insists only on the one amongst them which conduces to his own convenience, may thank his fortune rather than his prudence, if he do not miss them altogether. This reflection occurred, however, as little to the lady as to the gentleman. She felt shocked at a rusticity in her own ideas of which she had not till then been aware, and impatient to correct the impression it must have made.

'As to domestic good qualities, my dear sir,' she hastily exclaimed, 'nobody knows better than myself how very little value is to be set upon *them* in a certain sphere of life. But *autres temps, autres moeurs!* in our late confined way of living you have no idea how these trifles contribute to happiness.' Mr. Seymour did not think it necessary to answer, and the conversation fell to the ground, till Mrs. Cleveland, who had not yet recovered the alarm to her pride, made a desperate effort to renew it, upon a subject to which she believed herself perfectly competent.

'The gay world,' said she, smiling, 'will be quite a new scene to our Julia!' Mr. Seymour smiled also, and graciously inclined his head.

'I shall take care to give her my advice upon several essential points of conduct before she appears in it.'

'Don't you think you have been rather too long absent from town for that purpose?' replied Seymour, breaking from a very deep reverie. Poor Mrs. Cleveland was now quite thrown out; she could only stare. – '*Mode* is so variable,' continued Mr. Seymour, in the same indolent tune. 'Courage, however! We shall find some female friends to consult with; but the outset in these cases is every thing – every thing, my dear madam! and we must have her *dress* well, you know, at all events.' With a slight bow, he took his hat and strolled into the garden, leaving Mrs. Cleveland half angry, half ashamed; and so unjust to her future son-in-law as to suspect him of banter, when in fact all he uttered had been the fruit of decided opinion, and of his most serious cogitations.

Mr. Seymour, now satisfied as to the success of his wishes, thought it expedient to set out for London, in order to accelerate, by his personal influence, the splendid preparation for which he had already issued orders. He previously advanced to Mr. Cleveland a sum of money that considerably relieved his domestic embarrassments, and, under the sanction of future relationship, presented his lady with a bill that enabled her to make that figure in town which his own pride required. A splendid carriage, presented also by him, with the Cleveland arms painted upon it, quickly transported the fair bride elect to the scene of her future triumphs, and in less than six weeks from that time conveyed her to St. George's Church, where her mother, with much joy and all due solemnity, saw her bestowed for better and for worse upon Mr. Seymour's town and country houses, his rent-roll and equipages, with all the valuables or encumbrances thereunto belonging – the owner included.

Poor Julia in the interim remained bewildered and abashed. She was pleased to be admired, she desired to be beloved; she entertained a confused notion, indeed, that she should have liked her husband better had he been younger; but she felt that she did not hate him; and there were even some points in his character, independent of his very great merit, of which she never permitted herself to doubt, that excited her approbation. Minds of natural delicacy feel, without defining it, the charm of good-breeding. Mr. Seymour could be extremely well bred when he was in good humour; and Julia had acquired in the society of her father and mother, whose manners were still those of people of fashion, a taste for that polish which, as it appears to be the result of urbanity and sweetness of character, the unpractised heart readily conceives to be really such.

One circumstance, however, sullied the gaiety of those scenes which preceded the marriage of Julia. Neither her father nor her sister were in London to share them. She had promised the little Matilda mountains of trinkets, and fairy scenes of pleasure, when the indisposition of Mr. Cleveland, who was subject to an hereditary gout, put a stop to his own journey, and induced him to resolve on keeping his younger daughter at home for his companion and nurse. The parting was most sorrowful between the two sisters. Matilda was taken almost forcibly into the house, and Julia, 'like a rose-leaf wet with morning dew.' stepped slowly after her mother into the carriage. Among those who sincerely regretted the unlooked-for separation, the bridegroom himself was certainly not one, however complaisance might induce him to affirm the contrary. To say truth, the Honourable Edward Cleveland was, in his opinion, a very dull fellow: and though his name made a most desirable figure for a paragraph in the newspaper, his company was the last thing really wished for by his son-in-law; who even had it already in contemplation to dismiss the Honourable Mrs. Cleveland from his future establishment as soon as with any decency he could do so. An auxiliary he did not expect, however, saved him that trouble, by suddenly giving the gentleman an invitation to another world, and by summoning the lady to attend, not on his soul, but his body; for the soul had departed before she could arrive; and was indeed, except that it had been in the habit of setting the body upright upon two legs every day, as little to be missed as any soul that ever yet took a visible form in this nether sphere.

None, however, are so useless or so frivolous, that nature does not enlist some heart in their cause. Shame on such as take no pains to deserve her bounty! Tears of unfeigned affection were shed by the family over Mr. Cleveland's grave; and his son-in-law, in place of those which he found he could *not* shed, decorated it with a handsome marble and inscription. The widow and her youngest daughter now remained alone in the country, and in the country he intended they should remain.

'Oh, pray let us fetch my mother and sister,' cried Julia.

'My dearest angel,' said Mr. Seymour, willing any way to silence her, 'nothing could make me so happy as to oblige you, – but it really would not be decorous for your mother to be seen in town just at this crisis.' Julia sighed – lamented, – but she was too ignorant of life to decide upon propriety or impropriety. She wondered, however, that decorum and natural feeling should be so continually at variance. It was not indeed the first time that the delicate and timid Julia had wondered at this, though upon less solemn occasions. But her mother and her husband had never yet had more than one opinion: theirs had uniformly guided hers, nor did she in this instance suspect them of differing.

The death of Mr. Cleveland was nevertheless a terrible blot upon this brilliant era of Mr. Seymour's life. It seemed as though he had in very malice died at perhaps the only period when his son-in-law would have wished him to live a little longer. Seclusion and mourning were of necessity the portion of the lovely bride. Mr. Seymour, however, determined to shorten both as much as lay within his power; and here again his never-failing friend Fashion stepped in to assist him.

The grief of a young heart, in proportion as it is acute, is transient. Every possible allurement and temptation were displayed to dissipate Mrs. Seymour's nor was there a person or thing around that could perpetuate recollection. She sank, therefore, after a time, into quiet sorrow; and at length began to smile. The days of mourning had been limited by the impatient husband, and he already anticipated that on which he was to display his prize. 'There are secrets, however, in all families;' and before Julia was thrown into general society, Mr. Seymour deemed it advisable to give her some partial information with respect to a subject in which he was deeply interested.

'Have you any objection to driving on the Kensington road this morning, my dear?' said he, while putting her into an elegant new curricle. – 'I am going,' he added, as they passed through the park, 'to present a new acquaintance to you.'

'She will prove a pleasant one, I hope,' said Julia, smiling.

'The person of whom I speak is not a female.'

'Better still! I hope then that *he* will prove pleasant.'

'Time must determine that point: at present the gentleman is only twelve years of age, and – ' he hesitated for a moment – 'a distant relation of mine.' An embarrassment so marked conveyed some meaning, even to the unsuspecting Julia;; who would have otherwise passed on to the mere circumstance before her, without either comment or surmise.

'*How* distant?' returned she, somewhat archly.

'My dear Julia,' cried Mr. Seymour, 'I see your suspicious; but I give you my honour that they are ill founded. The lad is merely – ' they stopped at the moment at the gate of a large house, which announced itself to be an academy; and Mr. Seymour, giving the reins to his servant, inquired for Master Villars. Master Villars presently made his appearance.

'A very good countenance,' said Julia, in a whisper, – 'but he does not resemble you.'

'I swear to you, my angel—'

'Hush! no swearing, I entreat! It would be a dangerous example here, and if, by any terrible chance, I should discover that you were forsworn!—'

'I give you leave to treat me, in that case, accordingly.' Then, taking the boy by the hand, he presented him to her: telling him at the same moment that that lady was Mrs. Seymour.

'We shall improve our acquaintance,' said she, extending her hand very graciously towards him. 'You must be my eldest son.'

'I am a great deal too old,' said the boy, though not without embarrassment.

'Would you rather be my brother?'

'Yes, for then I would take care of you.'

'Very valiantly resolved at least, but I rather think my duty will come first in that way.' The boy blushed proudly, and Mr. Seymour closed the conversation.

'This young gentleman seems quite a hero in embryo,' said Julia, gaily, as after a suitable stay, they returned to the curricle. 'He did not seem half pleased at the offer of *my* protection. I believe that he thought you were jesting when you told him I was your wife.'

'He knows that I am not much accustomed to jest,' replied Mr. Seymour, with a little more asperity of tone than he had ever yet used in speaking to Julia.

'He looked so incredulous, that I am persuaded he took me for a school girl.'

'He was a senseless blockhead, then!' peevishly exclaimed her husband.

'His countenance in that case belies him, for I never saw one that pleased me better. And now,' she sweetly added, 'tell me frankly, dear Mr. Seymour, *how* nearly he is related to you; and believe that every degree of confidence which conduces to your happiness will always increase mine.' Seymour looked in her soft intelligent eyes as she spoke, and saw she was in earnest.

'Why, my love, will you persist in thinking that there is any thing more to tell? Charles Villars is an orphan: consanguinity, when it passes a certain point, is neither very easily understood nor explained; but he is, as I informed you, related to me. His patrimony is very small; and his friendless situation had thrown the care both of that and of his person into the hands of low people on whom he had no natural claims. I rescued him from them, and mean to give him the education of a gentleman; after which I shall send him to India.'

'Generous, kind-hearted creature! allow me to participate in your good works. Pray, bring Charles Villars often to see us.'

'By no means: it is not my wish to make him a fine gentleman, but merely to fit him for pushing his way in the world. I will very frankly acknowledge my reason for presenting him to you: I thought it probable you would hear that I occasionally looked in upon such a person, and I was unwilling to expose you to the risk of doubtful and disagreeable reports. Let us now change the subject.' Mr. Seymour cleared his countenance when he had finished his harangue; and, looking at the complacent one of his wife, he saw that she believed it implicitly.

A decent period had at length elapsed since the death of Mr. Cleveland; the days of mourning, therefore, closed, and the lovely Mrs. Seymour was brought out. But, alas! in the empire of ton there are many competitors; and some courageous enough to snatch that laurel which is not voluntarily presented to them. This was a species of courage in which Mrs. Seymour was totally deficient, and the success to her *début* was therefore not proportioned to the degree of expectation attending it. The disappointment was easily accounted for. However graceful her person and lovely her features, her address was still timid, and her manners somewhat reserved. She loved not crowded assemblies; she sought not adulation; she shrunk from gallantry; her eyes never canvassed the circle for applause; her husband's opinion long continued to influence her actions; and that husband might possibly, had he so pleased, have remained ever the happiest of men. But the felicity to which Mr. Seymour had aspired was by no means of this quiet and retired nature; and his mortification was proportioned to his hopes. He now, for the first time in his life, began to distrust his own taste and judgment, even in that point on which he had hitherto been most decided. Was it possible that he had deceived himself? Had he married a rustic, and fancied her a Venus? Where else were the eyes, the ears, the hearts of all his acquaintance? Truth was, they were just then pre-engaged – engaged by that strongest of all ties, their own vanity. Admiration, among the votaries of the gay world, is a traffic mutually understood; and no individual of the leaders of fashion continues to give what is not repaid. The fair stoic, therefore, who received the tribute without feeling its value, did not yet rank sufficiently high to secure it long.

Mrs. Seymour, however, careless and gay, was extremely well satisfied with herself, and with all around. She thought the world a very amusing place; nor was she at all indifferent to the desire of pleasing there, though too ignorant of the freemasonry of ton either to know or to care whether she were one of the initiated. A lurking sensibility, indeed, sometimes fluttered at her bosom, when men particularly gifted either by nature or education distinguished her with their applause; and not knowing, on those occasions, exactly how to silence the intruder, she had recourse to the remedies prescribed by her mother and her husband. She tried the expensive ornaments bestowed by the latter upon her beautiful arms and neck, and would not believe it possible that she could fail in attachment to a man so kind and so generous as the donor. She sat soberly down in her dressing-room to enumerate, and that with the utmost care and punctuality, his good qualities and his claims; and she finished the calculation with a firm resolution to love him with all her heart. Poor Julia was little aware of the enemy concealed in that heart. Nature, invincible nature, asserted her rights; and in the course of a few months, Mrs. Seymour had the mortification to discover, that though she had cultivated very successfully her attachment to all the splendid possessions of her husband, she could not, in spite of her utmost efforts, extend the fondness to himself. She was very seriously angry with her own perverse heart. No struggle, however, set it right. 'Wicked and ungrateful that I am!' sighed she to herself. 'But if I cannot love Mr. Seymour as I ought, I will carefully guard the secret, and will love nothing besides.' This appeared an excellent expedient. Arming her bosom, therefore, with triple steel, she deemed herself secure in her own impenetrability, and again sallied boldly into life. But sensibility, like every other gift of nature, may be too greatly repressed, as well as too greatly indulged; and the cold chills of the heart are always dangerous. They return its most wholesome impulses into the mental constitution, and the vanity that breaks out on the surface is often the least evil that follows.

And how did Mr. Seymour employ himself while these various shades of feeling and folly were passing over the mind of his fair companion? Mr. Seymour was by no means without his resources for pleasure. Although disappointed at finding that his wife did not dash at once into celebrity, he knew fortune to be a medium for attaining it much less fallacious than beauty; and on that he now rested his pretensions. Did taste introduce a new luxury, or vanity invent a new extravagance? Mr. Seymour piqued himself on being the first to display either. Profusion was the regular order of the day in his establishment, and the reputation of its being so his reward. All went now, therefore, according to his wishes, and the world was at his feet. His entertainments were talked of; his suppers were paragraphed; carriages were dashed to pieces in the attempt to approach his door; and crowds amused themselves with describing the elegance of his assemblies, that had never advanced further than the staircase. Seven years passed away in one uninterrupted triumph of fashion and gaiety; at the expiration of which time Mr. Seymour found himself to have been so eminently successful in all his undertakings as to have spent

The Canterbury Tales

every shilling of the fortune he brought with him from India, and to be under the necessity of dipping his landed estate, if he meant to pursue his usual modes of living. To this last measure he had only one objection; but that was sufficient – the title was defective.

When a man blunders upon an unlucky discovery with regard to himself or his affairs, he seldom makes only one. Mr. Seymour was soon too well convinced of this truth. He had toiled very hard for the last two years of his life to keep up the character of a *young* man; and it was amongst his vexations to perceive that the smallest discomposure of circumstances endangered that happy harmony of features on which he had rested his pretensions. Nor was this all: in spite of every exertion of his animal spirits, he frequently found himself asleep with his eyes open, at some of the gayest balls; and, what was still worse, as being more liable to observation, asleep with them shut, after the finest dinners. In short, age and economy stared him full in the face; and only one spectre besides could more have alarmed him.

During the interval that had elapsed since Mr. Seymour's marriage, he had had the misfortune to be twice disappointed of an heir. He could not with justice, nor even, as it happened, with injustice, arraign the discretion of Julia in either case; for he had himself been accessary to the dissipation that caused his loss. Both husband and wife, however, regretted it deeply, and each secretly resolved to be more guarded on any similar occasion; but no such occasion appeared likely to occur. Mrs. Cleveland, thus deprived of a pretext for coming to town, of which she had twice availed herself to make no inconsiderable stay there, was obliged to remain stationary with Matilda in the country. The gay visions that had danced before her imagination on the day when she bestowed her daughter on Mr. Seymour had faded almost immediately after. During the fortnight she first spent in his house she had had conviction that she never was welcome there; but Julia, fondly attached to her mother and sister, wrung from him by importunity an occasional exertion of complaisance which he was otherwise very little disposed to show. Matilda had reached fifteen when she last visited London, and from that time she was invited thither no more. The correspondence that continued on the part of Julia, though overflowing with kindness, was often dilatory; and a certain degree of reserve that marked her letters, as to all that related to passing events, was a source of secret disappointment to both of those who received them. Mrs. Cleveland loved the world for its own sake – Matilda for her sister's; but that sister had penetration enough to foresee that Matilda also might learn to love it too well, and sufficient experience of its dangers to fear that she should do so.

Time and circumstances that had performed such wonders for Mr. Seymour with regard to his fortune, had been no less propitious to his wishes in what respected his wife. Their irresistible influence, operating slowly on her character, had changed every thing in it but her heart. She had been led for seven years through the mazes of folly and fashion; had danced gaily on the verge of many a precipice; and, in the full bloom of four-and-twenty, was at length become all that he had once desired to see her: familiar with crowds; accustomed to homage; the model of fashion; and conscious, in all its extent, of the value of beauty, – not, indeed, of that beauty which is the grace of the virtues and the finish of the sex, but of that which delights to dazzle, to overwhelm, and is cherished as the substitute for every advantage besides.

'Where, Seymour, were you lucky enough to find that lovely creature?' was now the perpetual exclamation of half his acquaintance.

'Where I wish, with all my soul, I had been lucky enough to leave her,' was as constantly the internal reply of Mr. Seymour. – 'Psha! – she was Ned Cleveland's daughter.'

'What a syren! – hear how she sings!' Mrs. Seymour, however, could not sing; at least not scientifically. But she had now reached that pinnacle from whence her very deficiencies appeared to be perfections. Her knowledge of music was confined, but her ear was exquisitely true, and she had those low and melting notes in her voice which are always sure to reach the heart; perfectly informed how to add to them, by every grace of expression and every charm of feature, she delighted in this case, as in all others, to baffle sober judgment or critical skill. The women said it was detestable and out of all taste or time; the men thought it ecstatic: she secretly smiled at both – but she knew her power, used and abused it.

'Pray, Mr. Seymour,' said she one day, as by accident they found themselves for half and hour *tête-à-tête*, 'what is become of Charles Villars? – I am sure it is more than a century since you either saw or heard of him. Do you know that I think you treat that poor boy very ill?' –

'That boy is a man,' replied Mr. Seymour.

'Oh, frightful! A man! – By that rule I should be then an old woman. – Let me see! – one – two – three – four-and-twenty, as I live.'

'Time, madam,' returned the gentleman, not much charmed with the subject, 'is what we make it – some people will always be young in their conduct.'

'And some, dear Mr. Seymour, *would* be always young in their years. – But come – tell me what you have done for your son and heir?'

How should he be my heir, madam?' replied he, peevishly.

'Nay, that,' said she, smiling at the indirect acknowledgment of her first charge, 'the casuists must determine: I am sure that *I* hope he is not. But to ask the question more decorously then, what have you done for Charles Villars?'

'Obtained him an appointment. He sails with the first ships for India.'

'Heaven send him good fortune there! Be sure you tell him he has my maternal benediction, in case I should not see him before he leaves England.'

'Nonsense!' said Mr. Seymore, half subduing his features to a smile.

'I shall be afraid that it is such, if you look so well pleased with it.'

'And pray, madam, when did I ever fall out with good sense?'

'Fall *out* is a harsh phrase – but you must grant, my dear Mr. Seymour, that you do not much !ove to fall *in* with it – at least in the person of your wife. But come, do not be offended where no offence is meant;' and half rallying, half chiding, she restored him to apparent good-humour. This, however, was a sort of badinage a great deal more amusing to her than to him. He had naturally no great stock of liveliness, and years had not increased it. His answer was not always ready, and her sprightliness was, on these occasions, often resented as an impertinent pretension to wit, when it was in fact the mere result of youth and *gaieté de coeur*. It was not, however, always so innocent of intentional offence; and there were moments when, like Lady Townly, she could squeeze a little too much acid into the cup of matrimonial felicity: and this was the more provoking, because it showed off, at the same time, a thousand playful airs, which her beautiful person embellished, and in which Mr. Seymour could certainly not enter the lists as a competitor.

The last conversation, and all that related to it, had passed from the memory of Julia, when an accident revived it there. Her coachman was driving furiously home at a late hour to dinner, when, by turning too short at the corner nearest her own house, he dashed against another carriage. There was a heavy fog, and it was nearly dark: the shock was alarming, and the horses, which the man endeavoured to rein, beginning to plunge violently, left her in the utmost apprehension of what might ensue, when a gentleman who was passing and heard a shriek, forced open the carriage door with great risk to himself, and bore her out in his arms. She had just sense enough left to hear that her servants were around her, and on recovering, perceived that she was lying upon a sofa in her own house. The usual remedies had been successfully administered; and after listening to many lamentable exclamations and inquiries from her maid, she had at length recollection enough to ask if any one knew the gentleman that had assisted her.

'Oh, yes, madam,' replied the abigail, 'we all know him well enough; – it was Mr. Villars.'

'Mr. Villars!' said Julia: 'What Villars?'

'My master's Mr. Villars, madam. He had not left the house five minutes when the accident happened. Not finding Mr. Seymour at home, he told the porter he would call again. It was a mercy he passed by at that moment, for few people besides would have ventured to do what he did.'

'He is not gone away, I hope?'

'Not yet, Madam. He is waiting below stairs to know whether you are recovered.'

' Desire him by all means to come up, that I may thank him.' He presently entered; but she had no recollection of his person: it was full-grown and manly. Some traces, however, remained of the same character of countenance that had pleased her when she saw him before. He had an oval face, dark eyes, and features that harmonised in a manner which still struck her to be peculiarly engaging.

'Mr. Villars can hardly, I believe, recollect me,' said she, inclining graciously towards him, as he entered.

'Most distinctly, madam. It is not, I well know, the first time that you have done me *this* honour:' and he took the hand which she offered him. He then inquired, with some appearance of interest, whether she had suffered from the accident; and after a few minutes of very respectful attention, rose to take his leave. Manners so cold and so distant surprised, and a little offended her.'

'May I inquire,' said she 'whether you have any particular engagement – the dinner hour is very near.'

'It is for that reason I forbear to trespass on you longer – I am returning home.'

'Indeed I shall allow you no home in London but this house,' cried she, kindly; 'especially after so gallant a virescue as that you have lately performed.'

'Pardon me, madam – I had not Mr. Seymour's intation,' – and he looked surprised and embarrassed.

'Perhaps Mr. Seymour was afraid of his wife,' returned she, laughing. 'It is a very salutary fear, and I shall not therefore wholly discourage it. But I beg you for the future to understand that *I* order all these things. So put down your hat – you dine with us. We expect only gentlemen, and a servant shall in the evening receive any commands which you may think it necessary to send to your hotel.' She then rang the bell, and inquired whether Mr. Seymour was returned; and receiving an answer in the negative, gave orders that the housekeeper should prepare an apartment for Mr. Villars.

Villars found himself at once perplexed and gratified by this attention. He perceived that she supposed him to be just come to London; yet he had in fact been there nearly three weeks: but as Mr. Seymour had, on his arrival, given him to understand that a residence with them would not be agreeable to his wife, he had hired apartments at a considerable distance from that part of the town. Whether the apparent cordiality of her invitation proceeded from temporary good-humour, or might be relied upon, Mr. Villars was unable to determine; but whatever the cause, the effect was too pleasant, and she too engagingly peremptory, to admit of any denial from him.

Julia had on her side more delicate and decided motives of action than she suffered to appear. She thought herself indebted to her husband for the decorum which he had observed in not obtruding the young man upon her; since it was plain from the answer of her woman, 'my master's Mr. Villars,' as well as from other hints dropped by the former, that every servant in the family guessed the affinity in which he stood to Mr. Seymour. Independent of a partiality which Julia had early conceived for Villars, his present friendless situation, half protected, half disclaimed, on the point of being dismissed to another hemisphere, and thrown, during the interval, upon his own discretion and powers of entertainment in so gay and busy a scene as London, inspired a very kind interest in his favour. In addition to this, she found from her servants that he required some personal attention, as he had wrenched his arm very considerably in the effort of taking her out of the carriage, and the housekeeper had been bathing it before he could make his appearance above stairs.

'Your words seemed prophetic, Mr. Villars,' said she, 'when you promised to take care of me.'

'Did I ever promise to do so?' replied he, with great softness in his eyes and voice.

'Oh, a thousand years ago; when you and I first met.'

'I will hope, then,' he added, 'that the occasion is yet to come. As I did not know it was you whom I assisted, I shall not consider fortune as out of my debt.' – Mr. Seymour returned home extremely late, and hastened to his wife's dressing-room: he heard of the arrangement made for her guest with some surprise, and mused a little upon it.

'You have, perhaps, done more kindly than wisely,' said he, at length: 'but Villars shall not incommode you long.' He then withdrew to the dinner-table. Mrs. Seymour, though she had rallied her spirits, continued too much indisposed to appear there; but as she meant to confine herself at home for the evening, and was not much in the habit of courting solitude, she gave Mr. Villars an intimation that he would be admitted to take his coffee up stairs.

How dangerous to the peace of the young man were the hours, the days that succeeded! Mrs. Seymour, in all the graceful negligence of undress, soft – languid – interesting; – shutting out society, and resting only upon those resources which her own playful manners and naturally poignant understanding supplied, was ten thousand times more irresistible than if she had at once blazed upon him in all the splendour of beauty and fashion. He saw her indeed only for about two hours every evening, which was the time that Mr. Seymour usually passed between that of dining and of going abroad. She was not visible before, and she rarely stayed above a quarter of an hour after. This arrangement, however, was not the effect either of circumspection or prudence on her part. She did not entertain the least doubt that Charles Villars perfectly well knew himself to be the son of Mr. Seymour; for the character of the latter was not such as to induce her for a moment to suppose, that the invariable attention which he had hitherto paid to the education and interest of the young man could be attributed to generosity only. A sort of constraint that she observed in Mr. Seymour's manners and address, served strongly to confirm her opinion. He had not, in conversing with Villars, the easy and natural tone of a person who is conscious that he has conferred obligations, and shows exactly, even with ostentation, for such would doubtless have been been his method of showing it, the high ground on which he stands. He was like a man who constrained his own

The Canterbury Tales

heart, and veiled some powerful impulse there, which by turns induced kindness and distance between them. Mrs. Seymour knew that her husband much desired a legitimate son, and she hardly doubted but in that expectation he kept back from Villars the portion of fatherly fondness, which would perhaps, in any other circumstances, have been unduly lavished upon him. She had also great reason to hope that his wishes for an heir would not be disappointed.

Upon these two dangerous and intoxicating hours, the only ones now reckoned by Villars throughout the whole four-and-twenty, he nearly lived. Far from suspecting how transient this species of happiness was to prove, he was too new to life to be at all aware that Mrs. Seymour passed hers very differently. The elegant solitude of her magnificent house, the tranquillity, blended with taste, that distinguished every thing around her, and that graceful self-possession which is in fact only the result of elegant manners, but which seemed to him to mark the repose of the mind, all united to form an elysium, new alike to his senses and to his heart. It was the first time that Villars had ever known he *had* a heart. Removed, at a very early period of life, from every natural or habitual tie, without any companion but such as accident afforded him, or any relation but Mr. Seymour, his affections had undergone a secret blight. Nor was there one among them, gratitude excepted, that had ever been allowed an object or aim. Whatever therefore was the tenour of his natural character, his habitual one, was sedate, thoughtful, somewhat melancholy. He had indulged a passion for study, because to indulge any passion was delightful to him; but his very studies, although circumstances rendered him not deficient in the severer branches of knowledge, were of a nature to cherish the secret romance of an ardent character; and to bestow, on every object in which he could take the least interest, all the embellishments of imagination, and all the fire of sensibility. Such was Charles Villars; who now emerged from the house of a retired clergyman, in which he had passed the last four years of his life, and where nature and simplicity had been the sole objects around, to the brilliant habitation of Mr. Seymour.

The earth-shaking thunder that visited Mrs. Seymour's door every morning by way of civil inquiry after her health, was never heard by Villars. When he saw not her, he desired not to see any thing: and if business, either respecting his own affairs or those of Mr. Seymour, did not necessarily engage him, he passed his time in long and solitary walks, engrossed by that species of meditation which is of all

The Canterbury Tales

others most dangerous, because it has hardly any thing to do with the realities of life.

More than a week had passed in this delicious forgetfulness of the world, when Mrs. Seymour's brilliance and spirits returned. She stayed one evening much longer than usual in the drawing-room after Mr. Seymour had quitted it; and as Villars had a good deal of musical knowledge, she tried, accompanied by his flute, a number of passages that she was desirous to learn. They turned over the music books together, – laughed, – talked, – rallied, and passed the time so gaily, that Mrs. Seymour, looking at length upon her watch, rang, with some appearance of surprise and haste, for her maid. Mr. Villars very gravely wished her good night.

'Sober mortal that you are,' said she, laughing; 'is it possible that you are thinking of sleep? Well, – pleasant dreams attend you.' – Sleep was however very far from Villars at that moment. His mind was full of a thousand delightful emotions, which he did not even attempt to investigate; and he employed himself in trying twenty times the same musical passages they had run over together: then closing the books with disappointment, after a long reverie, he sat down, and attempted to read. Repose, far from seeming likely to befriend him, was every instant farther off; and a period of time, much more considerable than he was aware of, had elapsed, when, to his astonishment, he heard the voice of Mrs. Seymour on the stairs. She was carelessly running over one of the airs so lately learned, and as the door was thrown open by her maid, she entered the room before either could be aware that they should encounter the other.

'Heavens, Mr. Villars, exclaimed she, with great surprise, on seeing him, 'is it possible that you are still here! What on earth have you been doing all this time?' – Villars, dazzled by her appearance, had no voice or words to answer. Astonished, enchanted, he looked upon her as on 'some gay creature of the element,' and such as imagination only could present to any mortal eye. What her dress was he knew not: it was totally unlike all he had hitherto seen her wear, all, indeed, he had ever seen; light, elegant, gracefully disposed, and calculated to exhibit her in the perfection of her beauty.

'Are you asleep with your eyes open?' said she, at length, with a sort of smiling consciousness; 'or has my unexpected appearance locked up all your faculties in astonishment? Come – wake, I entreat, and tell me what you think I mean to represent – and she took her mask from the maid, who stood behind.

'An angel!' exclaimed Villars.

'Nay, do not be so ill-natured as to take my character out of my hands. It is one which suits me exactly: light, fickle, dangerous, and tolerably bewitching. What think you of *Flattery?*' And she held up a small mirror that was suspended by a wreath of roses from her waist.

'Armida, rather! said Villars, gently touching the mirror, to turn it towards her: 'the enchantress Armida!'

'With all my heart! Armida then let it be, and you my Rinaldo. But, unfortunately, you are neither a lover nor a coxcomb! – What can I possibly do with such a nondescript?'

'Make me – both, perhaps,' returned Villars; but not without some hesitation.

'Why, that is no bad project! A little of both would improve you, I think: but that sort of improvement devolves to other hands, or rather to other eyes, than mine: however, if I know any thing of your character, the day will come, – "the day decreed by fates" – and when it *does* come, remember Armida! – she was skilled, I believe in divination.' She then gaily bade him, a second time, good night, and, accepting his proffered hand, threw herself into the carriage that was in waiting. But, though absent, she left him not. Armida – the enchantress Armida, swam before his waking eyes, disturbed his slumbers, haunted him with a painful brightness, which he could not dismiss from his imagination. Mrs. Seymour had thrown wildfire around her, and knew not the mischief she was doing.

On the succeeding days Julia resumed her usual habits of life: he therefore saw her only at the dinner hour; and she vanished after that to some unknown, inaccessible earthly paradise, where *he* at least could neither trace nor follow her. Another, another, and another day still pursued the track of the former, and he learned too late, that every succeeding one would pass in the same manner; that to see her out of a crowd was a hopeless expectation; and that, though during the dinner hour she often smiled and addressed herself to him, there was not the remotest chance of any nearer communication between them.

The insupportable impatience, restlessness, and almost frantic regret, that now seized upon the mind of Villars, made it impossible that he should doubt longer as to the nature of his feelings. Honour, gratitude, principle, every thing rose in arms within his bosom to oppose the growing passion. 'What was Mrs. Seymour to him? What could she ever be? His wildest wishes, his most sanguine hopes, could hardly extend to the bare possibility of calling her his. She might, indeed, by the probable course of human events, be freed from those ties which now bound her to another; but how could *he* dare aspire to, much less hope to win her? Where was his consideration in life? Where the fortune, or even the merit, that should entitle him for an instant to indulge the expectation? In the interim, was she not the wife of the man on earth who had most obliged him? Was he not himself therefore bound by every thing sacred to an upright mind, to forbear attempting the alienation even of her affections? To extort from her one look of sympathy, one thought of tender partiality, would be to violate at once hospitality and honour.' Villars was too upright not to spurn the supposition. But the human mind is indeed strangely compounded. That idea which we reject with disdain in one shape, we embrace without remorse in another, and the severe, unqualified rule of right alone can steadily guide us.

'Can Mrs. Seymour be any thing to me,' he repeated to himself a thousand times a day. 'Yes, she may innocently continue to be the Armida of my imagination; the Laura to whom I consecrate my life; the realized image of a thousand visionary charmers, who have been described with visionary passion, while mine burns secretly and silently at my heart. This is an indulgence that can neither trespass on the most rigid honour, nor the most unsullied chastity.' Poor Villars, in fine, at nineteen, a lover and a poet, yielded to the chimerical idea that he might safely cherish a passion which should injure no one but himself.

Preparations meantime were daily making for his departure for India: an event to which he looked forward with a sort of calm desperation, that seemed to leave it to the moment to decide what his conduct would prove. The preparations were indeed so far advanced, that hardly any thing was wanting towards the completion of the business, but to secure the appointment; and Mr. Seymour, in the account he had given of this, when it was mentioned to his wife, had not been altogether correct. Large promises had indeed been made to him, and on these he had relied: but with his friends, as with friends in general, there was a wide distance between promise and performance; and so many obstacles had intervened to disappoint and chagrin him, that he began to suspect it would be impossible to secure his object, except by purchase. It was neither convenient nor agreeable to him, however, at that juncture to part with the money that would be requisite on such an occasion; and he, therefore, continued to hope for some favourable chance, long after the period when his knowledge of the world should have taught him that no such chance was likely to arise. What passed within the limit of his own house was the least employment of his thoughts. By that ill luck which too often attends the votaries of ton, he was become disqualified for enjoying his triumph at the very crisis when he had attained it. He began, therefore, to entertain a most decided enmity to fashion, in whatever shape she presented herself; and the state of his fortune made him secretly revolve a variety of new projects as to his future life, which in due season he intended to communicate to his wife. Till that period should arrive, be permitted her, though not without testifying sufficient symptoms of increasing peevishness on his own part, to run blindly on in the usual routine of extravagance and dissipation.

This dissipation, whatever might be its nature or extent, it now became the most ardent wish of Villars to partake. He found it impossible, as he believed at least, to live out of the sight of Mrs. Seymour, and as impossible to attain it except by mingling in her circle. Pride, delicacy, and a nameless fear that the true motive which influenced him would be suspected, for a considerable time chained up his tongue. But after long hovering around her with fruitless impatience and persevering attention, he at length found the opportunity of engaging hers; and with a reluctance that nothing but the temptation before him could have conquered, he ventured to describe the irksomeness of a life that was neither spent in business nor pleasure. A hint was sufficient for Julia; who in all that did not interfere with her own tastes and pursuits, was still delicately and anxiously alive to the power of obliging. She invited him at once to her box at the opera, and presented him with a ticket from among several which she had at command, for one of the most splendid assemblies in London. Mr. Villars was now enlisted in the gay world; but the gay world was secretly nothing to him: it was Julia, and Julia only, that his eyes followed, and his heart incessantly demanded. The romance of his character induced him to treasure up those words as indeed prophetic, which she had recalled to his memory: and that *he* would defend her, was the invariable dream of his imagination.

The evils against which Mrs. Seymour would require to be guarded, were not, however, such as Villars could avert; and he himself had soon too much opportunity of ascertaining this. The avidity with which he saw her plunge into crowds occasioned his wonder; the conduct she pursued there, excited even a less agreeable sensation. The presuming and the dissipated of either sex, if authorised by rank and fashion, approached her almost indiscriminately; and the courage with which when they trespassed beyond certain bounds, she either repressed or awed them, though necessary to her in discretion, yet took something from the charm of her character. 'It would have been so graceful to have shrunk from them altogether,' thought Villars. 'Why encounter men marked out by public censure, or private enormities? Why associate with women whose least fault is that they neglect every duty becoming their sex, and renounce every grace but that which externally belongs to it? Oh Julia, adorable Julia, can you voluntarily do this?'

The impression which Mrs. Seymour had made on his heart and his senses was not, however, to be superseded by succeeding events. As he took no interest in any thing that passed around him, except as it related to her, his attentions were soon noticed, and his person distinguished, by those whose jealousy was likely to be excited by either. The question of *who is he?* presently ran through various circles; and the report of the household soon made the conjecture respecting his affinity to Mr. Seymour be publicly whispered. An intimate of the latter, troubled either with more curiosity or more observation than the rest, resolved to satisfy himself and his acquaintance on the subject.

'Is the young fellow that lives with you, your son, Seymour?' said he.

'The world I hear has determined to proclaim him such,' replied Seymour, with an equivocal smile that spoke him not well pleased with the question. The point was now decided; Villars consequently sunk from the wonder of the day into the genteel insignificance of a half-acknowledged, half-disclaimed appendage to the family: and except that he was thought to make his bows with more or less grace in the different circles, and was more or less fortunate in opportunities of approaching Mrs. Seymour, his hours passed without being apparently marked in any calendar either of the pleasures or interests of life. But in his own bosom was lodged a source of ever-varying feelings, over which chagrin was but too often predominant. It was now among his frequent mortifications to be an auditor, and from propriety a silent one, of those indirect sarcasms which malice or ill nature delighted to level at Mrs. Seymour. Without being of force to justify resentment, they continually excited indignation; nor was it the least of his chagrins that her conduct too often seemed to sanction their utmost severity.

'You will drive me distracted, if you whisper again with that coxcomb,' said he, almost forcing his way to her one evening through a crowded assembly.

The Canterbury Tales

'You are distracted already, I think,' replied she, astonished at the abruptness and familiarity of his address. 'What can you mean?'

'It is impossible for me at this moment to tell you.'

'And it is impossible for me to wait another moment before I hear: so pray follow me directly.' And without the least attention to appearances she instantly broke through the crowd around, to pass a suite of apartments. – 'And now, she added, as they stood by the fire in an ante-room, 'tell me what it is that has thus disturbed you.' Villars remained for some moments in indignant silence, but perceiving that she still waited for him to speak, –

'Is he not,' said he at length, 'an intolerable coxcomb?'

'And are you to go distracted because I meet with a coxcomb? – My dear Mr. Villars, how have you contrived to keep your senses so long?'

'But this man is insolent – malignant.'

'Oh! now I begin to comprehend you! You have overheard him abuse me! I saw you stand near him between the doors; and had he been employed in observing you, instead of me, it is probable he might not have been very well pleased with some fierce looks you cast upon him. Well! – what did he say?'

'More than any one living shall dare repeat in my hearing.'

'Do not be too sure! – I am going to be that very daring mortal myself: and I believe I can give a tolerable guess at the crimes and misdemeanours alleged against me. You see I know the character of the gentleman, and I am afraid,' she added, laughing, 'I shall only prove that he knew the character of the lady. He asserted, perhaps, that I was vain – insolent – capricious! – that I trespassed against all rule and decorum. – Perhaps that I encouraged hopes!— Perhaps – more than encouraged them!' –

'*That* at least he ventured not to say.'

'Then he was very good-natured: for all the rest is, I am afraid, simple truth; and it is a rare thing when an angry man confines himself to that. – Nay, my dear Charles, do not look so like a knight of romance! – I *have* all these faults – ay, and ten thousand more! however, to console you for the mortification of having heard this coxcomb say, what perhaps fifty coxcombs besides are saying at this moment, I promise you to revenge my own cause. You shall see the very man in question follow me like my shadow, and obey implicitly the most absurd of my caprices.'

'Oh, for Heaven's sake, forbear so dangerous an experiment!'

The Canterbury Tales

'Dangerous to whom, pray?' – No answer. 'Mr. Villars,' she added, 'our acquaintance is, correctly speaking, of very late date; it may be proper at this period of it to hint to you, that I do not love advice – and never follow it.'

'Haughty – insolent beauty! thought Villars; and he continued almost motionless on the spot where she had left him, till her carriage was called. He then advanced hastily, with the hope of presenting his hand, but had the mortification to perceive that she had already given hers to the very man whom of all others he thought she ought to have avoided.

Mrs. Seymour was indeed very seriously offended: perhaps the more readily so, as her husband, by a transition neither uncommon nor unnatural, had lately passed, from sharing the pleasure of her celebrity, to jealousy of her conduct. Domestic dissension was, therefore, in danger of rising high between them; for the dissipation Mr. Seymour no longer chose to partake, he already began indirectly to control; as he did not, however, yet think it necessary to assign any reason for the change in his own modes of life, and as hers were only what they had been for several years past, she resented his interference with that tone of independence and indifference which her habits had taught her insensibly to contract. But though she could resent, she could neither forget nor silence his censures; and her home was therefore in danger of becoming hateful; delightful it had never been. The extreme disparity of years between herself and Mr. Seymour had disqualified the latter, in spite of her most anxious endeavours to the contrary, either to become an amiable or agreeable companion. It had been almost as little in her power to be such to him. Her personal charms were, indeed, such as no husband could see with indifference; but her ideas, during the first years of their marriage, had been girlish; she had read little, she had seen little: her acuteness of understanding was therefore troublesome to him, for it was not regulated either by judgment or experience; and her sprightliness fatiguing, for it was often ill-timed, and always ill suited to the measure of his abilities. What happiness, though she had proved herself the most domestic of human beings, could be hoped from such an union? Early tutored in folly as she had been, it now threatened to be productive of the utmost misery.

But although imperfection had thus imperceptibly tainted the mind of Mrs. Seymour, her heart, which had once been the precious home of the virtues, had neither discarded nor ceased to value them; and

The Canterbury Tales

it soon conquered the temporary resentment which influenced her conduct. When she threw the general herd of men to a distance, she was assured that she only returned them to another circle of society: but Villars had no circle – no place there – no existence, except such as her influence created, and she was yet ignorant that he desired not to have any other. Without exactly penetrating into his feelings, she had observation enough to perceive that he was silent, thoughtful, at intervals almost desponding: that though he did not absent himself from society, he addressed no one there; and she knew enough of the world to foresee, that if he continued to carry such an exterior into it, no one would long take the trouble of addressing him. She suspected his pride to be deeply wounded, and a delicacy in her own nature induced her to regret that she had probably added a mortification to that which his situation might, in numberless instances, expose him to. Her observations, however, were not confined merely to the manners or acceptation of Mr. Villars in society. There was something in the general tenour of his conduct, which struck her to be singular and mysterious. That she could be the object of any feeling in his bosom beyond that of gratitude, circumstanced as they were with respect to each other, had never occurred to her; nor did it now. She did not fail however to remark, that although he was to be seen in every place, he appeared to have no pleasure nor object of pursuit in any. Her own eyes, when she was in company, were too much engaged to admit of her making frequent observation upon his; but she saw enough to be convinced that they were incessantly and watchfully upon her; and a new idea, in consequence, presented itself to her imagination.

Mr. Seymour had for some time past withdrawn from the parties in which she mingled, yet he was peevish and inquisitive as to the persons she saw there. Could it be possible that, though absent himself, he had address enough to substitute Villars as a spy upon her actions? Her opinion of the justice, and even of the generosity, which she conceived to be blended in the character of the latter, could not shelter him from this surmise. She was assured that his ideas upon all points relative to honour and delicacy were romantically rigid; and therefore believed it by no means improbable that he was trying her conduct by some high-flown, speculative standard of perfection, which might dispose him to view it with eyes very little different from those of her husband. His own lips had informed her, unequivocally, that she stood arraigned for indiscretion and levity; and how easily might he, when thus prepossessed, be induced to believe that he did only

The Canterbury Tales

what propriety demanded, in becoming the guardian of Mr. Seymour's honour, and her reputation!

This idea certainly did not please her: but that which succeeded, did. It would be a whimsical project, she thought, to transform the spy into a traitor. It was one exactly suited to the sportiveness of her character, and to the habits of her life. At Mr. Villars's age, a smile, an ingratiating word, a kind and confidential glance, from a woman whose every glance was ambitiously coveted, would, she knew, he irresistible corruption: and why should she hesitate to practise so innocent an artifice? It was not concealment that she desired to obtain from him, for she had no secrets to conceal. It would therefore be mere badinage – *ruse contre ruse*; and she anticipated a whimsical sort of triumph in bewildering the judgment, and putting to flight the sober prudence, thus insidiously enlisted against her.

The plan once adopted, there was not the smallest difficulty to impede the execution: for she was really disposed to feel a partiality for Villars, and had only to indulge freely the natural bent of her own character, in order to let him understand how highly she thought of his. He was too anxious an observer not to read the very first look that announced him to be forgiven; and he felt that he should never repeat an offence, the consequence of which he would have averted at the sacrifice of his life. Nor was this all he felt. By degrees an uncertain and tumultuous pleasure began to agitate his heart, the nature of which he dared not attempt to ascertain. It could not be hope: he ventured not to desire that it should prove such. But it was irresistible, it was enchanting: it breathed into him a new life; it animated his character, it enlivened his faculties, made every place delightful, and inspired him with complaisance and indulgence for every person. Mr. Villars, in fine, now trod on ice: he had lost the vanguard of the virtues when he parted with prudence; and they are either a most sociable or a most cowardly band, for they generally steal off, one by one, when the foremost is dismissed from the service.

While Julia and Villars thus sported over the fairy ground of allurement and indiscretion, Mr. Seymour had been engrossed by a variety of contemplations. A more exact review of the state of his affairs had shown him, that he had been dangerously dilatory on some points of importance; and such was the constitution of his mind, that on those very points he was likely still to remain so. Turning his eyes, therefore, as men commonly do, from that which he was not disposed to view fairly, nor courageous enough to decide upon otherwise, he gave himself up to cogitations of a different kind. His Arcadian schemes were now perfect. Domestic ease, rural retirement, total seclusion from a world of which he persuaded himself that he was most philosophically weary; in a word, *otium cum dignitate*, was, to use his own definition of it, the plan of his future life. Impertinent people might have doubted its correctness; but it had been from the first his intention to take neither opinion nor advice; and he certainly showed more forbearance than is generally found in persons who have made that resolution, for he never asked any.

It was not, however, without a secret reluctance somewhat disgraceful to philosophy, that Mr. Seymour could finally resolve to give up that place in the world, which he had so dearly purchased, and so eagerly coveted. But our love of society is founded much less upon what we expect to find in it, than on that which we believe we shall carry there. Mr. Seymour could *not* carry the éclat he delighted in, and therefore he assured himself that he loved it no longer. It was precisely at this crisis of newly acquired stoicism, that all he had ever possessed was in danger of being demolished, by the expectation of an event which he had long most earnestly desired: he found that he was likely to have an heir. Pleasure, however, was not the only sensation by which his philosophy was now endangered: emotions of a very different nature had their share in his bosom. The homage paid to his wife had been a source of pain to him from the moment he had ceased to desire that she should receive it; and a restless suspicion, neither dignified enough for avowal, nor sufficiently timid to be totally disguised, had harrassed him for some months past. His mind was too gross to admit only a refined and limited jealousy, such as might have been excited by giddiness or indiscretion; and, without adverting to the real character of his wife, or scrutinizing her conduct, suspicions the most unjust and derogatory passed across his imagination. Yet the impression, though painful, was too little justified by circumstances to be other than temporary. Slander had not indeed spared Mrs. Seymour, who, on her part, had ventured to defy it with a carelessness, that almost amounted to levity: but that very carelessness was, in the eyes of dispassionate observers, an argument in her favour. The various tales which were circulated on the contrary side of the question, were all of them vague and incongruous, nor had they uniformly pointed to any individual of the circle she associated with.

But the triumphs of vanity are seldom to be indulged with impunity: hers too frequently imposed mortifications upon others, not to incur the penalty attending them; and among the credulous or the malicious, there were many who suspected her to be capable of error, though they ventured not to sully her fame with any decided calumny. In the former class Mr. Seymour himself was included. Yet the evil suggestions that clung in consequence round his heart, and blighted what had once been his most highly-cherished hopes, were such as he could only indulge in silence. The crisis was nevertheless, he believed, at hand, which must either confirm or remove his apprehensions. If Julia, without extreme reluctance, consented to leave London, and be domesticated with him, the conclusion would be obvious and fair, that she had no illicit attachments in it; if otherwise, observation, detection, and divorce presented themselves to his imagination in regular progress. Mr. Seymour, cold-blooded and worldly-minded, considered this mode of proceeding as due to himself; and contemplated without remorse the prospect of returning to obscurity, or marking with disgrace, a creature whose propensity to excellence he first had blighted, and whom he had purchased of herself, before she knew her own value: a value he, like many other husbands, had hitherto uniformly alloyed, by associating her with those whose follies degraded and whose vices might corrupt her.

The better angel of Julia – or rather, that which is the most angelic of all guards, a purity of character which might, under suitable circumstances, have rendered her happy, still interposed to prevent her rendering herself miserable. Lovely and admired as she was, the world could not fail to offer her attractions which needed not those of guilt to make her reluctant to quit it. Nor would it have been difficult for a mind of common generosity to have calculated and allowed for them. The fear of censure had, on this occasion, no share in deciding her conduct. She did not suspect the volcano that was ready to burst under her feet; nor dream for a moment that Mr. Seymour, however jealous of the gaiety of her manners, could seriously distrust her fidelity. Many a pang of vanity, and many a sigh of heart-withering indifference for her husband, agitated her bosom, therefore, as he explained the embarrassed state of his fortune, and the determination with which he meant to pursue his plans. The tone of Mr. Seymour's explanation was peremptory: for he knew his wife to be, on many occasions, of a character and manner so decided, that he had prepared himself to encounter her resistance, and was disposed both to calculate and prejudge its motives: nor was he aware of the different standard by which her conduct was at this crisis to be tried.

It was in fact neither the influence of temper nor habits that now acted on Mrs. Seymour, but one more delicate, and infinitely more estimable. She had indulged with secret and tender complacency, the hope of being a mother: of possessing a creature for whom she could live, and whom she would passionately love. The demands of her heart seemed likely to be gratified, and though she certainly did not wholly conquer those of her vanity, neither did they wholly conquer her. A few years later would, in the natural course of things, have found her a little more selfish and a little more vain; for the bowl that runs on a declivity will constantly have its motion accelerated; but at the period before her, it was possible to arrest its progress by the very circumstances in which nature had placed her, and its progress *was* arrested. With that grace and sweetness therefore which was among her early characteristics, she acceded without remonstrance to the determination announced by her husband.

This was a flight above Mr. Seymour's belief or comprehension. What! Julia – the vain – the giddy – the admired – the dissipated – consent at once to quit the circle in which she delighted! – Part, without hesitation, from all the pleasures of luxury, and all the triumphs of conquest, to seclude herself in the country, simply because it was his desire that she should do so! – For Mrs. Seymour, with a delicacy that always attended her conduct, when a favourite foible did not allure her to error, forbore to point out in its extent, the tender motive that most forcibly operated to effect her compliance. A black doubt, impossible to solve, struck at once upon the mind of her husband: too black and too remote to allow him to hint it: but which decided his conduct, while it was sedulously veiled both by his looks and his words. Gratified, as he professed himself to be, by her ready acquiescence in all that concerned the future, he expatiated upon it with an enthusiasm that was too artificial not to be by turns both dispiriting and ludicrous. Was it possible for Julia to forget that this husband, with whom 'her heart, her fortune, and her being were blend,' and all the delights of elegant retirement, and social leisure, was not in the least calculated to embellish either? Did no comparisons arise, no regrets embitter the sacrifices which situation imposed? Mrs. Seymour was a woman, not an angel; and she felt that, while discharging the first of all duties, they are most wretched and unwise who have not previously assured themselves that the heart will act as an assistant. Mr. Seymour plainly perceived that, in proportion as he continued to talk, his wife grew absent and melancholy.

'Let us now call another cause,' said he, 'and first, for that which of all our arrangements first demands our attention. It is time to think of dismissing Charles Villars.'

'Indeed!' returned Julia.

'Can you doubt it?' said Mr. Seymour, with quickness.

'I own I see no good motive, nor even pretext, for so doing. In what manner, therefore, can it be effected?'

'I, on the contrary, see both. And as to the manner – it is surely not more difficult to render a house disagreeable than agreeable, when the hostess is so disposed. Many reasons, however, may render *my* dismissing him a hardship, though prudence, under our present expectations and circumstances, may demand that he should go.' Julia's eyes filled with tears.

'Can I hope to be a mother,' said she, endeavouring to disperse them, as conscious that her sensibility was a tacit reproach to Mr. Seymour, 'and not feel for the situation of a young man to whose views that event is likely to prove so fatal?'

'What is it you mean?'

'That I am concerned to be the cause of ill fortune to Mr. Villars. Why then will you render me such? – Be assured that I am neither selfish nor ungenerous enough to wish that you should do so. On the contrary, you cannot oblige me more than by making some provision, or at least finding some situation, for him, suitable to his manners and talents, though not altogether to his birth.'

'It will be difficult to provide, madam, for one of whom you have made a fine gentleman.'

'Nature, dear Mr. Seymour, had spared either of us that trouble. I need not observe to you that she has been very liberal to Charles. – *You* surely will not quarrel with her for the kindness. And what is it that I have been able to do for him? merely to give him a temporary acceptation in society, which, I am sorry to say, my neglect would deprive him of to-morrow. If this has been an error, it has been a kind, I will venture to add, not an ungenerous one. But should it appear such to you, allow me at least to assist in repairing it.'

'In what way, madam?'

'On, twenty ways,' said she, gaily. 'Are you to learn the influence of a woman's smile or frown? only point out to me any professional line in which interest may serve Mr. Villars, and be assured that I love him too well to spare any solicitation in his favour.'

'You *love* him, madam!'

'Can that possibly offend you?'

'By no means. It is so natural that you should love and befriend an imputed son of mine!' and he fixed his eyes inquisitively upon her.

'I should be willing to befriend the son of any man, were he unfortunate; and yours in particular, whatever may be the prejudice that induces you to suppose the contrary. You *are* offended, I perceive; though *why*, I do not so easily comprehend. Pursue your own plans, therefore. Explain your own intentions to Mr. Villars. The art of rendering my house disagreeable to him is one which assuredly I do not mean to study. – Poor Charles!' – and, giving way to the impulse of her heart, she sighed deeply.

'He is in your eyes then extremely ill-treated, and very unfortunate, madam.'

'Is any being more unfortunate, sir, that one who is exposed to be humbled, though nor deserving of reproach? Who daily feels all the weight of obligation, without its being lightened bt the tie of reciprocal kindness? – Mr. Seymour,' she added, after a break, on feeling her eyes fill a second time with tears, 'we both seem disposed to be more irritable than the occasion can reasonably justify. You, I conclude, are decided: – so am I. – I gave Mr. Villars a voluntary asylum in this house, and my conduct had your sanction. Many motives of worldly prudence, and even if you please of decorum, were I much in the habit of considering either, might have prompted me to shut my door against him; but having once opened it, I am bound by ties that cannot be violated: nor shall any circumstances on earth ever induce me to affront or neglect him.'

'Take care of what you affirm, madam,' replied Mr. Seymour, with a wrath which he seemed unable longer to control. 'Many circumstances may induce you to curse – not only the hour that introduced him here, but that which brought him into the world.' He snatched up his hat, and before it was possible that she should answer, had quitted the room. Julia remained alone, lost in a fit of profound meditation. A vague and affecting similitude, that had struck her while speaking, between the feelings which she ascribed as incidental to the situation of Villars, and those which her own often unavoidably gave rise to, saddened and depressed her. Nor was this the whole subject of her reflections. Accustomed as she had been of late to paroxysms of ill humour in Mr. Seymour, she did not indeed attach all the importance to his words which they seemed to imply, but that something was veiled concerning the relationship between him and Charles Villars that pressed closely either on his honour or his conscience, hardly, she thought, admitted of doubt: and a remote, but very alarming one, had obtruded into her own mind, that urged her to a more particular investigation of the subject.

Bestowed as Julia had been at a very early age upon Mr. Seymour, she, of course, could know nothing of his previous connections or conduct. He had resided many years in India: her parents were as little informed as herself of the events that had taken place there, nor was it possible for either to guess at the nature of the tie that might bind him to the mother of Villars. Observation had made it very clear to her that he rather feared that loved the latter; yet in her eyes no being on earth was better calculated to be beloved. During the first period of his residence with them, Mr. Seymour's mind seemed often to stand rebuked in his presence, and to be sensible that it took a flight lower than that of the young man. This, however, was easily accounted for. Villars, when animated, was warm, energetic – sometimes eloquent: well-informed on most subjects, and capable of throwing over them that kind of light which a mind of vigour easily communicates when improved by education. Mr. Seymour possessed none of these advantages. He was indeed very far from ignorant, but his understanding was contracted and rendered trifling by a constant attention to the trifles of the world. His politics, his pleasures, his religion, the little portion of it he professed, took merely the tone of the day, and were affectedly discussed in the jargon peculiar to it. He had sunk all individuality of character, if indeed he ever possessed any, precisely after the same manner both in his mind and his person; and always said, looked, and wore, what ten thousand besides were saying, looking and wearing at the same moment: a sort of polygraphic copy of a man, that might be seen in some corner of almost every collection in London.

Constant association with Villars evidently contributed to wear off the impression with respect to the latter under which he had at first laboured: nor had this transition of sentiment any thing in it either new or peculiar. The comparing power that so forcibly points out the distinction which penetrating minds are capable of discerning between themselves and those that are highly gifted, is always a leveller with common understandings, whose blunted perceptions distinguish merely the coarser lines of the human character, in which each individual necessarily resembles the other: and long acquaintance therefore only enables such persons to make the ingenious discovery,

The Canterbury Tales

that they are much more like wise men than they had supposed themselves to be.

Mr. Seymour was exactly in this predicament. The advantages which Villars possessed over him, either of nature or education, insensibly lost their value and consequence in his eyes in proportion as he measured them with those which he displayed in his own person. From being silent and observing, he had insensibly passed therefore to contradiction and occasional arrogance; but he never permitted either to exceed a certain limit; and the temperance or forbearance of Villars – qualities very uncongenial to his natural character – proved him perfectly sensible of the respect due to that of the other, without ever allowing him to forget what he owned to his own.

Ingenuous, gentle, and upright, as the mind of Julia originally was, the surmises that had so lately presented themselves could hardly find a permanent footing it it. Her marriage she was well assured was valid, solemn; public even to notoriety; nor did it seem possible that Mr. Seymour could so have disgraced himself in the eye of the world, as to have produced her thus openly in it, while conscious of any similar engagement detrimental either to her or her children. She thought better of his heart, and certainly better of his head, than long to entertain the suspicion. Yet her natural gaiety was harassed and disturbed to a degree that made her impatient to enter upon some explanation with Villars himself: though such was the delicate nature of the subject, that she hardly knew how to introduce or to treat it. But she determined not to remain in uncertainty, whichever might be the party she should apply to for the purpose of removing it. Mr. Villars came in not long after.

Julia, in order to break from uneasy contemplations, had been writing to her mother. A sweet interest in the maternal subject of which she chiefly wrote, had harmonised her feelings, and restored the easy natural tone of her mind. She did not see him enter, however, without experiencing a painful degree of flutter; and though she continued to write, a fine glow, that denoted internal agitation, diffused itself insensibly over her cheek. Villars did not interrupt her, but leaned musing against the window.

'You are certainly in love, Charles,' said she, carelessly, and without looking at him. 'You have sighed twenty times, I believe, in ten minutes.' Villars hastily removed his eyes, which had been riveted upon her.

'*Out* of love much rather,' said he, – 'with life at least.'

The Canterbury Tales

'Nay, never quarrel with a beautiful picture because you have not yet discovered its best light. The world is a very pleasant place.'

'You have then found it so,' said he, advancing to lean over the back of the sofa on which she was sitting.

'I don't above half like your question. It is almost too serious, and touches a string which has just suffered a terrible jar. I will nevertheless speak to it fairly. Why – yes, then; I think I have found the world hitherto pleasant. *Only* pleasant, however; and it is in danger of becoming wofully otherwise. Do you know that we are going to make a most prodigious reformation in our domestic arrangements? Mr. Seymour and I are to keep sheep together for the rest of our lives. In sober sadness, and most sad I fear as well as sober will the experiment prove, I am to retire with him into the country.

'Oh, what exquisite felicity! exclaimed Villars, thrown wholly off his guard.

'Enchanting! – With a Corydon of sixty! My dear Villars, you have really some very extraordinary ideas! but I am not quite convinced that Mr. Seymour and I shall fill up to perfection this outline of pastoral felicity.'

'And what then induces you to resolve upon it?'

'Obedience!' – and she held up the hand on which was her wedding ring; by an impulse that seemed irresistible, Villars snatched and kissed it.

'You are more grateful, I see, than your father,' said she, laughing.

'My father!' repeated he, Julia blushed at her own inadvertency, yet raised her eyes with quickness, to observe its effect on his features. To her utter astonishment, she perceived that it took none; and an immediate conviction flashed across her mind, that, whatever was the secret attached to his birth, Villars himself was wholly ignorant of it. A strange confusion of ideas now at once assailed her.

'Sit down,' said she, after a momentary pause, and pointing to a chair at some distance. 'We must have a little conservation together.' Villars complied, but he did not take the chair. The evident embarrassment of her manner, an embarrassment for which it was impossible he should properly account, together with that soft and variable blush which perplexing circumstances had called into her cheek, created in him so strong an emotion of pleasure and surprise, as hardly left him power either to control or dissemble his feelings. All considerations that did not immediately relate to them, vanished from his imagination; all existing objects but herself from his eyes. Yet it was with the utmost difficulty that he understood what she said; the inadvertent expression she had used, passed wholly from his memory. It was her looks, her silence, that occupied him. The dangerous, intoxicating hope which he had so often sworn never to indulge, despite of himself engrossed his whole soul, and spoke in every glance. Could he dare to suppose it possible that his agitation communicated itself to her?

Julia was in fact disconcerted to a degree which the occasion seemed hardly to justify: but that Villars should not know nor conjecture himself to be the son of Mr. Seymour, presented so new and extraordinary a train of ideas to her mind, his conduct considered, as rendered it impossible for her to be immediately mistress of herself. She now felt, for the first time, that silence was embarrassing, and struggled to speak.

'Mr. Villars,' said she – and broke off abruptly. – Then resuming her usual familiar tone – 'My dear Charles,' she added, 'you and I are soon to part. Mr. Seymour has plans for you – '

'No, madam,' said Villars, starting from her with sudden recollection at the name of Mr. Seymour, yet as abruptly returning, – 'Mr. Seymour's plans are such as I cannot accede to. I have already been a dependant too long. But if my ingratitude be a crime, I am at this moment expiating it most painfully;' and he again withdrew to the further end of the room.

'I do not understand you.'

'You are probably not informed then of the proposal made to me this morning by Mr. Seymour. It is such as I cannot accept. I will be no man's pensioner, by whatever name besides the situation may be qualified. He has a project of sending me to India under patronage – *protection* he calls it! – where, – in I know not what character, – I am to render myself useful to I know not what persons. Let him add to the obligations he has already conferred that of giving me a commission: – to the East Indies – to the West – to any climate – any country – in any rank! – but let him give me the existence of a man, not of a slave, or allow me to find for myself that place in society to which my good or ill fortune may lead me.'

Vehemently and incoherently as Villars spoke, the tenour of his words at once explained to Julia all the meaning of the reproach which her husband had uttered, that she had made him a fine gentleman. What the situation might be that Mr. Seymour had proffered, she could not exactly understand; but it was evidently one which he considered as degrading; and which Mr. Seymour himself must have believed to be very far below the hopes and expectations he had contributed to raise, or he would not have forborne to mention it to her. Julia had now recovered her presence of mind. That earnest and impassioned attention on the part of Villars, which had, she hardly knew why, embarrassed and perplexed her, had been withdrawn by subsequent agitation of a different nature. He had quitted her side; he seemed lost in painful contemplations at a remote end of the apartment, and she had leisure to revolve the particulars on which she chiefly desired to converse with him.

'Surely, Mr. Villars, you are agitated very unnecessarily.' And again she blushed, at the recollection that twice in five minutes she had called him *Mr.* Villars. 'Whatever may be the obligations that Mr. Seymour has conferred on you, they ought neither to appear grievous nor humiliating: you can hardly doubt but that they are sanctioned either by friendship – or – nature.'

What friendship could possibly exist between a boy of five years old and Mr. Seymour?

'Hereditary kindness, perhaps. – Friendship for your parents.' –

'One of them I never knew: – nor did he.'

'But the other – you remember your mother.' –

'Not so. I remember my father indeed very distinctly.'

Again Julia looked up with astonishment. Villars was silent. He seemed thoughtful, restless, and willing to get rid of every recollection but of some secret and painful one that engrossed him. Now and then he raised his eyes to hers, but withdrew them again as quickly, with an air of apprehension and self-distrust.

'Come – tell me your history,' said she, forcing a smile; 'we have lived together like the hero and heroine of a romance, without knowing each other. You have no faithful squire to relieve you from the office, so pray undertake it yourself.'

'There is so little to tell!' – and he looked as if talking were irksome to him – 'The loss of my mother,' he at length added, perceiving that she persevered in expecting him to speak, 'I do not recollect. That of my father is still to my memory: I had been from my birth the object of his fondest affection, and all the heart I *then* had was his.' He sighed, and made another pause. 'I can hardly, even to this hour, recollect the farewell he took of me, I believe he was delirious at the time, without an emotion that would disgrace me in any eyes but yours.'

'Did he not then recommend you to the *guardianship* of Mr. Seymour?'

'They had little or no communication with each other, I believe. Mr. Seymour had been in Ireland some months before my father married, nor did he return from thence till after I was born: – he scarcely knew, therefore, that such a being as myself existed; – indeed, I doubt whether he knew it at all, till he was on the point of sailing for India.'

'Are you thought to resemble you father?'

'Judge!' and he drew a miniature from his bosom. There needed not further evidence than the features afforded. – In truth the perfect security entertained by Villars himself, in whom her questions seemed to awaken no other idea than that she meant to indulge a kind interest in his concerns, had already removed the force of her suspicious.

'One fact, at least, then, is ascertained,' exclaimed she, mentally: and her heart felt relieved from a strange weight of conjecture with respect to her own situation: in proportion as her apprehensions on that subject diminished, her esteem for her husband necessarily increased.

'You teach me,' said she, 'to think more highly of Mr. Seymour's conduct than I have ever yet done.'

'In all that respects Mr. Seymour's conduct towards me, this last proposal excepted, you cannot think too highly of him. Whatever were my father's professional abilities, he died at an age when he had but little to bequeath his son. I had no near relation: Mr. Seymour, with the most disinterested regard, rescued me, in childhood, from the hands of ignorance and vulgarity, and conferred the greatest of all obligations, that of cultivating my understanding, and of undertaking to point out my path in life. Kindness of manners is often the capricious offspring of temper and circumstances; and cannot perhaps be wholly commanded, either on the side of the obliger or the obliged; but the considerate prudence that bestows real benefits, is a virtue of the heart, and makes claims which none but a worthless one will forget. In whatever climate or country, therefore, I may hereafter be stationed, I shall carry with me such recollections—' He could not add a syllable further.

'Dear Charles!' – and, touched with that candour in his character which, amidst so many contending emotions, seemed irresistibly to assert itself, she extended her hand kindly towards him: he forbore to take it.

'We are absolutely making a tragedy of our conversation,' added she, smiling as she dried her eyes. 'Now ought I, as in duty bound, to tell you *my* history; but I believe it is as well left untold. Time and

The Canterbury Tales

chance, Villars, do strange things in this world: good, however, as well as bad: – *your* good is probably to come. Yet allow me to justify this last project of Mr. Seymour's in your eyes, by assuring you, that he is really at this juncture extremely harassed and perplexed by the situation of his own affairs. How we have contrived to spend so much money I cannot say, but he tells me that we have no more to spend. *I*, you know,' she added playfully, 'never cost him any thing! – The situation, therefore, he has offered you is, perhaps, rather the best within his power than within his will to secure. I will talk to him, however, further concerning it, and if it is really such as you ought not to fill rely upon me for some more agreeable project.'

The conversation then turned on lighter subjects; but Villars was still absent and distant. Julia's spirit, on the contrary, rose with most elastic gaiety. She was pleased with her husband: she was deeply interested for Villars. The world, viewed through the medium of her own disposition of mind, seemed all bright and delightful to her. She thought of nothing but of conferring obligation, of making happy, and of leading every one within her circle through a sportive labyrinth of pleasure and vivacity. Even her Arcadian scheme amused her; and had Mr. Seymour been present, she would have been very likely to have tried the experiment made upon Marmontel's Philosopher, and tied a riband, *couleur de rose*, round his neck.

Mr. Seymour, however, was far differently engaged. On leaving her, he had retired to an apartment on the ground-floor, which he called his study. A variety of gloomy suspicious perplexed and irritated him. The manner in which Villars had rejected his proposal of the morning convinced him that he had been too dilatory in pursuing his measures with a man who, by mingling in the world, had now insensibly acquired a knowledge of his own powers and ability of acting. It had been, from the first, Mr. Seymour's intention to remove Villars to some distance from England; but the circumstance that obtruded the latter into the house, had been wholly unforeseen, and his own irresolution had allowed him to remain there. Day had followed day, and month, month, without offering any situation for the young man, but such as it was necessary to purchase; and this, Mr. Seymour, who conceived it to be a measure always within his power to adopt, and whose liberality was of that kind that never extends to personal inconvenience, had delayed doing, even at the hazard of ill consequences to himself. The suspicions, mean time, that occupied his mind with regard to his wife, directed to the gay, the elegant, the fashionable men of the day, the only men who, according to his modes of thinking, were likely to prove dangerous, had never rested for a moment upon Villars. But he had persuaded himself that Julia would not accede to his plan of retirement, and her negative was to decide the truth of his surmises.

Considering her as a creature of habit and temper only, it was indeed little likely that she should comply: for in her habits and temper she frequently betrayed haughtiness, levity, and a proud confidence in herself, that would not patiently endure control. My. Seymour had not judgment enough to perceive, that under these defects she possessed a comprehensive understanding, as well as a generous heart; and that he had only to satisfy the one, and touch the other, in order to obtain the assent he demanded from her. Of this he made no calculation, and the sacrifice to his will therefore astonished him. Her subsequent tender expressions with regard to Villars, whose dismission it was his intention that she should appear to cause, fell like a thunderbolt upon his mind, with the united force of jealousy and conviction, and seemed at once to explain the enigma which he had before been unable to solve. He understood why the gay world was thus suddenly become indifferent to her; he perceived, according to his own judgment, a deep sense of past and future disgrace attached to him; and he a thousand times execrated the many entanglements which he too well saw he had created for himself, and which left him, on this occasion, no better resource than dissimulation.

While buried in ruminations of this nature, he heard a knock at the street door, which he knew to be that of Villars; who had dined abroad, or rather had, in fact, not dined at all, but had chosen, after the conversation of the morning, to avoid Mr. Seymour's table, in order that he might not betray the deep chagrin, as well as the hopeless suffering, that preyed upon his mind. Seymour heard him run up stairs, after inquiring who was in the drawing-room, with an alacrity that roused his own irritable passions to a degree that he could hardly control. It was because he could hardly control them, that he did not follow. It had been his intention to spend the evening abroad, but he now found it impossible to resolve on quitting his own house; and he therefore remained stationary, in a state of mind that grew every moment more gloomy. Several hours elapsed, yet neither Julia nor Villars quitted the drawing-room, or seemed to think of any thing but each other. The servants, however, passed and repassed as usual, without any appearance of mystery; and on the frequent

The Canterbury Tales

opening of the door, Mr. Seymour, at a late hour, caught the sound of the flute.

Had Julia's discretion taught her to stop at the point of kindness, obligation, and good humour in which she found herself after the explanation with Villars, all, as far as respected her conduct, had been well; but she was now unaccustomed to limit her influence by any steady and decided rule. To animate, to charm, to dazzle, was become habitual to her; she was nothing in her own eyes when she was not every thing: without foreseeing either the danger to herself, or the more obvious one to the heart of Villars, she gave way, therefore, to the impulse of the moment. Sprightly, elegant, bewitching, she insensibly departed from the character of the sweet and tender friend, the innocent-minded, yet dignified wife, and became once more the Armida, the captivating sorceress, that had almost overwhelmed his better reason. The mind of Villars, hitherto guarded by honour, and saddened by recent recollections, nevertheless took, imperceptibly, the colour of hers. How correct ought the conduct of woman to be, when the character of man becomes thus pliant under its influence! A few moments before, she had made him candid, generous, and capable of commanding himself! – In a very short period from that time, he was in danger of becoming an ingrate and a villain; while, without its being possible that she should not be ignorant of the state of his heart, she seemed to take a gay and thoughtless pleasure in asserting absolute sway there. After trifling till she could trifle no longer, she had, at length, recourse to music. The airs they had formerly tried, those they yet intended to decide upon, all were turned over; nothing was pursued, nothing engrossed them but each other; and Julia at length, to her infinite surprise, discovered that it was past one in the morning. She now inquired whether Mr. Seymour was come home, and found that he had not been abroad.

'He is sulky with both of us,' said she, turning to Villars, with the most indiscreet gaiety: 'but I shall talk him into good humour in the morning.' – So has said many a thoughtless wife, who never talked her husband into good humour again.

The next day Mrs. Seymour was to give an assembly, which was preceded by a splendid dinner; the domestic circle saw, therefore, little of each other. Mr. Villars was, indeed, almost the whole evening near her, but he had no opportunity of engrossing her attention; and, although she frequently spoke to him, their conversation was broken and trifling. Looks of familiarity, however, of which neither were conscious, passed between them, with respect to the persons and things around: Mr. Seymour lost none of these; and they sealed his opinion.

Villars did not appear at her breakfast table next morning, as it had been hitherto his custom to do; and, on inquiry, she learned that he had breakfasted by appointment with her husband, at an earlier hour than that at which she was visible, and had since gone abroad. Mr. Seymour came up stairs not long after: his air was extremely placid, and his salutation, if not very kind, at least very civil.

'You have carried off Villars this morning,' said she; 'I hope to a good purpose. What have you resolved to do for him?'

'Oblige him in his own way, since he will not be obliged in mine: – promised him a commission.'

'You are quite adorable! – Where is the regiment to be stationed?'

'At St. Domingo.'

'Gracious Heaven! Mr. Seymour, you would not premeditatedly send him to his grave? Do you not know that two thirds at least of the last detachment are buried there?'

'I may be permitted to doubt the fact. – Granting it to be true, there is more room in the world for the survivors.' Julia raised her eyes to heaven in speechless indignation.

'I understand the eloquence of your looks, madam. But Mr. Villars may, I presume, be allowed to decide for himself, and *he* makes no objection. He is heroic enough to profess not to value life.'

'Did he say so?' said Julia with emotion. Mr. Seymour made no answer.

'What rank is he to hold?' continued she after a pause. Seymour named it. She mused without replying for a few moments, and then directed the conversation to other subjects; affecting to run gaily over twenty different ones, many of which she knew to be unpleasant, and some very provoking to Mr. Seymour. Her carriage being then ready, she got into it, and drove out for the morning. The dinner was late, and only the family party sat down to table. Mr. Seymour was complacent, though not talkative; Villars looked ill and harassed; Julia alone was apparently herself, gay and entertaining. When the servants were withdrawn, she looked earnestly at Villars with a conscious half smile.

'Charles,' said she, 'I am going to put your discretion to a very nice test: you must decide between man and wife. Mr. Seymour offers you a commission at St. Domingo, where you may, most heroically, die of

403

the yellow fever. I have one secured for you in England, where you may live in inglorious safety: – speak for yourself.'

'I am little entitled to do so, madam,' replied Villars without hesitation, but with an emotion which he could not conquer. – 'Mr. Seymour must speak for me.'

'You are seldom, I conclude, in the habit of rejecting a lady's favours, sir,' said Mr. Seymour; but his countenance changed greatly as he spoke. Villars did not however look at him. He pressed his hand, with an air of suffering, upon his forehead, and leaned for a moment upon the table, as if taking counsel of his own heart, rather than like a person who either heard or noticed what was passing before him.

'The air of St. Domingo may perhaps do best for me,' said he, at length; and with a slight salutation to both, he arose and quitted the room. Julia felt indignant: she also felt a little embarrassed. Without previously weighing the impropriety or danger of the situation in which she placed Villars, she had depended upon his unqualified acceptance of any offer from her, and she had fixed her own determination to encounter the consequent resentment or ill humour of Mr. Seymour; both of which however, as the commission was to cost him nothing, she concluded would be temporary. Her courage nevertheless a little failed on finding herself thus suddenly alone with him. His looks denoted bitter wrath; to her great surprise however he uttered not a word, but coolly took out his pocket-book, and began to make various memorandums there with a pencil.

'Are you writing verses?' said she, striving to speak with unconcern.

'Not exactly that. I am making a calculation.'

'You choose your time and place well,' she replied, with a tone of raillery.

'Impossible to choose them better. When a man gets in with one friend, it is time he should release himself from his obligations to another. – Charles Villars is, I see, about two hundred pounds in my debt.'

'Which he can pay at a word,' said she, smiling.

'Which he will certainly pay before he accepts the situation you offer me, madam.'

'What is it you mean?'

'That it will be prudent in you to find some excuse for disappointing the gentleman of his commission, or that his first station will be in the house of a sheriff's officer.'

'It is not possible that you should be in earnest?'

'Most solemnly so.'

'And may I not tell him that the disapprobation—'

'No madam. You have *your* secrets, it appears – I have mine. It is your part not to send him to St. Domingo.'

'That I will never do,' said she, 'be the hazard what it may.'

'Not though it were that of your own reputation, and your child's legitimacy?'

'I don't understand you!' and 'a thousand innocent shames' passed over her countenance in a moment.

'You *look* as if you did not, madam,' replied he bitterly.

'Mr. Seymour,' she exclaimed, bursting into a passion of tears, 'tell me at once what it is you mean, what it is you suspect?'

'I do not *suspect*, madam; mine is conviction: but I warn you that I will no longer be a passive witness of my own disgrace.'

'Surely nothing less than madness can induce you to accuse me of an improper partiality for a man whom, till within these two days, I believed to be your son?'

'You have doubtless discovered the contrary *only* within the last two days.'

'Heaven is my witness, that I never even suspected it sooner!'

'Now, at least, then, you know it, madam; acquit yourself therefore in the opinion of the world, and, as far as may be, in that of your husband. Let it he *your* desire that he goes to St. Domingo.'

'No, sir! – I have said it – I will abide all perils rather. If acquiescence, indeed, will content you – afflicting as it will be to me under these provocations to acquiesce—'

'It will *not* content me, madam. I have now considered the matter, and find that it will be most discreet – most suitable – and, as *I believe*, most *conclusive*, that you should do again what you have undone. – Your persuasion, not my commands, must determine him to go.'

'Then he will never be determined.'

'You know the danger!'

'I despise it,' replied she, haughtily. 'You may be unjust enough, if you please, to attempt to disgrace your wife, and to shut up Mr. Villars in a prison; but I dare affirm that you will never induce either the one or the other to depart from what conscience and honour may dictate. Have *you* no sense of either, sir?'

'Madam!' said Mr. Seymour, and again his countenance changed greatly.

'And now for the alternative *I* shall offer. Either resolve to do justice to me, and act candidly by Villars – either receive my solemn asseverations of innocence, and restore to me that place in your esteem which my conduct has never forfeited, or expect me to seek another protector than yourself, and another place of refuge than your house! – decide.'

'I *have* decided, madam, and adhere to my first determination.'

Unable to control the excess of her emotion, and too proud to permit that he should witness it, she cast upon him a look of the most unqualified scorn, and rushed hastily out of the parlour into the drawing-room, where the first person she encountered was Villars, who had been walking about there from the moment he left them. On hearing a footstep, he had approached the door in order to make his own escape, and they were close to each other before either suspected it. Villars uttered an exclamation at sight of her, and extended his arms, for she tottered like a person who was fainting.

'Oh, Charles!' she exclaimed, as she fell into them.

'What has happened? – What is it has alarmed you?' cried he, eagerly.

'Nothing,' said she, 'nothing! – but I am going to quit the house this moment.'

'For what purpose? whither would you go?'

'Any where – so I may get rid of my husband and of myself!' and, without the least recollection or self-government, she wept upon his shoulder.

'Oh, let *me* be your protector – let *me* be your guide,' cried Villars, wholly softened and overcome. 'Is there a grief you can suffer that I would not hazard my life to avert? From the moment we first met I have lived only in you, and for you!' – and with the most impassioned urgency he repeated his solicitation.

The occasion now presented itself that was to decide the character of Mrs. Seymour's mind. Irritated on one side – softened on the other; with an inflamed spirit and a disappointed heart; perceiving, not merely in the language, but in the countenance of Villars, and in his broken tones, a passion strong enough to make him snap all those ties which seemed hitherto more precious to him than life itself, a wavering sensibility created by circumstances might, for an instant, have inclined the balance to the wrong side: but the mind of Julia, though warped, was unsullied, and in talking to Mr. Seymour of a refuge and a protection distinct from his, she had referred only to that home and that mother from whom he took her.

'Leave me, Mr. Villars,' said she, 'I entreat – nay, I command you to leave me.' Then, breaking away by a vigorous effort, 'Charles,' she added, turning to him with such self-possession as gave a sweet serenity to her countenance, 'I, like you, have forgotten what was due to prudence and to Mr. Seymour, – but the error has been only momentary. Neither you nor I are of a character to live self-accused, and therefore we must meet no more.' – The sound of a footstep on the stairs obliged them to separate immediately. It was only that of a servant. Villars quitted the house, and Julia retired to her own apartment.

Again Mr. Villars wandered silent, and half-distracted, solitary amidst multitudes, through numberless streets, revolving his past and his future conduct. He stood indeed self-accused: and too conscious that a similar temptation would again produce a similar fault. While engaged in this painful retrospection, time had insensibly passed away: and the recollection that, whatever were his feelings, it was impossible for him to break thus abruptly from every habit of social life, induced him reluctantly to turn his steps towards home. Having entered the house, he had neither resolution to inquire of the servants what part of the family was in the drawing-room, nor to satisfy himself on the subject in person, but passed into a parlour that was near the hall. He felt relieved, however, on perceiving that Mr. Seymour had quitted the adjoining one, which was the eating-room, and that consequently he should escape a meeting, which he found it impossible to encounter with any self-possession.

Here, a just, though painful, examination of his conduct, and of his obligations to Mr. Seymour, began at length to subdue the fever of the passions. Devoted as he was to Julia, it was impossible for him to disguise from himself that her behaviour had been indiscreet, and that his own had been dishonourable. He did not hope to retrieve the past, at least as far as respected the latter, if he attempted to see her again; – *not* to see her – all of life or man within him seemed to shrink from the effort. Yet, pass a few days, and the whole might be decided, as he was persuaded that he should find no difficulty in accelerating Mr. Seymour's measures for a voyage to St. Domingo; the only prospect to which his wishes now pointed. Death is always the desired refuge of hearts unpractised in sorrow, and yet ignorant how dearly they are to purchase, by a prolonged and well-sustained warfare, the privilege of dying as they ought.

The Canterbury Tales

Honour and reason having at length succeeded in restoring some degree of equanimity to the mind of Mr. Villars, considerations less important, but deeply interesting to his pride, now took their place in it. He knew that he inherited a very small patrimony, the management of which had been resigned into the hands of Mr. Seymour, by the persons to whom the charge of his health and safety, after the loss of his father, had, by accident rather than choice, developed. His father had died young, and somewhat suddenly, in a provincial town, where his views in life had stationed him, and very remote form the county in which he was born. He had had no opportunity to arrange his worldly concerns, or to do more than commit both them and his infant son to the care of the worthiest people within his circle. They had discharged the trust kindly, though ignorantly; but they willingly gave up both that and the orphan to a relation so opulent and so generous as they conceived Mr. Seymour to be. Villars greatly feared that the latter must have expended more than the income of his own very small fortune, in the education which he had allotted him. In this, however, he was mistaken. Mr. Seymour, although he loved ostentation, yet knew perfectly well the value of money, and except in the article of preparation for India, had spent very little more upon Villars than the latter was well entitled to claim. His arrangements had nevertheless been fortunate, as well as economical; for he had placed him in situations where it was possible for him to do much by his own exertion in the acquirement of knowledge; and the young man, having no other pursuit or use for life, had amply availed himself of his opportunities.

Whether Mr. Villars's calculations however were not just, with respect to Mr. Seymour's expenditure, he well knew that the principal of his little fortune had hitherto remained untouched: and, and small as it might prove, his pride, as well as the situation of his feelings in other respects induced him earnestly to desire that it might be applied to any present occasion, in order to obviate the necessity of plunging deeper in painful obligation. Yet how, without affixing upon himself the imputation of ingratitude, was he to demand any thing from the justice of a man to whose kindness he was so deeply indebted? He was lost in ruminations of this nature, when a servant opened the door, and told him that a person was in the hall, who, not finding Mr. Seymour at home, wished much to see him.

'He inquired,' added the man, 'for *Master Villars*, sir; but I suppose he can only mean you.' He had hardly finished his sentence, in the delivery of which he had some difficulty to command his visible muscles, when the inquirer, who had followed close upon him, made his appearance. Villars did not remember ever to have seen him before, neither indeed would the stranger easily have remembered that he had ever seen Villars. Nor was he a little surprised at finding the young gentleman whom he had inquired for as a boy, was a well-grown man; apparently older than his real years, and very capable, by his appearance, of imposing respect upon a much more important personage than his visitor seemed to be.

Many ejaculations, apologies, and testimonies of unpolished but sincere kindness, followed the ceremony of the stranger's entrance; from the general purport of whose address Villars learned that he was a tenant of Mr. Seymour's, who, having travelled, for the first time in his life, two hundred miles up to London, upon a law business, thought it necessary to pay his respects to his landlord before he quitted town. Why he should deem it necessary to pay his respects to *him* also, Villars did not so easily understand, nor was he in the humour to inquire. But that good-natured loquacity which is more frequently found in country manners than in those of the town, because, as the distinctions of rank are there more decided, and less liable to be confounded, it of course finds greater indulgence, did not allow him to remain long in ignorance, either upon that, or indeed any other point to which his visitor conceived himself competent to speak. He had now got the better of the impression of awe or surprise that attended his introduction, and began to be very diffuse upon the satisfaction he felt on hearing, after his arrival in town, a confused report of the residence of Villars with Mr. Seymour: a circumstance which, from some odd prepossession or other, he seemed to consider as an amazing advancement. From this subject he travelled back to the scenes and period of Villars's infancy, with a wild, motley sort of interest, which, while it proved him to be perfectly familiar with all he described, was compounded at once of the kind and the ludicrous.

Villars, who felt that a heart might be worthy and a head not barren, though the individual to whom they belonged wore a coarse appearance, made a greater effort over himself in his favour, than he would, at that crisis, have done for a much more important person; and strove to be civil and attentive. But the struggle was painful; and he saw, with chagrin, that a silence on his part, which he could with difficulty prevail upon himself to break, was in danger of looking extremely like pride, to his visiter. The latter, at length, took up his hat and stick, and seemed every moment on the point of departing. He had not yet, however, exhausted his stock of eloquence or curiosity, and the attention he bestowed upon the room in which they sat, seemed as if he was not a little inclined to take a survey of the rest of the mansion.

'A fine house, sir, – the squire lives away, I see, said he,' stopping once more to look around him, after having, to the great relief of his companion, advanced a few steps towards the door.

'Mr. Seymour has both power and will to do so,' replied Villars.

'A happy man, sir!'

'He has his cares, like other people, no doubt!'

'They must be of his own making then, I guess. What – perhaps he has no son?'

'Well! – the want don't break *your* heart, I suppose. But, pray, may I ask why he keeps you in his house?'

'What can you possibly mean by such a question?' returned Villars, with the greatest surprise.

'Only that he is very generous.'

'I don't understand you; you seem either drunk or impertinent.'

'No offence, – no offence.' exclaimed the other, still drawing a few steps nearer to the door. 'I meant no harm, and I see none. You need not be so close, sure! Most people will be of my mind, whether you are or no, that if the squire keeps the lawful heir in his house, like a gentleman, he does the handsome thing by him at last.'

'I am not heir to Mr. Seymour,' replied Villars, recovering his temper.

'Well, perhaps not: may be you're afore, may be after him. – I don't wish to talk of any secrets. – You may be both doing the prudent thing, for aught I know to the contrary. Law, to be sure, is but a ticklish business; and if the old gentleman means to give you your rights after his death, why, as he's pretty far advanced I suppose, the less said about it in the mean time the better.'

'You are under some mistake: I am but distantly related to Mr. Seymour,' said Villars, stepping forward, without further ceremony, to open the parlour door.

'Bless you, I am not talking of your relationship to *him*, but to the estate. I know well enough how near you are to each other. Your grandfather and his were both akin to our old squire as was: only his was *second* cousin, I take it, and yours was *first:* that's all the difference between you.' And he nodded significantly.

'Are you sure of what you say?' said Villars, with extreme surprise.

'Why not, as I may say, sartin sure in law; but I have heard so ever since you were a little strip of a boy, when the old family were in the manor-house, and your father and mother lived in our neighbourhood. To think what a power of children there was then to inherit the estate, and how they all died of! Nobody made any count of you, nor our present squire here, at that time: then your father went to settle in distant parts, I believe, and so we all lost sight of you.'

'Can you recollect any person that is likely to give me certain information on this subject?'

'Why, there's one Atkinson as used to manage affairs a pretty while ago. He and the steward did not seem to hit it much upon the occasion of the old squire's death: so now he lives a matter of sixty miles off us. Perhaps he'll tell all he knows when he's axed: perhaps more. 'Twas but t'other day that I passed his house, as I was coming up to town: so I thought it but neighbourly to look in upon him; and he was a saying – says he – "I wonder what in the world is become of young Master Villars!"'

'What is this person's employment? Is he a lawyer?'

'A bit of one.'

'Surely I recollect him.'

'Ten to one but you may: you knew him well enough before you were removed from our neighbourhood.'

'He comes confusedly across my memory like one seen in a dream,' said Villars to himself. 'It must have been as long ago as in my mother's lifetime. – An excellent fellow! – he has carried me on his back a thousand times! – Can you give me his address?'

'Can I give you what?'

'Give me a direction to this Atkinson?'

'Yes, yes, I can give you that easy enough! but have a care, sir, what you go about! Possession, they say, is eleven points of the law; and so, seeing that you have got no natural friends to stand up for you, and your pockets I suppose are not very well lined, I don't know that you can do better than continue to curry favour here.'

'I thank you both for you caution and your visit,' said Villars. 'Only give me Atkinson's direction, and trust to my own prudence for the rest.' The man complied, and took his leave with much rustic civility; assuring him that he should not forget to give young Mr. Villars's kind service to all friends in the country.

Villars was now less capable than before of deciding upon his conduct, or of seeing Julia; indeed, of seeing any one. If the intelligence which his visitor had communicated were true, there could be no doubt but his own right of relationship superseded Mr. Seymour's; even if incorrect, it was of force to create strong suspicion that he was himself the reversionary heir, if not immediate claimant, to the estate. In the disturbed situation of his mind, no eligible measure presented itself, but that of again quitting the house, with a resolution not to return till such an hour as should preclude his meeting with Mr. Seymour. He cast his eyes anxiously up to the windows of Julia's dressing-room a he passed: sighed, loitered, and, after a fruitless delay, at length slowly wandered on. Could he have known that that apartment, nay even the house, no longer contained her, how great would have been his alarm and astonishment! Yet so it was.

Mrs. Seymour, while contending with the stronger feelings of her mind, had not conquered the subordinate ones; nor had she discretion enough to recollect the necessity of conquering them. A chaste and delicate sense of what was due to her sex, and to the fundamental laws of religion and morality, was so much a part of her character as not to have been wholly expelled from it even by the trying circumstances in which she had placed herself: but habit had taught her a haughty indifference to appearances, and inspired a confidence in her own attractions that inclined her to believe she might do any thing with impunity that did not shock or offend her immediate sense of right. The resolution which she had announced to Mr. Seymour she therefore resolved to abide by. Her maid had a married sister, who kept a ready-furnished house in Lower Brook-street. Both the house and the person who owned it were of the first order of such as are to be hired; and Mrs. Seymour, on retiring to her own apartment, began instantly to make arrangements for removing thither. The house was not engaged, and by her command her maid caused it to be prepared: she also put together such trifles as were immediately necessary for her lady's accommodation, and for a residence of a few days: Julia, followed by her, then stepped into the carriage; and leaving a note upon her dressing-table, with directions that it should be given to Mr. Seymour whenever he inquired for her, was set down at the door of her new habitation within two hours from the period at which she had parted with her husband in the dining parlour. In this habitation she purposed to remain till the time that her mother and sister should arrive in town; and if the interference of the former did not bring Mr.

Seymour to such acknowledgments with regard to the injustice of his own suspicions, and consequent behaviour, as might satisfy both herself and her friends, she resolved to return to him no more.

Such, Julia persuaded herself, was her determined plan, and such her expectation. Yet the first was perhaps fluctuating, the second certainly so. However plausible the arguments which a temporary resentment dictated, she yet did not entertain any reasonable or permanent belief that Mr. Seymour would permit her thus to deprive him of what she well knew had been for many years the ornament of his house, and consequently the chief pride of his life in herself. She had indeed little reliance on his love; it was, unfortunately, because love had not been a bond of union between them, that all the present misery had arisen, and all the chance of the future had been incurred. Mr. Seymour, when he made his election in life, had not chosen a companion, a friend, in a word, a wife; one whom he could believe it possible should ever be disinterestedly attached to him: but a mere expensive bauble to decorate his house with, and outshine his acquaintance. He could make no such second purchase: and although Julia seldom considered her own fate, or his conduct, in this very bitter point of view, for bitterness was not a marking feature of her character, yet the irritated state of her feelings would not allow her now to overlook it. After having, as she supposed she should do, reduced Mr. Seymour to reason and temperance of conduct, it was her firm intention to make the best of their mutual lot: if it could not be happy, yet, if possible, to avoid rendering it miserable; and to console herself, by the sweets of maternal love, for all she had missed in life besides.

Decided and sanguine with regard to these various suppositions, she sat down to write to her mother and sister. The tenour of her letters to both, as far as respected herself, was uniformly the same; and the subjects on which she wrote too copious, as well as too interesting, not to engage her for a considerable time. Her letters were at length finished, and she had no longer any occupation but that of examining more coolly than before the occurrences of the day. Neither the examination, nor the sensations which, from the influence of trifling circumstances, took place in her mind, were favourable to tranquillity. When, for the first time, she looked leisurely around, and found herself solitary, comparatively unprotected, in a house not familiar to her, and, however convenient, yet very, very far inferior to that she was accustomed to inhabit; with no train of servants –

no chance of visiters or domestic circle to break the uniformity and silence of a long evening; when coach rolled after coach past her door, and knock followed knock at the doors of those around, yet Mr. Seymour appeared not, nor even sent to inquire concerning her, the tide of vanity, which but a few hours before had flowed so high, began rapidly to subside. In vain did she summon her reason to resist the force of local impressions: the solitude of the heart was not to be so soothed. She listened – she wept – she considered – in fine, she repented: but it was three o'clock in the morning, and her repentance availed not. She threw herself on the bed, much indisposed; and, striving to recall the resentment which had induced her conduct, as well as the hopes that encouraged her to pursue it, she looked with longing eyes for daylight, and at length, soon after it dawned, closed them in temporary but uneasy slumber.

Mr. Seymour, on parting with his wife, had quitted his house in a state of mind no less indignant than that in which he had left her. Secretly conscious of the dangerous predicament in which he stood with Villars, and harassed for some time past by the apprehension of such a discovery as during his own absence had in fact really occurred with respect to the claims of the latter to the estate, it had been his earnest wish to make her the instrument of driving the young man into the obscurity from which she had so unexpectedly rescued him; nor could he sufficiently regret that irresolution on his own part had prevented him, in the first instance, from interposing his authority to exclude him this house.

Mr. Seymour's situation was now indeed altogether critical. The embarrassed state of his affairs had induced him, before he went to India, to calculate every contingency that might affect his future fortune; and he saw that Villars, however remote the prospect then appeared, might one day materially interfere with it. By constituting himself guardian both to the person and property of the latter, he hoped to disqualify him for any struggle in his own favour, should unforseen chances inform him of his claim, – a claim at that time so little likely to be realized as to have had no place in the expectations of his father, and to be utterly unknown to the humble protectors of his infancy. Events had verified Mr. Seymour's calculations; but caution dictated to him still to continue the friend and apparent benefactor of the young man, that, attached by those ties, the latter might never be tempted to seek for either elsewhere. Nor was Mr. Seymour's heart so wholly tainted as to meditate crushing Villars to penury; for few men are completely villains at once – the speck becomes a gangrene only in proportion as we administer to the distemper. It was really his wish to provide for him in some station abroad, and he had brought him to London with that intention; nor, when there, did he treat him either unkindly or ungenerously, though to be liberal was not in his nature.

The first blow that defeated Mr. Seymour's plans was the accident that introduced Villars to his house. It brought his own professions of kindness towards him to a trial equally unexpected and dangerous; and when the unlooked-for proposal of rendering him an inmate there occurred, consciousness at once made him apprehend that the act of putting his negative upon so simple and natural a testimony of regard could hardly fail to excite disgust or awaken suspicion. He had therefore no alternative but to resolve on sending him quickly from England. Time, however, insensibly elapsed in unforeseen delays. The danger with which we are familiar loses it power over the imagination; and it operated less and less upon his, in proportion as he perceived that the error into which Julia as well as the whole of his family had fallen, with regard to the birth of the young man, was in the highest degree favourable to his own private views, by arresting all curiosity as to their object. It had therefore been his choice indirectly to countenance the opinion that Villars was his son, although he was too cautious to affirm what the inadvertent testimony of the latter might at once have confuted. He now saw, with the most bitter mortification, that he had, as he believed, been caught in his own snare; that while he had been looking abroad for evil, it had taken deep root within his very doors; and that, by a malice of fortune that made him at once ridiculous and miserable, the estate which it had cost him both his conscience and his honour to appropriate was in danger of being transmitted, under cover of his name, to the child of the very man from whom it had been fraudulently alienated.

Reflections if this kind engrossed Mr. Seymour's mind during his absence from home. He returned thither between ten and eleven o'clock; and had address enough to inform himself, without appearing to do so, that his wife was abroad. Retiring to his study, he there affected to be occupied in writing, and made no further inquiry concerning her. The project which, in a moment of resentment, she had announced as an alternative between them, had made no serious impression on his mind; and he did not entertain the smallest doubt that her habitual gaiety and volatility of character had easily induced her to fulfil some common engagement. When midnight approached he could, however, no longer resist the impulse of his curiosity; and, in a careless manner, he inquired where, and at what hour, Mrs. Seymour had ordered her carriage. The note she had left for him was then put into his hands. It was not because the servants were out of the secret of what had passed, that it had been hitherto kept back; but they were by no means clear whether their master suspected it or no, nor were they impatient to inform him. Her own woman being absent, they therefore abided by the letter of their lady's orders; and not, as she supposed they would do, by the spirit, which would naturally have induced them to give him the note as soon as he came in. Mr. Seymour on reading it, poured out a denunciation of the most alarming kind against his wife, and indeed against his whole household; nor had he recollection enough to avoid including Villars in his wrath. This, nevertheless, awakened not any suspicion in those around, except that the young man, involved in some domestic quarrel, had naturally sided with the wife, who, without relationship, was kind to him in preference to the husband, who, under contrary circumstances, was often much otherwise. Mr. Seymour concluded his burst of passion by ordering his doors to be closed for the night; and neither Mrs. Seymour nor Villars to be admitted, should either appear. Mrs. Seymour, indeed, her own note informed him, had chosen her residence in a house which he had seen, though he had never entered it; and Villars, he hardly doubted, was openly or indirectly her companion.

Mr. Villars's time was, however, far differently occupied. That more temperate frame of mind, to which reflection and circumstances had partly restored him, was perhaps confirmed less by the effect of either, than by a sort of sullen desperation with which he had prepared himself to acquit all he owed to Mr. Seymour, by leaving his native country, and the only object that he believed would be dear to him in any. The singular discovery which had recently presented itself threw, indeed, a new light over his situation, but it did not remove an almost insupportable weight from his heart; neither, after cool consideration, had he much reliance upon intelligence so vague, and founded only on the report of persons whose recollections were in all probability extremely incorrect. The story, nevertheless, bore some semblance of truth; and, if true, accounted for various instances of forbearance and generosity in Mr. Seymour's conduct that were not very consonant with his general character. Villars had therefore retired to a neighbouring coffeehouse, from whence he wrote to Atkinson.

The clock struck one, when, in pusuance of his wish of not being seen, he knocked at Mr. Seymour's door. The servants admitted him instantly, notwithstanding their master's prohibition; which, in fact, they considered in no other light than as the consequence of a temporary displeasure. That Villars could be an object of *jealousy* to Mr. Seymour, was of all circumstances least likely to occur either to them or to him; for as the suspicious conceived by the latter had, without passing though any graduation, at once reached their climax, they had not previously occasioned those inequalities in his conduct which might have led common observers to penetrate its motives. During the last three days he had been indeed unusually irritable and morose; but he had not rendered himself remarkable by departing from the habits of external civility; and Villars, least of any person, could surmise that he excited the resentment of a man who, while his own affairs were confessedly deranged, yet occupied himself in his service. It was, indeed, among the severest reproaches inflicted on Villars by his own mind to believe that Mr. Seymour relied implicitly upon him with respect to his wife; but of Mr. Seymour he now thought no longer. The intelligence he received from the servants concerning Julia awakened again all those heart-tearing emotions which he had lately, by so much effort, subdued. Uncertain what he ought to hope from a measure thus dangerous and precipitate on her part, he returned to the coffee-house which he had so lately quitted; where, without wasting a thought on any other subject, he passed the remainder of the night in a conflict of the passions that admitted not of any repose.

Weak as Villars was, however, in the presence of Mrs. Seymour, the more honourable part of his character was neither wholly extinguished nor dormant. The romantic wish which he had so long indulged he now perceived the folly and impossibility of gratifying. To have sheltered her in his arms, in his hearts, – to have guarded her happiness or her reputation, at the hazard of his life, would have been a felicity most precious of him; but to become a seducer, – to alienate her from the husband whose rights in that character, and possibly in every other, he was particularly bound to respect, – and to degrade her from the rank in society she had long been accustomed to embellish, – was a villany of which he was not capable. The man who is weak is, however, always in danger of becoming a villain; and Mr. Villars, by indulging a passion calculated to enfeeble his understanding and corrupt his heart, now nearly touched that point which the high tone of romantic refinement had once induced him to believe it impossible he should even approach.

As early as decency would permit the next morning he presented himself at Mrs. Seymour's door. But his most urgent solicitations obtained him no admittance there. Julia had now learned to view her conduct with respect to him in a far different light from that in which it had hitherto appeared. She too had had leisure to weigh all he owned both to Mr. Seymour and to his own honour: nor was it the least of her afflictions to have trifled with that, as well as with his peace of mind; nay, in some degree endangered his safety: that she had ruined his fortune, believing as she firmly did, that it depended upon Mr. Seymour, she could hardly doubt. Yet, though cruelly alive to all these reflections such was the nature of her own situation that she could neither sooth nor confide in him. Neither see him, nor write a single line of explanation. An imperious prudence that could no longer be defied, absolutely forbade all intercourse, or even explanation, till the arrival of her mother; and on her maternal interference she now rested, as on a certain resource, should no intervening circumstance render it unnecessary: yet that intervening circumstances would render it so, she hardly doubted. A short repose, and that renovation of spirits which morning produces, had again invigorated her hopes and her resentment. Many long hours were now before her. Mr. Seymour would have had leisure to weigh the injustice of his suspicions, nor could it be possible she believed that he should permit the day to pass without some effort on his part, either of kindness or resentment. It is not often that minds themselves suffering under irritation are aware how little leisure the same sensation leaves in the mind of others either for action or for thought. The long day *did* pass: Mr. Seymour neither came nor sent; and his wife experienced the heart-sickening pain of hope deferred.

The day that proved so tedious to her was spent by the two persons who chiefly engaged her recollection in a manner wholly new and unexpected by either. Repugnant as it was to the feelings of Mr. Villars again to enter a house of which she was no longer the inhabitant, he knew no adequate cause to assign for abruptly dismissing himself from that of Mr. Seymour. The occurrence of the night before demanded to be allowed for, in a husband whose agitated state of mind might reasonably palliate a temporary unkindness; and if not wholly excusable, it was at least far from being of force to cancel the recollection of past hospitality. Yet to Villars, Mr. Seymour, however little external circumstances might have varied, was no longer the same person he had hitherto appeared. He was a husband whose rights he had attempted to invade, a benefactor whose protection he had repaid with ingratitude, an associate, under whose very roof he was to dissemble; and to carry on a secret intercourse that tended eventually to deprive him both of honour and of fortune. Such were his claims and his character considered in one point of view. In the other he was a treacherous and insidious enemy, who, while he pretended to confer obligation, had been basely violating every tie of equity and feeling. Whether he was the injured or the injurer, the friend or the oppressor, it was equally adverse to the feelings of Villars to hold much further intercourse with him. Meet however they must. Since to insinuate motives for withdrawing, not authorised by any reasonable evidence, would have been an unjustifiable insult: to withdraw without assigning any motive was scarce possible; yet to preserve in thus meeting, that middle line of conduct which gratitude, delicacy, and prudence united to prescribe, was of all measures most difficult to a young man of the character and feelings of the one in question.

Nothing could be less expected by Mr. Seymour than the appearance of the person on earth whom he believed he had most reason to hate and to fear. A conjecture so degrading to Villars passed across his mind at sight of him, as the latter would ill have endured, had it been possible for him to have surmised it, and which none but a worldly one could have entertained. In fact Mr. Seymour hardly doubted but that he came prepared with some plausible tale, invented by Julia and himself, to induce a reconciliation that might extricate both from the difficulties into which her indiscretion had plunged them. Neither the countenance of Villars, nor his character, announced any thing, however, to support such a suggestion, It was possible, then, that he had himself extended his suspicions too far: and though the mind of Mr. Seymour was not acutely sensible either to the feelings of tenderness or pride, an emotion of pleasure to which he had for some days been a stranger found place in it at this supposition. The circumstances on which he and his wife had finally differed now recurred more dispassionately to his imagination. He recollected that Villars, from whatever motive, either of honour or caution, had not rejected the commission which *he* had proffered him; though, with a sort of equivocal conduct, he had waved all discussion of the subject by abruptly leaving the room. Upon his behaviour therefore on the present occasion, and more particularly upon his acceptance or rejection of the appointment at St. Domingo, seemed to rest the evidence that was to ascertain his views. Mr. Seymour had many reasons for temporising with the young man, and none, except those of ungovernable jealousy, for driving him to extremities; he therefore strove to throw something like cordiality into his manner, and, without reverting to any circumstance of his domestic history, affected to talk of the regiment in which he meant to place Villars, and to make, in a negligent manner, such a report of it, as should oblige the other to announce his determination. But Villars was no longer to be duped. He saw mystery and distrust in Mr. Seymour, though he wholly mistook the object at which they pointed; and he began to suspect that the concealment with regard to Atkinson, which he had imposed upon himself, was already defeated by some previous discovery. Even if that were not the case, he could not but think it a marking confirmation of some sinister design, that, of all countries, St. Domingo should be chosen for his station, and, of all junctures. Mr. Seymour should have fixed upon one when his own mind must necessarily be distracted with a variety of cares, to interest himself warmly in the hopes or the fortune of another. Occupied as both parties were by reflections thus mutually disadvantageous, the conversation could not fail to be cold and languishing: yet neither had the smallest suspicion of the real subject of distrust by which the other was engrossed. Villars, after a conflict of prudence and candour, suffered the former to prevail, and contented himself with declaring that he must decline the appointment tendered him by Mr. Seymour, as it was not his wish at *that juncture* to quit England.

'It is enough, sir,; replied Seymour, rising indignantly, after having anticipated a decision that thus confirmed his worst fears with respect to his wife. 'Spare yourself,' he added, 'the meanness of further duplicity. 'I am perfectly acquainted with the cause of your determination, and know how to draw my conclusions.'

'Draw your conclusions at least, sir, from what passes in your own bosom,' said Villars with some surprise, and no little resentment at the tone in which he was addressed. '*That* indeed may lead you to suspect, – or, perhaps,' he added, no longer doubting that Mr. Seymour was apprised of the vister who had been admitted the night before, and whose loquacity might have extended to the household, – 'perhaps your servants have given you ample information?'

'I have taken effectual measures to be informed of every thing that has passed under my roof, however clandestinely carried on.'

420

'Spare them then in future; and receive your intelligence from him who best can give it. The worldly prudence that enjoins my silence I am little practised in; but the dictates of honour are the same in all bosoms. I will, therefore, be explicit. – The information I last night, received, sir, has induced me to write to Atkinson. – This is at present the whole of my *clandestine* correspondence.'

'*Write to Atkinson!*' said Mr. Seymour, changing colour, and faltering at a reply so widely remote from the suspicions that occupied him. 'And what can Atkinson possibly have to say in the business between us?'

'That I am to learn. Mr. Seymour, you and I, as far as discretion is concerned, are far from meeting on equal terms. But as we may seldom meet again, I have no intention to conceal, in the present explanation, any part of my conduct. I wrote to Atkinson, because I believed no man could so well inform me who was the legal claimant to an estate, as one who so long had the management of it.'

And now Mr. Seymour changed colour, indeed! that Villars should be apprised of his own rights in life; should have taken measures to ascertain them; should decline leaving England for no other motive but to investigate their truth; were events at once so new and unexpected as to subdue all caution, and defy all dissimulation. Nor, indeed, was Villars much less surprised, to perceive that he had, himself, first unfolded that mystery to Mr. Seymour, which a pre-occupied imagination induced him to suppose that the latter reproached him for concealing. Yet concealment of some sort had certainly been alluded to. Villars, collecting his thoughts, was no longer at a loss to guess its nature; and he felt that Mr. Seymour's reproaches were not the only ones he had to contend with. Rising, therefore, with an expression of countenance more respectful and self-governed than resentful, –

'If, by a private application to Atkinson, I have shocked either your feelings or your pride, sir,' said he, 'recollect the peculiar circumstances in which I acted, and believe my assertion, when I solemnly declare that my respect for both, rather than any personal consideration, induced a concealment of the measure. You cannot but acknowledge that it is due to myself to ascertain the question of my own rights in life. – Be assured, on the word of a man of honour, that yours, whatever their nature or extent,' and a conscious glow covered his cheeks as he spoke, 'shall never be either contested or violated by me.'

'You dare then to suspect me of fraudulent possession?' exclaimed Seymour in great wrath; totally forgetting, in this coarse expression of jealousy for his fortune, that which he had before entertained of his wife; and as utterly insensible to the humiliation which Villars had imposed upon himself in his indirect concession.

'It is difficult to determine what a man *dare* do! – I have no answer sir, for a question so put,' replied Villars.

'Presuming and ungrateful! I suppose you know that you are in my power, sir.'

'A bad argument to dissuade me from getting out of it. – Mr. Seymour, one of us will owe the other a great reparation. It *may* be *my* part to offer it. You have *possibly* been a generous friend – be a generous enemy, therefore and spare me, for the present, an altercation extremely trying to my feelings. Allow me to thank you for your hospitality, for your protection, for all the benefits by which I have hitherto conceived myself bound to you, and to profess that whatever may be the event of my present inquiry, I neither desire, nor will receive, any future ones. Whether my acknowledgments for the past are a debt or a reproach, time will decide; in the interim I leave the question to be settled within your own bosom: – I must apply to some less partial casuist:' – he bowed and took his leave.

Dinner was announced to Mr. Seymour soon after the departure of Villars, but his conference with the latter had entirely spoiled his appetite, and it was removed almost untouched, – an accident that rarely happened. In truth, the whole circle of St. James's hardly perhaps afforded a personage more truly disconsolate than he at that moment discovered himself to be. His former suspicions had returned with additional force and acuteness in proportion as he began to believe that the plot against him lay deeper than he had hitherto supposed. He was convinced that he had lost his wife: he entertained very well founded apprehensions of losing his estate; and he already, in imagination, saw his town-house, with all its elegant embellishments, under the hammer of the auctioneer. After a very disagreeable contemplation of some hours upon these various particulars, he ordered his housekeeper to send him a basin of water-gruel, and retired to his apartment; where, while laying aside his Brutus wig, in order to tuck on his night-cap, he did not indeed make precisely the same reflection with the disappointed and celebrated hero whose name is thus abused, 'that virtue was a shadow;' but he so far resembled him, as to suspect that the great object of his own life would turn out to be nothing better: in other words, that fashionable celebrity would prove at sixty a very inadequate substitute for a good name, a good conscience, – or even for a moderately good wife.

Nor were the reflections of Villars more satisfactory. He had not been able, throughout his conference with Mr. Seymour, to feel the proud consciousness of an unsullied mind, nor to utter, with an unfettered tongue, the expressions of manly indignation, since sensible that he had himself resisted temptation very little better than Seymour had done: nor when he considered their different periods of life, did he stand much higher in his own good opinion, because to him the temptation had been of a different nature. The mental degradation this recollection brought with it was of all evils that which Villars was calculated to feel with most poignancy. The experience of a very few months had, indeed, as is often the case, rendered him both wise and miserable. It had proved, what all the moralists he had read never so feelingly convinced him of, that the man who qualifies with any passion which it is vicious to indulge will eventually be disposed to run the hazard of every ill consequence that may result from it.

Mr. Seymour, the next day, persuaded himself that he was desperately ill. He shut his doors, sent for his apothecary, and passed the interval between the morning and evening visit of this gentleman in considering what counsel he should advise with, most ingenuity and least conscience, successfully to litigate a bad cause.

But while Mr. Seymour was thus indulging the maladies of a distempered imagination, rather than frame, his lovely, though indiscreet wife, was suffering real and severe indisposition. From the hour that she left her husband's house she had hardly tasted food, in spite of every effort she made to attempt doing so. Sleep had utterly deserted her. Unable longer to support the inaction to which she had condemned her own heart, on the evening of the third day she wrote to him. Had her letter been received at an earlier period, it might possibly have produced the effects she expected from it: but Mr. Seymour was now thinking of his own griefs, and his own sufferings. The terms in which she mentioned Villars, whose fate and fortune she conceived to be in his hands, however cautiously guarded, kindled again all his irritable feelings. Another wound also lay festering at his heart, of which his wife was not aware: it was the look she had cast upon him when they parted. In domestic dissension any thing may be forgiven rather than scorn: other tokens of resentment are but common arrows; *that* is a poisoned shaft, and hardly ever ceases to rankle where once it has penetrated. Mr. Seymour could not pardon it. He contented himself therefore with signifying, by a short note, in answer to hers, that he willingly deferred all further discussion of differences till the arrival of Mrs. Cleveland: but he could not command his temper so far as to forbear adding, that the man in whose fate she showed so *generous an interest* was occupied by plans tending to impoverish her husband, and make a beggar of her child, if beggary on his own part did not prevent him.

Mrs. Cleveland arrived within four-and-twenty hours after the receipt of this note, and found her daughter very alarmingly ill. She had had a succession of fainting fits, and was reduced to a state of weakness that left her exposed to the utmost danger should the premature event take place, which was hourly expected. It was too late to remove her to her own house, had Mr. Seymour acceded to the overture for so doing; he neither granted nor refused it, however, but maintained a sullen silence.

The distracting intelligence of Julia's danger at length reached the ear of Villars. He had in the interim received a very satisfactory letter from Atkinson. The collateral degree of consanguinity on which the claims both of Mr. Seymour and himself were founded did not indeed appear so close in the person of either as his informant had reported it to be, but his own title seemed to have evidently the advantage over that of his competitor; he had therefore laid the question before counsel, who returned an unequivocal opinion in his favour. But what were claims, what was fortune to him, in the state of his mind at that crisis? The whole world would have seemed valueless if put in competition with the health or safety of Mrs. Seymour. He found it impossible to live from her door; nor did Mrs. Cleveland refuse to see him. Matilda was also present. He started at sight of the latter: it was her lovely sister, in the bloom of eighteen, that seemed to stand before him: but it was not Julia herself, and he quickly forgot her.

Mrs. Cleveland, whose interest and curiosity were both strongly excited by the particular circumstances in which he stood to her family, wrung from him by interrogation a confused account of what had passed between Mr. Seymour and himself. On her part she confirmed his worst fears with regard to her daughter; and he left the house in a state of distraction, to which the event that succeeded his return to his lodgings could hardly add. He found there a person to whom he was indebted for various expensive though necessary articles, which had been furnished for his intended voyage to India. He had no means to discharge the demand, nor patience to write to Mr. Seymour on the subject, and was therefore obliged to dismiss the intruder as he could. A second visitor, upon a business of the same nature, easily led him to comprehend that Mr. Seymour was in fact the man who thus indirectly threatened his personal liberty. Heart-rending chagrin constrained him therefore to address a few lines to the former, desiring an account of his small patrimonial fortune: but of this note Mr. Seymour, with most ungentlemanly insolence, took no notice. Villars knew himself to be under age, but his appearance did not denote this; it therefore remained to be proved; and what should, in the interim, secure him from the insults of a rich and powerful oppressor, who had plunged too deeply in injustice not to persevere? A prison – a grave would have been alike indifferent, but that Julia yet lived; and while she lived, to wander round the walls that enclosed her seemed necessary to his own existence.

Mrs. Seymour at length brought into the world a lovely boy, two months, however, before the time; but her strength was wholly exhausted, and little hope remained that it could ever be restored. Mr. Seymour himself was now roused to some tokens of sensibility: he did not, indeed, see either mother or child. The mother it was not thought prudent should see him; but he spared no demonstrations of respect to Mrs. Cleveland or Matilda; and the indiscreet and immoderate affliction of the former, whose weak character time had not corrected, too soon betrayed to Mrs. Seymour that danger which her medical attendants had carefully concealed.

Amid the great circle of human events, death had not presented itself to the imagination of Julia; none, indeed, according to their natural course, appeared less probable. She was in the very flower of life; had been, only a single fortnight before, in the perfection of health; nor could danger, in fact, have approached her but through the medium of indiscretion or accident. She had herself struck the blow, and she began to perceive that it would prove mortal. She perceived it with all the anguish of a young and unsubdued mind. Life was inexpressibly dear to her: her sense of pleasure was not withered; her heart was yet alive to a thousand tender and delightful hopes. It was indeed acquainted with suffering: but it had not passed through those melancholy gradations of disappointment and languor which palsy the feelings, and make all around joyless and vapid.

After drawing from the exclamations and tears of her feeble-minded mother such conclusions as left her no doubt with regard to the danger of her own case, she earnestly requested Mrs. Cleveland and

Matilda to withdraw; and amid the silence of a sick chamber, alone with God and her conscience, she now communed with both. The world no longer wore the same aspect to her that it had hitherto done. She saw it as a sphere of honourable and useful action, where every individual touched some point of moral obligation, of which that of example pressed most closely upon the great or the affluent. Hers had the negative merit of having never encouraged vice; but it had lent to frivolity, levity, and dissipation graces that might well have supported a better cause. Nor did her behaviour as a wife any longer appear to her irreproachable; for she felt that in ascribing to her own character an influence in society, a superiority over those of Mr. Seymour, the least duty she imposed upon her heart was that of rising as much above him in conduct as in self-opinion. She had failed in the trial, and it would probably be never more repeated. Yet she ventured to present to Heaven a mind sullied indeed, but not tainted, – one that had withstood the temptation to much evil, and had been disposed to much good. Heaven accepted the offering; for a soft and religious hope tranquillised her feelings, and restored an equanimity which enabled her to consider with calmness what yet remained to do in life.

She was worse the next day, and on that which succeeded, her case was pronounced to be desperate. Having extorted from those around a tacit acknowledgment of this truth, she requested that such medicines might be administered as would supply her with temporary strength and spirits; and her mother, by her desire, sent for Mr. Villars. She also signified it to be her wish, as the last act of her life, to see Mr. Seymour.

Villars, on arriving, was received by Mrs. Cleveland in the anteroom; nor had he, for a considerable time, either power or self-command enough to proceed further. The door of communication stood open, and the feeble light of a close-shaded lamp showed him the inner apartment. Mrs. Seymour lay on the bed, the curtains of which were only half drawn, and the folds of her long wrapper slightly marked her still graceful and elegant person.

'Is it you, dear Villars?' said she, hearing the low murmur of an anguish which it was impossible he should suppress. 'Draw near, and let me speak to you.' The unfortunate young man dropped in agonizing sorrow on his knee, while receiving the hand which she feebly extended to him.

'Control yourself,' said she: 'subdue this ungoverned sensibility, and hear me with calmness, if you ever mean to hear me more.

I am approaching a sad crisis, and you are among the very few in this world to whom I still wish to address myself; but your excessive emotion overpowers – it enfeebles me!' And she made a long pause. 'Yet, however painful the effort, I must speak, both to console you and to acquit myself. Do not believe, my dear Charles, that in this last, painful meeting, you are bidding an eternal adieu to a devoted heart, – such as yours seeks and deserves. Fluctuating sensibility, ill-judged levity on my part, and an unkindness still more ill-judged on the part of another, perhaps, induced you to admit so dangerous an illusion. But nature, dear Villars, had placed disparity between us. A premature knowledge of life made me even older than my years; and from the moment when the vehemence of your attachment obliged me to ascertain the nature of my own, I solemnly declare myself to have felt for you only that interest which a mother might have cherished for a beloved son, – an interest that taught me to grieve for your misfortunes, to palliate your faults, to suffer in your sufferings, but never to desire the possession of your heart. It *will* teach me' – and she feebly pressed his hand – 'if in another world I am sensible to any thing in that I leave behind me, still to share very honourable pursuit in which you may hereafter be engaged. We must part; and, assuredly, never *here* to meet again. But I give you one solemn, dying injunction,' and again she made a long pause both for breath and voice. 'Remember that you have injured Mr. Seymour. Had your influence kept pace with your wishes, you would indeed most essentially have injured him. Let that recollection made an eternal claim on your forbearance. At this awful moment, when his errors no longer palliate mine, I can pardon – can feel for him. It may now be his turn to suffer. – One thing, and only one more, I leave behind me,' – and she melted into tears, – 'a helpless and innocent child! I am told that, by some strange chance of circumstances, you, of all created beings, are the very one by whose claims it may be impoverished.'

'Never!' exclaimed Villars, starting up for a moment; then eagerly resuming him first posture, 'Angel of light!' he added, 'listen to me, while I solemnly imprecate every curse of misery or want on my own head, should any earthly motive ever induce me to litigate the inheritance of a child of yours!' Mrs. Seymour's lips and eyelids suddenly shivered, and her hand become colder: Villars was obliged to leave the room.

He retired to an apartment below, in a state of mind that unfitted him to judge either of time or place. He had been long there, when

Matilda at length entered. She came by the desire of her sister, who had not been able to prevail on Mrs. Cleveland to leave her, in order to inquire after, to console, and to request him to depart. But he was past all consolation; even that of the sweet creature who offered it in its best, indeed its only form – sympathy. He at length controlled himself so far, however, as to quit her with some small appearance of self-possession. In the hall he was accosted by Mrs. Seymour's maid: she had a cloak on; and he with difficulty understood that as it was nearly dark she desired protection. Without being able to ask or answer a single question, he suffered her to take his arm. She walked with him, by a way of her own choosing, to the door of his lodgings, and even followed him to that of his apartment. Villars, on turning round to shut it, looked at her in silence.

'I beg your pardon, sir,' said she; 'you think me very odd, perhaps very bold; but indeed I am ordered not to leave you without warning you to take care of yourself.' Villars shook his head impatiently, and motioned with his hand that she should withdraw.

'I must not go – indeed I must not, sir, till I have given notice – that – that we suspect there are some very bad men looking out for you. So Mrs. Cleveland and Miss Matilda, sir, – they were afraid – afraid—'

'Of what?'

'The men were waiting, sir, somewhere near our street. So Miss Matilda was very unhappy indeed; but she said that perhaps if two people went out together, and especially if one of them was a woman, they would not guess the other to be you.'

'Who are the men?' said Villars, at length finding power to articulate.

'I can't say I know their names, sir – but our William was the first to find them out, and he tells us that he is sure they are bailiffs, – and Miss Matilda did so cry at hearing it! for she says that it would be my poor lady's death-stroke at once, if she could but suspect that my master was capable of such a wicked action.'

'It is complete!' said Villars; and for a moment he walked up and down the room. 'Your ladies are very kind – and you are very kind. Say that I will endeavour to set some value on my safety, since they interest themselves in it. Oh, Julia,' he internally exclaimed, 'how immeasurably great will be the virtue of forbearance!'

On the following morning he received a note from Mrs. Cleveland. It contained a positive injunction to him not again to present himself at Mrs. Seymour's door, as it was utterly impossible that any person should be admitted there. Her husband was on that day to be with her.

To Mr. Seymour a death-bed was at all times a fearful and appalling thought. But the death-bed of Julia, – of that creature who, within a period so short that it seemed but as yesterday, had been bestowed upon him in all the lustre of beauty and health, – to approach *that* bed, was a suffering that nearly expiated his offences, those of the weak mother who had assisted so to mismatch her. The parting between them was solemn and impressive. He made no answer to the representations which she conceived herself bound by conscience to offer in favour of Villars, but he received and admitted a religious attestation of her unshaken fidelity to him, and he consented to take home the child.

On the following day Villars received another note from Mrs. Cleveland – and it was sealed with *black* wax.

* * * * * *

To the period of time that immediately succeeded, Mr. Villars was very little sensible. Julia gone! – eternally gone! – that fair vision vanished! – she whose image so long had gilded his anxious days! – his restless nights! – first and only object of his life, while life itself was yet new to him! – hardly could his imagination credit the idea! – much less dismiss from it the feeble light, the melancholy chamber, and all the dreadful ceremony of the last agonizing farewell.

'Oh that her voice, though low as then it seem'd,
Could reach me now!'

groaned Villars a thousand times a day.

* * * * * *

He was at length roused from anguish to a transient sense of gratitude, by the unremitting attention and kindness of Mrs. Cleveland and Matilda. His health had suffered very materially under the conflicts of his mind; and as they were on the point of setting out for Devonshire, they earnestly and perseveringly insisted on his promising to visit them there. Whatever might be the dictates of discretion, those of tenderness for her lost daughter, and even of gratitude to Villars, superseded them in Mrs. Cleveland's mind, and both had a powerful auxiliary in the person of Matilda: for she, as well as her mother, saw, or fancied they saw, a more than common degree of generosity in the total renunciation of his claims. The future line of conduct that Mr. Seymour intended to pursue remained doubtful; but it appeared that he had, for the time at least, withdrawn his persecution. Villars, therefore, set out on foot, a friendless wanderer, to go he knew not whither; leaving a power with his solicitor to rescue the little which he now deemed his sole possession in life, from the grasp of Mr. Seymour. But he left also a positive injunction to reject all compromise, all resignation of his own rights, and all overtures whatever, from the latter, that tended to establish intercourse between them. It was for the child of Julia, and only for her child, that he consented to be friendless and impoverished.

While art exhausts herself in vain and fruitless efforts, Nature has sometimes influence enough to stanch the wounds of the heart. Those breezes that invigorate the frame, penetrate with balmy influence to the soul. Nothing could, perhaps, be more soothing in the actual state of Mr. Villars's mind, than to wander alone through the solitudes of a beautiful country, to catch Nature in her wild, yet fairest forms; to hold converse with the dead, 'and entertain their spirits in his desolate bosom.'

After passing many weeks in this manner, he at length approached the retired residence of Mrs. Cleveland. Here, the tangled wood-walks and wild copses, that must once have been the haunt of her lovely daughter, became doubly interesting to him. After much irresolution, he presented himself at Mrs. Cleveland's door. Matilda was the first to recognize – the first to hear his voice, and to welcome him. Even her mother received him as one who had a claim to her hospitality; and the houseless traveller seemed in their society to have found that sweet home which fortune had hitherto denied him. No mention was made of Mr. Seymour; but the babe, so dearly purchased on one side, so dearly endowed on the other, was well.

Mr. Villars passed several days, that were never to be forgotten, in this retreat. He then quitted it, and, striking directly towards the sea, pursued all the irregularities of the coast for many miles; still indulging himself by keeping in view that element whose restless motion seemed most congenial to his frame of mind. Summer was far advanced when he reached Weymouth. Here, a feverish indisposition, that had been gaining ground fast while he was in London, and which continual change of air had subdued, returned with fresh force, and obliged him to remain stationary. He had been there more than three weeks, when, in the course of a solitary ramble, he cast his eyes upon a face which he immediately recognised: it was that of Mrs. Seymour's maid. She held in her arms a fair and delicate child, whose black sash announced its irreparable loss. Villars felt himself now bound to remain at Weymouth by a tie far stronger than any malady but that of the heart could impose. The woman knew him well: she permitted him sometimes to caress the lovely baby, and from her he learned that Mr. Seymour was himself on the coast for the benefit of his health, which had suffered considerably since the death of his wife. The shock that had occasioned to his nerves, had, indeed, never been wholly recovered by him. He was of an age when the sufferings of the imagination easily pass into the frame, and was indeed seriously, though not apparently very ill. Villars caught a glance of him one day upon the beach, but retreated from the view as from that of a basilisk.

Mr. Seymour did not hope to receive much benefit from his residence at Weymouth; but his own house had been a desert to him, since the gay world, and she who was once the gayest of the gay, were no longer to be seen there. He stayed, therefore, rather because he did not like to go, than for any other reason. The close of the season carried him at length away. Villars saw him drive from the town, and nearly on the same day received letters from the solicitor to whom he had intrusted his concerns, to inform him that Mr. Seymour, under the pretext of his not being of age, evaded giving up his patrimony into his own hands, except upon conditions which he had good reason to expect would not complied with. The letter also contained a caution to him to attend to his personal security, as there was reason to believe that Mr. Seymour, alarmed by the demand lately made, which he conceived to be the forerunner of other measures, would, as a desperate effort, employ every engine, however unjust, to reduce him to terms.

The event of this application seemed conclusive. Villars, too indigent to plunge deeper in law, was wholly without redress, nay, almost without present resource. The apartments which he inhabited were expensive, and made him too obvious to notice, to suit either his finances or his apprehensions, and he removed—

'*Where* did he remove to?' said Atkinson, frantic with impatience at seeing the break: for as the initials by which the story had been marked, had not to him disguised the names of the different parties, he had, at sight of his own, eagerly turned to the last page of the book, for the very intelligence that there failed him.

'Where did *who* remove?' said Mrs. Dixon.

'Mr. Villars, – my young master, Mr. Villars.'

'Why, sure you are dreaming! The name of Villars is not in the book.'

'But it is in my heart. Where is he, Mrs. Dixon?'

'Who do you come from?' –

'From Mr. Seymour.'

'Then I shall tell you nothing at all of the matter. I have read more of the book than Mr. Villars believes. Mr. Seymour is a wicked man, and I don't desire to hear another word about him.

'But he is a dying man, and he can't die in peace till he does justice. – I tell you that my business is a blessed one: it is to restore Mr. Villars his estate.'

'And why did you not say at first that you came upon a good errand?'

'What could possibly make you think that I should come on any other?'

'Bless my soul, sir, I took you for a lawyer?'

'Why then, Mrs. Dixon, learn to correct your prejudices; and to think that a lawyer may do a kind action as well as any other man. – I tell you that Mr. Villars is heir to five thousand a year.'

'Then I tell you, in return, that the heir to five thousand a year is at this moment shut up in my back attic, – and has been so, these six weeks. – Are you sure of what you say?'

'I will swear it,' said Atkinson, taking up the book.

'It is not a Bible, but it will do!' replied Mrs. Dixon. – 'We must not hurry poor dear Mr. Villars though, for he is not well.' So, because she would not hurry him, she ran breathless up the stairs, and, after two gentle but very hasty raps, threw open the door. Villars was reading. The appearance of health had indeed faded from his manly cheeks, but both his countenance and person were highly prepossessing.

'Here is Mr. Atkinson, sir,' cried Mrs. Dixon, speaking fast and thick. 'Your friend, Mr. Atkinson.' They looked earnestly at each other, but recognition was impossible. Atkinson, however, quickly made himself known; and informed Villars that Mr. Seymour, whose case was considered as hopeless, had employed every measure to discover his residence: measures which were constantly defeated; being imputed to very opposite motives from those which now influenced him. The child had rejoined its mother. It had ever been a delicate infant, and its death had been a mortal stroke to Mr. Seymour, both as to his feelings and temporal views; since, besides being passionately fond of it, the debilitated state of his nerves induced him to consider the loss as a visitation. He now earnestly desired to Villars, and had invested Atkinson with powers to make over the title-deeds of the estate to him, on the instant of his own decease.

Mr. Seymour lay sick at his house in town; but Villars found himself utterly unable to subdue his feelings so far as to enter that house, even though the refusal were to be attended with the worst consequences to himself. All there was Julia's – in *his* eyes Julia's only. Though it was now six months since the world had lost her, to him she still lived; and the spot in which she had presided, which she had embellished, it was impossible for him again to behold. Another Julia indeed in form and outward semblance, perhaps also in character, one deeply endeared to his heart, and to whom he was secretly most dear, was to be found there; but it was not the enchantress whom he had so passionately loved; nor could he resolve, in those circumstances, to see even Matilda again. She, with her mother, had come up at the request of Mr. Seymour, to console and watch over the latter.

The contending feelings of Mr. Villars's mind caused him to be an invalid himself immediately on his arrival; and during that period Mr. Seymour, by finishing his career in this world, left his competitor a brilliant fortune, of which, through the good offices of Atkinson, he took unmolested and immediate possession.

Time, occupation, and circumstances, at length succeeded in consoling Mr. Villars; but not till he had atoned for the weakness and romantic indiscretion of his early conduct by long and bitter regret. He was then permitted to indulge the overflowings of a heart still too tender and retired for the common intercourse of society, in the tranquil happiness of domestic life, and to cherish, in a fond and lasting attachment to Mrs. Villars, his love both for *Julia and Matilda*.

* * * * * *

And what became of the counterparts, Atkinson and Mrs. Dixon? Why, they had at length been fortunate enough to discover each other; a good fortune that does not attend all the counterparts of this world: in consequence of which, they agreed to make their little establishment in the friendly neighbourhood of Mr. Villars, and to have for the future only one fireside in common.